Finola Moorhead's second novel, *Still Murder*, won the Vance Palmer Prize for fiction in the Victorian Premier's literary awards when Joan Kirner was premier. A truant at school, Moorhead's view of the world was formed by the strong but unhappy women who dominated her early life. Never able to hold down a straight job for very long, and deciding to be a writer in the late sixties, Finola has survived by thinking, dreaming, learning to do what is needed and the fortunes of fate. First thrown down the stairs by the police demonstrating against the Vietnam war in 1968, then embracing the women's liberation movement in the 70s, and following the philosophy of radical feminism during the 80s, she joined a separatist collective in 1990 to put theory into practice. Since then she has lived on the mid-north coast of New South Wales. Her other books include *A Handwritten Modern Classic* (1985), *Quilt* (1985) and *Remember the Tarantella* (1987).

T0099384

What a misfortune to be born a woman! . . . Why seek for knowledge, which can prove only that our wretchedness is irremediable? If a ray of light break in upon us, it is but to make darkness more visible; to show us the now limits, the Gothic structure, the impenetrable barriers of our prison.

Leonora, *Letter 1*, 1805
Maria Edgeworth (1767–1849)

What power do we have over each other that has to be constantly guarded against for fear of annihilation? We're very easy to walk away from—there are no laws against it, and our pain and rage are no sort of weapon at all.

Denise Thompson, 'Freedom for What?',
Essays in Lesbian Feminism. Sydney, May 1984.

darkness
more visible

Finola Moorhead

Spinifex Press Pty Ltd
504 Queensberry Street
North Melbourne, Vic. 3051
Australia
women@spinifexpress.com.au
http://www.spinifexpress.com.au

First published by Spinifex Press, 2000

Edited by Janet Mackenzie
Typeset in Garamond by Claire Warren
Cover design by Wingrove Wingrove Design
Made and printed in Australia by Australian Print Group

National Library of Australia
Cataloguing-in-Publication data:

Moorhead, Finola
Darkness more visible
ISBN 1 875559 60 4

1. Crime – Australia – New South Wales – Fiction. 2. Love stories – Australia –
New South Wales. 3. Detective and mystery stories. I. Title.

A823.3

This project has been assisted by the Commonwealth Government
through the Australia Council, its arts funding and advisory body.

Dedication

My sister, christened Arthur Carmel Moorhead, known as Moodge, was born 30 June 1941, with a caul, and died 20 January 1970. Her spirit pervades this work as she could swim and play sport like no other and mentally she was brilliant.

Author's note

The people and places in this novel are entirely fictional. A lot of work went into making characters and locality seem real when they are actually products of my imagination serving the cultural purpose of story-telling. Resemblance to any living or dead person or district is an achievement; neither rip-off nor take-off. This work carefully avoids both plagiarism and libel, or hint thereof, for there is no intention or desire to hurt the feelings or reputations of anyone I've known or heard of. The art of fiction is not a representational one, since it must include fantasy. This literary venture is reflective, informed by my concerns and politics, limited by my talent, experience, time, education, brain-power, space, money, vision, and comprehension. Above all a novelist must have compassion and conviction, and be fully responsible for the words on the page and the world view propagated.

Contents

Book Six

transsexualism
Thursday Friday Saturday Sunday

Book Seven

money
Monday Tuesday Wednesday Thursday

Acknowledgements

This book was begun in 1990. Since then I have received invaluable help from numerous sources. It has evolved and transmogrified, risen, disappeared and come through at least seven drafts to the finished product. I have to thank the Australia Council for two Senior Writers' one-year grants in that time from the Literary Fund, 1990 and 1996. Individuals, also, have baled me out when I've been in desperate need financially. I hereby express sincere gratitude for this patronage.

As well as fiscal assistance, I have received invaluable help with the manuscript itself, reading, ideas, criticism, production, computer hardware, expertise, photocopying, printing, desk, books and talking time. Pencils, paper and paper-clips alongside hours of typing I recognise as donations towards this creation. While some aid was direct and practical, other incidental and general, it was all generous. At the point of saying thank-you it is difficult to know where to begin, how to quantify and qualify, how to make the priorities of give and take fall into place so as full an expression of indebtedness as possible can be put down. I am afraid I will fall way short of my emotion of gratefulness for the full gamut of support I have received. I am obliged to others not only for information and faith but also for knowledge, experience and tests of my self-esteem, from encouragement to challenge.

Earnest thanks to the following individuals for specific help in the time of my writing this book: Sandra Russell, Sue Standen, Janne Ellen, Jennie Curtin, Deborah Carmichael, Denise Thompson, Ticole Akuni, Shane Kelly, Robyn Martin, Cathy Lewis, Dot, Oshun, Dione McDonald, Kaye Moseley, Louise Lovett, Patricia Bodsworth, Liz Miles, Irene Bruninghausen, and the men in my life, Bill, Robert, Colin, Michael, Gareth and Garry Moorhead. Susan Hawthorne has been encouraging, considerate and invaluable throughout. I am very grateful for both her and Renate Klein's faith in me and that of all the women of Spinifex Press, Janet Mackenzie and Claire Warren especially, for close editorial work in the final drafts.

For the depth of philosophic perspective and cultural continuity from which I come to this fiction, I am indebted to publications of the following women: Virginia Woolf; Valerie Solanas; Germaine Greer; Ti-Grace Atkinson; Mary Daly; Elaine Morgan; Merlin Stone; Phyllis Chesler; Shulamith Firestone; Jill Johnson; Susan Brownmillar; Barbara Walker; Monique Wittig; Marilyn Frye; Andrea Dworkin; Kathleen Barry; Denise Thompson; Sheila Jeffreys; Robin Morgan; Adrienne Rich; Somer Brodribb; Renate Klein; Henry Handel Richardson; Miles Franklin; Leonora Carrington; Maria Edgeworth; and Christa Wolf. There are, of course, many other writers and artists whose work I have appreciated to the benefit of my own, with either sympathy or criticism, but a complete map of the mental process of thinking with a view to literary fiction is too overwhelming to undertake. I wish merely, by naming the above, to indicate the path to the point of view I embrace as real, as mine, authenticated and weighted by the authority of female perception available to all who would read the written word.

While I value the insights of intellectuals, I also cherish the worth of conversation and interaction within the community of my circle of friendship.

I honour the memory of Charlotte Moorhead, Badajos, Susie Stuart, Liz Lovely and Lors who lost their lives during the course of my writing this.

Book One

murder

Friday Saturday Sunday Monday

Friday's child is loving and giving

1

. . . body of a teenager . . .

Simply Margot was written on the manila envelope. The other letter had my full name, Ms Margot Ellen Gorman.

The moon was fat in the afternoon sky, affecting the tides. And my body. Restless with the agitation of PMT, I felt mentally tired after I looked at my mail. I scratched my head and distractedly wrote down 'hair-cut' above my address. I could not work,. so I made a list. Even though my quota of training for the day was done, I had to exercise, for my sanity. When I'm in the mood I kick and box a leather log of a bag hanging from the rafters of my verandah. But I wasn't in the mood to punch. I could swim. Or ride either of my bikes. A bit dangerous in the evening; it would be dark by the time I got in.

Or I could run.

Ten Mile Beach is five minutes' walk from my house. I live on the delta of the Campbell River. As soon as I saw this place, I realised I didn't need to live anywhere else. I can train along the beaches and in the surf. I can travel to competitions. As well as my racing bike, I have the mountain bike for off-road touring, and, maybe, for races in the future. Hundreds of kilometres of unsealed roads are only an hour away by car. I can bike into deep bush along Forestry roads and fire-trails.

Behind my property are paperbark wetlands. These become mangrove swamps closer to the estuary. A short walk over sand dunes is the sea. Canal development on the other side of the river enables wealthy retired couples to have a water road in front and bitumen where the back door is the front door. But these settlers in Paradise screen out all but the view of this nature because of the mosquitoes. Especially, the disease-bearing *Aedes notoscriptus*. Until the controversial bridge is built I am on the wrong side of the river.

The surf sounded like relentless distant traffic. The largest ocean in the world was banging at my door, calling me out to play, to witness the magic of seascape, dolphins riding the waves, sea eagles soaring, people walking their dogs. Whatever, the negative ions of the spray off the waves would do me good. Clear my head, blast my lungs.

Worrying about me is serious business. I strolled down to the beach.

When I had stretched my tendons I started out on the firm sand, heading towards the point, weaving up into the soft stuff now and then. As the body-work began to bite, physical aches concentrated my mind to disallow the idea of stopping and panting at the burning moment, if not, the chest will always burn here. I kept my eyes on the prize, got through it to the bigness of being. Being yourself and losing yourself at the same time is a rush. Eventually, my mind, my emotions, my knowledge, my past, my future were in my body. Everything was pumping. Rising and resiling like the sea.

Whiffs of exhaust and loud acceleration, brake-screeching and skidding indicated hooning kids doing donuts behind the sand-dunes. A woman who stood gazing at the horizon did not move when I passed. A dyke, I judged by her clothes, greasy wool, hand-spun, hand-knitted jumper, loose trousers of scarlet and purple tucked into socks and solid walking boots. As well as garlic, I smelt the earthy body odour of land-living. The evening sun gave her long brown hair a kind of golden aura. Her face was lined; she did not smile but glanced at me as if she had contempt for all joggers. Her straight hair fanned by the wind, she stared back at the waves in arrogant stillness. My grin of recognition froze to a grimace.

Why would a gurl acknowledge me? I stopped for a breather beside the track from the caravan park where four-wheel-drive tyres grooved a curve to the north.

Gurls was an acronym for Generally Unruly Rural Lesbians. A tribe of hillpeople who lived on a remote property somewhere around the head-waters of the Campbell River, high in the ranges, gurls had a reputation for being quite frightening. I found them friendly for the most part, though interpersonal relationships were fierce and they tended to fight in public. But there was a code of behaviour, a style of dress unique to themselves. I supposed a sort of quest was credited more than conventional success, commitment to women's freedom.

There was a pair of tiny sand birds, little bodies on longish legs, dashing about like miniature plovers. Coming onto the beach from the path was Tiger Cat, a woman I had good reason not to trust. Before I bleed I am irritable and I sniff out subjects to gripe about. I tried to get a grip on myself. Because she used to be a cop, Catherine Tobin could be a spy. I know they are keeping an eye on me.

Not wanting Tiger Cat to recognise me, I took off, sprinting until I hurt. The pain, eventually, leached from my calves and thighs and I began really punishing my muscles. Slowing down, I went back to the tide-line. Kicking my legs out behind, now up under my chin, I did not want to stop. The end of the surf's moving scallops showed the foamless sea rolling beyond the point into the mouth of the river. Another gash carved into the sand led to the road-access through the coastal scrub. I went up a pedestrian track of planks wired together and laid across the dunes to protect the coastal grasses.

Judith Sloane claims invention of gurls, the acronym, for bush-living radical lesbians.

Now she gazes at a tanker making its way along the horizon, thinking neither of the ocean nor what the container ship might be carrying, rather why she came to the gay and lesbian barbecue. She recognises Margot Gorman, the triathlete, but enjoys freezing the smile on her face. Times have changed. Judith wants a lover. That is why she is here.

As she stands, on the Paradise Coast, aware of the scene of herself on the beach, she refigures the past to a perfect picture. The original ideal of a utopian lesbian nation, Lesbianlands, is bleary with the sleep of memory. Judith contradicts any detail which doesn't fit her myth. All the facts blend with emotions and each telling is deluded by visions into a compendium from which Judith, appearing to meditate, chooses what to appropriate into her romance. She is rehearsing her next conversation. But she will not go back to the party.

Selfhood is a task, not a given clarity. Sex. Judith says the word to herself.

Touching the skin of another woman, entering the realm of intimacy, releases fluency into the hard boundaries learnt in antipathetic childhoods. Born into occupied territory. Judith wonders whether to keep this alien culture idea. The lesbian is terrorised into accepting a reality that simply does not accord with her feelings, thus she longs for congruence, a sense of belonging. Lesbianlands offers the place. The blessed bliss of being with another woman in bed, baring vulnerability, trusting and knowing and flying to erotic ecstasy, becomes a burden of knowledge. Judith tests the weight of this thought. We did not learn the way to be responsible at the knee of another, older, wiser lesbian. Living life itself is a trial. Utopian idealists claiming country, new country, travel through the experiences of each other towards community.

But the dream has failed Judith. It's free for all, now. Their behaviour is sleasy. Gurls have no more than their own minds to work with at finding the truth at the base of the intensity of being, among one's ilk, to fashion a culture. Romantic happiness of one love is too narrow a scope for the vast potentiality of the woman's heart. Lonely spinsterhood is not an option either. Judith doesn't stay with a partner, because there is always another woman to charm. Lesbians are everywhere. Gurls keep coming for one reason or another, refreshing her with new stories. New prospects for her lust.

The land is alive with spirits. She can pick her take on things. Does she believe the positive sightings of extraterrestrial craft which have been recorded in the large hard-covered minute book? She tries the witch image with words. Spells? Rituals of the old religion are scorned. Some secretly meditate with techniques learnt at monasteries or ashrams. Discipline cannot be imposed from the outside. Tradition is distrusted. Lesbianlands have also practical women, survivors, existentialists with materialist views. Judith has been all types. She generally prefers dreamers over liberals trying to rationalise the chaos. Judith can say what she likes. It is how she says it she is careful of.

The goddess is life, the earth, nature. Judith is disgusted. She would never get out of it, take drugs, drink too much or eat gluttonously. She has nothing in common with gurls any more, except the desire to relate to women.

When I reached the wooden path I began to jog. The late afternoon sun made the leaves of the trees syrupy with honeyed light.

There was the sound of skidding in the car park. When I emerged from the sandy seaward path I saw silver aerials, the top of a high cabin. Dust. What was a semi-trailer doing on this side of the river? There were no dairy farms here. In this parking area, nothing was happening. Just a couple of locked cars on the graded gravel and a rubbish bin near brick conveniences. Straightening my hammies on the limed log foot-high fence, stretching my inner thighs, warming down methodically, I could smell onions cooking and the smoke of fires. Invisible from where I stood, the barbecues were in a picnic area about half a kilometre along a track, taking the longest possible route through old banksias, new Little John callistemon and other planted natives, made by Council using a scheme for the unemployed. Sandy hills held off the sea winds. I needed to rehydrate.

The convenience block had its own tank. Rain water tasted delicious after the sharp salt air in my dry throat. I went into the toilet.

Lying half propped against the raw brick wall with legs splayed on the gritty concrete floor was the body of a teenager. Her eyes were black with either bruises or make-up, I couldn't tell. She was staring at me. Her skin was snow. Her clothes were black. Her mouth looked as if a pie had been squashed into it. Vomit. Her eyes were open but she was dead. I retched. I had to urinate and evacuate my bowels urgently. I burst into the cubicle and closed the door on the sight, sat and held my head in my hands with elbows on my shuddering knees. In a matter of seconds your whole world can change; comprehension of life and death suddenly throws all your priorities awry.

The girl was dead, no doubt about that. Her right hand was in a fist, holding something which may have been a crunched hanky. Her other hand rested in a small puddle near the sink was palm up, fingers almost blue. The floor was gritty. I stood for a few moments at the door, then turned away, shivering.

At the L-shaped corner of the entrance a hat lay on the ground. I picked it up. Black, spongy nylon comprised the front, the back of the cap was synthetic netting, an awful thing. Red writing said: NADIR Mining Support Services. My hand petrified itself into its grasp. 'Nadir' had been a name on one of the trailers of the semi which shadowed me in Queensland. I held onto this cap. Evil was palpable in its greasy, unnatural material.

Following the scent of meat cooking, going towards civilisation, I concentrated on the gravel of the path even though it wound in a ridiculously indirect fashion, figuring out my steps. My duty. I saw a ring of people around a fire big enough to roast a suckling pig. But nothing but a tin billy was on it. Further off a family group was setting up its meal on the table under shelter with the facilities provided. They seemed immobile. Time stopped. It was becoming dark. I heard my name.

'Margot,' Maria Freewoman called out. Amicable. Familiar.

Shaking my head, I couldn't respond vocally. I went silently up to the circle. There had been food. Paper plates showed the remains of salad, some sort of pastry. Nausea returned to my gut.

Maria began introductions, 'Margot, you know Alison?' I nodded.

Irrelevantly I thought why has Maria been ringing me up with her troubles when she has all these friends? I jerked to attention, searching to catch up with the formalities. There were a lot of people around, mumbling, talking, standing, sitting as if everything was the same as it was before I found her. Alison was a strikingly good-looking woman with awful dress-sense. She wore a wrist-band with studs, black leather pants and gold lurex top. The light made it hard to see others.

'Are you all right?' She asked and seemed to know why she was asking. I frowned at her. She came to my side. I nodded dumbly as Maria indicated others. I could not see Sofia anywhere.

'Dello and Maz,' Maria pointed to two with identical hair and dark glasses. I stared at them. I lost concentration, faces became a blur. Kids were running around. I heard a male voice. I was, momentarily, at a loss.

'Been training, Margot?' Jill, whom I had met at the gym, spoke. Jill David. I couldn't bring myself to tell these people what I'd just seen. I couldn't control my voice. They'd probably troop over and destroy the crime scene, anyway.

'Margot?' Maria addressed me, and said something else in a business-like tone of voice. I shook my head and moved my hands as if thrusting something in the air away from me.

There was a lull in the general noise.

'I need a phone,' I uttered.

'Anyone got a mobile?' A chorus of attention drowned Maria's voice. 'I think there's a public one at the caravan park.'

When I turned to run off, Alison was beside me. 'Easy does it. What's wrong?' Her hands were gentle, but forceful.

'Oh shit, I haven't got any change.' Thoughts and impressions were crowding my consciousness like refugees on the last ship out, stampeding my brain. Don't panic. Surely someone there had a mobile phone.

'Come on,' she called, and started walking decisively. I followed. We went up to the road. She reached into a red low-slung sedan and handed me a car-phone. I looked at her before I dabbed the number. We looked at each other. If she was this cool and she didn't have anything to do with it, she could be trusted to keep her head. Or she could be helping me because she knows exactly what is going on, what I have seen and what I have to do. I spun around with the car-phone and walked out of earshot.

My hand was still clasping the black cap. I rang the local cop shop, and then the Criminal Intelligence Unit for this part of New South Wales. I asked them what they wanted me to do, and I was told.

'Yours?' I pointed to the Saab as I watched her replace the receiver between the front seats.

'No. It's . . .'

I interrupted, 'Is one of these cars yours?'

Alison drove me to the toilet block in a heavy old Ford with the gear stick under the steering wheel. I wondered if she knew there, beside a dripping tap, near the basin, a dead girl lay against the wall. Before Alison had quite stopped, I jumped out. I pulled the door of the shelter shed shut. The Yale lock clicked.

'Can I give you a lift home?' What! I pressed my lips together. She reached for the hat in my hand. I couldn't let go of the horrid nylon. It was animated by some devilish fluency, it seemed to stick to my palm. Evidence. I was tense.

'I've had a shock.' When I said it I started shaking.

'Wait here. I'll get my son.' Alison ran along the path a bit and yelled. 'Lenny. Lenny,' she called, but I did not know why.

The cops wanted me to wait. I waited.

Judith Sloane, in the moonlit dusk, makes her way to her car.

Margot Gorman, now very cold, stamping her feet, watches her walk past.

Still without recognising me as a possible acquaintance, the woman I saw on the beach crunched by me in English walking boots, and, using her key, got into one of the parked cars. A shiny new four-wheel-drive ute with spectacular purple duco. I noted facts about the cars in the vicinity to keep my mind occupied. Usually I have a notebook handy.

After she went, I stared unseeingly at the locked amenities door, rubbing the gooseflesh on my forearms with the cap from the mining company. A few minutes later, turning, I saw Alison and her son walking towards me. Lenny's father was apparently Aboriginal. A tallish lad of about eleven, he had liquid brown eyes, long lashes and defiant eyebrows, deep brown skin, very baggy knee-length trousers and even baggier top. Alison thrust him forward.

'Lenny will wait here until the cops come,' she said. Confused, I shook my head vigorously and frowned at her. Why did she want to get me away from here?

'You were shouting into the phone. You're freezing.' Alison explained.

'Oh?' I looked at the lad, furious. 'Have you told him?'

She shook her head slightly. No, mouthed silently. 'Only that the cops are coming. That there's something in the toilet and not to let anybody go in. How long do you think they'll be?'

I didn't know. If she had told the boy, had she blurted it out to the people at the barbecue?

Alison queried, 'Who was that in the purple car? I thought I saw Judith.'

'You?' I started but could not find the words to ask what she had said to the others. For some instinctive reason I did not want them to know, yet.

'She used to have a mustard Landrover Series 3, short-wheelbase,' Alison continued, 'As well as an old grey Toyota LandCruiser.'

Fortunately, the police weren't long, or didn't seem to be, though minutes hung in the air with our desultory discussion about motor vehicles and the weather, meaningless half-finished sentences, scattered repetitions. The shock and the wait distracted me.

Uniform arrived in a squad car. They did not have the key to the toilet block. My credentials established with the local boys, I was allowed go. They took down my words on their incident pads and got the ranger by radio. My cotton training sweats were now icy. Leaving Lenny at the scene, Alison drove me home along the dirt road to my place. She came inside, asked for some paper and wrote on a used envelope. 'That's Chandra's number. Tilly and I are staying at Chandra's. I'll take Lenny to his father's. Should be back there in two hours if you need me. Or do you want me to stay?'

I didn't know. She was too much of a stranger, almost surreal in her leathers and studs. Slowly coming back to normal, I sat down in my own surroundings while Alison hunted for light-switches. She found the bathroom. I heard the water running.

'Have you any Epsom salts?' she called.

'In the cupboard, under the sink,' I answered.

The rushing water was comforting. Then she was behind me.

'You've been perspiring,' she said as she rubbed my spine vigorously. 'You're stiff with shock. Good idea to have a bath.'

'Yeah, okay.'

Alison patted my shoulder on her way out. 'Ring Chandra. Chandra Williams, she will help, I promise.' This was a caring, rescuing, effective Alison, not as I imagined her to be from the previous encounter when she was stoned out of her brain. She had to go. She had responsibilities elsewhere. She backed the old Falcon out of my drive and headed south. I wondered about the women, and the men, and the children, at their bonfire. Was the dead girl, so young and white, at their party? Or did she belong to the family at the gas barbecue? Why and how did she die? Her features under the gothic make-up were quite lumpy, large; her mouth open, slumped and misshapen with the muscle collapse of death. Not as good a look as fashion photographers imagine it to be. As I soaped my waxed legs, I had a sensation that this death was more than incidental to my life. Perhaps it would become a media bonanza, whipping up righteous indignation about the heroin epidemic, making one rural family suffer too many words, while many other tragedies go unsung and effectual policies don't get done. The war on drugs making the wrong people rich . . .

The bath did some good, but I was jittery and very alone when I got out of it. I put a soft tracksuit on and sat staring at the phone number. Chandra. I hesitated and thought of first ringing my ex-lover, Broom. I did ring her number. When I heard her voice come on the answer machine, I felt bereft. Nervously trying to cope with my need of someone, I pushed the buttons of Chandra's number, with a courage born of need.

While billions of hours of housework and husband-care are never paid for, when women do have jobs in poor countries, their wages are a pittance compared to the price of those goods for sale in America. These facts are what Chandra is reading on the Internet when her phone rings. The enormous profits made by transnational corporations and the salaries of their CEOs alone make Chandra as mad as hell. Recently, via the same medium, she discovered her good friend Meghan Featherstone was working for the conglomerate she is researching now. When she confronted her, they came to blows, literally. Each first shouted her passion but the words wore out as their emotions became ragged. Meghan's temper shot up like a geyser. She lost it and lashed out. Chandra, forced to defend herself, flattened her with a punch to the jaw. Although the fight and rupture of friendship is with her constantly—hence her ferocity at uncovering every ounce of information about this group of disparate operations—when she recalls the actual argument, she still seethes with anger. She is sore. She picks up the receiver.

'I've just discovered a dead girl in a toilet on the beach,' she hears. Chandra, having spent many years on the end of the rape crisis hotline, knows exactly how to deal with this interruption. She settles down to patient concern, welcoming the opportunity to be simply reacting rather than obsessively proactive.

A beautiful voice washed over me, like cool water over burnt skin, healing my crisis.

Chandra spoke with me for at least an hour. It was not only the timbre of the voice; there was skill in her approach to my distress. She calmed me down with intelligence, with belief, asking the right questions, soothing without saying anything false or sugary. I told her everything, or at least I thought it was everything. When I got off the phone to do as she suggested—drink some of the sweetest wine in my collection, as she had ascertained that I had no spirits to hand as a rescue remedy, then get myself some hot milk, again with some sweetening—I realised I had not told her that she had been a tremendous help. She was open and honest and chatty about herself after we had dealt with my discovery and shock. I asked her how she was so good at this and the answer came with a deep laugh. She had been a professional phone counsellor. The laugh was warmly reassuring. She said she was trying to place me. She knew my name from somewhere but I did not help. Curse my little PI socks. It was a sensible conversation as well. Alison would be asked to ring me as soon as she got in.

Soon after I put down the phone I heard a couple of cars race past my place, going north. No one goes that way at this time at that speed unless they are idiots or avoiding the ferry. The police? It is very much the long way round even if your intended destination is the coastal town north of here. And you wouldn't be speeding if you knew there was a series of hairpin bends two or three kilometres on. These cars were going too fast. The first one I didn't see, but the second was one of those souped-up six- or eight-cylinder numbers, with a heavy bass throb. A surfer's panel-van?

Alison rang. The ranger arrived, unlocked the toilet. The cops, according to Lenny, said, 'shit!' Among other swear words. They would not let him in. One went to call in details from his car. 'The reality,' said mother Alison, 'is quite different from the video games. He, all bravery and brutality in his head, suddenly needed his mummy and was scared. Glad to have his Mama.' The 'pigs' let her go after she had answered a few questions, a couple of which concerned me. She went back to get Tilly. The cops told Maria and company only that a girl had been found dead, and got their names and stuff. 'By the time we got to his dad's, it had become a story worth telling. His father was staying with his mother, Di Minogue, at Crossroads. Her house is full of extended family and supportive aunties who will listen to Lenny tell it over and over.' Alison raved on, as if the whole thing had been a buzz. I couldn't imagine her going to sleep. She sounded manic, and although she said she was concerned for Lenny and Tilly that was not how she had behaved. She had looked after me.

'Thanks,' I said, sincerely.

Natural curiosity wanted to know if anyone did it. Probably the girl committed suicide, but my intuition suggested dirty work in the background. If it turned out to be an overdose, whoever was at the barbecue will be under scrutiny.

'Who was still there?' I asked. Alison hesitated.

While her openness automatically took her off the suspect list, Alison confused me.

She replied, 'A few were staying overnight. Margot, you don't need to know this right now. It was a Spiders thing that turned into a bit of a fizzer. Gurls from the bush had camping stuff, tarpaulins, ground-sheets.'

Spiders is the name of the gay and lesbian coalition in the Campbell Valley and Paradise Coast. They organise dances, bush-walks, games, dog-shows, events and outings, and each year, prepare a float for the Mardi Gras in Sydney.

'Will they be there now?' I wanted to know, in case I felt like going down there later.

'I doubt it.' Alison snorted.

'There's a caravan park right there.'

'Fifteen dollars for a shower? No way. Not likely.' She laughed. 'It's not in their nature to pay. Just hoped the ranger wouldn't turn up. But, of course, he has.'

'Did you,' I began, 'happen to see a semi? In the parking area?' I finished, 'Anywhere?'

She answered very quickly, 'Nup. Why?' The police vehicles were banking up on the other side as she crossed on the ferry. My suspicions, my emotions, were way out of proportion with what I witnessed.

'Nothing.' There were actually too many questions, I could hardly expect

Alison to have the answers. It occurred to me, as we finished the conversation, that I could have been wrong; the glint of silver was probably just a big vehicle, a fisherman going on holiday.

To compound the distress of this upsetting night, shouting broke out among the hippies next door and was spilling into the yard. The language was foul. They were trying to get rid of someone. 'The fucking last ferry is going soon.' The violent words were masculine. The man's son from a previous liaison was a well-known trouble-maker. He was drunk. Maybe the father was too. Moonsunshine, Moo, will not remember a thing about it in the morning or she will deny that it was any big deal, just males working off their natural aggro to re-establish their karmic balance. I was about to go over and straighten them out when the boy suddenly left. His car skidded out onto the road and I watched its tail-lights go south.

All of a sudden, deadly silence. Unaccountably I burst into tears. Tears of fear and dread. And grief for the emptiness in some women, like Moonsunshine, who is simply not there, as if her self, her sense of being a person in her own right, had been annihilated for good. I was crying for the dead girl, too.

The stress drink I found was a beautifully rounded white port from the Rutherglen district in Victoria, wonderfully sweet without the slightest stickiness. I reached out for the bottle and noticed that I had already drunk a good third. I replaced the cork without pouring. Now to ease my nerves, as I warmed milk, I tried to believe it was possible she died of natural causes, not murder. Probably had too hot a shot. Jumping to conclusions offended my sense of logic. Without the fair play of evidence, proof, all one had was fabrication with no basis in fact or knowledge. I have to watch my imagination doesn't rush off into conjecture, which plays a role, sure, but not yet. I turned off the light as soon as I finished my Milo. I was nearly asleep when through the darkness my telephone belled like an alarm.

'Yes?' I answered the summons weakly.

'It's Meghan.' Her voice sounded very close. Meghan Featherstone was a client of mine. She had engaged me over the phone, from the recommendation of one of Broom's friends. We had not met yet. She sent her paperwork through the mail.

'Yes?' I repeated and looked down at the manila envelope which told me I needed a hair-cut. According to that she suspected someone was embezzling her money. But she did not mention it on the phone and I was too tired to ask.

'It's late, Meghan,' I addressed her thickly, formally.

'Margot. Would you like to meet my goats?' She sounded crazy, silly.

'Come over Tuesday. For tea.'

'What do you mean? What do you want?' I couldn't tell her what kind of a night I was having. 'Where are you?' I asked.

'Just off the Eyre Highway, in the Nullarbor Regional Reserve actually. The sky is so huge. The moon's magnificent but I can see the Seven Sisters.'

In the desert the moon would be bright. It would not be quite as late over there, but you'd think it would dominate the stars.

'Why? Why do you want me to see the goats?' Goats, I wrote under haircut. 'What are you talking about?'

'Just come and see my block. I'd like someone to meet you.' At least I think she said 'someone'. She may have meant herself, but that was an odd way of putting it.

To get to sleep again I picked up the closest thing to read, a magazine. 'Until recently, the Radiation Health Standing Committee of the National Health and Medical Research Council was responsible for setting Australia's standards and codes of practice in radiation safety.' Above that sentence was a map of the Maralinga Lands with small spots at Wewak and Taranaki where the clean-up of contaminated soils was taking place. Right near there was the Nullarbor Regional Reserve. Maybe Meghan was involved in that. I had not been told what this woman did. There were government payment slips and some from international companies. She may be a bloody nuclear physicist, an expert in the removal of plutonium from politically sensitive places to dump it in the outback where, according to the Europeans or Americans she probably works for, there is nothing. Did she work for the CIA? Eavesdropping? Spying, bugging communications bouncing off satellites, electro-magnetic waves flowing through the chemical gases . . . what do I know? She could be out there carbon-dating old bones.

Half-slept for about two hours then I couldn't go back to sleep, so I got up and began wandering around in the moonlit night, worrying about everything, why Broom left me, money problems, Sunday's triathlon, Chandra's voice, white face, sandy floor, streaky wall. Eventually, I went to bed.

The lone conspirator drives a lorry named White Virgin. It does not belong to him. Truckman surrounds himself with toys, gadgets. His cabin is spotless. Alongside the exhaust chimney, aerials of different shapes and intent point to the sky above the roof of the semi.

Ian Truckman is perpetually scared. He is afraid his boss will pull the truck one day and he will have no job and no pride. He has a computer terminal and a lap-sitting cyberman digital games controller shaped like women's breasts. He spent an entire year figuring out how to do it, but now he can do it. He can access the superhighway from the bitumen road. He has equipment to detect strange radio waves which may or may not (he keeps an open mind) indicate the presence of UFOs in the area he is traversing. Sometimes it is difficult to discern the static as he keeps his Citizens Band on at all times. In case. As well as monitoring extraterrestrial activity, he visits pornography sites because he does not want to be a man who is out of touch. He has opinions. For instance, when up to a million Internet users worldwide who downloaded pornography from a website lost thousands in telephone charges, he knew it was a feminist scam.

Ian is driving at exactly one hundred and five kilometres an hour. Dreaming. As soon as his head starts doing that he needs a coffee. He stops when he sees a line of semi-trailers parked in the verge. There he knows the walls will be decorated with mighty vehicles and blokes will be sitting inside. Before he leaves the semi-trailer he circles his load, checking everything.

The girl is there to serve him within seconds of his sitting down.

'Just coffee, love. Thick black, plenty of sugar.' Other truckers are discussing the bush. And pollution.

'Got a mate with cattle out in the scrub. Might turn up in the burning season. Give him a hand,' Truckman says, getting into the conversation with his bit.

The blokes keep talking. 'Up North they call it "shark shit",' explains the knowledgeable one. 'Putrid black muck.'

'No kidding?'

'That,' says the know-all who likes to chat, 'is the rugged farm term for the tonnes of the stuff which covers 600,000 hectares of prime agricultural land along the NSW coast.'

'How many acres is that?'

'Dunno, about a million.'

'Yeah, a million I reckon.'

'Heard about that stuff,' puts in Ian. 'It is basically pure battery acid which bleeds from cane field drains and farm canals. It causes periodic large scale fish-kills.'

'Farmers don't piss me off, developers do,' opines the big talker. 'They scrape the soil off too deep when they're grading. They have some kind of laser thing.'

'That's because they can't build properly any more. Everything's on a cement slab nowadays,' his mate adds irrelevantly.

'What I hate is these Yankee names.'

'Canisteo Bayou?' asks Ian Truckman, who recently passed that name.

'They call it canal development,' the know-all explains.

'Lovely, it is,' says his mate. 'You just step outside your back door along your own wharf straight into your fishing boat. The mother-in-law is rattling about in a bloody mansion.'

'Like fishing, do you?' Ian contributes, ready to talk angling his entire coffee break.

'Never get time, mate. Never have a holiday. The wife's old man died not six months after they built the bloody thing. And she's a pain in the neck, to put it mildly.'

Ian drains his coffee and he nods goodbye. It is eerily navy-blue outside. He has to make a call. Busy. Can't make this call from his own phone, has to be anonymous. Second try, the other end picks up. He puts down the receiver without speaking. Those were his orders. He visits the rest room and walks across the road to White Virgin gleaming ghostly pale in the still queue of darker vehicles.

Ian Truckman checks his Conspiracy Theory bulletin board before he presses the clutch and gets into gear. 'Flying saucers chase me down the road, hovering like a hover-craft a couple of metres about the tarmac,' he told a bloke once. The arsehole laughed. So now he shares his fears with like-minded folk on the World Wide Web.

He pours himself a glass from his iced water container and downs his no-sleep pills. The engine purrs, warming up. He reads about listening to *John Wesley Harding* backwards. He isn't sure about that, but he puts on *Highway 61 Revisited*. Bob Dylan sings 'Ballad of a Thin Man'. Ian considers the fact that John Lennon was murdered by a cabal comprising the CIA, MI5 and the aliens who escaped after the Roswell incident, and logs out. He looks in his rear-vision mirrors before easing the rig out onto the road.

The boss likes him because he is neat, on time and strict about the road rules.

2

. . . the shape of breasts . . .

In the catchment of the Campbell River water springs from the earth in trickles, finds ways to the creeks, which fall to the tributaries eagerly. Lesser rivers join the flow through flatter farmland then to break up into the delta of the estuary near the sea. Deep in the rainforest, high in the Great Dividing Range, where the rocks drip, Virginia White forces out of wood the shape of breasts. The uprooted tree lies on a steep slope to the creek. The upper branches overhang the stream. Twigs and leaves have long gone. All that is left is the trunk, once hollowed out in a bushfire, thick limbs and rearing lateral roots black with age and red with clay. The only path to this log is the one made by Virginia herself.

When she discovered the magic, mossy root system soaring from the ground like a chapel wall in a slightly different dimension, she returned to it time and again to gaze and enjoy a moment of magnetism. Until she climbed up onto the mighty trunk she could not understand the allure and why her gazing was not like meditation. Not peaceful at all. An impatience overwhelmed her. The timber had fallen out of the snigging jaws of the loggers' equipment in the days when the old-growth trees were huge. A lumberjack had died when this giant slid down the sheer descent into Deadman's Creek. There was enough wood in it to make a house, or a fortune in fine furniture.

The root-wall is a gateway, for Virginia, into a world, forbidden to the physical body, the breathing now of vertical time.

The day she carried her adze to this spot was shot through with inspiration. The red cedar was begging to be brought back to life as art. Chopping away, she cleaned, scraped, cut to find the hidden form. Lightning entered her veins. This work she must do: uncover the sculpture beneath the extraneous growth, decay and mud to find the permanent beneath the temporal. The seasons, the weather, fires and the industry of ants change the surface.

There is no going back from her blind journey of discovery. When she embarks the bush around her is a sea; the part-hewn log, an island, or a ship. Surrender to the super-normal knowledge buried within has her in thrall.

Virginia White is driven by some kind of karmic pressure, an under-standing that she must do the inexplicable. She is a long way away from the galleries and sculpture parks. The rainforest is her studio. She has no commission. No one will pay her. No one wants her to do this work. Yet she feels an exigency. Patrons with all the power and none of the talent are on her back, hounding her with deadlines and demands. Logically, intellectually, it makes no sense to be so obsessed. Except in the metaphor that the practice of art is an expedition to the continent of the mind where truth is beauty and beauty truth. The joy of creation is not the emotion she feels. Travail, rather. Consciousness of toil is what she is aware of as she carefully uncovers with axe, chisel and sharp knife what the old buttressed trunk contains. Female forms. One with the head of a horse. Where the truncated branches are, near the abrupt rockface of the creek, figures arch like archers.

Virginia is not averse to abstract sculpture but this gigantic piece must be realistic enough to tell its story. Hours, days, months now at work on the log reveal figures, possible weapons, a line of oars, instruments, the curve of a hull, the fold of cloth. Sometimes but a second before she gouges she sees what is coming, perhaps a piece of sail, a boom. She does not know. She must retain so much faith, so much discipline, she is in constant control of her wild ego, her impatience.

This Friday she works close to the base with some of the root and some above-ground tree where it is harder to determine what will emerge. The breasts seem to be pendulous but the character is not standing. Nor is the weight of a woman upon them though they hang as if she is lying on her belly. Nor are there arms to take the load. The breasts are not pendulous, they are tight, young, conical. It is a riddle. It is a monster. No neck. The head of a beast. She carves out five curling tresses. She moves away to attack it from another direction, behind, and finds crouching back legs; a dog, a large, muscular dog. Then she realises it is too chunky for the canine and the tail is all wrong. She is distracted and informed by the etheric, the esoteric, she must trust her body, her hands, the hemisphere of her brain that has no words. It is difficult. She goes off for lunch. Up before dawn and not necessarily early to bed, Virginia rests in the middle of the day. The light is better for books then, also. She reads through her siesta.

In the afternoon the waxing moon rides a clear blue sky. She strides back up the hill.

Instead of addressing the whole as she usually does, she dives straight into the detail she had worked in the morning. She knows now the whole is a boat with a female crew, most life-sized. She ignores appreciation of what has happened for her already because she is curious. The corner of the hindquarter settles her as she shapes it and the snake-like tail. When she is returning from a dip in the creek, climbing up the fallen tree, she spies what she has carved, the sphinx. She is finding a sphinx. She barks a laugh at the obvious and the ironic. The riddle all the time was the riddle itself. Chiselling the tassel of the tail takes the rest of the day.

At night, in candlelight, she looks up her books. Barbara Walker informs her: 'This glyph was . . . "the Lions of Yesterday and Today"'. Traditionally a monster, Mary Daly suggests, the sphinx 'invites us to Realise expanding Integrity, Harmony, Splendor of form/forms across Time and Space'. Virginia is gratified but not ecstatic at the possibility that someone else may understand what she does in another place at another time. She muses, all very well, but it doesn't dispel the lonely weight of obligation. Her friends consider her work a ridiculous pursuit, a hobby.

Although it is the most important piece she has ever attempted, she expects few ever to see it. The power of the process of uncovering, not making, is simply hers. The creative act a daily need for revelation. The inner and outer exercise makes her feel in control, feel capable of taking on all comers, an isolated happiness in the security of a hermit soul.

But Virginia White is in love with a woman in town.

The masked owl screeches and barking owls scream like humans. Ghosts are there for the feeling in the crying of the night. The bush is full of noises. Murderous sounds for the noctiphobic, Frogmouth ooms and nightjar grates, widow-makers fall like cannon-fire and crowns detach like pistol shots. Amid the galloping horses of butchering bushrangers, settler-women sing lullabies from Scotland. The past is alive in the present, Indigenous children play in the streams. Many gurls hear and see beyond the material plane for the first time in their lives when they stay on Lesbianlands. Whether with wonder or terror, either way, their knowledge of themselves as sentient beings is enriched. While money grows on trees and threatened species thrive, utopia it is not.

Hope Strange watches a spacecraft hover and land.

* * *

Gig is lazy and easy-going. She lives near the road on the lower part of Lesbianlands. Gregarious and hospitable, she loves women because they are not men, and generally accepts them all. Hope materialises out of the bush. It is the first time Gig has seen her. So she looks her up and down: slim, tanned, bald, about twenty-one; bare feet, ankle strap, bandanna round her forehead.

'None of it makes sense, no sense at all,' Hope says, crazily. Instead of sitting on the ground, Hope stands on the silver-grey log fencing the upper area around Gig's caravan, which has a roof and rudimentary verandah. Long grass in clumps hides the wheels. Her campfire is out in the open. Wood-chocks mark her kitchen.

'Everything is so unfair. How dare they dynamite our sacred site?' Hope goes on.

'That was a widow-maker falling,' Gig says. 'Happens all the time. They say this land made lots of widows. Which is cool with me.' Gig is not exactly blissed to have this mad visitor in her camp. But she rolls a smoke and pokes the fire under the billy. She has been away. Hope has come in the meantime, and she might as well listen for a while. 'I'm Gig, by the way.'

Hope is distracted by listening to the words in her own head as she speaks. 'The practising fascist contacted me again. That is to say, while he continues to be a fascist, he is no longer a practising father. But he'll bomb the shitter out of enemy craft from outer space. He'd love that.'

Gig hears her jabber, and recognises the particular madness: annihilation as a result of sexual abuse as a child. Many clever women come here with this experience. It results in a very personal hatred of men. 'Is he in the army?'

Hope nods, 'Chaplain.'

Gig sighs, 'My grandfather did it, dead in his grave now. I'd happily dance on it, if I knew where it was.'

'So gravely the dead are gone. Our father which art in heaven shall not be appeased. No pleasing him,' Hope comments, as she crouches, less like a highly strung deer but just as ready to spring into flight.

'Last time I saw him, he was so old and weak. The picture of innocence. He had dribbles on his chin that Granny wiped away with her hankie.' Gig repeats a story many times told.

And Hope continues raving, so both are speaking at the same time. Overlapping voices, concurrent silences. 'It is not good for me, this is not good for me. She took my passport from my head. I left it in my dresser. Snappy dresser, wasn't he? They love their polished boots and knife-blade pleats, the fascists do.'

Gig begins tidying things. 'Calm down,' she says. 'It was only a tree falling. It wasn't your father attacking the aliens last night.'

'Gig, Gig, listen to me,' Hope pleads. Then quotes: '"And to the woman were given two wings of a great eagle, that she might fly into the wilderness, into her place, where she is nourished for a time, and times, and half a time, from the face of a serpent."' Hope grins, 'Had to learn the Bible after he did it. Off by heart. My fault. I must be cleansed by the word of the Lord.'

'Let me guess.' Gig pauses in her slow housework. 'Your dad was a preaching hypocrite.' Gig fists her hands to her hips, akimbo, ready to discuss abusing men. 'Projecting his guilt onto you. Wasn't your fault, girl.'

Hope goes off on a tangent. 'She is hiding things. I'm telling you the truth. Someone took my passport so that I cannot escape. I haven't forgotten I know. What is it I haven't forgotten?'

Gig answers, 'You've forgotten to eat for days.' She studies Hope sharply, 'So it is you who has been stealing from other women's camps?'

'No, not me,' says Hope. And quotes again, '"I saw it was a sea of glass mingled with fire . . ."'

'Come on, own up? That's okay. We just like to know.' Gig explains, 'Like, if it's a matter of need, cool.'

'No no no.'

'Greed's another thing, see?' Gig cares about this distinction.

'Fire is the element of the devil. I saw two women on horseback and a dog with four legs on three legs. They smiled at one another. At the blast. You don't believe me.' Hope sounds hopeless as she starts to go. She has on a vest which her tanned thin shoulders swim inside. She arrived from nowhere, was the report, with a one-person tent and several packets of dried food. Plump, enthusiastic, young and too keen.

'You have to get it together and find your way home,' Gig decides, shaking her head. The fawn-like gurl backs away from her, the rag around her waist Gig recognises as someone else's scarf.

Hope steps forward menacingly. 'I have nowhere to go, but here. I have burnt my bridges. I came to a women's community, Amazons together in the wilderness, but what are you? A bunch of derelicts, with no spirituality at all. None.'

Gig gets tough. 'You are not the first woman who has come here expecting us to solve all your problems. You come to Lesbianlands wanting love, wanting women—because we are not men—to be perfect, to be your priest, to be your psychiatrist, to be your mother. But here, actually, you have to hold your own, give and take. Sure, we're all mad, but we're not all psychotic. Apart from giving you a lift to town, I can't help you.'

'You are rejecting me. "And them that had gotten the victory over the beast, and over his mark, and over his image, and over the number of his name, stand on the sea of glass."'

Gig watches as she goes to her woodpile and picks up her double-headed axe to put it under cover. Hope disappears up the track. Although Gig does nothing but think about it, the exchange affects her. She studies the she-oak in front of her. It is intriguingly rough. She imagines she sees faces drawn in the shadows of its grainy ridges. With the clouds overhead moving fast, she stares for a long while at changing expressions in the bark. Out on the plain, cooees and dogs' barking indicate the proximity of her friends. Self-obsession is a sickness, a transmissible disease in these parts, she opines. She walks to the creek with two empty buckets.

A white, late-model, long-wheelbase Toyota LandCruiser, white with toplights and primary red and blue decoration to broadcast the might of the law, cruised into my yard at seven-thirty a.m. As the copper parked, I kept stretching, taking my mind through the stiff areas as if it were a healing laser beam, warming my joints with inner heat. Focused, I stayed a moment in stillness at each sore spot while attention worked its cure. My body is my meal ticket. I would have to be a busy private eye, or a corrupt one, to make as much money at it as I do as a sponsored athlete. The few sportsmen who make a grotesque amount of money could fund a thousand dedicated scientists, I read recently. Quickly I touched my toes then responded to the knock on my front door.

'My my, keen dees,' I joked. Plain clothes, CID. He was alone.

The young detective did not look as ignorant as some. He shook my hand, said, 'Margot Gorman? Detective Constable Phillip Philippoussis.'

'Coffee?' I offered.

'Do you make Turkish?' he asked, wistfully.

'As if I would!' I led the way to my kitchen table.

My nose told me he and I were going to get along. Chemistry. I gave him a matey nickname. 'Do you play tennis, Pip?' I was trying to lighten up. 'Or do they call you Phil?' I showed him the fresh grounds and said, 'You make it how you like it.'

'Squash. Soccer, of course.' He shrugged. 'Phil,' he yawned.

He spooned heaps of coffee from the gold espresso packet I handed him into a mug from the sink and put a small amount of boiling water on it, resulting in a kind of mud that he thickened with sugar. We sat.

'You look as if you've been up all night,' I said.

'I have,' he affirmed. As I squeezed out my tea-bag and put it in the compost he talked. 'There was a fatality last night, on this road, as well as the death in the toilet block.'

Nodding, I glanced north.

Phil continued, 'I came over first ferry after logging in details throughout the small hours. I got a bit of shut-eye with my head on the desk.' He sipped at the sturdy rim of my Virgo mug as if it were a demi-tasse. 'Used to do it in the library all the time. Crowded house, my mother's terrace in Marrickville.'

We might as well get to know each other, I thought. Let him take his time. 'Did you get into policing after a bit of tertiary study? Are you a serious guy, perhaps?' The DC smiled artlessly.

Phil was polite and down to business after revealing some of his personal life. He must have checked on me while burning the midnight oil. He didn't say, but I could tell, there had to be a reason for the respect he showed me apart from the instant rapport. He noted my version of events in perfect shorthand. I was impressed. There may have been Greek letters in there, but no English except names. Pip was at ease in his body, at ease with me. I returned him the favour.

'Did you interview the gurls?' I asked.

He raised an eyebrow as if I were being politically incorrect, and queried, 'Women?'

Detective Constable Philippoussis, new to the area, straight and bilingual, did not twig to the word, gurls, hinterland dykes, according to local mythology, bare-breasted, knife-toting sheilas, but it won't be long before it is in his vocabulary.

'One of the new breed, are you, Phil? One would hope a stiff breeze is blowing through the NSW Police Force, rattling the windows and clearing out cobwebs, showing up corrupt coppers for what they really are. Maybe I am marked in the file as a potential whistle-blower?' Somehow he had put me on the back foot and I chatted nervously, still a bit shaken. Still premenstrual.

'I don't mind,' he confided as he drank the rest of his coffee. Ate would be a better word.

'Cleanskins might not be as universally disliked as in the old days.' This boy was a bright new penny, not guarded through fear of exposure; naturally arrogant.

As thorough as I would have been, he asked a few things about my surroundings, what was it like to live here, anything strange, and so on. Although he was tired, although he was into his job, he had all the time in the world, displaying, to me, the inquisitive patience of the natural detective.

'This broken-down cottage was quite expensive for what it is. So, plainly, the developers' plans to make a big bridge are seen by the market to be viable. For the moment, though, it is pretty wild. The dunes are saddened by bitou bush weed which native banksias try to struggle through.' I talked freely. 'There is a long stretch of National Park further north. Birds, frogs, even emu.'

'The Pacific Ocean, with all those rips breaking at acute and changing angles to the beach, would be too dangerous for most swimmers,' he commented.

Grinning, I said, 'I love it when the dolphins surf the waves.'

We got up and I showed him round. My house has a skinny verandah at the front with a door in the middle and a punching bag down the end near a neat shelf for hand weights and ab-frame. The internal walls are the same as the outside ones, vertical timber: inch-thick tongue-and-groove mixed Australian hardwoods. To the left as you enter is the big lounge-room; on the right, my bedroom. The kitchen, bathroom and laundry are all doorless behind the big room, opposite which are two cubes of space. Cubbyholes, each has a tiny window facing north. I've cleaned out one. 'My temporary office,' I explained. The other is my storage room. 'The closed-in back verandah was crowded with bunks and junk. A pair of those long gum-boots with braces fishermen wear angling for tailor from the shoreline hung from a nail I couldn't reach for months and swung in the breeze from the louvre-windows like a suicide.' The bedroom has french doors opening onto the east. 'My friends helped me to put them in,' I boasted.

We walked outside. Out the back is a large chook-house, silvered by age. 'Did the holiday-makers bring their chooks with them for the summer? Or did people live here full time in the Depression eating fish and eggs?' I asked his opinion.

'Fresh eggs,' Philippoussis reckoned, as he inspected inside.

'I am at present remodelling it,' I explained, following. The roosting area is like a hay-loft in a dairy in miniature with a higher pitched roof, like a squat tower.

'Cute,' he said.

'I have an acre of land,' I responded to a question which hadn't exactly been asked. He just stood surveying, listening. The loo is thirty paces from the back door along a narrow, winding path of cement. It has a pitched roof, too. The house does not. 'It is as if they have tried to lower the roof of the house so that it doesn't blow off in an easterly gale. Maybe the original one did blow off. Anyway,' I was in full swing. He had opened the floodgates. The house has a flat roof with hardly any slope at all with one long side and one short side. The long side has a strip of guttering feeding into a fresh-water tank, the short side has no guttering at all. The tap has a handsome bronze lever, so close to the ground it hardly fits a nine-litre bucket under it. We strolled around the yard. There is a 1950s tubular steel car port, free-standing plumb in the middle of the drive-way. The police vehicle was parked behind my Suzuki Sierra, almost bumper to bumper.

'My two sets of neighbours are completely different from one another. The old couple come about once a month to mow their acre with a ride-on he brings on a trailer,' I informed as we walked along my northern boundary.

'Herbert's conversation entirely comprises the progress of development. Elsie never talks. She just nods when he looks at her. To be able to do this she must keep her eyes on him all the time.'

'Strange,' opined Philippoussis. Herbert and Elsie have a roller door enclosing their sea-side, shutting off their front door and picture window, and one and only verandah.

'On my southern side are "alternatives",' I said, turning one hundred and eighty degrees. Honeysuckle covered the fence.

Together we proceeded to examine their paddock which is a field study in noxious weeds: lantana, thistle, ink-weed, fire-weed, Paterson's curse, morning glory, Spanish passionfruit, and madeira vine.

'It's a wonder Council don't get onto them,' said the policeman, looking at the climbers creeping over their outhouses and machinery wrecks.

'I want to kill this,' I took a flower, sucked out the sweetness and threw it away. 'But I am afraid of the consequences.'

Phil commented on the idiosyncratic nature of their house, which is mud-brick, pole timber and stained glass, all unfinished. Untidy.

'When they are here, they are noisy. The bloke has a beard, a pony-tail and no hair on top. He sanctimoniously declares all green is good, but he's basically too cowardly to chain himself up a tree. She wears dresses that drip below her knees and seems to have worn them for so long she is comfortable in nothing else. Style, in terms of cut and fit, non-existent. The number of kids around varies. I haven't got a handle on which exactly are theirs, theirs together or individually. Often other adults are with them. Sometimes they come only for the day. At other times, teenage boys are there by themselves. When the family stays overnight, she is usually hysterical by bed-time. To my face, she is as sweet as something sticky. One day when I asked was she all right she actually denied she had screamed. Although the sound had torn the night apart, she lied to my face. A tragedy waiting to happen if it didn't actually happen last night. Her name is Moonsunshine, Moo, for short. His is Jim or Jack or John, no, I forget. Jerry? I must stop myself at times,' I confessed to the cop. 'I get obsessed with getting the names of things right.'

'So what happened there last night?' He thrust the question like a swordsman making a hit after softening up the opponent. I didn't care if I dobbed in my southern neighbours and told him of the argument I had heard and the cars speeding up the corrugated road. Although Pip was going to be my man in the shop, I held back the solid evidence. The horrid cap. I had to meditate on its vibes and my paranoia. I could say I forgot it.

'The ones to the north,' I added, 'were not there last night.' He nodded and looked across at the dusty brown Volvo parked on the grass and said he would go and interview Moo and Jim.

'Expect lies, Pip,' I nearly said, but grinned, realising that they were probably drying a crop somewhere.

'Greenies are they?' he asked.

'That would be a matter of opinion. Hippies, alternatives, new agers.' I did not want to get too far into my attitude to passive-aggressive men who keep their women barefoot and pregnant.

Before he left, I made an appointment to formally sign my statement and told him to get some sleep.

DC Philippoussis drove the vehicle out of my yard and into next door. To get away from the temptation to be curious I took myself on a stroll through the paperbarks, stopping, stretching, listening to the birds. It was not a morning I needed the sort of high I get from pain. I had to think, be gentle with myself, although my verbal diarrhoea had worked out some of the stress.

3

. . . slicing at the head of a Moor . . .

The Shire of Paradise Coast is between the mountain range and the sea. River valleys and wetlands, lakes and bays, plateaus and escarpments, pockets of old-growth eucalypt and rainforest, koala habitat corridors, dairy farms, banana plantations, fisheries, timber industry rapidly giving way to the encroachment of tar and cement, bigger roads and beautifying palm trees. The development of brick veneer block-shapes, handsome villas, holiday flats and housing estates suggests increased population is changing the rural nature of the district. Craftspeople ply their wares at monthly markets. Oyster-farmers lease room in the estuaries for their racks. Both deep-sea fishing and fresh waterways offer recreation for tourists. There are seven lawn-bowling rinks. Resort-managers do well, if they don't over-extend their credit. Retirement villages are popular, with locked gates and serviced apartments. While there are mansions, there is also the highest concentration of unemployed youth in the country. Wealthy jet-setters pass through the Paradise Coast. Aborigines have succeeded in claiming some land back. Illegal immigrants could be, perhaps, forgiven for thinking they could disappear into the march of nomadic travellers.

Meanwhile, up-country, bush-folk stubbornly stick to seasonal habits learnt at their grandfathers' knees.

The exclusive romance with the challenging Broomhilda changed me. I cannot explain now why I had my head shorn. I no longer have long, straight, fair hair, and never will again. Keep it short. Styled when I feel like it. Dyed when I feel like it. I have a loyal hairdresser, or rather she has a loyal client. My muscles are hard, veins prominent. I am five foot eight. I wax off my body-hair.

In the Paradise Coast Pictorial Directory, my ad reads: 'Need a helping hand? Have a problem? Appropriate jobs accepted with discretion', and my phone number. Most of my employment, though, comes through word of mouth. If a male calls, I dismiss him with a single sentence. The simple believable fib, poetic in its perfection, is one of my stocks in trade. When someone asks me to do their ironing I say I'm too busy, but I've found often a woman needing domestic aid has a deeper problem. Usually I can tell from tone of voice whether I will listen, and I have done the odd spot of ironing. I can't think if I sit still, doing nothing.

Although I don't call myself a feminist PI or a lesbian detective, my rule in regard to clients is, I will not take on a job for a man. This is trickier than it sounds. As soon as you set something up for women only, some man makes it his life work to infiltrate. Does he do it for all men? A sole conspirator. I had one show up later, to smirk. I shake my head in wonderment at the duplicity of the woman who fronted for him. On that occasion, I took the money and said to myself, learn your lesson, Margot.

Ultimately I will discover the truth. It's a matter of practical application, examining the detail of each case and generalising often enough to remain sane. I'm a born blood-hound.

The phone rang. It was Lisa's mother. A regular client.

'Now at sixteen she is hateful, a criminal. I try to love my daughter, but she hates me,' she said.

'No, she doesn't,' I put in. But I don't think she heard me.

'I have my own needs. I need reassurance that I am doing good. She is my proof. I am defined as a mother. I am a failure. A sorry failure at that.'

She carried on, despite my denials.

'My Balmain bugs with coconut sauce make your mouth water. Where are they now? All over the floor.' Right, so they had had a fight. 'Her dark eyes haunt me,' she continued. 'They go black with accusation, as if I did anything, anything at all, to deserve it, except be a mother and be stuck in the endless ping-pong game between work at work and work at home. Then I feel guilty.'

'Where is the naughty girl now?' If she was not at home, I would have to go out and find her.

'Grooving in her bedroom. As if nothing's happened. Listen,' she continued. 'I bought her a computer. You see I think they need them these days. There was no way she wasn't getting the best start, the best chance I could give her, after the treatment she received from her father, if it wasn't quite physical abuse, it was certainly emotional abuse, and that was after I left him. The computer sat in its box in her room for weeks. All she needed to do was open it and set it up and say thanks. It cost me nearly a month's salary all up.'

How they hate the youth today, I thought.

'In the end,' she went on. 'I was begging her to unpack it and set it up. I was pathetic. Last weekend she did. She just suddenly did. And she did it quickly and efficiently and taught me the basics. And in our joint enthusiasm, was she playing me along? I ask myself. She demanded that I buy the Internet software, modem and get on-line. It was such a ray of sunshine I did it the next day and put it all on Visacard, and she said, "Cool," as coolly as you can. So again I was begging. We were surfing the Internet together, until I got hooked and she said, "Gawd, Mum".'

I began doing crouches waiting for her to get to the point.

'I moved it by myself to the sunroom, which is a whimsical word for where the ironing board is, some cane furniture and a north-facing window.'

'Oh oh,' I murmured.

'Yes, she did not like that!'

'She'll get over it,' I advised. 'If you can only afford one computer, she'll have to share it.'

'I suppose you are right. Thanks, Margot. For listening. I'm better now I've got it off my chest.'

Before Lisa's mother put down the phone, I said, 'Pick the bugs up and give them a wash. Don't waste them.'

When I turned up in Stuart on a push-bike with panniers, as soon as I swung my leg over the bar and let my long hair down from under the helmet, outside the local Greeks' greasy, I was addressed in formal German. 'What?' I replied, in broad Strine. Then she spoke to me in faultless formal English. The construction was sweet, the accent thick. She had a beautiful smile. My heart was in the palm of her hand by the time I had finished my toasted tomato sandwiches.

Broomhilda and I shared a yearning for the intrinsic relationship of nature and woman. I adored her body and the way she talked. Her revolt against mainstream society was eccentric. Not to say idiosyncratic: a kind of environmentalism and anti-racism mixed with an artless assumption that she herself was of a superior race. She would deny it on an ethnic basis but claim it as a woman-loving-woman. Her contempt for blokes made me laugh, mostly. She placed gurls at the extreme left of the political spectrum. Green concerns and outrage on behalf of the indigenous as well as a sense of injustice against the poor cloaked a more amorphous disenfranchisement, that of white women in Western society, which made Broom restless, scattered, exciting. Sometimes, movingly sad. Lesbian ethics, she said, was her philosophy. I wish she practised what she preached. Straight into the deep end; drama from day one. She was not, as I, unattached.

Nor was I, in this instance, going to walk away. My lesbianism was as fresh as a ruby cicada taking in life after the shell. My legs were brown and muscled, my hair bleached by the sun, my eyes very blue in contrast to the golden tan of my face. Ready for a new life, I exuded happiness from every pore. Broomhilda's real name is more Wagnerian than that. *The goddess is dancing* is written on the bumper of her car. Funnily enough, work fell into my lap soon after our affair began.

Within days Broom's friends had picked me as a cop. I had to come clean. 'I was,' I said, 'but not any more.'

Anke eyed me through narrowed lids and proposed that I help her fix up her immigration as she wanted to work and needed a tax file number. She had no legal status. In short, my first PI work was against the law, using my knowledge and expertise to achieve the illegal, successfully. It was a good job, well done. Not only did I get paid, I got respect, too. After that the work started pouring in. I managed to set up a moral framework for myself which runs a sort of parallel course to the law. The law stands there like command-ments, a big stick and a big oaf, and reality is over here in a different light, in subtler shades of grey. But I loved solving things, being surreptitious when I have to be, not because I believe the law is right and I am guilty; I just want to get the facts exact. Legislators pass whatever they want if they have the numbers. The law. Then it depends. You would not want to get too dependent on the moral standards of your law enforcement officers.

There are laws and lores.

Dykes in this district vary from those living in complete secrecy to those who flaunt their sexual preferences on the streets. We have your wealthy land-owning, wine-loving couples, your 'gays', your queers who prepare arty floats with the queens for the Mardi Gras in Sydney each March, your Christians seriously going about their ministry, your regular employed types, both in and out of the closet, your man-haters, refuge-workers, your anarchists, your bald girls with language, your tattooed types with attitude, your disaffected politicos, your genuine feminist radicals, your Koori and your hippie dykes, your thugs and your drunks. And the feral rebel gurls. In this area, as well, there are many women, not lesbians, who have plenty of cause not to trust the law. The local policeman, say, is a friend of their wife-abusing husband. The magistrate, maybe, is a child molester himself. There are women caught in the double-speak of social workers, priests, husbands, brothers, uncles, bank managers, fathers and lawyers. Their initial problems grow right up like Jack's beanstalk as they discover the binds they are really in. Too often the best scenario is they have been ripped off financially. I work, primarily, for women. Like Lisa's mother.

My poofter trainer, Sean rang, confirming our engagement for tonight. We are going to the Orlando dance. He will dress me in skin-tight bright

ORLANDO BALL

Come dressed up in the fantasy
you desire

Choose your gender!

Be in whatever bit of history/herstory
you want

Be free Be imaginative Be there

SATURDAY

Sunset / Moonrise

at Port Water Surf Club

colours to look like a jester. Not hard as I have a selection of lurid lycra to stand out on the highways. A fluorescent cyclist for the amusement of the kings of the road; would be if they weren't humourless and I wasn't scared.

My guide, my desert auntie, told me, with Scorpio rising, I should pursue the career of detecting because it would further my karmic path in this life. I don't have a private investigator's licence. As far as official income is concerned I am a professional triathlete, investments, savings and sponsorship monies from sports clothing companies, soap, breakfast cereals, fast food industry. I put in a perfect tax return each year. I am honest but I say what honest is. While people may use amnesia as an excuse, for instance, and get off in the court system, scot-free, someone is paying the price. I'm tough on accountability.

Take it easy before the dance, Margot. Hang around the house. Is the Nadir Mining Services Cap a real clue? Yes, I had taken something from the crime scene, but I could not let it disappear into department evidence-bags under lock and key, not until I understood something.

Spiders, the Paradise Coast gay and lesbian coalition, puts on a theme dance every three months. Fliers in the mailbox, stuck on refrigerator doors, in café windows, pasted on lamp-posts, all over the district the feeling among same-sex couples and singles is this is the do to go to. A real chance to fancy dress. Although the head-master does not know it, the new drama teacher at the High School is a gay activist. Giving energy as a way of getting to know people in the district, and building a life here, he puts his all into publicity, decor and costuming. This time, Spiders has really tried to involve their female membership equally. Even Hazel McDonald and Daisy Sweet are determined to enjoy themselves at least once a year. While Daze is reasonably recognisable as Romaine Brookes, Haze makes Radcliffe Hall look more like Gertrude Stein.

Couples in drag get into their cars. Gurls from the bush come out of the hills. Even Ilsa treats her peerless skin with fresh aloe vera and takes her tights and heeled high-shoes out of the closet. Gays make masks. Hermit crabs emerge from under their rocks.

Virginia wears her best black jeans to town. And her R. M. Williams elastic-sided riding boots. Cybil Crabbe is taking her miniature poodle, Puddles, on a diamanté lead, a touch which matches her decorative dress from Costume Hire and Rental. While copies of the video *Orlando* are being watched by gays and lesbians throughout the district, Virginia White reads the book by Virginia Woolf.

> Orlando—for there could be no doubt of his sex, though fashion of the time did something to disguise it—was in the act of slicing at the head of a Moor which swung from the rafters.

The thin paperback, having travelled with her through all her moves since the age of eighteen is now yellowed at the edge of the pages. The spine has held firm. Glad of the excuse, Virginia, lying on Cybil's lounge in the afternoon, hungrily devours the literature. The fiction.

'English,' Virginia White tells Cybil, 'has a lot to answer for. My twin brother, Jeff, the nuclear physicist, told me, it is the universal language of science and his colleagues from all over the world speak it. But they do not necessarily understand each other. Jeff runs marathons.'

'Tonight,' says Cybil, 'you will look exactly like him.'

Virginia laughs. 'No I won't. Jeff looks like Abe Lincoln, now he is fifty, stringy and tall, with his stiff hair and jutting beard!'

Virginia reads aloud the first sentence of *Orlando*. Then says, 'So English, Woolf's work,' and feels the power of many in her blood. She wants to be back at work in the wilderness, discovering. But it's okay to go out and have a good time, especially as Cybil is so excited. She glances up at the clean, ironed smock on the coat-hanger and the french beret.

Underground, not exactly buried, some Amazons hold on to the thread of existence in the maze of catacombs and caves beneath the Western world, to erupt at points of corruption and decadence in civilisation and flow onto the surface to proclaim the simple dictum: we are. Women warriors laying down lines to each other, marshalling forces, are gathering strength.

Rory happens to own an old-fashioned pair of khaki jodhpurs, flared at the thigh, bought at an op-shop. A brown leather bomber jacket and swimming goggles pushed up into her ginger hair complete her outfit.

Writing a long overdue letter to Auntie, I told her: 'We have town water, electricity and telephone. Sewerage septic tanks. There are several new brick houses clustered around the punt-port. The car ferry glides back and forth across the river on the simple pulley system of a submarine cable. If I go the long way around, which requires negotiating plenty of bends meandering over a couple of creek-bridges, I do not have to take the ferry. It's an extra hour into town, though.'

Auntie I met in the Kimberley, after I rode half-way round Australia. She could have been older than seventy, or younger. So tanned was she you could hardly see the scar on her face. We were introduced at Fitzroy Crossing where we were both staying at the hostel owned by the Ngar community there.

Her Landrover was covered in dust and mounted with tanks for water and petrol. She had been travelling for years, a geriatric gypsy, at home in the caravan parks and around campfires in remote areas. I'd set up a new off-road bike in Broome for my trip across the Top End. I rode to Derby on the sealed surface. I wanted to go to Tunnel Creek and Windjana Gorge. It was hard going on the rutted red road, the pindan soil got into my sinuses and the corners of my eyes. I was just about to admit defeat, luggage my bike and go by bus when I met her.

This grey nomad was an easy talker who seemed to listen and nod as she spoke. Auntie was prepared to take me to where I wanted to go: Gibb River Road, Napier Downs, King Leopold Ranges. Geikie Gorge. She turned me inside out and gave me an airing as if I were a stale sleeping bag. With my bike and gear on her roof-rack, we spent a few days together around the gorges of the Devonian Reef, swimming in its streams and exploring places of geological and tourist interest.

This character told me, 'You mustn't daydream, Margot. Your life is about crystallisation.'

In the shade at Tunnel Creek with brown falcons circling like buzzards, her hummock strung between trees humming with insect life, my thin blue mattress also my seat as I sat cross-legged, listening, she leaned forward on her camp stool, poking the embers beneath her billy. 'Prophecy is so terrible,' she said, 'I now bury my mind in the distant past. Knowing the obvious seems to break a rule,' she cackled. 'The rule of stupidity. The realists get so angry with us. But reality is created by men.'

Auntie moved in response to the hissing of the water and with a forked stick swung her billy off the heat and reached for her canister of tea leaves. 'The horror of prophecy,' she continued, 'is not only the deaf ears or the open aggression you get. It is also the anxiety you feel in your own body, in your nervous system.'

She shivered, sloughing out of a skin, and tossed her stick at the scavengers.

'Well, tell me,' I said, 'about the distant past.'

She glanced up from her methodical work with the tin mugs and hot billy, 'You have Scorpio somewhere but it is not your sun sign.'

'Virgo sun, Scorpio rising, Gemini moon,' I rattled off.

'Mars, Venus in Sagittarius,' she guessed. I shrugged. She continued, 'Earth, water, air, fire, good balance. Well,' she handed me my tea. 'Let's start with the invasion of the Indo-Europeans bringing worship of the father god, or, in some cases, the young warrior, to the Dravidians of India. This is attested, archaeologically and historically, to be about 2400 BCE but several invasions occurred earlier.' She talked like someone who had been alone for a long time as she drove the roads of the wide brown land, camping, reading, in discussion with herself, under the airy expanse of the sky. How much older than three millennia were the little stick characters painted above the entrance to Tunnel Creek?

Earlier in the day we had swum, walked and waded through the cool black water of the creek beneath the landlocked reef, seeing the paired red globes of fresh-water crocodile eyes watching us in the darkness. While she spoke of the Bible, the Koran and the Greek epics, I could have been in Gondwana where, 20 million years ago, fangaroo with dagger-like canines hopped like kangaroo in forests outside memory and science.

'And, of course, we,' she included me, catching my look with her own, 'go back to the Earth Mother of Willendorf, at least thirty thousand years. She is about four inches high and is a very fat woman, with big breasts and thighs and tummy.' She showed me the size with her hand.

The fantastic Fitzroy River, in the rainy season, flows fast enough to fill Sydney Harbour each day! We parted at Halls Creek. She drained her vessel for me.

My destiny was not in the desert, but I had met my karma in the Kimberley.

Sometimes I just long for her to be around, but our contact was of a moment. And letters from time to time.

Chandra Williams has no intention of going to any event which includes men; she finds even the word 'gender' offensive. She works at her computer, changing a page on her website.

Without control, Chandra wonders, how can one be responsible for one's actions? With constant clicks and quick movement of her cursor, her forefinger on the electronic mouse, Chandra Williams is a spider on the superhighway carefully weaving a revolutionary maze beneath it. As a spinster, she is as shrewd as a widow, making cobwebs to trap and protect, supplying threads through hypertext for those who would join her in subversion. Follow if you wish, she invites her cyber-sisters underground. In code. Political activity on the Internet is exhausting; information overload; keeping in touch. Email, news groups, chat sites take her time, tax her imagination. Her job is making the workable infrastructure. When she discovers the way to secure contact and interaction, what can be achieved?

Every woman, she feels, is different in her talent, but all share an enormous grief about loss of the female contract. She is establishing a special branch to her domain, <u>Wimmin</u>. Hoping to ensnare only the sympathetic ones, she knows that equally, or perhaps more likely, she will also attract the antipathetic. Lunatics and fanatics love to surf the Internet. She laughs as she types a quote from *Pauline Hanson, The Truth*: 'Australia could become a crumbling republic presided over by a lesbian cyborg president appointed by a distant "World Government".'

For the moment it is a joke. But why not call the bluff? Chandra can put in place mechanisms for quick connections. She had set up listservs dealing with Wimmin & Feminism, Lesbians & Amazons and simply Woman Be Whole, but, using some newly acquired game-making software, she can make a grid for the conspiracy. Her site—including guest books, drop-out menus, a reading list, a CD register, recommendations for decent entertainment videos, audio tapes—has firewalls to stop pesky hackers, encryptions for all the financial dealings as well as a real-time chatline house with different rooms open all hours. She figures out a way to call for *noms de geurre* and imagines that among the true believers there would be disappointingly few prepared to fight. She utilises Common Gateway Interface to execute her remote location with several web servers to add functionality to her site. Her avatar censors porn, boots out the less than sympathetic. She plays with seguing backgrounds. Chandra is the type of person who refuses to say the word 'impossible' until she has proved it so.

The Internet so accessible, she institutes etymological codes to cast her fine mesh as wide as possible, for the conspiracy to be significantly international. Chandra gets disgusted with the victimhood of women, and sees herself as a facilitator of vital feminism in the virtual world. She wants effectual revolution. What is really going on must be secret. Borrowing strategies and tactics from resistance movements, her warriors will be urban terrorists in the global cyber-village.

Chandra rolls back in her chair and reaches for her training bar, a piece of solid dowel secured from wall to wall in her office. She does ten chin-ups and another ten to the back of her neck. She then does five of each with one arm alternately. Though difficult, this exercise is necessary for her to maintain her lifestyle. She has been building her upper body strength since she was a child. The chair moves inconveniently. She swears at the brake, climbs back to comfort and returns to the screen. To command the nature of her recruits, she designs a hyperlink thread into her labyrinth using crazily mundane words, every *the*, *an* and *but* making adits to her mine. Ultimately only those who've read Gertrude Stein will find their way through her maze to the cell at the centre.

Now all she can do is wait and see. She checks the time on the screen and closes down.

Chandra wheels herself to the verandah which runs along the north, south and eastern walls of her house. Forward, back, twist and forward. Steely grey behind the lit limbs of the gums predicts rain for at least three days. Violet clouds deepened by yellowy lime leaf-tips complement her mood of excitement and trepidation. She decides to ride today. Chandra's horse answers to her call. Her Rottweiler bitch, Nikki, trained by a friend whose mission in life was to extend seeing-eye canine capacity to assist all disabilities, is erratic in her interpretation of instructions. Sometimes she actually brings the right bridle. Chandra exchanges chair for callipers and swings herself across the yard, accompanied by horse and dog and scattering chooks. Rigged up in the barn is a pulley-contraption from which a sidesaddle is suspended. When the knot is released, the rope lowers the tack onto the sturdy pony's back. A recycled dentist's chair provides hydraulic lift for Chandra herself to reach a monkey-bar so that she can twist herself onto the horse. All three have the procedure down pat: dog, horse and Chandra using crisp identical directions and murmuring loving reassurance until she is safely aloft.

Then they train in the dressage quadrant. Extended trot, collected canter, sitting trot, figure of eight, changing legs. Both horse and rider work up a sweat.

4

'Almost Gothic, isn't it?'

The surreal image of several lads roller-blading down the tarred lane to the clubhouse in Elizabethan hose amuses Virginia enough to intend to enjoy herself at the Orlando Ball. Unfolding herself out of Cybil's little car, she spreads her arms wide, taking in the round yellow moon above the horizon, the wild waves of the king tide and the thunder of the Australian surf. She looks around: it could be a scene from a Fellini movie shot on a hostile Peruvian coast, so many freaks about. Cybil, fussing with her dog, her fat skirts, struggling out from behind the steering wheel, placing money in her jewelled purse, tucking her serviceable handbag under the seat and, after clicking the central lock, trying to fit her heavy ring of keys in with her cash, is about to lose her temper. Country gays cannot quite manage the sophistication of their city brothers. Emerging from farm utes, trade vans with advertising, ladders, piping, gold card stickers, sedans, 4WDs with fringes of mud, in dresses, men have thick make-up on rugged faces, lipstick with moustaches and beards, eye-shadow under bushy brows. They are grotesque, tottering about the carpark on old-fashioned sling-backs. Cybil, usually so brazen, is bashful in her perfect pre-Raphaelite costume. Virginia wants to socialise and share jokes with her mates from the bush who arrive on the tray of Rory's army truck, clinging on as if they've just hitched a ride down from the road. Indeed, there are no spaces left in the Surf Club's parking lot. Rory drives over the curb onto the grass near the beach under the banksias. Cybil uses words as weapons and clings like glue, so Virginia just waves and yodels, then partners her lover up the steps.

There is a broad expanse of decking overlooking the sea, tables and a closed kiosk. The main hall is decorated for the ball in swathes of scalloped cloth. The entrance is narrow. There's a queue along the stairs. Cybil pays for both, plucking a note from her tiny accessory. Along the seaside wall are glass doors opening onto a railed verandah, higher and not attached to the kiosk area. Dogs are on the decking. Smokers on the verandah.

When the dance is in full swing, outside Rory squashes her cigarette butt with the heel of her boot. Other smokers puff and try to be witty. The path to the moon is shattered by ripples, its light exaggerating the whitewater of the breakers. Inside, cross-dressing wardrobe imaginings of times past are at odds with the music. Disco.

She shouts, 'Every woman knows Valerie Solanas is right! It is just suicide to say so.'

Virginia White, in her artists' smock, tight dark jeans and beret, hands her a drink.

'What a load of crap! You're a dinosaur, Rory!' Margaret Hall, who is dressed pretty much as she always is, crushed velvet top and stovepipe jeans, winds her up.

'Can you conceive of an Age of Solanas?' asks Rory, quite happy to argue.

'Ha ha. Deluding yourself. Solanas?' Their battle, which has been going on for some time, causes interest. Rory prefers to talk and smoke rather than prance around dancing and Margaret chain-smokes tailormades.

'Jesus was probably just an ordinary, gentle man with a good conscience,' suggests Daze. 'The writers and politicians made Christianity after his death.' Daisy is an old maid who knows exactly how the world should be run.

Rory respects Daze and addresses her. 'In his own lifetime Christ was— what?—famous for three years?'

'The age of Christ is fucking dead in the water,' Dee Knox contributes, then leans over the railing to check on her dog.

'Life is so full,' sighs Haze, who though she doesn't smoke, is never very far from Daze.

'The Age of Aquarius is, after all, here now,' Fi says. 'The Age of Pisces over.'

'Have you read Marija Gimbutas?' Haze asks Virginia. 'The language of the Goddess? Birds?'

'Yep,' Virginia clips her response and returns to the dancefloor.

'Well, we could overthrow Western civilisation as we know it,' Margaret speaks to Rory. 'But how? Involve ourselves in the surreptitious dealing of arms or other contraband, bring down the stock exchanges?'

'Character assassination of friends and acquaintances,' says Daze, 'is something we can stop.'

'Soon they won't even be able to fix the flu with a vaccine, the bug will outwit them before the laboratories can roll into gear,' Dee reckons. 'They're killing themselves.'

'Future shock already has me reeling back with the shudders. Cyberspace and virtual reality have those of us who struggled with Newtonian physics gaping in wonder and horror,' Haze confesses.

Daisy tut-tuts at the looming doom.

'Gunpowder will attack all the fortresses of the Western world in the third millennium. The financial castles will fall as cash crashes and plastic money turns on them,' Fi takes up the apocryphal theme.

'What I rue most is the loss of faith,' dear Daisy contributes.

'It might just happen,' Margaret is serious. 'The walls will come tumbling down. They're acting as if there is no tomorrow.'

Haze says, 'It would make a difference if they didn't make, um, plastic bags, for instance.'

'Good one!' Margaret Hall, like many of the cyber-savvy generation of feminists, thinks old warhorses incapable of humour.

Daisy plucks at her stole. 'I think the revolution is about changing hearts, I really do.'

'We came to dance. Let's bop, Daze?' Haze invites.

Rory enthusiastically harangues the pale Dracula at her side, Alison Hungerford.

Gurls hang together, watching and being watched, an identifiable group, laughing, arguing, brooding, flirting, playing, spatting, knowing, wearing the disparaging nomenclature like comfortable waistcoats.

'The SCUM Manifesto hit the streets, taking the establishment by surprise before it knew what feminism was about,' Rory proclaims. 'Solanas knew it all and drew the logical conclusions. She not only asked the questions, she provided the answers. Not only did she preach, she practised her doctrine. No privilege at all enabled or assisted her.'

She is interrupted by a jolly dyke from Coffs Harbour, trying to keep her filter-cigarette alight through a long cigarette-holder. 'So who are you birds dressed up as?' The gurls look at her without comment. Rory, passable as an early-nineteenth-century aviatrix, with goggles pushed up over a leather skull-cap, easy shirt, flared joddies and boots, looks at Ilsa for help.

Ilsa feels she has little in common with lesbians defined by sexual preference and in couples, confined by personal romance. She says, 'Her reading going no further than detective fiction, Lord Peter Wimsey apparently fits the bill as her Orlando personality.'

'Haven't read it, exactly,' the newcomer responds, completely without guile. 'Whatshername is too complicated for me.'

'Dorothy Sayers,' educates Ilsa, as she thinks. Amazons and Sapphists, lesbians of ancient Greece, the land-dwelling horsewomen with their arrows and bows, helmets and shields, were warriors while the sophisticated island people of Lesbos were into poetry and love-making.

'No one takes Valerie Solanas seriously any more, Rory,' Dee says and shakes her head, unused to tresses around her ears. She doesn't want to talk with the woman who calls women birds.

In the sea air, the mixed bunch on the balcony, come and go. Company makes Rory loquacious; she can't help herself. 'She was the most passionate woman of last century, but it didn't come from her heart. It came from her mind!'

'Is there a difference?' Ilsa asks, rhetorically.

'No,' Dee decides. 'Chinese medicine locates the mind in the heart, anyway.'

The electronic music suddenly stops. The ball is colourful, well-attended and camp. Pretence drowns pretension. Preening boys are silent while older poofters flirt. Gross, glorious darlings perform in the lull.

The drama teacher introduces a live act. Judith Sloane, dressed as a medieval troubadour, takes the stage, and with her acoustic guitar sings a Joan Baez classic. The smoking crowd cluster at the door and windows to listen. When she finishes her set, enthusiastic applause is laced with sarcastic mumbles. Madrigal music fills the speakers.

Rory wants to finish what she was saying. 'They called Valerie mad. Naturally, seeing she was a prophet.'

'A Cassandra. My mother used to say, "You're as mad as Cassandra".'

Alison leans her back against the railing and rolls a joint. Fiona and Dee wait to share it.

Ilsa, ever amazed at what she doesn't know, remarks, 'I never heard that expression, and I did Classics at school. Cassandra was Trojan. And . . .'

'Must be a class thing. All my mother knew about her was Cassandra was mad. My mum had lots of great lines,' Fi says.

'Yes, mine too. But, back to the point,' Rory wants to take control of the conversation. 'Solanas drew their fire and they have been firing ever since at any woman who pokes her head out of the hide and calls out the defects of . . .'

'Aren't we all mad?' Alison asks laconically. Dee notices, in the lighter flame, her pupils are like pins.

'The female must stay the second sex, or else. We fear for our survival. It makes cowards of us all.' Rory doesn't take any notice of the males stepping out in meticulous imitation of Elizabethan fun.

'And hypocrites. What are you doing here, Rory?' Dello demands, 'This is a gay and lesbian do and you're a separatist.'

'The separatist voice is, actually, the voice of diversity,' Rory explains. 'Anyway, there's not a lot to go to any more.' The ball has changed its momentum. She gives up trying to have a meaningful discussion.

Inside, lipstick lesbians and drag queens, young gays and heavy older women, in their fantasy of androgyny, melt masculinity and femininity into make-believe with their fancy dress. The recorded music after Judith's nostalgic performance is the special tape, prepared for the occasion. Rory goes in.

Alison, in her high-collared cape, gravitates to Maria, who is a motley and impressive dowager in a cloak in a fur hat. 'From Muscovy,' she pats her head. And smiles, warmly.

'Where's Sofia?' Alison's pale face paint is splashed with blood-red lips, and her voice is smouldering.

'She wouldn't come to anything men are at. But I can't resist a social,' Maria grins, becoming attracted.

Alison laughs, 'Same reason Chandra isn't here. Let's go down to the sand.' Dracula takes the dowager's hand.

When Rory finally enters the hall, she falls promptly in love. Margot Gorman, the harlequin, dances with the virgin queen, with swirls and bows, high hands hardly held. Totally made-up in Elizabethan garb, Margot's partner is camping it up for all to admire. Courtiers, youths on roller blades, circle around them as if on ice-skates, having studied the opening scene from the film, *Orlando*. The drama teacher looks hot and bothered in puff-sleeved velvet doublet, striped bloomers and tights. Dismayed and entranced, Rory muses on the authority of money, here the pink dollar, and class, the odd ignorance of the erudite Ilsa, with a side of her mind excited by the presence of others and herself a fool on the verandah, while she figures out how to catch the jester's eye. Her stare is direct, her feelings obvious. Margot herself is feeling cranky and bloated, although she is slim and attractive in skintight colour. She goes through the paces, steps gracefully, without enjoyment. Rory is confused by her sudden emotion: should she make contact or just stand back and admire? Whatever, her night is made. She watches and waits.

Virginia makes moves with Cybil whose breasts push into a peachy cleavage against the cloth of her costume. They hand the little dog to each other and laugh and carry on.

Rory thrusts her hands deeper into her bomber-jacket pocket as she stands, an island in a sea of moving people. Judith Sloane, the troubadour with her mandolin across her back, seductively arouses the interest of a handsome Koori from Kempsey, whom she introduces, charmingly, as if they are intimate already. A big-haired redhead grabs Rory's elbow and tries to make her dance with her. Rory solidly refuses.

'I'm Tiger Cat,' she growls, and flirts outrageously. Rory is not impressed at being thrown off balance by a body-builder in leopard spots.

Judith whispers, 'She fancies you, go for it.' Rory's fair skin blushes brighter red. Embarrassed, she reluctantly moves a few steps. Rory prays to the goddess, and is rescued from the attentions of the muscly feline by Margot, who takes her hand, raises it and swings her into a version of the Pride of Erin. She reddens again, and trips, and stumbles.

'You don't want anything to do with her,' Margot murmurs as she steadies her.

The disc jockey stops the music and the MC comes to the microphone. 'Now is the time for the judging of the best dressed.'

Rory leans towards Margot and says, 'Your friend will be sure to win.'

'Yes, he loves dressing up,' Margot affirms, watching Tiger Cat search out another loose gurl.

'Well, they do, don't they?' Rory is shy. 'Mind if I go out for a fag?'

Margot nods, distractedly.

Rory adds hopefully, 'Wanna come?'

'Okay.' Outside, Rory rolls her cigarette and mumbles, 'I'm Rory by the way.'

'That your real name?' Margot responds. She stands staring at the sea rolling like midnight silk disturbed by a draught.

'Well, it's really Rosaleen.' Rory again suffers verbal trots, 'O'Riordan. What do you think of *Orlando*?'

'Saw the movie,' answers Margot. 'I found it a bit boring. What was the point?'

'Something to the effect of . . .' Rory finds her fluency disrupted by her feelings. 'If you have a male body you are a human being. Orlando is not free when a woman, the dresses, strict rules of society etc. make it impossible for her to do anything. Go hunting and running and so on. Plus her property is entailed. Men got the money.'

'Oh, fair enough.' Margot's expression is sad. 'I can relate to that. I've always been pissed off that they don't have to suffer periods. Or pre-menstrual tension.'

'Well, that's related, of course. The pain, the crabbiness, could be about self-hatred. Simply not wanting to be a woman. Because we have it so hard. Even those butches who try to change gender. Males trapped in female bodies are given credence,' Rory explains. 'It's not an equal choice.' She notices that Margot is not listening. 'You know? I meant, men have always loved dressing up in female garb and they have the freedom to do it without loss of self.' Secretly Rory is chiding herself for her lecturing tone. 'What's wrong?' she asks.

Margot hesitates. 'I found a dead adolescent in a toilet block, yesterday.

Don't exactly feel like celebrating.'

Clapping inside is loud with whoops and squeals as the prizes are given out. Sean Dark as Elizabeth the First gets a magnum of champagne, and Virginia, a bottle of whisky, as the most believable Orlando.

'I think I'll go home soon,' Margot says but doesn't move. 'Look!'

Rory's eye follows her finger. Down on the beach, Maria and Alison make an eerie couple. The on-shore breeze lifts Maria's cape into a billowing balloon and Alison's high-collar cloak into fluttering bats' wings against the moonlit waves, a shot from a black and white movie.

'Almost Gothic, isn't it?'

Rory laughs in agreement. 'Very.'

Scraps of the evening came into my head, as I drove through the silvery night, sober and unaccountably angry. Tiger Cat prowling around the gurls: what's she up to? When I got home I just sat at my kitchen table leafing through the morning's paper. Not really reading. Sean, fortunately, is a small, wiry guy, and the drama teacher's boys positively Shakespearian, but most of those transvestites are so big, apart from being as ugly as sin, and half the women were awful. That Judith Sloane had a nice voice, but her choice of song made me groan. The other half, like my new friend, Rory, and the prize-winning Orlando, looked as if they'd be comfortable whatever they wore. Except, possibly, what most women wear, say, as wedding guests, stockings and frocks. Fashion. Rugby League bonding sessions are a bit of a worry. Newspapers are full of the doings of psychopaths. And the crazy things rich people do with their money. Eventually I bundled them up for recycling, cleaned the place and went to bed.

The phone woke me.

Maria screamed, 'I'm being murdered. Sofia has me by the neck and she's throttling me.' This would be hard to believe except Maria is a large woman who could maintain hold of a hand-piece and be shaken at the same. She would barely wobble, not lifting a finger in her own defence. Did Maria prefer the role of victim, or was she afraid of her physical strength? Fat people are frightening because they sit on you. I looked at the time, and that did not make me any more patient. It was three in the morning.

'What did you do?' I asked, assuming the attack was provoked.

'Nothing. Threatened to ring you,' Maria gasped. 'Which I am.'

Sofia hissed in the background. Putting in the effort to be patient, I wondered why Maria always rang me when in distress. What am I to her, a link to the real world?

I heard the receiver fall on what sounded like the marble top of the coffee table in their lounge-room. Vicious words were exchanged.

'Sofia! Sofia, pick up the phone,' I demanded.

Sofia did that but before she could speak she sobbed. I waited.

They began tearing strips off each other. I listened to their argument. Maria was called a sloth, a slug and a slob who made lecherous eyes at any young piece who came in the door, but this—whatever this was—was going too far. Sofia was insanely jealous. Maria couldn't even enjoy herself in her own house. Didn't Sofia have a life of her own? 'Pashing and slobbering, making a fool of yourself, Maria.' Sofia said she should call the police, 'It's perverse, pederasty.' Maria cried, 'She is not that young!'

Irritated, I heard the verbal abuse, the tears, the screams. I was, I guessed, being used. Relationship junkies. Energy-crawlers, people in these constant, repetitive relationships have an incredible sense of self-importance. That's what I felt in the early hours. Sofia picked up the phone and addressed me, 'She's right, Margot. I will murder her. I would be doing all the pretty girls a favour. It won't be my fault.'

'Put Maria on again, Sofia,' I commanded.

'She'll be the death of me,' Maria said quietly. 'I'll let you get some kip, Margot. Sorry.'

'Why did you ring me? What do you want me to do about it?' I asked, feeling that I should do something.

'I don't know. I thought you could help me, but, of course, you can't. I must have filed away your number in my brain as someone to ring in an emergency. A reliable person, just in case.' Maria laughed, deprecating herself.

'Okay.' Calmly, I asked, 'What did you do? Why is it so bad this time?'

'I slept with her.' There was a tinge of sarcasm in her voice. 'That's what Sofia thinks. Let her think that.'

'So it's not true?' I wanted to get the facts clear, at least.

'What if it is?' Maria countered, defensively.

'Do you want to hurt her? Why don't you have a break from each other?' I hoped I kept the exasperation out of my voice.

'We're like two thick planks stuck together, frozen solid. A paralysis.' Maria explained, then said hopelessly, 'I cannot leave her.'

Sofia began begging close to the mouthpiece, 'We've been eating each other for life-times, the gutless fat oaf makes me miserable.'

'For godsake, respect,' I pleaded. Exasperated.

After ruining my important REM sleep, they simply hung up. Back in bed, I tossed and turned, stewing, disturbed by my intuition more than anything else. Truly mad women love the night. Like vampires, they're feverishly conscious at night. So, the corollary holds: if you want to stay sane, let sleep reign at night. Let dreams work their magic and sort things out. All your worries are like fiddle-sticks to your subconscious mind. Maintain beauty sleep. I will buy an answer machine on Monday.

The telephone rang again about three-quarters of an hour later. Spookily, no one was there. Just silence. A nuisance call. It brought back my fear of harassment by a conspiracy of unknown operatives arising from my being a possible whistle-blower. Risky business, having worked for the Authority and knowing too much. They chase me in various vehicles, particularly semi-trailers. They bore down on me as I rode my bike on the open road on my round-Australia trip. Was the full moon making a lunatic of me, too? I am not paranoid. There was a semi in the car park on Friday evening. And what if Tiger Cat is working for them?

In the local paper is a map of parts of Great Dividing Range, including Lesbianlands, with a tender for lease to go about mining exploration. Fresh gurls freak out, but older hands say it happens all the time. The land was mined, just as it was logged, years ago.

'The goddess will protect us from the patriarchy outside, don't worry.'

The moans of long-gone Amazons, locked in the forbearance of rock, tell Roz, Pam, Olga and Nicole that in the denial of the strong female self is a misunderstanding of the entire human race. Out in the bush where gurls make up anecdotes, write poetry, create artefacts of little witches, the four who are not interested in stomping to acidhouse take advantage of the moon to light their way to eat a meal together and make their own music. The communal kitchen near the creek is no more than poles holding up a tar-paulin protecting wooden packing cases, with cutlery and crockery, blackened billy, three-legged cast-iron pot and fire. Odd musical instruments collected over the years, or left behind, have a box. Pam plays a pipe and Olga drums.

When Truckman arrives at the warehouse at four in the morning, lights are on. He does not move from his seat. Two men come out to direct him. The shutter doors rise, leaving him a foot either side to back the load in. Taking his time, he does it perfectly. He gets down from the cab, stretches, yawns, struts. The boss calls him over to a little glassed-in office. They exchange money and log books.

Ian Truckman is given a few days off. He decides to drive down the Campbell Delta and stay by the surf on Doon Buggy Drag near Lookout Point. His vehicle takes up most of the cable ferry.

The lone conspirator is fishing for salmon at the edge of the surf at dawn.

5

. . . fear of the abyss . . .

To: "chandra" <wheels@wimmin.com.au>
From: "O'Lachlin" <boobook@nadir.com.nz>
Subject: Annihilation
Date: Sun, 19 Mar 2000 17:07:57 +1000
==

MEMO: Revelation Ch. 20 Verse 7 "And when the thousand years are
expired, Satan shall be loosed out of his prison."
>> The Earth, that jewel among planets for cosmonauts and aliens to
view with wonder, astronauts say is dirty with smoke. Rainforests burn all
over the globe, smogging the atmosphere. The belt of coral reefs around
her equatorial waist died in a heated sea. That diversity and
interdependence of biospheric colour and organic life in the unique
oceans of our solar system, that epitome of phenomenal beauty, turned
to pale bone in the space of a few months in 1998. A thousand years of
breathing beauty broken by beholders who are blinded. Fire!! The last
horseman of the Apocalypse here. Can't you see?
>> Actuality overwhelms the dismal predictions of seers. But who listens
to prophets? They have only words! And language serves liars and
slanderers and flatterers equally as well. Probably better. Secrets,
dissemblance, even practised at home among your own, puts spies in
charge of the bear and the bald eagle.
>> The Inferno of damnation emerges from mythology onto the surface
of the earth in all its images of suffering. Unspeakable atrocities, rape of
the innocents, hordes of homeless displaced by neighbouring armies,
tribes and militias, dispossessed in snow and cyclone of food and shelter,
robbed of work, of purpose, of meaning, shattered by quakes and floods,
weakened by disease; their water poisoned, rivers of flame causing fish-
kills and die-backs, cyanide spilling everywhere, vegetables irradiated;
milk strontium-tainted; beef, contaminated through covetous
cannibalism, from cattle on the hoof to the final frozen mince, profane

all that was sacred in the once great Cow-mother. The sacrilege of transgression does not stop there, but it is so obvious.

>> Now Hathor's, Io's, whatever her name, the Celestial Cow's species is burping dangerous quantities of methane into the thin ozonic shield for the greed of carnivorous man. For hamburgers and dairy products: tell the masters by their wolverine teeth. Acid soils, salinated paddocks, toxic algae shrink natural resources as mega-production increases; beasts of mythological grandeur turn powerless as babes; words of apocryphal prophets mock their own kind in the deafening babble of brass drowning the music of the spheres; fine tunes of inborn talent absorbed by necrophilic porn; offensive greed honoured by obscene respectability making continuous capitalism malignant. Materialism is only one symptom: hark doomsday death cults!

>> Weaponry obsesses the chains of command and government at the cost of all that is priceless; the wild and the free colonised by nonsense, exploitation and criminal ignorance, if not destroyed. Pleasure putrefied by personal excess, perfection polluted by the very idea of itself perpetrated by sanctimonious paragons of hypocrisy, pettiness positions itself in the palaces of power and consigns wisdom to the sewer.

>> Paradise, that kingdom come, the Elysium fields for fools, opium of the people, dissolving into the white dust peddled on the streets and numbers on the stock exchange, is a chimera in the desert of commerce shimmering god and heaven as reflection, as projection, as justification for the abomination of all that is blameless. For fear of the abyss within, hell.

>> Supreme selfishness assails the subtle ecosphere of human character, attacking moral fibre, upsetting the delicate balance of soul, heart, body and mind as if a sick pestilence, the stuff of nightmare, escaped the fetters of geological time to wreak havoc in the brains of humankind. Evil at the end of the second millennium of the Christian era is as vigorous as cancerous tumours outgrowing the host-being. Sublime scepticism shrinks all knowledge to the dimensions of individual understanding, naming and numbering, casting the ineffable into banal backgrounds of grotesque shadow easy to ridicule.

>> In the same Western civilisation that produced the religions which rule our ways of life, the heavenly cow whose udder produced the Milky Way is shat upon. Birth-giving deities who existed when nothing else had being, who were believed to have created that which exists, while honoured through moon-worship in many cultures were never a notion of antenature, merely expressions of respect for that which is sacred,

joyous and bigger than us, beyond our capacity to comprehend, are divinities of the same history as now. Kali, Lat, Al-Lat, Audumla, whatever the name of the sacred wetnurse of humanity, is absolutely abused by bovine usage in the present time. Thus is Io angry. While jealous man endeavours to control the extremes of life, the moment of breath suffers for his search.

>> We cannot know what lies after the demise of consciousness, nor who peoples places we cannot reach, ever. But arrogance precurses its own fall. It is true that no amount of medical progress can check the extraterrestrial viruses, try as they might, and they will. In religious logic, therefore, the satanic is as viable as the godly. The spiritual dimension is beyond personal power. Fear of death is the province of the faithless who, in the dreadful irony of their own mortality, kill. Disastrous lack of love for life and living is poverty of the imagination, plain ingratitude, passionless lust, vice, little lies and major dishonesty, all within the free will and fate of being human. Robbing death of its dignity is treating life as a private possession.

>> Just as science has proved viruses rush through the hole in the ozone layer from outer space like molecules of water down a gully-trap creating mysterious diseases of the body, fantastic vision supposes evil erupts from the nether regions, the engine room of the devil within the material world, leaving circles of glass on the crust of the earth like pimples on the skin. Frightening the hopeless.

>> Isn't it tragic?

>> Tragic!

6

. . . white virgin . . .

After the dance and sleep disturbed by Maria's phone call, Margot Gorman is treating herself gently, sipping a herb tea, sitting on her front verandah in the sun, when she smells dust. Then she hears the approach of a powerful motor on her road. Travelling slowly, going north, the lorry White Virgin passes her house. It is a prime mover, no trailer. Overall fragile, and brittle, her uterus giving her hell beneath her flat abdominal muscles, Margot is not herself. Red clover or chamomile, she couldn't decide, now the mixture tastes horrible. She tosses it.

While 'white virgin' may have nothing to do with amazons or Valerie Solanas, it grasps the imagination of a death-crazed world. While being a code-name for a covert operation, the nickname of the figure-head of the extreme Right, the title of a pornographic interactive video-game, a new drug, a conspiracy, the white virgin is, typically, a victim. The words haunt Margot.

White Virgin. The two words bedevil me because Harry spat them at me because my courage frightened him. Harry said, with hatred, 'As far as I can see yo' nuthin' but a poor little white virgin.' Harry claimed a grandmother in the Pitjatjantjara tribe, but you couldn't see it in his face. He fancied the jive-speak of African-American ghettoes. He meant to annihilate me as a daughter of colonists. All at the National Crime Authority knew as much as I but were not going to do anything about it. He probably said it because I wouldn't go to bed with him. When the words 'white virgin' turned up on the bug catcher of a truck, the perspex shield mounted on top of the mighty engine, I couldn't see the driver whose driving was murderous but I knew they had sent him. As he tried to run me on my bike off the road, Harry's jibe echoed in the darker corridors of my consciousness where vulnerability sits and cowardice lurks. You have no bullet-proof vest, Margot. You're scared. The nuisance phone call, after Maria's, came from them.

There was a satanic cult up on the plateau, according to my neighbour, Moo. Satanists are always looking for a white virgin to sacrifice. Pagans may cry for respectability as a religion and honour old Gaia, the earth, but is it natural to have women naked and men overly dressed in cloaks? Most forms of erotica and soft porn I've seen say it's okay. Sexual fantasy is all right, but what is being fantasised? Penetration? Death? Sacrifice. Virgin indicates innocence, ignorance, youngness, potential, endless possibility. The cherry to be sucked, the fruit to be plucked. The work prostitutes put into looking as young and virginal as they can is mind-boggling. Happy, good-time-girl personas. What they love is the money and the brief power over men. They don't necessarily hate themselves, they don't know themselves. There's a hole where identity should be. All surface.

White virgin, that rig!, agent of my fear. I try to think of old, unmarried ladies, suffragettes, who did know themselves, in heavy tweeds with hunting stools as walking sticks, sensible shoes: have weapon, shall walk. Wise white virgins with a seat should they need one.

White Virgin, South Australian number plate. It could be a coincidence.

Mourning Tree-Lover's Cult. New Age witches and warlocks go out in the bush to moan and wail and ululate and weep over the destruction of the earth as they dance in their birthday suits, in a circle, playing drums and blowing pipes, getting high on the fruits of the earth. I bet they are as self-righteous as some Christian militia group which, on a neighbouring property, perhaps, gathers to practise shooting scum, aiming their guns at the enemy. It doesn't take too much of a flight of fancy to see the enemy as me.

Proud to be female. I am not paranoid. I saw White Virgin, driving along my road. I decided to ring Maria.

Virginia White is a striking presence. Tall, with a well-domed forehead, a Roman nose, high cheekbones and broad front teeth; her mouth is bow-shaped. Her eyebrows hawk-like, hair coarse and abundant, black now streaked with steel grey, her voice, although she speaks little, is deep and gravelly. Her face is expressive. She is big-boned and lean, athletic with stringy muscles and prominent veins. She moves with the grace of ease of action, with an energy that enjoys physical labour, but is otherwise still. She is a powerful thinker, capable of sustained mental effort.

Her charm is in the intensity of her smile, or frown. Being in love usually makes Virginia happy. Ecstatic, perhaps. Virginia never wanted lifetime companionship. Sexual intimacies are for her journeys of discovery, holidays from the terminal loneliness of the soul. Wholehearted in her commitment until the chemistry runs its course, she is not envious of greener pastures. Happy ever after is a make-believe that, even as a child, she considered a boring ending. A dead end. Stasis. She doesn't need power over the other woman, she wants her to be as free as she with a life to live and a job to do. She is with a woman with whom she has nothing in common.

Virginia is old enough to have had a significant past and young enough to want to create the future. She is at the change of life. Her twin brother's children's children she loves in a way no grandmother could as she has avoided the demands and resentments of motherhood. She is a great-aunt.

'Have you had an abortion?' queries Cybil, who wants to know Virginia's life story. The facts.

'I was married to a black man from New Guinea for two years.'

Cybil probes Virginia so much about this she even finds out his sexual technique, putting a soft cock into her vagina and letting it engorge inside. Did Virginia like it? 'It was okay. I was young. Doing the "right" thing.'

Cybil finds out that Virginia was in America when she explored the strawberry fields of sensual perception. Hallucinogens broadened her mind and on the whole strengthened her. She exhibited her sculpture in SoHo, Manhattan, and lived among the artists and intellectuals of the East Village. Having learnt Aikido in New York, she could sling aside a rugby front-rower if she had to, she says.

'I came back to Australia a celebrity! My work was in demand and money showered down,' she says, as Cybil takes croissants from the microwave. 'It nearly gave me a nervous breakdown. Through all this I was reading the publications of feminist theorists and absorbing that which gave me a sense of myself. Didn't bother to argue with what I did not agree with. Who needs it?' Virginia shrugs luxuriantly.

'What about your relationship with Jeff?' Cybil is an only child whose interest in siblings' lives is nearly prurient. Puddles, the poodle, leaps up on the bed. Cybil pushes the hired costume onto the floor to make way for the breakfast tray. Virginia and her twin were brought up by the sea in a poor family when violence as a means of managing children was the norm.

'My brother and I were athletes at school, he a pole-vaulter, a junior champion. And I won races running, swimming. It was a country state school, not a lot of competition. Kids did their own thing. There was no car. We rode our bikes to the events, caught a bus, or hitch-hiked, and had, at least, the encouragement of each other. There was always an excuse why the parents could not be at the presentation of our awards. Usually drink,' she tells Cybil as she pours coffee from the plunger. 'This sharpened the hunger of our ambition rather than quashed it.'

Cybil asks about sex and having a twin brother. Virginia thinks she cannot get enough of her.

'He taught me to piss standing up, but we fell out with our first sexual experiences. The same girl,' Virginia grins. 'Caroline.' At the age, for Virginia, of sixteen and, for Jeff, eighteen. 'They later married.' The twins' jealousy was mutual betrayal of a closeness that had seen them through a difficult childhood. By their mid-thirties, all three had healed the rift. Virginia had feminism and a vital lesbian life-style by then. She and her girlfriend came to Lesbianlands in the mid-1980s and built themselves shelters. Her lover, having built, moved on and, yes, they are friends. Even though she is open and truthful with her responses to Cybil's relentless curiosity, Virginia feels oddly distant from the facts as she relates them.

'What about now?' She interrupts herself. 'What about us, Cybil?'

But Cybil frowns. 'Why have you buried yourself out in the bush? With no money?' she asks angrily. 'Like turned your back on responsibility?'

Virginia loves a lipstick lesbian! 'To tell wearers of power suits, like you, to get stuffed.'

Cybil is not amused.

'Because it's about women.' Virginia relents. 'Woman's culture. The earth.' Virginia describes her vision and what she is doing with wood. Knowing Cybil's need for narrative contexts, she says, 'Perhaps I saw it once when I was nine. Jeff and I were on the rocks looking out to sea. The raft we had built out of planks and 44-gallon drums was floating away by itself. We didn't know why it was moving so fast. We only knew we had to get off. Sitting there wet and amazed, we made up adventure stories. The raft returned in my dreams. And daydreams. Never just a few boards on rusty drums. It was a ship. A galleon of pirates. A vessel full of Argonauts. A heroic thing. Sometimes it was a chariot pulled by six white horses. Jeff can't remember it very well. I guess the dreams stopped about the time Caroline entered our lives.'

Cybil's interrogation excites Virginia's sight; she stops speaking about it aloud. The urgency of her art dogs her every moment. She wonders why she is here with Cybil. She is bored with her own—and, if the truth be known—others' stories of childhood. All is fair in love and war, thinks Virginia White. She is as emotionally equipped as any woman for either. Mature. It is Sunday morning and they're having breakfast in bed, listening to Laurie Anderson and Marianne Faithful on Cybil's marvellous sound system. 'We told each other ghost stories in bed. That was good.'

Virginia feels that at the midpoint of her life she can truly love. Love with commitment. She is fascinated by this ardour as it is unaccompanied by the thrills of daydream and romance. It is in her breast like a knot, mysterious and heavy, taking the passion-room her work requires. She is in love, but she is not happy; she is divided. She trembles like a brumby in the yard, both fearing and wanting to be tamed. She is torn in two, aroused and desperate to be on her own. Unbelievably, Cybil wants to know her body and her story, not her being. She has never been close to anyone quite like Cybil before: can she really be as cruel and selfish as she acts sometimes? Or is there something Virginia does not understand?

Freewoman. I dialled Maria's number and waited. Sofia answered. Somewhat mollified, I dissembled on the purpose of my call. I wanted to check them out. I spoke to Maria.

'Hi, it's Margot. Do you mind if I come around to visit later on this morning?'

'No, that's all right. We might need some milk.' They lived on the wrong side of the railway line.

'Okay,' I jollied. 'I'll get a Boston teacake, or something, at the Vietnamese bakery on the way.'

'That would be nice. A tea cake or Neenish tarts or apple turnovers, apricot Danish, even custard pies will be fine,' Maria elaborated.

'Yeah.' I knew Maria was sending herself up, but I couldn't bring myself to acknowledge the joke. 'Well, I'm pretty sure they're open on Sunday. I like the buttery French taste in their pastries.'

'Wonderful,' responded Maria.

'Right, I'll see you before eleven,' I said closing the conversation. Overbrightly.

'Yes,' answered Maria. The stuffing sounded knocked out of her. A moment ago I thought she had made a joke, now she was dull. Maria was not stupid. She knew why I was visiting.

While we enjoyed the generous repast and sat over morning tea we talked. Sofia was unusually taciturn. Maria was warm, expansive. Very easy to be with. It turned out she knew my spiritual guide, my karmic auntie. This connection opened my flood-gates and I told them of our meeting, at Fitzroy Crossing. 'She knew all the tricks and the delicious value of air-conditioning; the privilege of being able to pay for it, or of being white; whatever, no hypocrisy or phoney liberalism.'

Apart from wattle-birds squawking in the grevillea near the window, it was quiet outside. Sofia sat with us silently, her head slightly bent, her blue eyes glancing at me through long lashes. Her honey-fair hair has a natural wave. 'I was drawn to her,' I finished. Maria chuckled. 'Noses,' I continued, 'were important to both of us. She said hers was about beauty, mine about duty. Mad people, she said, rhyme all the time. I didn't care whether she was mad or not. She told me to come to the hinterland of the Paradise Coast to "swim out of the pea soup of my confusion."'

'Are you glad you did?' Maria asked, buttering another piece of bun. Like Venus of Willendorf, Maria is a round woman, with big breasts and thighs and tummy.

'Geikie Gorge was the last place I bathed in the waters of the fantastic Fitzroy River. We parted at Halls Creek. With the last cup of coffee together in the morning at a service station, she reminded me. "Lesbianlands, Margot. From the town of Stuart, you take the road to the Cavanagh Gorge National Park". And "Give my regards to Virginia White". From Darwin I flew to Townsville.'

'Virginia White?' Maria sparked up. Virginia White was her friend. It was Maria's opinion, in Sofia's company anyway, as I watched the eye movements of caution, of appeasement, that Virginia made sculptures as others garden, or take heroin. It was her thing. Maria sounded particularly indolent, in indulging Sofia's drug habit. Not Maria's place to judge what other women did with their time or their money or their energy. Now I knew why Sofia was quiet; she was on the nod, as if she had had a hit immediately before I arrived. That must have been why I noticed how blue her eyes were. Big, like the eyes of a baby.

'Was Virginia at the barbecue?' I wondered.

'No. She came in on Saturday for the dance.' Maria spoke as if last night were a week ago.

Sofia shrugged. 'No, she wasn't at the barbecue on Friday. Cybil was.'

With all their attempts at physical description I could not picture Cybil Crabbe. Maria said she was gorgeous and sexy. 'Luscious. Surely you noticed her, she was the one with real tits.' There were so many people at the Orlando Ball I didn't know, it was all a blur.

Sofia clarified, 'She is overweight but carries it.'

'So, Friday?' I encouraged

'Anyway,' Sofia continued. 'Cybil Crabbe was making eyes at the new girl, and, you know, when Cybil does that, you can cut the air with a knife.' Sofia gave out a bitter, risqué laugh. 'Off they went into the arms of Old Man Banksia.'

'She wouldn't do that to Virginia!' Maria was sharp, and certain.

Sofia's body language implied she didn't care.

Maria enjoyed romancing about the goodness of women. Cybil was no exception. Nobody, according to Maria, would jeopardise a relationship with VeeDub. They'd need their head read.

Sofia had something to say and was debating with herself whether to say it to me. But she let it die on her lips. I described how it was for me, finding the body like that. They both nodded, listening with interest because they were hearing it from some sort of horse's mouth. I asked if they had noticed a semi-trailer or anything like that. Yes, Maria had. Sofia hadn't. Then we talked about the dance. Maria suggested I read Raymond's *The Transsexual Empire.*

Sofia groaned as if Maria's tons of books were a millstone round her neck.

'No matter how much men and boys wish to be women, they can never be women,' Maria explained. 'No matter how they change themselves surgically, or dress to be feminine. Yet by doing these things they annihilate the meaning of female sexuality and the real experience of women generally.' In her rave, Maria really hit her straps. She was clear. She was happy. She knew her stuff. I found it interesting enough. Rory was trying to tell me something similar last night. 'They will never bleed.'

'Lucky them,' I said.

Sofia repeated herself, 'I saw Cybil Crabbe take her into the bushes.'

Maria argued, 'Unless you followed them, you wouldn't know for certain. They could have been bird-watching.'

'Is this Cybil a bird-watcher?' I asked.

Sofia murmured, 'As a matter of fact . . .'

Maria chuckled. And contributed, 'Cybil knows her birds.'

'Tiger Cat handed out free eccies,' Sofia said.

'Why were they free?' The eagerness of my question startled them. I wanted to know what Catherine Tobin was up to.

Sofia shrugged, 'I don't know if they were eccies. I didn't have one, I was pretty spinny already. I have just avoided a really bad episode. I have to be careful.' Sofia looked to Maria for approval. The calm daytime situation was so different from the telephonic connection in the early hours. Whatever the nature of the power relations between them, they had come to some kind of truce. I would not like to guess what the conditions were.

I said, 'Tiger Cat is an old enemy of mine. Catherine Tobin. She was a cop. True filth.'

Maria eyed me ironically.

'Well anyway,' Sofia continued, unhearing, 'they were pills, and they were okay.'

Has Sofia such a loose relationship to the truth of fact that she could say two opposite things in exactly the same tone of voice within minutes? I asked myself, does she live entirely in a reality of her own making?

Maria clearly enjoyed the sensual pleasures of life and had no plans of denying herself when they were offered free. She complimented me on the food I had brought. And she really meant it.

'It is interesting,' she theorised, 'to see how drugs affect women in so distinct a manner. Chemicals seem like water off a duck's back for Sofia. Whereas, I am susceptible. She has such a riotous collection in her brain, that a little pill wouldn't make much difference. Sofia's mind is a wonder to behold, Margot.' She smiled, humiliating and praising her partner in one fell swoop. 'Whereas I,' she added, 'couldn't drive.'

'Well, Maria, you seem okay, today,' I commented as I slapped my knee and rose to my feet. 'And I had better go.'

Neither of them saw me out. Everything was calm. The house was tidy.

'Adios,' I called.

'Hasta la vista,' cried Sofia promptly.

'Ciao,' called Maria.

Watching the pelicans sitting and preening on the sticks of the oyster leases, the barge's slow progress, the fan-wave of its wake on the surface of the river, I thought about how I came here. A considerable while later than my encounter with Auntie in the Kimberley, I fell into competing in triathlons and Iron Woman events in Queensland.

After an enforced stress leave, I was transferred from Sydney to Adelaide to continue working with the National Crime Authority. Three years, then I walked out with full severance pay and an angry head of steam over misogyny, among other things. Within a week of my leaving, our offices were bombed.

Last words I said were, 'The name is Margot, not patsy.' I had just had enough.

The Sydney job soured me to law enforcement. They used the very best part of me on a phantom job, drugged me to oblivion, and, expected me to forget. They tried to send me mad, was Auntie's way of putting it. A good bloodhound never ever loses the exact scent of a track it's been put upon. Even when I was a cop, 'dog' was not an insult to me. Dog, detective, that's my calling in life. I have an exceptional nose. As for insults, is 'virgin' a dirty word? Maybe Broom and Harry think so.

Honest as I was, I thought I was part of the boys' club. I was not. No woman can be. The blokes communicate with winks and nods or deadpan looks beyond your ear at other males. They have a silent contract with each other. There is only one such club as mateship and women can only be associates. If you achieve membership, you're a token. I've been the honorary man, and, to that degree, I know how they think; basically all women are fuckable. What most of them don't know is, that all women are not fuck-over-able.

No job and in a very lonely situation, I left Adelaide. My only companions, a bit of money and my bike. Well, banks for all their daylight robbery can look after money and cars are made to be bought and sold. So I put all I needed in panniers, told myself I was as free as my body was fit and pumped my legs up the hills. In the Barossa Valley I took stock at a luxurious guest house and sipped wine. Since I have never smoked and found fatty foods yucky early in life, my palate is excellent. Discerning the grape, the vintage, the barrel, the time and the depth of tannin excites me. My sense of smell can taste on its own. Bouquet became my speciality. People who just pick a glass of wine and swill it straight down don't believe that ninety per cent of taste is smell. I stayed there so long I had to ask about their laundry facilities and purchase polo shirts with Barossa embroidery on the pocket.

Developing an appreciation for wine-making as an art began pulling me out of the hole I was in. It gave me a sort of preening pride, the one which separates the critic from the hoi-polloi, puts meaning into the expression, I know what I like. Statistically more women have supernoses, but men were employed by the perfume industry, I discovered. An enthusiastic amateur, I wanted to educate my palate and ride my bike. A body has to have a hobby.

As I crossed the Nullarbor to Perth, by train, I slept as if for years I'd suffered low-level depression. In my sleep, as the vast plain of no trees passed the window of the train, the anxiety of working for the authorities gradually trickled out of my body. The Margaret River vineyard district, though interesting and really beautiful, shaved the romance off my daydreams.

As free as I thought I was, I began to be bothered by my personal highwaymen, demons of my paranoia. Or, perhaps, real men had me in their sights. The boys who drive big machines which guzzle gasoline and screech their tonnage at a threatening proximity to a girl on a bike love ugly cuttings and road-works and open-cut mines and belching sooty smoke. They hide behind tinted windows in cabins you need a step-ladder to reach and think themselves inviolable in their almighty capsules. My imagination began obsessing about what they think about all day, so I guessed it was getting me, or someone like me and making her their servant; or killing me with torture and mutilation. When I caught my mind getting to these horrible meditations I realised they had half-won.

My progress was monitored even though I haven't spilled any beans and I haven't threatened to. Between leaving for the Barossa and meeting Auntie in the middle of the Kimberley, I reckon I was working through some sort of post-shock syndrome, for the misunderstanding of me among some of the men about the place was truly frightening. The blasted, aggressive ignorance of powerful people, barely in control of themselves and their fantasies, scares me in a really deep place in my psyche. Auntie reached in there, caressed, nurtured and okayed my being in a basic way. Instead of meeting an Indian with peyote to open my doors of perception, I met a women's libber with a chip on her shoulder, a scar on her face obliterated by the pindan, who released in me my confidence and allowed me to admit my real fear. I resolved to beat it out of my brain with punishing exercise schedules and fierce competition.

In Western Australia I was free-wheeling and so fit. Destination did not worry me much. I was going clockwise round the continent. Then it became I am where I am, which sounds much sillier than it is. It came out of the blue. I body-surfed in the warm Indian Ocean, and swam with some dolphins. Because I was outside all the time I saw so much. Birds, animals, trees, skies, rocks, scrub, colours, bottle-trees, beaches and deserts. Roads, lots and lots of roads, with trucks, lorries, road-trains, utes, semi-trailers, men in steel spoiling the air. Baobabs and ant cities are sculptures. I managed to have a fine wine with my dinner in restaurants in Geraldton, Carnarvon, and Port Hedland, which achievement pleased me, but damper, nuts and dried fruit were my main fare, and water, water, water.

I showed my residents' pass to the ferryman, gear-shifted my thoughts to the present and got on with my day.

7

. . . Myrmidons of Achilles . . .

Cybil has a flat overlooking the sea in the town of Port Water. At dawn Virginia is on the beach. The Myrmidons of Achilles radiate from behind ice-cream cumuli on the eastern horizon. Vessels are out on the water already: a large container ship, several prawn trawlers, a yacht under sail, one fishing dinghy, a launch, features dwarfed by ocean and sky. Low-flying terns and a high-soaring sea eagle are placed in perspective by the artist's eye. One other human shares the beach, a man with a rod and long rubber boots, thigh-deep in the wash.

The clouds entrance Virginia. Yet she is seeking the planes of the sea. Heavy grey beyond the curling tubes of the breakers. Water's slow lines rush towards the horizontal while wood's busy shapes patiently seek the vertical. Abstract circles and angles of straight geometry she draws in her mind, trying to find the impression of correct depth; the moment of sight to capture in her work, so boat and sea are distinct in a single chunk of timber. The container ship is not moving. Further down the coast, near Newcastle, sometimes as many as fifteen merchant ships are moored outside harbour. More if the stevedores strike. Its rusty squares are clear, close, ferrous cubes of iron floating. She moves on, distracted. Her unfinished sculpture in the rainforest has brought to the front of her brain the ancients as if they lived and fought today.

Achilles beat Penthesilea, Queen of the Amazons, who had brought her forces to the assistance of Troy. Some say he raped her corpse. The sea glitters like the armour that Thetis, his mother, had Vulcan make for him when, after one of his sulks, he agreed to go to Troy. Mummy's boy, she must protect him by all means in her power. Achilles was destined to die in the Trojan wars like Penthesilea, whom he murdered and humiliated. Even though Thetis knew Achilles' fate, she tried to defy it. She gripped him by the heel and dipped him in the River Styx to make him impervious to wounds. She hid him dressed as a maiden in Scyros to avoid battle. Ulysses wanted him and found him. Death culture.

Virginia has seen it for herself, mothers cheating for their sons. Fortunately, neither she nor Jeff took much notice of what their mother said, poor woman. She realises she has just experienced another burst of inspiration for her sculpture, for she has, actually, little knowledge of the classics. Only a children's book of Homer and ABC radio of the 1950s featuring the Argonauts. A few discussions with Caroline. The Greeks needed Achilles. Virginia finds it simple to imagine the court at Scyros, having seen the drag queens at the Orlando dance. Most looked like footballers amusing themselves with their hairy bear-like bodies in feminine clothes.

Jeff works with atoms on computers. And twins ruled Sparta.

Cybil delights in putting her into situations to see if she can make Virginia compromise her principles. Cybil had wanted to dress up as an oil painting as she feels her looks belong to another age. Her body out of fashion, Cybil enjoys camping it up as much as the queens, and flirting. But Virginia is grateful for the whisky and the experience as she understands more about misogyny. She feels she knows why Penthesilea fought. Clytemnestra did not leave her subjects, hence retained some power. Helen did and lost everything. If Jeff and Virginia were the Spartan twins, it would have been Virginia who went to war and Jeff who handled the political business at home.

Virginia frowns. She watches the surf and the powerful launch, bow rearing through the force of knots, slashing the goddess of the sea. Mothers who give their boys feminine disguises, inviolable armour, ultimately please the cheating general, Apollo. Daddy's girls. The art of the poets brought to the service of the death culture, glorifying war, manipulate sentiment.

The sun has risen higher in the sky, but it is behind pillows of cloud.

The Amazons' dawn is stolen and the sun's rays recruited in the fight against them. The Myrmidons are written into history from the ancient world to Gallipoli diggers' hats. Hellespont. The Dardenelles. Same place, for godsake. Virginia White reconciles her distrust of men with her love of her brother and his sons by admitting to herself she is but an individual being, a grain of sand. The wind whips up. It is about to rain. She is back at Cybil's flat by seven-thirty when she should be waking.

Off shore, the ship hesitates in its journey. The engines quieten, the gauge registers no knots, working merchant marines sit down for a smoke in the galley, turning a blind eye. All that is expected of them is ignorance. On deck, the activity is slick, quick. There are no coastal-watch Cessnas, no police helicopters, nor incidental vigilantes. The weather threatens. The few fishermen out on this ocean are one-eyed johnnies attending their hooks. The masters rely on their brutalised crew's obedience. The pay is good, the promise better than the normal expectations of their brothers at home. The crew have no responsibility. No power. Never would a woman be employed. Except as a prostitute. Then, only at port. The sailors on deck see a speedboat heading to shore.

Business done, the tanker makes way.

Alison did not come home to Tilly, who slept with the animals in the barn and woke with them, as soon as the swallows started nattering in the rafters. She dawdles across the acre through the dank dawn in her thin flannel nightie and bare feet to Chandra's house. She is decidedly damp when she cuddles into her mum-substitute and starts chattering. Rain makes life outside for Chandra three times more difficult than it does for anyone else.

'Hello, spring chicken,' Chandra greets her with barely forced gaiety.

They are into their day by seven a.m.: Tilly releasing the chooks, feeding them, giving Spotty his biscuit of hay, Chandra checking her email and going on-line to the real-time chat.

<MOP> Monkish living is not necessarily a sign of goodness & materialism is not the only evil.

<BLUESKY> Become a member of the fuck-up force?

<SKUMBO> To unwork is my aim. I hear you mujere.

<DEFARGE> Where do you mad sisters live?

<BLUESKY> Males, like rats following the pied piper, will be lured by pussy to their doom.

<DEFARGE> Identify yourselves. Where am I?

<BAC> Drug pushers and advocates are hastening the dropping out of men.

Chandra slides backwards: 'become a member of the fuck-up force'? She thought she booted out that nutter. Chandra doubts whether the revolution is as easy as that. It is possible to destabilise defence systems, but dangerous. Ditto, the money market. She knows she can set in place the infrastructure for war, create tools, but she needs unified commitment to strategies. The cells can't just go off, like free radicals, destroying what they please.

<WHEELS> consider the implications, she types. Because it is raining outside she will be at her desk all day. Especially if the avatar in Cellar2chat is failing. She needs to run a check throughout the whole site.

Cybil Crabbe sees the fierce pride in Virginia White's eyes and the deep, troubled groove above her nose as she bends down to kiss her as she wakes. She writhes with the self-indulgence of a cat and decides it is not wise to project onto Virginia the grumpiness she feels and identifies as her own guilt. Instead Cybil traces the long vein on her forearm with her soft fingers, then slips her hand between T-shirt and skin. She says nothing. She goes about exciting Virginia's sexuality with her tongue and her hands, aware of the effect she is creating. She reduces Virginia; she melts her. She is greedy for pleasure, as needy for Virginia's climax as her own orgasm. Cybil is a sensualist. When they are replete, they overflow and dissolve into the messy bedclothes. Cybil smiles cheekily. Virginia would like to tell her what she has been thinking as she would with most lovers in bed after sex, but with Cybil it takes an effort.

She tries. 'Transsexuals, according to themselves, are women trapped in male bodies. Was my Amazon soul trapped in a male body in a past life?'

'I don't believe in reincarnation,' Cybil says. 'It just excuses bullshit artists.'

Virginia adjusts her position in the big brass bed, and talks. 'Trannies who want to be lesbians appear less misogynistic than transvestites.'

'And, assumably, have less tacky taste in clothes,' Cybil plays with Puddles' ears.

'They are another version of Achilles at Scyros. Their task is to infiltrate the fearsome women's-only world for their own purposes.' Virginia's heavy eyebrows meet each other and she clenches her teeth. 'Sex and war. Rape. The pursuit of androgyny, for us, is pathetic.'

'VeeDub, you took the prize as the woman best dressed as a man,' Cybil likes an argument. 'How ironic!' They agree on nothing.

'As Orlando. You don't understand what Virginia Woolf was trying to say,' Virginia reaches for her book. But Cybil does not want to be read to.

Virginia herself cannot concentrate on the written words. Her mood changes. She remembers the lost raft. Forty years at sea. Flotsam. Driftwood. In Cybil's bed, gazing into the middle distance, unfocused. 'Disguised as a woman, Achilles fathered Neoptolemus. As a victor, he desecrated the bodies he defeated which was not a Greek custom, rather one of a more savage past.'

'What are you talking about?' Cybil interrupts. 'What's that got to do with the price of fish in China?'

'Achilles, the hero, is an immature person, a spoilt brat, a horror and a worry. The murder and dishonourable treatment of Penthesilea was unmitigated hatred. When he felt like it Achilles could heal injuries. What a weird irrational myth! He loved his boyfriend, Patroclus, so much he had to avenge his death by killing and abusing the remains and the family of Hector. He ravaged the Queen of the Amazons, arsehole! His final and fatal courage was inspired by his grief over the death of Patroclus. And they are such cheats, these fellows. Apollo disguised as Paris, or Paris himself helped by Apollo, fired a poisoned arrow from behind into his vulnerable heel. Achilles was vanquished by an act of cowardice on the part of a god. Makes you wonder; is cowardice central to the male myth?'

'Men are sooks,' Cybil, who suffers dysmenorrhoea, states, getting up.

Virginia queries rhetorically, 'How many living Amazons hate Achilles as I do?'

'Mummy's boys all over the globe have their battles fought for them.' Cybil wraps herself into her expensive dressing gown. She flicks underclothes off her computer keyboard.

'Maintaining sexual access to women, when their true love is men. Daddy's girls are inconsistent and vindictive, according to Valerie Solanas.' Virginia puts her arms behind her head on the pillow.

'What would you know about daddy's girls?' says Cybil quite viciously, as she checks her electronic mail. She sees herself as a superwoman, making it in the world. Virginia frowns at her lover's desire to hurt her. Suddenly, Cybil is late for work. 'While I have a shower, would you iron my shirt, my eagle? Please?' She raises her eyebrows.

Virginia shakes her head, 'No.'

Cybil shrugs then says, 'There is something I want to ask you. Won't be a minute.'

Virginia rolls out of bed, and touches her toes. 'You iron your own shirt. I'll make a coffee,' she calls passing the bathroom. As she sniffs the fresh grounds and waits for the kettle to boil, she realises she hates these demands of Cybil. The power game is pathetic. No contest. She pours hot water into the coffee pot and places the plunger carefully on its surface.

'I'm not going to socialise again, if that is what you want,' she tells Cybil as she emerges from the shower in a towel. Holding her mug to her, Virginia asks, 'What is it, then?'

Cybil irons with great care, like a dry cleaner, a perfectionist about pressing, and does not take the mug until she is finished. Then she laughs. She is warm and beautiful and Virginia grins. She feels sorry for Cybil.

Cybil clears a spot on her couch and says, 'Come here.' She reaches for Virginia's foot and massages it, glancing up through her lashes. 'Huge feet and your toes have little webs.'

'Yes?' Virginia is both amused and apprehensive.

'Concerns you. Mm. I'll come out with it. I have had a bet, well, I'm running a book. Will you compete in Sunday's triathlon?' she says quickly. She doesn't like divulging much.

'What triathlon? Where?' Virginia is taken by surprise.

'The only thing you have to do is compete. Please, it's only half-length. Swim seven hundred and fifty metres, bike, I don't know, fifteen kilometres and, run, about one or one and half. Like, you did all those things as a kid.

Will you do it for me? I want to see if you can do it now. Prove all that stuff about beating Jeff at bike races.'

Virginia laughs, and explains, 'The only bike race we had was at school. I did win it, but you had to come last. Anyway, why not? Sure.' The question of her age doesn't bother Virginia. Cybil will make herself unavailable if Virginia does not allow herself to be her toy. At the moment, she aches for her.

Virginia feels both abandoned and relieved when Cybil slams the door, descends the stairs and drives away. She plays on the computer, but is oppressed by the flat and goes soon afterwards, leaving the mess as she would never do at her own home. She doesn't care whether she competes or not. She likes a race and in that case doesn't mind playing this part in Cybil's scenario. Constantly on the make, constantly at some scheme or scam, always busy, Cybil controls Virginia's thoughts because she can make no sense of her. The triathlon is not all in Cybil's agenda, does she want to laugh at her? To show her off? To show her up? Her pride will not let her entertain the possibility of betrayal.

Shopping first, she heads bush as soon as she can.

Rory has a flattish, freckly Irish face. A favourite hat with the badges of the revolution pinned in all available space on the brown felt usually hides her thin ginger hair. Strong neck, low-hanging breasts and a penchant for the khaki and camouflage clothes from army disposal stores, Rory always has pockets, for torch, a knife, a pen, a pad and, often, a bit of reading. So dressed, and out walking, she is met by one of the gurls, Ella, who tells her the bridge is completely down and her car is stuck. Rory, the practical one, must be told of the broken bridge. Ella is on the edge of panic. Getting into Rory's truck, they drive towards the gates of Lesbianlands. Rory won't be blackmailed, bullied, bribed or bought, but she would do anything for anybody.

Because of the steep hills and gullies, Lesbianlands is far more than the three hundred hectares on title across the ground. Women have come and gone for twenty years and they keep coming. Many shelters constructed with love and excitement, now abandoned, can be occupied by lesbians who bring no inclination to become carpenters. Ella is a relatively recent arrival. Rory finds her timid, although her manner of dress suggests city-lesbian chic. Madly liberated by land-living, she wears a slip and lace bra with a leather jacket, high lace-up boots and stud in her nose. They don't talk much as Rory skilfully negotiates the bush track.

A number of gurls are waiting for them. A fire in a circle of rocks keeps the billy boiling. Rory pulls up and gets out and says yes to a coffee and hunkers down to listen. The story is unsatisfactory. A large heavy vehicle must have gone across the bridge, weakened it, and when Ella came screaming in too fast, still drunk and high from partying after the dance, it collapsed. The tin mugs empty, a few walk down the hill to examine the situation and inspect the damage. The huge logs thrown across the fast-flowing creek by loggers of yesteryear had given way. The planks of hardwood are severed in jagged, fresh breaks. The old Holden sits on the edge of these on its under-carriage, front wheels hanging over the creek.

Everyone's movements are discussed and reiterated but the upshot is no gurl hired a bulldozer or six-tonne truck in the last fortnight. The gurls laugh; disaster brings out their humour.

'No one has had a dam made,' Ci is frivolous, making a joke about an incident years ago when an individualist had brought men in to make her a personal dam so that she would have water for her garden. Like many who come too full of action, she had left. Her legacy, now, a pleasant billabong. There is always tension between the desires of the one and the consensus of the many.

'No,' Rory mumbles. 'But a bulldozer has been through here.'

'We expected it to last forever. Damn and bother!' Querrin jokes.

'Ella's car might have broken it. But who did the original harm?'

'It's a mystery. Looks like the planks were put back to hide the damaged logs underneath.' Dee points at evidence for her theory. 'That is malicious.'

'Not to say very dangerous.'

Gig says, 'Hope saw the Campbell women.'

'Well, it couldn't be one of us, could it?' Rory asserts.

'What we need is a detective,' Dee grins, winks, 'nudge nudge'.

Rory goes red, 'That may be so.' She kneels down and remarks, 'These are definitely bulldozer tracks.'

'A lot of them.' Fi asks Ella, 'Did you hear anything, I mean, like the big bits breaking?' Ella shakes her head.

'He backed away after he broke the bridge and went through the creek,' Dee says, again pointing. 'Over there.'

'He?' repeats Ci, with irony.

'Do you know any woman with a dozer?'

'Or an army tank, perhaps?' Gig joins the ironic tone.

Rory looks at Dee. 'You're right about a detective, let's hire one.'

'Yeah, Rory, you fancy the ex-cop, we know that.' Dee smiles.

'So, let's get her,' Rory argues. 'Let's ask Margot if she can figure it out.'

'Why?' Ti Dyer is aggressive. 'We do everything ourselves, we don't need her.'

'Maybe not, but, as Dee said, I'd like to give her an excuse to visit me,' Rory says peaceably. 'Does anyone know anything?'

'Judith was casual, when I spoke to her, as if it didn't matter,' Gig tells them.

'It might not matter to her, but it does to us, we don't have a four-wheel-drive and we need this bridge.' Ti Dyer maintains her aggro. 'You've got the vehicle to get around. Can we make a decision now to get the bridge fixed?'

'No, we'll have to have a meeting,' Rory responds.

'That will mean women coming from Sydney, Canberra, wherever.'

'Have we got any money in the bank?' enquires Ci.

Rory shrugs, 'Ask Judith. But I don't think so. We won't get the bridge fixed straight away, unless you want to pay for it out of your own pocket.'

'So, will we get Margot to come, get a full report from someone objective?' Dee finalises.

'Okay.' It always surprises Rory how the lesbians on the plain, the easiest part of the lands to live on, enjoy the prospect of a new romantic liaison.

She gets back in her truck, waving to the group of gurls. Perhaps they care that she hasn't had a lover for so long. She likes to think so.

8

. . . the World Wide Web . . .

The police station was a fancy new building beside a sweet little sandstone jail which could almost achieve a heritage listing but as it is islanded in the middle of a tarred car park, that would be unlikely. Patrol cars only—except for a tow-truck with oily dark duco, a mean-looking machine, American made V-8 engine and a vicious hook hanging free off a crane mounted in the tray—were there.

Uniformed officers were coming and going as I stood at the front desk. I didn't have to wait long. Philippoussis took me up to a bare interview room on the second floor. Alone we relaxed a bit. I signed the statement which he read out. It was close enough. When he asked, I did not expand much on the barbecue personnel. Apparently they had given statements. They knew nothing. In his mind, I had no connection with them, nor were any of the gays too drunk or doped. He shrugged when I asked disinterested questions.

We chatted. He was fixed on the coincidence of the two different deaths on one night, in one small part of the world.

A theorist, Phil. He said, 'It all seems consistent with an established profile of a manslaughter involving drinking, drugs, kids, the beach, a Friday night, careless sex, mixture of marijuana, alcohol and hopelessness. Car accidents. Violence happens. But in this case, I reckon there was a relationship between the two.'

'Girl overdoses in toilet block, boyfriend freaks out, takes off, totals his car and himself. Tragic but not unusual. Do you think she was raped?' I asked automatically.

He looked at me steadily for a moment. 'She was not really a she. She was a he. A lad in drag.'

'No way!' I was stunned.

Philippoussis had not been one of the cops who interviewed me on the night, so he was surprised I, with my background, had not examined the body, at least rudimentarily. I had not. Not a cop, just a civvy witness who wouldn't disturb a possible crime scene, I had gone to the toilet and closed the door on a very young corpse slumped into a concrete corner, slack and wasted, skinny legs in black tights spreadeagled out from a mini-skirt, hair black-hennaed, and make-up. Far too much make-up.

The words 'white virgin?' popped out of my mouth, as I remembered the grimy Nadir company cap I took home.

'It is hard to tell whether a boy is a virgin or not,' DC Philippoussis said, meditatively and ironically at the same time. 'We'll know more after the full PM. The body will be on ice for a few days. Because he was found where he was, and how he was, there will have to be a coronial investigation into the cause of his death.'

He was still pondering my question. 'But I don't think he was raped. No anal bruising. Could have had sex though. How would you know? Ejaculation often occurs in the death throes. Bodily reaction to leaving this world. But, as I said, we will have to wait for the pathologist's report.'

I rather liked the way he took my silly question seriously, without prejudice.

'Too many dead youths in rural New South Wales,' he continued. 'Wish we could do something about it, but resources, you know. They have to do an autopsy when someone dies in suspicious circumstances, but I want a full one for both boys. Forensic medicine is not a glam job among the medicos these days. Did a paper at uni on it. Stats show huge discrepancies between certified causes of death and post-mortem findings. Doctors are too scared of litigation to find out exactly how their patients die. But,' he said, uncertainly, 'they could try to put them both to bed and throw the investigation away. Save money.'

Phil, I guessed, would be about ten years my junior. I recognised the bloodhound in him. He wanted to find the answers, the complete picture, regardless of cut-backs. A matter of urgency, he wanted to be sure these deaths were not homicide. His first murder would be an important point in his career. I was friendly to this man, and not only because he was easy to look upon, easy to be with. Rather, my ulterior motive was to have, for future reference in my career as a PI, a trustworthy ally with access to Criminal Intelligence files. Not a bad thing to build up a network of contacts.

Lisa has been missing all weekend, according to the mother of the teenage girl. Since the fight she rang me about on Saturday. After the cop shop and before meeting Margaret Hall in the industrial area, I set about this paying job.

Heroin addiction is seen as sexy in the fashion industry. Stockbrokers and dentists and architects, who sit around their low-slung coffee tables on a Sunday afternoon, taking a line of recreational smack with their chardonnay and chilled bottled water, could lobby to stop the senseless, expensive war on drugs, but they don't. All charm collapses when you get among the teenagers trying to be chic. While the professionals' own cheeks are rosy in the mirror, they are entertained by the hard-angled shots of bony girls with black-rimmed eyes in slummy backgrounds, glossy art photography on their walls. Stoned and self-satisfied, they are cushioned by money. Corporate lawyers with mates at the bar of the criminal courts get paid so much for protecting the high financiers who knock out a few small economies with a stroke of the pen or a swear word on the phone, don't need their delicious, naughty pleasures to be cheap especially. No doubt, like clothes, the more expensive the better. If they could buy it like the Bollinger with a credit card at Liquorland I would be happier.

The war on drugs must be maintained! So many resources are bound up in it; manpower, money, policy. Not to say corruption. The black economy playing a game of chess with the white economy: pawns are dispensable; and there are pawns on both sides. I have been a white pawn, even though I thought I was a knight. We were, in the Authority, disgusted by the futility of our work when we got evidence against the high-flying criminal, often a respected man of money. We would get the case to court, only to be defeated by clever legal shenanigans. While everyone knew they had done it, they would walk away on a technicality, free, laughing. Not a blot on the copybooks of the oh-so-dignified, expensive barristers, their reputations stay pristine. The foot soldiers of the black economy, the cannon fodder, are addicts about the place who, however they got there, are in such pain there is no better thing than its obliteration. Whether, to begin with, it is physical, emotional, social or psychological—possibly feisty anger at political injustice—it becomes the addicts' personal problem. They need escape. They have a hit to get rid of the discomfort, and it's dreamy and cool. I have sat down and listened to their 'cool', and heard excuses, justification, cynicism and a lack of compassion for others which, as I thought of it, mirrored the scorn of the powerful with their total lack of conscience. 'Hey man, you're wrecked.' The victim and the victors are two sides in the one game, a mentality, a moral cancer in our society. In the victim's morning there's no ache worse than his, it's the worst—the starving millions in the world, well, knowing about that just contributes to his pain. 'Like you're travelling, man, in paradise lost, but you know where to find heaven, for a day,' a poet-junkie explained to me in an interview room once. 'You just have to score.'

Two dead boys. So much for heroin chic, glorified decadence! My high is health. I have seen heroin make heroines of the victims of incest. Fathers and stepfathers breaking the daughters to perpetuate the suffering cycle of worthlessness to make them available for the brotherhood later in life. Lisa, her mother has told me, did not suffer any trauma or abuse in her early childhood; she was more spoilt than anything. However, you never know. I went out to find the girl.

So far as a country's resources go, the war on drugs is a waste of money. And lining some very interesting pockets. I still consider blowing the whistle on a few individuals I have the facts about, but is it worth my life? I rode my bike to escape, but they chase me, keeping an eye on my every move, even way outback where there would be nothing but me and a road-train. In that cabin, a CB radio, 'breaker, breaker, she's here, she's there. Roger and out.' The juggernaut of corruption with mechanical tentacles electronically connected on all the band-widths lets its shadow fall on me whenever they feel the need to activate my fear. There is no way I can convince them I am no threat, short of working for them. And that, I will not do.

Lisa is fourteen years old. I had fetched her home before. The old crime, 'in moral danger', a case of the missing consonant, in mortal danger. It could have been she in the toilet block.

Down the streets of Port Water, into the arcade, up to the seats outside the foyer of the flicks, glancing at stills of Bruce Willis blowing up something in motion picture action, silhouetted in flames, I found kids were hanging around with not enough money to go to the movies. Among skateboards and drippy hair, I found no Lisa. Port Water, a town dedicated to tourism, has a big marina for ocean-going yachts, bars, cafés and motels, fun parks and little zoos, pleasures on sale everywhere, water-skiing with a parachute and, outside the breakwater, deep-sea fishing. One of the most popular places on the eastern seaboard, it is perfect for the dropping off of mega-millions of dollars worth of dope, cocaine and heroin. A rusty junk of illegal immigrants beached a few months ago.

The teenagers, wearing baggies so big both hands in pockets were needed to hold them up, bringing their shoulders forward in a hunch, but carefully showing bright boxer silks underneath, were not cynical or unhelpful. Their hair was parted in the middle to hang vertically over the cheeks, speckled with angry pimples from a diet of coke and french fries, which rarely bunch into a smile; it emphasised a kind of worried look, a worry in itself. I asked questions and got monosyllabic responses. Eventually extracting a clue, I went out to the new suburbs where brick veneer, road-works and roofscapes are replacing, at a rapid rate, the banksia, tea-tree, paperbark scrub of the coast. Houses on stilts dip into gullies of remaining rainforest. The natural contours of hills gently rising from the sea were covered by dwellings for humans seeking a view.

The schoolkids were in the rumpus room under the main part of the new four bed-roomed 'bungalow', beside the two-car garage. Five lads and Lisa lolled, half-standing, leaning, their eyes attached to the light of the screen, indifferent to my entrance. The computer monitor showed garish colour and jerky movement. The action looked pretty horrendous to me. Choosing the boy seated as the most probable line of articulation, I asked were they old enough for this stuff. I found out that this game had not yet received a rating from the Office of Film and Literature Classification. They giggled, proud as smart youngsters. It was only a trial version, freely available on the Internet. While the graphics were amazing, the depiction of competition and violence was horrifying. The boys with their loopy eyes were fascinated. Lisa looked bored. She had accepted that I had come for her, and, although not evidently keen, was acquiescent. For her I was an easy way home. We left the boys to their virtual aggression.

'Don't you think the nature of those games has some effect on how depressed you are?' I asked her in the car.

'I'm not depressed,' she said with dying fall.

'No?' I was incredulous. 'You look it.'

She whined, 'I was just having fun.' Her voice sounded morose.

'Whatever happened to swimming, playing hockey? Sports? I used to surf after school, or when I wagged,' I talked, determined to get something out of her.

'Like go groan,' she said. 'Computers are cool. Chat pages are real cool. Nerds are really cool. Surfies are dorks.'

I asked about the sexual material on the World Wide Web I had heard so much about.

'It sucks. I belong to Let's Wait. It started in America. You don't do it till you're married,' she explained, becoming serious. 'You know, it's about health too. You don't catch anything that way.'

Her mother figured it was cheaper hiring me than ending up with a daughter with a drug habit, health problems or criminal tendencies. Lisa's lift home cost her mother a hundred bucks. By the time we got into the shopping centre, Lisa had convinced me she would be all right, no matter what. Her mother worked in a travel agency, and walked with the brisk clippedy-clop confidence of a business lady. Her money was well spent. Lisa sloped off along side her.

Lisa, who stayed out nights without saying where she was, belonged to some on-line right-wing youth movement which restricted sex before marriage. How bizarre!

Chandra communicates with a woman from Thailand, initiating a signature campaign on behalf of a Burmese group. Then she emails

RAWA, the Revolutionary Association of the Women of Afghanistan, who have requested notes of solidarity to their office in Islamabad. Home and the world have become different places since the advent and expansion of the World Wide Web. Chandra hopes for no interruptions as she has so much to do. When she returns to one of her own webpages, someone has altered the background: how?

Virginia has an efficient vehicle, a white Holden Rodeo, four-wheel-drive, 2.8-litre turbo diesel dual-cab ute, which she services herself in the garage of a friend, sometimes leaving it there while she rides around Stuart on her bike. Recently she replaced the gearing on her old Malvern Star, and showed Cybil, which must have given her the idea about this triathlon thing.

A station wagon is hanging off the bridge. She drives through the creek, carefully avoiding large boulders. Because of the intensity of her thinking, she detours to Rory's place. They have a cup of tea together. Rory tells her about the bridge and the proposed meeting. Virginia nods. She, then, talks. They talk.

For thirty years, the SCUM Manifesto has been Rory's bible. Every time she rolls a cigarette, she imagines Valerie doing the same. It is a prayer ritual for her.

Rory shows Virginia a picture of Andy Warhol in the weekend newspaper's colour supplement, the 'weird, wigged-out creature who glamorised the banal'. She shakes her head, but she reads on, '"a void needs filling and one of Andy Warhol's objectives in life seemed to be to make himself exactly that: a void, a cipher, an empty mirror on which people could project anything and everything", a hollow man, a vacuum.' She nods. 'He was a working-class boy enamoured of the products and values of capitalist popular culture that the middle class take for granted, infatuated with the stardom of Hollywood's icons, less understandable as an evil genius than a compelling, slippery historical accident, a celebrity freak. This is the bloke Valerie Solanas chose to shoot, to practise what she preached. No wonder he did not die, there was no heart to hit.'

Virginia laughs, 'No blood in his veins but lies and hypocrisy, rip off and greed. The woman was a genius. You're not wrong. I met Warhol once.'

Rory enthuses, 'This little lonely avatar predicted the backlash world before the second wave of feminism. Before! She is a kind of John the Baptist to our new faith.'

Virginia, not the first to notice that ex-Catholics never lose the connection between behaviour and belief, says, 'Yeah, he was a scared man, but I was a post-modernist then.'

Rory continues, 'And Ti-Grace Atkinson is Peter, or Paul, the strategist?'

'Geez, Rory, it's years since I read those works. But I'll have another look. Could be interesting.'

'Before she could gather about her a tribe of apostles, before I could meet her, affirm her and hug her. Valerie's main friend was a drag queen! We have come so far,' she impresses her point with a fist on the table. 'We have land, we have community, we have visibility, we have strength, brains and some level of solidarity with her vision. But what have we done with her legacy?'

'The revolutionary movement has gone further underground, on the net. Discovered it on Cybil's computer,' Virginia reassures Rory.

'That's it,' states Rory. 'I have to get one.' They talk about solar power, battery hours, the nuts and bolts of alternative energy until Rory's decision has gelled into a number of pragmatic steps.

As she is about to leave, Virginia mentions Cybil's request, with a grin. 'Swimming, cycling, running.'

Rory says, 'She's trying to make a fool of you, VeeDub. They train for those things. She has you by the short and curlies.'

'That's going too far, Rory. It's chemistry, right? What goes on between two women? Who can explain it?' Virginia asks, dramatically.

'No, fair dinkum,' Rory is serious. 'She wants to publicly humiliate you. But don't worry. I'll organise the gurls and we'll be there. You'll have a fan club.'

Virginia laughs. 'Okay, I'll win.'

'Will you? Rory laughs. 'You'll never beat Margot, she's a professional.'

'Should be fun, anyway,' Virginia concedes.

Standing together, outside amidst the dripping trees, Rory asks, 'The Internet is a maze, a labyrinth, a safe underground for a Solanasite Conspiracy?'

'Why not?' encourages Virginia. 'Or you could call it Penthesilea's Revenge.'

'Yes, I'm working on getting on-line, already.' Rory rubs her palms together.

'Good, I'd better be off.' Virginia, finally, goes.

Unlike Virginia White, Rory passionately believes in written language. She avidly studies the IT sections of her newspaper. The female connotations of the World Wide Web, the words used, are spinsterish. She thinks this must have some meaning, as do those for the nuclear arsenal which are penile and phallic: missile erector and deep penetration of certain weapons. It is etymological.

In the supermarket a mother and teenage son were having a long conversation about bread. An exchange of rare interest to them both, as they didn't want to stop. They went from the merits of budget white to those of soy and linseed without argument. It was a discussion, a closeness. I felt as if I had dreamed this moment.

'What about genetically altered produce?' he said. Like mother, like son.

In a shed behind a fibro house near the industrial area, I bought a second-hand computer from a Mr Hacker with an electronic voice. Strange but true. He must have suffered throat cancer and had his vocal cords replaced with an amplifier. For a man who spoke through a tube, he was incredibly impatient. It cost the same as a dozen bottles of Leeuwin Estate Art Series, which offer from my wine club I had to decline. The printer is a new one, a laser. Very nice copy for my reports.

Margaret Hall came with me and we had coffee together afterwards. *Penthouse, Playboy* and various soft porn glossies, full of explicit photos, were the magazine reading for the customers of this place while they waited for their fast food. 'What if guys wanted to read something else? What if they were religious, family men?'

Margaret shrugged, 'They probably bring a cut lunch, prepared by the better half who will make sure that he has eaten it. Somehow. The brothel's just over there, busiest time when the wife and kids are at the movies. Weekends. Otherwise, the working week, lunchtime.' I watched her spoon sugar into the foam of her cappuccino.

She said then, with a laugh, 'It's basically useless, Margot.'

'Why?' I asked, indignant. 'Why did you let me buy it?'

'Because it is too old to get on-line, or collect email. That's where the action is. And you said you only want to have a filing system that doesn't take up too much room, for book-keeping and databases,' she explained. Margaret turned out to be the type of cyberchick who knows so much, she withholds all information until she feels safe. 'The World Wide Web is like a mine,' she continued. 'There's a lot of rubble to wade through but you can find some jewels.' A sudden, though slight, change came over her face when she glanced at me. Obviously she took me for an electronic age moron and dropped the subject. Or she really did not want me to have the latest equipment for my profession and my work.

But I let my suspicions ride, and shrugged. 'It'll do for financial records of my renovations, my hobbies and my personal life. Spreadsheets. Typing out reports, won't it? Don't want to download viruses from the net.'

'Sure,' she didn't care. 'This community is full of drama-addicts,' she opined, fishing for exactly the same gossip she criticised. Although she wanted to know my weakness, for some reason, at that time and place, being pre-menstrual, I raved on, carefully omitting gossip about Maria and Sofia, the dead boy and Meghan Featherstone, concentrating on myself. Our mutual friend was my ex-lover.

'Broom can't even afford the time to telephone me,' I concluded.

'Actions speak louder than words, they say,' she said. 'It is a matter of honour among lesbians to remain friends after a break-up. You've got to work at it.'

Margaret shook more sugar from its little paper package onto her palm.

'Well,' I allowed myself to express the anger of hurt, 'She couldn't give a flying fuck. What a hypocrite, what a coward! Witch!'

'So, it's over, Margot. You're dumped. And you're feeling all the abandonment you ever had,' said she, indifferently, as she licked her hand. I couldn't imagine anyone getting close to Margaret. She seemed to have a glass wall around her. Friends were species to be examined.

'Broom's just a lovable spoilt brat. Some women are sex objects very young, treated like little princesses by mild, smug patriarchs who do not have to resort to violent behaviour. They use a reward system, flattery, education, money, contacts, you name it. Broom hates her mother, right? I find, especially with spoilt brats of the middle class, the mother is cast as some bitch, either faceless and frigid or righteous and hidebound with conservative values. There are spoilt brats in the proletariat and some middle-class girls aren't spoilt brats. Viragos, misers, madwomen, nymphomaniacs, just women trying to keep their end up, trying to take power over their own lives, difficult when he has everything and she has to beg. I think Broom's parents were in the Hitler Youth.'

'I made a bit of an effort, but—' I hesitated, wondering what danger am I? 'Seems she can't be bothered ringing me.'

Margaret looked around as she spoke. 'I think she's into some eco-feminist trip, saving the trees up north.'

Jealousy stirred like a beast in my breast. After so much time.

Margaret picked up some loose packets of white sugar from a neighbouring table. Her face was pale, dark rings under her eyes.

'When you're the injured party,' I tried to explain, though it was stale news, 'everyone avoids you, you're a pain in the neck, no one wants to hear you bellyache.' I let myself open up to Margaret, to whom I was no more than a curiosity. 'Words get taken out of context onto the grapevine and one becomes a character in someone else's story.' I felt like bitching.

When we had said goodbye, I went off wondering why Margaret Hall had offered to help me buy a computer when the one I acquired was less than perfect. She wanted to make sure of that? She wanted to assess me for herself.

The industrial estate outside Stuart borders on a banana plantation and State Forest. The rain eased a bit and I took a run around its utilitarian streets. Broom made me love myself. She was this wonderful mirror who laughed at my jokes and excited my senses. I missed that.

Having the extremes in this area, you would think you'd have tolerance, but you don't. You have random acts of hatred, the odd brutal massacre and mutilation of wildlife, yet you have koala hospitals and FAWNA for the rescue of native animals and birds. Organised xenophobia in new neo-Nazi political parties as well as peace-love festivals of reconciliation attended by the wannabee Aborigines dressed in Red Indian clobber, exclusive gatherings, everywhere; multiculturalism within the monoculture of capitalism. Freedom! Primary staples of rural Australia were here: fish, fruit, beef, milk, timber, and mining. Service businesses. Diehard right-wingers share the grocers, pubs, clubs and video stores with way-out alternative types. Perhaps, I thought as I jogged along a fire trail, the diverse values can be expressed in attitudes to dirt. From neurotic cleanliness, attacking germs, and those people have gardens ruled off like school projects, with pretty flowers all in a row, coloured-in, to such blind passion for nature that to wash your hair or wear leather is criminal, so they go about barefooted and grubby in a uniform of ratbaggery, great for camping in front of bulldozers in pristine forests and endangered wetlands.

Serious rain. I drove through the new suburbs, windscreen-wipers thrashing, and decided to stop for a work-out and shower. When I got to the gym Sean was not there. Instead, Tiger Cat was hail-fellow, well-met, loud, friendly, too open, and too cunning. She was hanging about on the weights, watching the door. Expecting me? Checking on me? As soon as I entered, she was ready to leave what she was doing to come up to me. She brought my attention to the absence of my trainer and friend, claiming an intimacy with him that must have been exaggerated. I asked her if she was staying on the Paradise Coast. She smirked. I asked her whether she was working or holidaying, to which she responded, 'Always on the job, you know me, having a great time, wish you were here.' It was supposed to be funny.

Silently, I worked my stomach muscles, shoulders, neck; I did sit-ups and back stretches. Tiger Cat asked me if there was anything wrong. I didn't answer.

And, when I was leaving, she called across the room, 'Remember me to the mob.'

'I will,' I replied, and intended to.

No gym-junkie myself, I can work anger and loneliness out of the system in training and competition. Tiger Cat had less body fat than I; probably never bleeds.

Instead of taking the vehicular ferry, I came home the long way past the place where the boy was killed in the car crash. The river road has many bends and a covering of road metal. Loose stones lessen the corrugations you get on sandy dirt roads, but are hazardous. I saw the skid marks, the broken fence, a marvellous old twisted tree torn at the trunk and some shattered glass on the verge. I wondered who the lad was—one of the brave young men I heard hooning that evening?

Alison rang, telling me she really had to get away from Chandra's place, but she was not feeling safe in her own house. She rattled on about the corpse in the toilet block at the beach in such a way I found it inappropriate to tell her what I had discovered today.

'By the way, heard of a bod called Tiger Cat?' I probed, lightly.

Her voice changed. It dropped a complete octave as she said, 'There are undercover cops sniffing about.'

'So you know what she's doing here?' I made so as to ask.

'We are certain that someone creepy is creeping around. We don't know that it's not you, do we?' Alison sounded crazy.

'No, you don't,' I said sharply. 'What the hell are you talking about? And, who's we, exactly?' I asked. 'Are you at angry at me? Or pigs in general?'

'I can't tell you,' she answered.

Controlling my tone, I signed off with, 'See you then.'

Having eaten a bland vegetable pasta with a glass of quaffing chianti, mentally trying to realign my life from the self-interest of training for athletic events to the work of detective, I set up at my new second-hand computer.

The phone rang. 'Ready for Sunday?' he said, referring to the local half-triathlon.

'Yes, Sean, I know. End of season, and after one down the coast, then we'll see if I'm going overseas, won't we?' I fumed. 'Where were you today?'

'Sorry,' Sean said, then reminded me that my contract with Nike depended on my next two performances.

The rain resolved to a steady drumbeat, surrounding my house like a doona of wet down. I attacked the new keyboard. Figuring out the software, I contemplated the labyrinthine ways of cyberspace, but found it hard to share the manic enthusiasm of Margaret. I am a down-to-earth person. I need to feel things, taste them, see them to be convinced of their actual reality. Virtual reality is a puzzle to me because there is no smell. My intuition—my confidence—needed to be grounded. Apparently, computers are as addictive as playing the pokies.

Meghan Featherstone's financial papers were neatly clipped together at the top and unevenly stacked at the bottom. There were two signatures one above the other. In the sideways glimpse I gave the documents as I was taking them out of the file, I could see they were actually nothing alike. These autographs had been written by different hands. I sat back again and quickly rifled through, looking for other examples. As I focused it became harder to see the disparity between days, pens, moods and hands. So I had to track down the forgery. I placed the pile carefully in my Fair Dinkum Bargain basket. I picked it up again, shuffling through, frowning, rechecking her bank statements. Some months simply weren't here. A strange memo about world weather conditions.

With more interest in working with unfamiliar software than in Meghan Featherstone I set up a file. I listed descriptions of the documents I had been sent. The covering letter, typed on an old-fashioned typewriter, was hasty. It claimed she was being ripped off, that she was so vague and other-worldly she didn't keep tabs on things like she should and would I investigate for her. Strange way to speak about yourself. I went through the scraps of paper, mostly junk, incomplete, haphazard, thrown into a manila envelope and sent. As a matter of course I placed her signature against the one on a homespun contract. Touch and go. A weird document, a kind of pre-relationship break-up agreement made in the heat of love, this contract stated that the uneven income ratio obliged Meghan to look after her lover for five years after they had finished for all the housework, handiwork and gardening undertaken by the one without paid work. Worthless, really, as it wasn't dated or witnessed properly. There was here no evidence of theft, just a mess.

More than anything I was annoyed because I did not understand the job I had to do and the documentation did not help. For instance, a Post-it note with the words 'take the "f" out of life and you have lie'; so? The March and September bank statements were missing, although large debits were circled in other months. Only a couple of cheque butts accorded with receipts. I did not have Visa card statements, only a scribble on an invoice saying, paid by Visa. This was ridiculous. I imagined credit cards to be the easiest means for a stranger to steal one's money. Not having a lot of detective work at the moment, I took it on as a bona fide job. Paper chases were not my speciality. One telephone call, my handwriting on my notepad: Meghan Featherstone suspects she is being ripped off. Will send over paperwork. A phone number. A PO Box address. First, it seemed I would have to find out for myself if she was in fact being ripped off.

Half-way through this work, I decided my leg was being pulled. In one of the letters, a personal one with an illegible signature, the point was made about the new Family Law Act, which includes gay couples in the same category as de facto heterosexual partners if they have lived together more than nine months. I gave up and wrote in my diary from letterheads the names of her solicitor and accountant. Leg-work and face to face contact would sort out whether a joke was being played on me or not. Fishy business. Have to be on the spot to sniff out the red herring.

Before I wasted my time chasing her advisors, I would meet the lady herself. No one who earned that much money could be so stupid as to send me (or anyone) all this stuff.

The rain is pelting down. Quickly the creeks fill up in the majestic landscape of the Ranges; the escarpment of the Cavanagh Gorge National Park instantly turns into series of waterfalls; the flowing streams join the Campbell River with eagerness; the variety of wildlife, orchids, goannas drink to satiety; the dwellings of the gurls become hidden by over-hanging branches and low visibility.

As the moon rides wild horses made of cloud, Margot Gorman bleeds.

Book Two

motherhood

Tuesday Wednesday Thursday Friday

Tuesday's child is full of grace

9

. . . his mother's only joy . . .

Some time in the night, I bled. The gratifying stink of menses greeted me from my own bed-sheets. I woke up a different woman. No longer cranky but a bit ragged, I felt full of potential. Energy just around the corner from the ache, good timing so far as the triath goes. On the clock-radio, I heard a man's voice recite, 'he was his mother's only joy'. Because the rain was so heavy on the roof I switched it off. But that sentence stuck in my head. What a tragic life for the woman! The son could not give her sexual joy without breaking a really serious taboo, therefore the mother could have no adult relationship, not one with joy in it, or, anyway, she can't be a healthy woman because she's obsessed by her son. Yet, I suspected the line of poetry was considered perfectly beautiful and simple. It might be okay if 'only' weren't in it, but without that word, it would be too obvious to say at all.

The phone rang again after I had gone to sleep last night. No one was there. Just silence. Still tired, I began to read a detective novel about several pairs of English ladies staying in a chateau in France for a fortnight of self-improvement. One of each pair is taken in by bounder/cad/man. They have spinsterly tiffs. Meanwhile someone gets thrown over the cliff. They don't know this person, nor does the reader. In fact, it's not a person, it's the body. Fiction is supposed to be tidy, logical. Cosy, especially it's when rainy and dark outside. In this case, too cosy for me. Their good chaps are butch-dykes, if you think about it, bearing superficial resemblance to men. Harbouring a secret wish to write, I wondered how do these old dears get published. They wouldn't know detection from a hole in the road. Is it only Pommy ladies or do all female novelists have such narrow lives? I got up and did the washing.

The answer machine was still in its box. I unpacked it, read the instructions and taped myself, telling callers I would be happy to get back to them if they would leave their name and number. Minimal technology suited me. I should have a mobile phone and a more advanced computer, but there was a miserly side to me which refused to buy anything I didn't need. I fell in love with this place because of nature, the down-market coastal beauty. I cleaned the lenses of my camera. Everything neat, I went out to train after my warm-up. I did the routine a little too enthusiastically and felt a grab in my Achilles tendon.

The ocean sounded fierce. I have the deepest respect for the sea. Not a fool, blessed with some kind of innocent faith in its beneficence. No death wish. I studied the rips, which on this long beach change their position like a twisting tornado. The cold, embracing arms have shown me their strength. Getting whirled about in the centre of a wave was a terrifying experience; churned like ice-cream in a milkshake; finally, fortunately, poured out, virtually liquefied, among bits of detached salt foam on the hard wet sand. It was a wild day in Wollongong, I broke no bones.

The wind was biting and the beach absent of human life. My wetsuit reached my knees. I found a likely spot and jumped into the ebb. I was swept out beyond the breakers. I trod water to see how far I had come. My own little extreme sport! The foreshore was a narrow strip of yellow cadmium and the scrub just daubs of *terra verte* in an oil painting. The inland sky to the west was battleship grey, across which thin veins of lightning silently lit up and went out. I swam, breathing beach-side, as the rollers gathered their swell under me, elevating me and dropping me in a relentless sea-welling trench. I swam rhythmically as lazy jazz.

When I saw the surfers' signal post, I stopped the stroke and floated on my back for a while, watching the threatening greyness deepen, hearing slow thunder rumble, the clouds goaded by whips of fire coming closer. Sun lit the coastal weed, South African boneseed, to a bright lime. I turned and swam the other way, this time looking out to the crisp horizon, blue on blue and snow-cone cumulus. The sea was so buoyant, challenging, responding to the heaviness in the sky, it took my mind away from everything else. My towel on the sand came into view. The wave I body-surfed in took me all the way to the shallows. My right heel tendon was tender. Who the hell was Achilles, anyway? How would I know? Did he have the mental toughness of the sportsman? A hero in battle would have to concentrate his brain in hand-to-hand combat.

The temperature dropped when I was out on the road, doing the cycling leg of my training. Cold and stiff, I hung my bike on its hook just as the storm hit. Hailstones hammered the roof. In a hilarity of sound, my shower was a warm dribble amid the downpour.

Detective Constable Philippoussis waits in the foyer of the TAFE college reading the notice-board, feeling down. The weather is not helping. The advertising work in front of him reflects the aesthetics of the slum street glamorised in the claustrophobic corridors of music video clips, a style of untidiness that had come over students since he underwent tertiary studies. Litter as art. Litter as contempt. Student revolt?

It is Tuesday morning. Raining hard. Tired rebellion permeates the atmosphere, acne and hair in lank rats' tails or knotted ringlets. It's cool to be cold. Adolescents are underdressed and shivering, making it a style. Where had his moment in history gone? The clean-cut, short-haired, non-smoking, corporate commodity, addicted to nothing more than the adrenalins of the body excited by work-outs, driven by the ambition to have work and keep it in a competitive world. History's definition of his youth, nine-to-fivers, worriers. He stares at a flier about alcohol which is so nerdy it doesn't even have the allure of grunge. Philippoussis is also depressed at the prospect of a trip to the morgue, not because of squeamishness, but because of a morbidity in his investigation. Information he has gathered so far seems swallowed up in lethargy, left to congeal like old blood. His orders don't allow him the dynamism he feels. His energy is stifled. The boys' bodies are lying in a holding bay at the hospital like parked cars. The engines of the powers-that-be have stalled. He should be busier. Information should flow through CID, pieces of paper passing through the hands of the task force like water urgently finding its level. Knowledge spread, not contained. Especially at this stage of an inquiry. Facts soured in storage, corrupted like flesh. At the base of the DC's anxiety are fears about institutional corruption. Laziness is an ethical rot situation. The regional commander, Crankshaw, is antipathetic to the likes of Philippoussis who is not, in his estimation, Aussie enough. Not enough 'she'll be right' about him. Too eager, too serious. Not laid-back. Doesn't understand mateship. Phil's sense of honour would never let him be an Anglo-Saxon oaf for whom self-respect seemed to be lack of respect for everything, even his self.

The Greek heart falls another notch in his chest when he turns to greet Mrs Penny Waughan. The female equivalent of the mates, the helpmeet, she has the look of a soap opera mum: natural fair hair enhanced by peroxide, a neat cut strengthened by spray, a lot of make-up understated in colour, and buttoned-down lips. He stands about twenty centimetres taller. She tilts her face, its honed features sharp with curiosity. She does not hold out her hand to be shaken. He introduces himself and establishes her name and address.

'It's about Neil, isn't it?' Eyes widen as enlightenment strikes. 'What's happened to him?'

He nods affirmation and feels uncomfortable about telling her in the grotty reception area of the college.

Penny Waughan turns to the door, unhooking the shoulder strap of her bag. He follows, and is ready with a light when she fingers her cigarette from its packet. She needs to smoke, suppression. He huddles with her under the narrow awning. More litter. The flattened butts from smokos outside buildings look even more miserable on a miserable day. Her shoulders curl inward tightly. Nostalgic for the black and red hyperbole of the women he grew up with, whose emotions he could handle like flailing fists on his ribcage, Philippoussis has a cigarette himself, empathically. He smokes as a part of his job, never at home.

Penny Waughan blows out, ready for what he has to say. Detective Constable Philippoussis glances at the youths hanging against the wall watching. They walk away, patting pockets, with studied disinterest. Superintendent Crankshaw had given him a list of lads, known by some of his snouts to dress up as girls. Most of them had checked out. Alive.

He speaks. 'I was given the name of your son as a possible identity of a teenage fatality over the weekend. Actually I have two boys around fifteen years old, unnamed and unclaimed.'

Penny Waughan sags. She knew it. She had lived this moment before, her life suddenly switches from play to rewind.

'You could come with me straightaway if you like. It won't be very nice. Do you have a friend you would like to bring? Or ring? Family?' From staring at the ground he now turns to see her face.

Big tears roll lazily out of her eyes. She puffs on the remains of her cigarette, tosses it at her shoe and grinds it into the concrete. She bites her bottom lip. Although the faint possibility that it was not her son existed, she has a foreboding. But she says, 'It may not be Neil. Either of them.'

'Are there any friends you would like to have with you?' he repeats.

She shakes her head. 'It's amazing how few there are. How few there are when you are embarrassed by tragedy. When you really need them your idea of friendship, even family, changes.' The measured tones of one reading from a text book.

Penny Waughan fishes a carry-pack of tisses from her handbag. 'It's all right, I'll go with you.' She tries to stop the premonition tape with an effort at hope.

In the car, she is as still as ice.

They enter the back of the hospital, away from the comings and goings of nurses, of therapists, of visitors, sick people, live people. An orderly shows them the discreet door beyond 'Pathology'. The white room is still and silent, no sense of the activity elsewhere in the busy building. When the attendant removes both rubber covers, Penny stands, shock-struck. The men wait. She pulls herself together, shuddering.

She steps towards the car accident victim, shakes her head even though she recognises him. 'This is Hugh Gilmore. His mother, Gillian, committed suicide about a year ago. Hugh went off the rails about then. I suppose this was only a matter of time.'

She keeps her back to the other body as long as possible. The wardsman wishes someone had cleaned the lipstick and foundation off the face. As if physically pulling courage around her like a shawl, Penny Waughan looks at the dead face of her only child. She shivers.

'This is my son, Neil. He doesn't have black hair. It's a long time since we played with my make-up case, a couple of years. I didn't think there was any harm in it. How would it kill him? I'm sorry I'm not making sense.' She babbles. Phil listens.

She asks, 'Can I stay with him a little while? Alone?'

The men move back a step. 'Neil darling, I love you,' she whispers. 'What happened to you? How beautiful you were!'

The attendant shivers. 'It's cold.'

Philippoussis reacts to his insensitivity. 'Appropriate temperature I would have thought. Mrs Waughan, please try and not disturb the make-up. There might be a criminal investigation and we'll need a full forensic.'

'I just want to hold him once more,' she pleads.

'Fine by me.'

The attendant addresses Philippoussis. 'Detective?'

'Yes.' The policeman is introduced to a more senior medical personage, a serious man with glasses.

The morgue worker has something to say. 'We've orders from upstairs. You know. Do nothing. Duty doctor certified them dead. That's it.'

Philippoussis is stunned, 'Can't be. What about the official cause of death? Preliminary PM?'

'Very cursory,' the assistant says. 'The doctor had been on for eighteen hours.'

'So?' Phil tries to control his hot-blooded temperament.

'He just died. Overdose. System shock. Plummeting blood sugar levels. Teenage drug death. Plummeting blood pressure. Heart attack, maybe. How much work are you going to put into it? We've been getting too much of these lately. Not often dressed as girls, though. We faxed the interim report over to your office yesterday afternoon. You got the chemists, not us.' The man in the white coat adjust his spectacles. 'Weird, though.'

'My office? I didn't see it.' Philippoussis reaches into his breast-pocket for his notebook, and writes. 'Did their regular GPs come here, at all?'

'No, that was another odd thing. I faxed the death certificate to the police station, the detectives in charge of the case,' the man answers. 'I wasn't told names.'

Phil frowns. 'Sounds slack.'

'Sure does,' the other man agrees with the DC, then shrugs. 'But now they're identified, maybe—' The wardsman responds to his beeper, his senior nods and he hurries off.

'Have you got the page you faxed?' Philippoussis interrupts. 'Or a photocopy?'

The white-coated assistant goes into a small room off the morgue and returns with a piece of paper seemingly retrieved from the waste-paper bin.

'I'm intrigued. How did you know to ask for that? Some detectives are born and others made, I suppose. A lot being swept under the carpet these days. Cut-backs,' the man in white chats.

'Unless I can prove suicide, or the pathology report gives evidence of overdose,' the plain-clothes policeman promises, 'I'm going to worry this bone, mate.'

Neither man notices the quiet woman standing outside the nameless door.

'With email and faxes, privacy of official material is a thing of the past, and a lot of extra paper is shredded. And I took your shop for a shredder, a recycling establishment,' the policeman explains.

'My money's on OD and dangerous driving, taken as said,' opines the morgue attendant with the curious indifference affected by medical personnel.

They stand a moment in silence. 'Goes with the job, does it? No heart?'

Defensive about his trade, the assistant expresses his opinion. 'There won't be a full post mortem. Promise you. No money in forensics. Not enough doctors for those still breathing. Hang on, I'll see if the social worker's around.'

Philippoussis is in a trance. Penny Waughan is beside him before he realises the delicacy of the situation.

'Detective Constable Philippoussis?' The mother of the victim wants answers.

'I beg your pardon?' Phil shakes himself awake.

'How did he die? Exactly, I mean. And why?' Penny demands.

'I don't know,' Phillip responds simply. 'Depends on the Coroner. If it gets that far. It was most probably an accident, overdose, suicide . . . but they'll have to be proved.'

'I don't believe that, and you don't either. I can tell by the look on your face. You're worried.'

'I am, but at the moment, my job is to get the bodies identified, correctly.' Philippoussis cocks his pen. 'Could you give me the name of Neil's general practitioner? His regular doctor?'

'Dr Neville.' Penny Waughan supplies the address of his surgery.

'And, ah, Hugh Gilmore?' he asks gently. 'Family?'

Penny gives him enough information to find them. The morgue attendant and the social worker meet them in the corridor as they make their way slowly through the hospital.

The mother and the DC wait now for the other two to make conversation.

The social worker takes Penny aside, speaks with her, returns to Philippoussis professionally telling him he is free to pursue his work.

Phillip, back at the station, tells his sergeant the result of his work and before he types up his record of activity, asks, 'Shall I get onto the doctor?'

The senior detective is unforthcoming and dismissive. 'Complete the paperwork. Sure.' He looks up. 'Get the other ID as soon as possible. Take McKewen with you. Colleen is a local woman.'

Philippoussis is at his computer when Colleen sits down the other side of his desk. 'What do you want me to do?'

'Perhaps you could come with me to a farm with the happy news their son is dead. By the way, did you see the report from the hospital anywhere?' He looks at his watch, flicks through the handwritten list and his neat follow-up work on it, examines his desk for safe places. Shrugs, reaches for his brief-case, and slots the scrunched photocopy in there. 'Give us a couple of hours Colleen. Find out where and when we can get a four-wheel-drive and see you after lunch.'

'We are talking dairy farming here?' WDC Colleen McKewen raises her eyebrows. 'Then we need gumboots. By the time we get there they'll be milking. But that's all right. We'll find them home. The yards around the bails are muddy. A cow paddock actually,' she jokes.

He doesn't laugh, but watches her go, then picks up his telephone receiver, makes an appointment and lines up several interviews. He is determined to check details in all the statements, even though he has the feeling no one would mind if he was incompetent. He'll find basic inconsistencies if there are any. He will not be involved in a cover-up. Gorman was holding back something, he knew that. If these deaths were about drugs then Crankshaw, twenty years in narcotics, was the man who could provide hard information, contacts, firms, rather than an informant's pissy little scribbled list. He answers his desk phone, sighs, nods his head, 'Yes, sir. Yes. You mean now? Okay.'

Philippoussis picks up his jacket, leaves the trail of his own scent and slams the door of the office.

Chandra gives her walking fingers a rest and watches. The puzzle of the inexplicable fiddling with the background of the page called WebsighTlines, while intriguing, was past. Back to normal, except for a spot buzzing around like a bee. She counts the hits and intends to follow each up if she can. First she has to check which of her visitors have come to an evolution from the literal to the symbolic via the hypertext riddle, the language beneath the language. The thread through the complicated catacombs, which she calls 'the long march', is a progression through game software, news groups and email to a chatroom where the question of the practice of politics is discussed. Basement and Monkcells are, as yet, ideas for the freedom-fighters' safe refuge. Months of worming her grid for working, active women warriors, disciples, martyr-fucken-martyrs, placing hints in other sites, allowing input from understanders, interpreters of her scheme, is analogous with desk-top publishing on-line, in which design, while perfect in one's own fonts and high-standard pixel resolution, translates in untold ways according to output devices, monitors, computers, search engines of the recipients. The symmetry is lovely. Chandra sighs with satisfaction. The structure is viable if she stays in control. Even guerilla warfare requires a general. From the shopfront, her domain, Wimmin.com.au which is broad and interactive, the WebsighTlines begins the labyrinth to Kitchen.CellarOne can have the s 'n' m girls, CellarTwo, the ravers, beneath that Cellar2chat, which can be entered through the Den, ostensibly for serious debate, or the Bedroom, sexual angst and information sharing, confessions and disclosures, or the Bathroom, pleasure substances including those for your health. The Lab has branches named for activism in appropriate sciences and scientific current affairs. DinnerTable is meeting place for general topics of interest, dilettante in tone, and eclectic. Parties are often organised around essays posted on the bulletin board, accessed at various levels.

The immediate problem is language. Chandra is quite happy to keep changing the name of the site and her email addresses. For the moment with her web, there is a sigh and a T denoting a junction in her netting.

Chandra clicks on Kitchen to see what is going on. Any mention of white food is a revolutionary avowal, of character, not of theory, is a fast track to Cellar2chat.

<BAC> Is it okay to let Daddy's girls rule?

<ANNIEOAK> No. They are male females. You've read the bible! We need a code. Etruscan?

<CHE> Etruscan it is. A virgin alphabet. GMAB
<REDSHOES> To get beyond the vanishing point, we need to know the
nature of egg-white. Although he might know the nature of egg-white,
he does not know what we mean when we say we know the nature of
egg-white. Nor flour.
<MOP> Well the metaphysics of metacooking in the metakitchen, heh?
<DEFARGE> OIC.
<WHEELS> Male chef not the type to think beyond the food. And nerds
don't cook enough. Get me?

Chandra Williams settles down to program a virus as an experiment,
using various news services to scramble electronic communications on the
superhighway. She is testing the effectiveness of the code as language. She
wonders, can we rely on specialisation as a universal male trait? Someone
keeps quoting Valerie Solanas.

Chandra contributes to the chat enough to encourage women to examine
the proposition, then rolls into her actual kitchen. For the subterfuge to
work, of course, real recipes from real women with real problems must take
up a lot of time and space, like a wall of rock disguising the entrance to the
cave.

Although the travel of the morning is promising, Chandra feels a
niggling impatience. Inarticulate inspiration is burning her left palm
between the mounds of Luna and Venus. After she has checked the
marmalade bubbling on the stove, taken the temperature of hot sugar, and
reset the timer, she goes back to the page that had been tampered with. The
spot in her own design is now an eagle soaring. She tries to catch it with her
mouse. She is being led. Her digital skills are brilliant and it is a challenge.
When, finally, she does pin it, the entire text of the SCUM Manifesto comes
up.
>> Nothing wrong with calling the bluff.

It is a response to her joke. A Solanasite?

Chandra pastes a flag for a new room in the menu of <u>Cellar2chat</u>:
Life in this society being, at best, an utter bore and no aspect of society
being at all relevant to women, there remains to civic-minded,
responsible, thrill-seeking females only to overthrow the government,
eliminate the money system, institute complete automation and destroy
the male sex.

Well, thinks Chandra, I hope my structure holds, for the conspiracy is
born. She is amazed.

Colleen McKewen appears at the door of CID, tossing car keys from hand to hand.

'You're a hard man to find.'

Detective Constable Philippoussis says, 'I've been running errands for Crankshaw, interviewing boaties down at the marina, getting the shipping news like the lowliest reporter of all. Finding out the times of recent arrivals and departures. Names and registrations. If I knew why I would feel better. I thought the yachting world was a gossipy lot. The Crank wasn't even happy with the results.'

'What about the bodies?' Detective Constable McKewen asks.

'Leave them exactly where they are. Our boss lives up to his nickname.'

'Sure does. Let's go.'

Phil leaves his desk in careful disorder and takes his brief-case. When they are in the truck, he gives her his notes of Penny's instructions. 'Can you find that?'

She reads. 'That's Elias Gilmore's place. They are all Gilmores out along that road, except for a few Wills and Dickies.' In the long-wheelbase Land-Cruiser, police issue gumboots on hand, Colleen driving, Phillip mentions he heard the mother had committed suicide.

'Yep, Gillian Gilmore, what do you want to know? My mother was a Gilmore, different branch, same root stock. Soldier settlement, World War I.'

Flat paddocks of pasture run parallel to the river. 'Just talk about them, Colleen. Tell me. Whatever.'

'One day,' says the policewoman, driving competently and quickly through territory familiar to her, 'she simply gave up, took herself out into the garage and hung herself from the rafter with nylon rope. This son, Hugh, found her before going to school one day. Gillian kept her house neat as a new pin, her clothes, husband's, kids', pressed to a knife edge all the time. When she hanged herself with a length of green rope she hadn't even bothered to take the rollers out of her hair properly and she was dressed in a tatty old T-shirt and shorts.'

'Did she leave a note?'

'She wrote, simply, "No More".'

'Where?'

'Where what?'

'Where did she write "No More"?'

'Why?'

'Forget it.'

'No, why?'

'How did they know it was suicide then?'

'What bothered my mum,'—WDC McKewen, slightly older than Phil, wears make-up, and chats easily—'when she was telling me, was about how clean she was. Always proper. But Gillian just grabbed the nearest thing. Picked the rope off the floor of the garage. No preparation.'

Philippoussis nods. 'Go on.'

'Gillian came to the district as a teacher and ended up marrying a farmer. Hard to imagine that Elias was dashing enough to win the hand of the young good-looking school-teacher.' Colleen glances at her partner as she turns off the main road to see if she should go on in that vein.

'Was it printed?' Phil asks, suddenly.

'What?'

'The note?'

'I never saw the note,' Constable McKewen answers tartly.

'Tell me about the lad.'

'Hugh is the third of seven children. Marji is Hugh's elder sister and Daniel older brother, then boy, girl, boy, boy . . .' She hesitates, affirms herself and continues. 'Hugh was never the same after finding his mother. He was fourteen. Her suicide happened about a year ago. He went off the rails, stood up to his father's discipline, basically violence. Only a matter of time before he would kill himself on the road or through drugs.'

She takes another turn, and the police LandCruiser bumps along an even narrower road.

'Before she died, Hugh had heroes, Wayne Gardner and Michael Doohan, and wanted to emulate them. He was a good dirt-bike rider. Hugh liked the speed, been rounding up cows on a bike since younger than ten. But Elias puts local football as the only sport worth doing. He's a "hard-working" man, meaning his hard work includes having a drink on a Friday night and the game on Saturday and working the rest of the time— while the wife and children, as much as able, work all the time without the relaxation, except to watch. His drunken behaviour, like his mates', is dreadful but excusable because it is not every night. With Hugh, it was classic father jealousy of the son, too like his mother, too big for his boots.'

'If I were a school-teacher, I'd write a long suicide note,' opines Philippoussis.

'Gillian tried so hard. Always looked perfect,' Colleen remarks approvingly.

'What about the rest of the family?' he inquires, noticing new houses built within view of old as the road dipped and curved with the contours of the country along the valley of a creek tributary of the Campbell River.

'The older boy is the dead spit of his dad in taste and looks. He likes to be called Dan the Man. Marji, the older girl, also, her father's daughter, a farm girl, good in the dairy, left school early. The younger girl is ten now, bright and clever, small, fine-featured like Hugh, good at school and in command of her little brothers, changes completely in the company of her father or her oldest brother, according to my mother. Tons of cousins. Here we are.'

Colleen bounces the four-wheel-drive over an uncomfortably high cattle grid. While the dirt road is rocky, the sloping yards up to the cemented bails are grassless mud. The black and white cows mill about in slush, lifting their tails to shit down their legs. Line-dance music blares out so loudly that the police have to bend towards each other with their plans.

'Where's the house?' he asks.

Colleen gestures back and then draws a path with her forefinger over the hill. Abandoned calves bellow for their mothers nearby.

Philippoussis is a city boy, born and bred; sloshing around in gumboots is not his style. He indicates that he does not like the smell.

'Okay,' Colleen grins, 'I'll take the milker. Looks like it's Elias himself.'

As Phillip drives away he realises why the yard is so wet. A high-pressure hose to keep the concrete floor of the dairy clean is on full bore.

The home-yard is different from its surrounds. Over the gateway arches a bright puce bougainvillea. White painted chains stand on end like charmed snakes frozen at the moment of holding a shallow bird bath horizontal. Blue rocks fixed together in the shape of a basket handle over a circular garden bed of petunias and daisies. Decrepit wheelbarrows with their rust painted over put to use as standard plant pots for weedy grass and geranium. Flowers, exotic trees and rose bushes all rocked into neat corrals. Native shrubs flourish along the fenceline. Several gnomes confer at the side of the path. A pink stork stands on one leg next to a lonely palm tree. The lawn was mowed recently.

He mounts the verandah and knocks. Mammary glands to rival the Friesians', thinks Philippoussis as he is met with an instinctive hostility. Three younger children are mesmerised by a video screen in the room behind her.

'Marji Gilmore? I'm Detective Constable Philippoussis—'

'What?' she interrupts, truculently. A little girl beside her says his name perfectly. Polite and pert. A regular Lisa Simpson, thinks Phil.

'Shut up, Peggy. Right then. What do you want? My Dad's down the dairy milking, and Dan's down there too, I think. He should be.'

'Peggy, I want to speak with Marji alone,' Phillip says and watches the little thing in her socks and school uniform go back into the company of her brothers.

'Show me where your mother died, will you, Marji?'

Marji nods, steps out through the flywire door and selects a pair of Blundstones from the assembled boots and shoes on the verandah. She drags them over her ankles, and, as the elasticity of the sides have long gone, slops off.

'Follow me.'

Around the back of the house, where a vegetable garden green with produce has a fence to itself, are a couple of sheds: a big open one made of tin, another of earlier vintage erected with poles, and a lean-to. The third free-standing one is a typical garage with a door and pitched roof, strong and straight hardwood beams. Marji points upwards.

'Mum liked to look after her car, didn't want it to go off. Make it into a veteran one day, she'd reckon. It's mine when I get my licence.' Marji Gilmore pats the immaculate duco of a twenty-year-old four-cylinder Datsun. 'I put some polish on her now and then. That's Hugh's, she points to a bright lime motor bike decorated with an eight-ball number. He used to race. Won't let anyone touch it even though we never see him.'

Marji chats while she watches the handsome cop measure the depth of dust on the noggins with his finger, kick a tangled collection of old rope, examine rusty tools and note the air of neglect with the exception of the two unused vehicles.

'It's, er,' Phil interrupts, 'not your mum I'm here about. It's your brother, Hugh. Do you know where he is?'

'Nope. I do not. He's gone wild. Dad can't straighten him out any more. Dad wouldn't let him come home anyway, chucked him out after he tried to sell the dirt bike. Reckoned he stole it, it belonged to the farm, for the cattle. Hugh said it was his. He raced Motor Cross and kept it real good. Mum bought it out of her own money. But Dad reckons all the equipment around the farm is like, owned by the farm, it wasn't Hugh's to sell. So they had a row.'

The Detective Constable has no reason to stall the inevitable. 'There was a car accident at the weekend. We think Hugh died in it. The car was stolen. We have to ask you or your father or your brother or all of you to come and identify him.'

Marji asks, 'What kind of a car did he steal?'

'A yellow Charger,' Philippoussis responds generously. 'A hotted up Valiant Charger.'

'That'd be Hugh. Except I didn't think he was into stealing cars.' Poor

Marji holds back tears. 'Except, if it was an old one, a classic, like a Charger, I suppose.'

'Interesting,' replies Phil. 'Did Hugh find your mother's suicide note?'

Marji does not want to answer, so she doesn't. 'I'll go with Dad,' she says instead. 'Dan can finish the milking. We can take our own car. I've got to get the kids something to eat, first. They can have frozen pizza.'

The paddocks are emerald green. The distant hills are pure violet. The garish colours of the flowers in the garden stand out against a heavy sky. White clouds hang motionless in the front of darker ones. Cows straggle out across the near pasture, with eased udders. Marji slogs slowly towards the house. The policeman drives down to the dairy, and waits in the van. Marji Gilmore, more like his own peasant stock than the stiff-lipped Penny Waughan, was understandable. Stubborn, proud in a way. He can see the family resemblance in his off-sider. Colleen McKewen appears in whiffy gumboots.

'Colleen,' he asks, 'Is this a typical family, would you say?'

'Hardly ever leave the property, this lot,' Colleen confides.

'Marji keeps her mother's car in pristine condition,' he says in the same tone of voice he used when he remarked on the note.

Colleen removes the boots with the passenger door open and puts on her lace-ups. 'Marji would think,' she explains, 'life is not easy for me and it's not easy for Dad either, and it looks easy for those useless dole bludgers, dope-heads and blacks, and that's what Hugh became, a dope-head, dole bludger, nigger-lover, and, as Elias would say, poofter. But I don't know about that.'

Philippoussis studies the cattle egrets, like little snowy angels, as they follow the grazing cows, digging worms out of their footprints. He sees wading birds take off in a flock and make a design in the sky.

'Marji is bovine,' he says, knowing that Colleen McKewen, unlike Margot Gorman, will not to take him up on his sexism.

'Well, she's dumb,' agrees Colleen. 'Peggy's not. For Marji her father is god and god is her father and she will marry someone like Daniel, probably one of his friends. She won't get pregnant before marriage because that it is stupid and Elias would be furious. Anyway it wouldn't happen because he'd make the bloke marry her with his shotgun to his head. She only sleeps with Daniel's friends, though she's never got to actually sleep, usually it is done after football in the ute. She'll probably let herself get pregnant when the husband she wants comes along. She had nothing in common with her mother.'

'We'll see,' Phil notes cryptically, thinking his colleague could talk the leg off an ironpot. 'I hope she'll change her clothes.'

Colleen goes on, 'Don't worry. She'll be spic and span at the hospital. I liked Gillian, even though she was different. Old Mrs Gilmore, Elias's mother, hated her. Vicious old bitch she is. Thinks her daughter-in-law killed herself because she was mentally sick, neurotic. Probably why Elias slapped her around a bit. Marji has been too placid for him to find an excuse to hit her much. She has tried to save her little sister from it a few times, trying to tell her not to give him any lip. And her little brothers. Marji's all right. It's just that she knows she's a workhorse. Gillian's self-control made life uncomfortable for her because it brought out the aggro in her father, and probably Dan as he got older. It might be that, or it might be that Gillian came from the city. Marji and her father, probably most of the family, put mentally ill on a par with Aborigines and dole-bludgers. No sympathy. Too fragile. Things are tough. Shit happens. Life wasn't mean to be easy. Don't fix what ain't broke.'

He tells her she sounds like a cop.

'Always wanted to be one,' she says.

The fluorescent signs and sand-bags of road-work look sad and neglected in the increasing rain. The traffic is steady. People, just outside town, have small parcels of land for their one horse, their six steers or hobby protea plantations. They pass an ostrich farm with camera-toting tourists under an umbrella at the fence. Several wildlife parks are advertised. Other hoardings show graphics of resort-style accommodation with the ubiquitous palm tree emphasising the postcard syllogism of tourism.

'What do you think of our new regional commander?' she asks. 'If he is so into drug law enforcement, why isn't he pulling out the finger on this one?'

'Big reputation in narcotics, our man.' Philippoussis wonders whether they should discuss the unusual procedure of the investigation into the two accidental deaths as he does not trust Colleen one iota.

Colleen is cunning and gives her opinion. 'If he hates poofters as much as he is supposed to, why isn't he pulling it out, either, hey?'

'Yeah, well, call me politically correct but I don't think hatred is an incentive for proper policing.' Phillip Philippoussis turns into the hospital grounds past the pencil pines and dwarf cypresses and parks. Paedophilia has little to do with homosexuals, he thinks. 'Whatever,' he shrugs, 'my hunch is there are adult men in the picture somewhere.'

The police wait inside their conspicuous vehicle for the appearance of the Gilmores' truck.

'They won't be long,' Colleen assures him.

'Did you like Hugh?' Phillip asks.

'Nuh, not really,' Colleen says honestly. 'I'm sorry he's dead, but you know, he didn't fit. He was moody.' She continues fishing, 'Superintendent Crankshaw, who has just arrived, knew I was related to this kid.'

'He told you that?'

'Yeah, that's why I'm here. It blows me away how much that man knows. See,' she points at a muddy ute entering the car-park, 'Told you.'

Philippoussis turns the ignition key. The police car guides the farm vehicle around to the bay where it says, Ambulances Only.

'Been here before,' Elias Gilmore grumbles, scrubbed up like a garbo on holiday.

'Dad,' pleads Marji, equally crisp in ironed clothes and neat shoes.

10

. . . the warrior women . . .

Precipitation must have been heavy in the mountains. The estuary had great swathes of brown mud indicating rushing waters upstream, removing the topsoil from where it is useful and putting it where it is not, silting up the mouth of the river. I own a Suzuki Sierra with pretty surfers' waves painted along the sides with dolphins popping up. Hardtop, fortunately. In the afternoon, I took the river road to Lebanese Plains. The water was rising fast and carrying down to the delta whole trees, branches, plastic barrels, all manner of thing, dancing on flat swirls impelled by the surging and swelling. Like a parade. A cut-out drum looked like someone's letter-box had taken off to join the fun.

The world closed in, with adamant rain, all grey and green. Deafening at times. Newly formed puddles grabbed my wheels like a field of magnetism and twisted with the vicious intent to throw me off course. So I slowed right down, opening the window a little to lessen the condensation. I swear I could smell earthworms moving in the mud.

When the downpour eased a bit, further upstream, frogs croaked like a chorus of rusty hand-saws going forward and back. I had spent most of the day indoors making my way through a paper maze. Under different possible scenarios, I listed questions to ask Meghan Featherstone. Each headed: if, a, b, c. Then, why, what, where, who, et cetera. It was quite neat really. But as I drove west in the monochrome light, I knew firing them would be another story altogether, as I'd have to delve into her personal life. She had acted surprised when I called to confirm her invitation, as if she had forgotten about me. In a straight reading of the investigation, there was a troubling trend. Whoever was ripping her off was very close to her and doing it systematically. This thief was not acting out of passion. No. Clever cold cunning, not hot heart was behind it. At a T-intersection, I turned the corner and began climbing away from the course of the river which I saw rushing through a small gorge up from the bridge. Was Meghan Featherstone an A-grade fool, perhaps? Lump sums from the Federal Government, of that I could vouch for only March and August. Although not a salary, I suspected it to be a source of regular income. In the documents there was evidence of money coming from somewhere else, as well. Anonymously. Otherwise, she was transferring amounts from venture capital, stocks or debentures. No indication of an investment account but there had to be one. Big irregular deposits to her core savings, and consistent withdrawals, were circled for my benefit on the statements. The paperwork was so incomplete. I did not know whether, for instance, there was a joint bank account. No suggestion of share portfolio. There was the statement from a mortgage bank referring to a property in Brisbane with a note attached that it was partially paid by someone else. The tenant? If so, cheap rent. Considering her income she could have houses all over Australia. Why has she got a mortgage? Negative gearing? Why would she pay a lot more in interest, when if her deposits are right, she could earn the money in a month to buy it outright? Negative gearing is a concept I have never got a handle on; rich enough people buy property to rent out as a tax deduction? Indication of her 'incomprehensible' losses was in a typed note to me and circled debits on both credit card and cheque account statements. This in itself was not particularly odd. The cents and specific numbers in dollars meant that they would be easily explained as ordinary bills paid. A lot of used air travel tickets looked as if they had been retrieved from the bin. Again incomplete, but nonetheless a record of a hectic, haywire itinerary. She may be a trouble-shooter, out there in the world as some sort of Sigourney Weaver character, Captain Amazing, Ms Fixit. The trail of her expenses put her in major cities as well as outback posts. The Regent in Sydney, for instance. Eucla and Yalata, roadhouses near the Nullarbor?

Because of water on the road and limited vision, I drove ponderously, giving me ample time to dream up fantastic plots. If she did change personalities away from home, then she could have had all sorts of partners. Intimate folk would have access to her cards, whether she knew it or not. Whatever, this character was too casual with her money, I mean for someone with so much cash-flow.

Eventually I found the place through the forbidding curtains of trickles on the windscreen, steam inside and rain outside. The gravel track into her place crossed a creek in several places, one concrete ford and one wooden bridge. I sloshed through sheets of water and half-slid on the dirt road as I breached the hill overlooking the dismal shelter. But everything looked dreary in the dank dusk.

Meghan turned out to be one of those painfully shy, embarrassingly spirited people who, I've found, always manage to say the wrong thing. Her property was about twenty kilometres up river, twenty-five acres of ex-grazing land which, in energetic stints, she said, she intended to make over to permaculture, with goats for milk and ducks dispatching insect pests. Pigeon coop, a work-in-progress over there, in case sunstorms blew out satellite communications systems. She laughed. Nut trees here, stone fruits there, citrus, apples, vegies, all will have their place. Her hand shot out to draw on the muddy canvas of leaden weather the proposed wind-break, further back the 'canopy'. I could just make out the shapes of one or two dripping eucalypts in relatively close proximity. 'And beside the tank the shade-house,' she continued. I'm sure it looked terrific in her mind's eye. But it certainly had not happened yet. An ex-dairy in a scungy paddock going down to a creek choked with weeping willows was all it was so far. Goats with their scraggy necks in collars, knee-deep in weedy grasses wet around their delicate rock-bounding feet, looked vaguely freaked in the drizzle.

She greeted me with all this talk of bucolic harmony, as proud as Punch of several stunted carrots extended towards me in her long hands.

'My first produce, aren't they beautiful?' she asked, as if, for instance, the perfect human form were that of the muscly dwarf. Not bad if you like fat basset hounds and two-headed calves. But I didn't say that.

Nodding, I looked down the paddock at the forlorn goats and thin saplings caged in chicken wire and she rattled off their botanical names.

Suddenly she grabbed my arm. 'Come in.'

Inside was pretty rugged. The beautifying project, though under way, was not integral to the nature of the original structure. Cow-bails have gently sloping concrete floors and low roof, full stop. Standing in front of an Early Kooka gassed by a nine-litre LPG bottle was the girlfriend.

'You know Jill, don't you? Margot? Jill? Margot Gorman,' Meghan introduced, formally.

I inclined my head slowly. I knew Jill better than I knew Meghan, though not well.

'Gidday,' I said. I had seen Jill at the Orlando dance with someone else. I was taken aback at her being with Meghan Featherstone.

Jill's stunningly black eyes gave hints of caves and gas chambers. They had a dangerous quality, and they changed quickly. From threat to wicked humour. She might have borrowed the dress she was wearing from my southern neighbour, Moonsunshine, and over it she wore a daddy's barbecue apron, which could have come from my gentleman northern neighbour in his younger days. Jill David was over-playing the part of kitchen slut.

'Yeah, we meet at the gym, sometimes,' I explained to Meghan.

Not that I expected her to say anything deep and meaningful, but Jill's silence was disconcerting. My recollection was of last Friday. Seeing her reminded me of the death in the foreground of my memory.

Then she said, 'Margot, I've never known your name.' She was blatantly lying in front of Meghan. 'Not been formally introduced,' she continued. We shook hands. The sort of questions I had for my client could not be put in front of the classic main suspect. And this one was shifty. Of course, the black eyes could be a quirk of fate and genetics and not as full of secrets as they seemed.

There were only two other rooms beyond the kitchen: a lounge with half a varnished wooden floor and a pot-bellied combustion heater, and a loft-bedroom.

'Are you a vegetarian, Margot?' asked the cook.

'If I'm hungry and chicken's on the menu, I eat. Same goes for steak and roast. But basically my diet is a rigorous one and not easily described in one word,' I answered, turned and leaned on the kitchen-door jamb to relax. 'I have some wine in the car.'

'We don't drink,' said Jill. That puzzled me too. 'Megs? Find me some mint and parsley in the garden will you, dear?' I waited until Meghan was out of the room before asking Jill where she lived.

'Here,' she nonchalantly fibbed.

'All the time?' My astonishment was getting the better of me. Was she a pathological liar or what? My bullshit geiger counter was making a racket in my brain.

'Most of it,' she grinned. 'Sometimes I stay in my caravan on the coast.'

'Why did you lie about not knowing my name?' I plied awkwardly. Lying about little things suggested something as big as self-delusion to my suspicious mind.

'I haven't told Megs about it, yet,' she whispered.

This reply was supposed to satisfy me. 'What exactly?'

'It!' she rolled her dramatic eyes.

The deluge roared on the roof, coming off in cascades, startling me from my attempt to find words to describe Friday night, to skewer Jill. I skipped away from a splash on my ankle-high lace-up Doc Martens. 'Megs' came back in looking like a bee-keeper, so covered up against the weather was she, clutching a straggly bunch of herbs. A goat-kid was missing. Did I have a coat? she wanted to know. Dumbly I shook my head. Meghan was in a big hurry.

'Darling, would you lend Margot the Driz-a-bone I bought you?' she begged Jill, who shrugged.

'Sure.'

The jacket was so new it still sported glossy cardboard tags. I put myself into it, obediently, and felt as stiff as a shop-dummy.

'Have you got any spare gumboots?' I inquired hopelessly. I guessed that a trip down the soggy paddock was on the cards. Both said yes with their heads. But when they tried to find them, they failed.

Meghan Featherstone strode urgently off through the mud. Why was this idiot-woman worth so much money? I caught up with her. By the way she was behaving now, it was quite easy to see how she could have allowed signatories to her credit cards, or freely given out her PIN. Or lost one without registering it. This buffoon could be impossibly trusting. But she wouldn't answer any of the questions I shouted. My job was irrelevant, inappropriate. She swatted away my inquiries with 'what? what?' I wanted to know about specific times; where was she when her cards were used? She seemed a bit bewildered that I was interested in her credit cards, but shrugged it off with a frown, a minute hesitation, and then launched into a subject of her own. The land dropped sharply about thirty metres from the house, forcing us closer in our trek.

Meghan went into an indistinct diatribe through the squawl as we hurried down the paddock. 'My sister,' she stated. Was she giving me another suspect? 'You know? I think I hate her. I got a letter from her today. A response to one I wrote and she gets everything I said wrong. Backwards. She is so aggravating. She's always been like that. Do you think it's deliberate? Sibling rivalry?' She shouted, breathing heavily, 'I should love her.'

'Have you spent any time, like an overnight or a holiday, at your sister's place?' I yelled.

'No. Well,' she turned to face me, her hood making side vision impossible. 'Both of us were with my mother at Christmas for a few days. I paid. Sydney. Neither of us will go near Dad, the cold patriarch we call god. He's an utter bastard.'

'Wealthy?' I asked.

'Hear that?' Meghan interrupted, running around in circles like a dog on a rabbit's scent. Bleating.

I saw the little goat. It was struggling in the stream beneath the weeping willow. I ran, hindered by the slippery earth and the ungiving jacket. I slid into the creek. I was grateful for the caught tether. With one arm under its front legs, I used the other hand to yank the rope and pull myself and kid towards land. I thought animals panicked in situations like these, but this one surrendered like a well-trained victim of the sea to the heroine of the Surf Rescue. It took all my strength, then I managed to grab a tree root. Safely on the bank, I took a moment to comfort it.

Meghan moved another two goats to higher ground, squealing and wailing as she went. My goat was like a human child in my arm, trusting.

It and I walked slowly up the hill abreast. The heavy jacket was soaked, but, there's nothing like a bit of life-saving to lighten you up.

From being at the mercy of nature, the goats were now treated like the animals at Christ's birth in the stable, allowed into the little shelter beside the kitchen where the spout leaked. We told the story to Jill a couple of times and speculated what might have happened if Meghan had not noticed them missing. The young nanny had eaten through the sisal, probably wandered, then the frayed rope had tangled in sticks on the bank of the flowing creek.

Jill seemed impervious to our infectious enthusiasm, even as she uttered, 'Poor little thing.'

The fire was lit. While we were having mugs of tea Jill asked me had I read *The Female Eunuch*? I shook my head. *The SCUM Manifesto? The First Sex? Amazon Odyssey?* Negative, negative, negative. Instead of suggesting that I do so, she sneered a little, which expression I interpreted as my having failed a questionnaire. She whispered something in Meghan's ear, which could have been, 'Told you.' And went into the kitchen.

Where was this library of feminist thought? I didn't see any bookcases about the house she said she lived in. Just a coffee-table book on eagles and hawks, which I leafed through, as Meghan set the table. The book was new, the glossy photos of raptors stunning, but I was wondering what my reading taste had to do with Meghan's missing money.

Jill's food was not as good as I imagined it would be, considering her domestic persona. Boiled white rice, tinned peas steamed warm, and strips of chicken in a thin sauce with capsicums. It might have worked with a nice heavy bread, homemade in the rustic oven. Meg's compliments, however, were over the top. Jill was coy.

The huge jumper they lent me had sleeves down to my knees, while the body of it hardly covered my damp knickers. Rain on the tin roof made listening hard.

'The fords will be over,' Jill commented, transforming into a thoughtful Jill. 'You will have to stay overnight unless you want to lose your vehicle in a broadside of rushing water.' Her hospitality made Meghan beam with pride.

'In for a goat, in for a sheep,' I joked. 'Okay.'

We all relaxed. I was here for the night.

When the precipitation eased, Jill took charge of the conversation. She gave Meghan a sanitised and highly inaccurate version of the events of Friday night. One would have thought she was telling an anecdote second-hand, that she hadn't been there. Not even considering giving my version, I let my intuition wander. A visual of the cars came to mind. Red Saab. A van, Tarago

Getaway. A light-coloured little sedan. Maria's Holden Camira, Alison's old Falcon, a station wagon and a couple of others. And there was a motorbike. A Hyundai Sonata and Excel Sprint. A Daihatsu four-wheel-drive, a real paddock-basher.

'Who owns a Mitsubishi Triton GLS, cab chassis, ute with fibreglass canopy, four-wheel-drive, special purple duco and green interior?' I asked suddenly, remembering the woman who had passed me after I discovered the body when I was waiting for the police. 'With automatic power steering, V-8, airconditioning?' I pressed.

'Judith's new vehicle,' Meghan responded.

'The old bitch,' said Jill. 'How did she afford that?'

'Are you talking about the singer?' I wanted to know. I had not connected the gurl gazing at the sea with the troubadour at the dance. Jill went into a take-off of Judith Sloane, draping a silk scarf across her head like a nun's veil to indicate the Joan Baez hair and aping the smoky, lustrous voice with a familiar ballad. It was excellent, and Jill's voice, with a trace of irony, was equal to the send-up. I laughed, very impressed. She really was a very good actress.

'Judith is my friend, who lives out her principles,' Meghan took umbrage. 'And I like those old feminist folk songs. She would have missed me being there. She doesn't perform much any more.'

'I don't think so,' said her girlfriend, dropping the act by flicking off the scarf. For once I agreed with Jill. Judith was making a very obvious play for an Aborigine at the Orlando Ball. I encouraged her to do more impersonations.

Jill's art was contemptuous of nearly everyone. It gave an edge to her talent. Even though I was genuinely entertained, I found every sketch a little too cruel. Jill carries no extra weight but her Maria was fat and lazy. Wheezy. She did Sofia on medication. And then her refusing to take it, being hilariously manic.

'Drama junkies,' Meghan said when the portrayal of their carnivorous partnership was over.

'Really?' Jill mimicked.

My Broomhilda came in for some schtick next. The wink and nudge in Jill's voice implied she had had sex with the Germans, or one of them. Or was she just a good gossip? I got an uncomfortable feeling that I had been talked about.

Jill sat down and flexed herself into a broad-shouldered posture. 'Do you know Chandra?' she asked.

'I've spoken with her on the phone,' I smiled.

'Don't you dare,' hissed Meghan.

Jill obediently stopped. Her performance was finished. Her teasing ceased. She looked serious.

'Was she who I'm supposed to meet?' I put into the tense silence. Whether they ignored the query or didn't hear me I don't know. I felt there was more they could have told me about Chandra.

'Chandra Williams has a five-acre block near the local general store,' Meghan explained, gesturing the direction and dismissing the subject.

The mood had changed dramatically. It was time for bed. They gave me a futon to sleep on, dismantling the couch in the process.

While Jill could turn on the charm, be tremendously amusing, Meghan was plainly generous. The obvious discrepancy in their relationship made me suspect Jill's motives. She had lied at least once. The interaction between them fascinated me, like watching a snake beguile a dog.

The claustrophobia of the small residence, the restless ghosts of hungry cows, goat shit or the dampness disturbed my reliable sense of smell. I felt uneasy: there was a nasty scent somewhere. Something was off. The deformed dwarfed carrots hung around my mind as I lay on the floor near the heater waiting for the repose of dreams. When there's slime about you're liable to get slippery. One of them snored. Varieties of frogs chorused with drips on tin and trapped water while redolent leaf-mulch rotted. I drifted off.

The wrecked cattle-yards where Victoria Shackleton parks her horse-float with care and skill are boggy. She unpacks, repacks into back-pack her provisions and rides into Lesbianlands, intending to stay about three days. She rugs and hobbles her horse. With her Dalmatian, impatient to meet and greet friends, especially Xena Kia, Judith Sloane and Virginia White, old mates, she sets out in wet-weather gear on foot. Xena and she have been romancing over long distance for years. Neither wants full-time commitment. Both are big, strong women with clothes expressing their abrupt, aggressive presence in the world. Vee who looks like a cowboy and Xena part-Maori with green symbols of power hanging around her neck and ankles, they walk together through the darkening, streaming forest along narrow tracks to Virginia's house.

A branch of Virginia's sculpture is in the busy water of the creek. She fashions details of a horse's head on a human female body out of an ancient branch. She is using a knife; the wood is easy to work when it is soaked. Closer to the coast it is raining hard, here she is in cloud. The gloom of mist and the onset of evening suspend the artist in the fantasy of her solid wood. In the eerie light, time is of vertical essence: the present moment slides to a presence in the past, Amazons gather and argue.

Aella, that whirlwind of a woman, picks up her labrys; Antiope smirks as if she enjoys discord; Hippo stamps her foot and snorts, stutters in that absurdly high-pitched voice of hers; Hippolyta stands. Hippolyta commands attention from all with the force of her unquestionable beauty. The high curves of her cheek-bones and the breadth of her forehead find harmonious reiteration in the line of log, the turn of the grain. Virginia's eyes are playing tricks with her; she hadn't until this moment named the figures on her boat. Indeed, they are not formed yet.

'But how is history written?' Virginia asks herself. 'Did Hippolyta impress a single scribe or was it the careful archaeologist who brushed the dust away from her remains, who judged her skeleton perfectly proportioned?' The battle was on, whether Amazons liked it or not. Serene and statuesque, letting the tides of fate draw her in, still woman in the fluctuating world, a reed in the breeze, says, 'We have no choice.'

Virginia actually hears the voice in her head. The wet night closes in and she is, spookily, not alone. Marpesia eager to be military at any cost, Otrere nimble as a butterfly, carefree. In a warrior society the truly radical believe in peace, that there is no such thing as armed peace, thinks Virginia in her hypersentient state. Her boat is going to war. Amazons are an armed people, with many employed in the industry of beating out shields and fashioning arrows and dress-making the garb of aggression and defence. Omphale, heavy like Maria, dared to make Heracles her slave. The defence of Troy?

Virginia doesn't know what is true. Although she can hardly see her sculpture through the blackness, she is seeing another time, past or future. A future without freedom does not wash with the warrior women who spend their days sharpening their blades and expecting death, embattled. Penthesilea, Queen of the Amazons, Pantariste, Aella, Lysippe, bitter feelings souring her palate, Thalestris and Cressida, Amazons musing over the purple ranges of time, considering millennia. Virginia is with them in her reverie. She stumbles home, glad of the rain, the wetness, the reckless surrender to the continuum. Her vision is scored through with timeless aphorisms. Prophecy is memory. Stories of boats, of horses, weapons and castes, of when the sky-creatures invaded and rapid change came upon the earth, might triumphing over commonsense; invasion became adventure, in the songs of heroism.

'The trade routes of Bosporus are at stake,' says Cressida. 'It is all about economics. We must protect the Hellespont.'

'Colonisation is the name of the game,' answers Virginia.

Aella ceases her axe-work with the logs. Silver-tongued Pantariste leads her to the arms of the chubby Antiope. And Antiope looks like Cybil. Aella does not want to fight in man's stupid war.

'But the rules are set. Gods and goddesses play with human lives,' Virginia says. She doesn't even know these deities. She is going mad. But a yodel pierces the mystical realm of her mind and brings her into the present. That can only be Victoria. She gets up and goes outside with her torch.

Vee and Xena shake off their rain-coats. The black-spotted white dog enthusiastically makes muddy circles on the floor with paw-prints. Hugs all round. Vee's loud voice segues into her vision, which was, of course, an argument. Virginia lights her fire with the twigs and dry wood ready, collecting her thoughts. She activates the flames to warm her room, puts the billy on and settles into hospitality.

Xena makes tea and VeeDub and Vee catch up with what each has been doing over the past few months. Virginia cannot help speaking about her sculpture and Amazons. 'With our backs to the future we browse over the past, though we will never see anything distinctly except our present.'

'Come again?' Xena says. 'You've lost me.'

'I don't know,' shrugs Virginia. 'I really don't know how their society was organised.'

'I love talking about Amazons,' Vee Shackleton states.

Xena nods, 'Same for me. Fancy worshipping the scorching sun when the moon and the earth make more sense of our moods! That's why I live under the trees.'

'My dog's called Dike, after the goddess, Justice,' Shackleton confesses gruffly.

Xena and Virginia have both heard the explanation before. 'Did you see the full moon last night, here I mean?' Xena asks Virginia. 'Witches were flying across it. True.'

'Black, winged creatures. I did actually. Probably bats. I've been thinking about female cultures. They were done in in a short few hundred years. Amazons were at war for so long they couldn't see peace either in the future or the shape of it in the past.' Virginia is earnest. 'We're all slaves to it.'

'How depressing!' comments Xena.

'No, the war is still on.' The voices of the Amazons, though fading fast, continue in Virginia's head. And she speaks aloud. 'Penthesilea made a mistake willingly going into battle against the Greeks.'

'Snivelling hebephiles? I can live with it,' booms Vee. 'The idea that we're warriors. We have no choice.'

'Cressida sings our sorrows over the centuries, sealed them inside rocks for Amazons of the future to hear,' says Virginia, feeling relatively crazy.

'Didn't know Cressida was an Amazon,' Vee admits. 'I've heard of Cassandra, she was a prophet wasn't she?'

'Perhaps Penthesilea was in love with her,' opines Xena.

'Or Polyxena, her sister,' Virginia grins. 'She gets on quite well with Priam and Hecuba, too. Cassandra, of course, was given the gift of prophecy and then cursed with the bane of no one believing what she had to predict.

Victoria displays her knowledge. 'That is the men's story. The truth is more logical than that.'

'Ask me,' Xena scoffs. 'No one believes me.'

'Most intelligent people can probably work the future out, but few are prepared to act within that knowledge. They don't have the power! The political power!' Thus, Victoria is dramatic as she stands to warm her hands. 'Unable to implement policy.'

'I resign from the world,' Xena explains to two women who know very well the nuts and bolts of Xena Kia's resignation. Change of name. Off all electoral rolls. Embrace of dreams. No bank account. Cash-flow from the goddess-plant, barter.

'Reaping the rewards of Lesbianlands, mate,' Vee says affectionately.

Virginia smiles, 'It is easy to cheat.' She frowns. 'But what to do when you win. You haven't got real knowledge, you can't purchase knowing,' Virginia declares.

Vee nods. 'No power.'

'Amazonian intellectuals don't get spoken about much,' VeeDub says light-heartedly.

'Except for the nag,' Xena puts in, 'Cassandra, the scold.'

'She wasn't an Amazon!' Victoria erupts. 'Nor a lesbian!'

Three of them talk about the importance of wood to each individually and agree on the symbolic importance of the trees.

'I love trees. I love them like people, though. They're my friends,' Xena says proudly.

'Black wattles have shot up since I was here last. Fences broken in my horse yard,' sighs Victoria. 'Nicole's living there. Can I stay with you?' she asks Xena.

'Did you come for the meeting?' asks Virginia.

'I heard about it in Tamworth,' Victoria answers. 'So yeah, I guess so.' Xena and she are ready to go.

Virginia fixes the stub-ends of candles into a couple of rusty tin cans with handles, 'Here take these. The moon won't give you much light in this weather.'

'Thanks.'

Coloured light fell across my face as I opened my eyes. The day glistened. Puddles exploded with sunshine and reflected blue skies. The foliage was washed to a sparkle. Blades of lomandra shone clean at the edge of a square of cut lawn where dewdrops weighted the ends of grasses. Efforts had been made in this funny idea of a home. Specifically, stained glass: a learner's work of jagged daggers of leaded yellow like comic book lightning; and an art deco bubble-glass style, probably from a kitchen dresser picked up at a second-hand place, or the tip; but the third design was an impressively beautiful window. Rich apostles' cloak hues were rendered in a design of modern simplicity. I hadn't noticed them in the evening. An unfinished one of native fauna was leaning, unframed, against a wall, suggesting both had gone to class together. One talented in lead-lighting, the other not so good at it? If I had to guess the arty one, I'd say Jill.

A perfect cobweb pearled, seemingly suspended from nothing. I had slept well, considering the unsettling thoughts I was entertaining last night. They were no longer rank. The morning air was freshly pungent. Gaps in the data twisted with inconsistent personal impression made the sets of questions so carefully set in columns start knotting like strings. The job was not mentioned after the goat-kid incident. A simple financial search and discover, the fixing up of a glitch in accounting possibly had become complex with sexual overtones, and other components. Lying on my back on the futon, I saw a pale blue, artificial light come into the dark loft. More stained glass newly hit by the sun?

Daydreaming, I lay on my stomach, thinking. The window through which I was now taking in the dazzling outdoors was actually an aluminium-framed door. The light in the loft was not there when I checked again, must have a narrow angle to the east.

The enthusiastic strains of Meghan's vocal cords suddenly chimed like a clock, jostling my meditations.

'Morning, Margot,' she called as she backed down the ladder.

'Beautiful day,' I responded. She sat on the uncushioned frame of the couch and pulled on lace-up shoes.

'Coming?' she inquired.

Much as I wanted to get her on her own, as well as see whether the creek was still in flood, I am no fool. Recent soaking suggested slush underfoot. I felt like keeping my feet on solid ground and observing the wonder of nature from a distance. The green grass hid an underlying marsh, I was sure. Besides, over near the pot-belly I could see my Doc Martens really needed some tender loving care. Characterised by knobbly knees, her skinny legs disappeared into an oversized plaid shirt as she took off. The goats were being spoken to like children. I reached out for my bag which was within an arm's length of the pillow last night and did not lay a hand on it. That made me get up. Stretches. My mind took a Cook's tour of my body. The routine's automatic. I checked out the tendons, the shoulders, the neck: wherever there was tension I paid attention to it for a moment. No stiffness, muscles in order. I noticed my bag, while doing a couple of push-ups. It was the other side of the naked lounge. The notebook was dislodged.

Sometimes I hate my suspicious mind. I thought of dusting it for finger-prints other than mine. I was actually eager to do that soon because I could and I hadn't yet. In my chook-house studio I have fixed up a black plastic darkroom for my hobby, amateur black and white photography. So far I've had no chance to find out whether it is operative. I rifled through my bag, put it to one side then realigned the futon on the frame to become a neat sofa. And folded up the bedding. I was over at the pot-belly shaking out my clothes when I heard Jill's yawning voice.

'Hope you slept well, Margot. Like a coffee?' she invited, hospitably.

'Thanks, yeah. Please,' I replied. 'My boots dried.'

'Good.'

She had no clothes on. The vibe was sexy, but I was not provoked. Instead I slid the glass door aside and walked up to my car. The rain-cleansed air was so fresh and the distant hills such a dense blue-grey that after throwing my bag inside I kept walking along the stone and mud drive to the top of the hill, then did some deep breathing, chest-thumping, followed by tranquil observation. Their place was oriented the wrong way. The dwelling had a southern aspect, which might have been okay for a dairy, not a house. To the east a tall stand of eucalypts and she-oaks blocked most of the morning sun.

Meghan came up beside me, and whispered, 'Come, have a coffee.'

The birds in the timber were positively happy, raucous. Black cockatoos, bell-birds, spinebills, honey-eaters and fairy wrens. Meghan was better at identifying than I. We turned and walked together down the hill into the shade of trees, welcomed by the smell of freshly brewed coffee.

It was as if they expected a guest for breakfast, not for dinner. The coffee was really good. Quality stuff. We had English muffins from a packet with marmalade, and halved grapefruit. The sunlight speckled through leaves onto the picnic table we were sitting at on benches. The conversation was jolly. The goat I had saved yesterday took an interest. We roamed around easy topics: rowing, cycling, swimming, triathletics, coming events, the triathlon on Sunday. The pretty brown and white kid eyed me. I frowned back at it; does a goat have a measure of heroism?

The most interesting thing to report from the sporty talk was the change that came over Jill when I responded to a question about my trainer, Sean Dark.

'I don't mind poofters,' said Jill, 'but when I saw him on Saturday night cross-dressing, I decided never to trust him again.'

'It was a joke,' I supplied. 'A queen as the Virgin Queen. He's a radical celibate.'

'No, he's not!' Jill's tone was vicious. 'He's a transvestite and I hate them.'

Meghan interrupted, gently. 'Tell Margot why, Jill.'

Jill then told a bitter tale about the death and sickness of a number of her friends in Sydney. It was before the public recognition of AIDS and transmission of the HIV virus, but the guy knew he had it. He dressed as a woman and shared with a group of lesbians a smack needle, thus infecting them all. Jill considered it an act of calculated misogyny which gave her untold sadness through the loss of women she loved. Her hatred seethed with longings for revenge.

'It's just something a woman would never do,' she finished.

Meghan abruptly got up. It was time for me to go. 'Margot, you drive me down the road,' she commanded, 'and I'll show you Chandra's place.'

My polite thanks for dinner, breakfast and hospitality were met with sulky silence, as Jill slumped into the melancholic melodrama of her own feelings.

There was still a fair flow of water over the cemented ford. For the hell of it, I put the Sierra into four-wheel drive before we got in and was glad I did as we slid down to the wooden bridge.

'You could get stranded here,' I said with distracted concern, glancing upriver.

'When I have to get to work in a flood, I take off all my clothes, put them into a waterproof bag, hold it up and throw myself in and get swept down,' Meghan explained as if it were nothing at all.

'True?' I believed her.

'I land about there,' she pointed. Higher up the bank, beside the road, was her car, an expensive-looking sports sedan. I smiled, tried to match woman with vehicle. Both speedy.

'Then I get dressed and go to work. Don't have to today, but my car is always parked there.' Meghan told me as if assuming I thought the rusty navy-blue Nissan Urvan up at the house was hers.

'Tell me about your work?' I questioned politely as the Sierra splashed across the second creek-crossing, skidding dangerously. Was it locally based or Sydney? Was it urgent? Could she take flexitime?

She would not answer. So I kept rephrasing my queries.

'You seem to want to know an awful lot about me,' she said eventually.

'I'm curious by nature,' I smiled. We can all play the ignorance game.

'I cannot—cannot—*comprendez?*—tell you what I do,' she said emphatically. 'Can't even tell Jill.'

'I realise,' I said, 'that Jill doesn't know I am working for you, she thinks that I am just a friend, who is interested in sport, and, who was invited out to tea. There are discrepancies in your paperwork that I can chase up, but I need you to, at least, tell me where you were on certain dates. When large amounts of money went from your accounts. I can't believe you don't look at your bank statements when they come!'

Meghan Featherstone's face seemed to flick through a directory of personalities before it chose one. Then she brushed her head vigorously with her hands as if she had walked through a fine cobweb by accident.

'Does your work know about Jill?' I pressed.

'Good question.' Her reply was in that chirpy I-am-a-fool-can't-you-see voice that I was beginning to suspect was both incredibly honest and incredibly deceitful at the same time.

Impatiently, I said, 'I used to work for the Commonwealth, National Crime Authority. Stationed both Sydney and Adelaide. Previously with the New South Wales police force, rank, Detective Senior Constable. Served Redfern, Marrickville, and for a short time in Central Sydney. Trained Goulburn, graduating with credits. You think I can't find out where you work?'

She shook her head. Then spoke almost too quietly to be heard. 'I have access to more information than you've dreamed of, Margot.'

In a raised voice she gave me directions to turn right at the next dirt road, and finished. 'In your philosophy.'

Meghan changes like the wind, I was thinking, when she said, 'I am an idiot with money. Although I am a scientist, in reality I can't stand figures. Well, only in the abstract. I can't seem to whip up the enthusiasm. The envelope says bank, I just toss it. I know I have enough money to live,' she admitted, slapping her hands together, point by point.

'You can't be real,' I commented, slowing down so that I could look at her. 'Fair dinkum? You're short thousands of dollars and you won't tell me whether you were in the city, in the vicinity, at the time it was withdrawn.'

'Business can be done over the telephone. All bills I pay with plastic,' she said conversationally. Then blew me away with, 'I did not employ you to find out who is taking money from my accounts.' She said it so softly I hardly heard her.

'What did you say?' I was frustrated, confused.

'I said, I did *not* employ you to look into my financial affairs,' she stated.

We looked at each other, searching the eyes for answers neither of us had.

'What?' I demanded, incredulous. 'But it was your voice on the telephone, not a good line, mind you. Then the documents arrived, not a full set, mind you.' It was getting hilarious. I wanted to laugh.

Meghan looked as if she wanted to cry but didn't know how. Body language read, here was one stressed lady. I breathed in through my nose to the count of seven and exhaled to the count of four. Secrets were bound together in there like sticks of dynamite.

'So, you have my financial papers?' she asked.

'Yes. Here, you can have them back.' I reached over the back of the seat feeling for the folder.

She looked very unhappy for one moment. Then she was bouncing in her seat, saying, 'No, no. Keep them. Keep working for whoever me is. Find out what you can.' With that she employed me. 'There's Chandra's place.'

Whoever me is, what a choice of words!

She had me stop at a scenic spot. We overlooked bottle-brush in the foreground, an elegant sweep of valley, distant hills, wonderfully mauve, and in the middle, a sunlit north-facing hill, a small area of vegetables, dark glossy silver beet, beans on trellises, a large patch of sweet corn grown about six foot, tomato vines, passionfruit covered the two tanks either side of a shed. Herb gardens close to the house were interlocked with flower beds. A native fig the size of a house and post-and-rail fences gave perspective. A ride-on motor mower was being driven by a woman in a marvellous hat. We gazed for a moment. I opened my door. Meghan let herself out of the car. But she was not taking in the scenery when I glanced at her but biting her fingernail, perusing the ground. Jerkily, she sprang to attention.

'Okay, okay. I'll ring you. That is Chandra riding her mower. She is terrific, really,' she said, but stopped me asking anything by saying, 'She just has a problem with me.'

'Well I probably won't visit her, anyway,' I reckoned.

'I think I'll walk home,' she said in her artless way, as if we hadn't exchanged knowledge of a mystery. Viz, who employed me in the first place.

She started off. I followed her. 'Hey! You have to make an appointment with me. What's your sister's address? You got any other girlfriends in other parts of the country? I have so many questions.'

'I'll ring,' she brushed me away.

'You had better, or I'll resign from the job. And why aren't you introducing me to the lady on the tractor?' I skipped around in front of her.

'We are not on speaking terms at the moment,' she explained. I held her still. 'What I mean is Chandra is so in your face. I can't deal with her right now.'

'Why can't you deal with it now? Meghan, what is really going on?' I demanded. She side-stepped me and went quickly the way we'd come. As I waited for some kind of assurance, she turned and touched her nose with her forefinger. Then she grinned broadly, gave a hop and began to jog off like someone happily into a training routine.

Who was it I was supposed to meet? Meghan Featherstone herself, plainly. Whoever wanted me interested certainly had me hooked.

11

. . . bliss of being and non-being . . .

A little girl on a dappled grey pony rode up the hill on the other side of the house. There seemed to be no gate or drive-way this side of the property.

The land must have been subdivided in the last ten years into five- and twenty-five acre blocks, judging by the houses, which were new. Each looked like someone's dream of mansions, fancies of other places. There was the American clap-board look alongside the Southern States colonnades, a suggestion of Dutch African Colonial, a two-storey mansion, a manor house complete with rose garden. Early Australian imitation homesteads, in carefully combined heritage colours, of Hardiplank or aluminium siding or new wood glistening with paint. Some with no flowers, lawn or trees yet. Each of these homes aspired to a unique vision, isolated from one another. Brick veneer off-the-rack architecture with pretty English cottage neighboured Spanish ranch-style. Swimming pools galore. Here people plonked their individual ideas side by side with no recognition of each other's taste or the nature of the land. I wondered how it would look in a hundred years: would they have found some kind of unity by then beyond the general air of borrowed style? Would it say to future generations: here was a society in which citizens worked all their life solely in order to own a home? I could not criticise because I do it myself. We put a lot of energy into our relationship with a house. In ownership of land and dwelling, each person is so aggressive, obsessive and possessive. Yet I bet they are all similar people here. Tradesmen who have done well enough financially to be able to afford to live in their ideal chateau. Neat and new.

Chandra's block was quite different from the rest in that the residence was the original farmhouse. An ancient native fig dominated one side, while on the other the garden, designed for produce, was more successful visually than the bordering villas' picture-book appearance.

The Seaside Shopping Complex is a commercial village under a roof with air-conditioning. Dogs and skate-boards are not allowed. Sofia is horrified to discover that neither is smoking. She disobeys. She goes into the supermarket. She has it in mind to buy food, but she reads about food. She reads the small print on cartons of milk, on the tins, the cans, the boxes. Too much food. Too much packaging. She hates food. It is all poisoned, anyway. They do things without telling anyone. She tries to explain to shoppers the words on the packet can only be understood by the scientifically educated, but she can decode some of them. No one listens. She throws the things she has been studying into others' trolleys. She lights another cigarette, looks about for an official and gets ready to run. She suspects every person in a suit. There is a conspiracy afoot, poisoning not only people's bodies, but their minds as well. They have invented substances in the laboratories that get into women's souls. She must find out the secrets. The only people she sees in suits are women, power-dressing. Freaks rule! The one-eyed scientists managed to change an X chromosome into Y in the laboratories. Now the method has hit the streets.

Riding escalators in the Seaside Shopping Complex, Sofia is in the here and now of the brave new world. Nothing is friendly. The people are robots, pretending to be human, overacting. She can see through them. She spies a phone. She has an idea.

She rings Chandra. 'It is all obfuscation.' The place you go to find the truth is on the World Wide Web.

Chandra calms her down by making the basics simple. 'Do you understand?'

'Now I have a purpose,' she whispers into the mouthpiece and puts it down. She walks slowly towards plate glass and sees herself slim and beautiful; tosses her hair; shakes it back into place. But that is her disguise. She is really a hideous flying creature.

Sofia is thrilled to discover that in the internet café, CyberCage, they are not strict on smoking. She has a quick mind if she stays on a train of thought and does not disembark. She pays her money and types the address: www.webset.com.au/wimmin.htm. She has followed Chandra's instructions and she is a whiz. She is bouncing with excitement. She has to get up and pace a bit. Then she enters the <u>kitchen</u> chat.

\<ITSME\> Been cleaning the white goods listening to the radio.

\<SKUMBO\> Let's cook up a plan to assassinate the White Virgin.

\<MISS\> She is worse than the Iron Butterfly.

\<SKUMBO\> She's a woman, no. She's being used. BFN

Sofia writes down the number of a goods locomotive and has her say.

\<8202*\> If you imagine any woman has any real power beyond information you're fooling yourself.

\<ITSME\> If only we had the diamonds.

<EIEIO> But we cannot rob the earth mother.

<REDSHOES> Greed, one of the ways the men get you on their side.

<8202*> Real poison. I have proof. They're lopping a leg off an X, making wobbly Ys.

<BAC> We could put something in the water that kills sperm or makes them impotent. B.O.B. Okay, lesbian cyborg candidate for Oz Presidency logging on.

<DEFARGE> Gotta hitch-hiker. Cane toads! Anyone want a pet?

Me, me, me, wishes Sofia.

<8202*> But in a sieve I'll thither sail,/ And like a rat without a tail,/ I'll do, I'll do and I'll do. I'll have the cane toad, please.

<DEFARGE> Private room. It'll cost you a recipe.

Sofia types one out and arranges a meeting to pick up her new pet. Then she leaves <u>Wimmin.com.au/kitchen</u> and surfs the search engine for genetic modification and other food sites until her money runs out. All her fears are justified. There are aliens in the sky and lesbian cyborgs with an intent to murder. Murder. The OD at the beach was murder, intended victims, lesbians with the truth! Knowledge and no power, until now! It wasn't an overdose. Her mind is exploding. The electrons in her brain are leaping over the chemical arcs creating heat and distress. She needs a drink, a serapax, benzodiazepan. Not speed, she mutters to herself speedily. She needs a familiar of a particularly witchy kind, a toad. It'll do.

Chandra settles Tilly on the horse and lets her ride by herself. It is a beautiful day. The work in cyberspace is keeping her chained longer hours than ever at her computer, she needs some flesh and blood nature. After the call from Sofia, she decides to do a bit of mowing. She thinks she needs, also, a relationship. It has been a long while since Sofia but her sexy voice turns her on. Then, after the last, with Alison, she vowed never again and buried herself in revolutionary work. Love of women should make us full of self-knowledge and courage of conviction, broader of mind, safer, therefore able to explore more our radical thought. It should make us stronger because we have support, and freer and less selfish and more self-confident.

Chandra mows meticulously. She loves her ride-on. Sad irony that the goddess should give the gift of green fingers to the mobility-challenged; nonetheless, she copes, and the garden, as the sign says, is always a thing of pleasure. Being outside allows her to entertain lusty thoughts, while doing something useful. Bad experiences with mad, beautiful women have left her with a few responsibilities and expenses, but no great bitterness. Yesterday in the oppressive rain she did not know what she knows today. What she knows today with crystal clarity is: she is ready. It is a new morning. The chemistry of friendship, often left in abeyance at hot love times, requires phenomenal discipline. When to be kind. When to be cruel. What is needed is both loyalty and freedom. If she had let her stay, she would have had to give up so much freedom. Specifically, her choice to have no males in her environment. Tilly's okay. Most women are so used to being a helpmeet they don't know who they are or they are scared to be alone. Being indispensable is rewarding, Chandra concedes, but being a married couple does not challenge hegemonic reality. Unacceptable. Chandra doesn't have time. Ordinary lesbians can do it but not radical feminists because they're aware that there are no models for them to follow. We must forge a new path, of discovery, of sexuality.

As she turns, she glances up and sees the figure of Meghan Featherstone pointing at her, near one of those dinky toy four-wheel-drives. She is suddenly furious. Meghan could have been a sister-at-arms, but she works for a multinational, an earth-raping, secret organisation that Chandra suspects of being owned by the CIA. Meghan did not deny it. They had a very public barney, screaming at one another in front of a number of gurls. Chandra made her passionate position clear. She could not live with hypocrisy. Contradictions, yes, we had to, but deliberate, self-serving hypocrisy, no. Never. The betrayal of trust churns in her guts while she mows. She has lost sight of Tilly and Potsdam Harry. Gradually, with effort, she gears her anger to contemplation of the methods of war. The friendly mailing lists which she updates and checks with her email everyday are full of action. Known radical feminists are attacked personally. Brought down. The old troopers are starving in poverty somewhere. Not if Chandra can do something about it. Child porn. Coalition Against the Trafficking in Women. Women Against War. Zimbabwe International Book Fair. Sex is pornography according to Germaine Greer. It is not as though women aren't fighting. Forwarded messages keep her in touch. Social change does not come easy, pioneers pay dearly for what their successors take for granted. Well, Chandra is not finished, she is just beginning to gather a strike force.

A sealed ring road roped the mansions to Red Cedar Road. I figured that if I turned left, then left again, I could approach Chandra's from there. Like turning over in bed, the corner had the effect of taking the mind off one preoccupation and putting it on to the next. There was a rough track immediately to my left, I noticed, as I shifted up a gear. I glanced down it. Coming towards me at a confused canter was the dappled grey pony, without rider. I stopped, reversed and swung the steering wheel. I drove past the horse. Suddenly it came to a standstill and started eating grass. I was worried about the child last seen on its back. The little girl had fallen and was doubled up on the ground under a tree. I was beside her in no time.

'That branch knocked me off,' she explained thrusting an accusing finger upwards. 'Stupid branch.' Her voice was breathless as if she had been winded.

'Maybe you thought you were smaller than you are, you and your pony.' I was rubbing her hunched shoulders.

Her eyes shone. 'No, we were going faster than I have ever gone. We were galloping!' she exclaimed proudly.

'Then you must be very hurt,' I sympathised. Her muscles relaxed. Her breathing came back to normal.

'Show me?' I attempted to pull up her T-shirt. Kids usually show off their hard-won bruises. This one held down the front of her shirt with all her strength so quickly my hand slipped around and exposed her back. It was blotched with black-and-blues that were too old and inconsistent with either falling off a horse or being hit by a tree. It was only a glimpse. I lifted her to her feet.

'All right now? Hey? Let's go get your steed,' I jollied.

'Okay. He's really very naughty,' she chatted. 'A very naughty boy. Because when I tried to keep him on the road, he turned around. And then we went round and round. I tried to steer him off the road. It really pissed him off, me changing my mind. Stupid tree got in the way.' She held my hand walking towards the cropping pony, who turned and looked at us with mild interest. 'He was going so fast.' She looked up at me, and I grinned.

As we neared to her mount, her step got slower. She let go my hand and visibly gathered her courage and started talking like a schoolmarm. 'Now you come here, Spotty, and don't be a stupid boy.'

She castigated him while I picked up the reins and patted him on the nose. I've always liked the smell of horses and the softness of their noses. Now she was beside me, becoming more bossy as the moment of decision loomed. To relieve her of it, I whipped around, picked her up and placed her on the saddle. She winced as if I'd caught the fresh bruises. Weight, I'd estimate, twenty-five to twenty-seven kilos. I kept the reins and led them down the track.

The Suzuki was back there with keys in the ignition and my wallet on the seat. I let a twinge of worry come and go. Funny how eventually you check: car, keys, wallet. Forget it, I told my mind. Walking eased me, teasing out knots like some spinster at her knitting wool after her cat's had a go at it. The horse was a solid presence, a gentle giant of a person. The girl chatted on. Half the time her chatter addressed me and the rest Spotty got. I assumed the verbal trots were nerves, but when I looked back at her she was playing with the mane, thoroughly contented.

'What's your name?' I asked.

'Tilly. It's really Matilda. I have a second name and that's Jocelyn. And my mother says there's two reasons why Matilda is really good for me. One is that she used to carry me around everywhere like a swag and the other one I've forgotten. It is maybe someone who was alive and doesn't live in Australia. Who doesn't live any more,' the little livewire responded.

Whether or not she heard my name in response, Tilly began to give me minute directions, even options. I could go that way through the paddock gate, or open the one beside the main drive-way. I looked up to paddock gate and panned from there. Beside the cattle-grid was a magnificent picket with a wrought-iron contraption at the top. I realised the gate could be easily opened from the back of a horse, a complication of weights and counter-checks. Impressive. There was a horse-riding rectangle with recycled tyres and sawdusty sand on the flat part. Further down were white-painted little jumps between Xs. Neither conforming with this kid's ability to ride.

Tilly demanded the reins as we gained home territory. Instead of relinquishing them, I gave her my nasal rendition of k. d. lang's 'Tall in the Saddle' and she seemed to enjoy that as much.

'Chandra,' shouted Tilly. 'This is Margot.'

A big black and tan dog bounded up, barking.

The circular blades stop whirring. Chandra's meditations are destroyed by the appearance of Margot Gorman, untrustworthy by virtue of being an ex-cop. The triathlete, the summer Amazon, is a gorgeous creature. A jelly-fish on the phone, when she needed counselling, she is leading Potsdam Harry. Tilly's seat in the saddle is straighter than she has ever achieved before. No reins. Must do some lunging with her later, Chandra promises herself. The three of them are so beautiful as they make their way past the enormous native fig, the gravel road behind them curling away between overhanging gums and the true blue of the sky, Chandra frowns. Beauty melts her. Margot's physical perfection, completeness, makes Chandra aware of her-self, her imperfection, her resentment, and her system floods itself with a rush of embarrassment. Tilly has her mother's looks. Chandra has had to pay dearly for her own double standards. She is not attracted to other cripples. Why should others be? Especially those blessed by nature. Alison is exquisite, and Sofia a sex-kitten; both marred by mental fragility, they did not threaten Chandra's confidence. Margot stands gracefully. Harry pricks his ears. Tilly talks. Chandra, in self-protection, tries to be as rude and grumpy as she can. She did not imagine that the detective would have such an honest, open, bloody attractive demeanour. She tries to unsettle her.

Chandra's broad-brimmed hat came into view at motorised speed as we passed under the shade of the *Ficus rubiginosa*. She lifted the blades of the mower when she heard Tilly shout and drove up to meet us. I detected some hostility as she sighed and nodded, a gesture of impatience. I stood still, patting the horse's neck, but he didn't seem to tremble at the approach of the vehicle. Tilly started shouting explanations before the engine was cut. And continued after. We, the adults, looked at one another without interrupting the girl. Chandra remained seated, perfectly still, taking in what had happened and everything she could about me. I gathered that was quite a lot, from the intelligence in her eyes. She had one of those wide, brown faces, with big teeth and decisive lips. She was between forty and fifty. The lines becoming deep were those from the nose around the mouth and squinty-smiley crows' feet. She wore an ironic expression. She seemed little amused by the accident story. I let my gaze wander to her body and machine. The clavicle muscles were cultivated like a weight-lifter's. Her hands on the gearstick were strong like a musician's.

Tilly's story had changed. She was now an Enid Blyton-type heroine.

Chandra spoke educatively. 'That would have been his pirouette. You probably accidentally gave him the aids to dance around in circles. It is just not appropriate to do that under a tree, Tilly.'

'Anyway, he was really good, apart from that. And when we went to catch him he didn't move at all. Margot lifted me back on his back.'

When we shook hands, I saw the callipers. A pair of those arm-strap crutches was resting alongside the accelerator pedal. None of the gossip had mentioned that Chandra did not have the use of her legs.

For some reason allusion in words to Friday night's intimate phone conversation was out of the question. I had been pre-menstrual, uncharacteristically upset and on edge when I rang her. I couldn't use Meghan's introduction because it would have been clumsier than Meghan herself, and she had told me not to. I tried small talk. I felt awkward, I got everything wrong.

Spotty was not Tilly's pony. Potsdam Harry was Chandra's equine companion and one of her means of getting around.

'How?' I said. In for a penny, in for a pound. Abrupt.

'I ride side-saddle. And mount via a mechanism my father designed many many years ago.' Potsdam Harry was a very expensive animal with a pedigree back through Holland to Austria. 'The Lipizzan horses,' she lectured, 'have very strong bones, short legs, and thick, arched necks. They can make difficult jumps because of their powerful hindquarters. The best known Lipizzan horses are those trained at the Spanish Riding School of Vienna in Austria. These horses perform graceful jumping and dancing feats.'

'Okay,' I nodded. 'Once on duty at a special event in Western Sydney I saw them with police horses from all over the world. The Lipizzans were amazing. I can understand why he was offended by being seen as a dappled grey pony called Spotty.' He was an aristocrat among horses who could walk around on his hind legs, jump without putting his front feet down and be as trustworthy a child-minder as there is. Chandra did not like my anecdote of ordinary policing.

'Nice place,' I mumbled; it sounded like a grumble. I looked about with an idiotic smirk, hiding a sort of exciting discomfort. Wrong again.

She launched again, her piano player's hands unmoving on the wheel. 'I suppose you think I got all this with some compensation claim. A motor bike accident, perhaps?'

I nodded, even though I had supposed no such thing. I wanted to nod, I wanted to affirm her.

But she went on, aggressively. 'I have worked hard for everything I have. I had polio as a child, for which I have never received any compensation except the disability pension.'

'Well, better go,' I backed up a couple of steps, with my hands showing my palms, fingers wiggled goodbye. When she started the motor, she flashed a mischievous smile. I wondered what the trouble was; both the problem Meghan alluded to and the problem of my being there. Why was she so defensive?

Potsdam Harry accompanied me. Well, I was the one on foot. He was like a dog at heel. Hearing her scold him, I waited for Tilly to gather the reins and compose herself for riding. The canine had disappeared. Chooks and ducks pecked about.

'Where's your mother, Tilly?' I threw the question over the handsome arched neck.

'Chandra is really cranky with my mum. We're just staying here a little while. I don't mind because I have Spotty. And it's good sleeping in the barn. It smells like adventure stories. And my mum doesn't mind that. We're both sleeping side by side in the hay loft.' She gestured to a building that had not been visible from the place where I dropped Meghan. It was a closed-in barn, with big doors and a high roof. The side-saddle hanging in the rafters beside a trapeze and monkey bar confirmed Chandra did not lie about little things, which was what bothered me about Jill. A lean-to carport housed a Subaru wagon.

'I don't think I'd better go out on the road again,' Tilly said. 'I only wanted to see if I could open the gate and I could and before I could stop him, Spotty kept going. He's hard to stop if he doesn't want to.'

'Maybe he was glad to be out.' I gripped the reins near the bit and gently pulled them back. The highly educated horse stopped promptly and posed. I got the feeling that everyone around Chandra was well-trained. Probably even the chooks.

'Tilly, I think you're going to be a really good rider one day,' I reckoned.

'I ride bikes. Have you got a bike?'

'No,' she said uncertainly. 'Lenny has. We're staying here, but Lenny isn't.' The young intelligent face showed two conflicting emotions for a moment.

'I've met Lenny, where is he? At his dad's?' I asked.

Tilly nodded, 'Sort of. Chandra won't have any males on the property except animals, but they're not allowed to have balls. Like there's no roosters. Spotty and me are going now.' She pulled a long, loose rein and flung her little legs out in big painless kicks.

''Bye Tilly.' I smiled at the charming kid.

'See ya,' she yelled, still kicking madly to no great effect on the stately, gelded Spanish Dancer.

Still blushing from Chandra's brush-off and unsaid undercurrents, I regained the car. Wallet, gear, everything shipshape. This was a dead-end dirt road. I thrust a k. d. lang tape in the deck and her voice boomed from the four corners of the Sierra's quadraphonic acoustics. I sang the phrases I knew of 'Family Tradition' as I drove.

A milk tanker passed me. How can they get such a polish on white duco? Although I was thinking of something else, this semi jerked my recall. It felt like déjà vu, always an unsettling mental skip in time's game of ropes.

You would think gurls in the same neighbourhood would be friends. Whatever happened between Meghan and Chandra must have cut pretty deep.

Virginia White wakes up from a rest on her day-bed thinking of the Silk Road, the thin thread of money connecting East and West. The importance of Troy. Its culmination. The elegance and wealth of Troy, the gateway of the trade routes opening onto to the burgeoning civilisation of Greece, the markets of the growing known world. The fortune seekers, and adventurers, trekking the dangerous path. The whole thing had grown into a choking matted cobweb of commerce that threatened to destroy the earth.

While she was dreaming it was so clear what had happened. Her sub-conscious was capable of encompassing the lot in fluid images melting into each other in slick movement across time and space. The transference to being conscious is also generous in scope, though more confused and laced with ignorance, coloured by the memories and fancies of her own history. She and Jeff had played the stories of Marco Polo, Arabian Nights, Ali Baba, been pirates and thieves, on boats, on horses made of sticks, sword-fighting, charging like knights, been musketeers. And she listened with interest to Caroline's raves about ancient Greece, her specialty. Yet as she rises, she knows nothing of the trade routes and commerce, starting as a single silk thread, now stifling the planet with the madness of money. In the present, she has only the wisps of having dreamed something brilliant, her self as a restless being inhabiting transmogrifying bodies, freely flying through the ages. The artistic temperament, as the Surrealists tried to show, straddles the worlds of consciousness.

The mental work of her dreaming gives her energy to complete tasks necessary to living in the wilderness. Gathering twigs and bark, making the fire, boiling the billy, sweeping, washing up, placing things neatly, getting it together to go back to her work. Walking, climbing the rainforest track, her brain barely registers the brilliant day; the songs of birds seem like distractions. Drawn by a magnetism to her piece, she approaches a towering fortress, a rugged defiance in her own emotions, a dead tree teeming with life but not tree-life. It is black and green, impossibly inelegant.

She is fooling herself. Virginia wonders if she is going mad. So many women artists have gone mad, or got so depressed they killed themselves. A raging torrent of indignation, energy, righteousness makes them work their hearts out until one day their sanity breaks and they have no more to give. Without giving what is the point of living? Because Virginia is not mad, she fights her doubt with logic and righteous intention, but the axe falls leaden. She is afraid of destroying, rather than creating with her tools. Craft deserts her; she might as well be chopping fire wood. She considers killing herself.

She mounts the rudimentary ladder, sits down in despair. Soon, allowing the words of self-admonishing to cease, she is being transported to another place and time, by the fact of her work, by her imagination, by her concentration, by something beyond her. She meditates, she dissolves. She does hear the voice of someone called Cressida. Virginia relaxes. She poses, one of the forms she has not yet shaped, on the prow of the non-existent ship in the viridian shade and chill of the bush in a dappled sun.

'Because they do not know, because they were not there, they think old Cressida is lecturing when she speaks. The arthritis in my fingers cramps the movement of my hands which were once strong and supple. Such a calcification occurs in mentality too. My memory does not have the flexibility of

125

its youth. It has hardened around my own viewpoint, but I was there and I do know. The concrete accuracy of my recall is shaped by my personal vision, both my expectations and what I actually saw in my role as spy in the palace, plus, of course, by what I made of it all, later.

'Perhaps you think that Achilles dispatched Penthesilea in a back street, that there were skirmishes in different parts of the city and hand-to-hand combat happened in conditions of chaos. The crowds afflicted with mass blood-lust acting as a herd responding to rumours of where the action is, as if rounded up by the hounds and wolves of carrion hunger, is a possible view of events. It is, after all, how people behave during eruptions of rebellion and insurrection. The overthrow of Priam, the destruction of Troy and all her gubernatorial customs stemming from matrilineal descent, the control of wealth, the dispensation of justice, the secular and religious rituals Trojans enjoyed celebrating birth and respecting death, was not at all like a revolution, a people's uprising. It was a cold, calculated take-over, glamourised by a crude sculpture on wheels, Greeks bearing gifts, a wooden horse of grotesque size, an armour-plated tank, a military operation. The Aegeans insinuated a police force with the trickery of an undercover operation and proceeded, thereafter, to create war.

'Naturally the populace mobbed in anger, at times. Long had the hebephiles of Sparta, Ithaca and Athens converted the aggressive and competitive instincts of male youth into the arts of war, exulted these pursuits into the games of Olympus as if, indeed, the gods themselves enjoyed nothing more than the activities of might. Boys fight and compete. Give them weapons and they will go on a rampage. But, what do I, a single Amazon, know of the needs of greedy gods? Amazons could not hold back the tide. The ugly wooden horse collapsed slowly in the forecourt of the palace. It fell off its wheels and couldn't be moved.'

Like Gig's caravan.

'Even the Greeks were ashamed of it. Ulysses, military prodigy that he was, reckoned the real appeal of war was as a spectator sport. He had his troops construct an arena in the agora of their encampment for the matches of skill and strength. The hoi polloi did not, themselves, want to get hurt, and the politicians, councillors, bursars, priests, ladies of fashion, historians and court gossips wielded a power he measured as equivalent to feats of courage. Penthesilea will face the best, Achilles. Much fanfare accompanied Penthesilea's march to our camp, overlooking the River Scamander. The warrior-women's tent was a bigtop with the Amazonian flag flying from the mast of its centre pole. The dining board was a long table at which all Amazons ate, whether their jobs were cleaning, clothing, feeding or dressing wounds, fighting or carrying. Long-limbed dogs kept guard, lying watchfully at the four corners of our ground. I will record here and just once that there was never ever known entry by spies into the Amazons' living quarters. Although a spy in the court, full of its perfumed scents, I could pass in and out as I pleased. We did not question the acumen of canine discernment, merely used it to our advantage. Women collaborating with the enemy were immediately met by our diplomats and asked their business by an Amazon in control of her tongue. My counter-agent, the scholarly Greek, wondered how this could be. Failed attempts to penetrate the Amazon enclave to glean the secrets of our chain of command were subjects of endless interest.

'Did he not know that dogs only told the truth, or did he think that the dogs said nothing? Such trivial topics amused me for no more than a second. Achilles did not underestimate Penthesilea any more than he did any other opponent. Patroclus was slain after donning Achilles' armour, but there was, on this day, no mistaking the angry eyes, the fire of hatred behind the clouds of sultry arrogance. Seated ringside next to Briseis and Cassandra in an enclosure for females of a certain obtained standard of dress, I, Cressida, truly wished that my queen would win. I wanted to barrack and lend my energy and enthusiasm. I was caught up in the moment. The agora was crowded. Briseis and Cassandra reflected on the fate of Hector. Polyxena hoped, within my earshot, that Achilles would, for a change, fight fairly. For my own safety I was not privy to any tricks we may have had up our sleeves. The Greek princes, heroes, Nestor, Ajax, Diomedes, Menelaus and the rest of them each had his own tent, an entourage, servants and soldiers separate, and, although Agamemnon was supposed to be their chief, they operated along lines of alliances behind the goal of the shared outcome, the conquest of Troy, for the honour of Zeus, their father god. Or riches. Or domination. It's a rickety system if you want to keep intelligence secure. We all knew the secrets of their love lives, their passions, their weaknesses, what they had for breakfast, who was likely to betray whom, because their encampment was rife with spies. Everyone was aware Patroclus was the one who commanded the Achilles' heart. His boys, the Myrmidons, were god-given gifts. Achilles' armour, however, did not save his lover. Thetis made her son impervious. Wounds he sustained healed as they were inflicted.

'Penthesilea's arrow started the conflict. Amazon arrows stung the strident Myrmidons and pinged off Achilles' suit of brilliant metal. The skills of war were so refined and graceful at this pin-point in history that those not in battle had no fear of injury. Achilles was contemptuous of the arrows. They were as annoying gnats. What truly irritated him was there was nothing for him to do except march around displaying his splendour. Amazon arrows shot out from sniper's holes at irregular intervals as Penthesilea herself took her time arriving at the contest.

'Beneath the veneer of civilisation, the sophistication of both the Greeks and the Trojans, war itself is barbaric. Witnesses to this occasion were at a blood sport. The playful beginning would end in tragedy. The fate of the locals was in the hands of mercenaries shaping up against each other. Cassandra, beside me, was disgusted. She knew what was going to happen. Already the assembly was dispersing, muttering that the Amazons were not being fair to Achilles. The Amazons, other Trojans opined, had to stick to their nature. They were archers, and their lives were at stake. The city was in a state of siege and the residents needs must obey the curfew at sunset. This, I think, was what Penthesilea was taking into account. If she could occupy Achilles during the daylight hours, frustrate him by not being available at dawn, when he was fresh and his troops blinded one with the beauty of their pageantry, she could catch him in hand-to-hand combat with a minimum of distraction and have a reasonable chance. Our Penthesilea did not lack confidence, but she did know that brains play a big part in success.

'I snuck past the sphinx (the dogs) at the gate. There grew a lotus flower in these parts that was irresistible to Amazons who felt they deserved a break. I saw cleaners and cooks who had been busy for forty-eight hours sitting at the dinner board relaxing, taking a narcotic drink, because, they said, it is probably our last chance to feel proud. Already our medical team was treating wounded Amazons. Our jackal detail had brought in three bodies by the time I was there. How quickly disillusionment set in when the vision was glory!

'The detractors, however, were in the minority. For the most part unity was achieved because there was a common enemy and action. Amazons were in danger. The camp was busy. Outnumbering the pessimists were those with impossible optimism. When I found the crone I was looking for, she said, we have not been in this situation before and she did not know what I should do. It depended, she thought, on whether I believed my fate belonged with the sword or the word. There was a place for me in the last phalanx, the team of Amazons ready for clash of sword and shield. The smell of freshly oiled leather, the sight of polished steel, the industrious activity of other swordswomen, intoxicated me, infected me with the excitement of the fray. I stood in my court robes among Amazons clad in short tunics, tall boots, flexing their muscles, lunging and parrying, waiting impatiently for the call. We, warlike women, had been bred for this moment. We all had the training. I stripped off the soft fabric, and stood naked, letting the cold evening air ready my nervous system. Thalestris held up the suede jerkin for me to thrust my arms in its holes, quickly she buckled the shield holster into place. I stepped into the tunic. It was tight. I had put on weight in the luxury of the palace. My boots were worn and the leather worked with lard. My feet slipped in smoothly.

'We trotted out along the streets of the city of Troy in ranks of four, heading straight for the arena. We noticed some of our archers in position and others helping each other back to camp. Tears of excitement, pride, pressed on my lids. I jogged and chanted, carrying my sword in my right hand and my shield in my left. Achilles, by this time, was bored with the tricks Penthesilea was playing, yet he was not prepared to slay Amazon warriors whom members of his company were quite able to deal with. The man was furious, smelling blood. Penthesilea rose in stature as we formed an avenue for her entrance into the open-air stadium, shields clipped on our chests and swords aloft in both hands. Penthesilea issued the challenge to Achilles in formal and customary fashion. Her voice echoed and silenced the crowd. A bout between the greatest was more interesting to all concerned than the hacking of infantry into one another. Now it was Achilles' turn to play. His agility was a wonder to behold. His armour seemed to fit his musculature like a glove.

'He killed Penthesilea slowly, wound by wound. Her fight, her faith in herself, her determination to keep going until the end was gripping. As she had made him wait all day, he was going to make her suffer all night. All the myths were true. He could not be beaten. The sun rose and Achilles stood over his kill like a lion, not letting anyone near. Agamemnon called a halt. He was not heeded. Ulysses and Nestor realised they had brought a savage to help them overpower Troy when they again witnessed what he did to the vanquished. In the beams of the dawn light, Achilles looked around with a cunning gleam, he wanted an audience. The Greeks, in their under-shirts, watched. The local people took notice of him. He fanned his Myrmidons in staggered formation. He stripped the dead body of Penthesilea naked. The show pony became a vicious stallion. He reared and showed his erection. He raped her corpse in front of us and looked satisfied with himself. Agamemnon, who was apparently prepared to sacrifice his daughter, Iphigenia, to the gods for success in this war, by the lure of marriage to the great Achilles, made his way across the arena, with the pomp and ceremony of a magistrate, hoping to stop this abuse. He was checked in his tracks because Achilles had begun to butcher the remains of the valorous warrior Penthesilea, Queen of the Amazons. The hero charged through the pavements of the doomed city, roaring, "this is your queen, this is the carcase of the Amazon".

'The experience brutalised us. We had to absorb into our consciousness behaviour beyond our comprehension. Dripping with the red syrup of Penthesilea's vital juices, his argental armour, streaked and undone, darkening in the shadows of buildings, shining like jagged lightning when he emerged from the shade, Achilles carried Penthesilea like a slaughtered sheep across the vacant land, past our growling dogs to the palisades of the River Scamander, and tossed her over the bank. Then Achilles processed back to his camp, slaying any Amazon foolish, brave or angry enough to stand in his path as if she were wheat in a field. His men behind him slashing and stabbing, their active weapons catching flashes of sunlight in a spiteful show of heat. I divested myself of battle-gear and ran naked as a Trojan whore to my courtly robe, my passport to safety, and when I donned it I made my face a mask. I saw my sisters jailed and caged as the Greeks went forth to clean up in the wake of Achilles' wrath. They set fire to our bigtop. They burnt our fleet at anchor in the bay. They stole our horses.

'Surviving Amazons were scattered to the four corners in any camouflage they could muster. The conversation went on within the palace walls.

' "If only Paris had presented the golden apple to Minerva."

' "To be impoverished by Juno?"

' "Rendered loveless by Venus?"

'How come, I thought, the language had suddenly changed? Time was running like a swift river beneath the bridge of our still moment, ladies at tea.'

The bridge of our still moment. Ladies at tea, watching the river flow. Like time. The same and always different. Virginia moves along her slippery log to the creek and splashes cold water over her face.

'We, the Amazons, went underground. Some believe beings reside in the burning centre of this planet as beings exist in the icy reaches of outer space. The human mind is limited. The imagination, for instance, cannot go beyond the spectrum of colour, beyond ultramarine and infrared, beyond black and white. If I try to spread my understanding no one will believe me. Who listens to the rocks? Diamonds, rubies, gemstones and quartz? Who can hear the wisdom of the minerals? Zinc, gold, coal and sand? Molten lava turns to stone and bodies of humans turn to dust. When hell is furious, she erupts. It stands to reason. When she cools, rich mystery is left behind. Pure wealth. Knowledge of good and evil. Golden apples. A white stone. Earth. Eve.'

Virginia feels as if she has taken magic mushrooms or LSD, as if she had been tripping. She walks for several hours, choosing the steepest paths, feeling a thirst for competition, incidentally training for Sunday.

Her steel wool hair springing from her skull, Virginia returns to her house. She reads, still standing, Mary Daly who says that the courage of men is the effrontery to lie. 'As Shape-Shifting Witches shift focus back/ahead into our own context . . . We are aware that the gods of patriarchy are pale derivatives and reversals of ancient yet always Present Goddess(es).' Her body has no need for food; it is liquid, full of vibrant air, sinewy muscles. Away from clocks, away from calendars, weeks could disappear in the bush. Time is intense. Her work is immense. There is no room for fear, no personal place for boredom. Her internal life has magnified to the extent that her face seems strange to her, grainy, wrinkled. Her eyes, as she checks the mirror, are ferocious. 'I cannot be old until I'm old, and I am no longer young' she tells her image.

She does not sit down or contain her emotions: anger, anguish, adventure, yearning, love, distress, ambition, surreal fantasy, molecular-hormonal disturbance, the bliss of being and non-being; thoughts of time present, time past, time future, pushing boundaries of knowledge and security; sensations spinning around her spinal cord like fluids injecting themselves into the nerves and shooting up to her crown giving her energy to burn.

Unable to concentrate, or even do menial tasks, surrounded by the elementals, spirits pressing through her epidermis, Virginia wishes Cybil were here to anchor her.

'Margot Gorman? My name is Penny Waughan.' The woman on the other end of the phone sounded not so much desperate as inconsolably lonely.

I asked her to spell the surname.

'I got your name from Lisa,' she continued. She referred to the wayward teenager surfing the Internet rather than the breakers on the beach.

'Yes,' I said.

'My son,' Penny Waughan choked on tears. 'I need someone with this.' Drink had given her the dutch courage to ring. I heard the in-breath of a cigarette. She stumbled through apologetic explanations for her call. My own bowels went weak when I realised she was talking about the boy I had discovered dead last Friday, but I kept seeing the body as a girl.

'I hadn't seen him for three days,' she went on. 'That is, he wasn't home for three nights. And Monday.' She began blaming herself, telling me she was a stupid woman and a bad mother. 'Yesterday I was taken to the morgue and I saw his body. They think he took too many drugs, that it was an accidental overdose. I know he would not do that to me. I cannot believe he would suicide.' Tears strangled her speech while I uttered comforting words; sincere words because I felt the kid was no stranger to me. I was in danger of catching her tears and weeping myself.

'He is just a tragic statistic for the police,' she said, bitterly. 'I rang Lisa, asking if she knew where he had been. She suggested I ring you, she said you were a private detective. Don't think I'm hysterical, but my sixth sense tells me he has been murdered.'

I interrupted firmly, 'I don't think you are being hysterical.' I said, simply, 'I found him in the beach shed.'

She didn't hear me. 'Even though I work full time,' Penny spoke quickly, 'I would do anything for my Neil and that, since his father went, includes giving him as much freedom as he likes. Sometimes, though fairly rarely, he stays out all night, which is why I left it for the weekend. On Monday, I rang the school and he was not there. Or Tuesday. Then the police came to my work. They must have gone through the headmaster, attendances, I don't know. Or maybe his teacher mentioned something. It's not that I wasn't worried. I was because he always rings to tell me where he is. He didn't. I knew something was wrong but I didn't want to be a nagger, you know, an overbearing, smothering mum. I didn't want him to hate me.'

I interrupted her sobbing and asked her where she worked. She named the TAFE college which is part of Western Pacific University, Port Water campus. I looked in my diary and at the digital clock on my VCR. It was late now. Tomorrow I had an appointment at twelve-thirty at the cop shop.

'Perhaps,' I proposed, 'We could meet. At the Paradiso Cafe in the afternoon?'

'Fine,' she concurred. 'I have a class which finishes at three.'

'Three-fifteen, then?' I checked, writing it in my diary.

'Three-thirty? Okay.' She sounded reassured. Embarrassingly.

Il Paradiso, next door to the new CyberCage, subdivided the distance between the police station and the college. While I reassured Mrs Waughan that I would do my best, in my heart I had a horrible feeling.

I said, 'Goodbye, see you then.'

Now it was a job. I sat down at the computer and opened a file to note all that I remembered in chronological sequence. No matter what the pressures, it was important to keep my body fit. I must get the right amount of sleep. I employed a mental clearing technique to relax the tension and anticipation out of my autonomic nervous system.

. . . insane obsessions with nutso things . . .

To: "chandra" <wheels@wimmin.com.au>
From: "falcon" <solsal@silverberg.org.mt>
Subject: re: Annihilation
Date: Wed, 22 Mar 2000 11:18:13 +1000
==

MEMO: Rev. ch. 21, v.20: The fifth, sardonyx; the sixth, sardius;
the seventh, chrysolite; the eighth, beryl; the ninth, a topaz; the tenth,
a chrysoprasus; the eleventh, a jacinth; the twelfth, an amethyst.

The age of Christ is fucking dead in the water. The Age of Pisces—the
last 2000 yrs—was about chemical interpretation of human existence.
God's revenge on the sinners is the Age of Aquarius which threatens to
bring a virtual capsize of human existence. They're gunna download
brains! Freaky! Chemicals blot out experience of living or enhance it. In
the straight world chemistry explains every bloody thing from love to
skin disease, also the enormous problems of the modern world—
pollution, allergies, food poisoning, explains fear and is its answer.
Dependence upon substances for happiness, death and being able to
cope, being able to come—think about it: chemicals are like the water,
Pisces and the fish, Christ. A new age is upon us and it's about nerves
and electricity, fire and lightning, Uranus stuff, but who is the avatar?
Physics splitting up the particle of the neutron of the atom, indeed there
will be separation, a greater divide between rich and poor. The
information-rich and the information-poor. The virtual reality of the
mind.
Read this: Revelation ch. 21, v.23: And the city had no need of the sun,
neither of the moon, to shine in it: for the glory of God did lighten it,
and the Lamb is the light thereof.
Forget the mechanical, material, solid model of communication, bring in
the invisible but very real web rings. Internet, hacking and so on; puerile

conversations of chat pages, insane obsessions with nutso things which is shiveringly lacking in chemistry. Wonder whether love can flourish without smell and fluids, or are those who have married over the Internet deluding themselves? The Age of Pisces is senile. How can ya be postmodern without going mad? Anything goes, no history, no responsibility, greed, pornography, annihilation of women by clever whoa . . . men, get that! Sado-masochism is cool. Ever see the real fourth horseman, fire, as radiation? At the moment in chemical terms we see it as cancers, fallouts, acid soils, acid rain. Who gives a fuck about the precious atmosphere? No effective policies are diminishing the hole in the ozone layer, rather concerted efforts are made to maintain the conservative course of global warming. It'll take anything from 100 to 2000 years, and then it's cataclysmic. How could the apostle John be so blithe about the earth, the sun and moon? Messages in the birds' voices, the types of birds—we should have learnt by now how to communicate throughout nature because we are all in the same boat, in the age of water. Needing the earth to stay within a narrow window of temperature but radiation, virtual living and loving, non-physical connection, doesn't mind it hotter, so that you could have cities underground cooled and inhabited by nerds, modems, screens, processors, telecommunication lines, optic fibre, cable, satellite, generators, frozen pizzas, processed foods, microwaves, fizzy speed-drinks—air pockets in space stations with gates of gemstones? If there is not all-round integration of relation and communication in all biology we surely have extinction.
Signed,
Tragic.

13

. . . ripping off my wings . . .

Gophers, spiders, bots Chandra metatags the HTM of her webpage with her program, AdaLovelace, to attract material of potential constructive interest as well as pick up parallel pornographic activity: strain one, she downloads; and strain two, her computer automatically emails cryptic responses infected with viruses which transfer and dominate recipients' terminals. She is, fundamentally, more interested in constructive memes of radical culture than nihilistic destroying outright, although porn sites and those that perpetrate Christian, New Age and UFO nonsense are fair game for a Trojan horse. Not wanting her flaming to be obvious, she makes sure it is invisible. The avatar wades through, plucking the naive from the devious, the dynamic from the voyeuristic.

Going into the bulletin board CellarTwo, Chandra discovers another essay from the Annihilation Tragic. Chandra clicks her mouse on her FTP, downloads the text and arrows the printer icon. When the printing is done, she opens another window to email this woman who signs herself Tragic. She wants to give her hope, as well as recruit angry revolutionaries.
>> Can you conceive of an Age of Solanas? When women rule the hegemony? Ha ha. Deluding yourself is nothing new. What do you know about the Solanasite? Valerie made a splash, wrote the script. Check out this URL: www.1968/NY/Paris/scum/bi-L/ext.qu/sec729/TIRE/quest/ XW.Q/con.q/utterbore/X/yinco.html

Chandra clicks 'send'. Her maze of riddles and quizzes should test the resolve of potential conspirators. Her screensaver is a green tree frog, broad face and strong legs turning in three dimensions. A mosquito that she did not put there is buzzing around. Someone is meddling in her site. She packs up the hard copy and wheels herself to a patch of sunlight. In Chandra's house few chairs are in her way. She hates losing control. She has to think.

Dirt-bike boys are practising. The whines of their machines echo like chain-saws. Roughly written Xs point the way to Forestry roads deeper in the hills where the rally is to be held.

Chandra muses on the words she has just read as she gets herself a cup of tea. She is overwhelmed by a sense of synchronicity, as if the ersatz worlds of electronic technology and ancient telepathy brim together and lap at the banks of her physical being. Life is getting exciting.

Murder was the word Penny Waughan used. Thoughts of detection made me strangely nostalgic. Now that I had a murder to investigate, I wanted to run.

Dying moon lying high in the morning sky, the paperbark forest brought to mind an illustration of an enchanted world in a children's book. In water-colour and ink, tones washed in line drawings, were density and intrigue. The light was mellow, pale green and fine grey shot through with thin yellow sunshine dappling the ground and meddling with the reflections on puddled water here and there. Jogging along these paths, I was, also, reminded of films about the Everglades in Florida and the rhythms of Cajun blues. Fetid ponds full of wrigglies and tadpoles, frogs hid in swampy reeds, weeds and sedges watching mosquitoes. Ground-hugging orchids offered surprise. Black ducks and purple swamp hens disturbed the still water and reflections. Some of my regular running tracks were submerged. A short cut would be the long way round. I didn't want to end up wading knee-deep through hidden mires. Avoiding bits of horse-shit, I kept to the wider paths. On the flat between the mangroves of the delta and the sand dunes of the shore, tea-tree, wattle and she-oaks dominated but the occasional tall eucalypt grew beautifully big with nooks and crannies for owls and possums.

Banksia and callistemon, rushes and broad leaf marginata, lepidosperma, lomandra, acacia, naming what I saw, I sniffed. In scents is just delicious truth, recognition, requiring no consideration. No proof. Nor justification. After I crossed the road, paddocks veined by drains; dikes reclaimed the land. Cranes, egrets and ibis high-stepped, stabbing, and lap-wings squawked and ran in a hurry across the erstwhile wetlands.

My sponsors don't necessarily want me to win. If I broke down during a triathlon and the TV stations put the cameras on me, they got good footage—dramatic advertising. If my photogenic face grimaced in sudden agony in front of horrified spectators, viewers could groan in anguish with vicarious suffering while subliminally they taking in the logo on my trainer's towel, the make of my joggers. Primarily, I'm an athlete.

Running is different from swimming, which is more meditative. A triathlete at the age of seven, I competed in everything going, swimming, running, bike-riding; speed in the water and over the ground. I was best in individual sports, never excelled in hockey or netball. Cycling came later and became my passion, as did surfing. Decathlon was the Olympic sport I liked as a kid, but I was not much good at throwing. I pondered. I ran. The triathlon as an Olympic event was made for me but I am too old to go to the heights. Not that the body couldn't do it. I've left it too late, mentally.

First event, in Townsville, was a small one. I had been a year on the road, in the sun, away from offices and cities and work stress, and, when they told me I could make money doing what I did anyway, I simply glowed with white smiles. I was way ahead of all the females by the end of the bike, I thought I could walk in the run, but I was pipped at the post by a distance-runner sprinting. Whoosh, the ribbon was broken. A black girl she was and we had a good hug, but I never saw her again. She was ignored but I was surrounded by merchandising scouts: clothing, footwear, soft drink, cereal, even car companies wanted a piece of my body to write on. Even though I must have looked a royal dag that day, streaking out in khaki shorts. Suspicious because such attention might have been a trick by those who were chasing me, I played tough: 'Show me the paperwork and I'll get back to you.' They did, and I did. Although I don't have the dedication of Emma Carney, or Michelle Jones or Jackie Gallagher, I'm not bad and my sponsors have, so far, treated me fairly. The winners gotta have someone to beat, don't they? I am an also-ran, also-swam, also-rode, most of the time. But in small triathlons, like the one Sunday, I always give myself a chance. Australians love it when you lose trying your hardest. Fortunately, I look good doing it.

Fatal Friday night returned to my mind like a grey black and white photo in the studio of my memory. My brain snapped to attention, I ran home at a sprint. Things to do.

Philippoussis called to confirm our meeting this afternoon. And said, 'By the way, have you seen this week's *Town Crier*?' The local tabloid, mostly advertising, delivered free to all rate-payers, does have a few items of general interest but not the film program at the local cinema or television guide. I filtered through the unread junk mail and found the *Crier* still with an elastic band around it. Port Water's Gun Club will join the Four Wheel Drive Party in supporting the rally for the One Nation Party and the president of the Shooters' Party is not pleased. It can't be that story. Then I saw the ugly mug of 'the Crank'. Charley Crankshaw has a face so damaged by reconstruction, you could put him in a movie as an old war hero, or something. It has the charm of life lived, of laughs laughed. Of mischief.

'Superintendent Charles Crankshaw took up duties officially last Monday as the new local area commander, you mean?' I said to Philippoussis.

'Yes,' he affirmed. 'He has holidayed in the district.'

I laughed. 'No doubt he has a mansion here on Paradise Coast.'

When he rang off, I read:

Supt. Crankshaw, who joined the NSW Police Force in 1963, was a detective for more than 20 years in various Sydney metropolitan stations. The role of the commanders is different from the patrol commanders they replace by pure virtue of the area, number of police stations and number of police. He has a strong belief in intelligence-based policing and will be relying heavily on crime reports and accurate data to help dictate the direction of local policing.

Yes, the Crank always liked a healthy slush fund to grease the hand of the informer. He had as many of them as he did officers. Very good at covering his back, that man. The Commissioner has sent him to Mecca. I have no irrefutable evidence that he is not an honest and fatherly man; it is just that many of the men he worked with went down at the Royal Commission into Police Corruption. But why did Philippoussis bring my attention to his new boss?

Having showered and dressed, I rang Sweetness and Light and told him I was too busy to be at the gym at my usual time.

Sean replied with, 'Thank god.'

'Beg yours?' I intoned, astonished.

'Double-booking darling.' If I did not know him better, I would have guessed love interest. I didn't pry. I made a later appointment. 'Five, five-thirty?'

'Eggs and apples, Margot,' he quipped. Eggs as in sure as . . . and apples indicates, she'll be right. Sean is so bent, so blatantly queer, he can hardly say a straight word! I paper-clipped together my other pressing business and left it carefully squared on my desk. Tossed the greasy Mining Support Services cap into a box. Wine cartons I have aplenty. I stuck a sticky label on it: I.O.I., 'items of interest'.

Nadir, I looked up in the dictionary, out of a general idiosyncrasy of mine, to have the right meaning of a word: 1. the point of the celestial sphere vertically beneath any place or observer and diametrically opposite to the zenith. 2. the lowest point, as of adversary.

A group of gurls, including Margaret Hall, Jill David and Sofia Freeman are at CyberCage, an Internet cafe separated from Il Paradiso by a security grille, a gate and a couple of downward steps.

With a pile of two-dollar coins in a tower, Sofia discovers interactive story-telling. Like an Olympic equestrian on a steed who snuffs the barriers with delight, leaping over the irritating banalities of technology, she is in a creative lather. She mutters to herself; she says, 'Okay,' each time she successfully completes a jump. The marvellous maze of the webset.wimmin.com.au has inspired her. The hypertextual avenues to others' work presents a labyrinth of fictional possibilities that she previously thought only her mind was capable of, an absolutely mental space where the frustrations of daily life fall away is her dream venue. Split asunder, she is free to be.

Politically correct.

She doesn't need much money to do it; she doesn't get any money for it. It is the conscious arena she has been searching for beyond the power of men and their commerce to address the demons that oppress her beleaguered goodness. That little elf of a thing resides in her soul, usually too weak to beat the angry beasts that prowl about scavenging scraps of her being to devour, scattering the remains, leaving her demented. She doesn't need the drugs to keep her in control because, here, here, she has a powerful self. Out of it is the last place she wants to be. Nor does she have to deal with the nonsense that prances boastfully calling itself sanity, or the ignorance of those who have no idea. In the puzzle of this site, males can take a hike. She is safe. They don't know who she is so how can they lock her up?

'Now to express.' She ignores her friends who are doing something completely different together, and laughing. She shuts them out.

A chap floats like a slave, a servant, in the peripheral vision of her eyes. She allows him to assist her. He clicks up a draft page for her. Sofia types.

SOLILOQUY FOR THE FALLING ANGEL
When someone dies you have a requiem. This is for myself and for the girl who was killed by the inter-capital passenger train at the other end of the railway bridge on Saturday night. My neighbour, in her nightgown with her mop, called the news across the fence. She, standing at her back door, the angles of houses receding behind her, was like an impressionist painting, although the bright sunny day is photo realism.
A goods train percussed in our ears, locomotive number 8202, a rhythmic drumbeat. The XPT is quieter. This might be a reason. There was another girl hit by it at the level crossing last year. Both had the same Christian name. Incidental repetitions, in life, in music.
The girls' names were Melissa, I did not know either Melissa.
The river, the railway bridge, the station and the light industry comprise the rhymes and resonances of my outdoors, along with the closer squabbles of friar birds and honey-eaters in the grevilleas. I walk by the river. Brahmani kites swoop down on leaping bream and miss. The lofty eye, the heavy progress of freight, its da-dumb cacophony. Behind us, where we live, is a small farm with fat cattle. We had a flood across the river flats, made a lake of the paddocks, uprooted the casuarinas taking a whole chunk of the river-bank.

The sun climbed the sky, I had not slept although it was already dawn. The still river steamed in intriguing patterns of mist, unlike clouds, unlike anything but itself. Unlike snow crystals, unlike the swirling geometry of snails' shells, yet each eddy of vapour was unique, while the water reflected the sky and the trees on the other side.

The truth is the sensation of flying was approximated. But I had no feeling of suspension, no three-dimensional swimming with kicking feet, only a tearing pain on the inner edge of each shoulder blade, the weight of my body, the bane of my life, and my burden were ripping off my wings. The attachments, the muscles, the tendons, the sinews, were lengthening like chewing gum as I tried to fly like a kite, aloft, alone except for a single thread.

A memory. A solo thought of suicide, but murder was better. 8202 drags its freight forward, hopefully avoiding disaster and fatality. I am the loaded goods train, trying to fly up off the rails. I am 8202*.

Anything angelic was being ripped out of my body. I could hardly bear it. Why am I overloaded by gravity?, carrying a thousand things, when others walk along just fine? Why do I need to wing it?

Who needs a dogged description of the trials and tests, the contents of the large, grimy containers of pain, depression and oppression, the procession of hardships? I take the name, the loco name, as my cyber tag. I'm loco, after all. Manic and mad.

Something has been trying to kill me all my life. It, my enemy, has pierced my personality and is, at present, having a go at my character. I entertained thoughts of crashing to earth, of walking into the sea, boiling up the castor oil plant would do. There's enough of them around. I beguiled myself with means of killing, of letting go the final fine strings to my wings and watching them fly off like errant, erratic man-made kites.

At that time I smiled. I will smile. Now, I, myself, might destroy what courage and optimism built. I fight not to blame my mother, but it is all her fault. She surrounds and smothers me. One of us must die for the other to live.

As yet, by the river near the railway bridge, I am the falling angel. Present, and tense, expressing like a train. Will the driver go mad or stop? For Melissa, Melissa.

Eyes glittering at me, checking on me. Keeping me in check. Knowing eyes, her eyes are all that move. Giving me pills. Whether they're cunning like a vixen's or alive with a desire to control, they are kind. All for my benefit. What a suffocating trap! With my interests at heart, her own interests, are, well, not necessarily foremost. I am suspended on the thinnest string of gum. A falling angel is a winged woman with too great a load to lift into the sky.

'Margaret,' Sofia calls.

'Margaret isn't here,' says Jill David as she sits down beside her.

'Help me upload. I want to be a part of things. Happening things.'

Jill helps her post her story onto the <u>Webset.Wits.com.au/Cyberfiction</u> htm site.

Jill says, 'Anyone searching "angels" will find it, too.'

Sofia imagines strange cyborgs pressing the hypertext <u>angels</u> in the on-going novel of women's experience and flights of fancy and fantasy coming across her real experience, and be enriched by it. She has never felt so useful in her life.

Jill offers to give her a lift back to Stuart. But Maria is waiting in the park.

Phil and I were alone in the detectives' office, talking across his desk. Looking about for bugs with a silent question mark on my features, I asked what he felt about Crankshaw.

'I don't think I should tell you,' he said with just a touch of humour. The very black eyebrows frowned, paternalistic and macho. 'He's on my case, I don't know why. Hates Greeks maybe.'

If we were being overheard, neither of us minded. Bravado on my part. I did not want to be seen by the Crank. He is a nosy type, the sort that doesn't forget a face.

'Is he at this station today?' I asked.

The Detective Constable nodded bleakly.

'Okay, just testing you, mate. Stay honest.'

He queried, 'The ones at the barbecue? I would rather like to find out if they knew that the stiff was a boy. They all said "she". I never mentioned otherwise.'

Philippoussis wanted assistance. I half-smiled, sat, crossed my knees and took in the decor. New shop, pretty neat and tidy considering what these places are usually like. An old poster of missing kids hung on the pin-board.

'The women were crazy, anyway,' Pip voiced his opinion. 'They came up with conspiracy theories and other nonsense. We're all out to get them because they're lesbians. And gays. I backed off, Margot. I didn't see the need to unduly upset them.'

I nodded.

'But Commander Crankshaw does not have the same tolerance of life-style choices and gender differences.' A multicultural boy in a postmodern world, Australia the land of anything goes. 'I don't think they have anything to do with it,' he said. 'To tell the truth.'

'The Crank has them taped as marijuana croppers and dippy hippies.' Philippoussis shrugged.

I said, 'You are all fascists, only interested in busting small growers of a drug that should be legal for adult users? It would save a lot of tax-payers' money if the State let them grow their own, anyway.'

'You are not wrong. Getting close to the size of it. Actually the narcotic in question is probably heroin.' Phillip heaved a big sigh. 'I have two dead boys, died within five kilometres of one another and absolutely nothing similar about them at all. Except they are practically identical. If their deaths are primarily drug-related, or self-inflicted, they are small fry. Junkies chucked where junkies belong, in the junk box.'

'He wants bigger fish, naturally.' I got up, speaking to the bugs.

'So the man says.'

I paced around. Here was a veiled invitation to work closely with the databases, the computers, crime files and other useful amenities; to what cost? Be DC Philippoussis' snout?

In my gut, I didn't want Crankshaw to know I exist. Still we were baiting his eavesdropping devices and I was in the double jeopardy of trusting the young detective as well.

'Pip? Can I see them?' I begged.

'Phil,' he corrected. 'Who?'

'The bodies.'

'Why?' he asked.

'Perspective,' I answered. 'I'm employed by the mother of the corpse I found,' I explained, 'as of last night.'

'I'll see what I can do,' he rose to his feet. 'For you.'

We shook hands. A clean-living fellow, I could feel it in his pressure, see it in his eyes and smell it on his person. I can't know whether he is tough enough, though. He may buckle under. I have seen so many fellows change after the age of about twenty-eight. It is as if conservative values hit them as they become victims to greater forces. Whereas younger blokes can still have a fire for justice forging iron in their souls.

On my stroll to the coffee shop, I saw Maria eating hot chips from a greasy bag. I did not want to catch her attention. But she called me over, like Queen Victoria or someone, with a little movement of her finger. I stopped myself saying, 'You really don't do your health any good, Maria. Gobbling up that stuff.'

'Hello, Margot,' Maria said. 'I'm missing my doctor's appointment.'

'Why?'

'I know what she'll say and I don't want to hear it.' She licked her fingers.

'I need a good night's sleep,' I smiled, referring to her distress calls.

'I shouldn't bother you,' she admitted. She vigorously crunched up the paper bag. 'No, what I mean is, Sofia is, well, a genius.'

'Is she?' I wondered.

Maria was defiant, defensive. 'And you have to make allowances, don't you think? It's okay now, she has found a place for her work.'

'Her work?' I let my scepticism show.

'She's a writer. But, as a separatist feminist no one would publish her stories. Now, there is the Internet. Epublishing. She is creating!'

'Good. Look, I've got an appointment. Got to go, I really do.' I tapped my wristwatch.

'Yes,' she said, waving me off. 'I just wanted you to know. There is another side.'

'Sure.'

The Paradiso is one of a strip of cafés and eateries on the road down to the marina. From CyberCage I heard the beer hall Bavarian drinking song, rather than dulcet, tones of my Broomhilda's Germanic laugh. Trying to ignore it and not be disturbed by the thought she should be elsewhere, saving the trees, I parked myself in the garden. Sofia passed me on her way out with Jill David. She was, as Maria indicated, extremely happy and really attractive. Busy. Inspired. In a hurry. We exchanged a greeting.

Mrs Penny Waughan was a woman about my own age, slim with dyed fair hair and a clipped walk. She immediately lit up. The ashtray was beneath the sugar dispenser. We occupied fold-up seats either side of a moulded table. Beneath an umbrella, she talked and I took out my notebook.

'Nigel Neil Waughan, his father is Nigel you see,' she directed as I wrote down the victim's name. 'I'm Penny. Call me Penny. I called him Neil because every man I've known called Neil has been a nice person. I miss him.' She laughed self-deprecatingly, and fiddled with her Lights. I wondered what pharmaceuticals she had taken to keep her grief at bay. 'Call me Penny.' She kept saying that.

'Tell me a bit about yourself, your son, your situation, anything.' I smiled with my eyes, keeping my mouth serious.

'Well I'm a TAFE teacher. Computer studies. Basically it's, well, I started out. Um, I taught typing in high schools, sort of low on the academic rung if you like. Because word-processing was the next step and then computers generally, then desk-top publishing, I, I suppose, leap-frogged over my more learned colleagues into a relatively prestige position. I really only kept up with the secretarial demands outside education. My salary increased, of course.' She flicked her gold cigarette lighter into flame and joined a fresh smoke to it. 'If, if I'd known, I was going to end up with such a good career, I might not have had a child. Never felt particularly maternal. I was only ever a good average pupil at school myself, groomed for marriage from an early age, taking bookkeeping, typing, shorthand, geography, economics and English Expression, easy subjects. I got into Teachers' College and passed. A pleasant shock at the time. Still is, I suppose. My parents are humble folk. Ten-pound tourists, Nigel called them. They came to Australia poor, they stayed poor.'

A wistful look passed across Penny Waughan's face as she gazed into her past. I had given her a licence to talk which she grasped with both hands. For my own part I found it interesting. I wanted to know what happened to Neil Waughan. And why. Background was a start. I answered her melancholy with a gentle nod. She took a breath of nicotine and tar, and let all the smoke out in an accepting sigh.

'Nigel was the right man for me, the worst thing about him was his name. Can you believe that? We honeymooned at Hayman Island where they had a heart-shaped bed. We walked along the sand in the sunset holding hands. Happy. I was happy because Nigel was really happy.' She searched my features for irony or sarcasm. 'You want me to get onto the present?'

I nodded. I didn't mind.

'You see, Nigel really does love sand. He worked in banking with dry as dust numbers and always dreamed of sand, a Lawrence of Arabia at heart. Men have those sorts of silly dreams. It keeps them going. Neil was born in our first year of marriage, and I went back to teaching when he was about two because we needed two incomes to buy a house. Another child was put off, and put off, because of small practical things, at the beginning of each month. The pill suited my hormone levels anyway. I had had difficult periods before I went on it. After, well, regular and comfortable.'

I settled back with a cappuccino, gesturing thanks to the waitress. Penny is the type to partake in women-talk about the pill and babies, doctors and gynaecological matters in general.

'Tell me about Neil,' I suggested, taking the fluff off my drink with a spoon, dreading the love I was going to hear of and its loss.

'Neil was a good student at primary school, smart and popular. We, er, changed houses, suburbs. My salary overtook Nigel's when we had just about paid for our first home in Sydney. Prices were booming in the inner west and a few years on we decided we could afford to buy land and build on the Paradise Coast. It seemed okay for Neil as it would coincide with his going to high school. Nigel was over the moon, building, planning, bossing, landscaping and being on the beach. Out in the air. Closer to his daydream. Work became less and less attractive to him, even though he had a job. Banking had changed around him.' Penny seemed to pull herself under control, talking about her husband, as if it were an effort to keep her contempt from running amok.

'He was a hands-on, person-to-person, old-gold-standard type of money-manager. Really, I think he cannot grasp or won't accept the concepts of value the electronic world requires, with bull markets and bear markets and huge, inconceivably huge, debts and loans. I think I was more interested in the turns that capital and global economics were taking. Strictly a cash teller, Nigel. Likes to handle it. He really couldn't understand unsecured finance. He took redundancy. Off his own bat. Just like that. The burden of our new life fell on my earning capacity. Meanwhile, Neil hated school here. He was too sophisticated. He knew more about computing than his teacher, was more artistic than his art teacher and generally felt surrounded by boorish hicks who teased him. For a while he tried, hung around with the worst types in town, in the mistaken impression that they could protect him from the middle lot who for some reason loathed him, as did the teachers. Neil loves clothes.'

The present tense.

'Perhaps I should talk with Nigel sometime. Is he . . .?' I began.

Penny shook her head urgently to interrupt me, wanting to finish her tale.

'He left me. Suddenly, Nigel decided it was too much. He threw in the job. He lives with another woman. Unbelievably, neither Neil nor I meant anything to him. He told us both, at the dinner table, how happy he was, and went out the door, singing, "Don't fence me in". He has not taken any responsibility since. I have to finish paying for the house. I resent him. Nigel will demand one-half of its value because his name is there on the title and he can. I pay for his freedom in dollars and cents. He was never violent but I almost wish he was because then I would have something substantial. He will be devastated about Neil.' Conflicting emotions sent her searching for her friendly packet of cigarettes. 'Old romantic. Raider of the lost ark. In his dreams.'

'How did Neil take his father leaving home? I suppose you expressed this resentment about the money and the abandonment. Did he talk about it?' I probed.

'You know what teenagers are like. They keep secrets. So I don't know really. Not well. He liked his father sometimes, they played games together, but they are essentially different types of men. Neil is, was, more an indoor type and Nigel is one for the outdoors, if I am not putting it too simply. But, to tell the truth, Margot, I have been incredibly busy over the past few years. I have done everything practical for Neil and have kept our relationship relatively calm. I did not try to pry into his relationship with his father. I left it to them,' Penny slapped the words down, tossing in her hand.

'Did they spend much time together at Nigel's place?' I interrogated. 'Or camping, fishing, father-son holidays? Films? Cars? Whatever?'

She breathed out with a short, impatient huh. 'Do I know when I am lied to? Neil says, said, he spends time there, but he doesn't seem to know, or didn't want me to know, what Nigel is up to, what the people he lives with do with themselves or anything. I am kept in the dark.'

Again the present tense. She had painted the picture of a teenager who had no friends but his mother. An inoffensive nerd, it didn't wash. A very strange lad, indeed, would dress up as a girl all by himself. And go out to party.

'You said he started here with unhappy school-life, but surely he found pals?' Where are you coming from, Margot, The Famous Five? The Secret Seven? 'In the last few months?' I asked.

'Well, yes. He improved after he started drama this year. Here is a phone number. For Nigel.' She lifted her satchel from beside her, moved the Chemart paper bag, compact, comb and took out a small, black leather address book with a natty gold pencil attached. She ripped out a page from the back and copied a number from the front inner cover and handed it across to me.

'Oh, god, I hope you can find out what happened to Neil,' Penny Waughan said with an air of hopeless trust.

I read the number out aloud. 'Do you have Nigel's address?'

'He is always moving, but they will be able to put you onto where he is. If you are a private detective and I am hiring you, I would also like you to establish my ex-husband's permanent address so that I can pursue legal matters with him.' A little vicious streak snaked into her voice.

'Penny?' I caught her attention. 'I'd like to see Neil's bedroom, things. When would be convenient?'

'Ring.' The word snipped out of her lips like a scissor-cut. 'I have meetings some afternoons. I'm at work from eight-thirty. Should be home around dinner time. If you find anything, anything at all, please contact me at the college.'

Finishing up, I said, 'I'll be in touch, okay?'

She nodded.

We went together to the cash register and each paid for our own coffee.

The weather was still sunny, a lively wind in the light linden leaves smelt of sea. An easterly.

When Maria and Sofia get home, Sofia's imagination flies out of control, seeing all sorts of alien beings, important persons and net surfers watching her falling angel drop into their minds, dumping her cargo and bringing them down. Maria cannot make any sense of what she is saying.

She is happy when Alison arrives. She and Sofia rave together about cyberspace and the virtual world. Maria is glad that Sofia's words are out there. Alison assures her that Sofia does have an audience: who knows where her story is being read? Maria is bemused. Language in sentences Maria understands, not riddles and innuendo. But she hears the colour of imagery, and is proud.

14

. . . dog maidens . . .

Victoria Shackleton walks with Judith Sloane. The Lesbianlands meeting is at the site of the original white homestead where there remains no more than an old English oak, brick fireplace, half a chimney, a few stubborn blackened fence-posts and a flat clearing in the bush. In what's left of the silvered rosewood post-and-rail yards her horse noses a biscuit of lucerne hay. Judith tells her she is the last of the real dog maidens. Victoria swells with pride and imagines her bitch is not as disobedient as she is. The dalmatian is tied with a rope near the saddle so she doesn't make a nuisance of herself. Tess, the red kelpie, Ti's two bloodhound-dobermans, Dormie, the blue cattle-dog, Ilsa's butterfly-eared lap-dog, and various mixtures of tan, black and white canines pay attention to their owners and each other then settle down pretty quickly. The irony of Judith's comment is lost on Vee, who has the subtlety of a kettle-drum. While birds sing, cicadas ring, early evening is the best time to get the lesbians' attention. Judith Sloane has the large, hard-cover minute book in her hands, and the journal and ledger.

First there is an argument.

'Victoria should take the notes today.'

'Why don't you do it yourself, Rory?'

'Virginia?'

'I'll do it. I'm treasurer.' Judith grasps the book possessively.

'I'd like Victoria to do it because, as she doesn't live here all the time, she will be the most objective,' says Gig. 'And you're not the secretary.'

Judith turns the minute-book over when it is decided Vee will have least to contribute, so can concentrate on writing. The financial records she tucks away in her bag.

'Present: Rory, chair; Judith; Gig; VW; Xena; Hope Strange; Kay; Helen; Ti Dyer; Ilsa; Dee; Ci; Roz and Fiona. Shackleton,' Vee adds, almost forgetting herself. Bea arrives late.

Judith gives a rundown on the breaking of the bridge, the state it was in when she discovered it. Hope tells how she saw two women on horseback. Gig provides the anecdote of El Cohen's car teetering on the edge and finally drawn back to safety by womenpower. Pure might. Rory explains again why she thinks it would be a good idea to bring someone in to investigate. Ti, who can drive a bulldozer, romances how to fix it; she has the words, displays knowledge of details. 'It's only a matter of hiring one.' Judith dismisses her talk, which while full of meaning is hollow of action, with 'We haven't got the money.' Gurls must have their say. They do listen to each other. Some ready to pounce. Some of the discussion is way off the topic, for instance, the latest gossip from Sydney, about a man trapped in a male body who said he was a lesbian inside. General indignation at the transsexual annihilation of birth females is arrested by Judith's soft sibilant voice, 'Separatists are so fascist.'

Impassioned conference is her forte, thinks Virginia, who marvels at the way Judith wields power with words. It really doesn't matter what she says, whether she contradicts herself, speaks softly or shouts; the company hangs on her opinion.

'If the trannies say they are women locked in men's bodies, then around here I wouldn't be surprised if there weren't some jocks locked in women's bodies,' Fiona says mischievously. 'Cocks in frocks.' Ti and Victoria glare at her, and look to Judith for guidance.

'That's not what we're here to discuss,' she says gently. 'Someone destroyed the bridge, and it could be one of us.'

Not one among them believes that.

'There's an outside threat,' Gig reckons. 'I can feel it.'

'The male ego needs the reassurance of the female gaze,' Bea states slowly, irrelevantly.

Meanwhile Ti is fuming and Fiona says to her, 'Just because you're an Aries, doesn't mean you have to be angry all the time.'

'I don't want male approval,' Ti shouts. 'Hear hear' is the response and she is quieted by agreement.

Xena Kia brings up the matter of the explosions and suggests mysterious activity by UFOs. Hope nods. Dee tries to shut her up.

'It's a mistake to assume that lesbians are telling the truth, doesn't take into account manipulative behaviour patterns learnt as a child, or as a woman, to survive,' Dee is prepared to talk about abuse and lesbian domestic violence.

'Let's get back to the point,' urges Judith sanely. But the talk has gone onto how many trees have been falling down lately. Victoria taps the pen on the page. Rory mentions the need of a detective.

'Why should we employ a dick when we can work it out for ourselves?' Ti demands.

'Are you talking about Margot Gorman, Rory?' Judith asks.

'Well, I thought she could be impartial,' Rory says seriously. 'We'll need to bring men on to the land to fix it.'

A furore about separatist politics ensues. Why would women who want to live with men bother to come here when they've got the rest of the world? Open women's land. No one can change that. 'I don't like the term,' Ilsa comments quietly. But she is given no space to explain what she means. Privacy is paramount. The less outside interference the better. 'I'm sorry but you're not a separatist, you're an isolationist!' We are about pluralising the nuclear family model, the power structure of it, where the women and children are vulnerable, to violence, to slavery. We have to experiment, or start the experiment, with adult women, lesbians together. None of us can be totally private. Not here.

'Co-operatives are severely regulated.' Kay recounts her investigation into Lesbianlands going into official group ownership. Judith listens keenly. Then says, adamantly, 'I hate all that legal shit, it's rules and regulations imposed by the patriarchy.' Beneath words spoken, eyes exchange darts. Virginia is sure Judith contradicted herself, again. At the moment the title deeds are in the name of Ursula Tapp, a woman long gone from these parts.

'Just get the fucken bridge fixed. Why is it necessary to place blame?' Ci stirs the possum.

'I don't want the road open,' Helen confesses. 'If it means men on the land.'

'The majority, however, do,' Rory asserts. 'We have to make decisions about the way we live together.'

'In small communities, personalities matter more than ideas,' Ilsa pontificates sarcastically.

'You can have all the structures you like, it won't stop disobedience, lies, whatever,' Kay claims.

'Basically we have a club culture. Friendship's more important than outcomes,' continues Ilsa, as if the abstract analysis of what is going on is more important than the practical matter in hand.

'We can't afford a new bridge,' Judith informs. 'In fact we have little money in the account. Would you like to know who owes their fees?' She reaches into her bag, knowing that no one else on the collective is interested in the boring matter of money.

'Let's sell a few logs. We've got enough trees,' suggests Helen sarcastically.

'But you won't let the loggers in,' Dee argues.

'Power works at a formal level, leaders, committees and so on,' Ilsa informs. Virginia listens to her, wondering how gynaecocratic societies administered themselves, thinking of her Amazons.

'Once we let the men in, where does it stop?' Helen says to Ti, who nods furiously.

'But power is also informal,' Ilsa continues.

Virginia addresses her. 'Woman have had so little power, but as a group, we find it difficult. We have to change the notion of power. We should be flexible.'

'Power games,' Dee is disgusted.

'Resources, we use what we've got,' Gig decides.

'Not if it's just for the individual,' Rory disagrees. 'That would be chaotic and unfair.'

'No,' Xena vetoes selling logs, rocks, ferns. 'We're abusing the goddess, and we're here to protect the bush, not exploit it.'

'Do we even agree on our common ideas, ideals?' Virginia inquires.

General laughter. Victoria Shackleton gives her writing hand a rest. Gurls who have the most to say aren't necessarily those who have the real influence. Those who blend in, later to speak outside the meeting, in informal caucus, gossiping, going around slyly attacking speakers, creating an atmosphere of division, have effective power. Rory tries to formulate a way of saying this without whipping up anger, without causing the situation she despises, and despairs of. 'Do we?' she says simply, taking up Virginia's question.

'Why can't we just all be friends?' Bea asks.

Kay jumps on her, 'Because that is sentimentalising women's bonding. It's a false situation. I will not say you're telling lies, but you can't assume we all have the same goals.'

Judith pulls it all together. The English accent has a kind of imperial presence that silences the crowd. She expands on individual rights, being smoothly bitchy with her examples and concludes that it's okay to pursue self-healing practices.

Xena is the one who takes umbrage. 'Personal growth has been done to death, it covers over the political problems that are happening.'

Then Rory becomes impassioned. 'Personal growth can drag a group away from acting in its best interests. Collective ownership of land is the only way we can live in the bush without huge financial cost.'

'Feminists are all white and middle-class!' Ti hurls insults aggressively because every time there's a meeting she gets angry.

'Actually I'm not middle-class,' Rory says mildly. 'Are you Virginia?'

'I don't know what class I am,' laughs Virginia, recalling the violent poverty of her childhood and how far she has come as an adult. 'But I am white.'

Everyone, including Ilsa, has an opinion on class and race. And what it is to be called feminist. Patriarchal notions. Gangs. Lovers. Non-being. The absence of women in history. Mankind. Lying being part of the human condition. Honesty thus revolutionary. Negativity. Self-hatred. Sex as a commodity. Dominance and submission.

The free-for-all lets off a bit of steam. It seems vicious and serious until Hope says something no one understands and they all dissolve into laughter.

'Let's get back to the present problem,' offers Judith calmly with the authority of a head-mistress. 'There has been rubbish rotting up there on the road to Widow's Peak for weeks now. So, how are we going to get it down? The bridge is out.'

'The only car that could do that now, without a bridge, is yours, Rory.'

'I can't go around cleaning up after women, I am not your mother. I want to get to the bottom of this wanton destruction,' Rory declares. 'What if I asked Margot?'

'You want to bring Margot Gorman out here so that you can seduce her,' jokes Dee.

'Cool. She's a leso.'

'Well gurls, I have to go.' Victoria shuts the heavy minute-book. She extends the hard-cover book to Judith.

Rory says, 'Before you go, Vee, let's have a vote. Pass a motion. Employ a detective. Means we have to pay her. Those in favour?'

The vote is not taken because the atmosphere is ripped by an explosion. At first they think it is another tree falling in the forest, but the blasts continue. They echo in the hills.

Ti shouts, 'That's fucken dynamite!'

Women hold their dogs in an instinctive reaction and a shudder of fear ripples through the mob like a charge of electricity. Friends seek each other out to speculate on the whereabouts of the eruptions. Any damage to the earth makes Virginia fall into a rage these days. Hope mutters a verse from the Apocalypse. Roz and Xena exchange fantastic jokes about an alien invasion. 'Let's go,' Helen says, 'Before the helicopters come,' confusing, as always, any threat with a drug bust. Victoria Shackleton goes around hugging each and being farewelled before she saddles up, mounts her horse and rides to her car and float.

'It is probably on another property,' opines Gig, hopefully.

Fiona and Dee swear they are going to find out where it is, but they sit down and share a joint.

Ilsa and Helen go off together talking of terror. They convince each other that there is a firing range for the shady activities of a right-wing gun lobby group nearby. They scuttle home to their shelters.

Ian Truckman is the very picture of masculine serenity, standing in ebb of the surf with his long, thin rod arching with the flow of the tides. The lone fisherman receives the call he had been dreading.

'Bring in the Scania.'

He drives the rigid semi out of the paddock behind the caravan park and along the dirt roads to the meeting place. There he is given a sedan for a few days with instructions to be at the airport at five a.m. Sunday.

Lenny is with his father's mother. Tilly is still at Chandra's. Harold has gone west in his new car. Alison, free of her children, invites Maria to dinner in her Housing Commission flat in the old fishing port district of Port Water. Maria goes over the top with compliments at the effort she has made, as she tucks in to the salad and fish, rock melon and grapes. She tells her she is beautiful. Alison watches Maria eat with relish. 'You are like a South Sea Island queen,' she says.

Alison relates to her women as if they were all the same person, a huge enveloping mother-goddess, with many faces and body shapes. After such a lovely meal, Maria is dumbfounded when Alison demands, 'How did you get into my head?' As far as Maria is concerned they are only just getting to know one another.

'Are we in each other's heads? Is that why it's mutual?' Alison changes personality in front of her, from stunningly sunny to thunderously furious, as if she had whipped up a storm inside herself.

'Don't be so insulting.' Maria tries to regain some sense of comfort.

'How can we relate fully to each other when we are both mothers?' Alison lets fly. Maria is frightened.

Alison changes again, 'The way you let everyone walk all over you disgusts me. I don't want lies. I want the flattery to be thought out and accurate. I want you to die for your words of appreciation of me. I don't own my own beauty.'

'We have to prop each other up. What harm is there?' Maria begs.

'I'm not beautiful, really I'm ugly.'

'If this is self-hatred,' says Maria firmly, 'I don't want any part of it.'

The ebb and flow of argument and affection take several hours.

'Be free, Maria,' pleads Alison. 'That you are a victim is noxious to me.'

'That's going a bit far, Ali,' explodes Maria. 'Don't make me shout. I hate shouting. Don't do this, please,' she begs.

'I saw you as some kind of goddess, from a long-gone matriarchy.' Alison's dreamy words have a bitter edge.

Maria hugs the adipose eiderdown of herself, her protection.

'And that makes me murderous. I feel evil. I'm a bad person.' Alison sighs, 'Not to say, bad mother.'

'You don't mean that.' Slow tears roll down Maria's round cheeks. Will there never be an easy love? She just wants to relax into the sensual moment and leave her thinking to her times with her books.

Alison swings into a sinuous long-fingered pose. 'I am destructive like a goddess. Ruler of birth and death, Kali.'

'You're being dramatic.'

'No, if you are blaming me, I am,' Alison picks up a broom and wields it like a weapon.

'I am not blaming you, Ali. You are not evil. It's the mental illness, it's not you. Who you are.'

'Kindly get out of my head or one of us is going to commit suicide, or the other thing? Sistercide, perhaps?' She laughs, and flops. She drops the broom and lifts Maria's hand and places it on her heart. Trusting Maria allows Alison to spill so much bile, she cuddles up to her big bosom, trying to bury herself.

'So much of our time is taken up with guilt,' Alison whispers.

Maria experiences Alison's elfin presence like rose petals on her skin. Maria is both attracted and repelled by awareness of danger. Then gives in to passion. As they devour each other, she feels the thorns.

Alison is surprisingly cold and businesslike after the hot sex, not sighing with satisfaction. She cannot sleep. Nor will she let Maria sleep, who, irritated, simply gets dressed and leaves Alison's flat.

Maria, when she gets home, wants to talk to someone. She doesn't want to disturb an old friend in her sleep. Anyway, who? And what would she say? If she could afford it, she would call America. She often has nightmares. Maria rings Margot Gorman.

Sofia tosses and turns.

Ghosts people the swampy landscape of nightmares, sliding about like turds among dried apricot waterlilies. Sofia's subconscious plays filthy tricks on her. She, a thin wisp of spirit, is pursued and forgotten by the stream of humanity in dreams. She is the terrorist in the refugee camp, tortured by fascists who shine bright lights in her face, play deafening music, demand her time, wanting her to betray someone, but all the precious jewels of her intellect along with her insights fall before swine. She tries to tell the uniforms but they will not believe her. Credibility depends on what you wear, she learns.

Another distress call interrupted my sleep. Maria was in danger from her lover. The likelihood of actual murder was improbable. Because of incompetence caused by too much alcohol, vagaries of mood when tiredness meets drug, psychiatric drug meets sedative, sedative stimulant, the stumbling, the clumsiness, would make the threat of manslaughter fairly mutual. Sofia was in danger, too. The constant beer, the marijuana, tobacco, fatty foods; the nights with tequila, or harder drugs, or other people dropping poison, punchy people, gossip, rumour and accusations flying about. Frustration, I imagine, grew to rage, led to desperate phone calls in the early hours. With what they've consumed by three p.m. I'd be flat on my back. Even as a cop, armed and in uniform with a fair idea who was the victim and who the aggressor, I did not like going to domestics.

Margot assumes the lover Maria is so distressed about is Sofia. It is actually Alison Hungerford. While Margot harshly judges her, Maria is grasping at straws.

Multiple personality syndrome is Alison's excuse for the broken glass on the floor and the splashes of red wine like the blood of Ghengis Khan's enemies on the wall and in the carpet. Maria, a scorned witch with powers as well as wisdom, would never kill children like Medea. Or rivals like Lady Macbeth.

'But I could,' Alison talks to herself. 'I've gone off the track again. If I lash myself with the bit of barbed wire in the yard I can add blood to the mess I'm in. My guilt. Wasn't it a spot of blood I wanted to get out of the carpet? If I am hurting you, I can assure you, I will hurt myself even more.' So she paces until dawn. Then she walks barefooted to the beach in her loose night-gown. Alison returns a different woman. She showers and puts on her blue overall.

The phone rang again. The answer machine took it. No one was there. Just silence. I put on the boxing gloves and belted the bag for half an hour until I was dog-tired.

15

. . . the spaces beneath . . .

The wind was really up today, a snarling southerly. Lightning out to sea. Sand stinging the cheeks. Salt in the eyes. Sea pounding, spray thickening the air with a grainy mist. It made me exhilarated. Lean, hungry, willing to work.

When I was carefully grating carrot and apple to put in my muesli with yoghurt, the phone rang. It was Meghan saying she would be away for a week or so. She sounded lame, defeated or tired. Catching her before she speedily disconnected, I asked could she please send me a cheque for expenses before she went. I didn't really want the money but I did need her proper signature. And nothing like hard cash to get down to brass tacks. Facts.

'Meghan?' I said, 'Don't tell anyone about me. Don't give anyone your mail to post, okay?'

'Sure,' she sighed.

'Or collect,' I instructed, laying it on thicker, because I didn't know whether the 'sure' was affirmative or ironic. After breakfast, I found the names of her solicitor and accountant. Had she lost money on some property trust scheme or unsecured bridging finance? Paying off some mysterious debt, or loan? Best to get the simple explanations face to face. Get my nose into action. If I'm on a wild goose chase following the scent of red herrings of possible scenarios, then that is exactly what I'll be paid for. Her professional consultants were suspects in this cruel world. She struck me as a regular Pollyanna in rose-coloured glasses. But when forced to look at something she doesn't like, does she just cover her eyes, ears and blot it out, or turn into a vengeful virago? Is she really one of life's true eccentrics? A divine fool or a clever devil?

Busy day on the ferry. My neighbour and his extended family were in the queue. Behind their ratty-looking Volvo was an old four-cylinder sedan with the mismatched doors of amateur panel-beating efforts.

The solicitor would not see me. I had a little stoush with one of those sweet-as-pie, hard-as-nails receptionists who is just about to lose her looks and fears for her job. During our exchange, we both overheard an exasperated, aggressive expletive from the inner office, 'How incompetent!' Happy client? 'I'll sue.'

Pregnant pause, then, as cool as you please, the secretary intoned, 'I'm sorry Ms Gorman, he is unlikely to see a private investigator at any time.'

I had not said I was a private investigator, I'd said I was investigating a private matter.

Standing in the doorway, amused no doubt but glaring, were Libby Gnash and Lola Pointless (I don't know the correct way to say or spell her surname). I had run across Libby before in the course of a piece of detection I was doing a few months ago. Libby is less than five feet tall, became a lawyer in her forties having been educated in the school of hard knocks. Starting out with such underprivileged working-class credentials as could never be challenged, she was in the Communist Party, then into Gay Lib, battle-worn by anti-Vietnam and Women's Liberation street protests and still fighting. Her CI file was a meaty read. Going to the university through her thirties, graduating with a law degree, she carried on the struggle in the courts. She was the solicitor every woman with a legal problem on the coast wanted. She took the woman's side, no matter what. The ass of the law was Rosinante to her Quixote. A health problem forced her out of Sydney, where she had more work than she could deal with alone. Couldn't keep partners, apparently. She sold up, bought a hobby farm and runs her practice from a one-room office off the mall with her lover as office manager, the off-sider who hires and fires cute little computer operators at an alarming rate. Lola is tall and stupid, adept at making enemies, a gorilla on a rope. A formidable team. They hate me because I found out the truth that the woman was at fault in that case.

The receptionist set her jaw into a stubborn clench. A skirmish between Libby and her would be worth paying for. A sumo wrestle of female wills. I tried to pass shortie and lofty, but they blocked my way.

'Private investigator, hey?' Libby sneered.

'Got a licence yet, bitch?' hissed Lola.

'Have you, Lola? I believe if you're spayed they're fairly cheap,' I said sarcastically, referring her guard-dog role.

'Read the new tax laws, Margot?' asked Libby.

Beaten, I frowned and ducked between them.

In a new edifice, a monument to business, with carpeted stairs and framed prints, Meghan Featherstone's accountant was far more approachable. Rosemary Turner was a lady with big hair and little eyes as grey as ball bearings. And she had a big laugh, at nothing funny. The office was tastefully bare. On the desk were a foolscap, pink, lined lecture-pad, a Parker pen and a computer. She informed me that she was aware of the discrepancy in Meghan's finances. Still except for a restless hand on the keyboard, she exuded confidence.

'At first, I thought Meghan had a habit, you know?' she expounded. 'That she was hiding. Cocaine? Speed? Whatever, something expensive. What the hell, she could afford it. I only do her tax. She handles her investments herself.'

'Investments?' None of the paperwork I had been given suggested a share portfolio.

Rosemary dismissed my query as naive with a flop of her chunky wrist.

'After a while,' she continued, glancing at her screen, 'it became harder to write it off.' Big laugh. A big woman with a big laugh, and big bare office, so neat and grey there was nothing to gaze at but the large flowers on her shirt. Her focus pinned you in silhouette against the plain backdrop. I wondered how careful the lighting design was and how hard it really was to 'write off' money legally acquired.

'You spoke to her about it?' I urged.

Rosemary was not as generous as she seemed. 'Client confidentiality, Margot.'

'I mean,' I coughed, sensing that I was dealing with one of the best runners in the deception stakes, 'Meghan knew she was being ripped off?'

Broad, colourful shoulders shrugged. 'I wouldn't put it like that. Your mistake could be forgiven, on appearances,' Rosemary Turner said, patron-isingly. 'But she strikes me as clean as clean can be. Too nice.'

'That's the trouble. No vices.' I tried to indicate that I'd done more work on this case than I had.

'Well,' Turner appeared to give in, 'Meghan didn't know about it.'

The voice at the back of my head nagged, could this woman being lying to me? And if so, why? 'You're the accountant,' I said, 'Do people, clients, often not know how much money they've got?'

Apparently, I'd made the most amazing joke. Tears came to the accountant's eyes. The laugh and the loud shirt dominated the room. I felt small, as if my question were stupid. She reminded me, morally speaking, of one of those obsessively clean people who smoke, not a speck of dirt on the outside and filthy black lungs.

'So, anyone else could do it, you reckon?' I asked easily. 'Personal friends, professional advisers, credit-card hackers?'

'I doubt it,' Ms Turner said as if she were talking to a moron. I wondered if she were married. I'd hate to be her husband.

'Why not?' I let my confusion show, ingenuously. Instead of eliciting sympathy from Rosemary Turner for my ignorance, I got smug satisfaction. And the silent treatment.

'No kind of unsecured finance that went bust or anything?' I asked.

'Would I know?' she countered merrily. That was a cheerful mockery, since she knows money and that money is everything.

'What, exactly, was the discrepancy you brought up with her? May I ask?' I addressed the power in her steely eyes, and explained reluctantly. 'She has employed me to sort this out.'

A suspicious gleam in the ball bearings warned me to watch myself.

'Well, income and expenditure were not exactly tallying,' explained Rosemary Turner. 'To put it mildly. She could not produce receipts. Gifts to charity, according to her tax. Over the years. She was spending like mad!'

'But you said she didn't know,' I whined. Although I didn't trust this woman, I could think of no way to shake her. 'She is being ripped off. Surely? Not by you by any chance?' I had to prick this smirking dirigible.

'Nope. Afraid not,' she quipped, sharply. No big laugh now, I noticed her mouth, as it pursed, was too little for her face. I stared at it, waiting.

'My time is expensive, Miss Gorman.'

Summarily dismissed, I walked out, the phrase 'laughing all the way to the bank' jingling in my brain. Doctor M. Featherstone's previous tax returns would be interesting. I wondered how long it was since this accountant had been audited. The sulphurous smell of money for money's sake hung in the air-conditioning and permeated the whole building.

Alison Hungerford slaps the plastic gloves together in her palms before she sits down at the computer in the boy's room of the house on a canal in which she works. Canisteo Bayou is a relatively new extension to the town of Port Water. Although anti-static, non-streaking, non-abrasive cleaning wipes are handy, the screen is blotchy from familiar sticky fingers. She takes out of her pocket a pair of surgical gloves and lights up the computer after she has put them on.

She types www.webset.wimmin.com.au/WebsighTlines into the address field of the Internet software and loses herself. Alison never has enough time, yet she doesn't notice how quickly it passes.

<BAC> Finesse the bluff with a bluff.

<WHEELS> Of course we want to take over the world. BUT HOW?

<BAC> Be chameleon.

<BLUESKY> Crop circles are roped in with clandestine Government experiments in mind control and microwave weaponry. Ley lines are disturbed. Aliens have landed with their white stone. Women, u must ride our great eagle, honour/Jezebel, fly to the wilderness, be nourished from the face of the serpent.

<DEFARGE> God's vengeance upon the goddess.

<BAC> Colonisers and killers at heart are an introduced species to the earth. That they want the destruction of women and the planet is proved.

<WHEELS> Anyone had their home page tampered with?

Alison shoots her bullets through chevrons into cyberspace. If life from outer galaxies, or extraterrestrials of any sort, are making contact then the superhighway is their route. They will find no biospheric barriers there. Beyond the earthbound strife, the boring and depressing concerns of her own people, Alison seeks freedom through the radon gateway of the monitor. She clicks the Favourites icon on the toolbar. Then out of curiosity she looks up incoming email and regular sites. Messages from facilitator@whymen.com.vu she finds intriguing; why would such a young kid be interested? Soon she discovers the answer. Boy-Lovers, a photo album showing candid shots of youths in beach-wear, and a menu where the browsers can pick and choose. Code-words are required before she can get further into the channels of communication, but she deduces that the next step is credit card numbers. She finds the file set up to download material from the whymen site. Ach-Mem. She ponders the strange pages of numbers and abbreviations, trying to figure out what they could mean. 'Assholes' is the only full word and it is repeated at the end of each transcript. She feels her way through a stranger's mind as in an unlit house a newcomer searches for the light switch. Uncovering the lad's recently sent email, she notes his pseudonym, Innarestd, and service provider, Hotmail. From the tenor of his letters, the kid was posing as a pervert, boastfully claiming to be a lecturer in higher mathematics and electronic engineering. Anyone with a brain could see it was make-believe. The facilitator at whymen in Vanuatu, however, didn't seem to care as he responded to Innarestd as a bone fide client.

She carefully wipes and tidies the room the way a cleaner should. Alison goes into the kitchen and screams when she sees the time. She races to get the mopping finished, hares through the place with a feather duster, flashes around with a carpet sweeper, not bothering to lug out the vacuum cleaner, and has a lightning idea. Pay a friend to do the job she is being paid for so that she can access the on-line computers in the house. Iris, Lenny's aunt, is just the ticket. She has a key.

Ideas themselves are hits of speed. She is logs onto the other computer, because, for no other reason, she can't resist.

The phone rings. Alison is caught out. She shivers with a flush of guilt. It is Chandra. 'What about Tilly?'

Fucken meat street, Alison is furious, as she closes down and checks the house.

Public phones. Must ring Penny, with what? Reassurances. Must do a workout at the gym. I put the notebook down, brought out the little black book, flipped through, found Margaret Hall's mobile number and slashed the phone-card through the slot.

Margaret answered. 'Yes?'

'Margot here. How's the CyberCage?' When seeking information in the friendship network it is always best to ask how they are, what they're doing, how their friends, children, mother, whomever, are. It is excellent to remember the last thing they said the last time you met.

'Oh, cool,' she replied. 'Been teaching the Internet to women.'

'Anyone I know?' I bantered lightly.

'A few,' she acknowledged, then continued. 'I had Judith Sloane the other day.'

It did not strike me as odd that anyone would want to learn the intricacies of the World Wide Web, even though for myself it was only too aptly named, and I hate cobwebs. 'Judith Sloane? The singer?'

'Two old dykes from the bush. Virginia White knew what she was doing. But Judith, well, you know?, hates all things modern. Like we should live like the monks in the Middle Ages, growing, spinning, weaving, subsistence and all that.' Margaret dropped her voice. 'I got the feeling she had been on-line before and didn't really want me to know that. Could be bullshitting. Anyway, what can I do for you, Margot?'

'Nothing much,' I said. 'Just a couple of phone numbers. Jill David? An address will do.'

'Her caravan? She was in here yesterday. Ready?' Margaret Hall gave me Jill's mobile phone number and I carefully wrote it in my black book.

'And Alison? Tilly's mum?' I requested.

'Right. I've got two Alisons. I've got her work number. Hungerford. The phone was cut off from her flat after a month. Didn't pay the bill,' Margaret gossiped, being generous with information. I wrote down a number that seemed familiar.

'Do you know how I can contact Dello and Maz?' I prayed hopefully.

'Sorry, don't know them,' Margaret said.

I noted that and wrapped up the conversation with, 'Thanks. See you.'

'Yeah, bye.'

One mystery was solved immediately. I found I had written down Penny Waughan's home telephone number for Alison.

I dialled the college and asked for Mrs Waughan. While I waited, I saw Broom, Brunhilde Geiser, walking along the street with Libby Gnash. They stopped at the bus stop and sat down on the bench. As the diminutive solicitor was carrying a brief-case which she immediately opened to bring out papers, I thought they must be talking business. An odd coupling of women that I knew. Not seeing Lola anywhere I let my eyes rest on Broom as I waited for Penny to come onto the line. Her exaggerated hand movements and facial expressions were familiar, but now I found them overdone, like garish colours. Libby, in contrast, seemed to say little and moved her hands only to smoke a cigarette, a habit Broomhilda completely abhors.

Penny was speaking. 'Hello?'

'Penny? It's Margot Gorman,' I explained.

'Yes?' She sounded tentative.

'Are you all right?' I have a cop-educated voice sometimes that tends to step forward rather than backward when someone shows doubt.

'As well as can be expected,' Penny said. 'It's just that I am in a bit of a hurry. I have to get to the bank and pay my cleaner in cash before she leaves my house.'

'Okay, just one thing. When can I visit you at home?' I asked.

So Alison worked for Penny Waughan, as a cleaner?

'Sometime of an evening would be best,' she hesitated. 'I won't ask you how you are going, because.'

'I understand,' I reassured her. 'You get to the bank. I'll ring you either tomorrow or the following night.'

The grieving mother was sharp and hard all of a sudden, 'I must go. Goodbye.'

'Of course.' I jumped to attention. 'See you then.'

The dense bush outside Rory's house is busy with movement. Black cockatoos in a flock fly overhead squealing 'weird, weird'. Being close to the waterfall and perched on rock above the meeting of three streams, the place is full of tree-spirits.

The pixie woman, Hope, appears. Rory does a double take. Rory is really tired of all the incurably curious, incredibly stupid, albeit, often, immensely nice, young women who turn up all the time. Sometimes they are amusing. Always Rory offers a cup of tea and gives food if they happen to arrive when she is preparing supper. Lately, she has been very busy. As if she were park ranger, her home the café for tourists, not a counsellor, though a funda- mentally decent individual, Rory is forced to indulge their egocentricities, their untested fantasies, to answer their questions, even though, knowing from long experience, they will not take advice, anyway.

'Go,' she pleads silently, through the streaky window to the figure on her verandah.

She gets up and says, 'Hey, I am not in the mood for visitors.'

The gurl is mad with the monologues of wandering around

Lesbianlands alone.

Hope Strange says, 'I have a present for you, Rory.'

Another Kiwi accent, Rory sighs, where are the dinkum Aussies?

Hope hands Rory a white stone. This sort of gesture is not new. The land is full of gemstones and natural wonders. The white rock glistening with translucent green fits comfortably in her hand. The vibration is strong, but Rory has passed the stage of the rocks on Lesbianlands, just as she has dealt and finished with the circular Tarot cards she enthusiastically read a couple of years ago.

She thanks her and asks, as a matter of interest, how she got here. The gas roars from the bottle as she turns the knob. Rory strikes a match and holds it to the burner, thinking it is interesting to know the paths of gossip and personal contact which impel women to arrive in the remote Australian bush where man-hating dykes are said to live like savages. Whether or not this distracted seeker will respond logically is a gamble. You always make them tea. One, because long-term landswomen never know at first who is a sundowner and who a genuine swaggie. Sundowners arrive for the tucker and shelter and leave having given nothing. Swaggies chop a load of wood.

Hope replies quickly, 'Stayed a night at Meghan's and Judith brought me out, and left me at the gate. That was weeks ago.'

Putting the cup down, Rory nods.

Hope takes no notice of the brew in front of her even though she had nodded yes to honey. Hope begins talking about Virginia's sculpture. Rory fills her own mug and makes herself at ease in her chair, with a shrug. The goddess will provide. She hasn't been up to see Virginia's work herself. It is a steep climb. Lately, Virginia visits her, not the other way around.

'At first I thought it was just a fallen tree, magically showing the female essence of trees. Just nature, you know. But then, it was like an ancient wreck.'

Rory listens.

'Really weird experience. I felt like I was in a tomb. But it had a rhythm, a pulse, a heartbeat. Fluid and rigid. It was wood. Grotesque, but . . .' Hope had come to try and make sense of what she is feeling, Rory realises. 'Sitting on damp earth, the boundaries of my being opened like floodgates. I flowed about the curves and angles like water, investigating the spaces beneath. Like viewer like artist. It was a kind of key. I wanted to sit up there and play my flute, preen like a pussy cat rubbing its back on the snake shapes of growing things. Like the strangler fig. I saw a snake in a patch of sun, big lump in its belly. Trying to pull back my brain was like fingering water into a bowl.'

Rory's mouth is slightly open.

'I don't know,' the gurl's eyes question the middle distance. 'The mighty tree had been pushed over by loggers of the past, bands of men with bullock drays and long two-handled saws, chains and precious axes, but it fell into a difficult ravine and they gave up. Its girth is so wide Virginia has constructed a step ladder to climb its side to work in the centre, scrapping away the villages and towns of termites.'

'At least you're full of appreciation,' Rory says.

'I saw a classical symmetry in a flash then it was gone. This tree had frightened the men who disturbed it. It's like a ship. It has a vertical aft like a car ferry, and a bow narrowing elegantly with swimming limbs. Pitching in stormy seas. The squat lateral roots are being shaped into bodies. A couple, love-making, entwined about each other. Unmistakably, there is a proud figure holding a stringless bow up straight and high, the other elbow bent back to a quiver of arrows, yet she has no face. Her head is part of the tree itself. When she is finished everyone will know her.'

'Why do you say that?' asks Rory intrigued.

'Like the attitude is clear,' Hope trembles like a fawn. 'I will love her when I meet her. Then, like right away, I had to move, to go. Scuttled off down the hill in a hurry. I needed to run, to draw myself with me, like a clinging sheet, like lurex changing to water. And to blood, as it passed the portals of my skin. I needed to come here. To be one. Of many. Not insane.'

'I understand,' Rory says, solidly. 'Men are sculpted as they see themselves, women rarely.'

'Yes,' Hope nods. 'I find it freaky. It is a ship of fools.'

'Are we fools?' smiles Rory, rhetorically. 'Flopping about trying to create ourselves?'

'Yes, I reckon,' Hope frowns. 'Virginia was angry. It is an angry work.'

Rory shakes her head. 'Incredible.'

'But,' qualifies Hope. 'Brilliant really, that sculpture hidden in the depth of the forest, isolated and yet challenging. Because, like pain, it's the truth.'

'For women's eyes only, she told me.' Rory wants to bring the exchange to the level of her sanity.

In this, she is disappointed, as Hope begins quoting the Bible. 'And here is the mind which hath wisdom. The seven heads are seven mountains on which the woman sitteth.'

'I must look that up.'

'Revelation. Chapter 17, verse 9.' Hope drains her cold, honeyed tea.

Rory nods and keeps nodding. Grimacing. She handles the greenish white stone, feels its weight in her palm and asks, 'Where have you set up camp?'

Hope is so young, at rest there is not a line on her face. She makes her own furrows with her frowns and her smiles. They are there for a moment, then gone.

'Not far from here, just up on the ridge. In the burnt-out shelter. That is where I got that.' She points to the piece of quartz.

'Uh ha,' Rory knows where she means. 'That used to be Trivia's place.'

'Yes, I know that. I found her notebook in a tin.' Hope gets up, walks around and asks, 'Have you got a computer? Can anyone use your phone?'

'If you pay for your calls and note it down in the book there,' explains Rory. 'When I don't feel like trusting women, I lock it up when I go out.' Rory follows her with her eyes. 'Funny you should mention it. I'm getting a computer. I suppose you were a cyberchick at school?'

Hope nods. 'That's what I miss more than anything. Even cheese-burgers.' They stand at the open door, the threshold.

'Hope,' Rory asks, 'you didn't happen to see anyone else when the bridge was broken, by any chance?'

'All I saw were those two horrible women on horseback with their skinny dogs and stock-whips. One of the dogs had a paw tied into its collar so it had to walk three-legged. They had a look at the bridge, but that's all.'

'Wilma and Barb. That poor little bitch runs away as soon as she gets onto this property. That's why they tie up her leg, so she can't take off.' Both agree the dog would prefer to belong to one of the gurls.

Hope Strange leaps off the verandah with the lithe energy of enviable youth. 'Be seeing yer.'

Rory waves goodbye, wondering how she always has this settling effect on women, even when she does not feel hospitable. Wilma Campbell is Willy Campbell's wife and Barb is Willy's sister. Rory writes their names down for Margot. Because they're women, they come onto Lesbianlands whenever they want. Rory doesn't trust Wilma and Barb, but without proof will not judge them.

She sweeps out the leaves from her satellite dish, eventually warming water to begin cleaning the solar panel of birdshit, after which she makes a phone call. She wants Chandra to help her find the computer to suit her needs. Happy in anticipation of a new contact, she gets herself ready to go to town.

The cop shop was busy when I got there. People sitting on all available bench space and standing about seemed to be neither criminals nor coppers. I stated my business to the desk sergeant but before she responded, Philippoussis came out from an inner office, one arm in his reefer jacket, rattling car-keys and indicating I follow him. Standing with the passenger door of a late-model white Ford Falcon open, his hand on the handle, waiting for me to get in, he said, 'Recognise anyone?' I shook my head. I hadn't really looked, but a guy there could have been my trainer, which thought was so improbable I didn't give it credence. Philippoussis started the car. It hummed with comfort. He used the car-phone, affirming arrangements with the hospital.

I needed to see the body I found again. I needed to see him as a male. From the main entrance, we went down the corridor past the wards, then, after Radiology, took a right turn. The temperature seemed to drop. I felt as if I'd entered a time warp where things were different and workers in lab coats moved like robots. The mortuary. The two bodies were lying on parallel gurneys covered by rubber sheets, ready.

The hospital orderly removed the other boy's covering. Uncanny how similar the faces were, although they showed quite different deaths. The second lad's was cross-hatched with lacerations from broken glass and impact with sharp objects. Both had long unnaturally black hair, were about fifteen with pointy features and skinny frames. I suspected the lacerated one was taller. The bruising around Hugh Gilmore's eyes was real, the blackness around Neil's mascara.

'They are left, as if it just happened.' I asked quizzically. 'Why?'

'Why indeed?' echoed Phil.

'Actually,' the attendant butted in, 'I was just about to clean this one up for the funeral.' He was quite jolly. 'Just waiting for the word.'

'Phil? What about the post-mortem? What does the death certificate say?' I demanded.

'I don't know,' DC. Philippoussis sounded hopeless. 'I'm being jerked around and the kids are left lying here. Nothing happening.'

'Forensics is doing an analysis of the cosmetics, surely?' I got insistent. 'You've got to get an idea of where he got made-up.'

'There's more freezing going on than refrigeration.' Phil eyed the hospital bloke, who listened.

I exited the morgue and walked towards the front of the hospital, momentarily distracted by the colour and noise of the children's ward. The tall dark handsome plain-clothes policeman followed me. He didn't catch up. He didn't call me back. In single file we passed the main desk and waiting room and went through the self-opening doors. Instead of going back to the car, I sought a piece of grass and headed that way. I sat down cross-legged and looked up at him.

He lowered his long body and asked, 'Well?'

'I explained to you that Penny Waughan asked me to find out what happened to her son. She suspects he was murdered. Suicide very unlikely, according to her, and heroin-taking out of the question.' I sounded like a scolding big sister.

Philippoussis was distracted. If there were a soccer ball about he would be dancing it on his heel, toe, elbow, shoulder, chest, toe, heel, shoulder, foot, wall and back again, idly, thinking.

'They're pulling my resources on this one,' he told me. 'Minimum investigation.'

'What is the problem? It's straightforward. You have to investigate accidental deaths. The magistrate has to listen to the facts and recommend pursuance on your findings, doesn't he?' I insisted. 'Or she?'

'The Crank is a bloody riddle.'

'Drug War Baron Nasty. You know the joke. They get more than the Armed Robbery squad.'

'You're out of date,' he smiled weakly. 'What about the white-collar cops?'

'Computer fraud squad?' I displayed my disbelief with a snort. 'They haven't got a prayer.'

'He is on a drive to sign up informers. It's filthy policing. I hate the grass mentality. My grandfather was held by the fascists in Greece when they were in power. Police states finger the wrong guys.' While I chewed a blade of grass, Phillip kept talking. 'It's all politics. Ideally I'd like to be assigned to the coroner.'

'You had a run-in with the Crank already?' I tossed him a glance.

'Yeah.' He looked at his watch. 'About three-quarters of an hour ago.'

I sighed. Philippoussis continued. 'He is after pederasts now. He says.'

'But his contacts are drug-connected,' I contradicted.

'Crankshaw, our very own J. Edgar Hoover, amassing paranoid dossiers on everybody from job to job. Even us,' he raised his eyebrows at me. 'We could use this quirk of his, Margot.'

'You want me official, as a snout?' I asked, half incredulous, half eager.

'Well? It might put me in the good books, to play along I mean,' he said, apologetically. 'What do you reckon?'

'While I'm on the case. Okay,' I agreed.

Phillip leaped up feet first. Soccer-playing body angles.

'There is something I am not understanding here.' I tapped my head as if it were some sort of receiving transmission box. 'When you get the death certificates, will you show me? I want to know what the pathologist says, primary cause, secondary cause, and attendant conditions.'

'Anything else?' the DC obliged sarcastically. We strolled back to the new sedan, with its impersonal cleanness and two aerials.

I happened to say, 'I don't like rock spiders either. I know Sean Dark. He's not into it. I can assure you.' I wondered whether it was Sweetness and

Light at the station.

'It's not me you have to assure,' the detective constable said bitterly. The Crank was not giving his foot soldiers as full a briefing as he could.

'You've got to imagine a bigger picture, Pip,' I comforted, guessing what the regional commander was up to.

'Phil,' he corrected. 'Yeah, and what's that?'

'Money,' I reckoned.

'Maybe. Too much cloak and dagger for my liking.' He put his foot down sharply on the accelerator, proving, if the car itself didn't, that as a cop, he could go as fast as he liked.

'Not a healthy state of affairs,' I responded.

'I'll be in touch,' he said when he dropped me off near the Suzuki with its dolphin motif. Now, exactly how duplicitous I would have to be?

No need to identify the cause of her feelings of guilt, Alison Hungerford is in a mood to let it all out. They can't find Tilly. Chandra assumes she is hiding among the buttresses of the huge fig. They look and call and call, and no answer.

Alison loses it. Her eyes roll backwards. Her lower jaw juts forward in an effort to control her features. She releases a stream of obscenities in response to Chandra's censure about her leaving Tilly with her for so long. Chandra is cantankerous. The one place they haven't looked is the quarter-acre of sweet corn. To go in there will disturb the ripening cobs. Not on. This sends Alison to the edge. She rants. She raves.

Chandra quietly says, 'Let her be.'

But Alison is violent. Horrendous. She has no care for her own safety, let alone her daughter's or her friend's. Chandra tries to talk her down. 'Look at me. Look at me. What do you see? Who is there? Alison?' Chandra sighs with relief as Alison's eyes do focus and she sees tears. 'Alison, Alison,' she croons as she grasps at her with an impeded arm.

But Alison swings away, knocking the crutch out from under her elbow, shouting, 'You are a dose of poison, a capsule of antichrist taken with vitamins, go on, go on, destroy me. I can't carry responsibility. It cracks me open like an egg. Splat. Where is she?' She walks towards the corn. 'You drive me mad. Tilly! Tilly!' She turns to abuse Chandra, who has climbed back upright.

'Do you want me to deck you, like I did Meghan?' Chandra pants, catching her breath.

Alison suddenly laughs, 'Of course not. You could do it, too.'

'Tilly, there you are,' Chandra notices the pretty face peeking out from the stalks which are almost twice her height.

'Come here, sweetheart,' Alison calls her daughter. 'Kindly get out of my head or we will all get dirtier and dirtier until we smell like saints,' she says to Chandra, but with humour.

'What's the trouble?' Chandra asks in a business-like voice as she hobbles towards her verandah. Alison and Tilly follow. 'Not eating well is my guess,' Chandra calls over her shoulder.

'You have always criticised my diet. I had seafood and salad last night.'

'A change from chocolate and oranges.' Chandra continues, 'You don't eat enough, that's all. Your mind goes off its axis when you eat nothing.' Chandra goes into her kitchen.

'You don't have kids!' calls Alison.

'Oh, that's right. I forgot. Now, what is really worrying you?' Even though her dark moods suck out Chandra's energy like imploding black holes, Alison, being so dearly loved once, is allowed to claim her time. Chandra feels she can manage her. All the kitchen benches are lower than normal. Chandra heaves herself into her wheelchair and puts the kettle on. Tilly sits at the table, eyes wide.

Alison paces. 'Why can't you be Maria's friend?' she demands.

'Why,' says Chandra, 'should I?' She looks straight at Alison. 'I don't have to be everybody's friend. I don't have to like everyone you like.'

'You're sizist, Chandra. That is what you are,' Alison accuses, finally taking a seat.

'So? Who's perfect?' Chandra pours hot water into the pot.

Alison explains what has been going on and continues, 'She is burying herself. Too many of us nutcases buzzing around. She's eating herself to death. You don't know how beautiful she is inside. So nice. Grandma's feather-bed.'

'Why do you have to sleep with every woman you like? Maria loves being a queen bee,' Chandra claims stubbornly, putting milk, sugar and cups on the table. 'Excellent image. I'm no one's drone.'

'Stop being sarcastic,' Alison is annoyed. 'You're still in love with Sofia, right? That's why you don't like her!'

Ingrid Bergman looks with the grace of Grace Kelly, although skinnier than both, Alison could be playing a role in a Hitchcock movie, faking it. Chandra smiles as she sips her tea waiting for the scene inside Alison's mind to play itself through.

'It hasn't got anything to do with Maria, has it?' she eventually asks. 'Or my being "lookist"?'

'No. Yes. Too many things in my head. Real things, you know, things going on. Not delusions. Virtual things, as well as prophecies. Like it's, like, crazy. I feel someone's going to die.'

'Will Tilly be all right with you?'

'Why not? She's my baby, aren't you, darling? Go get your things, we're going back to the flat.'

'Has Harold been around?' Chandra asks when Tilly has run off to the barn. 'What's thrown you?'

'No, Harold's out bush, working, earning money. And,' Alison adds, 'you don't want to know what I've discovered. It's got to do with the mafia of rock spiders. I haven't worked it out, yet.'

'What are you talking about?' Chandra finds being with Alison in conversation is laborious work, separating insight from illusion.

'Nothing. Yet. Tilly will be fine. I'm going home. But Dello and Maz are taking Tilly for a couple of weeks. Lenny's at his granny's. I've got to be free for a while. So I'll be all right, okay?' Alison finishes her cuppa and bends down to give Chandra a peck on the cheek as she leaves.

Alison's two-bedroom unit in a block with other demented tenants is where, when she is unstable, Alison feels most at home, however unreliable the neighbours are. For her children, the opposite is true. Chandra is not happy when she is fragile and there. She sighs as she hears the old Ford rattle the cattle grid.

Outside the milky aqua, peachy pink and crushed strawberry mauve, tubular architecture of the accountant's building, where I had parked, I noticed that the girl holding hands with a handsome boy with tanned skin and the physique of an athlete was Lisa. I stood my ground, so they would pass me.

'Hi Margot,' she said.

I grinned and nodded acknowledgment. Nerds are out, it seems.

'Hey,' I called her back. The young jock posed against a parking sign, quite happy to be bored for a while. Lisa smiled at him and shrugged expressively. She came up to me. I fished for information about boys at the high school.

'Yeah, there were some cults,' she nodded. 'Before Hugh Gilmore left, he wore those creepy black coats like even when it was hot? Like der. Hello?'

'Sick group?' I confirmed that I understood with a question.

Lisa nodded. 'But dumb, you know.'

'Was, ah,' I looked across at the boyfriend, who still affected a nonchalance by the lamp-post, 'Neil Waughan one of them?'

'No, I don't think so,' she shook her head. 'Not at school. After Hugh left, I saw them together a couple of times. Which is weird in a way.'

'Why?' My query tried to pierce the shadowy teenage world.

'Neil was heaps brainy, you know, like heaps!' Lisa pressed the point as if she and her friends had discussed his death at length. 'Hugh and that just watched videos. That's all they knew about. They just loved death, you know. And fast cars. It was their thing.'

'Thanks, Lisa.' I glanced at my watch. 'You know they both died the same night?'

'Well, sort of,' she admitted. Her new boyfriend sauntered over to hang in the conversation.

'I take it the death-scene wasn't Neil's thing?' I asked them both, acknowledging the youth.

He shook his head and mumbled, 'Nuh.'

'Neil could be fun,' explained Lisa. 'Neil was nice. But real shy.'

The adolescents contained their energy with studied cool, moving as slowly as possible. I, busy middle thirties, proceeded to my car at a different pace altogether.

Seeing gurls on the road, on her way out of the lands, Rory stops. Fi screws up a leaflet that she had taken out of the mailbox.

'What's that?' asks Ana.

'It's for the Gun Lobby. The Right-Wing White Virgin is having a rally. I'm sick of all this junk that gets in our mailbox.'

Judith Sloane appears suddenly through the trees.

'Where did you come from?' demands Ana.

Judith, who never answers when she does not want to, stares back at Ana, daring her to crack her secrets. Rory watches the exchange and feels queasy.

Judith puts a postcard back in the mailbox and walks off. Xena stares at her back, but doesn't see further than the purple, appliquéd waistcoat.

Fi says, 'You've got to be joking.' She writes in biro on a used envelope. 'No Junk Male or Mail!! Pleeze!' The two other gurls admire her work before she goes to find a clothes peg to secure it to a wire.

'Hey, look at this,' Dee holds up the postcard Judith put in the mailbox.

'What?' Rory responds.

'Well, it's to Virginia White. And says,' she reads, turning the blue and white photograph over, 'Tierra del Fuego is cold. Be in Antarctica in a couple of days. Ha ha, Gina.'

'Her American friend,' explains Rory.

'Who's going to give it to the Beetle?' Dee holds picture of icebergs up, and comments, 'Judith had it.'

'I will,' says Rory. 'Why did Judith have it? But, hey, you lot are coming to the triathlon, aren't you?'

'Yeah, staying at the motel with you.'

'Well first I'm going to Chandra Williams'. See you there. Booking's in my name. O'Riordan.'

'Tell Virginia that Judith's running off with her mail.' With that, Fi, Ana and Xena get into their station wagon and head off along the gravel road.

Virginia White's diesel four-wheel-drive appears along the track from the back part of the lands. When she brakes, the Holden Rodeo idles with a tinny, low rumble.

When Rory gives her the postcard, Virginia frowns and says, 'Who's got time to go to Antarctica?'

'To leave more garbage in a pristine environment. Why do they bother?' Dee Knox tends to ask this rhetorical question quite often.

The three land-lesbians chat for a bit. About any old thing, books. The world. Dee reads fantasy novels, Rory newspapers. Virginia wants to discover the truth.

'Fact is a bit of a worry,' Rory comments.

'Fiction though,' Virginia wants to say, 'has got worse in an effort to provide escape. If it's not about psychopaths, writers are only showing how dumb they are, how narrow, by making sentences about what they know. Relatively, nothing!'

'The news is my horror story, it's got everything,' says Rory.

'The blessed focus, the overblown individuality,' exaggerates Virginia. 'That would enable me to spend my life with the beauty of the native orchid.'

'But it would be life with a magnifying glass, a self-imposed tunnel vision or an autism,' Rory objects. 'Anyway you don't mean it.'

'That's why I do massage!' Dee maintains. 'For focus.'

The three eventually get going in different vehicles at differing speeds. As Rory drives off last, the meditative old tank grumbles beneath her.

Sloane is so sly. Rory is amazed Judith gave the gurls any information at all. It was more Judith's style to let them drive in and discover the broken bridge for themselves. Ella came in the night, her dog howling at the big moon. Cohen, her surname, she said, means dog. Judith parks her new Triton outside the boundaries of Lesbianlands and walks in, so dedicated is she to secrecy. Rory has seen Judith grow more and more introverted over the years they have shared the deeper reaches of the property. Only four left in that part of Lesbianlands: Hope at Trivia's, VeeDub, Judith and Rory herself. No one expected Judith Sloane would last when she came, she was so English. She seemed, to begin with, hopeless at looking after herself. But everyone loved her and did things for her. They loved her for her voice, both her speaking voice and her singing voice, only to discover later that Judith holds some deep obsession. Exactly what it is, Rory does not know. Is it guilt? Revenge? Disillusionment?

Judith claims to have been involved in all significant feminist causes and ecological ones too: Greenham Common; Pine Gap; Michigan Music Festival. She has been in the Arab world, the Caribbean, India, New Zealand, knew members of the Bader Meinhoff and Greens in Germany. When Rory presses her in conversation for incidental detail of these times, she gets a succession of famous names and anecdotes. Like talking to the pages of a gossip magazine. No proof that she was there personally, no proof that she wasn't. Rory sustains the feeling that Judith is making a fool of her. The voice of a duchess, the soul of a guttersnipe, working-class Rory has been known to say, but only when drunk. The class thing is here, Rory admits, in our dealings with each other.

After she hits the Cavanagh Gorge Road, in the witchy way of the gurls, just as she is thinking of Judith, she sees her car. The violet four-wheel-drive is ploughing up the dust on the serpentine track across the paddocks denuded of trees to Willy Campbell's place in the hills behind. Willy Campbell causes the women trouble whenever he can, but he is a joke. The tiny, wiry man hates 'greenies' and swears every second word, and, in the pub at Pearceville, he calls the landwomen 'supercunts'. But he is their neighbour. He gets some sort of kudos from that. Judith is the most rigid of vegans and so green she criticises the gurls who kill so much as an ant. The sight of Judith's vehicle in that place at this time is further confusing to Rory as she has heard on the grapevine that Judith's latest lover is black. Willy is as racist as they come. However, there is probably an easy explanation, thinks Rory, she is probably just getting hay for her sheep.

Rory's vehicle, meant for difficult terrain, made to carry heavy weaponry during war, is not designed for the smooth macadam of highways. It rattles and shudders, requires the driver to use all her muscle power to keep it on the road, as if, like a wild thing, it strained towards its element, off-road. Rory is immensely fond of it, and, proud of acquiring such a treasure, named it Margaret-Rutherford-as-Miss-Marple, or Ma'am.

Putting herself to the arduous physical task of driving Ma'am allows her mind to roam unfettered and come across whatever it will. Rory thinks of Cybil Crabbe, the kind of excitement, anticipation, in the air, when VW is about to go to town. Rory cannot stand Cybil. Virginia's attention when getting close to Cybil in the near future is scatty, almost senseless. At home in the bush, they could spend hours together with nothing to say, while at other times, they would earbash each other to death. Rory pulls her thoughts around to Chandra.

Although both have been in the area a long time, acquaintance has never got beyond the nodding level. Chandra is fierce, Rory feels judged by her. But now, with the prospect of getting herself a computer, having set up enough electricity from the sun and installed a telephone tower, she has to face the new technology. Chiefly a psychological hurdle, she is sure. If she doesn't follow instructions to the letter, she will do something wrong. Unwise. Destructive. The ease with which the likes of Hope Strange and other whizzes swim in the electronic dimension mystify her. She must plod into that place herself and make her own way with hands-on experience. And Chandra is the woman, having had a computer ever since they were affordable, maybe before; her disability and energy probably helped. She is closer in age, therefore Rory hopes she will be able to grasp the concepts behind the jargon.

Logging trucks and semi-trailers have to drop to their lowest gear, their lowest speed, so as not to jackknife over the cliff into the river. She has seen some close calls in her time. The corner is haunted by the ghosts of bad drivers.

Rory arranged her IT lesson, formally, with Chandra Williams who teaches Artificial Intelligence to women. And gets good deals on hardware. Does Chandra, she wonders, like Judith Sloane?

Branches of thought stream together as she hits the hard bend cautiously. The explosions and the bridge disaster are run-of-the-mill for Rory, exciting her enthusiasm only in the prospect of seeing Margot Gorman in private, one on one.

Sean Dark, my trainer, has an inoffensive attitude. He knows his stuff, has a trim body tuned to understated perfection. But he is a bit of a motor mouth. So I know he gave up sex with others five years ago because of the health risks. With energy to burn he piles affection on clients with beautiful bodies, who enter competitions whereat he can feel a motherly pride. He is a sweetie. I call him Sweetness and Light.

We talked about a piece of correspondence I showed him from a sports-wear company.

'What do you reckon about my doing the TV ad? I'll think about it after Sunday.'

His opinion of my chance of getting the well-paid job was so-so. He thought I had the local triathlon won, though. He lacked his usual exuberance.

While hugging my leg and pressing the toe end of my foot towards my shin-bone, he chatted. 'Sponsor's letter? You're not the only one. They'll have to try you out. I think you've got to look right, present the superwoman image. They will be filming up here. Outdoor shots. Our tourist town will be an ambassador for Australia, Olympics and all. Your sport is glamour plus, darls. Muscle tone on chicks. You've got to have it but don't flaunt it. They are going for your age group lately. Have you noticed? Hair? Creams? They're using women in their thirties. Ah fashion! Love it. Always changing.'

He placed my leg down and picked up the other and pushed tentatively with an inquiring expression.

'Female body-builders are out. Speaking of which,' his tone took on a gossipy camp note, 'a friend of yours turned up the other day, nickname of Tiger.'

'Tiger Cat is no friend of mine!' I surprised myself with my vehemence. Bitchiness was catching around Sean. 'She was here when you weren't one day. Looked right at home.'

'Not hydrating enough. Those girls have got to make their veins stick out. Their faces, my dear.' He flipped his wrist. 'Haggard. She's entered the event, she told me.'

On the mat I started stretches, bending forward, head on knees, hands on ankles. Bouncing up, squeezing flexibility into my groin with the splits, I said, 'Well, don't discount her. She has an arctic will. In the late-night drinking days of being young and tough, she and I played poker with the boys. We held quite a regular school for a few months there. At the Police Academy. She beat me. Everyone else had thrown in. I was holding three jacks and two twos. She calmly upped the bet another two dollars or five dollars. All I had to do was pay it to see her. But, what can I say? I'm a miser, not a natural gambler. There was something in her eyes that wanted to grind me to dust. There was a lot of money in the middle of the table. I dropped my cards face down. She had nothing. Jack high. The whole group cheered, complimented her on her steel. But I was devastated. She has sneered at me ever since, mistaking gambling guts for killer instinct.'

Sweetness and Light was amused by the story, grinned a grin to match his name, 'Well, they don't want her for their marketing. And she won't come within a cow's moo of you on Sunday. She won't make it through a full triathlon.'

Bitchiness in others is so comforting. 'But what does she want? From you?'

He shrugged. 'She's got cosmetic muscle. No face. She keeps talking about you. And how she's a dyke. Methinks the lady protests too much.'

Sean knows his drugs, substances, pills and natural therapies inside out. I worked out for about an hour. There were probably illegal steroids in that well-stocked cabinet of his. As I went through my weights routine, I speculated on his comment about cosmetic muscle and came up with the suspicion that he was selling something to Tiger Cat. She had bulked up a lot since Goulburn.

When I emerged into a sunlit afternoon, Jill, the Featherstone partner, was in the car park aiming for her automobile. She looked like a business-woman in a new chocolate-brown pants suit with matching leather bag. She didn't seem to want to be recognised.

I yelled, 'Hey Jill.' She had to stop and turn. We exchanged pleasantries. It wasn't the time or the place to ask her the questions I wanted to in relation to the night Neil died. I wasn't ready and, anyway, I had her mobile number. The gymnasium shared the car park with the RSL Club and Seaside Shopping Complex. She could have been anywhere, with anyone. She implied she was on her way to pump iron. Whatever, the truth was too precious to waste on me. She had to say something. She had no towel, no drink bottle, no clothes bag. The car she was near was the red Saab. She turned towards Sean's gym saying she was determined to get up to lifting twenty-kilo dumb-bells. A gratuitous lie. Why? That gurl had something to hide.

On the western shore I stopped between a black Four Runner bristling with fishing rods and a white station wagon whose stereo was blasting a female voice singing 'You are my inspiration, I am everything I am because you love me.' Really? I thought about insurance: claims, and policies. I snapped open my brief-case. The discrepant signature was on an insurance policy. The car ferry clunked into its port. Motors in low gear straining towards second filled my right ear. I had not checked the coverage with the goods, although there wasn't much to insure in the place I had been to. I hadn't even noted the registration numbers of Meghan's car or Jill's. I drove on to the barge. For the ten minutes gliding across the estuary I played with the Featherstone file. There was a written agreement, between the two, promising each other the world with its horizons and rainbows in flowery language, signed a couple of years ago. Worth squat, as they say in the States. But it was the only document with Jill's signature on it: Jillian T. David. Firm hand, the J, T and D decided, definite.

If Meghan did not originally employ me, who did? Why did Mr Solicitor not see me when he was at work in his office, even if I had an appointment? Mistress Accountant said something that made me distrust her, but I couldn't remember what exactly. Was Libby Gnash more successful than I in getting into the Legal Eagle's inner sanctum? Why was she there personally? With Lola? Lawyers talk to each other on the phone or in documents mostly. And, why, incidentally, does Dr Featherstone have a male, incompetent solicitor with a brass-balled secretary? What is Jill up to? What was Libby Gnash talking to Broomhilda about? Or rather, listening to?

Rory goes into Chandra's house hoping it would be easy, to be met by a busy, distracted Chandra with a businesslike manner. She has a choice between a Macintosh and a PC, both portable.

Rory feels she is having to learn a new language, as Chandra impatiently runs through the two different operating systems.

'Wait,' she orders. 'If revolution is possible via the Internet, I must be in it.'

Her teacher explains about search engines and selections. 'Tell me a subject you are interested in.' Chandra puts a word in the field without waiting for the answer and continues, 'Here and click on here. Like this, see. You have that many sites, 19,342 in this instance. You can narrow it down, by specifying exactly what area of, say, environment, you want. When you get to a site, click on a highlighted word, underlined, called hypertext.' The movement on the screen is all too fast for Rory, but she listens and worries the stone Hope gave her with her fingers and palm. It does comfort her, cooling her fear of the new, allowing her solid-based brain to surrender while reinforcing her stubborn determination to learn.

'Solanas,' she says when Chandra takes a breath. The word and the way Rory expresses it spin Chandra around in her chair and she looks at her. Rory's mild blue eyes absorb all the urgency and irritation in Chandra's flickering brown ones: in the giving is the taking and in the taking is the giving. Both are equal. Plain, slightly pear-shaped, in unflattering clothes lumpy with filled pockets, Rory exudes the beauty of a rocky escarpment. Chandra has to change her prejudices and preconceived judgements in the moment of the exchanged stare. So much said in silence, in a tiny stretch of time, Chandra has met her match, the fire of activism meets the earth of love, both wrapped up in the name of Valerie Solanas. Chandra's well-learnt distrust falls away and her smile cracks her handsome face into friendly creases that show her humour. Rory feels as if she has said something brilliant, and raises her eyebrows. Ginger eyebrows on a freckly face; so much for appearances, shrugs Chandra, as she turns back to the screen.

'My domain,' she continues, 'Wimmin.com.au, is a house-like labyrinth of chat pages, MUDS, news groups, it has rooms for recipes, for sex talk, for counselling and the cellar, the radical feminist theory box, email listservs. The further maze I'm setting up is to band together Solanasites and conspire to do as Valerie would have wished through the use of a code using English language. Under the house, as it were.'

'Far out,' comments Rory, still trying to come to terms with what buttons to push.

'Multi-user dimensions work in real time. Mostly games where players, at their computers at home, take on characters, characteristics, whatever, and amuse themselves working out a puzzle and dispatching the enemy. I am trying to figure, configure one, that is, while virtual, in fact real. Using the game format to work out strategies and decide on tactics for, to put it simply, the women's revolt.' Chandra rattles on, excited by having Rory as a pupil. 'To get into the strategical MUD, there are various steps the women have to take to prove they're what I am calling cyber-warriors. They have to know their way, the virtual geography as it were. They have to know their feminism. After that, it gets more difficult. We're into the area of action. A lot can talk. A lot can act. Rarely is it the same being. And then, of course, nothing for women can be done single-handedly.'

Rory nods. 'This is world-wide? International? Or only First World, white, English-speaking?' Chandra responds to all her questions with clear explanations. She cannot make it simple because intrinsically it is devious, and complex, and while Rory, through her avid reading of news, understands the politics and possibilities, she is slow at grasping the techniques and actual operation of the cyber-world. 'Let's call it Penthesilea's Revenge,' she suggests.

Relaxing, now, in Chandra's company, Rory explains Virginia's obsession with Amazons at Troy.

'Okay,' replies Chandra, quite happy to expand the conspiracy to embrace enthusiasm such as Rory's. She tells her about the hypertextual threads using the simplest words in the English language. But when she is showing her, she finds the meddler in her site has been at it again and underlined 'which' wherever it appears in the text. Without revealing to Rory, at this stage, her concerns, she pursues the link. It goes to the chat page. So whoever is doing this is playing with her.

'Chat occurs in real time,' she explains. She allows it to scroll on the larger computer screen as they speak.

'What does <BAC> stand for?' asks Rory, bemused by the nyms.

'Bullets and chevrons,' replies Chandra. 'This individual calls it the language of aliens, female ones.'

'Aliens? Are you kidding?' Rory is jolly as she is sceptical.

'Takes all sorts,' Chandra says. 'But they are like computer short-hand, smileys and so on.' She points to what she means. Then she clicks out of the chat, wanting to discuss the Memos of Annihilation. 'I've been fascinated by this woman who keeps posting essays on the bulletin board. She signs herself Tragic. A pretty serious Solanasite. Hopefully.'

When they are having a break and sitting at the kitchen table, they leap-frog over the initial hurdles of getting to know one another, small talk, and settle into a friendship which could be life-long.

'Andy Warhol was about emptiness,' Rory seriously states. 'Is that why

Valerie chose him?'

'All men are empty,' spits Chandra showing her contempt. 'He was certainly symbolic of his time, but I don't know if she knew that. Probably.'

'You bet. Celebrity. But, you know,' Rory, thinking of the implications of a genuine revolution, decides to be honest. 'I don't think I could shoot anyone. But what you're doing is so far out. A Solanasite Conspiracy was a dream of mine.'

'Well,' says Chandra, 'you can share it with others on the net. If you can afford this.' She indicates one of the lap-tops. Rory pulls a cheque book from one of her commodious pockets, and they decide which one she will have and talk about how she will set it up and so on.

So many questions stream into Rory's consciousness, she doesn't have room to hear answers. She asks, 'Do you mind if I call in, like often, say Sunday? Or tomorrow?' Chandra doesn't mind. She is actually keen. Gratified, Rory keeps questing.

'Isn't it vulnerable? Couldn't a spy infiltrate?'

'Yes, of course,' Chandra explains methods of encryption and schemes for booting out suspicious types.

Rory literally rolls up her sleeves. 'I understand your structure and control. But when it's under way what do we actually do?'

'Who knows? Carpet-bombing?' Chandra explains the method of flooding the target address with thousands of emails. 'The server is overloaded and the entire system collapses and shuts down.' They go back into Chandra's home office. 'Think up a name, introduce yourself, chat.' Chandra spins out of the way, and offers Rory her place. Rory pulls up a chair and types, ANNIEOAK.

<EIEIO> Eh? Has anyone barged into mixed (male-female) couples to bust 'em up? By making love to the woman making her a lesbian.
<MOP> Need you ask?
<CHE> There are girl porn channels for the likes of you, sister. Wheels ICQ

'That's me,' Chandra murmurs.

Chandra leans in front of Rory and types in EMML, BAC.

Rory asks, 'Who is <MOP>? Another acronym?'

'Moments of pleasure, can you believe?' Chandra remembers, 'She came through <u>CellarOne</u>. Here, let me show you.' She brings up the pattern of her virtual house and explains the make-up of the basement. 'I didn't want to exclude lust, just as I didn't want to judge those with a passion for cooking, so you can get to <u>Cellar2</u>, which is based on the Anarcho-Syndicalists' model of cells, from there as well. Anyway, let's have a look at what's going on in <u>CellarOne</u>'.

Rory reads.

>>i can write a love letter with juiciest sex-pets lines a canal dripping with slippery slime glides slides into darkness tunnel & hark! marvel at u at me sound & bound by white knuckles fierce & fire spits me up it spins me out about billets-doux to so many unworthy individuals of both sexes who diddled my und(erl)ying lust as long as my flu(id)ency controls imagination waxing lyrical with waxen rubies & stacks of lace & what i am capable of in private! & in private parts my knots tight tighter as lazy muscles spaz erectile tissue strutting its stuff my whip can crack smack & whack cries enough surfeit suffice & surfacing no one believes her singing for help minuscule pearls of adoration form at the tips of eyelashes flaxen flames of innocence as sadly i shake my golden head & say let's go to bed let's fuck & suck but the silence the violence clinging without apologies with no thanx

'What?' she shakes her head.

'Yeah, I know,' grins Chandra. 'Let's have a cup of tea.'

Chandra enjoys Rory's interest and gives her the secret code language of white food to access the revolutionary group from the <u>kitchen</u>. First she has to learn how to use the technology. 'Yes,' Rory says. 'I do. Be back tomorrow or after the triathlon, on my way home.'

'That's okay,' Chandra says.

Catherine Tobin checks her email at a booth in the post office. She angles herself so she can see who comes to wait in the snail mail queue, which moves at snails' pace. Her contact's instructions are clear. She notices an interesting customer dispatch a large manila envelope. This could be one of the women she is in the area to get to know. She follows her out into the street and watches her unlock from a distance, with a gadget in her hand, a late-model car.

Jill David cruises around Port Water in the borrowed Saab, playing a part. Wheeler-dealer, power-woman, undercover agent, drug-courier. She grins and waves to Tiger Cat. Anything but an unemployed actress with nothing to do, an artiste, performing roles in the drifting world indifferent to her gifts, Jill keeps herself fit. In case, some day, she needs to perform on stage. But all the money she has is a few coins in her pocket. Change. She drives round the block.

She pulls into the curb outside Il Paradiso. Margaret sees her sitting down at a table, taking a newspaper out of her brief-case. She waves. Jill calls her over.

'Want a cappuccino? Macchiato? Long white?'

'Mugachino. Lots of froth, please,' Margaret says to the waiter.

'Just the woman I want to see.' Jill is charming.

Margaret picks up the key-ring from the table near Jill's purse. 'Nice wheels.'

Jill shrugs. 'I'm doing a favour for a friend. Got her car.'

After their coffee, Jill and Margaret go into the room with the computers.

'Sofia's right into it.' Margaret points at one intense user.

'Don't mock.' Jill fires her defence of another frustrated talent with the passion of her own disappointed ambition.

They stand behind Sofia for a moment.

'Bit gross, Sof,' comments Jill.

'Got work to do, see you later,' says Margaret.

Jill sits down at another computer and starts surfing the net, wondering if Sofia has found the hidden cave or is she just an intelligent woman spinning out? Another net-nutter.

Jill drives Sofia home.

'Has it ever occurred to you, when doom is foretold, those with most to lose are the most into denial?' Sofia expounds, freakishly picking up thoughts in the air around her but not hearing direct questions.

'No imagination,' Jill says, humouring Sofia, whose political stance is total distrust of the male of the species.

Sofia nods. 'Everyone is crazy. Merde. It's too big. It's too boring. Maybe nothing. Eh bonne.'

'She'll be right, mate.' Jill takes off the Aussie bloke perfectly.

'Say, for example,' Sofia is intense. 'The Thredbo disaster. Whose car is this?'

'My brother's,' Jill lies. 'Thredbo?'

'A ski lodge collapses,' continues Sofia. 'You want to build on a piece of land which those who don't want to build on it but have knowledge, say, is unstable, dangerous, and you still build on it? You are into denial but nothing happens to you. So denial was okay.'

'Then something does happen,' Jill prompts as she overtakes a truck with effortless acceleration.

'The sooth-sayers were right. You lose your building, your assets, the rent and whatever was inside and people are killed, money is lost and personal tragedy. The earth has caved in,' Sofia clings on to her point. 'Who takes responsibility?'

'That's the question.' Jill asks.

'Precisely. The earth has quaked. You were wrong. All you have to say is, it seemed like a good idea at the time. But, you see, no one is responsible because denial is not a crime and warnings are not currency.'

'Sofia, you sound coked to your eyeballs, but you're not wrong, you know. Are you okay?' Jill has never heard Sofia so lucid.

'Images, visions. There's my locomotive.'

Jill stops at the level crossing for the goods train to rattle past with various shapes of freight on the carriage trays.

Sofia talks, 'Leviathan of the new age, sleek, cylindrical and phallic, or a sleeping secret rocket launcher. Aliens turn up like the Blessed Virgin Mary in a balloon, their interstellar caravan. Maybe it is a prone silo disguised as a tanker.'

'Have you taken any drugs today?' Jill asks in the voice of a nurse. 'You're different.'

'It doesn't matter how much I use, I still think. My head's about to blow off.' Sofia continues, 'Did you know we are on the bottom of the pond of the future?'

'What do you think of the white virgin?' asks Jill, responding to a bumper sticker for the gun lobby. 'A woman fronts the most masculine organisation. Like, most guns are used in domestic disputes.'

'She is an expression of the mediocre. She is a product of the multiple, the mean number, not the average, the mean.' Sofia is speaking quickly.

'The media love her,' Jill comments.

'There are thousands like her out there, Mary Smiths, Joan Cains, Molly Abels, so many in fact that one had to be made into a star. She is created out of brains, thought is an energy out there. It creates things. It is as solid as shit. She is quintessentially ordinary Australian. She is just the catalyst, not the one to fear. She will probably be assassinated. The mediocre somehow find a place in history and wise witches are burnt. Unsung.'

'She's a puppet,' Jill states. And starts the car as the long train leaves and the red light stops its dinging.

Sofia shakes her head, 'Like god, people only adore images of themselves.'

'You're as mad as Cassandra,' Jill laughs.

'Don't ever call me mad.' The tone of Sofia's voice is threatening.

'Okay, cool.'

'The idiocy is that only partisan interest is taken for real.'

'You could have a point there.' Jill parks in front of Sofia and Maria's house.

'When god is in your image, or your image is in your face all the time, it doesn't matter how shallow or what the image stands for is, because it stands for you. You then go out into your own life and be as fascist as fascist can be. There are no controls, none whatsoever, because you are right, even though, everything you say contradicts yourself. Even in little ways. And, ohmygod, you won't shut up. You understand what I am saying, Jill? There are these people in our own community. Now it has to be about women, because the fundamental, the basic, the firmamental contradiction, is that the leader of the ratbag right is a woman and fascism can only benefit the patriarchy.' Sofia's monologue goes on, even as Maria prepares dinner, serves it, eats it, feeds her, listening. With Jill who stays for tea.

Having done a lot of running round today, I felt I'd worked, but had got relatively nowhere. Two investigations and the meet on Sunday, my life was full, fulfilling in fact. I told the boxing bag, left hook, right jab, left hook, right jab. Goodnight.

Book Three

madness

Saturday Sunday Monday Tuesday

Saturday's child works hard for a living

16

. . . greenish glass . . .

Ian Truckman is never late. It is pre-dawn. The six-cylinder Commodore, with only 30,000 on the clock, is uncomfortably low and fragile, frighteningly fast on the uptake: a feather-touch on the accelerator and she's off. As vulnerable as the Man from Ironbark or a bullocky on a race-horse, Ian speeds along the airport road, takes the corner, hits the cattle-grid, and, with an expletive yelp, is flying. Eventually he pulls in beside the truckie who is picking up the morning papers. He identifies himself as a fellow of the road fraternity by mentioning the size of his rig in the small talk as the first plane of the day lands. Back in the sedan, he drives to the commercial strip of oversized aluminium sheds, where transport companies have their warehouses, and several hangars are up for rent.

Truckman consumes the fast-food items of Saturday's paper like crispy chicken wings, until headlights pierce the mauve early morning. A tow-truck brakes next to him. The engine, a V8 Chevvie, is tuned for super-acceleration. A bulky, black-haired bloke jumps out. The guy is jittery.

Ian nods good morning.

'Hey, man.' The tow-truck driver opens the Holden's door before Ian does it himself. 'Ian, right? My name's Paul. Boy, are you going to be pleased! All your Christmases at once. Wait and see.'

Ian is unsettled by the looming closeness of the big chap. 'Where's my rig? Don't see it here anywhere.'

Of South Sea Islander appearance, Paul could be a lock for the All Blacks so impressive is his physical size. 'Keep your jocks in place, man. She's right here.'

'But my gear? I spent a lot of dough setting myself up in that cabin,' Ian says feeling small. 'He promised.'

'Hey, man, you gotta remember you don't own her. But,' Paul concedes confidentially, 'Don't worry, china. Settle down. Where's your bag? Pop the boot. This it? What's this? What are ya? An executive? They said you were pernickety.'

Truckman, already grinding his teeth, picks up his mobile, his paper and his overnight bag from the back seat and follows Paul. The chrome-glistening semi-trailer is radiant even in the low sheen of coming dawn. They approach it from behind, twenty-four wheels in the back, some bald, and ten brand-new on the semi, seven and half thousand tare. His name in elaborate brush script on the right hand door near the bottom, near the step, gives him a shock. Spooky. This FreightLiner has more horse power than the Scania he had so recently called home.

'Usually do that myself,' he complains grumpily. Something's going on and he doesn't know what it is. Why are tanker-trailers at the freight terminal of an airport?

'What are we packing?' Ian asks Paul who has bounced ahead, pointing out all the aerials, including a tiny satellite dish and miniature solar panel which protrude from the cabin-casing. Mounted above the front of the engine, which juts forward in the rounded lines of the brand-new, is his own sign: White Virgin.

'Go on, get up inside, take a deco,' Paul pushes the keys into his hand. Ian Truckman puts down his port, turns and, swinging the smooth door wide, mounts with care.

Paul jiggles about, wanting to get up, but truckers take their time.

The interior is immaculate. Radio, stereo, tape deck, computer screen the size of a piece of bread, dash modem, aerials everywhere, VCR, CD player, phone, fax, CB, TV, bed, bar, leopard skin, pine forest aerosol spray and new box of cleaning materials. Ian inspects every nook and cranny, and finds a butterfly knife and his own rifle as well as a 0.32 calibre self-loading pistol. Whoever installed the gadgetry knew what he was doing. Truckman cannot find fault. He dismounts backwards and circumnavigates the vehicle. Everything on the FL112 is new.

'Can I?' Paul, surprisingly, has the manners to ask if he can look inside. Men respect each other's boundaries, and White Virgin, with 'Ian Truckman' hand-painted on the door, is out of his bounds to the uninvited. Ian nods distractedly. Hearing noises of wonder and praise, his own bliss rises quietly up his body.

'What do yer need a video player for?' yells Paul, impressed with a VCR in a moving vehicle.

'We do stop and rest,' Ian replies, impatiently tolerant. He has questions but he doesn't want to ask this guy. He'll take orders from the boss, Hannibal.

Against his better judgement Ian finds himself chatting with Paul. 'The two-lane black-top is my home,' he explains. 'Cruising. Sleeping in the cabin.'

'Yeah, well, mate, it is my hunting ground.' Paul flexes his muscles like a boxer. 'But shit, man! Gaming in the truck, soft porn interactive software.

Plus your long-barrelled hardware.'

Ian swells with pride as if the size of his penis has been praised by another man.

'We have to wait.' Paul changes his mood, his tone has a tinge of menace. He picks up Ian's newspaper and goes over to the step of the side door of the building to read. Truckman is reluctant to join him. The beauty of the new rig is better savoured alone. Ian tries out the IT in the cabin. He is no sooner on-line to his voyeuristic website than the screen runs by itself. Eerily reacting to thought patterns in his head, as if he were grabbing snacks of news from hard print, which he was a little while ago, the words scroll.

A Sydney man accused of murdering his wife and dumping her body in a bin of acid, he reads, was 'extremely exhausted and distressed' after police questioning. The judge in a different trial was told that Leonard suffered from a severe and extreme personality disorder from his early childhood years, when he spent school holidays with a grandmother who bought him kittens and taught him to torture them by cutting off their ears and tails. This father, worried that he was not creating a world for his four daughters, was acting under a delusion when he cut their throats and then killed himself, the coroner found. He used a meat knife. Sara and Rebecca suffered wounds to their hands, indicating they had struggled. But it appeared neither Georgina nor Anna awoke before being attacked.

Ian expected pictures, not old news of a murder-suicide in Tasmania. But why is this coming up on his screen? He switches it off, and reboots.

An icon flashes a military hat. Australia the lucky country is transforming itself into Australia the shrinking country, retreating from the rest of the world, unable to come to terms with its past, frightened by the future and with a political leadership lacking strategy or direction. There's no telling what Asians and Jews can do, they are so cunning. All this Japanese hardware does not work the same. Intelligence agencies in the United States have stepped up their campaign to control the flow of information over the net, counteracting an unholy alliance of civil libertarians and business chiefs who back the introduction of secure encryption technologies to protect personal privacy and commercial data on-line. Must be something to do with that, Ian is unsettled by powers beyond his control. But, at least, the modem works through the truck's telephone connection. Must be satellite, that Echelon business. Ian keeps in touch with conspiracies around the world through his users' group. Wherever he goes while on-line, news items of the murder of women and girls scroll like credits at the end of a video.

The man accused of one of New Zealand's worst mass murders admitted yesterday killing six people and trying to shoot four more but pleaded not guilty on the grounds of insanity. A youth dragging a wheelie bin believed to have contained the body of a murdered Japanese tourist through peak-hour traffic was seen by scores of motorists on their way home from Cairns last week.

Truckman sees the tow-truck driver throw his newspaper down in a mess of uneven pages and unaligned folds. Ian detaches his wireless connection and goes over. He ostentatiously picks his *Telegraph* up and tidies it. He is not going to confide his mystification to the aggro brute named Paul. He goes back to the truck.

If he does not key in his presence, the sound card reminds him in an electronic voice: Still on-line?

Most GPs grossly underestimate the numbers of women suffering physical, sexual and emotional abuse by their partners and believe in an average practice they would see 10 a year when a more likely annual figure is 250. And many doctors are missing the one in 25 women who have suffered severe abuse.

The worm addresses him by his Internet tag. Those Lesbian cyborgs and their secret world government have to be contained with the threat of biological or atomic warfare. He tries to go to his other favourite, the UFO site, but the same thing happens. He is not surprised, it proves all his theories: they're out to get him. They put things in the microchips these days. He climbs out of the cabin. And wanders around until he finds a toilet, relieves himself. When he emerges, the boss is there. Truckman is officially given the Freightliner, FL112.

The boss's American accent goes with the expensive stuff and reassures Ian on all counts. You gotta admire the rich. Ian takes orders and he takes what he is given. He does a good job. He is conscientious and imagines that that earns him rewards, rather than admitting to himself he is an owned man. He wants to ask what he is carrying, but the money is too good and the FreightLiner too beautiful. He does say he finds it very strange having tanker-trailers at an airstrip.

'A temporary arrangement, Mr Truckman,' assures Hannibal. 'This depot was cheap and vacant. An expediency, you understand?'

'So what's the cargo?' Usually he doesn't ask questions. 'I'm just curious.'

'Nothing that is freighted by air, my boy. Hired the hangar, that's all.'

Satisfied with the explanation, Ian walks back to the loading bay where his pride and joy, White Virgin, is parked. He slaps a mosquito on his forearm. Beyond the runway are mangrove mud flats beside the river. Little boardwalk piers at the end of winding dirt tracks serve the oyster leases. He does not like being bitten by mosquitoes because he knows they carry diseases medical science has no cure for.

The artificial intelligence has him sucked in. Ian has never been so spoilt in his life. He tests the satellite dish for multi-media on-line. On top of the digital images, the unbidden worm keeps wriggling.

Ian plays with another gadget which gives him his exact longitude and latitude, a global positioning system.

Australia is the natural home of the road movie. I'm just a living movie. Regardless of that jerk, Paul, he is happy. Tow-truck drivers are bloody cowboys, anyway.

After cleaning the tanker he heads towards the interstate highway. The trailer is loaded, he feels, but not with milk or oil. The weight is more like water than anything else. He adjusts and becomes familiar with its carriage.

PCYC constables organise the marquee, the district division of the State Rescue Squad assigns jobs; their wives and good-hearted volunteers handle the various crises of organising the local triathlon; club officials mark the course; fanatics and triathletes prepare themselves psychologically and physically to punish their bodies for the greater wealth of media barons and, possibly, the entertainment of lounge lizards; cameramen check their stock, and power-brokers exchange words and make decisions beyond the imagination of even the most paranoid nobody. Meanwhile, Chandra Williams reprograms her trojan horse virus to insinuate itself past the portals of porn sites.

A run, a swim, a cycle. Breakfasted, I went next door to discuss the commotion there the Friday night of Neil's death. My barefoot southside neighbour was breast-feeding. I wanted to know whether the boy who had driven off at high speed after an argument with his father had any connection with the lads in the morgue. She was an unsatisfactory woman to talk to generally. Her brains seemed scrambled by too much yani and half-baked New Age ideas. But, breast-feeding, she was relatively coherent.

'What was the fight with your son about?' I asked, getting down to the topic with little preliminary explanation.

'He is not my son. He is my partner's by one of his other ladies,' she ducked my query with irrelevant fact.

'Other ladies?' I repeated, going with the flow. She implied her partner was presently polygamous. I really don't understand these people.

'Yes, why not?' She was defiant and defensive, as if I was a member of the moral majority intruding on her space and railing against adultery.

'Anything unusual going on?' I insisted.

'Hopefully,' she replied, as she adjusted the moth-eaten soft silk shirt and gave the infant the second breast. 'We don't like being bored by banal routines. Son and father, you know, have to work out their aggressions on each other.' She lectured me on the needs of men, how they are at the mercy of their testosterone chemistry.

I cut into the psychobabble with, 'It's hardly a fair contest, his dad's twice his size. Don't you feel threatened or frightened? When male aggression gets out of hand, it's women and young children who get hurt.' I looked at her babe in arms and saw the pleasure she experienced from the contented sucking, and darkly imagined the man being possessed by jealousy throwing a tantrum. Not an arduous creative exercise.

'It was only about mullah,' she dismissed and gazed at her baby.

Those who profess to care little about money tend to get very passionate on the subject, and again I was aware of an inequity in the classic battle. The boy probably had none at all.

'Weren't you worried when he drove off like that? Another kid was killed going the other way. He wasn't driving safely.' My words fell over each other.

'Tell me about it. He doesn't even have a licence,' she said, as if there wasn't adult responsibility involved.

'Why was his father so angry? I interrogated. 'Don't you care?'

'No,' she said vaguely. 'The cops found him. There was bad karma about that night. Someone had to die.'

'What?' I nearly shrieked.

'A Mars-Pluto transit.' Talking about truly spurious stuff she was very definite. 'And,' she added eagerly, 'remember there were strange lights in the sky.'

'The moon,' I commented crystallising her weird illuminations to solid rock.

'Moon in Scorpio, yes. At first we thought it was lightning out to sea,' she went on.

Paranormal phenomena was not the topic I needed. Even if I told her of my involvement in finding the dead youth and investigating his murder, she would probably offer no sympathy. If she did, it would be shallow or sugary with a touch of arsenic. Guessing I was distressed, she reached down into her huge patchwork and denim bag and shuffled about until her free hand emerged with a rainbow purse. She detached the infant from her nipple to examine the contents, a large variety of pills, herbal, pharmaceutical and round black Chinese ones all mixed up together. She chose a yellow Valium and gave it to me.

There was nothing to do but hold out my palm and say 'thanks'. I may even swallow it later. After the triathlon, perhaps. Relax the muscles.

I had to go to town. A work-out. Shopping.

A couple of Koori friends stopped me in the street. Dannii held out a flier about the racist white virgin. Violet, pulling at her dachshund on its lead, said, 'Stupid gubba gin.'

'Don't take any notice of it. It's unmitigated rubbish!' A bit of guilt always seeped its way into my system when I spoke with Indigenous Australians. The way I speak English is different. Perhaps the experiences of being a law enforcement officer branded me for life.

With hands swinging free, her red dog at heel, Rory joined us. 'Just the woman I'm looking for,' she said to me.

The canines took some interest in each other as Violet told us that the black community was organising a demonstration when the racist caravan rolled into town.

Rory laughed, 'Okay. Cowards creating myths and paranoia to get power. They're empty, ignorant.'

'Well they don't know what they're in for.' Violet looked fearsome for a moment, then grinned. The frown, however, didn't leave Dannii's face.

Rory continued, trying to express some kind of solidarity with Dannii's justified anger. 'It's not simple. Their slovenly intellect is simplistic, and they want revenge for mistaken injustices.'

'Well, they going to get a fight when they come here,' Dannii promised.

'They don't think. They wouldn't know injustice if it bit them on the bum,' Violet's laugh was mean with menace.

Locals busy, visitors strolling, violent forces were undercurrents in the pleasant sea and river-mouth environs of civic pride dedicated to tourism and Saturday-morning consumerism. The sun was shining. Sparrows hopped about the tables. Seagulls mobbed those eating take-away on the grass. But I thought of the east Kimberley. The sight of the blacks from the outback communities wandering around drunk, impoverished; expensive cartons of beer sold by whites and discounted only in numbers of forty-eight cans or more; council signs not allowing them to enter playing fields or parks with alcohol, thus forcing them onto rubbish dumps and vacant housing blocks under spindly trees, to drink out in the open, getting punchy and argumentative by night-time, empty cans everywhere. How quickly culture goes when you lose self-respect! Self-respect, I thought self-critically, is probably a white term for a white set of values. Aboriginals have respect for the spirits of the land, the Dreamtime, each other, the children, the elders, family, kinships. The litter I automatically found offensive made sense when a generation or two before one ate off bark. It's actually white society that doesn't deal with its own garbage. The pub at Fitzroy Crossing had cyclone fences inside separating the bars from each other, making it look like a pound.

Rory kept talking about the rally while I silently felt shame. Sitting in the dirt by the river, fishing, drinking, lighting little fires in circles of rocks to cook the fish or to ignite a bong or a cigarette, hanging together like any mob of drunks, or assiduously admiring their dances and paintings, whatever we do, we can't really know what it is like to be Indigenous.

When I tried to get to Cape Leveque, I was turned back, something about their law. I went onto Community land without permission. When I was confronted with my whiteness, I realised, my being, my courage, my honour, are all wrapt up in autonomy. My singular independence. I feared dissolution in the ratbaggery of community. Rory was asking about a local land rights issue.

So many places on this island continent I have been without invitation. I don't even know the names of original nations. In Sydney and Wollongong the Darug, Gadigal and Gandagarra.

Daanii and Violet were talking about a land claim not far from my house. I was not invited to buy it. I didn't know what massacres it cost to pass into white hands. We stood together on the pavement. Tourists in pairs in matching clean shorts and walking shoes stepped around us. Even though Dannii's sentences were spattered with swear-words, I listened earnestly. Deep down I felt confusion about my place in the world. As an ordinary Australian with little idea of her ethnic mix, I was as uncomfortable with her hate-filled threats as I was with their cause. Such discomfort, exaggerated to a kind of inability to live with such unease, might be why ill-informed extremists latch onto the notion that Indigenous people are different, not within their definition of 'human', hence deserving of scorn. If I never opened my mouth, or let my eyes rest on their faces with an attempt at understanding, if they did not know me personally, these two Koori women could see me as the same as any ignorant, gubba gin. I, after all, am not giving up any of the advantages of being white in this society, nor am I likely to. The neo-fascists may as well be our storm-troopers, if you go only on skin colour or background. I am European Australian, therefore I am racist. Nor did I fully understand what Violet and Daanii said. It seemed repetitive and scattered. But I was not sincerely in the conversation. Our interaction was superficial unless, I realised, it was about an exchange of favours or some kind of trading. The silences beneath and between the words contained implied knowledge that was not shared.

'Margot, have you got a moment?' Rory pointed to tables outside the fish co-op. I nodded, okay.

'If you need my help, at all,' I offered heartily as we parted, 'call me.'
Rory and I crossed the street.

Rory had a job for me. Unaccountably, a bridge on Lesbianlands had been
destroyed. There were bulldozer tracks. None of the residents had a dozer nor
had ordered the use of one so far as she knew. Rory wanted me to interview
neighbours and women and discover what had happened. She smiled as if the
whole thing were a joke, so I took it seriously, not wanting to believe her
merry eyes were conveying what I think they were.

My notebook out, I asked the names of all neighbouring people, their
interests, their attitudes and her possible explanations as to why these people
would do it. It seemed, as she talked on, a rich canvas of motives and malice,
a touch of the wild frontier.

'If there really were explosions, why no police involvement?' I asked a
routine question. 'Surely, it's illegal to use dynamite on someone else's land.'

Rory shook her head. 'We won't have men on our property. We try to keep
a low profile. Anyway, we have no proof. We don't know where they blasted.'

Rory showed me the Forestry map. Lesbianlands is a whole swathe of
mountain range between two river valleys; a huge property. Tributaries to
the Campbell, and in numerous little gullies, creeks feed into them with the
wonderful symmetry of geography. The Wurrumbingle Highway, weaving
along the contours then bisecting them, made least sense to me. I would
have to be on the ground to understand the climb. Cartography was a
discipline I had never mastered, the abstract pattern of landscape describing
altitude in closeness of wiggling circular lines simply did not compute in my
brain as hills and peaks. I would have to see it physically. An escarpment, for
instance, would give me an idea of what is accessible.

Neighbours. The Campbells live up the Campbell Road, which is on the
other side of the highway, but on the map almost adjacent. Willy, Wilma,
Barb, sundry cousins and nephews, parents dead. This family owned the
place as a cattle run before they needed money, so sold it to the gurls. Several
members still think it is theirs. Willy leases the Crown land bordering
Lesbianlands.

'Why?'

'Because their spread is on the dark side of the bluff,' Rory explained.

On another boundary, the National Park side, a South African dentist
from Newcastle was an absentee landlord. His name, Vanderveen; owned a
helicopter. Two single mothers, very tough girls with a tribe of wild
children, rented the cottage up there. 'They shoot their own supper, wallaby,
rabbit, brush turkey and wood duck. Vanderveen refers to the eldest sons as
'white boys' in his funny accent as he orders them about.'

'Meaning?'

'Meaning they're not black, but they are peasants. Those girls don't like it,' Rory said. She had never met the wealthy dentist, but described the single mothers as fair-ground types who may at any time take up with some new jock, pack up the kids and hit the road. Tenants probably wouldn't stay long and haven't been there very long, I noted.

'Who knows what kind of prick will insinuate himself into their lives?' Rory asked rhetorically as though shady moral character was a given in any new boyfriend.

There was an Indigenous claim in concerning the Crown land. The Cavanagh Gorge National Park is just beyond. There, Rory suspected, very large marijuana crops were grown by criminal syndicates. 'Big operation. Very dangerous to know about. On the river flats, the neighbours nearest Lesbianlands gate are honest dairy farmers, Christian folk, who hand out Country Party voting cards every election.' The criminal syndicates, we decided, are not so stupid as to use occupied land rather than the deep, dense rainforest of the National Park. They use local lads to tend their plantations.

Willy Campbell looked the most suspicious to me, I commented, but Rory said, when I met him I wouldn't be so worried. 'He's a little chap, with all the aggro and filibuster of being short, fundamentally terrified of big strong women. Including his wife and sister. Actually, in his strange way, puffed up with importance through his alliance with the frightening pack of witches with attitude. Gives him kudos.'

The names of the gurls on the land would mean nothing unless I went out there. Visit, listen, gossip, find out what I could, stay a night at her house.

It seemed a reasonable job to me, but I could not get over the feeling that Rory was using it as an excuse to get me into her environment. In fact, she said so. But in such an overt and flirtatious way I didn't have to take it on.

Finally, I got down to the fundamental motive of money or gain. In the past there had been a bit of mining. Gurls had found pretty nice gem stones. If I found a big crop of marijuana well and good, because they did not want commercial growing on the place, just enough for women's own needs.

'Another reason for no police?' I grinned.

Rory nodded, saying, 'We can rely on your discretion, Margot.'

'You can,' I replied. I shut my spiral-bound shorthand book, having enough to go on for the minute. I would to get back to her as to when it would be convenient for me to go out there. I needed to get to the gym, do a work-out, to sweat. Rory intended to attend the triathlon as a spectator. 'Well.' I got up. 'I'll see you tomorrow then.'

In the desert, Dr Meghan Featherstone stands up. Her American colleague, the metallurgist, kneels, scraping the earth.

He says, 'It's like the elephant's foot.'

'You mean Chernobyl? Where the nuclear meltdown baked the sand into radioactive glass in an enormous solid column?' Meghan humours him.

He looks up sharply. 'Well, what is it?'

Meghan frowns. She examines what appears to be an unbroken expanse of greenish glass, about five metres in diameter. Under shifting grains of sand and the restless twigs of desert oak is, 'a circle,' she answers.

MacAnulty removes a small pick from his tool belt and begins chipping. 'I wonder how deep it is,' he ponders.

Meghan stops him digging. 'You want radiation poisoning?'

'Where's your geiger counter?' he asks, still scraping. He is not afraid of death or disease, he is looking for buried treasure.

'In the jeep.' Meghan lifts her hand to her forehead to make a brim. The jeep seems a long way away, spiky with short-wave aerials in the sketchy shade of a single tree. The heat shimmer makes it look like an insect on water. 'Loren, we have something here. It's pretty extraordinary. I can't be sure, but I don't think it was here last year when I did this area. There was a lot of rain in the wet season. I don't have a good feeling about this.'

'Oh, sure, we pay you for your female intuition, Dr Featherstone,' MacAnulty replies sarcastically.

'You men are so bloody careless.' Meghan scratches her temple. 'Well anyway, we have to check. I don't want you disturbing any more dust, you gung-ho Yankee.'

'Hey, what more damage can I do? I'll go over to there, okay?' He points. 'I'll see if I can get a handle on its depth. Whatever,' he laughs. 'I wouldn't be surprised at anything we found out here.'

'I'm not your nurse or your mother, you can poison yourself if you want to. Please yourself.' Meghan turns on her heel, still frowning, and strolls back across the red earth to their vehicle. The Elephant's Foot was an inspired guess: the circle of hard glass could have been made by a nuclear fuel meltdown. Five metres in diameter, not a crack in the surface, Meghan calculates mentally. It's either cylindrical or semi-spherical beneath the surface. Too geometric. But then again, Stonehenge is geometric. Dr Featherstone's stroll becomes a stride.

The car-phone rings as she comes within earshot. She runs to pick it up. 'Megs?' Judith Sloane's voice.

'Hi,' she responds, taking in the ridiculously blue sky. 'What is it?'

'Megs, there was a fight here last night,' Judith says with the sly confidence of a tale-teller.

'Anyone hurt?' Meghan wonders why she has rung her at work and how she got the number. 'Where are you, Judith?'

'In Stuart. Your place. Between your sister, Trina, and Jill.' Judith relishes the gossip. 'I wanted you to know it from me, not Jill. Or Trina. You know, third-person witness.'

'Trina is in Stuart?' Meghan sits in the open passenger's door watching the activity of Loren MacAnulty of Kentucky shimmering like a Drysdale figure loosened by the watery filter of heat. She considers Jill David's trustworthiness or its lack, her propensity for practical jokes and her capacity to ape Judith Sloane's accent. This conversation is a surreal. The chimera causes Loren MacAnulty to disappear altogether. She likes being Judith's friend. She sees her as the wild, uncompromising aesthete living on Lesbianlands, standing against the tide of time, spinning or weaving or shearing with hand-clippers, her twin soul, the ideal being who hides inside Meghan's breast. Her own ambitions of the future—to live on brown rice and bush herbs, away from the civilised world's rat-race, at peace, with one sole piece of technology, her highly magnified binoculars—are on hold until certain work is finished.

'I feel totally unsafe here,' Judith whines. But it could be Jill taking the mickey.

'Any reason?' Meghan asks.

'She was furious.'

'Who?'

'Jill.'

'Jill?' Meghan smells a rat. Loren materialises not very far away, walking towards her. Meghan speaks into the mouthpiece. 'Look Judith, I have to get back to work.'

'I liked Trina.' The English voice sounds patronising. 'She is so like you to look at, she even speaks like you.'

Loren sees her holding the phone and nodding. He smiles, 'Whatever it is, Meghan, we have got something. And it's big.'

'Big' being the salient word in every American heart. Meghan says good-bye and finishes the call.

Jill can't lose her temper, that is why Meghan has hit her on occasion: to get some passionate reaction. Heroine on the stage, she is phlegmatic in real life. Meghan fell in love with the actress, and she still loves her to distraction. Trina is a thorn in her side. Admiration for Judith, adoration of Jill, Meghan feels responsible for all three women. Jill has mimicked for her, acted for her, amused her. Her own falcon, helmet on, chained to a perch, it stands to reason that the creature pecks, painfully at times. Trina, always jealous of her lovers, hates Jill more than most. But why, Meghan quizzes herself, is Judith involved? She puts the questions out of her mind and starts attending to what Loren MacAnulty is saying.

'Big Money still overrides domestic laws, NAFTA and CER. None of your concern, my girl. You are in our employ. And I'm thinking this find might very well be one we keep under wraps.'

Meghan snaps open the instrument case, absently shaking her head. She runs the geiger counter casually over her own person. Its constipated click confuses her. 'Come here,' she orders. She stands him straight, and, starting at his feet with her ear close to the amp, she swipes the sensor over the air about an inch from his body. Again, the half tick. A cough.

'What is this, Loren? I don't understand,' Doctor Featherstone says meaning to worry him.

She puts the instrument down and reaches into the back of the jeep for a bag. Dressed in an overall the colour of the desert sand, she hauls the pack over her shoulder. Offering no explanation, she makes her way back to the site. When there, she crawls all over the surface of the disc, rapidly reassessing her first impressions. Disc, column or semi-sphere? The geiger counter reports exactly the same stifled burps, indicating, at least, there is not a dangerous level of radiation here. She removes other testers from her pack, and begins tapping and knocking and scraping, putting dust and chips in plastic forensic bags. She chisels out a specimen.

When Meghan Featherstone returns to the vehicle, the beaming MacAnulty is eating a sandwich.

'So give,' he pleads through a mouth full of food. 'Rutile, ilmenite, maybe zircon?' He would believe anything, this scientist. 'A bit of a comet or something?'

'I can't say with absolute certainty, but my guess at this stage is pretty bloody weird,' Meghan says seriously. 'You'll laugh at me. I have to get back to a lab to make sure. Hydrogen fluoride is the only known substance to eat glass.'

'Extraordinarily toxic,' Loren grins evilly. Destructive substances give him a rush like no other. For all his faults, Loren MacAnulty is unfailingly cheerful.

'So tell me the intuitive news first.' He hunkers down on the sand in the shade of the Jeep. Meghan removes her gear and arranges the samples carefully in a case for the purpose.

'What impressed the physicists about the Chernobyl disaster was the effect of huge heat on the sand and rock,' Meghan says as she packs up their camp. He laconically rises to help her.

Loren lifts the tent poles onto the roofracks. 'Go on,' he yells.

'Well we know the earth is a shell over molten lava, and is skin. Geologists have only ever drilled, what?, eight kilometres down?' She, too, shouts, as they move about.

'You know what? What we have here is one beautiful object that our lords and masters will be very happy with. Are, I can say. I described it over the phone. Couldn't help myself,' Loren MacAnulty, the lovable redneck academic, says deprecatingly. His lords and masters are probably CIA.

Meghan doesn't care. 'I don't know what burnt this soil. It happened quickly like a nuclear event, but fusion not fission.' Loren slams the back doors of the truck.

'But it is not particularly radioactive. It could be a fuel we don't know of,' he says as they get in the jeep. He drives.

'It could be natural, a kind of pinprick in the earth's crust, a pimple of the inner inferno, an emission on reaching what it would see as a cold atmosphere flattening out,' says the humourless Meghan. 'Or it could be evidence of a small alien craft, rocket-like, taking off vertically.'

He grins, the odder the better.

'I imagine that when I get to the lab and analyse this stuff it will be ordinary sand glass, with the geological constituents we have around here. The oldest continent out of water,' Meghan shrugs off zany conjecture.

'We could be looking at something that is scientifically spot on, an elucidating, genuine discovery.' Loren MacAnulty slaps his thigh.

'Which will make you and your company famous, Mac.'

'Yee ha.' A genuine cowboy. 'We might be getting closer to the answers: why we are here, and where we have come from and so on, the meaning of life.'

'The life of rocks, the life of the earth,' Meghan says earnestly. 'What about the locals? You don't care about the Australian government. What about the community here? We could be on a sacred site, but when one is working for the white man one hasn't got freedom of conscience,' she finishes primly. 'For the moment.'

'Point taken,' Loren floors the accelerator. 'Anyone tell you, you're a genius!'

Meghan Featherstone suddenly laughs at the absurdity of it all. Or the bumpy ride.

The sheds of the outback station, owned by a multinational pastoral company, come into view. After a polite tea with pumpkin scones with the manager and his wife, they take a fixed-wing aircraft back to Darwin.

Raptors and reptiles entertain Meghan's mind during the flight. With glass one would expect some refraction, some luminosity. All she can see is a dull greenish shape in the pindan, not even the clear circumference they had determined at close range. Her brain files this inconsistency along with the others. Organiser of data, paid for her excellent work on detail, she looks at her big hands. Alison once said that meant she should be a jeweller. She has funny hands, long, but chubby at the base of each finger, a life-line split in two. They pass over a settlement, shapes of new corrugated iron blazing the sun back up at them. Of course the locals will know we were here. The Aborigines probably know the green glass is there also, or some of them will. They will have the best explanation of all. Something mystical, mythical, religious. But it is not in her charter to ask them. Let's hope the company thinks to compensate them, but what does money do? Buy souls?

Raptors and reptiles, she is an enthusiast, has loved them since a child. She sees several whistling kites outside her window for a moment, and down below a flock of brown buzzards lurk around a camping ground. When they reach controlled airspace, Meghan is asleep.

My body was zinging after a work-out with my trainer. He stretched my tendons, pummelled my muscles, and merrily gossiped about one of the top female triathletes having an eating problem which he, in his wisdom, considered was actually a character problem. The girl was so self-obsessed she was a joke.

'How is it,' he questioned rhetorically, 'your sport is so full of weirdos, fanatics and der-brains?' He answered himself, 'Money and television, multinationals and advertising. And Mickey Mouse games. The real challenges are on the track, in the field and the pool.'

'For an aerobics chappy, that's a bit rich, Sweetness and Light.' I pointed out his hypocritical prejudice.

'Aerobics is for housewives. Bread and butter for me, darls.' Sean spoke, unfazed, as if he didn't take the aerobics classes himself; as if the housewives didn't adore him. 'It is not as though the girl was a gymnast. Anorexia among gymnasts, now that was a genuine worry. They have to stay young and pretty.'

'You're an ordinary misogynist like the rest of your gender? Aren't you?' I mumbled into the towel.

His verbal diarrhoea annoyed me. I tried not to listen. My cerebral pores had already absorbed the reality of fascist stupidity and racism in Australia with the possibility of ugly violence in the near future. Lack of generosity of spirit tends to get me down. Even my own. Detective work did something to satisfy a righteous zeal in myself, yet I needed self-absorption, focus, single-minded concentration to swim, ride and run, keep fit, have a chance of winning. Later it occurred to me that he was nervous about something, chatting thoughtlessly so as not to say what was on his mind.

On a dry part of the property which was bought to become Lesbian Nation, Ilsa lives above a lake in an old Bondi tram, set up on sleepers, and now chopped fuel has a neat place beneath the floor. A skinny crooked chimney puffs smoke from a pot-belly stove. The lake was a dam, a controversial piece of work at the time it was dug. The tram was pulled in under the scornful but amused scrutiny of radical gurls by the same unwelcome men, but not for Ilsa. Now there are wood ducks and cranes as well as other migrating birds. She keeps a conscientious record of them all. A brush turkey regularly scratches up her vegetable garden and generally makes a nuisance of itself.

'Endangered my fat foot!' Ilsa abuses the native fowl affectionately.

Ilsa Chok Tong is spectacularly chair-minded; she reads a lot. Books line the walls beneath the windows and make little towers on occasional tables. She has a wing chair and an armchair placed for the angles of natural light. A little kitchen is at the driver's end. At the back a bed hides in a muslin tent. Five kilometres by winding walking track connects her to Rory's house on Lesbianlands. Both women can trace their ancestry back to the same goldfields in Victoria. While the male O'Riordans still treasure their Eureka flag, Ilsa's father's family is part of the Melbourne establishment. Her mother is Latvian. Ilsa reads *The Accidental Tourist*, and then reads *Miss Macintosh, My Darling* and doesn't miss a word. She reads *The Dream of Red Mansions*. She also reads the science fiction and detective genres. But is equally entertained by chaos theory and quantum physics. She has read *Utopia* and *Herland*. Handy's *Gods of Management* and Plato's *Republic*. She reads legislation if she's curious about an Act and orders it through the mail. She studies the algebra of artificial intelligence, the biology of botany. She uses the common names of trees only to explain. She does not read Chinese, but both French and Latin are easy for her. When other gurls are getting high, Ilsa reads. She is tolerant and serene. Mostly silent in company, she can be impatient and passionate, high-handed and arrogant. She walks carrying a staff. Through *Lauraceae* and *Myrtaceae*, *Pittosporaceae* and *Urticaceae*, *Moraceae* and *Dilleniaceae*, today, she makes her way into the rainforest.

Ilsa comes across the fallen *Toona ciliata* that Virginia White is working on. Ha ha, she barks. She peers down the deep gully; not even modern equipment would get it out. The forms that both Virginia and the wood itself suggest unsettle her. Majestic and classic, evidence of hours and hours of chiselling, axing, shaping and sanding. What is the point? Ilsa loses interest and turns back.

Inside the cosy draperies of her den on dusk, she sits down and reads
Shakespeare, anywhere: the sea being smooth,
How many shallow bauble boats dare sail
Upon her patient breast, making their way
With those of nobler bulk! But let the ruffian Boreas once enrage
The gentle Thetis, and anon behold
The strong-ribb'd bark through liquid mountains cut,
Bounding between the two moist elements,
Like Perseus' horse; where's then the saucy boat
Whose weak untimber'd sides but even now
Co-rivall'd greatness? either to harbour fled,
Or made a toast for Neptune. Even so
Doth valour's show and valour's worth divide
In storms of fortune; for her ray and brightness
The herd hath more annoyance by the breeze
Than by the tiger; but when the splitting wind
Makes flexible the knees of knotted oaks. . .
Ilsa decides to read *Troilus* and *Cressida* from beginning to end. Aloud and
alone, tomorrow among the acacias.

A high carbohydrate meal, piles of pasta. To bed early, up early.

A phone call from Meghan Featherstone's ex-girlfriend came just as I was
about to retire. She dumped some pretty dire emotional baggage on my ear-
drum, which continued to vibrate for some time afterwards. Unlike the nose,
the ear does not share tissue with the brain, and words themselves don't
necessarily convey factual or logical truth, especially not when they're shouted
with vindictive spleen. When I replaced the instrument, totally flummoxed,
I had no idea whether this outpouring of swear-words was water off a duck's
back or heavy shit. For Meghan. It did strike me that if you were a well-off
lesbian living the ups and downs of serial monogamy, there could be quite a
few girls with whom you had lived long enough, who had a right to half your
assets. But this woman did not even give me her name or that of the solicitor
she threatened, a character who did not sound real at all, rather constructed
from American network TV.

Before bed I went through a few yoga positions. Then, sitting still,
emptied my mind by concentrating on the breath going in and out of my
nose.

17

. . . the Port Water triathlon . . .

On any ordinary day, Virginia is up with the birds, always using her body as much as her mind. For Cybil, rising out of her warm and cosy bed before light, dressing at speed, down at the paddock at dawn like a strapper or bookie's scout when the horses' breath is steam, it is special. The quest for the best of the best, the Aussie battling competitive spirit starts in the playground and ends in the bronzed god of the surf, the Ironman, she reads in the Paradise Coast Triathlon Club newsletter. She notes the times of the winners in last year's event for each age and sex group. Virginia overhears technical jargon and talk of tactics, the instruction of coaches, the encouragement of friends, lovers, spouses, kids and family. She senses the nervous anticipation of others as she puts her old Malvern Star on the stand. She marvels at the professional bicycles with their elbow-rests and spokeless wheels. She listens as an official spells out the rules.

Cybil loves to hustle. She is all coquettish charm as she takes bets from doctors, dentists, mothers, sons, gamblers, health nuts, used car salesmen, fishers and gawkers. Having aroused the attention of the officers at the PCYC tent, she manages to laugh off her illegal activities as a bit of harmless fun but she wasn't going to tell the cops who was who or how much. What could they do? Give the money back? To whom? Five dollars here, ten dollars there. Keep it? What about the form of the runners? Doesn't matter, she will take any bet; against the time, against the field. She allows the punters to suggest their odds, except in obvious cases where she has to cover her stake; in other instances she cajoles folk to risk a bit. She rakes in the money and writes slips, tearing the pages from a receipt book with a flourish, all signed CC. Making the most of her brush with the law, she comes away with policemen's bets. She gathers in quite a few dollars against her dark horse with the rusty bike. Into the romance of running numbers, she scurries about with her leather pouch and tickets in her hat. Busy as a bee.

Whether out of blind loyalty or knowledge, the gurls back Virginia, though. Cybil won't take a large wager from them. Her odds are short on Margot Gorman in the open section. She has a quick chat with Tiger Cat, glances at the pupils of her eyes, takes in the six-pack of muscle between the two pieces of her outfit and shortens. Anyone from out of town is an automatic favourite. Virginia, amused by her industry, sits by her bike and daydreams until it all begins. Looking forward to the sheer fun of competition, her mind is more relaxed than it has been in months. The tension of younger women around her recalls her trepidation before her opening in a lovely sculpture park south of Perth. The exhibition was composed of abstract pieces that she named after parts of the human body, formed from chunky jarrah. Giant elbows, shoulders, foot and knee, the smallest three cubic metres. The nervousness she felt then, even though she had a commission—or was she nervous because it was commissioned?—she doesn't feel now. Sensing failure, she prayed the wood itself would save her skin. The black sculptures were scattered around on green acreage with white-limbed gums screening the modern gallery where her drawings, her aesthetic philosophy, her notes and photographs were mounted in frames. It happened to be a success. The toast of the town and ecstatic, the artist herself saw a dismembered giant-woman, Gaia in bits.

The man with the megaphone is speaking. She strips down to her Speedos and has a number painted on her thigh and upper arm.

The Port Water triathlon was 750 metres swim, bicycle road race eighteen kilometres, and the foot race ten. Sean's cynicism about those young athletes who take triathletics too seriously contrasted with my envy. Although the sport began in 1974 in San Diego, California, I did not start until I was in my thirties. Full of zest and charisma. Great for television, specially cable. Gorgeous competitors, not wearing many clothes, plenty of places for advertising logos on the buoys, the clothes, the barricades, the tents and hospitality marquees make the companies happy. Today plastic colour flapped in the fresh breeze. State Emergency Services personnel in bright orange and red did point-duty, on the water in blow-up life boats, on the road in fire trucks and rescue vehicles, and on foot around the bike enclosure and running course. Spectators were a pretty fit mob themselves, casing the sport for a hobby? You actually don't get a good view of a triathlon if you are there to watch. Women are of particular voyeuristic interest, but I think they're just as attracted to the beauty of the boys' bodies too. Australians, a journalist wrote, are exceptional at it. And he was right. It might have started in California, officially, but it's quintessentially Australian. We have the climate, the lifestyle and the culture for it. Coastal country towns and tourist destinations host different series and championships during the season. The ocean backdrops make great vision too. Big names are always threatened by newcomers with the lights of future prizes in their eyes. It's egalitarian, and hard at the top. Someone like me, on a good day, could take out a triathlon.

Specialist bikes have narrow hard tyres like compacted rubber. They have aluminium frames or light steel, broad aerofoil moulding and plenty of room for advertising, suspension seats, worth a lot of money. Tiger Cat had a new one! Handlebar rests, long tube drink holders in the middle of them, so there is virtually no movement of your head while racing if you want to wet your whistle. Mine is a good road-racing bicycle, with a detachable elbow-bar for the crouch and balance adjusted to my style. Tiger Cat was at the gym the other day, batting her eyelids at Sean Dark. He prefers to perve on young boys. She is the type of woman who achieves power through sex. Cat fucked the men at the academy, not because she was a nymphomaniac, as they said, but because, as she said, she was claiming power as a woman. She does the seducing, hence she is proud. Cat enhanced her feline name for the television show *The Gladiators*. And kept it. But why is she hanging around? She said she left the Police Force years ago. She said she was competing to give me a run for my money. Wearing her beach volleyball outfit with enough advertising showing off her midriff, she was strutting her stuff. She looked the part because she was the part; dedicated to her body; on the same wave-length as the cameras and the viewers in their lounge-rooms. Trim, taut and terrific from all the power work, sun-lamp tan and blonded hair corrugated like a male lion's, curled into wrinkles, everything is in proportion, except her eye sockets, which are too close together and too small. Incredibly, the eyes seem to swim inside the lids. Gives me the creeping willies. Bitch. She was prowling around the lesbians, talking the talk. To give the gurls their due, they didn't look impressed.

Rory and crew were there in the park in the dawn light, setting up a picnic breakfast. Had they all come to watch me compete? Shy of the bike paddock, looking the same, even though hair might be long, drippy or dyed while others were bald, or so unkempt they wore dreadlocks, dressed in unironed, darkish coloured clothes. I noticed one of Rory's mates had entered the race. A lesbian-of-the-lands oiled the chain of a rusty five-gear ladies bike, wearing a woolly, striped poncho over togs with Australia in caps across the bum. Club triathlons attract all sorts of competitors in all sorts of costume, some with mountain bikes, a hobby characterised by enthusiastic amateurism. Like the city-to-surf in Sydney, they all have their own goals. It might only be to finish. About five of us were on the professional female circuit. According to the local TV station, I was the favourite. My riding slippers are already attached to the pedals, I checked the clips were secure. I lined up my Nike Airs neatly for the run. I am as fast with lacing as I am with changing tyres, but I don't like having to do either. I chose and used the Velcro pair.

Sweetness and Light hovered around, side-glancing the lads. Rory came over and I asked distractedly where she stayed.

'Got the gurls to gather after a night of luxury in the Coast & Country Family Motel!' she responded cheerily. 'Some dykes who were at the Orlando Ball also stayed there. They're here to help decorate the Gay and Lesbian Mardi Gras float, and when Dee asked how long they had been dykes, they said, totally affronted, "We're not lesbians, we're gay"!'

Sean laughed, and informed us that he was going over to the float when he was finished here. But I was psyching myself up to win. Rory slapped her daydreaming mate, 'Good luck, VeeDub,' and wandered off. Winged Victory gets a small invocation as a bit of a ritual before every race from me.

The marshal with a megaphone called all competitors to the jetty. Tiger Cat had greased her hairless limbs. Virginia, I remembered her as Orlando, was all skin and bones and stringy knots of muscle and veins. Goose-bumps, hairy legs, huge feet and hands, rubbing herself. I smiled. She whispered, 'I feel like a kid again,' and grinned. Several young ironwomen horsed about. I stretched. The instructions. The gun. For the first twenty metres of a triathlon, bedlam in water, other swimmers' splashes get up your nose, the jostling for position is brutal. By fifty metres, the ones with a chance are hitting their strokes and you have a moment to look around. Tiger Cat's swimming was all shoulders and paddle-steamer arm action. She was beside me, to my right, my better breathing side. I decided to breathe to the left every third stroke and the right now and then. It slowed me a bit but I kept my rhythm. Having racers in front of me gave me a route to the first buoy. I ignored her antics, figuring they would wear her out before me. For all her pretence, she had trained for this event.

When they dive from the pier into the marina of the Resort Yacht Motel, and swim straight out to the first buoy, Virginia feels the bliss of a moment in linear time. Light, afloat, as the weight of the past and the future lifts off her shoulders, leaving her free to roll them through the smooth brine of the estuary, totally involved in the present. She spreads her toes. Her webbed feet flip her along like an outboard motor and her knotty hands, muscled by woodwork, throw bowls of water back with ease. Her arms skim the water like gulls' wings. In the long stretch to the second buoy she overtakes all in front of her. She has to pause to gauge her way: another length and then straight back to land, she remembers to concentrate, and goes for it.

Confined by the conditions, the course, she is unfettered. She is not mad. She is in tune. She is so thoroughly in tune she busts through the melody to the rhythm of chords. Within the safety of the race, having to make no choices other than those she could execute, having nothing to do except go fast, Beetle, go fast. Go fast. She might have been racing Jeff when they were nine, or eight, or seven. They did it all the time, on grass, sand, rocks, sea and bikes, most of the daylight hours of their childhood. Taking spills and getting up, no tears, no adults fussing.

The gurls on the land see the water as a mess of splash and arms. When Virginia, hardly a ripple on the surface, breaks free, they give voice with uninhibited energy. 'It's as though she's swimming with flippers on,' 'Come on, Beetle,' 'Don't slack off, you mole,' they yell. 'Beetle, do it.'

Between the second and third buoys I spied a couple of swimmers a fair distance ahead. An iron-girl, myself and Tiger Cat were within five lengths of each other as we went around the last buoy. I looked up at the shore to choose my line and go for it. Rory and her mates were cheering. I couldn't believe it, not an amateur. She must be a mermaid. 'Beetle'? The short, compact body of the girl left the water neatly, immediately in front of me. She ran through the sand on her toes, thighs working beautifully. I did not push myself for this stretch. Two-thirds of the race to go. Tiger Cat passed me.

By the time we were wheeling the bikes for the road, I was ahead of both. Rory's friend was way up the hill. Bike was my best leg. I accelerated out of the company of Tiger Cat and the young pro. I thought I could reach Virginia on the downhill or through the tricky acute-angled turn into the factories. Legs pumping, all the rest of the body centred, I closed in when we came to the sharp corner, about ten metres behind. Her old bike handled nicely but was awful to look at. She rode like a kid. 'She's got to skid,' I thought. I calculated to stay on the bitumen even though it sharpened and lengthened the bend. She went right into the shoulder, through the gravel, no sign of using her brakes, no weight on her pedals, a brave lean into the curve from her seat effectively cut the corner, making up a lot ground through sheer, careless guts. She was happy, free and fearless. So balanced, she took her hands off her handlebars to glide down a slope and give her back a rest, casually pedalling. I passed her at that point and sprinted through the town, back to the bunting of the bike yard.

Slapping together the Velcro of the runners, I was ahead of the women when I began the last leg of the Port Water triathlon. Virginia just dropped her bike and ran barefoot; Tiger Cat and sponsored girls were right behind her. Three or four men were in front of me. I took the last of them as my mark and stretched my stride. The run was a straight two kilometres up to the breakwater, a circle through the surf club car park and back along the road to the last 100 metres in the park. I made the turn and could see where the other women were. The stocky girl with the glittering lights of future success in her eyes was running fast and scheming to overtake me if I stayed at my present rate. I more or less gave the race to her when I saw that. However, I upped my pace and was really pushing it when I reached the path to the finish line. I got a burst of barracking from the feral lesbians and broke down.

There and then, my Achilles tendon tore. Agony. I hopped, groaned and fell. The gurls ran to help me and officials screamed at them to get off the track. They kept egging on 'Beetle', as they helped me. I looked at her back out of curiosity as I lay, moaning. Her gait was funny, heels flinging outwards, the soles of her large feet black and leathery. Tiger Cat was puffing furiously to catch up to her. The little, serious triathlete from the Gold Coast broke the tape for the Open Women's event, but second place was so exciting it was ridiculous, Virginia, Tiger Cat, and one of the teenagers neck and neck.

The TV cameras preferred to photograph me in my distress than the place-getters; no doubt to get shots of the logos on my dress and towel. I felt like giving the shoes away. Two strong gurls armed me to Sean's table. He rubbed his magic potions into my injury, ice, warmth, ice, warmth. He made me drink something. It relaxed me. As I was being massaged, Rory came in and asked me how I was. Her sincere concern was touching. I developed a soft spot for Rory and managed to ask how Beetle finished to confirm what I had seen.

'Second,' she grinned. 'First in her age group by a mile.'

Sean affirmed that with a happy laugh, 'Yeah. The cat is positively spitting french fries.' He fluttered his hands as he hissed. With mischief. I laughed.

'I don't want to blame my track shoes,' I lied, 'but here, Rory, take them. If they don't fit you, give them to one of the gurls. Compliments of Nike,' I added bitterly.

Jody from the Gold Coast wins, Beetle second, the doctor's daughter beats Tiger Cat for third. Officially. The cardiac specialist and his family gather round, a tribe of beautiful people with two cars, the Beamer and the Range Rover.

Cybil Crabbe pays out with stubby fingers. She manages to score a good sum of straight dollars; having targeted some macho males, she flirts as they tear up their bets. Rory watches her with distaste as she strolls back to her crowd with Margot's expensive footwear.

'Hardly one of us,' she comments.

'I don't know,' boasts Ti Dyer, her two large dogs straining at their collars because the local inspector made her tie them up. 'She gave me twenties outright on the swim leg. So I'm laughing.'

Virginia White is chuffed. Dee grabs her for a massage before she sees the thunderous scowl of her girlfriend.

'So you bet on me, hey?' she asks, her head in the towel.

Dee says, 'I'll take a lesbian any day. You know me.'

Virginia exclaims, 'That was satisfying. I was totally inside my body, forty years of worry dropped away! No doubt, no ambition and absolute concentration.'

The gurls have a billy boiling on the gas barbecue, but the party-minded have already popped a beer. It gratifies Virginia to know that she has a fan club. It makes up for all those meets that Jeff and she went to together without their parents. She grins like a Cheshire cat. Their breakfast picnic is a distance from the sponsored area. Dee Knox gives Virginia a rub-down on a thin camping mattress. They are the only people in the whole place to sit down, let alone smoke.

'The speed did it, my personal pace did it,' Virginia goes on permitting herself to skite, knowing the put-down will come soon enough. 'If I let my mind wander I would have hit something or broken a leg. I loved you gurls geeing me up.' She smiles, now, with affection, and like a yobbo hero, she wants to punch the air.

Rory rolls a cigarette, and opines, 'Women are from the sea, as Elaine Morgan said in *Descent of Woman*.'

'Don't get serious.'

'Shut up about evolution, already.' Yvonne says, 'Let's celebrate.'

Dello and Maz turn up when the race is over. The presentation is at the local Bowling Club at half past eleven, two and a half hours after it finishes. Bea, Zee and Gig arrive with sausages.

Jody, the feisty girl from the Gold Coast, with the graciousness of winning, comes over to congratulate Virginia. She is tiny, maybe five foot one, a solid, tanned body. The lesbians clap her on the back and call her a champion. This good humour is interrupted by a thunderous Tiger Cat in her short vest top like a sports bra, flat stomach showing her navel dead centre and briefs like men's swimmers held up with a draw-string.

'Very form-fitting,' nods Bea.

Zee reckons, 'Don't know why she's got 'em on at all!'

'Hang on, that's not cloth, it's acrylic paint!'

Tiger Cat is accompanied by one of the 'sweepers', volunteers from the SES, in bright overalls, who was warning traffic at the factory corner during the triathlon.

'I'm putting in a complaint,' she states. 'To the committee.'

The gurls go silent. The official looks uncomfortable. Rory's hand plays with the stone in her pocket. Virginia is resting on the massage mat.

Dee, wiping the apricot kernel oil from her palms with a rag, asks, 'You're a cop, aren't you?'

'I was,' she says with dignity. 'This is not about politics, it is about illegally cutting corners. As this gentleman will attest, this competitor,' Tiger Cat points rudely at Virginia, 'went off the course by going up onto the verge.'

The gurls scoff and deride, 'Talk about sour grapes.'

'Sore loser.'

The SES volunteer is not so sure it was against the rules and assures them that correct and just procedure will be undertaken. He walks away.

'You cheat!' Tiger Cat accuses.

'What? Virginia cheat?' Rory closes a fist about the rock that Hope gave her and feels a surge of power.

'Nu-uh, mate,' Ti fronts Tiger Cat, 'You were just too chicken. Afraid you'd fall off your al-foil wheels.' Her dogs growl in sympathy with her aggression.

'You know,' Rory says with quiet menace, 'People who criticise others for something are generally considered guilty of that thing themselves. So Constable Loser, do you cheat?'

'Ask the marshals,' says she and storms off.

Sean put me on crutches for twenty-four hours. A tendon injury needed absolute rest, not strapping. Nor he would he let me drive, which meant I had to go across town with him to where the Spiders Coalition were putting the finishing touches on their Mardi Gras float. Bananas in Pyjamas at the Seaside, would you believe? Actually it was a fairly impressively decorated truck with lots of foam rubber shells and things. Lola Pointless was active, no Libby Gnash. Barry, the school-teacher, was without his boys, last seen on roller blades at the Orlando dance. Poofters and dykes in blue stripes trying on yellow heads in a fever of frivolous creativity amused me as I just sat and watched. Alison's two younger children were running around. Tilly said hello. Alison herself was a centre of interest, as she was reading palms. Maria sat on Neptune's throne, which would be put on the float at the last minute in Sydney; no Sofia. Pissed off about missing the Forster Minolta World qualifier, I did not feel like being socially out-going. I waited until Sean finished his fluffing around in a fug of self-pity.

18

. . . like a kid again . . .

'Dawn, for crying out loud,' Rory cries fairly loudly as Chandra is in the kitchen and she is sitting comfortably outside and taking in the view. 'Virginia was ageless. Her bicycle by no means state of the art! Although the frame is an old-fashioned female design, the gears are new. Tyres blown up.'

Chandra produces tea and listens.

'Margot and the others are ploughing up the sea smashing into the water and splashing. VeeDub is cruising. Hardly a ripple, then she rides in wet bathers, bare-headed, and runs barefooted. Near the end Margot tore her Achilles tendon. Reminded me of primary school, you know, dashing about with all the energy of insects. Margot has a beautiful body!'

'Yes,' says Chandra. 'She does.' Rory becomes expansive on Chandra's verandah, giving her a full account of the morning's event. 'There were no smells. I expected to smell sweat. By the river with mangroves on the other side there were not even mudflat smells or sea smells, strange. Port Water is so sanitised. Little treated pine walls separate the dirt from the sand. Glamorous pelicans in groups on the water. Moored yachts. A cheesy little meet, really. For Margot to injure herself.'

Rory just wants to keep talking about Margot and her sport. Chandra spins her wheels round to lift the cosy from the pot and pour some more.

'This cat-woman accused VeeDub of cheating! So I said, that must mean you cheat, sister,' Rory effuses. 'Like I thoroughly believe that, maybe not in the sports event, but you know, something? Margot's rival from the old days, Tiger Cat, is an ex-cop. We want to watch her. She is a worry.'

Chandra nods. 'Probably on drugs. How can you, Rory, trust one ex-cop and suspect another?'

'You've got to meet Margot,' Rory offers as an explanation.

Chandra nods. 'I have.'

Rory grins, 'See what I mean?'

'I don't know.' Chandra suspects the prejudice of sexual desire beneath Rory's argument.

Rory looks at her for a moment, recalling the ferocity of the barney with

Meghan. Chandra is prepared to lose friends over principles; to use her fists, something Rory herself could not do. But she goes on, enthusiastically.

'One chap was running alongside his bike, having had a puncture, later I saw him finish, second last.' Rory continues, laughing. 'He had plainly fancied himself. His buzz seemed higher than most.' Rory puts her cup down, 'Virginia second, hey!'

'You don't know Virginia if you don't think she's competitive,' Chandra says sharply. 'Takes one to know one.'

'Yeah, I suppose,' Rory frowns; in fact, she hadn't thought of Virginia as competitive at all.

'I have competed in equestrian events,' Chandra confesses.

'True?' Rory makes a show of looking at the lovely dappled grey horse in his paddock. Rory doesn't really know Chandra, tries to cover her nervousness with talk, but Chandra says quietly, 'Come inside. I want to show you something.'

Virginia White has her back to the window of Cybil Crabbe's flat with its ocean views. She is great, feeling inviolate. Plenty of cyclists tried to cut through the sharp bend as she had and some had come to grief. Virginia, at the presentation, was given a caution about not wearing a helmet, but the placings remained the same. A triumph. Gurls were thrown out of the club for unruly behaviour. Although Virginia is excited at her success at the triathlon and the progress of her artistic vision, from the dismembered Gaia to the group composition, and full of herself, she does not feel she deserves the shit Cybil is laying on.

Virginia laughs, and boasts, 'You're just jealous.'

Dangerously vicious, Cybil tries to rattle her with insults Virginia cannot believe. 'I'm not the one who's jealous.'

'What do you mean? What's this all about? You're acting like you're guilty of something. You're picking a fight. It doesn't make sense to me,' Virginia leaves the windowsill to stretch out on the sofa. The poodle sleeps in a tight ball in the armchair, making a pair with the woolly cushion. Cybil is trying to make her feel like a loser.

After niggling and bickering most of the afternoon, eventually Cybil loses it, screaming, 'You hate women.'

'Me?' Virginia cannot imagine what is motivating such violent passion. Cybil had made her money. Virginia proved herself an Amazon! At fifty, she was as brave as a nine-year-old. But Cybil likes a stouch.

'Women's culture is in the realm of your imagination, somewhere between Amazons and aliens. In the clouds. You don't care about ordinary women.'

Cybil ends her tirade with, 'You actually hate women! You won't admit it.'

'I don't hate women, they just disappoint me sometimes,' Virginia says patiently, assuming that beneath the verbal abuse her girlfriend is trying to find her own truth. 'I do judge and analyse other women because I want, at least to see, the ideal. It's so easy for women to work in the male cause without, sometimes, even knowing it. All that good lesbian energy nurturing gay men, for instance.'

The relentless argument goes around in circles without Virginia believing that Cybil is mean-minded. 'What have I done?' she asks. 'Do you really think only victims and losers are real women? Well, I'm here to prove they're not.' But like a spoilt child playing its mother's patience to the end of the tether, Cybil keeps at her, following her about the cage of a flat. Virginia tries to prove strong women are not trying to be men.

'You are a hypocrite,' Cybil goads. She finally hits the mark. Virginia cracks.

'A hypocrite?' Virginia yells. 'I've already been called a cheat today!'

'You are a hypocrite because you are the most androgynous woman I have ever known! You're practically masculine. All that women's culture stuff, it's a pipe-dream. You don't even know what it's like for women. You are really boring. Not living in the real world.' Cybil expresses her humiliation, 'Getting us chucked out of a club!'

'Is that all? But, as I was saying,' Virginia continues, 'lesbians who think androgyny is the way to go, I mean as a philosophy, are fucked. It white-ants the foundations of whatever female culture we have. You let the male into your head, you have a spy there.'

'I felt so embarrassed, bunch of drug-taking, drunken deros: how can you call them your friends?' Cybil cleans a clot of lipstick from the corners of her mouth. 'You don't care about me. Or anybody else but yourself.'

Virginia refuses to cry, but her fists want to smash something. 'I do. Who don't I care about? There's nobody I don't care about. I have to care. I can't create unless I care. I care deeply.'

'You don't care about your mother. You dismiss her along with your father, you call her a lush. You care about your brother more than your mother.' Cybil keeps winding her up, pumping her handle like a spinning top.

Virginia throws a plate against the wall. Suddenly, definitively. Puddles takes off, yelping. The shards of crockery, globs of dolmades and pink dip sticking to the plaster give Cybil some measure of satisfaction. Although not one for cleaning, she makes a show of picking up the pieces she can see. She loosens her pressure. Virginia watches her as she giggles at her poodle running up and down the doona on the double bed, yapping. Now, having made

Virginia angry, she is quite happy. Turning soft and longing, she kisses VeeDub on the mouth; and the Amazon melts. She then gossips about gurls she hardly knows; curiosity without judgement, but without tolerance either. Cybil is a postmodern being.

'Catherine Tobin,' Cybil conveys, 'works for a gay and lesbian merchant bank, an investment business. The idea's not bad, but I would not sign over my hard-earned to that one. She said she is really successful, getting more women every day.'

'We don't have any money. Why she was hanging around us?' Virginia says, sighingly. And begins cleaning the wall.

Cybil chats about Tiger Cat. 'Her latest client is from the land, she said. Judith Sloane is interested.'

'That weasel,' Virginia scoffs. 'Every time I pull a weed I think of her. Well, that makes me feel better about the body-builder.'

Cybil resumes her attack. 'What's wrong with this Judith anyway? From what I hear, she is a vegan, she sings right-on songs. She is politically correct. You're all about political correctness.'

'All bullshit,' Virginia decides. 'She makes me so angry it has kept me from topping myself. At times.' Virginia becomes impassioned as she remembers her rages. 'Fucken Sloane Ranger, Poms, what a fucking arrogant race of barbarians! It's the colonial attitude. See something? Just go and own it. Self-serving shop-keepers, Uriah Heeps with their grasping fingers and abject sly classism, why am I cursed with their bloody awful language?'

Cybil, sitting solidly in her armchair, refuses to be amused. 'Aren't you one to talk?'

'We are nothing but custodians of the earth we stand on. We can't have anything, except respect and gratitude. The perfidy of Poms,' Virginia tosses the sponge into the sink from the doorway, 'is the idea of ownership. They stole it in the first place.'

'See! you're prejudiced. You're not perfect yourself. You're prepared to muddy her name.' Cybil's little dog leaps onto her lap. 'What are her crimes?' she asks.

'Plenty of gripes.' Virginia has difficulty knowing where to start. 'The feral pigeons she's got. Her fucken sheep. The bloody honeysuckle, it's destroying the bush. Oh, you name it. She's got no damn soul.'

'You should hear yourself,' Cybil calls and hears what's left of the plate clatter into her kitchen tidy. 'Listen to yourself. Judith's just a moody feminist whose day is done. They can't change.'

Virginia does listen to herself and doesn't like what she hears. 'Don't make me say things I don't want to. I'm feeling unreasonable. Unlike you,

I don't like this constant arguing.'

'Admit it, feminism is a dead horse,' Cybil laughs. She reaches across the arm of the chair for the phone. 'I'm going to order Thai take-away. They'll deliver.'

Virginia gives in. 'Speaking of dead horses. The Clydesdale. It happened years ago,' she begins.

Cybil listens.

'We came across the skeleton of the horse, Trivia and I. It had no teeth in its mouth. He had one tooth left in the back set when he died. This noble beast. He was a magnificent animal. I remember her leading him up the track, young, handsome, gentle.'

'Who?' Cybil, when hearing women's stories, wants names.

'Judith. He had the eye of a gentle giant, though he was not trained. She was going to break him in herself. He would drag the logs in from the forest for her log cabin. He would not need grease for his clutch, oil for his differential, nor need a road through the trees. He wouldn't spoil the ferns or elk-horns. All the little girls could line up along his back and get to primary school ten kilometres away. There were plenty of kids on the land then.'

'Really?' Cybil is surprised. Virginia's speech is sarcastic. 'Sounds like Judith's heart was in the right place.'

'He was probably cheap because he wasn't broken in,' Virginia continues. 'Little girls never lined up along his back. He never got his feet trimmed or his teeth filed. Judith pronounced that he was a loner, that he liked being wild. Domestic animals have to be fed. They're like us.'

'Disillusioned, probably,' Cybil comments, glancing at the time and looking about for her purse.

'On the day we found the skeleton, Trivia stood there feeling her own regret. She said she should have done something. Now it was too late. Far too late. One tooth.'

'How sad,' Cybil says softly, flattening the note, ready for the doorbell to ring.

'It was,' Virginia nods. 'Feel the truth, and remember this is what Trivia said.'

'Go on,' Cybil urges.

'There were always vegetables in Judith's garden. She was a star, she had groupies. They would come from the city and dig and plant, and feel privileged. The food was left to rot, never even given away to gurls, her neighbours. Nor even to the horse. Like all her bullshit, she probably didn't have a clue. Yet she wouldn't let anyone else have him.' Virginia is still furious. 'Meanness is pathetic. Never feel sorry for a mean person. It is not wise. They shall not have that as well.'

'Why didn't you just take him?'

Virginia shrugs. 'A number of times I asked her. I would have trained him well, and fed him hay and oats. Horses are not native to this country. It is cruel to set them free. For the land and for them. Hard-footed animals destroy the bush. Compact the soil. Trivia agreed. But I kept away, then I had good manners, timidity in the face of Judith's power games. The big horse eventually died of starvation and neglect. I hope her dreams are rotting in her chest.'

The bell rings. Cybil leaves Virginia with her memories and regrets while she goes down the stairs to the security door with the cash and returns with a plastic bag of sealed containers. She makes room on the table and puts out plates and chopsticks.

Cybil and Virginia converse as they eat, Cybil gently teasing out the details and Virginia talking.

'I don't mind killing. If I kill the right person,' Virginia replies to Cybil's curious question.

'The right person is the absolutely innocent or the absolutely guilty, yeah?' Cybil eats energetically.

'True,' Virginia nods. 'I could deliver euthanasia.'

'We're not god, we're not the judge.' Cybil wipes her hands with the paper serviette.

'If I'm free you're free, we cannot police each other,' Virginia jokes. 'Beware, liar in your lair. Vengeance is mine. I watch and wait.'

The food is finished, the evening wears on. Cybil switches again. 'You have hatred and racism of your own, VeeDub. And you won't shut up.'

'It is not racism when you're talking about the English.' Virginia is on her feet, pacing the confined space of Cybil's flat.

'You've often boasted that you are as free as your twin brother,' Cybil probes with an untruth. Cybil's refusal to understand makes Virginia frustrated.

'I'm not. That's the point. I don't want to compromise and serve like most women, mother, whore, nun. Not of my own free will.' Virginia remains patient. 'Jeff has, like the English, all the privileges of being intrinsic to the hegemony.'

'Sounds like the politics of envy to me,' Cybil interrupts. She feels her power is secure when she can get Virginia to throw something. Or shout. Having this power proved again with Virginia punching the wall, she begins to cry. She wants Virginia to cuddle and comfort her.

The weeping doesn't move Virginia; this time her heart turns to stone.

'You are the hypocrite,' she says, provoked. 'It is easy for you to claim the pain. My frustration is like a padded cell with no lining. I hurl myself against the walls, and the walls are muscled monsters with no compunction.' Angry tears sprout from her fierce eyes and she becomes passionate. 'The powers that be truly want me not to exist,' she insists. 'They taunt me with their ignorance and the next bit of horrendous behaviour. Mine pales beside the brilliance of their violence, and you don't care!'

'Yes, I do,' says Cybil, softly. 'I care too much.'

'What?' Virginia listens to Cybil relent, ratonalising her outburst in terms of the Change. 'I don't control the chemicals in my brain, let alone the bloody hormones. Menopause, what a ride!'

'Come here,' begs Cybil.

'Look, I can't stay in this place,' Virginia says, feeling trapped and burdened by the duty of work, by the onus of love. 'Because you're not admitting your part in it.'

19

. . . ghostly rapists . . .

Sofia frantically looks up fish recipes. She has Mrs Beeton's *All About Cookery* and the Heart Foundation's *Guide To Healthy Eating*. She is attracted to the recipes Mrs Beeton tactfully parenthesised: Jewish Dish; Passover Dish; Jewish Invalid Cookery. Her duty to Maria whips her into action. She will feed her low-fat food. Intending, at the outset, to get Maria's weight down, she now worries about '2 pennyworth of gingerbread' and the meaning of the word gill. Showing off, obsessed, she begins talking aloud, assuming Maria is within earshot.

'The Jews have different tastebuds, chosen ones, I suppose. Apart from the gingerbread with fresh salmon, it combines cayenne pepper with golden syrup. We shall eat kosher from now on. Good prana. God will whisk the obesity away. No sacrificial lambs. No cloven-hoofed meats . . .'

Maria, seated in an armchair, shuts the irritating chatter out. All she can imagine is a kitchen blasted by Sofia's culinary efforts looking as if a bomb hit it. She would not only have to clean up, she would have to be grateful. She does not want to eat fish and salad, she feels like fried tomatoes and lamb chops and two slices of bread tossed in the hot juices. And she wants to do it herself in a kitchen scrupulously clean and efficient. As Sofia calls out about exotic pairing of flavours, Maria thinks wistfully of bubble and squeak, of mashed potatoes browned in a hot pan, of bacon slowly manufacturing the pig oil that makes everything taste so satisfying. She recalls a moment in a film, possibly *The Color Purple*, or maybe one set in South Africa, where the black woman who slaves for the whites is allowed to take home bacon fat. A solid white block. The shot of the pure lard portraying contrasting possessions brings tears of sympathy. A victim of bathos, Maria feels the sentimentality as hunger in her stomach.

Maria must not allow herself to get depressed. Andrea Dworkin's *Intercourse* is the book on her lap, but she needs science-fiction, fantasy. She imagines she could give up smoking and drinking before escapist reading. But not, she sighs, food. The genre novels on the table are due back at the library today.

Sofia, having decided on the Jewish recipe for her expensive fish, is manically throwing together the ingredients for gingerbread.

Oh no, Maria heaves herself up and glances around the surfaces for the car-keys.

Respecting that Sofia in these moods is highly sensitive, she speaks politely. 'Well, a kosher lunch will be another two hours I suppose. I have to take the books back. All right?'

Sofia doesn't hear her until the front door slams, when Maria's words echo in her brain a clear repetition. She is panic-stricken. 'Maria, Maria. Where are you going?'

Like a yacht with heavy ballast and a light wind in its sail, Maria is not about to turn around. 'Library,' she yells.

Sofia strung like a violin string could spend money in ludicrous amounts. 'We are aristocracy! We have to have the best, even if in genteel poverty like Anastasia Romanov.' Sofia, having spent some of her childhood in a wealthy diplomatic family, has wintered in Moscow. An adventure with Jill and Margaret in Rosemary's car to the Fishermen's Co-operative down the coast at the weekend turned into a spree. In the fridge are crabs, lobsters, cod, and being dealt with now, a large chunk of salmon. Monday morning came and Sofia was down at the deli before Maria was out of bed.

Now there is caviar, as well as pâté and cheeses, bottled eggplants and artichokes, exotic spices and herbs, but not, Maria noticed with a groan, one slice of cold meat. No one to turn to, not even Margot. She trusts Gorman because she understands confidentiality. She won't talk, and is, possibly, the least damaged woman in her circle. Alison, who intuitively reads her palms, perceives her needs, is dangerous. If Maria confronts Sofia with her extravagance, all this beautiful food, fit for a banquet, will end up all over the house, not a shred would be left to eat. Tonight it will be loud music and seriously sadistic sex, if past experience is anything to go by. Everything has drama, importance. Small things have exaggerated significance when Sofia is the heroine in the art-house movies in foreign languages that she loves. Maria turns the key in the ignition and revs the engine to warm up in the old-fashioned way. Then, using only the rear-vision mirror, she slowly backs the car out of the yard and into the street.

Sofia is a genius, her mental associations so fast the strings of insights come in rhymes. In riddles. Although life is full of humour and commitment, the relentless entertainment tires Maria. She does not mind doing the work of cleaning up, tidying and keeping the ship steady. Really. She is committed to Sofia's welfare. The dysfunction is a fault of society, other women must rescue and care. No one else will. Maria has been through it many times, helped many women. Sofia cannot take extra stress. But something must have happened to bring it on. The Internet? Sofia has been known to blow light globes when she enters a room. Screens emit electro-magnetic radiation, disturbing the delicate balance of chemicals and neurons in her brain. She lives on the edge, her nerves cannot take strain from the outside world. It was okay, yesterday, for her to go for a drive. Maria spent the day with Alison. Was it the girl who had gone to the toilet and never come back? Maria thinks. But Sofia did not know this girl before. No one knew her. Dello and Maz had picked her up hitch-hiking and, as is Dello's way, invited her to stay and party. Dello runs Maz through the ropes of sexual jealousy as a game of keeping them together, making life interesting. Yes, a death, an accidental death of someone she was just getting to know would prey on Sofia's mind. Sofia loves new people on sight, later she is suspicious and scared, sometimes vicious. On that Friday, she was fine. Maria puts importance on death, as if drawn by a morbid empathy.

'I have you, Maria. I need you. I know you are always there for me. I am worried about your weight and I'm going to do something about it.' Sofia yabbered on in the car in the moonlit night. She had been clever with the cops, though. Maria waits for a train to pass in front of her at the level crossing. Then without warning she had been callous. Sofia switches mental tracks as a traveller changes means of transport, leaping from one obsession to the next. The obsession itself the destination, the being. Maria read Chessler's Women and Madness when it first came out. It is not Sofia's fault. Male power in families is reinforced by violence or its threat, by religion, by set moral and legal systems; even his absence gives weight to his point of view, ensuring his patrilineal line, his sexual rights. Some girls are denied childhood altogether by becoming sex objects very young while treated like little princesses by mild, smug and rich patriarchs. Maria is convinced Sofia suffered sexual abuse at the hands of the diplomat or a member of his family. Maria takes the direction to the coast, to gaze at the sea and think.

But before she sits in the car overlooking the ocean, she must get take-away food.

On the footpath outside the take-away, she meets an old friend, hurrying about her shopping. Maria stops Virginia White, who is always good for a rave if you can ever find her.

Maria grabs her arm, pleads, 'Sit down in the park with me, VeeDub. Tell me how you are?'

'You heard about the race? Yesterday?' Virginia fills her in.

They walk to a table beneath the Norfolk pines, and talk—the tall Virginia, thin and strong, beside the short, round Maria, breathing with difficulty. Virginia can unburden her woes on Maria, who, even if she doesn't actually understand what she is talking about, can absorb it all in the subcutaneous blubber.

'Then Cybil turned on me. An individual lesbian may suck out the very life force of her partner. It's never happened to me before,' Virginia prefers to take the incidental to an abstract, broader canvas.

'Unless her partner is prepared to ape the model of heterosexual perfection and be a wife,' responds Maria. She sits down, and, comfortable with generalities which disguise personal gripes, continues, 'provide, succour, listen, edit, admire, be a saviour. Long-suffering, or be a husband in virtue, loyal, faithful, bringing home the bacon, flattering, taking out to dinner.'

Virginia nods agreement, 'To holidays in winery valleys listening to classical quartets. Cybil would truly love that. But I have neither the time, nor the money.'

'In the 'seventies we thought we could break the mould. Create a new paradigm. Do it anyway,' Maria advises. 'Cybil's so sexy.'

Virginia means what she says. 'Where am I going to get the money for that sort of a trip? Borrow it?'

'Indulge yourself,' sighs Maria. 'Pairs of dykes, both working at shared projects, like gardens or businesses or in the arts or wherever, they seem happy just with each other. It is too easy to criticise.'

'True.' The last sentence is what Virginia expects from Maria. 'That's it, she doesn't share my art, but I don't choose that happiness. You disappear in the morass of the patriarchy, like one of those kids' games where you have to find Mickey in the picture.'

Maria, long past her own menopause, listens to VeeDub's account of her ups and downs with sympathetic humour. She doesn't bother to point out that she has never seen the kids' game she's talking about.

Virginia confesses, trying to understand herself. 'She says I get violent, in cycles. She says she sees it coming on. I get depressed, anxious, the darkness descends, then, she says, I let her have it. Not physical, I just get intimidating. Something inside starts to curdle. It feels like gastric juices gone awry, souring in my guts, right up my gullet so that I want to spew bile but I don't, I spill it in language. Dump it. Drop it. Like a hot pan of boiling fat. I am swearing at the same time, am furious that it has all got so out of control. I try to blame myself but that does no good whatsoever. Then I see her shivering in fear, spitting out defensive aggression like some lizard, crouched in the corner, threatened. I am not a violent person, Maria. I hardly know myself.'

Maria smiles. 'So, what's wrong with the wine-tasting?'

Virginia does not have to explain to Maria that Cybil is a sensualist. She recognises it as well as the fervour for art. Her passion is for politics. Maria can see their conflict with the clarity of one who is not involved, then, perversely takes the conversation to a different relationship situation.

'If a rescuer is in a relationship with the rescuee . . .'

'If the lesbian is a rescuer in a relationship with the rescued?' Virginia echoes and arches her heavy eyebrow with irony. 'The rescuer is killing herself. You get a mutual dependency situation where she has a stake in the other's illness.'

Maria goes on, regardless of Virginia's analysis. 'And, at the same time, she can't get sick.'

'But, she can get domineering. Or self-destructive,' Virginia puts in. 'Don't punish yourself.'

Maria tears her chicken leg. Virginia swigs her mineral water. A toddler runs ahead of a mother pushing a pram hung with bulging plastic bags.

'If the lesbian is working, preferably in one of the worthy fields, where she is paid, she can afford a partner, often a younger prettier one, who doesn't have to do anything except pursue hobbies of an artistic sort or a useless sort,' Maria says wistfully.

This, for Maria and Virginia, is funny. They laugh.

'Then they can be equal, as one is kept and the working one has an economic sort of power. The other one has emotional power.'

'Sounds co-dependent,' Virginia implies Maria has lost her. 'I'm spending far too much time in town staying at Cybil's. I have to go out home and work.'

Virginia, although she is not aware of it, reminds Maria of the good old days. The demo days. The roneoed rags put out with a lusty zeal to change the world. The dances. The music. The days when common purpose among women led to easy friendships.

'Hey, the dance the other night was good fun. Should be more of those!' she enthuses, sadly.

Virginia wants to give Maria something. Hope? 'Nevertheless, it's good to be us,' she says heartily. 'I wish you could see the work I'm doing. You are a woman who might appreciate it.'

Maria lies and smiles beatifically, 'Some day, some day.'

Virginia knows that with the obese state of her body now, Maria could not walk on the uneven ground to her house, let alone up a rainforest goat track through a rocky gully to get to her sculpture. 'I would make a great effort to get you there, you know that. You only have to ask.'

'Well, I will then,' Maria says firmly.

Virginia tells her where it is, how she found the tree on one of the steepest slopes, then flashes fire. 'But that is the weird part of it. There's this tremendous thing I have to do, but it's a ten-tonne secret. Even I cannot answer why it's inaccessible. It just is. And I'm free enough to make the choice. But only there. In the heart of Lesbianlands.'

Maria's eyes express polite regard for Virginia's words on the matter of her sculpture. But, as she truly does want to see it, she asks, 'When?'

'Wednesday? Why not Wednesday?' Nostalgia takes up no room in Virginia's emotional arena whatsoever. It's action, or nothing.

'I'm busy this week, but soon. Soon,' Maria promises. She sighs, and says, 'I have to go to the library.'

Goodbyes said, Maria pulls the remaining chicken leg out of the greasy bag and watches Virginia skip over the little chain fencing off vehicles from the lawn as if her stuffed back-pack was no weight at all.

At the municipal building, faced with prospect of a frantic Sofia, she knows why she came to the larger town. Maria decides to score for Sofia. It is, she rationalises, the lesser evil. Maria chooses seven fantasy novels to take herself into another reality, then drives up to the Hornets' Nest, where deals are done.

In the morning I could walk, but I couldn't train. Well, I had other work to do.

My visit to the property of William J. Campbell was unproductive in the extreme. The road off the Warrumbingle Highway is called Campbell Road and many mailboxes at the junction sport the same surname. There were also several Williams. After the first couple of cattle-grids, the land rose steeply. Conditions deteriorated quickly and my four-wheel-drive seemed to putter into the backwoods locale of some savage splatter-flick. The first house I found had twenty-odd starving, barking, under-sized cattle-dogs chained to the tank stand. It was difficult to figure which of the roofed structures was the residence. The canine chorus would surely have signalled the presence of a stranger. However, no show. I noted the address to report them to the RSPCA.

The second dwelling I came to was hardly bigger than a pump-housing with a tin chimney. There was a mountain of beer cans and bottles within throwing distance of the single door. Dogs, here, roamed free among rusting wrecks of cars and tractors. A man in shorts wet with recent piss staggered out. 'Got a beer?' was the only full sentence. All my questions were answered with a negative or positive grunt.

My third stop was a group of buildings. There I spoke with grossly over-weight women of different ages. Willie, I discovered, was probably out on the 'lease'. As the place we were standing was ringed with close hills, still in damp shade, I had no idea where her gesture indicated. A loose arm movement was all the explanation I was going to get. I hoped to hell Lesbianlands bore no resemblance to this. 'Crown land?' A shrug. 'Wilma?' They stared back at me. 'Barb?' The fat women closed ranks. Or didn't know where they were.

The track called Campbell Road was a travesty of the synonymous magnificent river. My clutch was lucky to survive it. Let alone my person. Younger male members of the family emerged from a side track in a ute chockablock with glossy rainforest ferns. Fancy footwork impelled by pure survival instinct on my part got me out of that situation.

I said, and I didn't stop talking, 'Hey fellas, I heard around these parts there was the—um—lesbians' land? I must be lost. Like heck, I'm always getting lost. I thought I could take a bush-walk? I'm just passing through the district. Like, hey, what's the name of the shire? How do I get to Stuart? Left or right down here. All these bush trails look exactly alike to me. It's nice to take in nature, get some air in your lungs. Actually, I was looking for some hippies, greenies, just to see how they live? Like I come from Adelaide. South Australia's dry. Like so different?' Et cetera. They were identical to the women in their dumb approbation of me, and let me go without moving.

Along the highway on the way back to the coast, I passed a butcher shop which had no companion businesses within close walking distance. A couple of kilometres further on was a cluster of houses and a general store. Pearceville, an old timber town. I pulled in to pick up a paper and a bottle of mineral water. As I was leaning on my car gulping, I noticed, set back from the road, the nice wooden architecture of the pub and a beer garden shaded by big trees. A deep verandah overlooked the river.

Still gazing around, I recognised some of the cars; the Larrikin's motor bike, Alison's Ford, a van and a big old-fashioned four-wheel-drive flat-back. I strolled within view. Rory, my client, waved. She called in tones to recall an obedience dog, 'Come here, Margot.' I reached into the car for my wallet and plucked out of the ignition the jingling keys. Half-way across the car park I hobbled back for my notebook.

The beer garden, with a view of the water rippling over pebbles, glamorous river-rocks and sparkling rapids, had equal access to both bar and car park. The lesbians were sitting around a table with a couple of empty bottles on it. Alison was there, being intense, curled up as if someone had punched her in the ribs.

The Larrikin, who had picked me for a cop the moment I stepped into the love-life of the community, to whom since I seem to have proved my credentials by doing under-the-counter work while being honest, treated me as her buddy. A rough diamond, probably common quartz, she thrives in company. I have never seen her alone. Tattoos trumpeted down her freckled arm and finished off at the wrist like a cuff. The paisley skin showed naked females on winged horses and wonder women in suspenders slaying dragons amongst the swirls. She wore a plaid shirt with the sleeves ripped out, her unwieldy hair knotted into half-worked dreadlocks. Known as anything from Larrikin, the Larrikin, the Rik to Rik, there were strict levels of formality with her: steps of familiarity, whereby you eventually earned the right to call her Rik. If you try Rikky, your continued health depends on her famously unstable mood. She was drinking with another who might have shared membership in the same Bikers' Club, who had one tattoo per arm and a number-four-blade haircut. Alison ignored my arrival but she looked drunk or sick. Possibly stoned. The Rik, with sudden and unusual largesse, offered to buy me a drink. I looked at my watch.

'A bloody mary wouldn't be too bad at this hour. Yeah, okay,' I said. There was no way Rik was going to pay for my drink, but she fancied the effect of saying it. I handed her the money. Everyone except Alison watched with ironic eyebrows until the exchange was complete. These women knew each other like family and controlled each other's excesses with similar mechanisms. Rory's image blended lesbian butch and hard-bitten country woman. I wondered how much effort went into it. Maybe none. She spoke with rugged toughness, which could have been genuine, and wore a sweat-stained, weather-beaten Akubra covered in campaign badges. She seemed so much a caricature of herself, that I smiled. She grinned back.

She, thoughtfully, inquired, 'How's your foot?'

I said it wasn't too bad. Considering.

Then she asked, 'When are you going to come and do my job, anyway?' She was not aggressive-sounding, rather a little urgent. 'You've lost your crutches I see.' All I had got from my trip up Campbells road was a vow in my vigilante self to notify cruelty to animals. But before I could expand on the immediate past, and tell them, gurls interrupted.

'Scared of the bush, Margot?'

'Frightened the cute Suzuki might get scratches on it?'

'Been too busy, have you?' The Rik was always sarcastic to me.

'It's the wild west up there. They've got guns and things.' Laughter.

Their shots were hitting close to the mark. 'I believe you,' I responded, recalling the farm ute with its illegal load of luscious orchids and ferns, and I said, 'Well. I better get around to it, hadn't I?' I picked up my notebook and went around behind Rory with my pen poised. 'Tell me how to get there. I don't want to get lost in them there hills, never to be seen again.'

They thought it was a joke.

'Here. Give those to me,' Rory commanded. She reached out for my imple-ments, found a clean page and began a map. When she had finished, I registered surprise with wide-open eyes. This map was a piece of art, with roads and houses and bridges drawn and beautiful handwriting. Not remarking on that, I wanted to be sure I knew exactly where to go. We went over it together.

'This anywhere near Willy's Campbell's lease?' I pointed to the line she'd drawn where the bridge damage was done.

'Hell no. That's way over there.' Her hand went over the edge of the book to the west. There was more Rory wanted to tell me, but all she said was, 'We have a real mystery on our lands, Margot.'

As we settled the appointment, I planned to take my off-road mountain bike and go into the hinterland that way. Rik was right, I didn't want scratches on the Sierra. I sat down next to her.

Booze. Drinking was a culture in the Police Force. Ironically, it was seen to be liberating for a female to get as blind as the blokes. The pressure to be a hard-drinking mate was enormous. If you didn't drink, you couldn't be trusted. If you were a woman, you had to drink twice as hard twice as fast to prove yourself. Drinking somehow saved you from being harassed verbally. Like any drug of addiction, alcohol has corrosive effect on the moral fabric of any group or individual. I know. I've been there. There were some bad car accidents. We knew what was to blame, but we kept our lips buttoned. That was part of our code, our pride. To be able to drink and do the job was a measure of your physical fitness, another contradiction in terms. You were hardly hale, but you had a kind of strength in numbers. The myth of mateship. Bonding. Tell me another.

When I was a teetotaller, I became pretty ineffective as a police officer because I couldn't get decent co-operation. In cleaning my act up I was distrusted, used, played with and finally moved sideways into the NCA. That was a two-edged sword but I am alive and I have memory. I didn't like getting drunk, but here I sat among another bunch of dedicated drinkers quite at home, opining about the nature of existence around a collection of empty beer bottles and dirty glasses. Philosophers all, the problems of the world imbibed then forgotten. I watched the light on the rippling river and sipped my tomato juice, taking a look at myself. Having a background in the pub scene, I know the ethos. Instead of leaving on rattling the pink ice cubes, I sat for a few moments, half listening, half thinking.

Alison spoke intensely about a film. 'Old man, Robert Redford, with yet another young female lead.' Conversation turned to the familiars of witches. Sofia had a toad. Laughter. The Rik was performing in the way Jill had aped the other night, but not nearly as well. Vienna at the turn of the century, a thickening of the voice.

'Sofia puts on the Austrian accent because she wants to be part of a milieu of intellectuals. Sad really,' said Alison.

Suddenly she looked at Rory, and asked, 'Do you think it was aliens?' Men, I supposed she meant.

'I don't know,' Rory shrugged. I was intrigued by her lack of censure. In an aside to me, she explained, 'The explosions.'

'Before I never believed in them, now I do,' a big, taciturn gurl called Bea stated.

'Before what?' I asked.

'Before I nearly died, but in my near-death experience I saw them. Glistening beautiful creatures. Standing about three foot tall in cloaks made of bats' wing.' She spoke adamantly. 'They said I could join them if I wished.'

The Larrikin expounded, 'Xena says they can transform themselves. From people to wolves, birds, mythical creatures with wings and four legs, to slithering snakes.'

Bea said, 'The Lands is a known landing ground. Plenty of dykes have seen them. Or lights. Just say, "Excuse me, I mean you no harm" and keep walking.' She laughed in an easy-going way.

'The black holes in space are portals,' supposed Alison, speaking with difficulty, 'They say black holes absorb matter. I say material transforms in the interface and you enter another reality. Virtual particles.'

The nature of aliens and the speculations of outer worlds with ghostly rapists, the Holy Spirit and Zeus as a swan over Leda and so on bored me. My mind wandered. I remembered Tilly's bruises, the phone call from Maria about Sofia killing her, then the second one, and dancing with Sean dressed as the Elizabethan queen, the tedium of the Meghan Featherstone job, two boys in the mortuary. I did not have time to be here. I had wasted my morning going to Campbells, I'd be lucky to be paid. These gurls were certainly crazy, talking about how dogs see extraterrestrials and ghosts and elementals, spirits of all sorts.

'Because Sofia has a toad she is a witch,' Bea finished complacently.

'Why?' Milt, the short-haired biker, demanded to know. 'They're fucken poisonous.'

The Larrikin slapped down her large glass after she'd drained the last of its contents. I grabbed her by the swirls on her forearm and tugged suggestively with a slight toss of my head in the direction of the bar. With elaborate courtesy I removed my hand from her tattoos and begged for a few words on the front verandah.

'What is it? Schooner of New?' offered I, and bought myself an unspiked tomato juice.

When we had seated ourselves on the hardwood benches and faced each other over a matching rough-hewn table perpendicular to the car park, I asked the Rik what she knew about the Spiders barbecue, who was there and anything interesting? I described the ugly headgear I picked up in the toilet. I managed to glean a few facts. Jill David was wearing a cap, but she couldn't remember what colour or whether any writing was on it. The kid who died had a cap on backwards and so did the big bitch dealing out the pills. Tiger Cat was dealing drugs?

A Scania 380 interrupted my interrogation. I stared at its heavy herd bars. The windows were dark-tinted. I looked down at the number plate, South Australian. I must have gone pale. The Rik started taking off Thelma, 'That man done gone and raped you down in Texas, Louise? Let's you and I just fire his little ol' rig and steal his hat.'

'Actually,' I started. I wouldn't confide in Rik, and skirted around my brain for an easy subject. 'Actually,' I repeated, 'it's more like that older movie, *Duel*, remember that? The guy gets shadowed by a huge, big, evil, anonymous semi on his way home.' I choked on my drink and began to cough and splutter.

'Shit, what's the matter?' The Rik was aware something had made me gasp.

I explained. 'I've seen it in West Australia, Northern Territory, Queensland, now here.' My throat was still catching. 'The first time I was on my pushbike. I'm sure, at least once, it deliberately tried to kill me.'

Rik scoffed with disbelief. 'It's just a milk truck. Or is the tanker on the back full of toxic waste? Get a grip, Margot.'

'In WA, it had double articulation, full of cattle aching to be out of there, crapping with fear and claustrophobia.' I took a swig of drink to clear my throat, to avoid the eyeless gaze of huge windscreen.

'Road trains are different from this vehicle. Gotta be more powerful,' stated Rik.

The rig drove out of the car park and headed west. My Achilles tendon started throbbing. 'No matter how strong we think we are, each one of us has a weak spot. I've known robust women turn to jelly when their thing happens. One cop I knew, it was traffic. Being held up more than three minutes really sent her. We'd have to go the long way round. She was okay, provided we kept moving. Apart from that, she was great. Brave. For the three months we were partners.'

The Larrikin laughed, derisively, 'I had to save Milt, over there, from her own sleeping bag. Screaming as if she were being bloody murdered. The fucken zip caught.'

'My weak spot is someone is always following me,' I maintained my point, seriously. 'This phobia is not exactly an irrational fear. I know too much, and they want to, silently, one day, give me an accident, good and fatal.'

'Why?' The Rik was all ears, a sucker for the excitement of undercover work and intrigue.

'So I don't blow any whistles,' I confided. 'There are too many of them, their contract with each other too clever to be spoken, their conspiracy a matter of a wink. A word and I'm gone. They're everywhere. I know the extent of their subterfuge and how necessary it is.' I exaggerated to Rik, to make a story of it.

The Rik got up saying, 'Truckers are okay. They gotta code.'

She removed a brick from a pile of papers on another table, took one, held it up and waved it at me as if it explained everything. She brought it over. It was a flier for the gun lobby. Shooters were gathering to protest the government's anti-gun laws. I glanced at the date and let the offending material float down. Rik picked it up again.

'Now tell me,' she was tapping the page with her finger, 'You would know one firearm from another. What's this?' She held out the picture, ostentatiously covering the caption.

'That's a .243 calibre repeating rifle. It's been picked up in suicides and domestics quite a bit,' I answered the quiz question.

'They love their toys. Need semi-automatics to protect our wives and children. And kill wild boar,' she said. The Rik was smarter than she let on.

'But actually they are used to shoot wives and children,' I argued. 'Murder-suicides. Easier. With guns,' I expanded, rubbing my heel.

'Yeah? What about gassing? In cars,' Rik seemed prepared to express the opinion that guns don't kill, people do.

'Bikies are fairly fond of killing each other,' I said.

'Me, I reckon,' she puffed with bravado, 'What a way to go. Pow!' She used her forefinger to illustrate. 'One clean shot, and it's all over Rover.'

'What's the word among the gurls on the barbecue night, the evening the kid died, Rik?' I leant forward confidentially.

The Rik eyed me with cunning, wanting to talk and not trusting me at all. I told her I was investigating this death.

She said, 'It's fucken fishy if you ask me. We left before the action.'

'The new regional commander, he wants a war. On drugs.'

'Marijuana. Or what? Big stuff like the shit landing on the coast?' The Rik probed as if she thought I had inside information.

'I don't know, but his track record is stacks of informers. It's the way he works. Surreptitiously, cards close to his chest. He's ex-Vietnam. Wouldn't be beyond him to order a massive helicopter operation out here.' I swung out my arms to include the distant ranges. 'Would he have a cause, do you think?'

'Last time they did that, it cost them twenty-five million dollars and they got twenty-odd arrests. No shit!' The Rik showed her contempt for that particular incompetence (or corruption) at the same time as being impressed by the figure spent. She mentioned the names of the growers caught, the pathetic size of their crops, and was about to spread rumours when I brought her back to my question. 'Dello and Maz said the girl was crying, freaked out. Maz has got a rescuing side to her. They think she was dropped out of a car, near the mangrove swamps, on one of the dirt roads.'

'You happen to know who owns a red Saab?' I shot the question without waiting for a beat.

'Nope,' she fibbed. 'Some rich bitch. You'd be surprised who uses and who deals on the coast.'

I nodded. 'Probably,' I admitted, too cool to ask for names. We went and joined the others, who were talking of explosions heard by the gurls on the land. Rory was having the least to say.

'I wouldn't put it past the old Judith to have ordered a booby trap through a catalogue to keep marauders off her crop,' the Rik proclaimed. 'Or Virginia.'

'You don't know Virginia. She is not like that,' said Rory.

'She frightens me,' Bea put in unconvincingly. It didn't look like much frightened Bea. But the Virginia I saw yesterday could be capable of anything.

'Nuh, she's like a big black crow all the little birds are shitting on to protect themselves or their tucker. That's how little birds get rid of them, you know. Flying above shitting on them.' Bea was impressed by this fact about little birds.

Virginia and booby traps! I noted on my pad. Judith?

'There are recipes for bombs on the Internet,' informed Alison. 'Any one could make one.'

I got up to leave. This was going round in circles. I said I'd be seeing them. Rory accompanied me. 'I'll meet you at the mailbox, Margot.'

'You bet,' I jerked my head efficiently. 'Saturday. Two things before you go; what's wrong with Alison? And, you wouldn't have any idea who owns a red Saab, would you?'

Rory folded her arms and leant her back into my car, and replied, 'Fortunately, she hasn't got any broken ribs. Just sore. And, I can't say for sure, but I think the car Jill's been driving around in, a red Saab, belongs to a woman named Rosemary Turner.'

'What happened to Alison?' I asked urgently. 'Beaten up? A car accident?'

'I'm not dobbing anyone in, Margot. She'll be all right.' Rory slapped the roof of the Suzuki and said, 'See you.'

I sat in the driver's seat and wrote: Alison bashed, who? T.C. dealing hard drugs? R.T., surely not? An attaché case on the passenger's side floor looked invitingly neat, even though I knew nothing much was in it except a few loose threads in the shape of papers relating to four diverse topics. Clicking it open I tossed the spiral notebook inside, virtually entangling the lot into one knot, to be dealt with later.

In the couple of hours' drive home Virginia White's mind carries on its tirade, only the tip of which she expressed to Maria. Virginia backs up and drives through the creek, over the rocks and up the slippery bank. She takes her reliable vehicle down the side track to have a chat with her neighbour, Rory. Rory is not home.

Virginia strides through the bush, stopping at her cabin only long enough to drop off her shopping and collect her leather satchel of tools. As she works the wood with her adze, taking out hunks of rot, trying not to interpret the shapes that emerge too soon, Hope gazes silently, wondering whether to make her presence felt.

Eventually she does. Although Virginia doesn't want to be disturbed, she listens to Hope's monologue of woes. The younger woman, her limbs as smooth as saplings, her tanned legs and arms streaked with mud, the bits of clothing that she wears green and brown, merges with the bush around her. Her being there in fact doesn't interrupt Virginia. She keeps working, forming female musculature as if Hope is posing for her. Rather than having to imagine the Amazon beneath her chisel, whether she is glancing back over her shoulder or staring intensely towards the future, Virginia will pause and look up as Hope moves enough to give the idea, to assist the perception of the secrets contained in the cruddy old wood. Each is in awe of the other. While Hope knows she is witnessing the great artisan at work, Virginia appreciates the mere youth of the girl, the naivety, the innocence, the flexibility, the language of another generation, like a patois from a province she can never visit. Understanding those coming after along the path of linear time is like stepping in the same river-water twice, impossible. She, the older, must bend backwards in the effort to impart the wisdom of the wiser. But the discourse is distressing. Hope's life, just the tale of a white girl struggling for identity, has a degree of suffering; coming to the sanctuary of a women's only place, to find lies told her, all the official documents of who she is in the world stolen. Gurls out to have a piece of her, why?

Virginia tries to wrap the detail up into packages of generalities which apply to us all. The childhood rape, the poverty, the perversity, the non-sense, the mother's betrayal and brutality, the lesbian sexual experience of being made into a slave, and so on. Horror. They talk as furiously as Virginia applies her sharpened blades.

'Women betray their knowing frequently. I don't know why mothers such as yours—such as mine, actually—do not protect their daughters with, at least, truth. Telling. Except to analyse their position from a feminist, theoretical position. That, dear Hope, requires that you read for yourself,' she says.

Hope lets go of her depressing tale, or rather, stops the sad past influencing her mood. She is actually happy with the present moment. Privileged. She, as Virginia forms her bold likeness out of jutting root, asks questions pertaining to the quest both are on, seeking answers.

'Mothers don't have the freedom the fathers have to give you a cultural place. They have their own worries, they're no better off, emotionally, than their daughters. Their selves are stolen, and, depending on the woman herself, she behaves in compensation of that. Whether violently, like mine. White-washing, cleaning, scrubbing, protecting the man, like yours.'

'Annihilation?' Hope smiles. 'Motherhood.' She climbs easily up into the sculpture of a boat and sits on the beam, two arms by her side supporting her balance.

'Spiritual annihilation, I mean annihilation of the female spirit,' Virginia lectures. 'Like, it not only includes massacre, murder, outside attacks. It's a job women do on themselves inside, because, for the most part, it is too hard not to. To survive. It's better to pretend.'

'You don't pretend,' Hope comments, simply.

'Yeah, but look at me.' Virginia implies she's a failure.

'What do you mean? I think you look great. And this,' Hope pats the timber, 'is brilliant.'

'Precisely.' Virginia picks out a chisel and digs out the curve of a cheek-bone and the hollow of an eye, and then stands up to stretch. 'Where am I doing it? Who will see it? I have come to a place I had to come, both physically, and, um, politically. Nowhere. Off the map. No money. No influence. No standing, even among the alternative world. You see, a sculptor influences culture in a really subtle way. Like you need a whole civilisation around you, for your expression—of self, of knowledge—to be understood. You're not a trail-blazer. Theorists and on-the-ground activists are that.'

'How do you stop the annihilation?' Hope leans back and takes an upside-down look at the bush.

Virginia changes to a broader chisel, and says, 'Just don't be annihilated. Don't allow it. You don't have to. But, it requires constant thinking and absolute honesty. You kind of attack each trial as you come to it, then try and practise what you know. Express your real self.'

Hope seems to have lost concentration as Virginia wants to go on thrashing it out. She says, 'I saw the aliens land last night. It was really clear. A bunch of lights. Right in front of me. Then, in seconds the craft was beyond the hills. I see tree spirits, too. Bunyips, dark shapes, sneaking about.'

Virginia's mood plummets. 'I don't see them,' she says grumpily.

Hope swings her body upright, hops along the log, slipping and keeping her footing in one fluid movement. 'Time to go,' she calls from the creek end.

'Hope,' Virginia murmurs to herself, 'has led me on. Nonsense, madness.' She goes to an untouched part of the fallen tree where all she need do is hack. She picks up her labrys and swings forwards and backwards, getting down to the red wood underneath the crap.

Virginia tires. She drops the axe and wants to cry, but boiling blood burns the tears into steam. Like sweat. Angry energy overtakes her like a sudden wave breaking, but she will not damage her work. With a discipline borne of faith, she leaves the site.

The rainforest, in places, is being choked by lantana, an introduced species gone rampant. She slides down the mossy slope to a hedge of lantana. At the weed's scratching edge she digs its roots with her fingers; with the power of her arms, planting her feet, she pulls and yanks and hangs on with all four limbs, a monkey of fury. The large dynamic weed begins to loosen. Blood makes her grasp slippery, but she wants to rip this thing out of the crumbing soil of the hillside. She crawls belly-wise, following every lateral root fighting its hold on rock and ground. She hurls herself at the new sprout. Her weight alone dislodges the huge bush from the precipice. She is glad of the danger. More of the same species smugly creating erosion feel her weight. With fists, elbows and knees hooked around the stinking, abrasive spines, suddenly, she falls. Together they fall into the next lantana bush. She crawls through its spines to its roots and begins again with bleeding bare hands. Falls again with the weed, dangerously, eventually making the hillside bare. Stupid. Heroic. Alone.

Ecstatic. She talks to the goddess, laughing. 'My rooting ability rivals the wild swine. I am a feral pig and I am digging, tearing, pulling until the last tug brings the thing from the earth and, gravity and I bring it down together. And another. And another. I am exhausted, trusting mother earth as I tumble cushioned by tangled growth right down to the creek.' The bruises and grazes she hardly feels, splashing water into her armpits. She finds herself in a beautiful part of the creek with high walls either side and huge rocks. Flat rocks, native ferns and orchids, the spot has the immense charm of humanlessness. Across the creek is a eucalypt with a low enough hanging branch to suspend the uprooted weeds to die and behind that a big fig. Now she is methodical with a mixture of righteousness and intimacy with the earth, is-ness. Then, spent, in torn clothes she lies in the stream, contemplating her work, full of wonder. The way she came is just about sheer and almost perceptively breathing with relief. She makes her way home via the creek. The bliss of menopause is that its fury supersedes the egotism of needing flattery, self-congratulation.

At last, inside, in the dark, Virginia crisply unscrews the top of the brandy she bought and stares at the provisions on the table. She thinks of Cybil. A stone-heavy ache of her love weighs her down to her seat. Yet a magnetism draws her to dreams of seeing her again. She forces herself to stay put, as if she were in a train looking out the window, letting thoughts come and go. Jeff is a good man, Cybil, and our mother was not a good woman. 'He and I would be equal were it not for the war against women,' she sighs. Cybil is not listening. Cybil has heard the stories already. Jeff and Virginia suffered so much parental violence, corporal punishment, physical discipline in their young years, what would be criminal abuse now, toughened them. Virginia is thankful it wasn't sexual, nor reinforced, like Hope's, with religious bigotry. The bruises, the scratches and gashes on her body are no big deal.

The phone was ringing. I propped my brief-case beside me and sat down to answer it, idly picking up a pen, reaching for the note pad. It was my hair-dresser.

'What's wrong with me? Got the plague? You coming or what?'

My hairdresser is a Koori who works out with weights. Her scrawny white husband looks incongruous at the gym. Her salon is a light airy room above the store opposite the ferry landing. Its big aluminium-framed windows give a grand view of the river and the mangroves. The husband, who used to work in a family timber mill until it was auctioned for peanuts, whose father worked with logs out in the bush with his father before him, does delicate inlaid craft. Lois's benches are a sight to be admired, her mirrors small and beautifully bordered in patterns of different wood-grains.

The local village, if you can call it that, consists of a two-storey brick veneer building. On the ground floor is the shop, which sells newspapers, groceries, milk, cheese, ice-cream, fresh fruit and vegetables in erratic selections, mostly locally home-grown. Videos for rent. Cut and Thrust, my hairdresser, is above it. Her neighbour in the darkest of the upstairs rooms is a dental prostheticist whose door proposes every other Thursday in the morning hours for false teeth fittings. I have never seen anyone go in. I imagine it is very Dickensian in there. The other door upstairs is also sinister, saying MASSAGE. At odd times, an unhealthy looking man sits in there behind a desk before a narrow window. An older, wooden building has outside two petrol bowsers of an old-fashioned variety. On peeling paint is written BAIT. Lois's husband hangs around a lean-to aromatic with wood-shavings behind it. Often he is out the front exchanging grunts about the river. Twenty-five kilometres away along the coast is the Hawks Head National Park which has rudimentary camping facilities for dedicated bird-watchers and eco-tourists. The other caravan park, picnic area and surf-beach are on the ocean side of the peninsula.

Lois must have seen me drive off the ferry and not stop at the time of my appointment. Then she would have waited for me to get home. Hence my phone was ringing just as I came in.

'What?' I responded, 'What day is it? What on earth am I thinking of?' I had forgotten I had made the appointment. Most of my adult life I've had long straight blond locks maintained at little expense. I would patronise the local store more, except that it never has anything I want. I had already picked up a newspaper. If I had stopped I wouldn't have had the extra aggravation of driving back there because Lois would have yelled out and reminded me. Five minutes home and I was out again.

Even though I was quick, I had to wait at Cut and Thrust and sit in a low cane chair. Unlike all other hairdressers in Australia, Lois did not have the *Women's Weekly*, *New Idea* or *Latest Hair Styles* to browse through. Her coffee table carried an assortment of brochures about things to buy. Outboard engines, Bolens Tractors and Riding Mowers. The enormously thick *Deals for Wheels*. I read the Bolens booklet because that was the ride-on Chandra was driving: 'Now, we've taken the vision and foresight that invented the riding mower, the mulching mower, the rear-line tiller and the chipper/vac, and turned it to the needs of home owners for top-quality tractors and riding mowers. Convenient cruise control lets you set and maintain a comfortable pace by pushing a button.' Safe for the disabled? The right side pedal could be easily worked with a crutch and the only shot of the left showed the man not using his foot and all gears were on a handle attachment.

'Gunna buy a ride-on, Margot?' Lois was shaking out a floral piece of cloth and her customer, an elderly woman, was easing herself out of the comfortable chair. Another sat stony-faced, her hair stretched into tiny rollers, stinking of permanent solution.

'Come on. Get yourself in here. What do you want? Same as usual?' Lois always offered 'the usual' and it invariably came out different, but similar to everyone trimmed around the same time. My thick, straight fair hair responded well to changing styles.

'Make it sexy, will I?' she asked. I nodded as I smiled at myself.

She pursed her lips and raised her eyebrows in the mirror over my head, hands on my shoulders. 'You got it, sister-girl.' She was a rough and ready artist at work. She shaved my skull from the nape of the neck to a neat line from the top of one ear to the other. I could hear and feel it with my head bent. When I looked at myself I saw that Lois's 'sexy' was 'cheeky'. I was going to have a straight fringe almost to the eyeball that I'd have to flick out of the way, while the back was a basin with a few wispy long bits hanging over the breezy pituitary-cerebellum area. As I was getting used to this, I wondered what the bit of paper in my pocket was, and brought it out.

I chatted. 'There's an ex-gladiator at our gym.'

'You have to have upper body, yeah. And balance. But it is so stupid. Bring back mud-wrestling I say.' Lois laughed with real amusement.

'I can see you as a champion mud-wrestler, Lois,' I answered. Lois had challenged once on *The Gladiators.* Her big moment. She had spoken of it before. In fact, she spoke about it a lot. 'They filmed that in Queensland. You have to go to Queensland. I wanted to go to MovieWorld. But, too big a mob of us went. Who wants to go to Queensland? Needed my head read.' But she was proud in retrospect, of something. She pulled a face.

She makes me laugh, Lois. And when I laughed, in the mirror, the hair-do looked great. Would she remember Tiger Cat?

'It was like a blown-up kindergarten plastic play area. Only they don't make it as interesting for kids. You don't get hurt, though.'

She stopped trimming and took in the mangroves. I mentioned the Gun Lobby Rally.

She lent down and whispered in my ear, 'Someone's going to kill that goon of a white virgin.' Then she let out a squeal of self-fulfilling laughter. Ripping Velcro from Velcro, she carefully removed the hair-filled floral smock.

Not only is Lois a hairdresser, she is part of a community within a community and that ensures that she knows all the gossip. I wanted to talk to her about the night the boys died. But not in front of the ladies with their dyes and perms. I flicked about my new fringe and complimented her. 'Got to go fishing with you soon, Lois.'

She said she would call me and I paid. As I left, she called, 'I didn't like those gladiating sheilas. Stuck up.' Racist she meant.

Outside I ran into the teenage son of my southern neighbours. When I spoke, he snarled in a hostile manner but his eyes were vacant. Stoned or shocked, immediate intelligence seemed blown away. Ignoring his aggression, I asked if he were all right.

He stared back. Simply didn't answer me. I couldn't find the right question relating to the activities of last Friday night. 'Did you know either of the kids killed?' He shrugged, turned and sloped off to the park across the road to be with a few of his friends.

Lois's husband, whose ancestors appear in sepia photographs in the salon beside logs of a diameter over the height of two tall men, earned the nickname Thrust on the river. No one called Lois 'Cut'. Thrust stopped me to talk. He was worried about the upcoming rally, blokes were coming all the way from the Western Plains to create hell, and hatred went two ways.

'Trouble brewing in Vegemite city,' he mumbled.

'I beg your pardon?' Although I knew he was referring to a part of town chiefly inhabited by Aborigines, the familiar slang gave me a shiver.

The water looked silky in the afternoon sun as the cable lugged the ferry towards our bank. The vehicles on board seemed mostly bound for the camp sites, with a couple of familiar station wagons of residents coming home from work. The boys were smoking dope at a picnic table through a hooker made of a little plastic bottle and a few centimetres of garden hose.

Thrust went on, 'I've known some of those blokes all my life. Bullies at school, they're still at it. They'll come around to my place and make mayhem. World War Three.'

'Don't worry, Thrust. You are always worrying. Why would they bother you?' I asked, trying to sound indifferent and casual, as I guessed by naming a real outside threat, he was actually talking about the effect anticipation of that was having on the individuals he knew; conflict with each other.

'You know.' He shook his frowning forehead from side to side. 'I don't know if they know where I live these days. Unless someone said. And there's Lois's sister's family, they're closer to town. Crossroads won't be a place to go if you've got a white face, girl.'

'What's all that about threats of assassination to their white virgin?' I joked.

'She said that, did she? Oh no. What am I going to do?' Constant anxiety seemed to be Thrust's major mood. 'Wouldn't put it past her city cousins, no I wouldn't.'

'It's a worry,' I said brightly, 'but don't let it get you down.'

'Danny.' Thrust actually identified who he was talking about, 'As sweet a fella as you could meet, when he's sober. A bloody meat-axe with a skinful.'

There followed a story of domestic violence. I did not know the people by name or face and felt uncomfortable participating in loose-lipped gossip, especially as an outsider. But he apparently wanted to tell me. 'Lois promised me we'd go fishing,' I changed the subject.

He placed another durry between his nicotine-stained fingers, and nodded, 'Plenty there. The mullet are jumping.'

'Gotta go, mate,' I said.

Thrust worries, but does nothing. A foot shorter than she is, he is devoted to Lois, to fishing and to his woodwork. Her people have taken him in as one of their own and their three children are polite and energetic.

As I started off, he wandered over to the jetty to stare at the water. He could watch the river for hours, quietly watch and smoke, thinking about blackfish, bream and schnapper, a mystery to me. But I like enthusiasts. There is always something for them to find contentment. Happiness? The damaged Achilles tendon grabbed now and then on the accelerator pedal.

20

Dishes for the Quick and the Dead

Mouldy Rice Bread
Cooked rice gone mouldy. Excellent ferment.
Mix with flour and warm water and sachet of yeast should you have it.
Chuck in a handful of sugar if you feel like it, if you've got plenty of sugar left.
Knead. Leave near fire.
Come back later. Punch it and knead again.
Have fun. Grease camp oven. Build up fire.
Place sculptured dough in 'dutch' oven. Put lid on upside down.
Find a nest of red coals for it to sit in.
Shovel a pile of hot coals on top of it.
Turn every now and then, don't hassle it.
Remove when you think it's done.

Black Coal Chapattis (or bread substitute)
Flour and water.
Make into a firm dough. Shape into flat dinner plate.
Throw onto black coals of fire. Turn once.
Remove embers and eat as unleavened bread.

Pip's Eggplant Dip
Medium-sized aubergine
Garlic
Yoghurt
Lebanese bread, 1 pkt.
Put whole eggplant in microwave for three to five minutes until eggplant is soft right through.
Chop fresh garlic finely.
Get bowl and yoghurt out of fridge.
Peel eggplant, mash with garlic and two generous tablespoons of yoghurt.
Dip into it with Lebanese bread while getting on with your work.

Sofia's Dope Cake

½ lb of unsalted butter
½ lb of useless male leaf
All the ingredients of your favourite chocolate mud cake.
Place leaf and butter together in heavy-based saucepan, leave on slow heat for ages.
Remove and strain off stalks etc. Allow dope-butter to cool.
Use in straight recipe in place of butter.

VeeDub's Anything Patties

Anything that can be mashed can be made into patties.
Place in bowl, break in one egg.
Combine with nice heavy fork. Sprinkle flour, mix in until all is firm.
Crumb stale bread and spread out on dinner plate.
Spoon patty mix onto bread-crumbs and pat into rounds.
The secret is in the patting.
Fry on cast iron frypan in salt or little oil, keep patting, turn until golden on both sides.
Serve hot.

Camp Oven Stewed Vegetables

Have time, good fire, commitment and company.
Fresh produce from recent shop at the growers' market.
Vegetables: pumpkin; potato; sweet potato; parsnips; carrot.
Peel and cut into equal size (bigger than chips and smaller than baked).
Fire should have built up a reasonable heat so there is no need for kindling. Not too hot as you must be able work close to it for a few moments at a time.
Place clean, empty camp oven on fire (have handy either very long sleeve on jumper, or *topflappen* i.e. any old bit of heavy rag or superannuated gardening glove).
Tablespoon of virgin olive oil.
Onion, chopped, whisk with wooden spoon until softened.
Turn fixed vegetables into onion, with wooden spoon, generously splash in soy sauce or tamari, grate black pepper and mix in.
Add a cup of fresh spring water, or tank water.
Put on lid and leave for twenty minutes.
Get ready green vegetables: broccoli; peas; beans; zucchini.
Rest in water with white vinegar in it.
Cauliflower, turnips, brussels sprouts optional (according to taste).

Carefully remove camp oven lid. Sprinkle with plain flour.

Stir vigorously, add more water and the other vegetables.

Toss in handful of roasted sunflower seeds and dried mixed herbs.

Replace lid. Leave for another twenty minutes or whatever.

Serve when pumpkin is unrecognisable.

Chandra's Strawberry Jam

Pick strawberries, wash and remove green bits.

Put in saucepan with a cup of sugar and cook until jam.

Bottle in sterilised jars, identify and date.

Victoria Shackleton's Fried Tomato Sandwiches

There are no grillers in the bush, or on the road.

Thickly butter the bread on the outside, sliced tomato in the middle and put them on the skillet. Nearly burn, turn once and nearly burn the other side. Yummy.

21

. . . murdered by those bastards . . .

Ian Truckman is enthralled, playing with his Pentium. He types 'sport' and he can see in digital resolution anything from caber-throwing in remote Scotland to kick-boxing from Thailand, anything. Amazing.

Sometimes, he is given words he does not type with his forefingers even though the thoughts are probably in his head. He suspects the computer is reading his mind. When he goes to his pornography site, he gets the *Police Gazette* advertising pages.

AFP spokesman said in Sydney yesterday that the flying squads, to come under the banner of 'Drug Task Forces—National Mobile Strike Teams', would be open to applications from officers experienced in the field of anti-drugs operations with State police services.

Tracking his UFO buddies, he is totally out of control of his screen. The CB radio crackles, Breaker, breakman, trucker truckman! Your rig looks like a Russian Topot-12M mobile missile, just a mighty big phallic threat.

His fart is wet. Ian Truckman pulls into a road-house before his long haul south. He will have breakfast at noon.

Lois and Thrust do not live at the Koori settlement out of town, Crossroads, where a rare moment of enlightenment in public housing resulted in interesting, energy-efficient roof designs among the cheap shanties of an earlier generation. Kids, bikes, broken-down cars, weeds and spindly scrub occupy the space. At the turn-off is a large petrol station, restaurant and highway general convenience store. In this brightly lit establishment, which is half-way between their places, Chandra is having a cup of tea with her busy friends, Haze and Daze, who are a pair of hard-working women's libbers of the old school. They have been together so long they finish each other's sentences and sometimes talk at the same time without noticing. Daisy is about ten years older than Hazel, who is sixty-odd.

'Male violence and money conspire in the annihilation of women.'

'It doesn't matter to him,' Haze points at a truckie, 'what the material he is carrying . . .'

'Provided he is getting good money for the job,' finishes Daze. 'In today's world, even women's morals go to pot under the overriding need for money. As an ethical being . . .'

'It explains, excuses, enslaves, buy souls, is unavoidable,' interrupts Haze, 'Above all, it is dangerous. Male violence is essentially cowardly and fascist.'

'So he does have bosses,' Daze takes over.

Haze butts in. 'His having bosses releases him from any responsibility for this stuff. As he has bosses so does he boss, or oppress; as he lives in fear being a coward so he delivers fear.'

'Enjoys other's fear,' Daze elaborates. 'When he stops at a truck stop, likely as not, there is his picture on the wall.'

Daze displays a knowledge of trucks that surprises the amused Chandra. She nods towards a gleaming silver and white outfit, 'So in that small world of fanatical, big-gutted men, he is an aristocrat.'

'They are all going to call him "mate" whether he is or not. It is the class of his rig that matters, its petrol consumption and its natural enemies . . .'

'Retirees on their round-Australia getaways with caravans or furnished vans.'

'One day, dear,' Hazel reaches for Daisy's hand and gives it a squeeze. Since they started this routine of meeting once a month, Chandra finds the environment they've chosen features in the conversation for a while.

'Essentially he lacks imagination and is lonely and too stupid to know it.' Chandra decides, 'He is proudly able to express his inadequacy in whatever way he chooses.'

'Boys do not criticise each other for having toys,' says Haze.

'They die of envy,' laughs Daze.

Haze frowns. 'He constitutes a threat to women, the ecology and reconstituted men merely by being. He will live unchallenged until the planet runs out of oil because no one in power has the slightest interest in re-educating him.'

'It's funny you should mention annihilation,' Chandra says. 'It is a word that has come up a bit lately.' Chandra trusts Haze and Daze completely. They are crones to her middle age.

'Oh, the restless white man,' proclaims Haze, 'searching for the place to fight for his rights. The restless white man is the hungriest thing on earth.'

'He thinks he is heroic if he fights for his rights,' contributes Daze.

'But he has everything there is to have,' comments Chandra.

'Yes,' Haze suddenly hears her, 'Words do come in and out of fashion. We hardly know we're using them.'

'There is this net-nutter who has this theory of the trials of annihilation, and I don't know whether she is full of hot air or dangerously fanatical.'

Chandra feels safe confiding in these two.

'It's all beyond me, I'm afraid. Solid Newtonian physics is what I understand, gravity and all that.' Daisy is the picture of solidity, indeed, solidarity.

'When I studied,' Haze looks back into the dim, dark ages, 'I found it hard enough to understand George Berkeley who said the table wasn't there unless you were looking at it.'

Chandra is truly fond of these two, tireless old hags. 'There are some cyber-friends who want to do something revolutionary.'

'Ah ha, Haze, we're too 'seventies, again.' Daisy looks affectionately at her long-time partner. 'Our refuge is old hat.'

'We work, Chandra. Where it matters, where women are suffering.' Haze is defensive almost as an automatic reaction.

Chandra sighs, 'Well, I wasn't going to tell you the whole conspiracy.'

'What you clever hacking girls should do is get at the banks. They are criminal. Immoral,' Daisy says with what, for her, would approximate hatred. She is a gentle soul.

'Precisely,' agrees Chandra. 'We're working on it.'

'Why don't you slip in a virus that redistributes wealth?' asks the impossibly romantic Daisy.

'Great idea,' agrees Hazel. 'To everyone with under five hundred in their savings, rather than slugging the poor with bigger charges and rewarding the rich under the great forgive-all, the shareholders' interests.'

'Take it away from this late capitalist shenanigans, subvert the stock exchanges . . .' Daze is interrupted.

By Haze, 'Stop the weird scientific brains running around in search of the be-all and end-all answer of why are we here?'

'The nonsense of trying to take birth away from the female. That's what it is all about,' states Daisy seriously.

Haze is also serious, 'Modern science is detail, immense and minute detail. Even scientists in the same field can barely talk to each other . . .'

'Let alone the rest of us,' interjects Daze, 'Because their expertise either doesn't overlap or they're in competition.'

'Or conflict,' clarifies Haze. 'What about medical technology? Women's bodies are there to be explored and probed like outer space. Forget about the female as a person, she doesn't exist!'

'Meghan is one of the genius-types running around searching for the be-all,' comments Chandra. Chandra tells Haze and Daze about their vicious disagreement and why it happened.

'Meghan, a charming lass,' opines Hazel.

'I like Meghan,' agrees Daisy.

The double act bubbles on. 'When the brain needs a logical and complete answer,' Haze finishes a previous thought.

'Like God was,' understands Daisy. Chandra is lost.

'It can lead to conclusions which are nonsense or are made nonsense of,' Haze is apparently back on the subject of science. 'It is a question of truth and belief.'

'And what we are forced to believe,' expands Daze. 'Germaine Greer says that women will never know themselves as well as a girl of three!'

Haze jibes to a different tack, 'The devious doings of Dionysian-type guys!'

Daze joins her. 'Their mission is women's madness.'

'You're a couple of mad women,' Chandra teases affectionately. 'But saner than anyone I know.'

'And, one would have to suppose, that, for all her genius, Meghan is too,' Hazel jumps back into the slipstream.

'But many characters qualify for madness because, in one way, the sensitivity of a woman can present as madness simply by being misunderstood by everyone else,' Daisy explains.

'That's right, Daze,' Haze turns affirmatively to Daisy as if it is the first time she has heard her say that.

All three of a piece know time's up and start fidgeting for their things. Chandra holds her sticks still for a minute staring at her friends, then asks, 'Do you two still have sex?'

'Of course.' Daze is indignant at the question.

Haze raises her eyebrows. 'Regularly. What about you, Chandra?'

'I'm thinking about it,' Chandra grins.

'You wouldn't be Robinson Crusoe in that,' remarks Hazel.

It takes them at least another ten minutes to get into their cars and go their separate ways. Chandra feels nicely warm having been in the glow of passionate female friendship.

Resisting Chandra's number for about half a second, I did press her buttons but the whine of the fax machine replied. I put the handset down, knowing I had no idea what I was going to say, anyway. Work to do.

First, on Penny's job, I had to speak with the lad's father, and I could find him? On the beach. With the camels. And Cybil Crabbe? I found out where she worked. Le Cote de Paradiso Holidays, cottages, caravans and cabins. I looked in the *Yellow Pages* and decided to turn up in person.

Instead of heading towards the ferry crossing, I turned left out of my driveay. I drove very slowly for the next hundred metres, trying to see if a car had turned into next door. There were no tyre tracks in the black mud off the shoulder of the gravel before their gate. I backed as if I had forgotten something at my place. Yes, tyre marks would have shown if he had been there last night. I continued north. As I came to the corner where the accident had been, I had to brake as there was a police car on the verge. A uniformed policewoman and a fat female teenager were planting a white cross. A narrow young girl with sharp features stood nearby with a bunch of plastic flowers held in two hands watching.

White crosses on the roadside where teenage boys lost their lives have become almost iconic about the country. I mused that probably most were young drivers and passengers, not only because of their high road accident death rate but also because the incidental, simple crosses begging remembrance spoke of the grief of life unlived, an innocence, a real loss for a real family. I drove out along the surf beaches road to the tourist end of Port Water. Where are the poppies for the babies who die from domestic violence? Boys' reckless despair or brattish arrogance monopolised my thoughts as I passed alpaca, ostrich, deer and angora in paddocks looking for camels. Welcome to Australia! We shoot wallabies, don't we?

Neil Waughan. I did not know him alive.

I turned at a sign on a fence 'Camel Tours Beach Safaris 10 a.m. and 3 p.m.', and was relatively surprised to see native fauna in the shape of kangaroos grazing about the edges of the scrub.

Nigel Waughan was preparing his beasts for their afternoon walk. Apart from being barefooted with grey hair braided down his back, he did have the bearing of a bank clerk. Perhaps it was the words he said, 'May I help you?' We went into his office, which was hardly more than the tin shed it seemed. A noticeboard was thick with fliers of ecological concerns with detailed accounts of Council's misdoings and a plea to demonstrate against the racist rally and the visit of the white virgin.

Nigel addressed the woman behind the desk, 'Susie, let's swap jobs.'

Susie, dressed in ranger-like gear, was plainly eager to be with the camels. She strode out, a dykey type who wouldn't come within a bull's roar of a lesbian. Nigel sat on the table with his feet on a chair, his posture in complete contrast with his manner, which retained the unerring 'have a good day' efficiency of the teller who crisply hands you freshly printed currency notes.

'Mr Waughan, I am the one who found your son. I was jogging near the beach close to where I live and I stopped at the toilet block. I thought at first it was a girl and that she had died from heroin overuse or overdose. I called the police and was later told his actual sex,' tumbled out of me in a stream. The man had to know I cared.

Nigel interrupted me with a hand gesture. Easy tears came to his eyes. He snuffled them up through his nose.

'Can you tell me about him? What he was like?' I asked, concerned. 'What was your relationship with him like?'

Nigel would talk, he was a feminised gent. He did.

'Where to start? I could talk about that lad for hours, he blows me away. The greatest kid a man ever fathered. I bothered to father, you see. I parented. Supermarket, childcare, play. What a kid! It changed my life being a father. Penny wanted to work, wanted to study, and teach. I went to the bank each day and did not work or think about work a second longer than I had to and I was home, picking up this perfect little person from day care, throwing him up on my shoulders. We walked, we went places. Penny dug it. She flew, the new woman, the superwoman. Her salary went from a standing start to passing mine halfway down the straight, so that, with both of us working, we soon had enough money to do what we wanted. I wanted the sand, well, that's how she puts it. She said I have gritty old sand in my blood like the books on my side of the bed, *Lawrence of Arabia* and *Seven Years in Tibet*, adult adventure books. Neil was so bright. He could talk in sentences when hardly more than a year old. And when she started bringing home computers! Well, I tell you, I felt like Biggles overtaken by Luke Skywalker, rumbling along in an old bi-plane in goggles, while the boy wielded the Force and piloted spaceships. But we shared something at the bottom of all that. Do you ever think about good and evil? Well if there isn't a devil creating merry hell on the planet, how do these bastards get away with it?' He waved his knuckles at the noticeboard. I assumed the bastards were mining companies, the logging and chemical industries, local councils, estate agents, developers and politicians. My eyes followed his directing arm and I saw an announcement about a Men's Group Gathering in the forest. I nodded.

'Neil was a fucking hero. He was going to change the world. Can I get you a cup of coffee?' he suddenly offered.

'Okay,' I accepted.

Nigel filled the kettle with spring water from a large blue plastic container with a little tap. 'The devil's not stupid. It's no accident he died,' he said. Waughan plugged in the cord and swung around, standing over me. The gentle gent became a he-man. 'She tried to castrate him! I never thought it would happen. That we would grow to hate each other over Neil. Women should not have boys after the age of twelve!' he said with conviction.

'Really?'

'Really. After we moved up here and I finally decided to make my life my own. Penny is a mean, bitter pragmatist, while I am an impossible romantic,' he shrugged. 'She won custody.'

'You fought for custody?' He didn't answer my query.

'She's sick. She would dress him in girls' clothes and put make-up on him. She was playing with this kid like he was a doll. But he was beyond primary school. Sometimes it happened when I was still living in the house . . .' This man had learnt to talk about his feelings.

'I had an affair,' he confessed. 'I was guilty. She threw this at me. I had no moral courage. I wanted to stop her putting that green stuff all over his face. But I got angry. The two of them laughing! At me!'

I looked meaningfully at his beautifully plaited long hair.

'Grotesque, it was. I've always been a sort of SNAG, but I felt the rage. When I look at it in the cool light of therapy, I only saw it a couple of times but they are exaggerated in my memory because of the suppressed anger I held inside me. And jealousy, I'll own that too.'

'You both loved him so much,' I said mildly.

'Oh, I didn't fight it. I did love my son!' Nigel made coffee from a jar of instant de-caf and offered me soy milk. He, however, did not wait for my refusal, and handed me a mug with 'Men Are from Mars Women Are from Venus' decorating its heavy porcelain. We heard Susie call from outside. The camels were lined up head to tail with glamorous Arabian cloth across their saddles. Gold, maroon and aqua tassels festooned their noble heads.

'It's time to go to the beach. We do all our business on the beach. This,' he implied the shed, 'is only for telephone bookings. And a change room.' He closed the door, pushed off his shorts, he had no underpants on and turned my way when he pulled off his T-shirt. Then I tasted the lukewarm concoction in the mug. From the back of the door he took down a set of robes, like sheets, and a sheik's headgear. The bank clerk was now T. E. Lawrence, or Peter O'Toole in the role. Still barefooted, he opened the door and emerged into the sunlight of his dreams. Susie's face was thunder. She grumbled as she handed over the caravan of tourist camels and stamped into the office to man the phones, picking up my dirty mug as she passed. We had not been introduced, so I didn't say goodbye. I followed Nigel and standing beside him I was taller. He tapped the knee of the leader with his riding crop. She sank slowly down to mounting height. Nigel smiled with seductive generosity and told me to get onto the back part of the saddle. I shrugged okay. He took the front and we hit the track to the beach at a swinging walk.

It was a pleasant trip through a patch of coastal rainforest on the dignified ships of the desert. The luxurious pace fascinated me. Nigel, aloft, did not talk much. When we arrived at his station on the beach, he erected a flimsy Bedouin tent with bamboo poles and cloth matching that on his camels, advertising his safari in gold lettering.

Now, on the sand, he began talking again. 'You would have thought that Neil was going to grow into a poofter. Well he wasn't. Even during the divorce, Neil and I shared what we had when he was a child. I don't think Penny knows how much time we spent together. At first, she was kind of morbidly curious and would grill him every time he got home about what he did with me, apparently suffering each word with self-flagellating envy, until he began to feel sorry for her. Then he lied about where he had been. Well, what we said to one another was still Biggles and Luke Skywalker. We talked of heroes and heroism. He had so much information and such a head for it. It didn't, like, stagnate either. He wanted to do something. The last time I saw him . . .'

Nigel stopped speaking because tears overtook his voice. I looked up and down the beach for paying customers. They still had half an hour to arrive.

'Ever heard the inside story of that Dolly Dunn business. The one where reporters discovered that sick man in his motel room in the Bahamas or wherever?' These New Age men who gossip were a worry. 'Ever wondered where their millions came from? Neil found out on the Internet that not only were they using and buying boys for pleasure, they were testing drugs on them. This got up Neil's nose. He told me, "Dad I've found it".'

'Found what?' I inquired.

'The battleground where he could fight evil!' Nigel was overcome with sentimental tears again, 'Fucking fight evil. All my best parenting ends in this. He was bloody murdered by those bastards.' A tourist couple were examining the camels. Automatically I cautioned the hero's father, with a jerk of the head at them. He lowered his voice. 'We bloody enjoyed our tales. I didn't think he would really take them on. But he has, he did, and they did him in. His name should be put alongside the great failures of Tobruk, Gallipoli and so on. They should erect a statue to him.'

A brightly coloured double-decker bus parked on the cliff above us. Equally effulgent trippers giggled their way down the steps onto the path through the coastal scrub and grasses. I strolled along the row of kneeling camels, patting their necks and saying hello to their eyes and superior noses before their customers arrived, checking out the too-obvious tourist couple. I went down a hole someone had dug in the sand and put my Achilles tendon injury right back on the agenda. Shit.

T. E. Lawrence, the bank clerk hippie, aka Nigel Waughan, was now greeting tourists like a professional actor, his voice taking on the ring of a town crier and the warm concern for frailty and fear that the magnanimous manage for lesser beings.

Back beside him, I said, 'Thanks for the conversation, and please accept my sincere condolences for the loss of your son. Goodbye.' I was responding to that bank teller side, a readiness to accept formality as a means of chatter, of dismissal. A large American woman overheard me and proceeded with the renowned tact of that nationality to demand to know why our sheik was accepting sympathy. I limped away, not wanting to hear Nigel's reply.

It was a painful walk back through the rare remaining rainforest to my car. I did manage to think between 'ouches' of Neil and Nigel. I could not decide whether the latter was worse than my greenie neighbour, the same or better, but there was something about these libertarian men that gave me the creeps. A woman couldn't feel safe around them, they would be always wanting it, like apes in the zoo. Their sexuality was slimy. I find macho boys like Philippoussis easier.

Neil, the cyber-spy, going under cover to do what, exactly? Give me a break. I preferred the bitter, pragmatic superwoman dressing her boy in women's clothing to the unmitigated romance of this man. My heel hurt like hell as I backed my car towards the shed-office in a three-point turn. Susie benefited me with a look of undisguised envy, which I didn't deserve beyond not saying hello or goodbye. I have no interest in your sensitive New Age guys, they're not my cup of tea, nor my soy de-caf.

Right along here somewhere was the Le Cote de Paradiso caravans, camping, cabins and whatever. It was tucked into the back of the very same rainforest I had walked through. I pulled up beside a recent model Hyundai Excel with the number plate, CC. Cybil Crabbe. Iridescent pink-mauve in colour, the small car was shiny clean on the outside and a tip inside. I entered the office and saw a caricatured image of myself. She had exactly the same haircut, same hair really, colour, weight and straightness. Here was a me who had sat down all my life, eating. She was chubby with heavy legs and about six inches shorter.

I registered shock with my eyebrows and said self-deprecatingly, 'And I thought Lois did me an exclusive.'

'Excuse me?' She pretended not to know who I was but she had the kind of eyes that soaked in everything. She had seen me break down during a triathlon. She was the one who egged on Beetle to keep running and leave me be. She said the 'excuse me' to disconcert me, or make me blush. I was truly lame again and asked if I might sit down.

'Lois,' I repeated, 'you must have the same hairdresser, Lois.' She looked at me and didn't reply, wondering what card to play from a hand held close to her chest.

'I'm afraid my Achilles tendon is still a bit of a worry. Remember a couple of days ago?' I reached over her desk to shake her hand. 'Margot Gorman, you're Cybil Crabbe? Yes?'

A softness about Cybil was reinforced by fleshy bases to the short pointed fingers. She smiled and became quite pretty.

Cybil was obviously comfortable seated; her elbows rested on her desk but she didn't seem to lean forward.

'What can I do for you, Margot?' She looked me up and down, all the boldness of middle-class confidence.

'You could probably do a lot for me, Cybil. If you told me what happened in the evening of Friday before last.'

She barked a mirthless laugh, 'I doubt it.'

Notwithstanding the educated voice, this was no lady. This was a brick wall. Posters detailing Marine Life of Eastern Australia described and identified fish to be caught in the area. One for sea. One for fresh water. Tackle for hire, and purchase. The office catered for holiday-makers' needs very efficiently. Even the camel tours had a brochure. I began to talk about Lois, and her cousin and Thrust, and fish, fishing. I let my knees slip apart and leant back in the chair with my hands behind my head, just to watch what she did with her eyes. They went to my crutch and up to my face. I lifted my sore foot onto my left knee and began rubbing it and talking about the barbecue and the women who were there. 'You were there.'

She busied herself with a pen. 'I was?' Before she was going to give any information, she had to know what I knew.

'You know Cybil, the funny thing about secret-keepers, is they think they keep themselves secret . . .' I let the sentence hang, to watch her reaction. Her eyes went blank. She won, I lost. I explained. 'Well, possibly they do keep secrets, but they don't know much.'

'So?' She had not stopped work on my account. She addressed an envelope.

'They haven't got the mental room, if you see what I mean?' I went on.

'I'm sorry, I don't,' she remarked disinterestedly. She was riveted.

'Their secrets are relatively easy to guess. Their lives are narrow, you see. Ninety-five per cent of a person you can read from the outside, body language, behaviour, aura, more if you have a good nose. Less than five per cent is controlled by the will-power of the individual. Less than that by someone presenting an image of herself, especially if it's false. It's rather pathetic when you think about it.'

She put that envelope aside and picked up another.

'You have a nice new car out there. Now here's an example. I bet it's fully paid for. I guess that it's fully paid for, no loans. No loans on the car.' She had a choice here, whether to crack that laugh that would fool a lot of people into thinking she saw the funny side or lie about the car.

She laughed, really jolly. 'You're right. No loans on the car. But I don't know what interest it is of yours.'

Looking straight through her, I frowned. 'This is not a social call, Cybil. I am an investigator.'

Cybil got up busily on her solid legs and went to a filing cabinet. An admirable way she had with files, her fingers quick and eyes busy.

'My other guess is,' I continued—she brought out the butch in me—'And this one also doesn't matter, while most people who own places like this work them themselves, you don't own it or part-own it. You are just a worker here. I measure you as a worker, a worker anywhere, a woman who has a job most of the time.'

'So?' She shrugged.

'It doesn't matter, I'm just showing you how much I could know about you or anyone who chooses not to say anything. A big white silence about the other Friday night looks to me like a great cloud of guilt.'

She stopped fiddling with the manila folders, but grabbed one anyway. Cuddled it to her breast, her eyes greedy, her lips sealed.

Getting up, I said, 'I've just got to go and find out what you're so guilty about.'

She didn't move until I had opened the door and then she said sweetly, 'Margot? What are you investigating?'

'That's not hard to answer. The death of a boy that night there. His mother thinks it was murder,' I revealed. 'And so, incidentally, does his father.'

'Boy? Who hired you?' Cybil Crabbe stepped towards me. She flicked the long fringe out of her eyes and let the hair fall back. I have been known to do that one myself.

'The mother,' I threw over my shoulder with a glance. I saw Cybil pale slightly. I knew she would stop me so I moved very deliberately, limping, to give her time to think, to make up her mind, to keep me talking.

'Lois did a lovely job of your hair. I've been with Lois ever since she got her certificate,' she turned chatty. 'She used to be at Liz's Scissors?'

'I've never been there. If you don't want to give me any information, I'd better let you get back to your invoices.' I acted, for want of a better word, hurt.

'What exactly did you want to know?' She opened the door for me and followed behind. Clever now she'd had time to arrange her disinformation.

I shot a guilt trip from left field. 'Well, for instance, was Virginia White there?'

'Virginia was out in the bush. Virginia is too obsessed to party,' she explained, strangely defensive.

'Ah,' I exhaled with comprehension, 'To party. Drugs were there, hard ones, thank you. What drugs, exactly?'

'The usual, I suppose.' Cybil conveyed that she didn't indulge, even though she was hip with the jargon. Which means, she could well deal.

'I saw Alison, Maria, Sofia,' I said. 'Not you. Dello and Maz, who else was there, Cybil? Do you know Jill David?'

'Well,' she turned back to the office, 'Tiger Cat was big-noting herself giving away designer drugs for free, a sort of combination E, acid, crack, I don't know. I don't do them.' The wire door sprang itself shut.

I followed her back in, 'Yes, you do, sometimes. But did you that night?'

'No. I don't do drugs. Your instinct is wrong there,' she said smartly.

'Why were you there?' I almost begged, 'Cybil?'

'As it happens, I heard it was on, and I was on that side of the river. Having a haircut as a matter of fact. I saw the gurls come off the ferry and, well, I went.'

'Okay,' I took my notebook from my pocket. Cybil described Tiger Cat perfectly, dishing out the pills. Ingratiating herself to all and sundry. That was the most accurate thing Cybil had to give me. She had gone to the Spiders' do out of curiosity, alone, and went home alone. She would not reveal her private address, or phone number.

As if I couldn't find it for myself! I left her place of work dissatisfied, but not as much as she would have wished. Staring at the iridescent mauve car, its bubble shape, its polish, I felt she could be guilty of something as simple as not cleaning the car. Just then I saw a red Saab leave the caravan park, but I wasn't quick enough to follow it.

Sofia stares at the train passing listening to the messages in its percussion: excuses, excuses, excuses. Her crop has turned to weed. The goddess plant has betrayed her and turned into a boy with balls. With the money she could have bought the computer with a modem. The Internet was going to save her sanity. It gave her Shulamith, her toad.

Old feminists, like Maria, romanced telepathy, pathenogenesis, trans-spatial, trans-temporal connection of the sisterhood, but here was a real web of electronic and instantaneous intercourse, a network. Clogging up the esoteric ley lines in the earth's natural magnetism, no doubt, but on the tangled World Wide Web, she can move like a spider. 'Why should SCUM care what happens when we're dead? Why should we care that there is no younger generation to succeed us?'

But the crop is a loss. Cyberspace is the safest place. Who knows if you're stoned? Everyone is stoned. The only place she can be herself and tell the truth, gone. No money this year. Sofia lives in an urgent present, a deep, intriguing, eternal present. Her world is collapsing.

Excuses, excuses, excuses, rattles the train.

Maria smothers Sofia. Everyone thinks Maria takes drugs, but she doesn't. Sofia knows. Maria wants to appear cool, tolerant, so both keep up the pretence. Maria does not want to be judgemental, moralistic. But she eats. Food without manners, food without rituals. Although she sits like a monolith and mouths off, Maria lives in the dead past. She swallows Sofia. 'She munches away, consuming me.' The feminist history Maria devours sucks Sofia's future, creates a hungry gorge that sits like a hiatus. Maria knows her so well, it destroys Sofia, while it sustains her. A good mind making excuses; what kind of conversation is that? Sofia loves and hates Maria, the Internet is her chance. Was. Escape from breaking bread, discussing Andrea Dworkin, another fatty, sorting out resentments, getting down to party lines and agreeing. Sofia's individuality, her rampant creativity, is sat upon by dinosaurs. Cyberspace is pure, crystal clean, away from the vomit and shit, the germs and mould. If anyone needs a computer, it is Sofia. She cannot be a have-not. It is not fair. Sofia is as radical as Maria. More so, she has talent.

Fat is a feminist issue. Schmissue. Sofia picks up the bag of useless leaf and goes into the house talking to herself.

'The need the greed to heed. Hunger? Thirst? Quest? Thrills? The impatience for it is driving me over the edge. I'm sick of waiting. I'm sick of fear. I don't care. I want to get to the fling of not caring, not caring a fig, doing a jig of not caring. I know, I've got it. By jingo, Dingo. I've got it. With the pounds of leaf, male leaf, I'll make this cake, I'll bake this cake. It's something to do. Why should I care? I don't care. It'll blast us off our little rockers like rockets. Get off this planet and fly back home.'

Sofia is careful and thorough. When it is in the oven she feels she can face the world again. She has a weapon. She can socialise.

Making a date with Alison proved difficult. Perhaps I could pick up Tilly for her from school and bring her around to an address she spelt out. I asked, 'Do you recall any other vehicles in the carpark near the toilets before I arrived?'

'Lenny was impressed by a suped-up Valiant Charger,' she said. Her voice changed. It dropped a complete octave as she said, 'There are spooks sniffing about.'

'Yes,' I affirmed her suspicions, 'but what are they interested in?'

'Drugs, what else?' She put down the phone abruptly.

I gazed at the greasy Nadir cap I had perched on top of the Waughan file, trying to vibe out its secrets.

Alison rang back, explaining that Tilly, her daughter, thought she had a part in Neil's murder. 'Murder?' I queried. She told me that Tilly was a baby witch. All she has to say, is: I hate you, I wish you were dead.

'All the kids say that now,' I expressed my disbelief.

'But Tilly felt she could point the bone and someone would die.' Alison pleaded with me: could I explain that I was looking for the real killer? And do it convincingly.

'I guess so,' I said uncertainly. No one had established that it was murder yet.

Dello and Maz were picking up Tilly from school. These two conversed in a way which implied that there was something to tell but they were not letting on. They didn't give me much of an idea of who else was at the barbecue either. Tilly was to be dropped off at ballet practice.

When I took Tilly back to the car after asking her formally what she said to Neil and when she heard that he died and how she felt about it, and reassured her that she could not have been responsible, I quizzed Maz, 'Did you have any idea that the girl that night was a boy?'

'No way,' said Maz. 'We talked with her.'

'Nuh, her politics were too good for a jock,' Dello agreed.

'For one so young. For a male. What was it she called men, Dell?' Maz spoke. 'Something right on.'

'Her father?' asked Dello, 'She called him an emotional miser.'

'She said, "Never met a wise man, if so it's a woman."'

'She also said something really sweet when we picked her up. What was it?'

' "Maybe I'm to blame for all I've heard but I'm not sure." and "I'm so excited to meet you",' supplied Dello.

'How did you come to take her to the barbecue?' I acted innocent confusion with facial expressions.

'You don't know Dell,' said Maz. 'Dell picks up strays. Cats, dogs, kids, you name it.'

'No, well? Was she stoned?' I asked. Dello glanced at me through the curtains of her hair, then moved a strand from her face and shook it all backwards.

'She chatted on about the G7 and GATT, the Third World and the International Monetary Fund and how the rainforests are being fucked by loggers and plantations taking people's food to put a cup of coffee on the tables of cafés,' Maz expanded.

'So you picked up a stray hitch-hiker and took her to a party? Just like that?' I sniffed, raised my eyebrows in wonder.

'Wouldn't have done it if we thought she was a trannie,' Dello grumbled.

'No way!' asserted Maz.

'Who exactly was at this celebration? What was it in aid of?'

'Equinox. There were gay girls there, you know, from town. Not a lot of them stayed around,' Maz explained.

'When us mob turned up in numbers with our kids and camp ovens, they were out of there. Some stayed. All the cool doods took off, leaving the riff-raff.'

'There was a kind of fight. Poofter buddies weren't welcome so the cock-suckers boycotted. We were supposed to pay and all. We didn't, of course.'

'I guess, gurls ruined it for them. Again.' Maz laughed.

'Did many poofters go?' I wanted to know.

'Yeah, I think there was one car-load. We pissed them off with ululations, brown-eyes and other disgusting actions. Jeez, I didn't know the kid was a boy. No wonder he killed himself.'

'Do you know that?' I took Dello up on her suicide theory.

'Well,' Maz expressed her opinion. 'She was awfully depressed. We thought it would cheer her up.'

'I thought she was scared,' Dello said. 'We could heal that, the company of women, you know?'

'Were there a lot of drugs?' I queried coyly.

Dello and Maz looked at me as if I were stupid then changed the subject and talked to each other. 'The white man's ideal woman.' I didn't know what they were referring to until I saw the poster on the schoolyard fence: the political face of the Extreme Right, the white virgin.

'She could be worse. She could be a man. In drag.' Maz laughed at her own joke. I did not join in the mirth.

'My brother says,' Tilly piped up, 'She wants to kick Kooris out of their own country. Auntie Iris reckons, You don't have to pay for things twice.'

'Who do you work for, Margot?' Maz gunned her motor, all humour gone.

'Different people. Professional confidentiality, you know.' I grinned. 'I'm not the undercover cop you're worried about,' I called as I waved to my little friend, who was sitting quietly in the back seat of the van fiddling with her ballet clothes.

If Maz did not trust me, I certainly did not trust them. The teenager had quoted lyrics from Nirvana? Kids don't usually articulate very much to adults; saying the words of his favourite songs was clever. I gathered from Penny, he was a smart lad. And whatever else, his father wasn't an emotional miser.

Later at home, filling in a couple of hours gladly, doing formwork for the cementing around the chookhouse-studio, I thought about Kurt Cobain. Didn't he commit suicide by overdose? Was it a trend, an end of the century nihilism among young men, to glorify their own death? Or was Kurt murdered? I will check Neil's CD collection tonight when I go there.

I tend to imagine that everyone has a life they haven't lived, a kind of parallel possibility, something that would equally have fulfilled you. With me, it is geology. I could have been a geologist. I am amazed by the properties of minerals. Earth. That concrete can be made from sand and lime and water and sometimes gravel is amazing. I needed to spend time with the ground, levelling it out, thrusting a crowbar into it, digging. But I didn't know anything at all about geology. I wondered what time I should go to Penny's. Perhaps quite early, immediately after dark.

Canisteo Bayou, a suburb of Port Water, is built on mangrove swamp converted into canals. Successful people in this world can have as much as the rich, it seems. Palaces, boats, except they've got neighbours and borrowed money. Rich in the red. I parked in the circular drive-way. When I entered the brick veneer mansion, I was moved by the atmosphere of emptiness. Penny was, of course, tragically lonely, devastated by the incontrovertible fact that her boy was dead. She adored her son. He was her emotional life. 'His mother's only joy'? She wore her grief like a cloak of the same colour over an underlying despair. Her face was lined by the frowns and squints avoiding the cigarette smoke as it hung around her head. I took one of my best bottles of wine with the quality of an art piece that will make you remark upon it even if you don't want to. A gesture of comfort. She found a corkscrew in the well-appointed kitchen, having opened and shut several wrong drawers.

'My cleaner knows more about my things than I do. Here it is.' She handed the designer wine-opener to me and turned to a cabinet which had many shiny and purpose-shaped crystal pieces inside. She picked the right-sized stemmed glasses and checked for smudges before she sat them on the coffee table between us. She lied about the cleaner to cover her distraction. Her place would be a dream to clean.

'What a nice idea. Chips and cheese, too. Good.' Penny nibbled a bit, but could not eat and smoke at the same time. Easier to talk with a cigarette. The lighter was closer to me so I held the flame for her.

'You know I did everything I did for Neil. Everything. He wouldn't thank me for saying that. He was a beautiful person. Although he dressed as one, he would hate to be called a vampire. But it was my blood he drank. You don't realise how invading motherhood is even when they are almost grown. Now he's gone I have no blood at all.' Penny did not ignore the wine. 'An exceptional red,' she said.

'Things are never the same after you have a child. You are not the same. Then childless. The death of a child is worse than worse. I've, well, for the last fifteen years, complained, I suppose. Now, despair, utter, hopeless despair. Oh, don't worry, I'll go on. I won't let grief entirely destroy me. I am not a coward. I am hollow, now. Teaching gets me out of myself. Adult students are so appreciative. Giving of yourself and that not being trampled upon, well, it's the best you can expect out of life, don't you think?'

I said, 'Yes, teaching is very selfless. I reckon. Generous people are great teachers.'

'You think despair would make you give up, but it's the opposite, despair drives me, like a demon. Despair means I will never give up. Why did Neil do it?'

'You think he killed himself?'

'No,' she shook her head. 'Why did he paint his face and then die?'

'Can I have a look at his room, Penny?' I asked at an appropriate pause.

She took a sip of wine before she got up. We went back to the foyer of the house near the front door. She switched on lights. To our right was the study, a small room with a computer on a specially angle-designed table. We turned right, through a big bedroom which looked unlived in to a smaller one behind it. Neil's room was superficially untidy. Books and disc jackets were on the floor near the sound system. There was another computer in here.

'How many computers do you have?' I asked.

'Three. It's my job, of course. There is another one in the garage, pretty well exclusively for playing games on. This is for school and surfing the net. So is mine. What did you want in here?'

'A look.' I picked up a CD, Regurgitator, and pulled out the booklet with the lyrics and sped-read them. That accounted for the lines about the G7 and GATT. The Nirvana disc was there, as well. Maz and Dello were word perfect.

'If you play that I will certainly cry,' said Penny.

'Why don't we play it, then?' I smiled.

'Okay,' Penny put it in the player, pressing buttons. We stood for a while and then there was the song I wanted, 'Never met a wise man, if so it's a woman.'

'Neil played this over and over. He has a lovely voice this young man. Are you making some sort of parallel? Teenage male suicide . . .' She spun on her heel and exited the room saying, 'I must have another taste of that delicious claret. Excuse me.' She wanted to be alone for a minute.

I sat down on his bed, imagined myself to be Neil, idolising the singer. I took off the CD and put in Regurgitator. 'Couldn't do it' . . . possibly for myself. It's a favourite of mine.

Penny had pulled herself together using cigarettes and wine. Was his death the sum total of a disappointing life? She began talking as soon as I entered the living-room.

'I want to know why he died where he died and why he was dressed like that. I don't want it to be a mystery. I teach desk-top publishing. I am going to write a tribute to my son, a statistic of teenage suicide, blame it on society! No. I want to know what happened to my reason for being. It doesn't matter now. Nothing matters, so I might as well work hard. I don't mind paying you, Margot. You provide me with every detail. I am haunted also by Hugh's face, cut all over with abrasions. I knew Neil loved make-up. It was a game we shared together, of a Sunday morning.'

We finished one bottle of wine and in a moment, Penny was opening another, talking all the time. 'Gillian Gilmore was a friend of mine, but she hardly had room for friendship, or for herself actually. I didn't have much, either, I suppose. But Gillian wasn't allowed time.'

'Were your sons friends?' I pulled my notebook towards me. 'I mean, good friends. Would they spend time together?'

'Hugh,' sighed Penny, 'was a very unhappy boy. After Elias threw him out he had nowhere to go, nothing in the future. He came here a couple of times. I couldn't get two words out of him. They would sit and watch videos; or he would sit down there on the other computer shooting things. When he got into stealing cars, I put a stop to it. Neil had to study.'

'And Neil?'

'Neil seemed quite relieved.'

'I have to ask you this . . .' I began.

She interrupted, 'I know what you are going to say. Marijuana is the only drug Neil ever touched and that rarely. I know they are saying he had drugs in his system. But it's not Neil. He wanted to be an adult. He wanted a life. I know that, we talked about it. He loved the idea of university. He had ambition. He was not a loser!'

I drove very carefully back to my place between the paperbarks and the sea. Back inside, I handwrote: who was wearing the black cap? who was driving the yellow Charger? ditto ditto the red Saab? was the second car that sped past here 'the carload of poofters'? As I wrote that the sounds of that night came back to me. The throbbing muffler, the suped-up Valiant, the one Hugh died in, the other was simply speeding, not necessarily a heavy car. It went by first. Didn't it? My memory was not clear. What was it Cybil wasn't saying? I had to spread out the jigsaw pieces before I could put them together. Form-work.

Book Four

nonsense

Wednesday Thursday Friday Saturday

Wednesday's child is full of woe

22

. . . boredom is a function of evil . . .

Playing in cyberspace is so sexy. Power, pure eroticism, a Faustian contract, worth it. The user of the pseudonym, Moments of Pleasure, MOP, appears as if she has not eaten proper food for a week. She is tired. Her whole body expresses one corporeal sigh. The many windows, directories and sub-files she has on her home computer are a tangled labyrinthine web. Her desktop is clogged with state-of-the-art software, what she downloads from the Internet, give-away CD-ROMs in bought magazines, program for encryption and fast-pace hacking, but that is not the real problem. She is too tired to dispose of the rubbish. The installer, an inoffensive nerd with a limp and a harelip, has unlocked the secret, which is inexplicable. Satisfaction and frustration are the complementaries of the palette of her life, as others swing in the health-sickness duality. The controller is silent. Or stabbed in the back. Gossip is that she has died, defected or, simply, decamped. That yarn having been spun for all it's worth, speculation moves on to who she was anyway: some powerful rich woman working out of the Bahamas, Norfolk Island or from a cruising yacht; she had been a baby lover of Valerie herself and was dedicated to avenge her death, her mistreatment, to advance her thoughts from paper to action; she was a young Valerie, a teenage genius, with computer skills beyond any adult's.

MOP has to be creative. Her finger hammers the Delete button, a function she usually presses with utmost caution and forethought. She has to simplify the subversive stuff, to disguise files, favourites, parents and passages to camouflage the conspiracy, itself a blind for her solo activity. Revenge. Fisherman's hell, she can crack and hack wherever she wants. The embarrassment of riches has sucked her humour. She needs to focus her vengeance. Express her hatred. She intends to ride the conspiracy to its demise, to surf its wave for her personal ends. Alone at three a.m. in her room, she opens her tool-box with its array of illegal programs. Her fellow Solanasites are not up to speed. The chat has become ridiculous, gutless women backing off, mouthing off.

<MOP> Boredom is an expression of evil in the inner being.

<BLUESKY> Evil is banal.

<SKUMBO> Those with the knowledge don't have the power.

<MOP> Those with the power are ignorant of practically everything.

She leaves her desk to go out into the moonless night to think. Boredom, of course, isn't women's fault. The whole fucking society is so pornographic, boredom is a healthy, not to say, sane reply to the muck dished out. Without control, the net-gliders are uncensored. It doesn't matter now, MOP decides. She returns to her keyboard, standing, frowning, to read.

<McHEAT> I came into this room for some hot sucking sex and what do I get, boredom. You're all boring about boredom.

<MOP> Get a life. GAL.

She is sick of messing up porn sites and perpetuating nonsense in UFO newsgroups. Flaming was fun for a while. She wants bloody revolution. She settles down and brings up a search engine. Wearily she types an E, a V, an I, and L and S. She is too tired but she cannot sleep, exposure to the electromagnetic field has made her feel electric through lack of negative ions. She wakes with a start. Her screen turns as magnificent as diamanté and the sound card starts blasting nostalgia from the king. The sites are numerous and colourful, and all conceivable Internet applications are utilised by the undying Presley fan club, clubs, fanatic fringes, lunatic land, suburban circles, the impersonator societies and so on constantly chatting about his resurrection in different forms and immanence.

MOP hits a gold-mine. She fists her hand and punches the air. To reclaim evil, she has to seek cover in the court of the king.

She typed EVILS, got Elvis. With this she can certainly carpet-bomb the enemy, gum up emails everywhere with the fractals of graphics. The king will overtake the world. The mistake was using text. The centre core of the really radical Solanasites will find this useful. Evils, first a general category, evil, which became too cumbersome, is so obvious. Wrong. A hammer and tong. They simplify with the added s to slim it down, then twist. If the goddess of inspired coincidences is working with her this morning, then other Solanasites might have typed, or mistyped evils. It is a matter of going into the Elvis maze to find her, or them.

Suddenly her system clears up. Cyber-conversation gets going. The first and most obvious place is food, white food, hamburger buns. Ingredients. How to get away from the real fanatics, the Presleyites? She gets the ingredients of the hamburger buns. She sifts a lot of data on how to make them exactly as Elvis would have loved them, great contention.

MOP has found the big girls, the cadre in their hide-out in the mountainous bullshit of Presley-mania, screened by the enthusiasts of the diamond-studded momma's boy.

<OWL> Philosophy is not allowed; it's about what you do, not what you think or how you feel.

The goddess is working with her. Boredom she links with evils. An action of evil is the absence of any meaningful action, truly without feeling or thought, let alone passion and interest in others. Forget compassion.

<MOP> But what about the crushed pills? The white powder?

She waits for a bite, closely monitoring each indignant or drug-crazy sentence.

<MOP> White Virgin?

She sits, hovering like a goshawk over its prey, watching all the other reactions as they come up. Some smart alecs even give chemical formulas for White Virgin and how it could be masked in hamburger bun dough. The two words repeat with a question mark, masquerading as a glitch. Slowly losing the dills, but new idiots come on-line as Americans get home from work. Her mind flips file cards of produce.

<REDSHOES> milk?

MOP's fingers are busy wings, but she doesn't dive. She is hungry but she must wait for the misspeller, glitch-user, to come on line. Whether or not that happy happenstance will be hours or days later she can't say. She believes it will occur soon.

<BLUSUADE> WhiteVirgin is the name of a particularly nasty software program.

<MOP> AOK.

<ANON> What a gurl!

MOP frowns: mistyping backfiring?

<ANON> That is 'anon' as in soon, get it?

MOP stays in the conversation, using nonsense, but she is not sure of the right input, so she simply puts U in imitation of a virus, with a question mark. She uses one of her illegal programs to ensure continual interruption. It doesn't commit her one way or the other. An acronym is MOP's only reading. What's that doing in the Elvis maze with her? She waits. The other conspirators scroll.

<SKUMBO> Hey Soon, how soon?

<MOP> Boredom is an indication of evil.

She wants to check to see if anyone on line at the moment was with her earlier in the Solanasite cell.

As an angler rests the baited line, not expecting a fish to get hooked immediately, she leaves her desk for a cigarette. The sky is pale in the east. She watches the clouds' abstract designs with faint violet and washed yellow cadmium.

Most women don't know their boredom is a function of evil, she muses idly. The fisherman's hell, she recalls, is where, for eternity, the line is thrown, the fish is caught and the fish is perfect, the catch immediate and the shore is pleasant, the tide is right. Am I fish or fisher? She wishes her system would crash to give her a break. When she goes back to the screen, sure enough, a message:

\<YM\> Hear you've got what you wanted, bitch. We're talking daughters of Eve, right? A servant to sleep with. A youth to fuck.

Beautiful beautiful rock spider, is sung through the amp, by a rugged, amateur voice.

\<MOP\> Anon come back, Private chat. Private chat, MMIMR.

Not only Solanasites feeding off the Presleyites, but paedophiles as well. Charming. MOP wonders if the intercourse is still taking place between that of the conspirators and innocent recipe-writers because she cannot find out for herself. Her gear is reacting sporadically.

\<MOP\> Miss Peller seeking entry, Please.

MOP feels her way humbly. Anon allows her in. MOP is caught off guard. She is in a space of direct language. There are four in the private chat room, hidden within the glitter and sentiment of Elvis fans' networks, a continent away from other political lesbians.

\<SKUMBO\> You're righteous rattling about boredom. I've been following you. Wonder how far your greed for power will go. The personal is political. We can't trust you any more.

Moments of Pleasure, sure her net-name was secure, is now convinced the other three know who she is. She doesn't know exactly who or what they are. She feels cornered. Cyberspace had been her romping ground. The higher political purpose of the serious Solanasites, really worthwhile, exciting and violent though it is, is not her obsession. Computer savvy gives her an edge. She could, on behalf of the boss, deliver orders. Take orders. There is money. There are schemes. There are contracts. There is intelligence. MOP feels compromised, scared. She is trapped in readiness to being used. They tease her with nonsense.

\<REDSHOES\> Your boss is really a Russian cosmonaut, a woman in a rogue, broken down space-ship, circling the earth, interfering with telecommunications, organising her own revolution. We need you out in the world. You will wait for instructions.

\<MOP\> This techno Amazon does not want to surrender.

\<MISSPELLER\> Don't think 'surrender' MOP. Think collective good, Get some sleep, ozzie.

Something is seriously wrong if the congress is sacrificed to an individual, no matter how 'good' that person is. On the other hand, how does anything actually happen if there is not chain of command? She will be able to implant a bug in the arsehole's pace-maker, detonate him from the inside. MOP wants these orders. She wants her strength and acumen co-ordinated with others all around the world. 'A small handful of SCUM can take over . . . within a year by systematically fucking up the system, selectively destroying property, and murder.' Solanas' list of targets and objectives are rich men with pea-brains, the captains of industry, bloated with power, gambling with other people's money and lives. And specialist doctors on the cutting edge of medical science and IVF technology, experimenting with women's lives. For MOP there is no doubt these people are bad. Other SCUM will destroy all useless and harmful objects, like Great Art.

MOP coolly deletes all unnecessary software from her desktop, feeling the load of better revenge lift off her brain and leech into her muscles. She turns off her computer. And before she puts herself to bed in the day-time she checks her wardrobe for her uniform, her jewel-box for her name-pin and brief-case for her registration papers. Something to look forward to: the real world.

23

. . . the information on the monitor . . .

This morning I had a hunch: if I dropped in on Meghan, or Jill, or both, without warning, I might get one or two of my questions answered, simply by wrong-footing them as it were. Passing cloud weakened sunlight as I drove along the narrow strip of bitumen between tall tree trunks. The patterns of shadows came in and out of sharp focus. The weather was cooler, fresh. I liked slow driving in certain moods in this kind of terrain. The road's bends dipped down to creek bridges to weave up again, requiring constant gear shifts. Beyond the fringe of gums were farms and houses, cows and horses; barns, some on the lean, others shiny galvanised steel. And beyond them the washy outline of distant ranges. Foreground features. Idiosyncratic letterboxes. A person on a tractor. Children waiting for the school bus. Xs and arrows indicating the way to the dirt-bikes' trail painted on boards tacked at turn-offs for the next Motor Cross meet. Two men chewing grass over a gate. Stacked white boxes of bee-hives. Honey-coloured limbs of grey gums newly stripped of bark. A small mill with its pile of sawdust smoking.

The rhythm of the road had me cogitating. A car approaching, driving too fast, hugging the centre, narrowly missed my fender. Woke me up. Attracted my attention. Altered my meditation. These maniacs drive as if in a constant state of panic. The interface of death shimmering like some celluloid cloth glistening with temptation to enact contempt for life with the lure of beyond, every near accident must give them a rush, a glimpse of some exciting, fear-some unknown. It is immaterial whether these boys are suicidal or homicidal. The glorious edge of death, either way, has them entranced. The survivors became truckies, I supposed bitterly. Or tow-truck drivers. I recalled the video game, *Carmageddon*, in Lisa's friend's rumpus room and wondered about the difference between virtual driving and real driving. Maybe they saw death as an entrance into another reality where they became supermen, able to fly, jump tall buildings, have fire-power beyond their wildest dreams. Cybergods. Neil Waughan: how could I hope to understand the hormone-crazed youth, the testosterone teenager, with an electronic superworld at his fingertips? How normal could he be in my comprehension of normality? Taking into account my ignorance of the information, entertainment and communication revolution, how could I assess the norms? How could I know science fiction from what was technologically possible? Theoretically in the pipe-line or actually happening?

After the sign for Lebanese Plains, following the arrows, coincidentally, pointing down the same gravel alley, I fell into the same trap as Philip-poussis. Because the two boys died on the same night there had to be a connection. Hugh Gilmore was none of my business. Neil's GP was away on leave for a month. The receptionist was busy and would only answer basic questions: I would have to wait until Dr Neville returns. The death certification was signed by the locum. Very fuzzy, the behaviour of the busy medical profession! My guess is that signature was no more than a formality.

A tickle on my tongue made me glance towards Chandra's property. Meghan Featherstone's white Daewoo Leganza SX 2.2L (I had this detail from an insurance form) was not in its place on the safe side of the water-course. The creek was much lower, babbling nonsensically and innocently across pleasant-looking stones. I achieved the hill after the last ford in two-wheel drive. As the sun was well risen, the dark clouds away to the west and near cumulus as jolly as dollops of ice-cream, the valley did not look as depressing as it did before. When I got out, however, there was a dankness about the long runners of kikuyu climbing the fence-wire, thick around the posts. The smell of choking grass underneath did not have the nice pungency of dead mulch rotting. The goats were on tethers, forlorn with drooping ears and arrogant noses; silly, sad aristocrats. Curly Cue nibbled the air in my direction. Assuming no one was home as Jill's old Urvan was not in its spot, I walked down past them to the stake which held the rope and pulled it out to take them higher, near the gate where the feed was untouched. Instinctively, I noted the tyre marks on the driveway: broad defined off-road treads were unlikely to be the van's. The goats were like dogs to lead. I saw a couple of buckets under the tank-stand. They drank thirstily, then attacked the scraggly vegetable garden.

The door opened easily. The place had been ransacked. The living-room looked as if a hurricane had come and gone. A tantrum? The kitchen was undisturbed, just a little dirty. I went up to the bedroom and instantly knew this was where the force of the storm hit. A small filing cabinet was overturned, each drawer emptied. A bedside bureau had spilled its contents: photographs, pill jars, repeat subscriptions, lotions and oils, discoloured bandages, dental floss. An unwound yoyo with tangled string. I moved slowly, surveying, frowning. The perpetrator was not necessarily trying to intimidate—pillows, for instance, had not been torn open; no loose feathers for cinematic effect—so, was possibly alone. The night cream and moisturisers had not been splattered in the tempest of personal spite. It was more like a search which had grown more frenetic as it became unsuccessful, perhaps. The papers in the main room had either blown from the loft or been thrown, some were scrunched. In the middle of the eiderdown I discovered the key to the house, along with the telephone, another article in the mess. Did I have Meghan's work number on me? The connection was dead anyway.

My silent mouth open, I abruptly sat on the bed, processing it all for a minute. She would have to be ringing from a cell phone if she were camping out under the stars on the Nullarbor? The concurrence of reading about the Radiation Health Standing Committee and seeing a map with the Eyre Highway and the Great Victorian Desert, Pitjantjatjara Land and Maralinga Land with Meghan ringing from the vicinity had me believing she was a nuclear physicist. But she could be any of those exotic scientists: anthropologist, archaeologist or palaeontologist digging up fossils from the Jurassic period or whenever. The more spurious, the more madcap the scientific exploits, the more generous research grants were, it seemed.

One of the pages was a birth certificate. I expected Meghan Feather-stone's and Jillian T. David's names on the papers. I reached down and read it. A female was registered as coming into the world on the 18th day of the fifth month in 1981. She was called Hope, Hope O'Lachlin. Her parents were married to each other and then resided in Auckland, New Zealand. I picked up a handwritten note on a piece of pin-feed computer paper 'Our agenda is pretty clear. The elite of the elite is divided up into spies and killers.'

Suddenly I was absolutely furious. I kicked around the balled papers some more in the bedroom. I found no further evidence of the existence of Hope O'Lachlin, but I scribbled her name in the little notebook I carry with me in my hip pocket when the spiral one might be too obvious, speculating about Christian names chosen by parents across the Tasman Sea. Perhaps a Prudence and a Patience completed an uptight Kiwi family. Faith, perchance? Charity? I knelt down to look at the scattered photos. Most of the snaps were of lesbians in various states of undress with backgrounds of bush or desert. Several I recognised. There were far too many shots of the goats as kids to be of any use to anybody. Some prints had been ripped. Interesting. To settle my disordered mind I tried to piece together severed parts. Unusually boring was one of a rear-view window filled with high-beam headlights of a following vehicle taken from the driver's seat of a car. It brought to mind dodgy UFO pictures.

The pot-belly stove seemed to have been pelted with bits of documentation scrunched by hominid hands. A rate notice from a municipality in

Queensland, Brisbane, the suburb of St Lucia. The address the same as the mortgage for that property. Another, a letter, was from the solicitor who had refused to see me, angrily discarded. This was about a power of attorney. A photo fell from a pile of envelopes I picked up. Another black and white snapshot of a saucerish white shape against a background of a two-lane black-top lit by car tail-lights. An actual UFO? I slipped the picture into my pocket.

Before I left, I sniffed the air indoors with my eyes closed, each area. It was pretty much the same as the night I had stayed except for two scents. There was a lingering drift of greasy wool, fleece, in the bedroom. Downstairs, something so familiar the word for it was on the tip of my tongue and I couldn't catch it for a while. Then the membranous brain clicked, in one single pouch, female-sweat-perfume-filter-cigarettes, as you smell in clubs full of poker-machines or the casino-rooms of pubs. Neither I identified as Jill or Meghan.

Outside, I patted the nanny goat's snobbish snout, vacantly murmuring reassurances. I went over the rough map of Meghan's financial situation that I had. Her source account was a cheque and savings into which went her pay, in uneven sums; from that flowed a key card and credit card which dealt with property expenses and everyday living. A debit account with another bank which could be the mortgage on the property I was now standing on. Yet why would she take out a mortgage when in a few months she could have bought it outright? About eighty thousand in the red being paid off at about six thousand six hundred per annum, but something funny was going on because someone was also taking money out of that account. Meghan's two hundred a week was automatically transferred and Jill's $60 p.w. was more spasmodic. There was financial neglect here, as well as physical. There was hole spreading across the two: where was that money going? Thirdly, she had a hunky-dory superannuation nest egg into which the government and she paid equal amounts. What I needed was evidence of a share portfolio. The ATM dockets I'd been given showed that money had been taken out in town X while Meghan said she was in town Y. Proof that something was up. She was too otherworldly to keep a proper track of her bank statements, this I had been told. The accountant probably got copies when she needed them on payment to the bank in question. There was a lot of money somewhere. Where? Other properties, apart from the flat in Brisbane? Buried cash in case Armageddon crashed the banking system? Rosemary Turner would have to know if Meghan had any other income. How did she write off the deficit?

Who was Hope O'Lachlin? Or more appropriately, why was her birth certificate here? Who was in the Brisbane flat? I could find that out.

The goat nuzzled me. I did not have time to stay around there. I went back up the stairway to get the key, ignored the papers and mess, and, locked the place. I hung the key from a nail in the laundry. I found the goat feed and gave them heaps, leaving them near the house and vegetable garden. I pulled a trough under the overflow of the tank and filled it up with a hose.

As I got in my car and drove away I had the silly thought of the goats leaping inside that half-finished dairy house and eating all those papers I had left as I found them. I wondered if they, like dogs, sensed ghosts and other spirits, well, I felt decidedly spooked. I needed information on electronic banking, and I knew where to go to get it.

The actual chaos I found at Featherstone's half-finished mansion-in-the-mind's-eye was yucky internal muddle surfacing in profligate abandon: a physical depiction of 'I don't care about the consequences I want something now', or, just horrible carelessness with someone else's stuff. My gut feeling was that the ransacking had been occasioned by my investigation. Money is a sore spot with most people. Number two feeling was that whatever was searched for was found and the state of the place was mere mess-making. Used cheque books. Cheque stubs. Whoever it was did not want me justifying cheque stubs with bank statements. If Jill wanted Meghan's money, she had only to take it out of the card account. I gathered that Megs would give darling Jill anything she wanted.

Alison sits at Neil Waughan's computer trying to tat the strings of her fraying personality into a doily, into one viable piece. A circle of perfection. The face of the screen changes with the alacrity of her forefinger and the click of the darting mouse; web pages dissolving and building images. Her seeking ship docks in one of the harbours of her brain as if her quest is Homeric. Then she is hunting down the back lanes and alleys of a virtual city. To her side on his workstation is the cryptic crossword at which, every now and then, she glances. Or stops to handwrite a word. Puzzles relax Alison, release the pressure valve in her brain. A lump of guilt in her guts prevents her eating. The relationship is too intense, too karmic. Maria's loyalties? An old aunt had said to Alison as a zany, brilliant teenager, 'If I had the courage, girl, I would scar your face with a carving knife, to save yourself and others from tragedy'; the double barb, it had happened already, dissociation from the shame. All these strings, her beauty, her destiny, she tries to knot and separate; Medea, Helen and Cassandra she has been; now she is an impoverished, dysfunctional single mother on a pension with one job, cleaner.

'Does the cycle never end? Things happen around me, people dying. Because I wish it. And I see them before they do. I do not wish her dead, yet

I wish for my own exorcism. Demons overtake me like succubae. There are my blackouts.'

Suddenly her eyes hook onto the information on the monitor. To avoid the pressure banging on her brain, she has been searching Neil's favourite websites to solve an enigma. Now she is looking at what she knows to be a major clue: <u>www.Whymen</u>, Hebefilia International, Sail to the galaxy, boys, on our yacht. Boys who love nature, boys who love sport, adventure, ecstasy, pics and places! The pornography paths through the Internet, she interprets as a teenage boy thing, a geek's adventure into cybersex. Boy-lovers' societies. Okay, lads have egos and like to be called beautiful. Galaxy is highlighted. She clicks on it. This is beyond libertarian porn. Trips like you wouldn't believe, kid! All free, all we want is your body, for a heavenly moment. Using Neil's cybernym, she joins the chat. This is tacky, rings false, she mutters. The tatting of purpose falls into place. The *Argo* is rigged and ready. She takes command of the fleet with a thousand oars.

Soft porn slime won't get Lenny, Alison determines. These guys claim they are not interested in prepubescent boys, but mid-adolescence, where a child turns into youth. Beauty, love and truth, as classic as ancient Greece. Smooth as lines of snot. And wealthy. She has a link. The date coincides. This is Neil's computer and his cyberfriends would push him places whether or not he wanted to go. Do the boys hate what the older men love? Something doesn't gel though. She looks at the cryptic and sees that she had written the wrong part of speech, *'tion* ending, instead of *'ting*. The Neil puzzle is flashing the same amber light. Caution.

She is interrupted by the pink palm of a black body. 'You owe me sister-girl.'

Alison pulls fifty dollars out of the pocket of her blue uniform, and smiles at her friend's face. 'Thanks Iris.'

'No worries. What's this shit you're reading, sister-girl?' demands Lenny's auntie.

'You got it, shit,' Alison responds, working fast. 'Have you noticed any fancy yacht berthed down on the pier, or anywhere along the river in the past couple of weeks?' she asks, not moving her eyes from the computer.

For some reason, the Aboriginal woman does not answer, but asks, 'Do you want me to pick up Lenny or what?'

'Iris? Answer me.' Alison turns around.

'Oh, they are probably just fishermen, you know, rich buggers after marlin and fame.' Iris stands with her arms folded beneath her breasts, speaking as if there is so much she has noticed over the years that white people don't see that she could just fish out any observation and it would do as well in answer to the question.

'Who? What? Who? Yes, I do want you to pick up Lenny and can he stay overnight? Listen here's another twenty bucks for pizza. Tell me where it is.' Alison pleads.

Iris shrugs. 'What about Tilly?'

'She's okay. She's with some friends.' Alison wants to shake the information out of the nonchalant woman. 'Where is the yacht?'

Iris grins. And explains, 'You have to go by boat, too muddy to walk, the mangroves are thick there. Behind the oyster leases. That's what makes it funny, sticks out like a sore thumb, but I suppose they can pick up anchor and motor off anywhere anytime. To Tahiti, perhaps.'

'Perhaps. What does it look like?' Alison has to interrupt her own interpretation of Iris' expression; she has the odd impression that Iris dreams of travel.

'Well,' Iris fills her in, 'it's like a three-storey speed-boat with two bloody great outboards about 800 horsepower each, and it's prickling with aerials and rods. It's a flash motorcruiser all right. A bit like that one on the other side of the canal here, only bigger, I reckon.'

Alison, indeed, hadn't taken much notice of the surroundings of Penny Waughan's house, usually entertained more by mental visions than outside observations. Iris pulls her to the window which overlooks the brown canal. Opposite, moored to a private jetty, is a cabin cruiser, shining white and blue and looking brand new. 'Would you call it a yacht?' she asks.

Iris laughs with a gust of amusement. 'A yacht has sails, and a stick up the middle they call a mast, and the wind blows it along the sea. This one up the river could reach 30 knots out of pure diesel power, girl. Reckon it would cost more than a million dollars.'

Alison frowns. 'Well, are there any strange yachts about?'

Iris shakes her head, 'I don't know. The marina is like a closed shop, you know. Like a locked paddock full of racehorses, they can tell the difference between them. I don't know if any of them is strange. They pay money, they get a mooring. What we couldn't do with one of them, you know?'

Alison nods, 'Of course. Thanks for your help.' She goes back to the computer. The screen-saver is Bart Simpson who says, 'Yo Ninja!'

Iris, at the door, asks, 'You ever tell your boss that I do the work?'

'Hell no.' Alison picks up her fresh rubber gloves and sniffs them. It is a habit. 'And don't you!'

'Helps to be a white girl, don't it?' Lenny's auntie comments without bitterness.

'Don't it, just? It's not that, Iris, you can have all the money she pays me. I need this.' Alison slaps the keyboard. She covets Neil's IT equipment and plans to use it more.

'Nothing wrong with sharing.' Alison goes back to the dates and times, reaches for her crossword pen and scrabbles about for some paper. She writes them down. Then she refigures the material on the computer and attaches it to an email to Chandra. When she shuts down she is desperate to see Maria; not to touch her; not to have sex with her; just to ground the sparking wires in her brain.

When I got to Chandra's I found her on the verandah flipping through a PC magazine. 'Can you believe this?' she said, as she gestured me to sit. 'There is a video game called *Blind Pedestrians*.'

'Heard of *Carmageddon*?' I asked, struck by how weird it was when something you have been thinking about comes up in someone else's conversation.

She answered, 'Yeah, you hard-shoulder your opponent and ram a competitor from behind as he corners and watch him flip over your head in a terrifying roll.'

'That's funny. I was just thinking about that.' I fished the paper out of my jeans pocket.

'They have a lot to answer for, these guys.' Chandra claimed mildly, belying the heat she probably felt about it. 'What's that?' she demanded abruptly.

'Nasty,' I said, and unfolded it. 'Nutters.' My confusion led to frustration, then to a quickening anger as she did not say anything, implying that she did not agree with my judgement. I told her where I found it.

Chandra said, 'Betrayal makes us vulnerable.' She who trusted felt betrayed and feeling betrayed, paralysed. 'Fuck Meghan.' She ignored me and went into her office and started manipulating the computer screen. I heard the dial tone of telephonic connection. Then, after a few rapid screen changes, a page of chat came up. Chandra typed, waited, typed, waited. I stood in the doorway.

<MOP> Surely we didn't really think we were invulnerable? Stay smart, (re)sisters!

<WHEELS> We set up such a labyrinth. Put so much work and ingenuity into it, spent on the creativity credit card, maybe reached the limit?

<BAC> This is all beside the point, who did it and why?

<BLUESKY> Consequences fatal.

<BAC> The Etruscan is scammed. Bastard . . . or Bitch!!!

<MOP> GF Be cool. We have our spirit. Revolution. Our reason for being.

<WHEELS> And our set-back. We have to fight back. We have to stay alive.
<MOP> Some internet surfer cum hacker cum nosy parker has seen our harmless nattering and probably thought meaningless equals meaning, let's go white sauce.
<DEFARGE> Kaput.
<WHEELS> Not by a long shot.

'What all that about?' I asked.

Not responding straightaway, Chandra eventually confided, 'My enemy.'

'Mine,' I said, as I debated internally whether to show my hand, 'is on the tar and cement highway of life, in control of gasoline power and tonnes of weight, smelling in the fumes, perfume to himself. The muddy clouds of coal chimney fires look fine to him. I prefer to see and hear the foe I fear.'

'Wait,' she said.

I started to converse, but she interrupted with, 'Hang on, there is something I have to check on.'

I gazed out the window at Potsdam Harry, who was grazing between the white-painted tyres in the exercise yard. She opened her palms to the screen, 'This is truly weird.'

The sentences rolled up like the credits of a film. 'So?'

Chandra looked at me and shook her head, then said, 'Someone's playing with me.'

She began thrashing her keyboard rather hard I thought. No change, just a scroll, like the work of a fast typist monopolised the screen. The icon moved with Chandra's hand, but the click on the mouse wasn't having any effect. She pulled the switch on the whole thing, which I'd been advised was a big no-no. 'RSA cryptosystem, invented twenty-five years ago, was considered impregnable. Now it's no longer safe.'

'Have you cracked it?' I asked Chandra, the hacker.

She said, 'Time to make a move in a more serious direction.' She took a laptop from a brief-case and brought it to life on her knees, leaving the desktop computer without power. 'Let's see what the RAD method can do. That is,' she said for my benefit, 'rapid application development.'

'I knew that,' I muttered in the slang that meant I had no idea what she was talking about.

She went on. 'If I email myself, here,' Chandra clapped her desk, 'I'll discover whether I have been sent a defective, infected, message. Ah ha! Someone has just loaded my computer with crap. Virus attached. What is bizarre is, it does nothing. Except.'

She looked at me, doubtfully. I nodded, encouraging. 'What does that look like to you?'

'Dates and times?' I guessed, relatively alarmed by her mood. 'Can't you de-bug it?'

'Cross-tool. Easy if you know what you're doing,' Chandra leaned back, gazing warmly up at me. 'You utilise a file replication service. Works like a chain letter. Or an office distribution list. Oh, forget it.' She switched on the desktop terminal, found a program from a very long list and set what she called a defrag in motion, the computer arranging its pixels into neatly colour-coordinated squares. And wheeled herself out of her office. Chandra, apparently, plays by her own rules.

'What do you think of this?' I sought her opinion. 'Meghan's place has been ransacked. Gear everywhere.'

'Why were you at Meghan's?' Chandra seemed suddenly astonished, picking up the note I'd shown her.

'Doing my job.' I grinned. 'Have you any idea of what else Meghan owns?' I asked Chandra, meaning property. She shook a negative with a her handsome head.

'There is a huge hole I'm trying to get to the bottom of,' I explained, being as vague as vague. 'I like digging,' I admitted. Client confidentiality prevented me from dealing in nuts and bolts as regards my investigation.

'On-line banking, perhaps? Have you considered that, Margot?'

'Wouldn't that show up in credit card statements?'

'I suppose,' Chandra replied, still holding the handwritten chit. 'Meghan, and/or Jill, plainly know their way round the Internet.' She wiggled the pin-feed paper. 'Can I copy this? I'll give it back to you in a minute.' Chandra scooted back to her office. I followed. She fiddled with her electronic equipment. Scanner, fax. I didn't know. I wondered if Chandra was as rude to everybody else as she was to me.

Determined not to let her fob me off, I entered her home office and said, 'Tell me what's going on here.' I myself was struck by the tone of my voice.

She glanced at me sharply, narrowing her eyes. I saw trust and distrust of me slide across the surface of her irises like wind-driven clouds. 'Just a glitch.' The facsimile regurgitated the page and she thrust it at me. 'Nonsense.'

'How does the information get there, anyway?' I leant against the wall with my thumbs hitched in my front pockets.

'Three basic ways. You know computers "think" in noughts and ones? Well on the CD-ROMs they are read as pits and dashes by optical fibre. Read Only Memory. Then there is RAM, random access, which is built-in, electro-magnetic, and then there's electronic communication. Phone lines et cetera. Leaps and bounds are being made in wireless, completely wireless, communication. What's happening here is some kind of cross-over. Beggars reason.' A natural teacher, Chandra, I felt she said all that nervously, as a way to attract me or, perhaps, to divert me.

'You can say that again,' I said softly. 'Well, best you get on with it.' I bent down to kiss her cheek. She presented her lips. A wholly sensual woman with serious concerns in cyberspace.

'Let's have dinner?' I suggested.

'Let's,' she accepted.

'Okay,' I smiled. Departed. Seated in the car I noted down in my Spirax the pseudonyms of the chat page, Chandra's odd reaction to the 'elite of the elite' note, and as much as I could under the title she had given me, nonsense; I neatly tucked the UFO photo and the spies/killers memo in between the pages. Betrayal, I wondered if there were any way one could find out who the real people were behind the virtual names, whether the anxiety Chandra felt on that score had anything to do with my business and why, finally, she did not recognise the numbers as dates and times.

But as I drove again through the picture-postcard scenery I let my thoughts loose along lateral lines. Lesbians ought to be independent women. Freedom. They have no reason to compound their lives with each other's, making avoidable clutter. The unaccountable fury I felt back there at the nanny-goats' dairy was at how Meghan and Jill had intermixed their domestic, financial, emotional, sexual dealings and dreams. The mess in Meghan's place seemed symbolic. Chandra was disabled, but independent. I liked her for that. I really liked her. She was hiding something from me but she liked me too. The ability to love another woman and the freedom to do it was a sacred gift, according to Broom; therefore, if profaned, it turned very bad indeed. Once on the highway, I opened the throttle on the Sierra and wondered, as I sometimes do, how I could update it to a Vitara for more comfortable and speedy road travel. Sponsors. Should write to Suzuki. My appearing in a commercial for a politically unsound multinational company would not overly impress Chandra Williams.

Wednesday afternoon aerobics were in full swing. Music as hype echoed through the building. High-cut leotards and leggings were reflected in the wall of mirrors. Mainly women were stepping on indiviudal portable steps, flinging their arms and wiggling their hips to the bellowed rap-rhythm directions of a pair of instructors. Tiger Cat was a gym junkie. As I did not have her phone number or an address, I figured I would find her pumping iron even though all I could do for myself was exercise the upper body, bench press, arm weights, abdominal rolls and, seated, shoulder work. Sure enough, she turned up when I was lying on my back. Not wanting to stay in canine submission, I lowered the bar to the stand and called her over while I stayed in a sitting position. I asked her a few questions about the evening Neil died. She wouldn't answer directly until I told her I was working on the case. Tiger Cat respected employment whatever its nature, provided it was paid.

'You want to interrogate the fat bird,' she said. 'That chick is a bottomless pit.'

As she would incriminate herself in no way, denying that she distributed any drugs or pills or knew the names of who did what, descriptions such as 'fat chick' were all I was going to get and what she meant by 'bottomless pit' was up to me to interpret.

Tiger Cat herself carried no flab, even to the point of ingesting little fluid, and judged all those who did as beneath contempt. 'Couldn't get enough, really sus,' she went on. 'She's your one, Gorman.' She made a few snide comments about sex, which I dismissed as sour grapes.

I would have taken everything she said with a grain of salt, except there was something in her tone reminiscent of corrupt cops: while they are careful to cover their own doings, they have a good nose for moral stench and their clandestine activities can expose insights into the guilt of crooks invisible to those of us who are straight-dealing. Although Maria would not necessarily want mind-altering substances for herself, she could easily have been stockpiling for Sofia. I knew that Tiger Cat had really given me something, but she was not about to speculate for my sake as free-ranging deduction and induction from known facts would finger her. I did not let on that I knew what she was distributing at the barbecue. But I walked away from the gym having to reassess my opinion of my friends in the light of the search for truth, regardless of the likableness of characters and personal loyalty.

24

. . . her dead body . . .

The wind is lively. In the swampy paddock behind Maria's a sparrowhawk hovers. Crows shriek to each other, suggesting the flock fly to the large gum tree near the fence. They are raucous, black and well-fed. The may bush in the backyard is as white as a bride in a wedding dress. A bay laurel dominates the herb garden, along with rampant spearmint. The sage bush is a shrub of sticks. Rosemary survives neglect. Pumpkin, a Queensland Blue, winds its vine around everything in its reach. The house is busy with the blow-ins of cheque day. Cars queue in the drive-way, brushing the hedge. The gate is shut to contain a pack of dogs. Helen and Ti Dyer are in from the land. Yvonne arrives at the same time as Alison. The comings and goings are haphazard as if swept in and out by the fresh, seasonal wind like the leaves of the English maple. Sofia is at home. Eddies of gossip, accidental encounters, incidental invitations, transactions and odd dealings occasion an impromptu congregation of souls in the ebb and flow of company. Maria is having a great time with Libby Gnash and Judith Sloane, talking of the past.

Maria asks, 'What are you doing now, Libby?'

'I'm a lawyer,' Libby replies, lighting a cigarette. A grey crane alights on the back lawn, folds its wingspan and begins high-stepping, its bony neck trembling; its dagger of a bill ready to stab the ground.

'Oh, that's right. I heard.' Maria gazes out her window at the bird, wondering why she had forgotten that.

'But,' Libby searches for the phrase that will bring Maria's attention to her. 'I'm still a believer.' She winks at Judith Sloane. She has known her since Judith first came to Australia. Stunning then, entertaining women in the smoky bars with her glorious voice, Judith has shrunk with time, not only in status but also the muscles of her face. In the 1970s Judith was a radical working-class Pom with plenty of grassroots experience of fighting for the rights of women on the streets of Bradford and Leeds and London. An energetic activist. She was journalist, photographer, film-maker, anthology editor, festival director, conference organiser, weaver, quilt-maker, wool grower and spinner, you name it. Most of all, she could sing like an angel.

'Yes.' Maria watches Sofia make a fuss of Alison. 'Believer? Strange word, these days.'

'Gotta keep the faith, Maria. Remember,' Libby lectures; it is her tone of voice.

'The word warms me. Cuppa?' she offers. 'There is still tea in the pot.' Libby shakes her head in refusal. Judith pours herself a cup. A harsh ring echoes in the hall. Sofia responds to the doorbell. More gurls with their shopping in the car. Maria Freewoman is gusty. She likes an audience; she likes to be overheard. She loves the good old days and conversation pushes away a silence she feels creeping inside her. She, Judith and Libby fist the table to emphasise points in a trivial pursuit of their own memory, the less certain of the facts the more adamant the statements. They compete. A progressive barn dance on the floor of history speeds up to a fandango of enthusiasms for politics, consciousness-raising, conferences, concerts, past loves and infidelities. Alison from her spot on the lounge sees through the door that beneath the cheer are old sores, and she wonders, will they end up settling old scores. Indeed, Libby feels a waft of pain as Maria laughingly rides roughshod over her tender heart in a boastful recounting of her having a lover for every day of the week, except Sunday. Like tourists in another country, the 1970s, they taste and take in the scenery, watch the natives, themselves, being fascinating.

Lunchtime is lost in the hours between eleven and four. Plenty of women move about the house, indulging their own cravings and appetites. Gurls open the fridge, and shut it; use the toaster and scrape the plastic tub of canola-butter mix with a rinsed knife; answer the door, use the bathroom whether or not it be for a hit; smoke nicotine, marijuana or coltsfoot; appease cramps with pain-killers, alcohol or food. The dogs outside or sneaking in, Sofia's pet is not to be seen. Friends throw in the odd witty comment, or sarcastic taunt. Now and then, they loosely relate stories of their own. Libby, Judith and Maria pause politely. In the sea of the spoken word, Maria is in her element, a whale gliding with swordfish and shark.

The discussion swells and resiles. 'Individualists,' Libby remarks critically. Maria nods. Judith says, 'Times have changed. It will never be the same.' As if analysing their generation were vital, they are back as quickly as possible, thrashing out old theories and disputes, recreating the forum where the personal was political, the oppression of women the fight. They talk, recalling the dynamics of the old wars. Libby relishes the indulgence around Maria. The opinionated listener, she is used to being the most intelligent woman in the room and is as pugnacious as a pug dog. Judith glamorises the scenes in perfect word-pictures that Maria appreciates as one does a film in which one starred or was an extra. It is, surprisingly, the first time their three paths have really converged since the activist times in Sydney, the heady days, Libby skinny, small and tight, smoking, Maria fat, loud and unbound, Judith, soft-spoken and serious.

'You can live in the past,' says Sofia, 'But you can't breathe.'

Libby Gnash yearns for the hungry, angry times of solidarity. She drums the table with brown-stained fingers in the rhythm of horses galloping. The fag and the way it is lit is reminiscent of the moments when urgency and excitement rippled through the air and cigarette smoke was exhaled with a vengeance and purpose to hare off to graffiti a wall, or slap up posters, hurry down to a hall or a tin shed to sew banners. In fetid rooms, where thrill-seeking females were too impatient to wait for the de-brainwashing of millions of arseholes, she could take on other women with a tongue as sharp as a tack and tell the men exactly where to go. She puffs now, but not from hot-footing it away from a cop cruiser. Words are all that remain, and Judith reminds them of slogans and lyrics. Sentimental in her recall of her salad days, Maria laughs with moistened eyes. Maria's tears are easy. Unashamed. She wipes them away to recall the joy. Libby frowns, hiding her own susceptibility for nostalgia, and remembers Maria as a broad ox of a woman, megaphone to mouth and loose tits in the latest right-on printed singlet. She wades into the tides of time and dives for a swim in its bay having the conversation with Maria.

'When the political devolved to the personal, we lost the plot,' she says. Maria has changed. Her muscles are flab, her mind lazy, yet, now she absorbs. Libby does not remember Maria listening, like this. She didn't have time; she had to change the world.

Maria recalls a show, begs Judith for a scrap of music from a piece of theatre. When Judith sings a line, Libby suddenly can hardly wait to put in her bit, her patch in the quilt. They make a fabric they find fascinating and Maria invites the other dykes to view it. Libby's smile of pride cools to a mild embarrassment. Judith is unconcerned, superior. These younger women seem to be waiting. Filling in time. 'Do they expect it to happen again, and sweep them up?'

'Well, it won't if they just sit there and do nothing but try and feel good,' states Libby, prepared to argue with any takers, for as well as the past she lives in the present. 'Dropping out is not the answer,' she grins at Maria. 'Fucking-up is.'

Judith says, 'I can't believe you are still quoting Solanas.'

Contemplation of the present flattens Maria's mood for a minute. 'Out of what?', she asks sadly. Tolerating behaviour, because there are valid excuses, is her way of life. Her body, lately, has been giving her trouble she is not admitting to Sofia or even Alison. She is swelling. Maria accommodates all at cost to her frame. Her knees are giving way. 'Things have not got better for women, who can blame them wanting to get out of it? It is a sickness. Society is worse.'

'I don't agree,' states Libby, shaking her head, looking down. 'No, they had more than we did.'

'You're sure of that, Libby?' Maria reaches over and bots one of her tailor-mades.

'You've lost the fire you used to have, Maria,' observes Judith, unsympathetically.

Maria is offended and calls to Sofia to put on k. d. lang because she wants to listen to 'Constant Craving'. The sharp eyes of the cool gurls exchange glances.

Libby goes into the toilet, leaving silence between the other two. Maria does not know why Judith has come to her house by the railway. 'Tell me, are you into computers? The very thought tires me. I'm happy with my handwriting and my books, but if I were younger I'd miss out. The world will divide further into the haves and have-nots, and it'll be about knowledge, the poor are becoming poorer.'

Judith nods, knowingly. Libby, gingerly stepping around a grumbling canine, responds, 'Of course. I have to be, but I know what you mean.' She doesn't want to make Maria feel left out of her working world, or shatter the illusion of class solidarity, or sacrifice her status of a comrade in arms. Judith stares at her. 'It's frustrating, sometimes,' Libby concedes. Frustrating, like interesting, is a useful word if accuracy is not what you're after and experiences so thoroughly differ. Although Libby's computer crashes frequently, it is not her ignorance which causes it, rather an overcrowded desktop or software failure. Or viruses. Email is a part of her everyday life. And at least two hours a day on the Internet. She works most of the time. She is well-off. Maria remembers Libby as the archetypical humourless feminist, frowning into TV cameras, haranguing, with energy to burn. Her mild expression invites confidence. Libby leans towards her and lowers her voice. 'Even though the good old days have gone, there are still some of us into activism, the revolution has gone underground. We'll make things happen soon.'

Maria raises her eyebrows. 'Good for you.'

Judith exchanges a meaningful glance with Libby Gnash. 'The legal documents are in my car,' Libby says to Judith. Her secrets are safe in the waters of the past. But now Judith and she have business.

Lola's comment 'Cool gurls don't smile because their teeth are bad' comes to mind as she passes through the other room. Bossy in herself, Libby wants to inform these younger dykes on the responsibility of anarchy. Her remark to that effect is laughed at. She didn't intend to be funny. Maria abhors moralism, the past is not such a blast. 'Alison,' Maria pleads. 'Come and give me a kiss.'

Alison gives Maria a cuddle, whispering into her ear, 'I am worried about you.'

'Don't you worry about me.' Maria says.

The dogs are barking, blocking up the doorway.

Sofia, passing Libby in the hall, says, 'Turning into quite a party.'

Sofia's harried voice consciously changes when she greets the new arrival, 'Cybil!'

'Cybil,' says Jill. 'Why are you following me?' Jill David has a six-pack under her arm, coming up the steps.

'Jill,' Sofia greets her with a hug. Libby and Judith, speaking softly, go out the front door.

'Who's following who?' asks Cybil. Alison feels some sort of wave is about to break.

All newcomers crowd into the kitchen. Responding hospitably, Maria says to Alison, 'Put on the kettle will you. Another cup of tea would go well.'

Alison finds the kettle behind some recipe books and the plug hidden by the canisters. She fills it at the tap through its spout. 'Strange place for a fudge cake,' she says, 'on top of the fridge.'

Maria cries, 'Let's have some chocolate cake.'

'Yeah,' affirms Sofia. 'Be careful, Maria, it has dope in it.'

'But we couldn't get much of a rush from it,' calls Ti. Helen agrees.

Maria queries, 'Anyone for tea?' There are no acceptances.

'It is not hard to pick jealousy in the air when it is there,' Alison says and leaves Maria alone in the kitchen. Maria sees the steam rising from the kettle, and heaves herself up, taking some of her weight on her hands.

Alison chases after Libby and Judith, foiling their attempt to talk business. A manila folder is handed over. Libby's car is a silver-grey Volvo. Judith tosses the folder into the purple Mitsubishi Triton with its sheila-na-gig on the dash. 'Wow,' Alison whistles, 'Nice wheels.'

Ignoring her, Judith drives off.

Libby has more to do, Meghan Featherstone affairs. She is a terrier. She needs to talk to Jill David. She smells a rat. Gorman won't outdo her, not twice. She and Alison go back indoors. Libby refuses cake, settling for one of Jill's beers. Cake eaten, dope smoked, along with cigarettes, while water, tea and beer drunk, Maria has a second helping of cake. She is the only one with a hot drink. After a parley with Cybil outside, Ti and Helen pass through the lounge-room saying, 'Goodbye.' Yvonne has gone.

Kay and Em discuss addiction. Libby, comfortable with a beer as well as her cigarettes, contrives to believe she was not a part of the addicted set. She is fighting a fogginess that is catching in the lethargy of sitting around. Jill will not talk about Meghan or what Margot Gorman is up to.

Kay says, 'The more you have, the more you need. You get used to it. Your body chemistry changes.'

Em laughs, 'Yes, Ellie nearly died when she had a taste in a buy we divided evenly. Couldn't take it.'

'What happened?' asks Jill.

'She dropped, fitted.' Em describes taking her to hospital.

Alison contributes, 'I aspire to detachment, like a yogi. Detachment is the complete opposite to addiction. All Western society is addicted. There's always something everybody needs, the whole thing works on that. Gotta have it. Everyone is hanging out, or grooving away without having shared it, or angling to get whatever it is they want. Because that's what it is, wanting and wanting and wanting.'

'Yeah, but some addiction is worse, like hankering, like, you know, hell.'

'Hanging out is hell you mean.'

'De-tox,' Jill advises.

'You ought to talk,' Sofia says sarcastically to Alison. 'I mean you know detachment, you're detached from yourself half the time.'

'But if you're really detached, you're dead,' comments Kay.

Libby watches her keenly. Kay looks interesting. Hash-heads goon out on the fudge cake. Cybil does not like eating in front of others, especially skinny women. She sits quietly in the armchair, longing for chocolate cake, but denying herself. The social dynamics are centred now in the lounge-room. Libby looks at her wrist-watch and cannot believe the time.

When she goes into the kitchen to say goodbye, Libby finds Maria collapsed on the table. She stifles a scream. Sofia comes into the room, giggles and cannot stop giggling. She hears someone behind her say, 'Greedy Maria. Naughty, naughty.' Everyone is in the kitchen.

Cybil asks, aghast, 'What did you put in it?' She stares at the mud cake.

'Better get her onto her bed,' Libby mutters.

'It'll take all of us, come on.' Kay mobilises the troops.

'Shouldn't someone call an ambulance?' Alison asks Cybil, who shakes her head, shivers with shock and pulls herself together. 'And get Sofia for criminal negligence or something? Hang on a bit.'

'She has just gone into system shock,' says Em. 'Blood sugar has probably shot down.'

Jill wants to escape. 'I'm out of here.'

'If you don't call an ambulance I'm going to,' Kay declares. 'I don't care if they report it.'

Alison says, 'Let's call Margot Gorman.'

'Why?' asks Cybil, confused by the idea of the detective.

'Give her some honey,' suggests Em.

Dee arrives in the midst of the commotion.

'No!' Libby is responding to Alison, 'Margot Gorman used to round up Aborigines in Redfern, put them in nice police cells so that they could hang themselves.'

Alison is horrified at the insensitivity of the foxy little woman at the same time as wondering what Cybil Crabbe was doing here. Maria begins gagging. Dee puts her head to the side and pulls out her tongue, calls for the honey. Cupboard doors are opened and slammed.

As Jill makes her way out she nearly trips over Sofia, rocking on the front step with her head in hands, rocking, rocking. Jill drops down to put her arm around her shoulder. Sofia does not respond when asked if she is all right. She shakes her off angrily.

'No, go,' she orders. 'Go.'

Then, hearing the echo of her own strength, Sofia gets herself up like a woman with a purpose. 'Get out of here, all of you,' she shouts. 'Go go go.'

'No Sof, calm down,' Em coos. 'We've got to get her onto her bed.'

Kay, crouching, slaps Maria's face, 'Maria, wake up. Please.'

Dee pleads, 'Maria, come on. Have some honey.' She spoons some onto her tongue. The sweetness slowly brings her round. She looks up to the others who are galvanised in horror, reflecting her own terror.

'We'll have to lift her,' Dee directs. 'Sofia, where?'

Sofia flaps her hand, 'There there. Down the hall and to the right.'

It is such a job moving Maria's bulk to the bedroom, the gurls stifle guffaws. While there have been episodes of unconsciousness in many heroin lives, no one really believes she could be dying. Sofia's cake was mild. In the dance with the devil, death is the ultimate drama. The edge in a culture of death is genuine fear of it. Cybil is paralysed by her morbid curiosity, fascinated.

'Just get her to bed and she'll sleep it off,' Em pants.

Back in the kitchen gurls hover around the filter-tips, roll tobacco into papers with trembling fingers and thumbs, make jokes, stand up, pace to keep their anxiety in check.

Alison freezes in the doorway of Maria's room. It is just as she saw written in the hand. She calmly finds the self in her who can cope. Maria is breathing, but white.

Her son, Lenny and daughter, Tilly, are suddenly at the front door, being brought in by a big black woman, who begins, 'Tilly . . . What's going on here?'

Sofia brings the sugar bowl and begins dabbing grains onto Maria's tongue. Alison sees her repulsion at touching Maria. There is hatred there.

'Get away,' Alison yells, 'You are trying to kill her.'

Maria tries speaking. 'I am dying, I am going. I can feel it, floating away, no reason to stay. Alison? Sofia, where are you going?'

'Be back,' Sofia says, hurrying out.

When she sees her friends standing around in the kitchen, Sofia pulls at her hair, saying, 'Freaking out, freaking out. I'm losing it.' Her hands are shaking. 'I need a hit.' Kay pushes a joint between her fingers.

'Mummy? Mummy?' Tilly's voice tinkles.

Alison responds, 'Yes Tilly, hang on darling. Is it important?'

'Lenny said you said we could have Maccas tonight, can we?' singsongs her daughter.

'Yeah, but not yet, sweetheart. You go with Iris, okay?' She gently shoves her into the arms of her auntie. Iris ushers the kids out of the hallway. 'This is an emergency.'

Alison, feeling waves of panic crash through her nervous system, takes Maria's hand as she lies on her bed.

'Ring Margot, Alison,' Maria gasps. 'I told her it would happen. Get Margot. Keep police out of it.'

Alison responds to Maria's urgency, 'What are you talking about? What can Margot do?'

'Got to protect Sofia. Don't tell the police about the dope. The cake.' Maria's voice is thready. Alison is amazed at her self-sacrifice.

'This is about you, sweetheart. Don't go.'

Maria shakes her head in distress.

'Okay.' Alison asks, 'Do you want to talk to Margot?' Then she pleads, 'Don't sail away, Maria. Tilly,' she calls, 'grab the phone for Mummy, darling. Bring it in here. Maria, we slept together, yet you never told me much. It's okay, don't worry.'

Maria's voice is scratchy. 'I'll live. She won't let me go. She holds it over me. I abandoned her. Trapped in guilt. I love her, but I don't trust her, I have to watch her all the time. Don't let them lock her up.'

'No, no,' Alison assures her, 'Stop speaking now.'

'It would kill her, to be locked up, Ali.' Maria's eyes cloud over. 'I am going to die this time.'

'Here's the phone, thanks Tilly,' Alison keeps hold of Maria's hand. 'Has she tried to kill you before?'

287

'It's not her fault.' Maria's breathing is ragged, as if her throat is burning.

'Don't die,' Alison says gently. 'You don't have to die.'

'You understand.' Maria squeezes Alison's fingers, 'I didn't need to tell you.'

When she lets ago, Alison dials. Margot answers. She puts her hand over the mouthpiece and says, 'Do you want to talk?' Maria nods. She hands over the phone and leaves the bedroom.

In the kitchen, Kay, Em, Dee, Cybil, Libby, Tilly, Lenny and Sofia stand around the table. Iris is in an armchair, waiting. A normal conversation goes on, made reasonable by the presence of kids.

Sofia asks indifferently, 'Is she all right?'

Alison wobbles her head numbly.

Em pipes up, brightly, 'How's the drama queen?'

Kay suggests seriously calling an ambulance. 'What's to worry about? Don't want to bring attention to the house?'

Sofia leaps up, 'Okay okay, I will call an ambulance.'

'Maria's using the phone,' says Alison and, as she does, she feels it is so absurd. Sofia disappears. Cybil tries to think of a way to leave. She catches Libby's eye. When Alison comes into the bedroom she sees Maria, certainly dead, with the telephone in her slack mouth. Those in the kitchen hear a blood-curdling scream. A telephonic voice is appealing, 'Maria? Maria?'

Sofia delicately picks out the receiver, and Alison takes it, calling 'Margot?'

'What's happening?' inquires Margot on the other end.

'Dead,' Alison says abruptly. 'Maria.'

'She's dead? How? I'll be there as quick as I can,' Margot promises.

Alison sees Libby scuttle off down the path. 'Like a lizard,' says Sofia, who is beside her. The sane women are still in the kitchen reassuring each other and chatting with Tilly.

'You got Maria's last words,' accuses Sofia.

Alison's person begins splitting, addressing Sofia as she were herself. 'And I understand because I, too, have trouble with the chemicals in my brain. It doesn't make me immoral, Sofia? Why did she say I understand? Did she mean Harold? What am I saying?' Alison turns back to the lifeless Maria. 'I could have loved you. I see sides of you that you have buried under mountains of . . .'

'Obesity,' Sofia says coldly.

Alison rakes her hair, musing, 'It may not be your fault, she has been slowly killing herself. What kind of guilt is that?'

Sofia and Alison stare at each other, mutually accusing. Big, generous Maria's spirit hovers above them. They kneel either side of her dead body, murmuring, grasping a hand and stroking it. Sofia on the right and Alison on the left. They stay that way until the ambulance arrives.

When I got to Maria's the ambulance had come and gone. Sofia had a glazed look about the eyes. Alison was not there, she had taken her kids to McDonald's with Lenny's auntie. Cybil was a little bit sarcastic, but I think it was just her manner. Although she was not an intimate of this household, she explained that Sofia had made a dope mud-cake. They thought Maria had eaten too much of it, that her body had toxic overload. They needed me to liaise with the police in case Sofia should be had up for manslaughter. All the heroin had been removed from the place and they had stashed the marijuana. A bottle of brandy was on the table. Em, Kay and Dee sat around it. Jill David had been here, they said. And Libby Gnash. Alison again, always there when there is a crisis. Judith Sloane. A similar crowd to the barbecue.

'The hospital will have the cops around here in no time,' I said. 'Don't touch anything in the bedroom.'

Sofia was locked in a kind of stupor. I looked at the brandy and said, 'You don't need alcohol now. You need something hot and sweet.'

'Chocolate is brain-food,' opined Kay. 'I really believe that. Maria loved to talk, she was having a great time,' she continued.

'Maria was just a porky when it came to food,' Em said, affectionately.

'She had a great sense of humour, of symbol, of the dramatic,' Dee commented.

'But,' Kay still had a point to make, 'she was highly educated and political. She ate more cake than anyone else because she was thinking. Brain-food.'

'She's dead. Died with a phone in her mouth!' blurted Cybil.

Dee reckoned, 'I wouldn't have put it past her to have sucked the means of communication to represent how she had been silenced by this community, which is as good as death.'

I went over to the kettle, took off the lid to fill it up and exclaimed, 'What's this?' In the kettle were lumps of flesh and little bones. 'Someone has boiled a frog!'

'They're toxic,' informed Dee.

Sofia leapt out of her stupor, saying, 'Shulamith. No. Not my familiar. Oh no.'

'Your pet? Sofia, you didn't really get that cane toad?' exclaimed Em. 'You idiot!'

'My cane toad. I needed auric protection, powerful enough to take on demons on the astral plane, a grey landscape where I have been, where hulks, and sculls, and cloaks are all moving, automated by inner emptiness. I have been there, when the devils transport me.' Sofia raved on. She got up and paced up and down. We stood horrified, looking at each other. The madness was so sudden. Sofia grabbed our attention, pulling at our clothes with her fingers. 'She killed herself.'

'Are you saying she suicided?'

'I don't know. I don't know. I mean, no. No. She didn't do herself in. She didn't have to. No, I don't think she meant this. All I was saying is that she could have put the thing in her mouth to say something to me—I saw it— by saying nothing,' Sofia was nutting it out, slapping her forefinger on her other palm.

Cybil asked me. 'Why was it so important to ring you?'

'I don't know,' I replied. 'She rang me when she was in trouble. All the time.'

Moments like these I wished I smoked. My wonderful fitness does not need smoke or nicotine or tar or whatever, but if I smoked, I would have had something to do, like sit down, roll it and light it. Instead, I went into cop mode and told them what I thought would happen in a practical sense. Realising what I had to do, I leapt into action, unplugging the kettle. 'Admit something, though.'

It was best the gurls dealt with the cops who turned up in their own way, as if I hadn't come and sanitised the site. I advised that they get rid of the cake, crumbs and all. This caused panic as they didn't want police finding them digging or anything. I thought of the Crank and his extreme crime-fighting methods in his personal war against drugs.

Kay went through their story. I accepted her dissemblance. 'Dispose of the cake. Absolutely.' Cybil was in two minds. Eventually she departed with the offending food in the boot of the Excel.

'Excuse me,' I went to find the phone. I called Philippoussis.

'Margot?' He was cagey. I took the kettle with me when I left, leaving Kay in charge of a group of stoned women in disarray. Uniforms in a patrol car passed me as I crossed the rail at the level crossing. I went straight to CID. The kettle with the remains of the cane toad was suitably placed in a plastic evidence bag and my fingerprints taken as a matter of routine, but they would find nothing definitive down that path.

Philippoussis filled his immediate superior in on the details, including Maria's weight.

'That would be about twenty-five stone,' the older man said. 'No, mate, no worries, forensics won't want to deal with that, unless they have to.'

'It was an accident,' I assured them. 'There is no point in considering foul play.'

The detective sergeant agreed with me. 'Yes, we won't waste valuable resources on this, Phil,' he said. 'However get the toxicology report, witness statements and wrap it up. Crankshaw will want a neat summary to release to the press, it being an odd way to die.'

Provided they stuck with their story my friends would be saved from over-zealous scrutiny and police harassment. Without giving her the exact details of my deal with the detectives I rang Chandra as soon as I could, and fell under the spell of that counselling voice.

'What could I have done, anyway? All she said to me was, I am being murdered, nearly two weeks ago, a life-time,' I said to her midway through our telephone call.

'Murder, suicide, accident, what had happened? How did she die?' Chandra was distressed but keeping cool.

'What could I have done, anyway?' I asked heatedly.

'Alison predicted it,' Chandra said thoughtfully.

'Did she?' I asked, while thinking I, too, had a premonition.

'You okay?' comforted Chandra.

'Maria signalled her fears to me, but,' I repeated myself, 'what could I have done, anyway? She died with a phone in her mouth, speaking . . . trying to speak to me. Why? Why me? Did she need to tell me something about Neil's death? I don't know, except she kept wanting me to do something. She rang a couple of weeks ago, saying someone was trying to kill her.'

'Don't worry,' Chandra soothed. 'It's a metaphor. Sofia has said Maria tried to kill her, too.'

'Has she? Well, yeah,' I went on excusing myself. 'That's what I thought, you know, that it was all psycho-drama, indulgence in lesbian relationship, you know, how women get inside each other, abuse substances and take it out on each other, you know, the whole frustration of being, you know, a woman, or bored, I don't know. I thought it was all theatrical bullshit. She rang some time in the early morning, like dark. She sounded drunk. She sounded stoned. I thought tough.'

'Listen,' she said quietly. 'I'll come over tomorrow night. Remember? Dinner date? Meanwhile, try and find Alison. Okay?'

'Yeah, 'bye.' I hung up, bemused. Alison's different personalities were something like Blindman's Bluff, you're spun and you don't quite know where you are going to end up. Was one of them psychopathic?

At McDonald's I discovered the Rik and Milt on their motorbikes in the drive-through talking to a little girl who ran back to the slides as I came up. They would know soon enough but I smiled, weakly. 'You know Tilly?'

'Of course. There's her mum. Alison?' Rik indicated the group at an outside plastic table and I couldn't believe it. The white-faced, older version of Tilly caught my eye. It was Alison, so drab, defeated and weak, she was unrecognisable. Drugs? The drama of death was exhausting. I couldn't move.

I had not asked Rik for her explanation of Tilly's bruises last time, and didn't want to now. Alison looked too unhappy. The rest with her were Kooris. A man had his arm in a sling. Alison shook her head. I walked back to my parked car.

When I set out for my Cliff Young shuffle along the road, which my Achilles heel did not need, but I did, I noticed there was no car next door but the female half of the couple was there. She had been as quiet as a mouse. I calmed myself by listening to the birds as they settled in their nests in the paperbarks, stopping, stretching. Not allowing myself to think, I walked, naming things: trees, birds, weeds, cars.

25

. . . the empty bed . . .

A hole appears at the core of Maria's reservoir of acquaintance, with her death. A sucking emptiness, as if the plug was pulled in the basin, turning love into a vortex. All floating friendship and kinship rush to the place where Maria had been, unless strongly attached otherwise.

The ethereal Sofia, whose classic prettiness could inspire lust, whose erratic behaviour arouses distrust—indeed—hatred in those not prepared to comprehend, is spinning from individual to individual, as they gather about her. Words, hysteria, tears have her going in circles, in a mania of activity. Within the sadness something is important. Maria's room is the centre of the whirlpool, the vacancy, containing not only the empty bed, but an archive of an unusual life lived in unique times, priceless documents should a moment of feminist history have value and brilliant books now out of print. Secret papers, pills and plans. Sofia's job is to keep the grave-robbers at bay. No one trusts her judgement. She oscillates between eagerness and anger. Her chilling insight and egotistical warmth make stormy weather of discrimination between the worth of the women who come to her aid. Not grateful, fully expecting and anticipating the attention, she hunts them away from the door of Maria's room. She is gracious in hospitality. Be anywhere, be everywhere, but not on her sacred site. She is as ferocious as a hound. She doesn't howl. She doesn't cry. She growls. There is plenty going on. Telephone calls from far and near. With each new woman come new thoughts at what to do. Sofia this. Sofia that. Real jobs. Real fears. Although the significance of Maria's death is nothing to the outside world, it is a tragedy for the gurls. Rumours, speculation, paranoia and opinions outweigh sentences of concern which, even when expressed, seem to involve intrusion on Maria's voided space. What a disaster!

Helen, of those who were with her yesterday, took the tale to Lesbianlands in her fast Subaru. Now Judith Sloane sings dirges in the yard. And Tiger Cat turns up. Cybil Crabbe and Lola Pointless. Ti, Kay and Em hold the fort. Dee, who stayed overnight on the lounge, prepares herbal teas, washes up, then goes out to shop. When Jill David comes, Sofia grabs her arm and says, 'At last.' Maz takes a drum and beats a rhythm to Judith's music. 'Dello,' Sofia instructs, 'don't let anyone in here.'

Jill emerges now and then to give reports, each more horrific than the last. Sofia is in a nest of papers. Has taken everything from the shelves. It is a mess in there. Dello and Jill let Sofia wallow in the tomb, becoming more and more confused. Other women want to see. Gurls gossip and mourn, hang about, hang out, inform the interested, work out a pecking order of power to swing into operation when Sofia finally lets them in. For now, they indulge her every whim.

People have a need for stories when a life is finished, stories fed from fact and memory. The aggrieved want to know why, where, when and how. The significance of death is the depth of intercourse among the living, a savage short-cut to knowing and being known.

Chandra's ideals are connected to her emotions by a very thick cord. When principle is at stake she cannot be dispassionate. Analytical thinking, while not beyond her, requires, in her, determined discipline. Few know of the control and difficult dedication Chandra puts into being a logical woman. Often criticised as hard for her strictness, it is herself, not others, she is keeping in check, her wild emotions, her sensuality. Duty is onerous for her. Yet she takes responsibility on all levels.

Rory rings. Chandra is glad. The shock felt with similar disinterested regret and genuine sadness moves the two into recognition of mortality. They agree. They share enthusiasm for the work and the excitement of life itself, which encompasses death, and exchange along the band-width an energy of the intellect. Love for their own kind, despite their differences, makes the conversation vitally present. Despair, depression, loss, felt by others, exist in a perfection that can only be achieved in a past, or a future, or other pastures. It is better to know the truth. The Valerie Solanas in us all, knowing herself as a 'dominant, secure, self-confident, nasty, violent, selfish, independent, proud, thrill-seeking, free-wheeling, arrogant female', is unashamed, defiant of conventional condolence.

Not lacking in sensitivity, Chandra mentions the Solanasite Conspiracy. 'For now, we can only do what we can do. Remember and live. *Vive la révolution!*' Answering Rory's doubts, she asks, 'Any younger women out there to help you?'

'Yes,' Rory describes Hope Strange to Chandra, and, incidentally informs her that Margot Gorman is going to Lesbianlands at the weekend. Chandra does not tell Rory she is having dinner with her in a few hours. Perhaps she will when she arrives. 'See you soon.'

Sofia's number is engaged each time she rings.

Rory goes to get Virginia whose dual-cab Rodeo, always tuned and full of fuel, has a nice quiet diesel engine. Virginia's level head and speedy driving are what she needs.

They head off. To Chandra's first.

Fiona, Ci and Gig, immediately on hearing the news, jump in Fi's car, pick up Yvonne and drive to Stuart to be there for Sofia. The drug culture has been around the lesbian movement for years. Fi and Gig are contemporaries of Sofia, and, at times, have harshly criticised her relationship to Maria; how suffocating ! Nonetheless, a death, often an overdose, speaks to some fundamental sense of community, a deep desire to be of service, to be an aunt, a mother, a sister, a daughter, at a family tragedy. Downing tools, they go, not knowing what they will, in fact, do, just confident in the knowledge their presence is needed; their friendship is real. In the car, on the highway, they talk over each other, verbalising the hurt and the generalisations which come from experiencing living with and loving addicts.

'The annihilation of the self dissolved in the feel-good moment of heroin, that is the problem,' Yvonne rationalises, not really admitting to herself that Ti went to town to score.

'Junkies don't care,' Gig bravely, yet vaguely, states the obvious as if it just occurred to her. She says, 'What I hate is the lies, the theft, the conning and the cunning.'

'Ignoring and adoring the irresponsibility where the compulsory realigns itself behind the god of happiness at the end of a hit.' Yvonne sounds academic when she expresses herself.

'Moral dilemmas,' says Fi, 'are solved by craving. Oh the painless pleasure of being so alive to feel so pleasant! The self is dissolved, "gone".'

'I didn't know Maria used,' says Gig.

Ci is sure she didn't. 'Sof's cooking had something to do with it,' Fi says, not speeding, keen for the conversation to mean something. 'The hatred of self paralysed behind a set of problems arranged around the knowledge that there is a way—one single way to cope: "get out of it".'

Ci plays along, 'Fill the selfless hole with selfishness.'

'Oh yes,' Yvonne remarks sarcastically. 'Revolutionary that is.'

'Helps a lot.'

'I think not.'

'Revolt!' comments Fi.

'Grasp at any old slogan as at any piece of electrical equipment and take it and hack it or hock it!'

'Become sick and mutilate the body.'

'Risk accident.'

Fi takes a curve carefully. 'Painlessness,' she continues, 'A pattern, a meaning.'

'They all hang together.'

'I think they're afraid of meaning.' Yvonne leans forward to look at Fi.

'There are all the excuses under the sun!' Fiona responds.

Yvonne, whose present lover is Ti, not a one known for brains, speaks as if she has been there and done that, with freedom and honesty her companions have not heard from her before. 'The beautiful high flies like an angel above the grotty mess below, individually and culturally, from a very early age, what the penis wants the penis gets in the phallocentric world. So she takes the penis given her, the pin, the needle, the fine dripping line and is an honorary man in a man's world, grovelling in the gutter of that world begging, stealing, borrowing, surviving.'

'But it is really self-hatred.

'Or hatred of women by women. Less than human without the addiction. The cockroach-infested kitchen of liberty, walled away from the real pleasures of life by service to a demon who holds divine painlessness within reach. An inch of time, enough money, the inclination. Information. It's easy to die or smile idiotically.'

'Ain't life a drag when you love an addict?' Fi grins impishly at Yvonne.

Yvonne acknowledges Fi's remark. 'You can't help loving someone.'

'Pity I didn't hear all that,' comments Ci.

Yvonne continues, 'Drugs suck out the goodness of good women. Nihilism: I am worthless therefore the future is worthless.'

'Death is a pretty final annihilation,' says Gig. 'Maria of all people!'

'The risk is always there,' Yvonne frowns. 'But when your self is drained, it seems more likely somehow.'

'You can get addicted to anything, I suppose,' reasons Fi.

'Like relationships?' Gig tolerantly jokes.

Yvonne takes out her tobacco. Gig offers her some hooch to go with it. She shakes her head.

'Nicotine's legal,' Yvonne has given up smoking and taken it up again more times than she can count. They pass through Pearceville.

'The teenage girl thinks it's cool, keeping her slim to fit the slut cut of dresses exposing belly-button studs, rings or chains.' Yvonne feels she can choose her poison but she cannot choose her meat. The extremities of her limbs are cold at night when Ti is dead to the world and she searches for some pleasure of her own which will flood the dark with tinkling lights. Poker machines, the attraction of town. Worries drowned by the chattering of strangers, deadened by alcohol followed by another drink, hoping for a win. Yvonne, the victim, wishes she wasn't intelligent.

'And food is a chemical addiction, too! Fats and preservatives, long lunches and sweet treats, beef outweighing rice in the diet, bombarding the mouth-watering taste with images of gluttonous pleasure as if that is all you need to be happy in the phallocratic society!'

As they come through a succession of curves and bridges over named creeks, Gig recalls Maria, in the light of their discussion. 'I used to see her at the surgery, trying to interpret her troubles with self-diagnosis, so that she didn't put the doctor to too much bother.'

Yvonne sounds off again. 'Not putting him to too much bother is what women do. And what the medical profession does is deal in prescriptions. Legally doped into submission.'

'Domestic violence.' Fi slows down at the speed sign, entering Stuart.

'Poisons they sprayed at the school fence.'

'Such stress,' says Ci. 'The woman of the 'nineties! Superwoman!'

Fi, Gig and Yvonne become spirited as their bomb of an automobile makes the turns through the exurban streets of the country town. 'And a mother as well.'

'Offered hormones, hysterectomies, creams and cosmetic choices in bewildering array; hospitalisation, *in vitro* fertilisation and caesarean section, but not for nothing.'

'Nothing for nothing!'

'For everything, her soul is paying all the time!'

'Agricultural monoculture of the moronic!'

Chemicals concerning the annihilation of a woman's self having taken their attention for the entire drive, they climb out of the car. Yvonne says, 'Search yourselves, girls. Have a look. If chemicals don't get you, motherhood must.'

Sofia wanted to show me something. I felt calm floating on a rather turbulent sea of mysterious undercurrents. The depth of hysteria and herstory was beyond me. Women stood in haphazard groups, wandered outside, squatted on the front steps, were in and out of earshot, restless. The telephone kept ringing: people were coming from as far as Adelaide, Melbourne, even the Pilbara and Alice Springs. A meeting was needed to organise the cremation, the wake and ritual. If Maria Freewoman was so widely loved and admired, how come it had been me, whom she hardly knew, who she turned to at the end of her life? Death had created, in some, a kind of obscene energy, a morbid curiosity, the pitiable self-importance of their own mortality. The majority of these characters were complete and utter strangers to me.

Batting flustered acquaintances away with flapping hands, Sofia took me into Maria's room and closed the door. The drawers of the desk and filing cabinets were all opened and we were ankle-deep in papers on the floor. Dated posters, old newsletters, roneoed theses, handwritten correspondence, fliers, leaflets, sketches and exercise books. Sofia pulled volumes out of the bookcase and fanned the pages under my eyes before throwing them down and thrusting other written matter into my chest. 'Nothing,' she said. 'No mention of me.'

Obliging her distress, selfish though it sounded, and, not actually believing it, I knelt down and looked at bits and pieces. I did not discover, as I had hoped, disproof of what she claimed. We spent a while on the quest for her name, even going through the wardrobe. Chest of drawers. There was no diary. Standing by the dressing table, I let a wave of sincere sadness wash over me, staring unseeingly at little bottles. 'Nux vomica' came into focus. I picked it up.

Sofia, who had scrutinised my every action, and reaction, explained, 'Homoeopathic. She took that whenever she got drunk.'

I knew that strychnine was poisonous alkaloid, derived from nux vomica, which has a powerful effect on the central nervous system and was formerly used in small quantities to stimulate the appetite. I pocketed the jar. Sofia did not mind.

'How can someone know you all your life and not really know you at all?' she asked me.

As if I could answer that!

Grief. Maria. Chandra's tears flow, swamping, choking her. She sobs with her head down, grasping the steering wheel. Shoulders heaving, she repeats her old rival's name over and over, remembering. Twenty-two and half years ago, Maria broke her heart. She stole the love of Chandra's life ten years after the death of her mother. In those days, Maria was big but not fat. She laughed a lot and took the podium at conferences. At demonstrations she loved to rabble-rouse and wear the marshal's armband, and lead the chant: what do we want; when do we want it. Maria could sing and knew all the protest songs. Maria, then, like Dolly Parton's Joylene, could have had anyone she wanted. But she took Mary Smith. Mary Smith was slim and other-worldly, with a sly sense of humour, skin colour she said she got from moon-baking, and a very sharp mind. Every so often, Chandra hears Mary Smith on the radio talking about the latest sociological study in the area of her expertise, a cautious interpreter of statistics. Then, she was cheeky, witty. It was at a dance. Maria had a hearty ego, though in later years you wouldn't have guessed it, really. Maria and Mary fell to kissing on the dance floor. Chandra could not kiss or even hug on a dance floor. In fact, she rarely danced. When she did she needed her sticks. A great pleasure of her life, up until that moment, was watching other women dance and move their bodies in rhythm. Mary and Maria snogged the night away and all the time Chandra had to see it because, at that time, Mary and she lived together and she did not drive. In the car going home that night, Mary told her she had been having it off with Maria for a couple of months but she didn't know how to tell her. She guessed she had to see for herself. Chandra was devastated. For three years she troubled herself over the cowardice and profligacy of Mary Smith. Her broken heart galvanised her mental processes. She threw herself into reckless and endless activities to shatter the bones of her Saturn Return. Worthwhile years, she now realises, as that is when she really developed her edge, on the eve of the Age of Aquarius. Released from chains of Saturn onto the wings of Uranus, she kept abreast of technological change, updating hardware, facile with software and, incidentally, earning a good living as a programmer.

Now Maria is dead. The tragedy of Maria was that she would never face her own guilt, preferring relentless compensation out there in the world. She had a daughter at the age of sixteen whom she had to give up. Even when she got her back, she would take off, trying to live a life of her own, come back with presents or apologies and promises.

In the thirty-seven months and eight days, Chandra was getting over Mary Smith, Sofia was a young dyke of eighteen and nineteen, who lived with Maria and Mary on and off. She idolised Mary and copied her in everything. She came around to Chandra's quite often because of her recent closeness to Mary. She became more Mary than Mary, not so white in the skin, with fairer hair, but in identical clothes; Virginia Woolf grey cardigans and drippy skirts. Chandra heard the story of her childhood and comprehended, later, a component of Maria's guilt. Mary betrayed Sofia's devotion with cowardice and scorn and lying. Sofia learnt to hate. Chandra grins to herself now: there is no hater on the circuit quite as good at it as Sofia. Without Mary, Maria and Sofia took different paths again. Maria went to America for a few years, and Sofia sank into the rough trade of heroin and alcoholism and mental breakdown in various Australian cities. About seven years ago, Maria took Sofia out of the asylum where she was tortured by psychiatrists, the claustrophobia and psychotropic medication. She promised her she would never go back inside again. Or be locked up anywhere. Since they have lived in the area, Chandra has very little to do with Maria. A short affair and a long friendship with Sofia, notwithstanding. After Mary, Chandra never forgave Maria, until now. The biography of her contact in Maria's life plays through Chandra's head like a little wake.

Her tears are spent. Life goes on. Death means change. Now is the time to step out of cyberspace, where she is fleet of foot, back into the community, where she in her chair can be relied upon. She toots her horn. Rory and Virginia respond, walking slowly up to the car.

They organise a gathering, with the gurls they find at Sofia's, to arrange Maria's funeral, for tomorrow. Dee answers the phone from Margot about when the body will be released. No police interest. General relief ripples through the mob. Virginia leaves in Cybil's car; she can pick hers up at Chandra's after the meeting. With Chandra and Rory there, Jill David gone and Dello and Maz still playing music out the back, the dynamics change for Sofia. She goes outside and finds they have lit a fire in half-barrel. Rory and Dee close the door on the chaos Sofia has made of Maria's things.

As soon as Mary Smith arrives from Sydney, along with others from Lismore, Tamworth and Brisbane, Chandra leaves for her appointment with Margot.

There was a particular energy running around my nervous system like an electrical current as I readied myself to be taken out to dinner by Chandra. She said, her car, disabled parking spot. She was in my driveway within a minute of when she said she'd be. I went out to greet her. She swung herself out of the driver's seat of her Subaru station wagon, taking most of her weight on the right stick and using the door frame.

After a few words about Maria, I said, 'Let's forget that for now.'

'Yes,' she concurred.

Lightly, then, I told her I was fascinated by her sticks. They were beautiful red wood snakes. I expected the hospital callipers. These were hand-crafted and individual. The right one curled right up to her elbow, the left just over her wrist. Although the straight parts were a little bent, they were extraordinary pieces of wood, and wonderfully carved and polished, with solid rubber butts. Her going-out sticks!

'Virginia made them for me. She searched for months in the rainforest for the perfect shaped branch, this one is a branch. This is a sapling. She has an affinity with wood.' Chandra said proudly, 'These are the product of a labour of love.'

I wondered whether they were lovers once, but not aloud.

'Sculptures,' I admired.

'Well, she is a sculptor. You know Virginia? Of course you do.'

'Not really,' I shook my head, 'Not well.'

Chandra, for her part, was determined to see every bit of my property and took great interest in my renovation of the chookhouse. I laughed when she noted as I had that the people who built it must have loved their fowls. The pitched roof and hardwood frame, the proportions and balance, all gained her attention. They probably had show hens, she decided. She spoke of agricultural shows, her mother, and horses. She understood the pride people have in the breeding of livestock. She named exotic types of chooks. Then she was curious about what I was going to do with it when I finished.

'Wine cellaring and photograph-developing, I don't know. I might learn something else.'

She cross-examined me on the wine and photography. 'A pity to waste such a beautiful studio spot.'

I knew she was assessing my artistic potential, as if every woman worth her salt had to be in some way creative. While I was humble about cameras, I could not hide my arrogance about wine. So we discussed cellar potentials for a while. And then triathlons.

'Rory told me all about it.' Chandra searched for somewhere to rest her arms.

'I thought Beetle was a mermaid,' I said. 'Swim! At first I thought she had a lazy left arm, but then I noticed the right hardly cleared the water either, and fast! What a lovingly cared-for bike! An antique.' I called as I went to get two bottles of wine from beneath my bed. I showed her the labels. A McLaren Vale 'Futures' Shiraz, 1994 Release. The crust had developed near the neck. I shook my head as I saw it.

'I really should decant this before drinking,' I sighed. 'But it is a sensation.' The other was a Traminer White for dessert. I anticipated, because Chandra couldn't, at this stage, her pleasures in these tastes.

Margot and Chandra are attracted to each other, sexually. Both being happiest with honesty and intellectually excited, one by investigation, the other by organisation, Chandra decides, they could not be in bed together, after having made love, keeping secrets from each other. Not for long. How can she trust Margot? She fraternises with men, reasons Chandra, counts them, or several individual males, as good friends. She sees humanity as one grouping and would consider it insanely criminal to want to kill half of it. Her philosophic question comprises: are people fundamentally evil, or good? Boring, but Chandra likes her.

'Sure it is right to fight evil, but look at the facts, girl, see the inconsistencies: every man benefits from the evil of other men, and the evil of women, from the good of men and his god. And women don't!'

They argue vigorously. The delicious taste of romance on Chandra's tongue, there is nothing so erotic as knowing someone fancies you. Physically, Margot is gorgeous, each line, outline, profile, the hue of her skin, the way she moves, the grace of fitness. Chandra could eat up that Amazonian beauty. Chandra knows she would throttle Margot, eventually, if they ever became intimate partners. Or lose her own higher purpose.

The seaside looks peaceful for a moment. A woman and two children walk along the water's edge calling to each other about kelp and shells. The sunshine is on its last rays. Margot is showing her where the beginning of her first murder investigation happened. The toilet, the car park, the beach.

We had already decided on the restaurant. We went in her car, stopping where Neil died, because she asked me and I was gratified that she recalled the night she comforted, counselled, me, in such detail. After dark we took up our booking and made ourselves comfortable, starting with a light beer and a plate of entrees while we examined the choices. Giving the menus to the waitress, we settled back.

Wine works wonders for conversation, over dinner. 'There is a vitriolic side to Meghan,' Chandra told me, in the midst of my speculation on the cause of the ransacking of her house. 'Not to say, a vicious and violent one. Ask Jill.'

Megs had beaten Jill up, at least once, but then she had probably provoked it. They had sought counselling. 'Lesbian DV is an issue, Margot.'

Later, she asked me about Penny Waughan.

'Perhaps her son died because someone else was meant to,' I said.

'Who?' Chandra's eyes were very direct. Even though the matter was serious, Chandra and I managed to laugh. 'Someone with fat fingers, according to Alison's predictions.'

We went through characters with chubby fingers. Cybil and Maria being the obvious ones. Had Maria been murdered? Chandra did not know Cybil, only that she was Virginia's lover and Rory could not stand her. Even the lanky Meghan had chubby bases to the fingers of her hands. Rory has long, artistic digits, I had noticed when she drew the map.

'But Maria.' I told Chandra of my arrangement with the cops and how I managed to arrest suspicion from that quarter. She called me a smart alec, but the warmth left her eyes.

'Maria? Her own fears, her phone calls,' I said. 'Do you think she had a premonition?'

'Doesn't make sense.' She poured some more wine into our glasses.

'I had heard on the grapevine that Maria had a thing going with Alison. Where did I hear that?'

'I heard it quite recently from Alison herself.' Chandra lapped up lemongrass sauce with a spring-roll. 'If we keep on that subject, we'll destroy our appetites.' So practical.

We talked and talked over expensive Thai food and my wines, and while snatches of what we said, of what was exchanged, come back at me when I least expect them, it is all, if I try to put it in sequence, a bit of a blur. A pleasurable blur. Chandra seemed to despair of most of the bush women and admire a certain stamina at the same time. 'Virginia,' she said, 'when accused of being left high and dry with her moral outrage, responded that she would not like to be swamped in sewage and dragged down by the quicksand of gossip.'

'But,' she continued, with different emphasis. 'It's the hub of the community we have here, a lesbian community under siege. Not a healthy community but a community nevertheless. Our own reality, a shared reality of living and inter-relating, is better than being in bourgeois units invisibly notched in the grids of the malestream.'

While I did put short notes in my brain to follow up at a later stage, I did not tell her what I had done so far about Rory's job. Although the bulldozer and the bridge and the explosions came to mind, I tried to slough the job. There would be paths I could chase starting here, but it felt like the ground had shifted. I felt I could go back to Chandra any time and ask her to expand. I didn't forget, but I looked into her eyes, and somewhere in the subliminal sense of smell, the chemicals started adjusting those in my head and heart, and so on. I was getting off on this woman.

She helped me sort through the details I had of Neil, in between long diversions into her past loves, last of whom was Alison. She had worked out the glitch; the email had come from Neil's computer. Alison Hungerford, apparently, had several distinct personalities: witch, nymphomaniac, genius. She was abstract, earthy; political, amoral, inspired, weak, energetic. But could she trust herself? No. Could she pursue the puzzle of Neil's Internet life? Yes, for a while. The print-outs intrigued Chandra. She was going to bring them but, of course, forgot, the greater event of death in the community having overwhelmed incidental things.

'Plainly, the boy, and now Alison, were onto some kind of ring of boy-lovers who are not nice, and possibly preying on lads, not only for sexual favours, but also testing drugs,' Chandra opined. 'I have heard that doctors, lawyers, magistrates are in some weird cult around here.'

'There is also the coastline, being a landing place for big-time drug importers.'

Looking in her bag, she said with some excitement, 'I found one of the sheets.'

And handed it to me. 'This is a yacht. The name, the identification number. This could be code for place, and time.'

Chandra using a highlighter pen had signalled out the dates. 'This one, look, that is the day you found the body!'

'Which would explain all this activity near the beach and the mangroves. They would just have to motor up the river, weigh anchor and hide in one of the side-waters.'

'Separate the dates before and after Neil's death,' she suggested.

'And Hugh's,' I added. Instead of being enthused by my work, I wanted her to look at me, in the eye. But she was avoiding it, like crazy.

'Yes, what exactly did he know?' she asked, fiddling with a pen and a serviette.

'Where had he been before Dello and Maz picked him up?'

'The yacht!' We said it together.

The passion for detecting infected Chandra and swamped the need to physically dissolve into our mounting mutual attraction. As soon as I mentioned Philippoussis, she cooled off, told me she had to be home in the morning because of the demands of her farm, her commitments, the meeting, and made too many excuses.

When she dropped me off at my front door, Chandra pulled me to her again and gave me a big, sympathetic hug. I responded. Chandra came inside.

'They were mother and daughter you know,' she whispered.

'Who?'

'Maria was Sofia's mother.'

'What?' How could I have been so stupid not to have seen that? Or simply known it, somehow? Could it be the difference in their relative size? Am I that conventional? That was what Sofia's search was about!

Chandra left about three in the morning. We did not make love, although, I think, both of us wanted to. While we had been fond and kissed, I was confused about how Chandra felt about me. Certainly the evening had connotations; indications of something she was not sharing with me. Could be anything. I placed it in my head, hoping my dreams would sort through the material of the day. Conscience is corruption, meaning? Because Chandra distracted me when I wanted to pursue this aphorism, my mind hung on it. What did she distract me with? It worked. What was it? Something theoretical: drugs and paedophilia were boys' war games which negated women yet again, sapped female energy, further preventing self-realisation. I think I wanted her to stay, for me to say, 'I need you more than I let on tonight.'

Maria is dead. Gone, on the dark side of the moon.

26

. . . institutional corruption . . .

Not long after dawn, Detective Constable Philippoussis drove through my gate in a sporty convertible. I poured about half a packet of Italian espresso into the plunger and put on the kettle, thinking how fortunate it was that Chandra did not stay overnight. That would have placed me in the difficult role of double agent. Here I was playing footsy with the Crank's 'strong belief in intelligence-based policing' which relies on informers, spies and moles. Cops turning up at my house when they know I'll be home, like in bed, in their personal vehicles, for a chat over breakfast coffee would not have impressed Chandra one little bit.

He had with him a laptop computer, and the ease with which he balanced it on his knee and accessed files and cruised cyberspace made me doubt any other cop in the region had as a good a facility with it as he. I wondered what kind of advantage it actually gave him. On screen he showed me the results of the analysis of the kettle's contents. What I guessed turned out true: poisoned water; remains of cane toad; unfortunately boiled, occasioning death. A rudimentary forensic test of Maria's stomach contents proved a match. Accidental death. Police surgeon and her regular doctor agreed: no suspicious circumstances. General condition of the immune system pretty low. High cholesterol; a heart attack waiting to happen. They weren't interested in taking it further.

'That was fast,' I said.

'Expedient,' he replied, plainly trading swift shifty work for whatever I was going to get him on the boys. He knew exactly what he was doing, and quoted a statistic, 'In this tolerant country homosexual men and women are about four times more likely to be assaulted and about as twice as likely to be murdered as Australians in general.'

'But not in this case,' I affirmed our understanding.

'No.' He looked at me, letting me know he knew I was a lesbian, out and in his face. 'I could, of course, add this file to the others I have. See if there are any parallels.'

He zoomed in on a page labelled Chemist's Report, obliterating the identifying details at the top. His fingers slid on the touch pad. The words 'unknown drug' came up in a different colour. Philippoussis scratched his dark stubble with a long forefinger. I glanced away frowning, my eye catching the Nadir Mining Services cap, sitting in a box near the phone. When my attention returned, another chemical report, again the words 'drug unknown' underlined: Neil Waughan.

'And a third,' Phil said, as he indicated Hugh Gilmore's chart.

'Same unknown drug?' I asked. 'All three were around Spiders' barbecue night.'

'Amphetamines, pain-killers, flu tablets. Looks like a mix to me,' the police detective deduced. 'Heroin, only in Gilmore's. My hunch is some new pill. But this, of course, is a superficial, not to say cheap, analysis. Small traces of strychnine.'

'Rat poison?' I exclaimed, and asked, 'In all three?'

'Not that much. And most in the big woman. LSD has strychnic effects. Hallucination, stiff jaw.'

'Ecstasy was there,' I dobbed Tiger Cat in, without proof, on the strength of personal animosity and hearsay. He tapped out the relevant details as I spoke.

'Well, with those party pills, only some of the constituents would stay in the blood. Insulin, for instance, would be used by the body. They're a combination, anyway, analysis would only isolate partial contents.'

'Was Neil diabetic?' I asked, wondering whether he had managed to get hold of the general practitioner.

'Dr Neville is on leave, overseas. But no, not according to his mother.' The Detective Constable shut down his machine, and pulled the extension out of my telecom jack. 'All that,' he said, 'was off the record. My boss is freezing me on the question of the boys.'

'Why?' Whatever my dubious moral position in relation to the abstract concerns of hypocrisy and practising what you believe, which I was sure mattered deeply to the woman I wanted to love, I was going to do a good job for Penny Waughan. And helping Philippoussis was invaluable. Especially, as there was a rift in CID.

Phil shrugged 'Commander Crankshaw is a great hero in the war against drugs!'

'Exactly my point.'

'His background in narcotics means he is all about drugs in this area. Like any war it has frontline troops who are no more than cannon fodder, in this case, the users. By their very using they are suffering a self-fulfilling punishment. He needs to go for the big guns. Governments turn their expensive cannon on the addicts. As well as being pointless, it's cruel, mean and greedy.' Phillip sighed as he clipped his electronic notebook into a passable brief-case.

'Mean and greedy individuals through all strata of society stick together like shit in a blanket,' I agreed, wondering where the pharmaceutical reports we had just read had been, actually. The virtual world has the substantiality of holograms, a shimmering consistency. I would be happier reading the lab results on solid paper and checking the authenticity of the signature. And, if necessary, checking out his qualifications.

The little brown jar of nux vomica rested in the cave of the grimy cap. The Neil Waughan folder and my spiral notebook were beneath them. All tossed in the carton in the lounge waiting to be dealt with properly.

'Where's the long-wheelbase LandCruiser with its bold red, white and blue statement of police presence?' I asked to bring attention to the clandestine nature of this meeting.

'Let's go the toilet block,' Phil suggested. That was a good idea.

'Give me twenty minutes,' I begged as I needed to brush my teeth and put some decent clothes on.

A surfers' panel van and a fisher-person's vehicle were under the shade of banksias on the picnic area side. My man's MGB Roadster was very well-kept, light blue with white upholstery, 1969. Obviously garaged, it was pretty special. No doubt he loved it. I parked beside the sports car. Then I hesitated, leaning my elbows on the steering wheel, trying to assess the situation: what was he up to? The botched investigation into the Leigh Leigh murder was in everybody's mind lately due to media coverage. Officers in that instance were even accused of sexual harassment of witnesses. Could Philippoussis suspect similar slack standards in this division? He came jogging up the slatted path, adidas socks and head-band, and, as I had on the fateful evening, he stretched his hammies on the limed pine foot-high fence. He splashed water on his face and thirstily slurped a palmful of water from the tank. Was he recreating my aspect on events? If so, how was I going to respond? When in doubt, Margot, I told myself, tell the truth. I had already decided to give up the solid evidence, hence lose a bit of credibility so far as my own honesty went. But the devilish influence of the mining cap wasn't infusing my file with fiery inspiration. In fact, it was spreading a dank pall over my papers, depressing my intuition. So, with bravado I gambled on the whole kit and caboodle of revelation, because I was working for Penny Waughan, didn't want to cut off my nose to spite my face and, fair's fair, I expected the same from him. The homoeopathic remedy still on the seat, I got out of my car, carrying the offensive headgear, and apologised, 'I didn't give this to you because, mate, I am guilty of lack of trust.'

'Okay,' he sighed, still breathing gustily from his exertions. 'Where was it?'

We reinvented the scene. I put the cap in the L-shaped corner. He balanced a few SOC photos on the tap and along the walls. I told him my exact movements and he walked them through. We came outside, and I went into the detail of Judith Sloane passing me and getting into her four-wheel-drive.

'You know this woman?' He caught my tone and fired the question at me so quickly I nodded, 'Of her, not really. Can follow it up though.'

'What about the others?' I nodded again. We agreed on a few names, then he went back inside. The photos were a sad exhibition, both in matter and style; ill-lit, grainy, ugly. The block itself looked better in the morning, lively with proximate bird sounds and crisp sunlight. He picked up a photo and knocked his forefinger on a smudgy impression near the foot of the body. Then he kicked around the sandy floor.

'A footprint?' I asked.

'That's what I think,' he said. 'You said you didn't go near the corpse?'

'That's right.'

'Well someone did.'

I studied the photo more closely. Something had made Philippoussis sure this foot had been placed in the frame after the boy died. Slight indication, but, like those three-D puzzle pictures, it popped only when you saw it.

'Was there anything else shown up by the scene-of-crime chaps? I assume they were male. Any objects, you know?' I rubbed my smooth chin. I seemed to remember a hankie or something in the young transvestite's hand, and now that I was thinking as an investigator, that was pretty strange. I examined a relevant snapshot. Cloth was clasped in a fist. Death, thus, some sort of spasm.

'Yes,' he said. 'The deceased was on top of a used syringe. But,' he continued, 'prints suggest that this was not handled by the victim.'

Slowly it was coming together for me. I speculated, 'Whoever was wearing the cap was near Neil before, possibly, after he died?'

'Well, I didn't know about the hat, did I?' he said peevishly.

'Have you measured the size of the footprint? It looks bare to me. Not large.' The grainy shot had stopped popping for me. 'The boy had shoes on.'

'Yeah,' said the detective, 'a kid's or a woman's.'

'Have you talked to the family? The ones cooking onions?' I reminded him of my story.

'Yep, no joy.' The tall man suddenly grinned down at me, 'You are not going to believe this.'

'What?' I was intrigued.

'The family,' he said slowly, 'was that of a colleague of mine.'

'A cop?'

'And some.'

'You're pulling my leg.' I played up the incredulity.

'They weren't on duty. Some fishing. Then a barbecue with the mates, wives and juniors.' He laughed. 'Hadn't got a clue what was happening until the following day. And,' he was sharply serious, 'I wasn't informed until some time later than that!'

When we were about to go, standing at the door of the conveniences, he thanked me for my co-operation. I, however, wanted to know why he turned up at this hour, what was he doing in shorts et cetera driving his own car. 'Are you working or not?'

'I have a squash date,' he glanced at his watch. 'At eight. As for the rest. Put it down to mischief. I may be new to the area but I'm not going to play in any cover-up games. This death is crying out for an inquest. I am going by the book.'

'What about the cloth? What was it?' Instead of watching his eyes as I asked this I registered the progress of the surfer, an older bloke than you would expect. Beyond him was the path I took. I frowned. 'A handkerchief?'

'That's just it,' Pip hinted sibilantly. If he weren't so fresh and keen, it would have been a bitter spit. 'Evidence has unaccountably gone missing.'

'Incompetence or corruption?' I wondered.

The surfer strapped his board, a malibu, onto the roof-rack of his van, and, with a glance our way, got in and took off. People busy in their cars, part of the landscape like the flutter of wings of birds in the trees all around; what do they see? what do they know? what do they care? If they do see and care, what power do they have? Phillip was watching me watch the anachronism, no drifter I decided but a servant of the clock who had to get to work, and apparently thought I was staring towards the picnic area. 'Come on.' He strode across the gravel, intent on finishing a trail like a hound on a scent.

We walked along the weaving path, indulging in clipped conversation, incidentally observing where the fenced-off regenerating coastal bush had been disturbed, deducing together. We found a little cubby through the bitou bush and lantana at the end of the green corps' activity. A cleared piece of earth with the litter of used condoms, cigarette butts, lolly papers, methadone vials, a bed of brown bracken and tussocky grasses beneath a big, old banksia tree had all the hall-marks of a teenagers' hang-out. A T-shirt had been there a long time, a torn rag half dug into the sandy earth.

'Cosy,' said Philippoussis. We discovered a narrow track from that leading to the beach. There had been plenty of rain and wind since Neil died, but if this had been found and analysed closer to the time, foot-marks and activity would have been evident in the sand dunes. If the Spiders crowd were aware that the straight barbecuers were police in civvies those among them shooting up would have used the conveniences that serve the beach, not the ones in the picnic area. Had the investigating detectives searched the other toilets? We went along the scrub-line until we found another path, plainly the regular access to the sea from the park. It came out near the loos and covered barbecues where the meat was being cooked. Standing in the relatively clean, newer amenities, we looked across at the site of the Spiders' bonfire, now a pile of half-burnt, blackened logs.

'Someone in that crowd,' Philippoussis nodded in the direction of the empty space gays and lesbians had occupied, 'knew the families here were cops.'

Alison saying the word 'pigs' came to mind, along with the fact that Tiger Cat was big-noting herself giving out free party drugs.

'Or,' I added, 'someone in this crowd knew what was going on over there.'

'You're not wrong, Margot,' he nodded. 'So, it might be neither incompetence nor institutional corruption, but a deliberate attempt to keep me ignorant. I wondered why so little forensic evidence was available on my request.'

'Why would that be?' I asked as we walked back to our vehicles.

'I guess I'm a pain in the arse,' said the rugged individualist.

An angry, arrogant pain in the arse, a spoilt Greek boy, who learnt his righteousness at his mother's knee while women served him moussaka, no doubt. Not a team-player. Even though I was his senior in years, he treated me with the paternalistic attitude of a brother in a culturally sexist family set-up, magnanimously. I bet his sisters couldn't afford such a car. He skidded out of the parking spot spewing a fan of gravel into the air. I was a mere bystander, a witness, not a fellow detective. I didn't envy his squash opponent; that black rubber ball smashing into your thigh or back would leave quite a bruise. But, I assured myself, I didn't want his friendship, just his help.

Dr Featherstone takes an internal call in her lab. The words Meghan's assistant hears her say are, 'Ah ha, I'll be ready in no time. Have you? Yippee. Send him down.'

Her overnight bag packed, the shipment of equipment organised, the specimens locked in a cupboard, official documentation on the terminal of the mainframe, which, although firewalled, is never one hundred per cent secure, there is one thing left to do. Transfer the secret analysis from one notebook to the Inspiron. In cyberspace nothing completely disappears.

While she exclaims 'Ooh ah!' to the high resolution and seems naively impressed with the extra battery time, the techie points out its faults. 'You might find it a bit heavy to carry. Heat pipe's large and fan in the back, to cope with the heat of the power.'

She begins loading the mighty gigabyte capacity with stuff from her other computer and encodes it among the multi-component bays. Before she relinquishes the portable PC, she apparently accidentally crashes its hard drive. Apologising profusely for her clumsiness, she wipes it clean. The poor boy groans, but is confident he can retrieve it. Given time. He leaves her with the opinion, 'Some people get all the perks.'

'Pays to be part of the game,' she responds. When Meghan has been driven to the airport, she inserts the axial equations she had committed to memory. Without those particular experiment descriptions, salient information when recovered, as it surely will be, won't make sense. They will not be able to follow her thought patterns, certainly not through the progress of her logic, anyhow; even if they do have the bright idea of crossover checking with the desktop in the laboratory. What they will make of the nonsense of hanging conjectures and sublimely complicated hypotheses, she is not at all sure. All she knows is that cybercops, the CIA et al., mistake the unauthorised entries achieved by hackivists, who not after their own reward, merely want to show up systems' weaknesses, as having a criminal intent such as blackmail or some other form of exploitation. Microsoft's Explorer has an inherent unreliability, easily open to serious abuse. The laziness of programmers left debug labels on their free software such as Hotmail, keys to the secret door of Windows lying around for anyone visiting the Cult of the Dead Cow website to download. If Black Orifice is loaded without user's knowledge, it can sneak in the back unseen and literally take over; can change files, delete data, relay information; can switch off your computer, lock you out and wipe your disks. Her misinformation can slop around in the wash and wake of all this activity in the pretty safe murk of governments' and corporations' paranoia that their interests are at risk and unassailable assumption that everybody thinks like them.

As usual Dr Featherstone has to wait at the windswept aerodrome. Having finished her multi-list planner, written a program which will interpret jargonistic data into reader-friendly lay language, she tests the digital modem, a sort of inbuilt mobile phone. The world is at her fingertips. All so incredibly puerile. The one thing Meghan cannot comprehend is stupid people. Stupidity makes her angry. Meghan has been known to lose it. Big time.

A fox in the chook-house makes Chandra glad not only that she came home, but came home at the hour she did. Ordering Nikki around in the dark and minimising damage to her prized hens excites and gratifies her so that before she goes to bed she checks out her site. New hypertextual links guide her to an essay entitled The Trials of Annihilation, dealing with, under sub-titles, Chemicals; Madness; Motherhood; Male Violence; Nonsense; Transsexuality. Beneath Chemicals is the word, addictions, and included under Male Violence is money. She doesn't read it fully, but wonders whether the writer is also the one the Solanasites have been trying to boot from their chat-room. So far she has not been answering Chandra's emails. Before she goes to sleep, she writes and sends another. >> Annihilation tragic! Been reading your work. Like your ideas. Are you into action? Contact ASAP. Wheels@Wimmin.com.au.

No literature, fact or fiction, history or fantasy, no escapist reading, helps her sleep. She visualises the raver, shitting out her disgust at the female predicament in a verbal analogue of a tricky bowel. But why is she using Chandra's personal website? Or so carefully disguising her identity and where-abouts? The unedited essays are done in quick time with rapid fingers and contain unrelated gripes and bug-bears such as the voice-overs in nature documentaries which, in her view are masculinist, anthropomorphic projection onto animal, especially ornithological, behaviour. Obfuscation of truth being her general worry, Chandra decides to trust this person as having the courage to go against the law if need be. And the subtlety, a virtue Solanas herself lacked, to use the tools of the techonological age for revolutionary ends. She is not, Chandra discerns, the frivolous imp who posted the recipes.

Busy in preparation for the meeting about Maria's wake, and terribly tired, Chandra resists the temptation to ring Margot Gorman because it would be indulgent and her purpose requires some measure of sacrifice. Chandra, who believes all women are capable of loving another woman, knows the anger that flares in individuals like Margot, honest, autonomous, lonely fighters for justice, when a lesbian dares to express and live a separatist lifestyle. It's ferocious. Let alone what she herself is up to. The cyber-network is, thus, necessarily surreptitious, a cobweb. But when ideological differences pierce the blood and wine of day-to-day, of face-to-face interaction, well, feathers fly.

27

. . . down the dirt road . . .

Sean Dark also drives a Suzuki, a 1.3-litre Mighty Boy, with glistening duco of British Racing Green. He is heading for the hills, even though he should be at work.

Sean is losing money, trying not to feel guilty. He is thinking about Alison who read his palm and said, 'Beware of secrets and tall dark men. Or a contact from the past.' On the Gay and Lesbian Mardi Gras float-building day, the float began to resemble its title: Bananas in Pyjamas at the Sea Shore. Her own hands are long with knobbly knuckles and the softest skin. Psychic. 'Your skin,' Sean, had responded, 'has calluses on prominent mounds at the base of the fingers.'

Beyond the Hippi Sitti plateau immediately before the Gymea National Park is the Firagyra State Forest, at the edge of which is a picnic area for travellers from east or west. Several barbecue spaces have chopped wood provided, bench tables and toilets. There is a short bush walk beside a creek, which spills over a wall of rock. A longer trail winds its way through rain-forest species to the bottom of the waterfall. Near a deep pool, is a smaller and almost wholly shaded picnic area and toilets. This is a beat for bush poofters and gay network trippers, reps and truckers. From an earlier turn off the highway, it is possible to drive to this area along a gravel road.

Sean had told Alison, 'The cops picked me up. After twenty bloody years. I was in the '78 Gay Mardi Gras, and arrested. With tons of others. You know what they would do then? They would arrest you for disturbance or some such, then go and search out all your unpaid parking fines and lump them into your rap sheet. Well, darl, I had a mile high of the pink slips. Well, then you could pay them off behind bars. Me with all those brutes! As it happened there was this cute butch by the name of Paul. I was only in clink for a fortnight, but you know, it was enough.' His own words come back to him. 'I was heavily into the sauna scene, the Turkish bath scenario, haunting the streets at midnight and such, you know, it was such a buzz. Before the epidemic put a real bitch on the whole business. Well, Paul took me under his muscled wing, used me and protected me from the nasties.'

'Then,' he'd said to Alison, 'this Commander Crankshaw interviews me, out of the blue. I am as pure as the driven snow now. Chaste cookie. I had the devil of a job understanding what he was getting at until he brings up my record and this fellow, Paul. Suddenly I am a spattered lily with the guilts. For a start I would be too scared to rat on Paul, he is heavy metal. This police bruiser is clever. He knows he's got me shitting myself and suddenly even in my own eyes I don't look so clean.' The parties in his gym were so covert, such a delicious, camp romp, clandestine delight, he kept knowledge of them even from Al the Pal to whom he was opening his heart. Well, how could any woman understand? 'He knows I'm a sprat and he's stringing me along. So he has a proposition which is upside down if you ask me. He'll lay off Paul if I dob in my playmates. This is too weird, I'm thinking.'

Alison had taken Sean through the details of his fears and suggested that he find Paul, make a date and get a reality check. Paul was in the area. The date is today at the beat at Firagyra State Forest. As he revs the little motor and ascends the ranges, Sean wonders exactly what he wants to say to Paul. He does not dwell on how easily he found him. The tiny utility takes the bends easily and the hills weakly; fortunately it has light petrol consumption and everything in working order. As for his games, all they do is get together and dress each other up. The young lads look so beautiful as girls. The way they preen in front of the mirrors, in tutus, in petticoats, in feathers, in glam and in doud. There is nothing sexual. Gorgeous youth. Pretending has its own allure, the fascination of the fiction, the delicious filth of being women. The worst thing they do is language, speaking of legalities, but no one was being hurt by that. Men, telling the boys about the wigs of the old days, the stockings and powders in Baroque society, the opera and bitching about divas, educating them about Oscar Wilde, Charles Baudelaire: 'I've always been amazed that women are allowed in churches. What sort of conversations can they have with god?', give them witty quotes like adolescent toys to play with. And the Orlando dance was pure class.

When he goes down the dirt road to the waterfall pool, he sees a farm vehicle facing the forest. A man sitting behind the steering wheel by himself is waiting. Sean parks, gets out, stretches, then goes for a run along the track. As soon as he moves, the bloke in the ute opens his door. Sean passes at a pacey jog. Twenty minutes later he emerges neither sweating nor puffing. Now there are three vehicles parked. A tow-truck has joined the Mighty Boy and the ute. Paul is lying on his back on a picnic table smoking a cigarette.

'Well, Nancy, how are we?' he mumbles as Sean joins him. All macho South Sea Islander.

'Good. Thanks. And you?' In those days all the bitches had girls' names.

Paul swings his legs off the table top and faces Sean. 'Take a seat. Fag?'
Sean smiles, 'I don't.'

'Well, I'm here. Shoot.' Paul is all broad grinning charm.

Why would the police call him in and bring up their relationship with
each other? Paul responds with reasonable theoretical guesses. Sean begs.
'What is going down? Paul?'

'Heaps, you name it.' Paul exudes confidence and Sean notes the shirt
on his back is expensive.

'Why me?' Sean hears the old whine in his voice. 'Is it because of you? Like
next time, he's going to get what he wants out of me, even though I don't
know what he's after. Can I say something like I'll get you to ring him?' Sean
pleads.

'Why not? I'm cool. Got all bases covered, mate,' Paul smiles in an encouraging way. 'She'll be right.' He used to do that when Sean was threatened,
or Paul told him he was threatened in goal. 'Anything else?'

'They're investigating a murder,' Sean betrays a justified fear. 'I don't
know anything.'

'God's on our side, Nance,' Paul thrusts out his chest with infinite confidence.

'Can you get him off my back? Ring him.'

'Sure.' Paul moves towards Sean. 'Hey, let's do it, for old times' sake? Let
me fuck your arse, I'm getting a hard-on. Making wood, getting big, man.
Come on. Lemme bone you. You're looking good. What do they call you,
Sweetness and Light?'

'How do you know that?' Sean screeches. 'Paul, I don't any more. I just
don't do it. I'm into health.' Sean backs away.

'I don't care.' Paul moves in, at least a foot taller and wider than Sean.
'I don't mind a bit of rape.' Sean resists the temptation to take another step
back. Resists the desire to scream.

'Hey, mate,' he shoulders away, 'we've always respected that we're different.
In stir we had an arrangement. I've changed. The world's changed. AIDS is
everywhere.'

'Don't I know it? My black brothers are rife with it. Pity. White man's sexually transmitted diseases have been decimating the people for centuries,'
Paul no longer grins. 'Do you think I care that you want to stay clear? Now,
dear, I can feel a rage coming on.'

'Please,' Sean reaches out his hand to touch Paul's arm. Paul sweeps it off
him with contempt.

'Don't touch me, slut.' Paul's eyes turn cold, gleam hatred. He pushes Sean
so suddenly he falls backwards. He lies on the ground, still. Paul is now intent

upon raping him. Sean neatly eases himself into a crouch. His celibacy had never been so seriously challenged before. He prepares to fight. As Paul comes towards him, he shouts, 'No, definitely no.' The shrieky sound comes into his voice.

'Don't turn me on, girl,' Paul is sarcastic. He lifts him, shoving him towards the toilet. Sean spins around and begins punching. He visualises he is in the gym, the bag rolling and swinging to meet his fists. It is a shock to get a sharp jab right on the side of his face. But reflex anger helps him now and he extends through a feint with a fast uppercut. It is on. The other man watches. Although Paul makes more of a mess of his opponent, Sean is not tiring as much. He is still dancing on the balls of his feet when the man in the stubbies gets out of his car, uttering racist slang. Paul ignores it, but Sean responds with a surprised turn of the head which means he receives a savage blow which hurts his neck, bones crunch. Two men pummel Paul for a while before he throws them off in disgust.

'Get fucked. I got better things to do than hang around with white trash.'

Sean says, 'Paul I'm not racist. You wanted to rape me.'

'Look at the colour of your skin. You're shit.'

'No, I'm not. You're a brute.' Sean leaps back into the fray trying to land a decent strike, but fighting carelessly now, for crying and anger. He knows he is pathetic.

Paul turns to the other man slowly and inquires, 'What did you call me? Say again?'

'Boong, fucking boong.' He raises his hands ready to protect his face, but Paul doesn't punch him.

'Repeat please?' Paul towers over him.

'Boong,' the man repeats, grinning idiotically.

'I'm not a boong, man. I've got Polynesian blood, proud Pacific blood.' Paul's frown is savage.

The man takes off. But Paul catches him by the band of his shorts. 'I think you probably meant to insult me, was that it? I don't know whether to knock you out or rape you instead of him,' he says it arrogantly.

Sean sees that they both begin to enjoy themselves, sharing insults and threats of violence. He sneaks slowly to his car and softly opens the door. The ignition catches straight away. He skids in a semi-circle of dust and gravel as he beats a retreat up the corrugated road. Sweating and swearing and keeping his eye on his rear-vision mirrors. Tow trucks have V8 motors and their drivers are faster than ambulance men with sirens. Sean prays to god that Paul is not really interested in him. He is afraid all the way home.

When there, he locks all his doors and windows.

Tiger Cat was at the gym, not Sean. She is there five hours a day. Lois was pushing a mean two hundred kilos with the leg-press. I slapped her chummily with the end of my towel. 'Gidday.'

'You too,' she puffed.

We three were the only females using the seriously weighty equipment. Down the other end, on walking-mats and push-bike frames, several women in leotards and tights obediently pursued gentler regimes, telling each other Sean Dark's orders with constant reference to a personal sheet on a clipboard. Thrust sat on a bench talking to local footballers in singlets who grasped hand-weights and flexed their biceps while idly gazing at themselves in the mirror.

When the bench beside Tiger Cat became vacant, I chose a hand-weight and sat next to her.

'Sean should be here,' I worried. I stretched hearsay to fact as a tactical move. 'The gurls think you are a spook.'

'What I tell the cops I tell the women,' she replied mischievously. 'After all we both can be suspected of undercover work.'

'Yeah, who do you talk to, Cat?' I pushed up, waited, and added, viciously, 'Rather, who would talk to you?'

'That's for me to know and you to find out.' She got up and compared the numbers on our rounds of steel and sneeringly remarked on the contrast, easily to her advantage, proving she was stronger in the shoulder.

'Sweetness must know you are not to be trusted. Never were. Never will be.'

'Your loyalty is lovely, Margot,' she grinned, as I lifted.

She wandered off towards the office where the drugs are kept. An argument erupted. One of the white males working out said something insensitive when Lois claimed her man in her customary high-handed manner. She swore at him.

'Just because you're black, it doesn't mean you have a patent on all suffering,' he said in a disconcertingly educated voice. 'You don't have to be white and male to be a bad bastard.'

Superior command of language notwithstanding, I hoped he could look after himself because Lois would deck him if he went too far. I faked an attack of deafness and worked gently lying on my back, strengthening knees and ankles. Keeping a keen eye on the clock, I noticed the footy lads shaped up on Lois and Thrust's behalf and the bloke minced off, miffed, to the end with the ladies to warm down on an exercise bike down there. Lois, when I left, was angrily beating the life out of the punching bag being held by her husband for better resistance. Tiger Cat had disappeared.

This sort of thing simply did not happen when Sean was around. How could he be so stupid as to leave Tiger Cat in charge? But I couldn't bother about it then. I had to get to Chandra's for the meeting, which was relatively uncomfortable as Chandra does not have enough chairs. Surprisingly, Cybil took over the funeral arrangements and the cremation was arranged for Tuesday at Port Water, the wake out at Pearceville. Jill took Sofia home before it all finished. I spoke once, reassuring the crowd that the police would not be involved any further, a full post mortem would take a couple of months but the prelim indicated accidental death by poisoning.

'Log-book. Can't put 13. Hours straight. Me and him. Doing North Coast to Melbourne. Passing each other. CB. Keeping in touch. Keeping awake. He is watching me. Matching trucks. Matching loads. Keeping me pumped. Noon sightings. No, too many pills. Super lorry, flies by itself, bristling with equipment like a 747. That's black,' Ian mutters to himself.

'Breaker, breaker White Virgin. Fucking thirteen, mate.'

'You're dropping out.' Static. Interference. Ten ways to communicate and nothing doing. Nothing. No contact. They pull into the side of the road, parking closer than cars do.

Truckman steps down from his rig thinking he'll go for a mixed grill, or fried eggs and chips. 'Booby farm girl gotta appreciate a man's gruff compliments.'

'She won't last long in a place like this if she don't know the rules. Something they're born with, you can't teach it.' Samurai semis, enforcing the rules.

'Get shirty if my table is occupied by anybody but the fraternity. Same table. Same tucker.' The lone conspirator carries on a conversation as if in monologue with himself.

'They left their newspapers. Broadsheet. I get my news from tabloids and off the Internet. What I call news. But I look at the pictures and headlines.'

The other trucker says, 'Look at that!'

'The photo? Man in a suit looking up at a flying saucer, name Dr Seth Shostak: THEY'RE OUT THERE BUT THEY DON'T WANT TO EAT US.'

It scares Ian. He yells at the waitress, 'Why don't you fucking clean up my table properly?'

'Take it easy, comrade.'

'Didn't mean to. It slipped out.' Sudden aggression, urgent defensiveness. 'She's gotta learn, blokes like me. We do long hours, and we got a code of honour, demanding respect from little cars and little girls.'

The driver of the Scania 143 stares at the master of the bigger Freight-Liner FL112. Ian shows him the picture, and says, 'Just like mine.'

'You see 'em too?'

'I never bought this! They left it. They were here five minutes before me, pretending to be people. It spooked me.'

'You're not wrong.' His partner humours him, listening.

'Lucky I didn't get tossed out for swearing at booby waitress,' he confesses.

'Fucking thirteen on the dateline, mate.' Jittery, high on speed. 'We'll be there. You know what we're carrying, Ian?'

'Did ask myself that, Michael. It's not petrol. It's not milk. But it's a tanker, right?' Ian Truckman calms himself, tackling the question.

'I reckon we've got toxic waste.' Partner's voice too high.

'Hey, keep it down, you dork,' says Ian.

A cunning gleam in Michael's eyes; the creep likes it, thinks Ian Truckman, essentially a solitary man.

'Toxic waste, flying saucers. You ought to get a grip, Ian.' Partner, grinning at other blokes, speaks under his breath.

Ian nods. 'Don't know about you, but I am going to get some kip. About twenty kilometres down the road there's a shady rest stop.'

'You're my man, Ian. It's not as though they don't provide us, eh?'

'Stopping too?'

'You betcha. You're the senior man,' he shamelessly flatters. 'If you do, I can.'

Ian Truckman does not know what being the senior man involves. He was never told.

'Yeah well. I take it you're watching me.'

'We gotta keep an eye out for each other, man.'

28

. . . no stasis . . .

The gathering of many women focused on the unequivocal climax of a funeral, the swell of their strength and weakness lifts Cybil to an unfamiliar sense of belonging. She comes into her own, being helpful, generous, articulate. Her overt sensitivity to the observance of the occasion is appreciated. Her practical advice, her knowledge of the area and the options on offer saves the assembly from becoming a shambles of hysteria and histrionics. Sadness. She is a natural chairwoman.

Spontaneously, Cybil wants to stay at Virginia's overnight and to see her work, the ship in a fallen dead tree, although she is terrified of the bush. Puddles, the poodle, will enjoy herself. She roots around the bottom of her built-ins for her oldest sloppy-joes. Her shiny car safely locked in the basement of the block of flats, she puts her weight in the passenger seat of her lover's turbo-diesel Rodeo. Virginia is thrilled. But it is not her only emotion. Maria was her friend. They share a voyage of discovery through myriad deaths and rebirths; there is no stasis, no end to the parabola of reincarnation. Dying and living are one. All time is now.

Virginia drives fast, negotiating the bends she knows like the back of her hand with, what seems to Cybil, too little attention, and talks.

Cybil cannot listen when she cannot see the road ahead. She is basically an urban woman for whom rainforest is jungle, full of snakes and poisonous vines. A sophisticated, cool woman, she is suppressing her fears of tumbling over rocks and disappearing into ravines. On separatist land, where men with their emergency services are not allowed, you could lie under a log with a broken leg like an escaped convict in colonial days and be maimed for life, that is, if you live. Starving to death. Listening to Virginia is making her feel worse. She shuts her out. She taps her new mobile phone. It won't work, out of the range of the air ambulance. The little dog paces and pants on the bench seat of the dual cabin, going from window to window, from all fours to two paws. And back again.

Virginia is speaking too much. 'Made, unmade and made again through the ages, the connection of fighting women, a network of ferocious, bitter women who usually only wanted somewhere to live, laugh and work but were forced to fight. Indeed they were—we were—heard laughing under the full moons in the months and years that preceded the agrarian revolutions. Strong females met with the other peasants to organise action for justice, under the best light they had. Once a month in a safe natural light. Night light. Subversives know the magical humour of such occasions which must seem mysterious to fascists. When revolutionary cells are described in films or books, they are greyish earnest gatherings. That is not true. I guess you had to be there. Comic imagination is fired by hope and readiness when revolution is brewing. Well-intentioned peasants were feared, called names, groups of women became cults, sheeted home to the poor old virgin goddesses, Diana, Selene, Artemis, or to animals. Herbalists, witches, madwomen, bedlamites. Women with a modicum of power, even if it were among the powerless, were blamed and accused. As soon as an alliance among females could be proved, or provided, be it kinship, or mere acquaintance, let alone passionate friendship, not to mention—never to mention—sexual devotion, the sword descended to slice it apart. The cowardice of men rationalised its way into law so they could act out its worst fantasy, and destroy with impunity and indulgence. Legally, culturally.'

'You are so naive,' Cybil comments, 'All this crap about goddesses is a lot of hot air'.

Virginia is definite. 'In another age I would be burnt as a witch.'

'Pleasant thought.' The highway is straight, at this point. Cybil glances at the speedometer.

'When I chip away at my boat, my muscles powered by hatred and resentment, indignant with knowledge, I work furiously. My head gets full of voices. Trying to counter the process of cultural annihilation.'

'Annihilation?'

'Yes. What is the opposite of that?' Virginia asks in an effort to make Cybil think about what she is saying.

'Preservation? Conservation?' Cybil mentions a few more words. 'Continuance. Maintenance. Upkeep.'

'Exactly, you understand. But it is discovery as well. Life,' Virginia philosophises, 'which includes death.'

Cybil sparks up. 'Hey! Did you remember to bring my crossword puzzle?'

'What? Yes, today's paper is there. Why?' Virginia is disconcerted.

'Because I have to have something to do. You brought insect repellent? I am allergic to bites.' Cybil is fearsome when fearful. Bossy.

Virginia feels a kind of impatient yet gentle protectiveness. When she turns off the tarred road and continues to speed, Cybil's knuckles go white as she grasps the dash and barely contains her panic.

'Socially I am wooden, stiff with the energy of past and future,' Virginia continues. 'A Luddite, I live as Europeans did after the gutters and viaducts of Rome's superlative plumbing were grown over with weeds. Collect my water in tanks, cook over an open fire, carry fuel. Except for the chain-saw. I eat, simply, grains, rice and lentils, potatoes, yabbies and eels I catch in the creek. Bush tucker, lilly-pilly berries, native fig.' She laughs at her perverse boasting. 'Woodworm.'

'For godsake, slow down!' Cybil orders. 'You're making me sick.'

The cows move out of her way with plenty of room, two or three feet, so Virginia thinks she must be talking too fast. 'It is a covenant. I must be mad or in contact with another who knows as I know that it is dire. Ghosts, perhaps. The ectomorphic presences dressed in wisps of mists visit in silence. I am grateful for my eyes to dissolve. Then I work again, furiously. When I spin I think of spiders and when I weave I think of schemes. Who can know that I am like this? Seething like a nest of killer ants . . .'

'Slow down!' Cybil shrieks.

'Okay,' Virginia turns to her smiling, one hand on the wheel, eyes off the road. 'So I don't spin or weave, but I could. It feels as though I could do any craft reasonably well.'

Cybil screams, 'Watch where you're going!'

'Don't worry, it's okay. It's okay.' Dawdling is too much of a compromise for Virginia to make.

At the gate, Virginia introduces Emma Ledgerwood, and her daughters, Serena, Venus and Cassie, big, bland Bea Valiante and Olga with her dog, Owtchar, and Dee Knox, whom she has met before at the triathlon, to Cybil Crabbe, formally with pride. 'My tribe.' The gurls are pleasant and chatty.

Bea says, 'You're a member of my clan. I like you.'

Cybil notices how awfully dressed in rags they are, almost indecent. She frowns, no longer feeling at one in the company of women as she had a couple of hours ago. Virginia finishes the interchange with a claim for the pressure of time and the explanation that Cybil has never been bush before. Gurls and girls grin knowingly.

'What was that about?' Cybil demands as Virginia skilfully jolts her vehicle through the creek and up the bank, commenting on the broken bridge as she does so. When she is back on hard road, she answers, 'Bea is a member of the elephant family, according to herself. She likes all women with no knees or ankles, with straight elephant legs,' Virginia elucidates.

Cybil is not exactly pleased.

'So do I, or, at least, I love you.' Virginia is blatant as if a skin of civilised language has been ripped exposing raw meaning.

At home in the wilderness she fits, Cybil loves her too, but doesn't say. As the territory becomes more hairy, she trusts her more. She has to. She is in Virginia's hands. Soon she feels the thrill of a pioneer as they climb into the range, and stunning vistas appear when cathedral walls of tall timber part to reveal the expanse of valley they have already travelled through. 'Wow,' Cybil mutters. The tension in her hands has become a tremble throughout her being. She lets it happen. She lets herself feel. At the edge of her terror is excitement; any sort of thought would torment her.

Virginia's house is primitive, comfortable and clean. It is cosy. Cybil enters a realm in her emotional landscape past death's crossroads; she moves into a hyper-sensual place, a sexio-spiritual fantasy she can express no other way than making love. The darkness of a moonless night is darker in the bush, and deeper with echoing sounds of barking owls, dingo howls, close and distant nocturnal activity. All superlatively sinister, Cybil shivers with the menace of secrecy, her own and that around, and delves into Virginia. Savage in her lust.

While Alison's bowels bleed with emotions among women she thinks love her, she does not want them dead. She is too busy to go to Chandra's. Alison goes to work without Penny Waughan's knowledge. She sits down at the computer and logs in. She finds peace in the community in cyberspace. There in freedom her alien spirit can fly.

The lesbian cyborgs are chatting. They are discussing whether women can be as psychopathic as men. It is a hot debate. She is just about to enter a private chat room when the telephone rings. She closes down and puts on her cleaning gloves. The action and the texture help her get into the appropriate character.

In Stuart, on my way back from Lebanese Plains, realising I should have spoken to Jill about the mess at Meghan's and admitted I was an intruder, I pulled up beside the public phone-box, pushed in my phone card and punched out her mobile number. She responded within seconds. At first, it was hard to hear her voice. She was speaking softly and the unmistakable ring, ting and din of poker machines was close to the mouthpiece. As we spoke I was conscious of the fact that she kept playing, although she made no mention of it. I asked some questions and was not satisfied with her concentration. She was putting me off with vagueness, and short answers to my wordy questions. I rang off with only one useful piece of information: Meghan Featherstone's girlfriend is a gambler. You never win at that game.

It is more an addiction to losing as addicts tend to send good money chasing after bad. It is a fixation, an obliteration, I cannot understand. I have seen women's desperation turn to despair as the last wager is lost, the last cent in the kitty gone. Then they kind of pack up their devastation with their handbags and force their heads high as they walk out of the club. Something is seriously wrong in a society where the absentee landlords of old with their back-breaking rack-rents, their cruel wringing of blood from a stone for their tithes, their taxes, whatever, is absorbed into the mentality of the peasants so that they do it to themselves. Worse still, when the waves of feminism have brought some modicum of freedom for some women, those women go and flush it away down some toilet: heroin, gambling, god knows. Financial independence in a capitalist system must be the first step, not the end of the story. Wasting time and money is wasting freedom.

In a more tolerant frame of mind I could rationalise that if it were your way of dumbing out when emotional strife got too much, then poker machines with their hypnotic mandalas turning could make you forget. Whatever was happening for Jill David, apart from the trauma of Maria's dying the way she did and Jill being present, then the intensity of so many women talking, shouting, feeling, some of whom may well have been intimate with her in the past (or present?), drove her post-haste to the comfort of the casino room. So where was the other gurl who was at the scene of both demises? She was not among the mob mourning for Maria. I was lucky, in the end, to find her.

Alison answered as I was speaking to Penny's answer phone and sounded overjoyed to be invited to join me for afternoon tea at the surf club kiosk. The deck overlooks a longish beach with rolling surf scalloping in between two cliffs of spectacular rock formations. The surf was murky with the red weed. I sat with a mineral water, letting the wind bounce my fringe around. Each time I have seen Alison she has been dressed completely differently. Walking towards me on the boards today she was in a uniform like a nurse's aide and low lace-up shoes. She carried a purse and a pair of rubber gloves. Even so she is a striking woman with black hair and dark eyebrows, high cheek-bones and exquisitely shaped mouth. After waving recognition she leant on the railing before coming over to the table. She inhaled in the sea air and turned towards me with an expiration of appreciation. She raised her brows and I smiled.

'Why the rubber gloves?' I wondered inquisitively.

She said she cleaned for Penny Waughan, as if I didn't know, and hadn't rung her there. We did the business of ordering, then Alison was silent. I explained, patiently, how I was going in the work for her boss.

She frowned. It was a pose that brought to mind self-portraits of Frida Kahlo, with the entrails of pain exposed on the viscera and absent from the face.

'Neil?' she asked, though she had to know that.

'Dressed as a girl,' I encouraged.

'I didn't recognise him,' said she so vaguely I doubted her mind was in residence.

It occurred to me, in a flash of intuition: she saw the body.

I sighed, 'How's Tilly, my little mate?'

'I've sent Tilly away with Dello and Maz. Had to. She still thinks she killed him.' What she said, or rather how she said it, had about as much emotional connection to the matter as a story told in animation with elastic cartoon characters. Playing with her gloves in a way actresses convey idle days in a pension beside Swiss lakes, she sighed. 'I was never cut out for motherhood, you know. Not a part of me as I know myself. I threw up every time I had to clean up shit, or vomit. Even baby milk burps made me retch. Have you ever thought about homosexuality and parenthood, Margot? Feminism never had the time to understand the freedom it was asking for women, of women, nor did it ever have the power "to let women down", as it is accused of, or enough power in the face of the status quo to establish any infrastructure for its theories. Amazingly, perhaps, they believed they could do it all, thus their disillusion is superbad.'

'Who?' I replied. 'Who is they?'

'Us, you and I. The next generation, those whose mothers are contemporaneous with feminist second-wavers, who are themselves now beyond youth. Perhaps you are older than I am, anyway. Penny is.'

'I reckon.'

'Safe houses, refuges, abortion reform, child care and women's health centres was a mop-up operation, intelligent women soon got bored with it. Even though the need is as desperate as ever. Penny and I, we share knowledge of motherhood, the blame and the glorification. Maria and I, too.'

'You knew Maria was Sofia's mother?' I felt angry that I did not have this information sooner.

'Uh ha,' she nodded. 'Maria died of despair. No, she couldn't change and times changed. Feminism itself didn't expect us to be superwomen, work and have children. Maybe they didn't think about it. While the men turned out to be wimps, absent, sperm donors or SNAGs giving up the responsibility for opening doors and bringing home the bacon, crying at the drop of a hat . . .'

Alison's passion was dissociated, distanced. She continued the mannerism of gracious ladies with time on their hands taking tea on a balcony, fiddling with long gloves, faking supreme disinterest in the affairs of men, and conveyed it so well I almost believed the rubber was fine kid. Yet, she seemed duty-bound to educate me.

'Has Chandra asked you to feel me out about my sexual politics?' I interrupted.

Imperceptibly affirming my suspicion, she went on, 'Crumbs were tossed towards cultural activities, as if to keep the libbers happy and in a small group, growling at each other.'

'For godsake, Alison!'

She continued, serenely. 'So feminism became a generational fashion; similar to the suffragette era. Faddish in the sense of having a style of dress and thinking, easily caricatured. The thread of discourse remains, of course, but it's a skinny thread from before and persisting through Matilda Joselyn Gage and continued in embattled publishing, reading and writing. Of this string a small percentage is fresh, most is research and recovery. So the discourse is penned in the patriarchy. If you look at *The City of Women* or Gilman's *Herland*, or the lives of artists and doctors, women scientists, the expression of female human brilliance has a small paddock on the planet. So small each woman is close to the fence.'

She got up and strolled to the rail. To the edge. 'I wonder who Maria left her library to,' she murmured. Her body was like the character of self in dreams, an expression of mentality. Her thoughts were running away with her.

'It's all a trial, it's all so bad,' she finished a sentence I didn't hear. 'Motherhood is under attack from the birth doctors.' She floated back to me. And stared into my eyes. 'One is actually called Dick Seed, Margot. Dr Richard Seed said last year something to the effect of "reprogramming the DNA is the first serious step in man's becoming one with god".'

That was so ridiculous I laughed. A smile would crack Alison's poetic persona so she looked serious. She put her thin hand to her chin like a lady writer in a photograph with eyes that penetrated surfaces. She was certainly away with the fairies.

'What amazes is our ability to live fooling ourselves.'

'Perhaps they don't really fool themselves, mothers I mean,' I said. But she was carrying on a conversation with someone else.

'Mothers are alone. Surrounded and alone. Out on a limb with responsibility which no one else ever shares. To get help we must compromise, bend over, beg, belittle ourselves, become tyrants or bitches and help is generally exactly what we ask for. No more. Not an inch extra.'

We were the only customers at the kiosk, the gusty on-shore wind too cool for swimmers and idlers.

'Penny and I, though we speak and touch hands, cannot be friends, ever. We are mothers and our hearts are taken up, with grief, with worry, whatever. Maria . . .' she choked down on whatever she was going to say, and pulled herself together. 'Tilly, I told you, thinks she killed Neil. Normally she would have been with me today. In fact Penny asked me where she was the other day. I lied, naturally. Tilly is so open, she would have spoken about Neil, taken the blame. You see, they hated each other. Neil would dress up in his magician's cape with black lipstick and red paint and false fangs and frighten her with tales of vampires. You could see he enjoyed it and any other kid he may have amused.' Alison sighed. 'But Tilly said, "I hate you, I wish you would die." Fully believing, as I have told her, wishes come true.'

A sudden fear for Tilly passed through my mind. I recalled the distress I felt when I saw the bruises on her back. The anger, the desire for revenge, must be far deeper for her mother. How much did Neil hurt Tilly or how much did Alison think he did?

'I can't share Penny's grief. You see?' She sat down. 'For Neil.'

Our cups and saucers came, with serviettes and assurances that it wouldn't be long. It was, actually, taking ages.

'That's an odd thing to say,' I frowned. Alison was almost insane with sorrow, but was it for Maria or the woe of motherhood?

'A woman like Penny Waughan's needs are greater than she realises. She does perceive they are not really met and that she'd better bloody put up with the best she can get. So she lays down the law, convincing herself that her real needs are nothing. Indeed, she couldn't say what they were. She is a sad sack. Now it's okay. There's a cause. The charade gets deeper, more embedded in phoney connections. How can you share feelings with a woman like that?'

My hot water and pot of tea arrived. I pulled out my spiral notebook and wrote: A touch of the viper about Alison Hungerford! 'Go on,' I suggested, making it obvious that now I had a pen in hand.

'No naming does not mean no essence, no reality, no existence, no meaning. Hormones have their expression. The female self as a physical organism is in constant change. It has a rhythm which responds to the needs of the moment, to the seasons of time and the flux of the moon. Because of the paucity of words these feelings are not communicated in the woman's daily intercourse. The actual demands on her time often fight with the ups and downs within. Temper, depression, guilt, dismay, maybe even enviable bliss, are there but never accurately said in words, so a language of excuse, apology, cunning, cajoling disguises truth.'

Theory reflecting personal experience, I put in brackets. She sugared the froth of her cappuccino without stirring it in. Watching the sugar slowly sink grain by grain through the sprinkle of chocolate, she continued, 'Ideally the conditions of the birth of a person should be a topic of conversation throughout the individual's life, a constant reference, an intimate knowledge, as people refer to their stars in dealing with emotional upsets in their lives, or accidents. But, like breast-feeding in public places, it is embarrassing. Like the slimy bloody placenta, the details of one's birth are buried soon after and life is carried on with in ignorance. Or lies. Parallel stories of their children's babyhood is all once removed, just chatter, not real connection. Even in their absence, it accommodates men and their eternal ignorance of the experience of childbirth. Also it takes away from the child his birth, as it were. He just lands in life. The womb as real to him as the pouch of a stork. His mother, a cabbage. If he were culturally required to carry in his mind the details of his birth, as an ancient mariner carries the caul he was born with, he could not hate women as much as he does. To come to the ideal, I imagine, would mean overcoming the thick strata of prejudice and tradition to ritual cleansing. He washes his hands of his birth. He washes his hands of the woman's labour, he washes the blood away.'

She performed the famous Lady Macbeth scene trying to get the spot of blood from her palm. Alison is so versatile, so riddled with talents, I reached for her hand to search for the stigma. There were small calluses on the ridges—from scrubbing Penny Waughan's floor?—no deep hollows or spongy mounds, plenty of shallow criss-crossed lines. I remembered she read palms. I made a joke about the lecture, my taking notes and encouraged her to go on.

'As the ever-present male fibs about his birth, amnesia washes through the woman's brain. She is left with strange feelings of emptiness and fullness that have reason but no rhyme. She is not given time to ponder the problem, she is beset by practical demands. Motherhood is busy. Chandra made me read the books. She thought it would help. It made me hate. Most mothers have no time to read. Whether or not we have the mental space. This is all leading to the fracture in relationships of women to women. A mother is alone, but she is always relating, not necessarily out of love. If she loves another woman, her ability to express that love is limited by the freedom she has to do it. Even adult children make demands on her that she is mostly powerless to refuse.'

Eventually we did talk about Maria and the night Neil died. 'I've been around too much death lately.' Again the abstract contemplation drew her eyes to gaze at the clouds.

The sails of a yacht listing in the stiff breeze moved swiftly along the horizon, a modern mariner.

'Did you have any of the pills that were handed out so generously that night?' I asked.

'I had Lenny. I hadn't been there very long. I didn't. No,' she shook her head.

'Why not?' I persisted.

She shrugged, plainly thinking it was a stupid question. 'I'm like an orchestra. Sometimes I can't stand the din in my head. I know how to play every instrument, but I don't know how to conduct. Or when I am a fiddler I am not the percussionist. Neil was going to die young. I already knew that.'

'How?'

'His palms. I did not tell Penny, but I thought Neil was a marked boy. There's more death to come.' How mad was this Alison? How much do I believe, or merely believe that she believes? I raked back my fringe. 'The gods love those who die young. They're special, really special. There is another death.'

'Whose?' The waitress came with our sandwiches and asked if everything was all right; did we want anything else? Alison ordered another cappuccino. I thought about herb tea and settled for water. I trained my eye on a surfer who was braving the red weed. The wind whipped up ponies' tails behind the breakers. Alison wanted to tell me about this hand, so she asked to see mine. I said there are only four lines, two across and two down and nothing much else. 'Tell me about the hand you have read?'

'Maria had thick short fingers, puffy at the base, meaning, ironically, she considered her own comfort before others. Small, weak nails, broken lifeline in both hands and equivalent breaks in the head and heart. But she was a goddess, as well. The health line pierced the lifeline. When I read her palm I knew she was going to die soon. And, of course, she did.'

'Do you want me to do anything?' I can't help myself; if I can prevent a tragedy I'll try.

'I don't know what to do with all the knowledge. It makes me sick.' She looked at her own palms. 'There is no sickness here, but I am racked at times with chronic fatigue syndrome and Ross River fever.'

'Are you okay now?' She nodded. 'By the way.'

'Yes?'

'How come you're carrying your cleaning gloves?'

She laughed, 'What's the time?'

I told her and observed the surfer carrying his board up the beach. Alison drained her coffee. Abruptly she got up, grabbing her gloves. Distractedly paced, forth and back. The wind started to get fiercer, from the south. 'Not enough money, never enough money. Look at me! Should I have to deal with the grubby necessity of money?'

'It's okay, Alison. Calm down. I'll pay. Don't worry.' I had to think of something pleasant to ground her. 'Do you play a musical instrument?' The smile I expected came over her face; she nodded.

She pointed her finger at me. 'The sleuth! You're not stupid are you? Yes, I play the Irish harp and sing in Gaelic.' She put down the gloves.

'Here is a nice place to sing me something. Stand over by the railing and I'll imagine I'm in Galway or somewhere.' It was an inspired guess: if she used orchestra as a symbol for her inner being, I just wondered whether that was anchored in actual musicality. It had the desired result of removing Alison's agitation.

'Okay.' She laughed. She shifted personality, purpose, as a driver moves a gear-stick.

A serious singer, she did a couple of vocal exercises, took up a position with the ocean behind her and sang in the highest voice I have ever heard live. It wove in and out of the wind in the overhead wires and the waves' crashing. When she finished, fading into the rhythm of the rollers pounding the shore, the waitress clapped behind me. Her voice came from somewhere in the mists of Erin, too airy to anchor anything.

She sat down again. She looked directly into my eyes. I could see she was worried. The waitress came over with another cappuccino, 'On the house,' she smiled. Alison thanked her quickly and blushed. She looked down at her palms again.

'What would you do? I mean, if you were me?' she asked. 'We slept together. She was elemental and self-indulgent, but solid in generosity. She was so much like a rock, I felt like the sorrowful Ariadne cast upon it in hostile seas.'

If I said anything at all, it would be misinterpreted because I saw she was mad.

'I am jealous, mischievous, meddling. Violent, so likely to get bashed up. What time is it?' she asked again.

Looking at my wrist-watch, I answered. She felt for her gloves.

Alison's shoulders sank into a kind of despair, a gesture that added years to her age, 'Harold! I have three children by three different fathers. Harold is my eldest. He is like his father, a barbarian.'

She grabbed her purse and showed me a photograph of her children. Only Tilly looked at all like her. Harold was big and blond. Lenny, except for his blue eyes, Aboriginal and fine-boned. She spoke speedily. 'I rejected him. He became violent. He went away. He came back, threatened me, hit Tilly and then we went to Chandra's for refuge. Lenny stayed with his father's family, who are just great. The stress of it all exhausted me. Now, it's beyond all that.' She got up. 'Look I've got to go.'

She ran off along the boardwalk.

'Where can I contact you?' I called after her. She spun around with the timing of an actress, gestured with her arms: another stupid question. I had contacted her today, hadn't I? Alison made me feel so dumb.

I walked along the beach ruminating. I could see a fragile and beautiful teenager, Alison, made pregnant by a large, fair-haired brute of Northern European extraction. First, in a domestic violence situation, then, probably a single mother eaten up by the demands of a rapacious son, whom she probably loved to distraction. I could see this boy spoilt with mother love for a few years, then rivalled by the arrival of a half-brother, a light-framed, dark-skinned boy. I began to feel like a profiler, but I had had some training in this method as it related to the criminal mind. The boy has a boy's anger which, at first, probably expressed itself in tantrums that, while he was small, adults could control. Then his mother stops relating exclusively to men, she is changing, maturing. Her music and whatever else she is into does not impress this growing lad; he demands more. When Tilly comes into their lives, he is probably at the difficult age of thirteen or fourteen. He has the choice to adore his little sister or hate her, to protect her or abuse her. The lad has a moral choice, a dilemma, but he is like his father, a barbarian—strange word, she used. He has barbaric solutions. Something must have happened and he goes away. He comes back demanding, and, if he does not get satisfaction from his mother, punishing. Tilly is the spitting image of Alison. Tilly takes blows intended for Alison. I created the personality of a committed misogynist, Harold, Alison's first-born.

Then, making my way between the ebbing surf and the drying red weed on the tide line, I thought about this Ariadne cast upon the rock. What an image! I began to think Alison some kind of genius. Where do such self-destructive leanings begin? Whose is the imminent death? But I don't know whether I believe in fortune-tellers of any brand.

Superstitions actually bore me. I set my imagination aside for practical purposes, inspired guesses. The Gaelic song washed in tide, smoothing the sand, enabling me to leave concerns about Alison's welfare there on the beach, find my way to my car, and be on with my business. Life is a gambler's winnings, held in the fist for a minute, then lost. Or like fingered names written in the sand between the ebb and flow of time. I stood and wrote 'Maria' between waves and watched it slowly wash away.

Sean Dark's dinky ute was not in its usual spot and the main gym was locked, although Friday evening basketball training was under way. I considered stopping at the RSL Club; would Jill be there? The casino room was lively with the tinkle of poker machines. Family groups played their weekly flutter. Meat trays were being laid out on trestles in readiness for the raffle, and the man on the microphone was encouraging people to buy tickets, offering bonus specials for scattered aces and the like. As I was driving away, I saw her further down the street. I did not need to be told here was a woman who had lost all the cash in her wallet. Jill was fairly cagey but she did confirm that Meghan had beaten her and they had been to counselling. I did not reveal that I had breached privacy codes by being in their house when no one was home. She refused a lift.

At home I rang Newcastle, hoping to catch the absentee landlord, the neighbour of Lesbianlands, at dinner time. As it happened, the South African would be checking out his property tomorrow. We made an appointment. Before bed I rang Chandra who expressed the opinion that all intelligent women who had the time should educate themselves on fundamental feminism. It was, according to her, necessary for their self-knowledge. While it was a veiled criticism of me, I dealt with it lightly, not interested in abstract philosophising but confirming that, at least, part of the Alison act was fact. Chandra made her read the books. Ergo, Chandra made all her lovers read the books?

29

. . . the colour of gingerbread . . .

The delta was lively with craft fanning out from the marinas and canal developments of Port Water with tourists, trippers and retirees aboard; a flat-bottomed house-boat; an adventure launch called Campbell Discovery; guided fishing excursion vessels and numbered rental dinghies; small and large speedboats with outboard motors. Saturday morning. It was positively surreal seeing an airborne water-skier suspended from a technicoloured parachute glide by in the sky above the muted olive greens of low-lying bush.

The dentist had a thick South African accent, a Dick Smith-ish character. The tiny packet of humourless energy actually did own a whirly-bird. He landed it away from the main terminal, at an end of the airstrip I had never had occasion to visit before. Hangars, warehouses for hire, joy-flight operators and flying schools were along a road parallel to the mangroves which fringed an arm of the estuary. I went the back way from my place along rutted tracks gridded across the wetlands, chiefly servicing oyster leases. That, in itself, was an education: wooden bridges I did not know about. All this was inland from the ferry-crossing I usually took, yet within the other route which meets a major black-top further north. I supposed that there were worlds within worlds; even familiar stamping grounds were full of surprises and the mystery of others' lives, priorities, hobbies. Topped by the appearance of a private helicopter, a bubble of glass seating two at most, my appreciation of wealth, the things and activities that money can buy, begged questions that insight had yet to answer.

Arriving by helicopter to tracts of land bought because he could afford it and for no other purpose than to keep it pristine, he was obsessed with conservation, an eco-maniac, an environmentalist. A man with a mission. To protect endangered species. To discover some parrot, last sighted in 1972, or something. To disprove, or prevent, extinction. To snap up every opportunity to spread his message. To put his binoculars to his face to name and note, discard with impatience if the specimen were common. To speak nineteen to the dozen. To get rid of all cats, especially fat suburban moggies, who live near bushland, as here, and kill for pleasure, thus dispatching more lizards and quail than feral cats. To lobby against the interests of cattle-farmers, cotton-croppers and rice-growers. Why I needed to know this was anyone's guess, but I expected everybody who came within range got the spray.

'Yes, Margot?' As busy as a bird, he eyed me with an avian gleam for the second he interrupted himself, then grasped his binoculars and studied a speck in the true blue distance, said, 'Kite. Brahminy,' and expected me to continue without wasting his time.

I thanked him and agreed with his passionate sentiments and asked if he had noticed anything odd happening near his property up in the catchment of the Campbell.

'How would I know what is odd? I have only owned it a few months. And it's all odd. Odd, my dear! This country—I mean the land—is managed by the stupidest people on earth!' His commitment to his cause was over-whelming. 'Nothing they do is right. Fancy giving this magnificent estate, unique on the planet, to morons!'

'You mean cattle-farmers, your neighbours?' I pressed.

He aired an exasperated sigh, 'And ferals! People ferals. Pig ferals.'

'Lesbians? Are you referring to them? Your other neighbours?' I stood with my weight on both feet and crossed my arms.

'No,' he said, 'when I say pig I mean pig. When I say feral I mean feral. I do not mean tree-sitters. I bought that place because it is the last known habitat of a rare marsupial.'

I listened with interest to the description and Latin name and when a pause presented itself I told him about the explosions. When he heard a fact that was not already in his encyclopaedic brain he was silent.

'You know about them?' I sounded surprised.

'No no no,' he denied. 'I do not know about explosions, or any mining explorations in the area, although, of course, I have had a geological survey done, and the place is rich in mineral. Gold, tin, copper, gemstones, precious metals. That is not unusual, necessarily. But if anything is done in that regard, for the moment, it is illegal.'

Now he was itching to go. I had worried him. He saw no need to disguise his mood-change. I, too, had to be on my way, so I relaxed my stance and began, incidentally, chatting on his favourite subject. What methods he would use to improve things? He was forthcoming on organisations and projects, successes here and there. One north Queensland sugar farmer had incorporated owl boxes to keep his rodent pests down, et cetera. We strolled across the tarmac to his flying machine, which reminded me of a small sedan, except with rotors and landing plates attached.

'Margot,' he said in parting, 'if you think something is vermin, it is very easy to kill. In fact, it is thrilling.'

'Really?'

'Ask any gardener,' he tried to smile. 'They pull weeds, and poison insects, with righteous zeal. But, my dear, it is a matter of proportion. How big is your garden?' He was on board and waving me off before I could reply. 'An acre.' But I took his point. He was a zealot and I could only guess at how large he considered his garden, his own hectares, his adopted homeland, the planet?

Cybil leans up against the pillows on Virginia's bed in state with her cross-word being brought treats from the kitchen, saying things like, 'My pooteeful poodle,' to Puddles. Virginia, for a while, lies beside her, cuddling into her soft curves. She reads other parts of the paper before she folds it neatly to put it in a box near the fireplace. Cybil does not want to get out of bed all morning. Originally, Virginia tells her, she wanted to make her home half in and half out of the ground, an organic house, the rock and daub walls a dome made from the rocks and clay removed. She saw it in a book. If nothing else, Lesbianlands is a place where adult women come to build cubby houses dreamt up in the restricting time of tomboyhood. Cybil says she was never a tomboy. And outside doesn't interest her.

Amazed by such an admission, Virginia White must get away from Cybil's sticky presence lolling in the warm sloth of the doona, to find herself. She walks through the lilly-pilly forest, scanning the ground for brown snakes which look like sticks. She does not step on any twigs or broken branches. Cybil's sensuality is alluring and, here, strange; almost exotic. Virginia comes to the hole she dug for her cubby. It is now a place she meditates. She watches the tiny beauty of insects on the walls of her depression. Intense menopausal moments have Virginia questioning everything while her chief concern is her sexual relationship with Cybil.

Sex, she won't talk about it. She just does it. For Virginia it is as if her body betrays emotions in and of itself, as if feelings originate in the hormones. She suffers a churning sort of unease, only marginally related to outside stimuli. 'These days,' Virginia speaks quietly, but succinctly to the insects around her, 'I am so serious, laughter and jokes not so easy any more. I've got to accept something about myself and am resisting it. At menopause I should be getting dry and tight. I am very sexual, open, wet, but not all the time. In fact, at this moment, my cunt is aching as if a hot poker is up it, and has been since she entered me, sawing, pushing, forcing my orgasm which was as hollow as outer space, hardly allowing me to manipulate her clitoris. My way.

She had to have all the giving, the power. When I am making her come, my vagina opens and is lubricant and likes being occupied. I should be happy. She is here. But onanism leaves me dry. Yet my need for sex, as if my body is boss, is good, because I am discovering something in my nature that will rid me of doubt and shame of being a woman, disentangle what is learnt from what is truly there. And Cybil is my vehicle, she knows something I don't. But I am sore.'

Cybil in her bush shack, probably getting angry at being left alone, is a magnet, and Virginia has to force herself to think. Female orgasm without the male organ entering to propagate the species happens independently of any other need apart from pleasure. And that pleasure seems to need love. It is, too, the sensual excitement of nerve endings and erectile tissue, blood rushing around sending messages, melting feelings, swamping thought. 'With this involvement I've allowed myself to be open, to dive into my femininity, and feel a pain I've not known before. I will have to keep it entirely to myself because I don't want to damage her ego. I can't tell her I feel as raw as if it was a rapacious man inside me. Relations between women are so delicate, so strange, so strained we are too quick to blame ourselves, hence hurt each other.'

She goes back to Cybil determined to reveal herself, to nut it out.

'More coffee?' she calls.

'How about that milky sweet cha you make?'

'Okay.' When she brings the mugs to the bedside, she starts, 'I am not good at talking about sex. Individual difference, talents, education, tastes, hang-ups all come into it, so that the one who has, say, biology or a medical background might be better at understanding some aspects of sex than another, though that woman may not be so good at the relationship side and so on.'

Cybil enjoys her embarrassment, but Virginia continues. 'Power in a lesbian community enters our personal sexual relationships. The private does in fact remain private, as public as the gossip-merchants want to make it. Fear of truth is relative but, I'd say, pretty general, because so much is painful when women are so damaged and so quick to slide into the habits of that damage.'

Cybil says, 'It goes with the rest of the self-indulgence. Why should anyone care? This place is off the map. You're in a world of your own.'

'My inability to discriminate what is damage to my female being from the society and what is my real self matters! There are assumptions made shared by others that I'm not aware of even though I've been all ears and attention in most of my encounters. I must understand,' Virginia pleads.

But Cybil shakes her head, 'You are so critical, you're obsessed. Worry is the old maid's curse.'

Her troubled mind fails to arouse Cybil's interest, yet Virginia herself is refreshed. Too energetic to lie down again, she begs her to come and see the sculpture.

The walk up the hill to the log has never been so slippery or so slow for Virginia before, but hilarious. When they eventually reach the spot, Cybil asks, 'Where is the boat?'

'This is it,' Virginia opens her palms to the mossy wood. The lines of the figure she now calls Penthesilea stands tall in the stern, her windswept hair a suggestion of Medusa, the chunky tiller-woman beside her dipping her long oar into the sea of mud on the forest floor; the gestures of the half-formed figures down the trunk of the ship express a breath-taking variety of personality.

'Where?' Cybil says, 'I don't understand. There is nothing here.'

Virginia is devastated. She explains. She shows. She leaps around. She sweeps her arms around elongated limbs and stunted crones. But Cybil stays blind.

'Don't worry about it,' she concedes, eventually giving up.

'I'm not.' Cybil smiles, conciliates. 'Maybe when you've done a bit more work on it, I'll see what you mean. Look at those beautiful stag-horns, are they? Elk-horns?'

Virginia stares at the figures on her ship, never clearer to her. In this light, from this angle, from this stunned stillness, she sees more definition, more need for scraping away, uncovering, than ever before. Yet she can't do it. Not only must she take Cybil home, she hasn't the heart. She collects her heavier tools and secures them in a cabin of the vessel, a hole in the log, half-way to the creek. She dislodges the ladder and lies it flat. Cybil does not seem to understand that she has dealt a blow that has taken the wind right out of Virginia's creative sails. The discoverer feels a lesser woman. She is Cybil's lover. The cramp is in her emotional muscle. She lets Cybil enjoy herself skidding and sliding back to the shelter. She accepts that she is her servant, her guardian, protector.

Stuart was busy. I bought torch batteries, candles, plenty of fresh fruit, a packet of dried fruit and nuts, some biscuits, pâté, brie and a supermarket fruitcake. I had brought a bottle of wine and I remembered the newspaper.

After an hour and a half on the highway, I spied the turn-off just as I was about to pass it and breathed a sigh of relief. I stopped after that for a few moments to look at Rory's lovely map. The temper of my thinking changed with the terrain. Now I was entering the Great Dividing Range, hills started falling steeply either side of me. While some were thickly wooded, others were paddocks of stumps. Herefords blocked my path, occupying the roadway as if they, like humans, preferred to stand on flat land. One heifer with a creche of calves proved particularly mulish. I had to almost run into her before she slowly took herself to the right, glaring at me all the time. I travelled along the graded gravel for a fair while, going up into one ridge of hills then down to rise more steeply into another, the road getting increasingly rougher and narrower until it split into two equal dirt tracks. I braked, picked up the map for clarification and discovered that, for all its artistry, this map did not tell me which prong of the fork to take. I gazed around me.

The mailbox was plastered with purple stickers, like My Other Car Is a Broom, and Magic Happens. These were remote parts, no houses in sight. I got out, stretched, took an apple from the box, munched and figured north, south, east and west from the position of the sun. A passenger plane high in the sky seemed, thus, to be carrying people from the Pacific Ocean to the Western Tablelands. A sight to enhance my better mood appeared around the bend of the track to the left, a dense rectangle of colourlessness, no windows, no delineation except for the manic movement of a sharp-eared dog.

The vehicle lumbered towards me, rattled over a wooden cattle grid and pulled up. 'A most unusual truck,' I commented.

'Land Rover Guntractor,' Rory answered succinctly. Proudly. It had no roof and a serviceably large tray carrying short logs and a Farm Boss chainsaw. A galvanised steel lock-up tool box was bolted to the floor. My Suzuki Sierra looked like a little girl in a tutu. Rory reached into it and picked up the box of goodies and the paper and wine, without instructions. My empty back-pack became unnecessary. All I had to carry was my jacket and change of clothes. She asked about the bike.

'I was going to ride it around Lesbianlands,' I explained. 'I didn't know you meant to pick me up here.'

'That's why there were no more directions, just L and R.' Rory was wearing khaki pants with numerous pockets and a camouflage-patterned shirt along with her badge-proud Akubra. I smiled as I enjoy irony and appreciate big statements. She was appropriating the military, so there.

'I see', said I. A bit embarrassed.

She laughed good-humouredly. 'You'd be better off walking, any rate. Follow me and I'll show you where to stow the wee beach buggy.' She jumped into her Guntractor and forwarded and backed until she was facing the way she had come. We halted near some cattle-yards where one white Holden and two near identical brown Ford panel vans were parked. I locked my car and climbed, using both hands and a big hop with my good leg, into the passenger seat. This was a woman who loved being bush, a kind of joy came off her. She changed gears carefully and the engine ran smoothly, if a bit rattly. She told me again the story of Rory, R.O'R, her initials. Having been christened Rosaleen, she got Rory as a nickname early in life in country Victoria where she was as good as the boys at Aussie rules footy. She could talk the leg off an iron pot, once she started. Nervous, I wondered. I watched the track get more and more difficult and the trees close in and the sun set and rise again as I listened. My ears popped as I swallowed saliva. We passed a Combi van parked in a clearing that looked exactly like one parked at the beach. Being reminded of the corpse made me go cold. I glanced at Rory as she chatted and decided not to interrupt. When I looked beyond her to the view, it was as if Maria had lain down and become land mass; the boobs, the belly, neck, chin. A matter of proportion as the man said.

Evidence of fresh grading, uprooted trees preceded a bridge we crossed. Rory pulled up and got out. 'Now this one,' she was saying, 'needed doing. It collapsed last year. We had a bloke in. He brought down a couple of iron-barks and straddled the creek. Hardwood planks. Cost a thousand dollars, and we paid. The creek was invisible before. We didn't really know there was a spring here.'

'Beautiful place,' I said. A clearing in woodland defied time and seemed as if it could be found anywhere on the earth, the rustic bridge a mere mention of European habitation.

'Someone just piled a few logs across the seepage and filled it with dirt a few decades ago. The wood rotted, of course. It's not a bad job, pretty hairy for riders. Horses could rear up and go over the side if they panicked. The next one collapsed. After the main gate. It didn't need doing when we had the work done last year. Floods gully-raked it into bunches of rocks that were really dangerous, because your vehicle could get stuck on the top of them. Anyway he fixed that. No big deal. This next bridge is a different story. Tracks are very recent.'

We got back in the Land Rover Guntractor. Rory took off her hat and slammed it down on the seat.

'It makes me roaring mad. Excuse the pun. I do have a temper. And I get stubborn. This bridge was perfectly all right to take the weight of my truck. Which is the heaviest car that gurls have. What we reckon is someone drove his bulldozer over it. Broke it. Wanton damage, deliberate. Saw his chance. Crunch. Why did he do it? No reason, I can see.'

'Who saw it happen?' I asked and frowned. I didn't have this information.

'Pam. She hid.' Rory laughed. 'She said she was hiding behind that white mahogany.'

'There?' I pointed. 'Majestic tree!'

'She should have leapt out at him in her bejewelled nudity and cursed him in abracadabra, that would have frightened him out of his boots.'

We stopped again after a few bends, dips and rises.

'Judith came in soon after it happened,' she mused as we were looking down on the scene. There were the jagged remains of an incomplete bridge. A track down to the creek and over the rocks and water was visible.

'Lazy. Or ignorant. Or thoughtless. Or greedy. Or malicious. I don't know people's motives for this sort of thing. But now we've got no bridge here. If Willy did it, we want him accountable. He is the one we employ when we need work done.' She turned away and pulled out some rolling tobacco. I walked over to the broken bridge, bent down and reached out my hand. The lichen was thick, moist and soft. There was rot inside the log and the break was spiky, following the weaker grain of the wood. On the parallel partner the damage was minor. 'Where were the tracks in the mud?' She replied that it had rained heavily since. The planks had fallen off one side and lay for the most part propped against the other. Whatever had happened, the offending bearer was going to go sometime. I returned to my transport and client-friend who was sitting behind the incredibly skinny steering wheel. 'Marvellous pebbles in the creek,' I said.

'What I need,' Rory stated as we plunged over the side of the track into the creek, 'is a helicopter.' She laughed when I told her the South African guy did have one. 'I'd like a whirly-bird like that.'

The English army vehicle seemed to walk across the rocks like a bandicoot, first one corner, then the next, then the next, and the fourth, then she climbed the rise with a roar. This Guntractor could take punishment and come through with good old British grit.

'Vanderveen mustn't come up here much, then?'

'I've heard him once or twice. To tell you the truth, I thought the helicopter was National Parks.'

Putting the damaged civil engineering behind us, we entered the rainforest and progressed through dripping green darkness. Like a dwelling in a fairy tale is Rory's house. I gasped. It had hand-formed curves like Gaudi architecture and the serenity of a Tibetan temple, jutting out from the rock face, made of rock, clay and rough-hewn timber. Organic to its surrounds, the colour of gingerbread. The afternoon sun caught its higher windows with an orange wash, both house and land looked burnished. The shade was deep negative space, a jungle of vines and luscious growth.

Standing on the swing bridge and gazing, I said, 'There's one a bit like this at Nimbin, but that woman had a pulley and a flying fox to get the rocks up. Yours doesn't seem to have one. I'm just struck dumb with its charm, Rory. What a place!' She was again carrying my carton of food and I could only see the back of her but she seemed to swell with pride. She turned.

'Well, we carried everything. There is a bush path down to the road over there. Plenty of women helped. I couldn't count the number. Visitors, residents, everyone lent a hand.'

When I came up to her I could see why she had stopped right there. We had a view through the valley a little way to a waterfall. Rory blushed when she said, 'I'm glad you like it, Margot. And I'm glad you came.'

I wondered how long Rory had fancied me. It's funny how you suddenly absorb the obvious.

Rory dropped my gear and took me on a reconnaissance walk of her surrounds, presenting everything with broad gestures and enthusiastic explanation. I smiled and asked about the smoke coming out of her chimney.

'China and Jo, a couple of campers from the city, are here. Arrived today. Go tomorrow. Happens all the time.' She laughed. 'I really should charge.'

We stood still and let the evening become quiet around us. Sherry flagons set in mud-brick made a feature as we climbed up to the door. The early settlers and writers always referred to the Australian bush as silent, empty of noise. They must have been deaf. It was so alive with constant sound. Inside, the dwelling was basic. The bedroom reached out from the rock-face on sort of horizontal piers and rock stumps. We entered at ground level through an earthen kitchen-bathroom space. That led to a hexagonal-shaped main room with a fireplace built out of stone. A solid, stunted staircase joined the sleeping eyrie. Its windows let in the last beams of the western sun which streamed light onto the varnished floor where we were standing.

The holiday-makers from the city, China and Jo, were seated either side of the fireplace leaning forward in deep discussion. They turned reluctantly away from each other and nodded on introduction to me, whom they plainly expected to dislike. They continued their dialogue immediately after the introductions.

'He/she/it, followed me around the back of the church, which was really dark and spooky, like a rapist. She/he stalked me, like a stereotype of a man. I mean they learn to be masculine, they can never be male.'

'There's a difference,' China was saying.

'Deliberate mutes,' put in Rory who picked up the topic straightaway.

'To think I knew her when she was a baby butch!' Jo was indignant, personally affronted. Then they explained to me they were talking about a female-to-male transsexual.

'Changing gender is easy because it is a sociological construct. Masculinity and femininity are learnt behaviours, and both, both of them, serve the patriarchy.' China's accent was pure Melbourne.

'It's like she has been given one right to act like a man,' Jo wanted to hammer the subject. 'To stalk a woman. Yet this was an all-female party. She had only completed her transformation a few weeks before. After the invitation.' Jo was Joanne, but I couldn't help but be struck by the pair of words which are colloquially mates in the male mateship game naming two very radical feminist lesbians.

I began speaking to Rory as I got out the cheeses and fruit. She asked me about my Achilles tendon, genuinely interested. She opened the wine, a Grants Gully Estate Premium claret, a velvety soft dry red.

'Let it breathe, Rory. It was matured in oak hogsheads prior to bottling. And it's such an easy drink, you may not realise its fine fruity blend of grape varieties. From south-eastern Australia,' I sounded pretentious.

China and Jo said they had to go to their camp site, but Rory invited them to stay for the meal. China offered to do *reiki* on my heel. I accepted and sat down by the fireplace. The pain went as I gazed at the bare uprights and noggins of the stud-frame wall. This healer could be an escapee from justice or a professor of theology for all I cared. Although they had finished their earnest discussion of transgender operations and moved onto sports injuries, Jo apprised me of Achilles' sojourn in the court of Scyros dressed as a girl to avoid Ulysses' call-up to Trojan war duty.

Then China said, 'Priests wear women's clothing to obtain some level of divinity. Like Heracles, Achilles, Dionysus and judges. And men into witchcraft.'

When she had finished, my heel felt better. Rory stewed vegetables in the camp oven. The Grants Gully 1993 tasted like ambrosia in this magnificent setting. We had hardly more than a glass each and yet the conversation didn't lag. It broadened in subject matter as the night wore on. My mind felt pleasantly drunk though not from alcohol. China and Jo were leaving in the morning. 'More's the pity,' Joanne opined. 'At least I've been able to help you with your new computer, Rory.'

'A great help.' Before she went to sleep, Rory settled down at a desk in the corner. The Chinese antique, made for the travelling aristocracy of some mandarin period, seemed in harmony with its rocky alcove. I got cosy on a mattress on the floor, completely bushed. The space was lit by a cold blue glow, not the warm flickers of candle or oil lamp. Within the sylvan surrounds good taste seemed nothing more than the intelligent placing of things, the odd piece of art or sculpture catching the eye, crafts of amateur ingenuity, quirkiness, unified by the blatant female theme. Comfortable as the house was, an invisible mite bit me and made me itch my armpits and pubic hairs. There was movement in the ceiling. Rory saw me glance upwards, and told me about her welcome swallows. Presuming I was wary of nature, she boasted about her fifteen-foot python, Nygella. 'Keeps out the rats in summer. And possums might walk over your sleeping bag in their nightly peregrinations. If you are afraid of spiders,' she shrugged, 'there's nothing much I can do. They're everywhere.'

'I don't mind spiders,' I said, 'but cobwebs bother me a bit.' Red-backs and funnel-webs. Eek.

She wanted to kiss me good-night but I think she was too shy. I slept as if the air was enhanced with something narcotic.

Virginia chauffeurs Cybil back to the coast, driving conservatively and not saying much.

Cybil Crabbe is positively confident in the car.

They quarrel. Virginia cannot sleep and Cybil can. Too thoroughly awake, she drives back to the bush at three o'clock in the morning. The highway is black and empty of traffic and the bush tracks are like the tunnels of a Luna Park Ghost Train ride. Virginia feels she has accommodated Cybil's limitations by not demolishing her self-esteem with ardent argument. She does not want to destroy her. But for Cybil it is not an investigation, rather a battleground with winners and losers. Words as firepower get loaded and shot from the guts until there are victors and vanquished, not an arrival at an understanding, for instance, of the difference between love and like. The mechanics of, and the distinction between, intimacy and friendship, are immensely interesting to Virginia, not a matter of life and death. Debating the role of spoken and written language and the way it obliterates womanspeak, for Cybil, is a crock of nonsense. Virginia has no idea! But the lack of words for much of what women feel and know distresses Virginia. She tried to tell her, 'We are of nature. It is not an out there, not an enemy: the ecology is our environment, our habitat.' 'Dream on,' Cybil had replied. And when Virginia said, 'Perhaps when computers and Internet technology synchronise our activity further we will communicate as well as ants', Cybil scoffed, 'You are so full of bullshit, it's unbelievable.'

A rock lodges beneath her undercarriage as she crosses the creek where the bridge is broken. The Rodeo is stuck.

chemicals

Sunday Monday Tuesday Wednesday

But the child that is born on the Sabbath day
is bonny and blithe and good and gay

30

. . . not known at all . . .

In the morning it felt pleasantly eerie. No one was about. The forest had disappeared overnight. I had to check my watch for the hour, nearly nine. The luminous greyness was fog. I did not wander far after relieving myself for fear of going over a rock face. Mist was mystery in the trees and structural shapes embraced by the white blanket of dampness were the antithesis of the boxes and grids of the rat-race. My mood was to dream and be conscious as well. The vaporous air was energising, exciting. I breathed in wonder. Rory was boiling water on the portable gas stove, wrapped in a great woollen dressing gown when I came back into her house. I looked out all the windows, watching the hazy wall break up gradually. Sunlight caught the high branches of the gums behind the darker, closer lilly-pilly and coachwood. Birds began to sing. They must have been quiet, because now I noticed them, close and busy. One sang, 'Oh oi I, am in situ, wanna be wit you.' I turned back to the interior for human contact, afraid my anthropomorphic projections were bending my brain.

Rory queried, 'Tea?' Her robe was royal blue; angled patches of sun on the noggins and varnished floor made complementary shapes of sharp orange. Where was my camera?

I accepted, and began stacking the plates from last night's dinner which had been left where they were in the dimness as, I was told, it was a waste of light to wash them then. The oriental desk merged with all the other dusty clutter in the daylight. I found the washing up table outside in a place now warmed by the sun. What a pleasant task at this time of day!

When I sat down to drink tea with Rory, I was surprised by a change in her. Her eyes were under-shaded by dark bags and bloodshot with weariness.

'You look as if you have been up all night,' I commented.

She nodded. 'Been surfing the Internet. Did you know there was a big trade in counterfeit labels of 1990 Penfolds Grange?' she asked evasively.

'Well, I did actually, but it seems awfully irrelevant right now.' I smiled, shaking my head, listening to the birds and glancing as often as polite through the windows.

Rory good-humouredly acknowledged my point. 'Do you know anything about the Internet?'

I shook my head.

'It's addictive,' she frowned. 'I'm like that. I worry things to death.'

'Like this bridge thing?' I asked, getting her concern into a subject I was involved with. 'It was going to break anyway, sooner or later.'

'It's the intrusion, really,' she explained. 'The invasion.' She leaned back and stretched. 'Farmers, it's an endless uphill battle against them! Ownership of land has made me angry ever since I was a young child.'

'How the country got given over to the most ignorant and stubborn people in the world really riles Vanderveen as well,' I imparted, referring to the passions of the conservationist with all the possessions money can buy, transport through the air and property in this range.

'Who?' Rory was confused for a minute, 'Oh him, he didn't do it.'

'You think it was the farmer, Campbell, too? I had made up my mind about the dentist. 'Why would Willy do it?'

'Trees, wouldn't he love to log our trees!' She gestured towards the arboreous abundance in the mist.

'He couldn't do that without permission.' I felt indignant that the female feel of the place had been penetrated by foreign bodies.

'Well,' she remarked, 'I wouldn't necessarily put my money on that. Who could stop him?' She yawned. 'I need to give my head a rest. Why don't you take a walk? Maybe go up to Virginia's. See her sculpture.'

'Okay, that's fine with me. Point me in a direction.' I was bright from a terrific sleep and this experience of being away from it all, being in 'her' land, not 'his' land. And I had a job to do. Rory took her cup and mounted the stairs to her bed.

I had a bowl of muesli, did the dishes in the sun, then put a bag of nuts and dried fruit in my pocket with my notebook and pen and set off. The mountains in the distance were being brought out in purple relief against a sky as fragile as a light-blue eggshell.

During the bush-walk, the pain in my heel was only spasmodic. Everywhere I looked I was surrounded by views that could make you weep for love of this country. Forsaking the vista, I saw a path through the lantana; lantana was everywhere. It became very thick. The way through it was like a hallway or a tunnel. It branched like a maze, or a labyrinth. I went up with the climb, hoping to come to a high point where I might see where I had come from and where I was going. Rory had been tired, her directions rudimentary, dismissive. I suspected she left out mentioning a hill or two. Too bad.

Virginia sleeps in the back of the ute under a silver tarpaulin until dawn. Then she works for an hour or so by herself, moving rocks and assessing the situation. Fortunately, although the exhaust-pipe is caught, most of the load is resting on axle and the front diff. To find some help, she walks to Gig Brisson's, the closest, then up to Ti Dyer's, because she is strong. Individually, they light their fires and, after making tea, come to her aid. By mid-morning the vehicle is out of the creek and a rough and ready ford made. Yvonne, Helen and Ci hang about, rustle up food. Jay and Fi do a bit.

Gurls can deal with logs across the road, landslides and, indeed, cars stuck on boulders, without dramatics, taking their time. Unlike a meeting or a party or having personal visits, a gathering focused on a necessary job is treated with good humour. Fighting bushfires, for example, brings out genial, generous interaction, the primary concentration being the physical exertion. Incidental chatty gossip is couched in companionable lack of intensity. Virginia hears about an altercation outside the Pearceville pub in which one of the Campbell fellows threatened Helen with rape, and later, when Pam came through, they ringed her and repeated the intimidation. 'To teach us a lesson,' says Yvonne, 'All we need is a good screw.' Ci makes light of the rumpus caused by the gurls themselves, describing how the males butted in. 'It turned them on, you reckon?' 'You're kidding.' Jay is of the opinion they meant it this time. 'They always mean it.' 'The men had singled out a "good looker".' 'I saw it in his eyes.' 'It can happen any time, to any woman, any-how,' says Fi.

Virginia eats with the mob, thanks, talks, drinks, shares perceptions, comments that without co-operation coercion is always imminent and gets up to move on. Says and is told how lucky she was as a flock of rainbow lorikeets descends into flowering wattles and bottle-brushes, chattering with high-pitched urgency. Her motor has no oil-sump which could have cracked, leaking a slick into the creek. 'Didn't happen.' 'Thank the goddess.'

'Be careful, you old diesel dyke,' Ti Dyer jibes, offishly. Virginia glares at her through beetling brows. The would-be if could-be bulldozer driver, Ti, who gets her pride at the end of a needle not from her enviable strength, with her low-brow pun intends a compliment, and given Ti's set of values, it is sincere warmth: VeeDub is as butch as they come. It does not please her. Gig, in contrast, sensitively offers commiseration for the loss of her friend and recalls a little of the time Maria and Trivia were on Lesbianlands. She makes her way up into the clouds, which metaphor Cybil would approve, that'd be right, and Maria would say, why not?

Gossamer veils still cling in the trees of the higher gullies with sunbeams banding rays through them like direct intervention from god the father in religious art. Virginia seeks her sculpture. It is breathtakingly beautiful. Cybil simply could not see it, and Maria never will. Virginia runs her fingers through her coarse-grained, streaked and black hair, making it stand out from her head like steel wool. She arches her fingers into a cathedral, then various rectangles framing details, imagining camera angles, and goes home, stepping on twigs and stones, seeking pain, but the soles of her feet are as hard as dog's pads. The rainforest weeps. She stops at her woodpile, picks up her block-buster and begins splitting sawn hardwood into chocks for her stove. Disbelief like an iron ball swings through her rib cage into the solar plexus damaging the edifice of self-respect, wall by wall. It must have meaning. Incredulity crashing and thumping, Virginia keeps trying to understand. Chopping fuel is where her axing skills are at, right now. Cybil makes her crude, telling her that she is not who she thinks she is, but someone worse. 'Involving all my time in confused emotions, I can't find the me in me, I stew over the impossible task of pleasing the unpleasable. I cannot be her idea of perfection. Am I her projection? How could she want to annihilate me and my work? No, I am not nothing, but Cybil, do you loathe yourself so much you loathe me even more for loving you?'

The woodpile grows. Virginia expects conversation as well as sex in the gift of selves in intimacy. 'Why won't you let me know you?' But one or other is withheld with Cybil. Virginia refuses to feel despair. 'I'm not a loser. She is afraid nothing is there. No person. She could not be more wrong. The self in her is so strong all her life it has been acted upon, reacted to, plundered, defined, presented back to her as something she does not want to be. Self-knowledge, in Cybil, is self-hatred.'

Having finished splitting what wood is there, Virginia finds her chain-saw and energetically pulls the starter three times. It whirrs to angry life, bites into the horizontal log as she presses down. She zips along creating rounds which fall on the ground. Her blood pounds in her veins. Creativity is deadened by the monopolisation of her feelings, so she makes good use of her time completing chores. The mind is a deep pool and she is not aware that her distraction, her feeling that her genius is being sucked out of her has, also, to do with sadness and incomprehension of grief. Her vision is blurred. Cybil could not see it for the object it will become. Dead lumber hacked a bit, the expression of our future and past culture, a sort of sacred presence, an honouring labour, a struggle for meaning, is something Maria would have seen the value of, for Cybil not more than a place lichen clings to, indistinguishable from the living decay around it. The mossy growth, embryonic fern varieties, ignorance of the analogy of growth, of learning, Virginia wishes for the logic of wordlessness in what she is showing, in what she is doing, muscle throbbing alongside the electrical pulses and chemical carry-on in her brain. Driven by set tasks, seven superhuman trials, heroic initiations to the next level of awareness, she is always a reaching towards a sense of things as they really could be. Each test is a mortal challenge requiring courage. But Virginia has forgotten that each must be dealt with always, including the corrosion of self through lack of money and the deviousness of others.

The sawing done, she uses the axe again, thinking of hubris and humility as frail faults, when the nature of community is interdependence reliant on the independence of each entity: an individual is intricately woven into the white woman's quilt, a torn fabric fraying for centuries. In need of repair. Virginia picks up the wood piece by piece with one hand, making a load in the crook of her other arm, believing that she works at the artistic end of cultural needs, importantly occupied in full accord, past present and future, as still as a mountain ash and as busy as an ant.

Taking the fuel inside, restless, questing, she makes her way, again, towards her art, tossing tin over the pile of firewood as she goes. The boat of seven trials is a personal voyage, yet she wants to dedicate a moment in the log to the shape of Maria. Her figures are objectified women. In the distance, the rounded mountains furry with old forest growth and rearing above clouds backlit by sun are too familiar for Virginia to see. She cannot find appropriate stumps on the tree to mould the classic fat goddess. Herself is the subject. 'Who will know if I starve to death, if I hide, wrap the forest around me in splendid isolation? Will they find me in the lovely lichenoid boat, an ancient tree fallen long ago, alive or as bones? I could arrange my bones and let heart, mind and flesh detach and leave. Dead white purity.' She thinks of suicide.

Eventually I came out of the prickly thickets and, climbing over a stile, proceeded into a paddock. Smoke came from a hollow. Walking that way, I saw the rusty roof of a dwelling, and a tin chimney. Several brown-fleeced sheep gazed lugubriously at me as I passed them, ripping at their pasture. The little humpy was surrounded by stands of sweet corn, a pumpkin vine, balls of parsley, salad burnet and other English herbs, within a barbed and chicken-wire fence. I found a gate near an exotic cactus plant and entered the garden with a rather weak cooee. As Rory had pointed me towards the home of Virginia White, once a famous sculptor, I thought I had found it.

'Remember me to Virginia White,' Auntie had said in the Kimberley. The woman was sitting in front of the fire, black logs smouldering on a ploughshare; half the smoke went up the chimney while the rest hung in the rafters. She was spinning, not wanting to be disturbed yet commanding attention in the way she ignored my entrance. She acted like a famous person. In the gloom long hair hid her features. It was Judith Sloane. I made all the play at small talk while she spun and uttered pearls of abstract wisdom. For such a grand natural environment, it was stuffy in there, with the heady smell of fleece and my back to the view. I turned around.

'What's that?' I asked, seeing something silver glimmer through the trees.

'Rory's phone tower. You would have passed it on your way here. Or did you come the low path? Powered by a solar panel? You didn't see it?' Snobby voice sneering at either my justifiable ignorance or Rory's need to maintain contact with the real world, she wanted to put me in my place.

Laughing it off, I said, 'I must have been watching the birds.'

Judith smirked a little and put the brake on the wheel. 'Would you like some cheese?'

It was such an odd request I accepted. I was quite happy to have encountered Judith instead of Virginia. Not only was I on a job here, I remembered her signature when I was looking at the handwriting on some of Meghan's papers.

'I used to make my own,' she began piously. 'But . . .'

Her voice faded out, I didn't hear any more. She had turned away. She was not kidding, cheese. A block of cheese with bits of blue mould on its hardened outer edges was placed in front of me. She watched me until I had some. As I did it quickly, I ate mould as well.

'That's how we live here. It's hard. It's the frontier, your cheese goes green. That's why I got myself a cow. Fresh milk, protein, calcium. And a herb garden. Greens. Yoghurt, cottage cheese. Women should stay healthy. The revolution starts with the self. Subsistence. Discipline.' Judith Sloane apparently thought she was being educative.

I recalled the bright purple duco on her car. New, that vehicle would have cost about thirty thousand. She had a mesmerising, prohibiting way about her. 'You don't have a phone?'

A puritanical look of disgust passed over her features as if having a phone were the height of cowardice, the root of all evil. She pointed out the cooing of carrier pigeons in a loft close by. 'There are other methods of communication.'

'Rory has bought herself a computer,' I said, cheerfully.

'Does Rory deny herself anything?' Judith asked rhetorically, hardly disguising a bitterness. 'She has to have roads and bridges, for her convenience. Why did we come here? Wasn't it to live in the wild?'

'I don't know,' I said simply. 'Why did you come here?'

Judith had the dark-haired good looks of someone who was photogenic. She needed a kind of staged lighting to be at her best advantage, and this effect she was trying on me in her shadowy shanty. She had not, herself, touched the mouldy cheese she offered me.

'To be the noble savage, raw in tooth and claw,' she answered enigmatically. 'Be self-sufficient.'

Unlike Rory, she seemed weary of welcoming guests to Lesbianlands. Her hostility was palpable, but I could not see its purpose. I said thanks for the cheese and complimented the view. I did not feel like becoming any more intimate than a wandering visitor but I had to ask questions. It was why I was here. She was there the day Maria died.

'You're a singer, aren't you? I'm sure I have seen you perform. At the Orlando Ball?' I was inspecting the guitar on the sheepskins on the couch.

'And you're the detective, Margot Gorman,' the smart-arse countered.

Her English voice was sweet with super-sensitivity, but spiked like arsenic in old lace. Her skin was very tanned, but without sun would be very pale, no freckles; her eyes slightly too close together. She pulled her hair back into a ponytail and tied it with wool from her spindle. Burnt poles held up this rugged shack.

'So what is your story about the broken bridge?' I asked cheerily.

'I'm not prepared to gossip.' She watched me take my notebook from my pocket, and sighed with forbearance. 'It's the hobgoblin of small minds.' I lay my book down on the oddly rocky Laminex table, wondering what a hobgoblin was.

'Spell Sloane with an e,' said Judith. 'I was walking out and I found the bridge had been destroyed, and when I met the gurls coming in I told them, but I don't know anything.'

'Well, could you speculate for me? What is your theory?' If she was a cactus I was a daisy.

'As I said, I don't gossip.' She stated a rule. I could tell she wanted me to go away, but she had to charm me as well.

'Gossip, I should have thought, was a responsibility for women.' I spoke in the broadest Strine of my working-class roots. 'The passing on of knowledge and wisdom over the back of the fence, in the market places, around the kitchen table, waiting in queues, spending time with one's peers. Gossip keeps women informed,' I said grandiloquently, responding to her facial expression. 'Probably men too.'

The seductive side to Judith Sloane appeared. 'But if gossip were our only means of learning it would have to be the truth. I actually don't know what happened to the bridge.'

'That's not what I heard on the grapevine,' I threw in a fib as a bait.

'I can only go by my experience,' she intoned, piously. Her voice was measured, gentle.

Deciding to use a similar tactic that of talking to Cybil Crabbe, I opined, 'If I were to seek a recipe through the channels of gossip, I would not expect the aunt, friend, acquaintance, mother, to deliberately add a tablespoon of chilli to spoil the menu for me. However if an erroneous piece of information were added with the intention of, say, ensuring that dish could not be effectively made by anyone else, I would suspect the giver, the perpetrator, of some degree of nastiness.' Judith looked at me sharply.

'All types of information are put on the conveyor belt of gossip, but what oils it and keeps it rolling is the interest we have in each other. We write our own scripts of, and enjoy, others' stories in the same way we might watch *Neighbours*, say, *Days of Our Lives*, perhaps?' I continued. Judith went back to her spinning wheel, using it as smokers use cigarettes, as something to do with their hands, something to fiddle with. She expressed ignorance of TV soaps and would not catch my eye.

'Yeah, it's a form of entertainment. We talk about others, and in talking about others, we can entertain or inform. Often we colour it with our personality, our language skills and our opinion,' I lectured, self-importantly.

'You judge as you talk, you mean?' A bit of insight from the spinner.

'Most of it is okay because we have checks and balances and arrive at our own evaluations. We have memories. We instinctively know whether it's fact, or accurate knowledge,' I said slowly, and added, 'or considered opinion.'

'Deliberate lying is as nasty as throwing an extra tablespoon of chilli into a recipe?' She was playing me out like the yarn across the warp and woof of her mechanism.

'Deliberate lying, actually, is slander. Using the daisy-chain of fair dinkum gossip to convey false information, knowingly, either about character or fact, leads to false judgements and ill-considered opinions. You see gossip loses all its intrinsic interest if it is known to be made up. Slander lives off the trust inspired by gossip, like a parasite,' I finished as I felt something furry under the table. An elderly cat I had not noticed before adjusted its position and went back to sleep.

'Well most gossip is slander,' Judith concluded pompously, concentrating on her craft.

'So, what do you think happened to the bridge?' I lifted my voice.

'Mistaken judgements of women can go on for years and pass through a lot of mouths in this community, Margot.' She was determined to make me feel like a new girl at an English boarding school.

'Yeah, that's what I meant by irresponsible gossip,' I said. 'The more it is repeated, the more it is believed.'

'And the less it is true,' Judith said, bitterly, 'Women can be known for ages, and not known at all. Which is a sad thing, because the dreams and myths are beautiful and nostalgic, as memories.'

I got the feeling she was watching her ideals disappear over the horizon on the beach that evening. What do people who gaze at the sea like that really see? A straight line, a stasis? 'If we lie to ourselves, we are lying to others,' I reckoned, trying to grasp the exact origin of my dislike of her and her views. Why this defensiveness? Was she sad, or bad? 'You sound depressed,' I offered.

'I've lived here a long time, and been very hurt. It's hard to trust when you have been as burnt as many times as I,' she said with a perverse relish as she got up.

'Your dreams and myths make great songs, though,' I tried encouragement.

Judith said she doesn't write songs any more, balling wool into a skein and throwing that into a basket.

'What about friends? Meghan Featherstone?' I heard my voice ask.

'Who?' She stopped in front of me, eye to eye, very close, staring, intimidating. 'Of course I know Meghan. I've know Meghan for years.'

Taken aback by her sudden aggro, I asked, 'Perhaps you could tell me what she is a doctor of?'

'She is a forensic geologist, an academic,' Judith replied, with pride. 'What's Meghan got to do with the bridge?'

'Nothing that I know about. I hadn't connected them.' But it was interesting that she did. And, in my admission of ignorance, I had obviously annoyed her. A lightning flash of vicious suspicion crossed her eyes. 'Geologist? That's interesting.'

'Is it?' Judith quipped.

'Seeing I'm investigating this matter on the part of your collective, might I have a look at the books?' I followed her outside to a little cabin which was like a woolshed in miniature. I inspected it. There were tin chests underneath the greasy fleeces. She put her key in a padlock and removed a heavy minute hardback and an exercise book.

'The journal, ledger, bank statements and cheque book are in my car,' she explained helpfully, and if I had asked why she would have had a lengthy tale to tell about the business she had done in town which would have been totally credible. As I simply did not believe her I nodded, glanced at the notes of the last meeting, the lines of figures and names in the school book and saw that a lot of gurls were behind in the yearly payments.

'Thanks,' I said and watched as she returned them under lock and key. Ignoring me was a positive and complete act. I was thin air.

'Cheerio,' I called, as I walked off across the paddock. No ciao, no adios, no goodbye came back at me, but I was gratified because in this instance nothing was something. Mention of Meghan roused her hackles. She was annoyed I had not dug deeper into the accounts, thus not seen what a responsible and reliable treasurer she was. I don't know, I just did not want to give her the pleasure.

Climbing a knoll in the sheep paddock, I surveyed the country. I saw the way across the hill towards the waterfall, and the solar panel that powered the phone transmitter, the tower, the satellite dish and a much easier path back to Rory's eyrie. The spines of ridges reared like the backs of a herd of dinosaurs. Deep rainforest greens merged with the lighter limes of lantana infestation where evidently there had been pasture, but higher up the bush looked impenetrable, brightened now and then with the red of flame trees. I heard a chain-saw rev, whine, cut, rev, whine, cut. It sounded quite close. I set off towards the higher path. Once I was below the tree-line I became disoriented. The mechanical noise ceased. I had only now the sound of water falling to guide me. If the worst came to the worst I would walk in the creek and follow its flow. Then I heard chopping.

My instinct served me well. I came across a beaten track, which led to a neat rectangular cabin in a small clearing. Functional, unadorned, surprisingly bright and dry inside, considering the setting. European and Asian herbs here were in terracotta pots on a specially constructed window-box within arm's reach of the kitchen bench, looking glossy and fresh. I chewed a sprig of parsley. The structure was open, airy, but closeable, and everything seemed to have its cupboard, books behind glass, food protected by steel mesh, matching jars of dried food lined the shady wall. Cups and utensils hung from hooks, plates, saucepans were shelved. A slow combustion stove separated kitchen from sitting-room. The bedroom opened onto the bush, facing east, wardrobes screened it from the lounge. One long couch and an armchair, a table and three straight-backed wooden chairs, the whole place was uncluttered, each space had a unique feel related to its use. A balance between tension and relaxation reflecting work and contemplation had been achieved somehow through the placement of furniture, attention to detail. Yet all so artless and unaffected my bought house seemed messy in comparison. Virginia interrupted my appreciation. The hectic, tall artist, her hair standing out from her head, her eyes direct and searching, although an imposing figure, she was in no way intimidating. Even though I was standing inside her home, uninvited, she smiled.

'Take a seat, Margot,' she pulled a chair out from the table. 'I assume your Achilles tendon is still sore?' Now I was the detail she was attending to and she remembered everything she knew about me; not much, but pertinent.

I sat down and gave her Auntie's message. I told her about meeting my destiny in the gorges of the Devonian Reef. She sighed and said she had never been to Western Australia. The grey nomad was important to her, she wanted to be reassured of her welfare. Being with Virginia White gave me a sense of the powerful sisterhood reputed to be about in the 1970s. Unlike Judith Sloane, trust was not an issue with her. She gave it as freely as the date loaf and coffee that appeared in front of me. She must have prepared it, jiggered up the fire, found plates, cake and cups during my account of my travels, and then we spoke about Maria.

'Lesbians who are only after a good time get my criticism because we have such a lot of work to do,' she said as she sat down at the table ready for discussion. 'But.'

'What about all the hard work and heartache and effort their lives demand?' I countered with a twinkle of humour.

'This is where I disagree. I think "I just want a good time" killed Maria,' said she rather dramatically. 'If I commanded the minds of the masses, I would allow them small time in which to indulge what they think their needs are.'

'If only those needs weren't controlled by a sick society,' I grimaced, exaggerating my facial expression. Did this noble-minded lesbian ever stoop to consider the lowly matter of the fiscal running of the place, or did she leave all that to the goddess?

She nodded, earnestly. 'Generally, addictions that blot out lives. Real living. That doesn't mean you can't have fun, the most sublime fun is had in cultural sincerity. Can't the beauty of women's achievement be celebrated without expressing, in behaviour, the damage, the sexual violence internalised into a cynical put-down of the women who try? We women who try are seen to be privileged and I suppose we are. And that is what it is inside of me, privilege makes you obliged.'

Throughout our chat, I felt that Virginia's intensity was ignited by a clear and present personal hurt but the heat generated concern for a larger problem.

'The lesbian and ethical way to grow and create community and culture, and consequently greater happiness for ourselves, is to get to know each other as well and as fairly as we can,' she theorised. How well did she really know the women she lived with, Judith, for instance? Could any of them have anything to do with the broken bridge, and the inexplicable explosions?

On leaving, when she was showing me the way to Rory's, I asked what she felt about it.

'A bloody nuisance,' she replied. 'And no, I don't think anyone has booby traps. Though, once, I did go on-line to see how they're made.'

'You surf the Internet?' I displayed my amazement with a gesture of opened palms indicating the authentic integration of her full-time home in these remote mountains, so plainly without the mod cons of Rory's residence.

'My brother is a nuclear physicist,' she informed me. 'I've been mucking around the technology since its inception.'

'Really?' I was sure neither Chandra nor Rory knew this.

'Yeah,' she affirmed casually.

The walk to Rory's was relatively flat, mostly downhill, and easy because Virginia had taken me to where her car was parked and all I had to do was follow the road.

After a late lunch I put my triathletic body in the icy shower of the waterfall and squealed with the pleasure of it. Rory paled when I suggested Judith could possibly be dishonest. There was no sight nor sound of the other women from last night. They had gone, she told me, about eleven.

Virginia, even though she enjoyed the conversation with Margot, is restless. Over-tired, she walks up the mountain, taking the steepest path, forcing herself to step firmly on the jagged blue copper rock. The grass trees bend in frozen communion with the land. She looks down on the canopy. The bones of a wallaby catch her eye. Death.

The skeletons on the ground on the spiky new growth, reflect her emotional state. A weight. A non-flowing. She recalls smelling and seeing the smoke in the distance in her forwards and back race to Cybil's flat by the sea and is disgusted with herself, for her neglect of the land. She walks down from Widow's Peak, feeling an aching sorrow. The fellowship of trees is accommodating beyond words.

Every spring the Campbells light the bush, and don't care if it gets out of control. What an act of huge self-hatred on the part of humankind to set fire to the jungle and let it rage destructively. It is massacre. One man's excuse is the justification for decimation of millions of living life-forms. It doesn't do the rock or the air any good either. The ozone. Life. Mystery. Life, from that of the tiniest ant in its tireless work to the majestic serenity of the mountain ash whose life ant-industry helped to create, Virginia's love of the surrounding beauty turns to a righteous wrath. She wishes she were a simple soul, like Olga, the hours of whose days are dictated by care: for women, for children, for dogs, goannas, snakes—always something, a kookaburra with a broken wing—

whose heart can dissolve in uncomplicated bliss. Anger is her ready mate these days. If she could duel with someone, as she and Jeff did in the make-believe sword-fights of their childhood, using home-made blade and shield in fair combat, she would like nothing better.

Murder? Aggression? Like? Love? Hatred? Power? She has heard gurls call each other stupid and ladies call themselves stupid women. Why does someone like Dee turn herself into a doormat? The dutiful daughter obedient, even to the demands of her dog, Dee relates to all with powerlessness as an integral part of her character. Everyone's her mother. The world as a household is the only way to cope. She wishes she could be as sober as the weather-beaten, old-fashioned Vee, Victoria Shackleton, who comes and goes with her horse-float. Or Pam, for that matter, for whom black is black, and white is white; what to be devoted to and what to despise determined by her feelings; the natural eternal teenager. Gurls call Pam Roxburgh a baby VeeDub: she looks so like her physically, but twenty years younger.

But Virginia doesn't actually feel envy. She is in love with a woman she does not like, who says what draws her to women is lust, no more. She cannot work. She goes, instead, to lie in the lap of the goddess and let the pensive persona assail her, heal her. She lowers herself down onto the crunchy bed to let the ants run over her bare skin, not noticing whether they nip her or not. She tries to mourn for Maria but trivial history intervenes, the immediate past, the busy day, little sleep. The light love of the commune, lending her support, rests like a fine cotton blanket over the heavier passions in her heart; it is a kind of dearness, an essential caritas in the anima of society, which is a need to give, and in the giving, take. Margot's wholesome, whole-hearted appreciation of her shack. Her mind wanders to what has been built as she touches the spaded sides of her original folly. Each woman's dwelling has the singular charm of her own creation.

Now she cries. She sobs, lying among the tree-roots. She feels annihilated as a female artist by the tongue-lashings Cybil spits out, assuming superiority. Telling Virginia she has no idea! Cybil's voice was as cold and cutting as stalactites and stalagmites of ice. All the polished dreams of separatism fade away. Her work is undermined by the plight of ordinary women, the lies they live with, while for Virginia, it is inexplicably courageous. A butcher bird's sublimely beautiful whistle inspires a smile. It occurs to her that Cybil is jealous of her famous past. But Virginia wouldn't have looked at her then. Succeeding in the gallery scene, rewarded by grants and engagements and exhibitions for being known, exposure of safely understood work is the past. Virginia's personal progress is that her art is a spiritual vehicle, not a product in the commerce of capitalism. Logically, it can be no other way. Black cockatoos scream overhead, squealing of coming rain. Rain-birds, so many of them living in the tall casuarinas which comprise the flora of the steepest gullies, it is hard to believe superstitions. For the moment it is dry.

The insects go about their lives, perceiving the long limbs of the woman too big to bother about. 'Cybil does not even know me, and that is what it is all about. Being known.' Virginia looks at the side of her misbegotten dream-place. The acacia and the she-oak intertwine with each other beneath the skin of the earth, while above the ground they are separate. She does not axe or saw living wood. The roots relate in a different way from the branches, the leaves and the flowers. The bushfires were, for them, a short trial. Virginia rests the flat of her hand on a rock which she feels, almost vibrates, and she cries, 'Hell!'

Rory, when I recounted my discussion with Judith, commented, 'The past is dead if it's stuck in a freeze-frame and doesn't change, like the future is dead already if you live in it today. If Judith is stuck in the past, then her present is a lie.'

'The bank books were in her vehicle,' I said. 'Why?'

She interrupted my mundane concern about the financial condition of the collective with, 'Her past is rewritten.' Did neither Virginia nor Rory care that Judith controlled the money?

When I had heard about big-winged creatures, lights in the sky, space-ships landing, goddesses dancing, that ghosts sang haunting melodies, cyberspace and other high-flown matters, I asked, 'Where are the deeds to your property?'

'In a safety-deposit box,' she replied. 'At Stuart's remaining bank.'

'Perhaps I could come out again? I seem to have been busy with every-thing but detection. Willy Campbell wasn't home when I called,' I said lazily.

'Wilma and Barb, too,' Rory reminded me. 'You've done Vanderveen. That's good.'

Eventually, I said I would walk back to my car.

'No, don't walk with your bad heel, I'll drive you,' Rory offered. 'When do you want to go?'

'Pretty soon,' I said. 'But I wish I could stay longer. I have an appointment I have to keep in the morning.'

On the drive through the bush, Rory asked me about the Friday night Neil died. I told her the bare facts of my involvement, complimenting the cool efficiency of Alison, and the strange coincidence that I had been engaged by the mother to find his 'murderer'.

'Alison,' Rory smiled with all the features in her face. 'A more unsuitable woman to be a mother I have never met. She is brilliant, but she shouldn't have children. They will kill her, or vice versa.'

'Are you serious?' I asked, remembering how flaky I found Alison.

'Not really. It's a hell of a life with boy children. Harold, I heard, was working for the syndicate, growing dope in the National Park,' Rory casually imparted. I took note.

'I met Lenny that night. What a handsome lad!' I commented. 'And Tilly is delightful.'

'Different fathers. Harold is handsome, too.' The big vehicle murmured slowly along the stony road. Rory became uncharacteristically quiet and short after mentioning this boy's name. 'We had a lot to do with him when he was younger.'

Gone were the explanations which flowed from her complete with embellishments from history and theory, peppered with anecdotes from life. Silence. We passed the wreck of a Toyota Cressida rusting away in the bush. I mentioned it, and Rory's said it was Trivia's car, and left it at that.

'You're like the landscape, Margot,' she said suddenly. 'Things happen upon you but it would take an earthquake to tangle you up the way of lot of us are. Everything about you has a sort of evenness, if you know what I mean? So bland and honest and there.'

'No,' I admitted. 'I don't know what you mean.'

'Can anything shatter your complacency? Your Protestant work ethic, your tough physical regime, your immaculate diet? Early to bed, early to rise, healthy, wealthy and wise.' Rory was not so much sarcastic as slightly sour, yet with a bark of a laugh she seemed to apologise. 'The rest of us are bickering at the breakfast table, grabbing the marmalade before anyone else, yelling to Mum to settle the sibling squabbles, but Mum ain't there. The provider is off having a nervous breakdown,' she joked.

We passed a stump with Girls Rule OK burnt into it. Dogs barked with hysterical squeaks in their woofs. 'Someone visiting. First the dogs warn, then they greet. They don't have the vindictive feuds which follow intimate relationships in their memory of friendship, so their enthusiasm can be embarrassing. Sometimes.' Rory felt to the need to explain.

Dolphin Suzuki came into view before I was prepared for it. It stood on the road in front of us like a gift box, a shining cube of Western civilisation. The other cars had gone. Seeing it shocked me back to who I really was: a cyclist, a swimmer, a runner, an investigator, an independent lesbian. A worker. The afternoon sun lit up the aqua car with golden lights. I keep it polished, not from vanity, but to preserve the duco as much as I can, living near the sea.

Rory was not so wrong about me. I looked after things, myself included. As I searched the mountains with my eyes for what it was I felt there, I thought perhaps I look after things too well, am too straight, cautious, careful and that my staid qualities might prevent me from knowing that which has no scientific basis, no logical staircase to it. I even needed proof that there were such things as a goddess, a spaceship, ghosts, aliens invading the planet, visitations from the nether-world. All that sort of stuff left me completely cold and relatively bored. But I had a sense of sisterhood, both fractured and potent.

'Fear is fear of fear. I know that,' I said.

Rory grinned at me and shrugged as she reignited the sturdy engine of her tank. She tugged on the slim steering wheel and waved. There was a little sadness in her farewell. I felt brittle as I unlocked my car, got in and turned towards the road to the coast. On the drive I let my mind float about as I looked at the countryside changing colours. By the time I got home it was after dark. No moon. Houses both sides of mine were empty of light, almost invisible.

31

. . . the thrill of killing . . .

Africa, a woman Sofia does not know, has taken over the cooking. She is tall, statuesque, with a neck as elegant as any swan's, like a model in the glossiest fashion mag. The house near the railway is busy with the warmth of women coming and going, creating friction, music and story-telling; myth-making. All nothing to Africa. She relates to the gurls as sisters, cousins and aunts grouped for a family tragedy, elegantly walking about, quietly performing chores like an actress being filmed. Sofia tracks her, making her fingers and thumbs into a camera-viewer, framing her shot by shot. Africa disturbs her.

Sofia speaks intensely, 'Who is she?' Grasping the hand of any listener, her grip is amazingly strong. When she is told, she says, 'No, that isn't right.'

Africa pours fresh coffee into the mug proffered, and says vaguely, 'Women are bound by chains of have-tos, it doesn't matter what society you are in.'

The conversation she bent into continues without her as she moves on. 'Maria was everybody's friend.'

'Look at her pride, her head held high,' Sofia whispers to Fi whose is the closest ear. She chases the stranger. 'Who are you? Why don't you speak to me?'

Africa replies in an American accent. 'Betrayal of the inner self has no words in any language,' she says, and pats the head of the younger woman with gentle indifference. 'Why speak?'

Sofia would prefer her humiliation covered up with a large number of euphemisms. Yet the noble beauty remains cryptic even though it is plain she has the knowledge. Her silence pisses Sofia off. She wants her to talk with her of Cajun dishes, of anything. How dare she take over the sink and stove and not say why? Then Sofia thinks she has it: the magnificent creature is disgusted with herself. She sees it so clearly, her story, as well, is the tragic tale of being too beautiful.

'She hasn't done anything wrong.' Mary Smith takes Sofia aside to explain, 'Africa is staying with me a while, travelling the world. She is passing through, and came, because, er um, Maria and she had a short affair a long time ago.

I thought it would be all right.' The eyes roll in Sofia's head, and a flood of memories laden with unresolved emotions threatens to swamp her, but Cybil has an announcement to make. She addresses the whole company from the top of the steps.

Having just been on the phone, she shares the news, 'That was Jake and Jessy Freeman! Maria's parents!'

Sofia, jolted back to reality, expletes, 'Ohmygod, they are so creepy.'

'Anyway,' continues Cybil, 'We have a problem. They are Christians and for religious reasons demand that Maria be buried, not burnt. We, as you know, have organised a cremation.'

The peace and serenity, the companionship of conformity to their own rules, their plans and excitement at creating a gurls' ritual, all shatter. Shocked stillness. Cybil goes on, 'As compensation for our dreadful deed I offered them a compromise.' She pauses to take in what is around her, and sees curious faces. 'They can choose the words for the memorial. The alternative is . . .'

Sofia interrupts, 'No, I object.'

The calm of the throng becomes intense discussion, division, as if the paddle-wheel suddenly starts, churning up the mill-pond of subdued mourning. The eruption of contention and tensions, noise, disagreement, movement, changed atmosphere takes some time. Each gurl has a point of view. Eventually the decision is made on a vote. Sofia loathes her grand-parents. She has her supporters, but they are in the minority. Loyal but useless. Cybil is back on the top step.

'You want to hear the words they've chosen?' Of course, everybody does. 'I'm sorry. There was no alternative, because we would have had a legal wrangle on our hands.'

'Quaint.'

'Don't want that.'

'We couldn't keep out the cops then.'

'Disobedience was unconscionable,' Sofia says. 'They tortured her!'

'Do you want to hear or not?' asks Cybil, taking command. 'They wanted something simple, took ages to decide.'

'What is it?'

'"Gone to live with God" it is.'

'You can't be serious.'

'That is, like, the worst?'

'Bullshit.'

Sofia feels a horrid loneliness, complete rootlessness. Yet her house is full of faces, overrun by control-freaks making alliances with the grand-daddy of them all. She goes to curl in the caucus of her peers, to toke on a joint, to pop a serrie, to mutter and listen to impotent criticism, to feel better than frazzled and hassled. Sofia fights the pressure to surrender her rights, but what can she do? Her allies offer the space-ship. Africa notices her vacant eyes and says, 'Dear, that is not the sort of trip you should be taking right now.'

Ilsa Chok Tong waits on the road near the mailbox, expecting a copy of *The Man Without Qualities* in the post. She is eager to read a novel about a world, a hegemony, a lifestyle that disappeared into the vaults of history before the novelist finished his book, to be thoroughly entertained by her own questions. She is studying the turn of the last century and may be fascinated by the way that fact is regurgitated in literary form. Her thoughts are disrupted by the clip-clop of personal transport that has survived millennia. A mounted figure rides towards her. Ilsa sighs. Every time she emerges from her reclusion, she anticipates being annoyed by social interaction. She really doesn't know what to say. Small talk is not her forte.

'Whoa,' says Wilma Campbell to her horse.

Ilsa and Wilma discuss the Sydney Blue Gum. Both agree that it is becoming a weed, though for directly opposing reasons. Ilsa has decided, after much love and observation, that the silver-grey eucalypt is intruding on the diversity of native forest, while Wilma sees bush out of control and better cleared with a heavy chain strung between two bulldozers. Ilsa's domestic squabbles with her stubborn possums and brush turkeys taking many hours of her daily life, and her noticing greater trees being replaced by lesser species, are expressed with gentle impatience, giving Wilma the familiar impression of the naive attitude of dickhead greenies. Would not know a grey gum from a blue gum, especially now the new bark is ageing. In this instance she is tolerant. Cunningly, with a broad smile, she takes what Ilsa says as an arrangement. It's okay with the gurls to fell that variety. The sophisticated, serene escapee from the wealthy middle class of Melbourne probably doesn't quite understand the truncated, monosyllabic language of the Australian bushie. Ilsa simply wonders why the equestrienne is so friendly. Wilma, on her muscly steed with its shiny coat, is as impressive, to Ilsa, as the chivalric knights of the Crusades. The horsewoman making dust as she canters away is as idyllic as a Hans Heysen oil painting.

Having finished typing up notes of my meeting with the dentist, and my visit to Lesbianlands, I dealt with my mail. I dashed off a reply to the food label, subsidiary of a corporation probably listed on Wall Street, expressing my interest in the audition for the television advertisement. If they also harvest tuna to can, killing dolphin by the thousands, then I had to consider what part of my soul I was selling for use of my body. But I needed the money. Meghan Featherstone's work lay neatly by. I flipped through it again, looking for the scrap of envelope I had assumed was Meghan's scribble before I noticed it was signed another name, Judith Sloane, to check it against the other dodgy signature on an insurance policy. Different hand again. Or Meghan in another mood? But there was something else worrying about the message: Thanks, Judith. Unlike Rory's elegant script, Meghan's handwriting was an unattractive scrawl. The dollar sign was the only bit readily legible. She paid an awful lot for a greasy wool sweater. One, at least, was a false Meghan signature. I slipped the two relevant pages into a plastic sleeve, ready to photocopy, along with the ridgy-didge example on my cheque, and send off to a handwriting expert.

What the hell is a forensic geologist? Forget forensic for the minute. Judith noticeably changed when we talked about Meghan. Meghan is a geologist and geologists know their stones. The very small actions and omissions indicate the inner workings of a being. Liars are conscious of what they say and what they obviously do, but not usually the incidental. The little thing, and it could so easily be overlooked like a Freudian slip of the tongue, was her putting my two investigations together: 'What has the broken bridge got to do with Meghan?' She should not have said that to me because it is my job to suspect everybody. Rory told me the place is rich in mineral and gemstones. And so did Vanderveen.

Out in the chookhouse—busywork helps me think—I was mucking around with this thought, picking up old newspapers which I had put to work in my renovations and now did not need, when I read in bold, PACKER SITTING ON A RIVER OF RUBIES.

> The search is on in earnest in the remote backblocks of the sprawling playground of Australia's wealthiest man for subterranean riches of biblical proportions. The ASE confirmed yields of 1,600 carats of ruby from a relatively small alluvial sample from the easternmost point of Packer's Hunter Valley polo retreat and cattle fiefdom. And ground magnetic surveys indicate the presence of a far richer volcanic gemstone reserve within a 10 kilometre catchment. But there's nothing the mogul can do to get his paws on his own gem-quality rubies, unless the small exploration company empowered by exploration licence decides to deal the big man in, harnessing his persuasive powers to counter the mining's bureaucratic maze to promote their product. The ASE has reported the recovery of 1,630 carats of ruby, 250 carats of blue sapphire and 390 carats of green sapphire from 223 tonnes of alluvial material.

If 'subterranean riches of biblical proportions' were in the Hunter region, then the likelihood of equivalent wealth in the catchment of the Campbell was pretty bloody strong. Beneath the subdued greens of that unsullied bush fire-red rubies waited in the ground glistening with tempting allure. The gurls' commitment to their collective ideals, their freedom in commune, their joint ownership, whatever their reasons for living that difficult life, would be severely challenged by the availability of personal fortune a stick or two of dynamite away. I felt I could vouch for the moral character of Rory and Virginia, but what did I really know about the others? And I needed my time over again searching Meghan's ransacked ex-dairy, maybe there was an exploration licence I missed.

Dropping the yellowing broadsheet on my unfinished work, I decided to verify my intuition on site at the Featherstone mansion-in-the-mind's-eye. And drove straight out there.

The dairy was still in the shade of the hills to the east. There were no goats about. No car was there. Neither a white Daewoo Leganza nor a burgundy Honda Integra, both currently and comprehensively insured in the Featherstone name, on one side of the creek, nor Jill's van on the other. Both doors were secured. The kitchen-laundry was padlocked. I looked in through the windows. All signs of disturbance were cleared away yet it no longer had the semblance of a home. Things were missing. Bits of sculpture, a picture on the wall, a poster, I couldn't quite place the exact thing missing. A presence. Habitation? Gumboots, raincoats. I returned to the little porch at the back. One pair of boots and one coat, old goat tack and a few rusty tools. Staring at the wellies gave me the idea of funnel-web spiders, which like dark places like that. There were no new tell-tale webs near the doors and windows on the ground floor. I checked. The bedroom loft window, which must surely be open when anyone sleeps there, showed signs of a cobweb at the corners of the glass.

Back in the car, I reflected on the spiders' art. The logic of it. Now you see me, now you don't. The Featherstone job was a wretched cobweb. Sticky and tricky. If I had been set up, whoever was doing it had not taken into account my uninvited visits, or if they had they were too clever by half. The problem of the financial maze of disorganised book-keeping was compounded by the riddles from my surreptitious ingenuity in discovering first, a tempestuous search and second, a soulless cleaning. Beside the murder investigation set me by Penny Waughan the whole thing looked immature, silly. Even if Meghan were vague about money, she must know her own movements. Her whereabouts might be a mystery to the whole damn world but not to herself. Unless more obscure forces than money and relationship were at work. UFO snaps. Now that was going into fantasy land. The Twilight Zone! Why does she need a detective at all? If she is up to something, why draw attention to herself? Why is someone else drawing both her and my attention to her finances? Someone's spinning a net to tangle me up. I hate being jerked around by nonsense. Evidently the dairy-house was not the primary place of residence for either party. It was what it is, a folly.

As I was close, why not call on Chandra?

There was no answer at the main door so I went around the other side, through terraced and trellised gardens. I looked about and heard her wheel-chair on the verandah boards. She spun away when she saw me. Chandra was a prickly character. Angry at being interrupted? I found the steps to the front door, even though they were plainly not used, being for the most part support for a tangled passionfruit vine. Her hostility may have been about the illegal plants bristling with fat heads. I could allay her fears on that score.

'Enter if you must.' The call came from several rooms away in the rambling old farm-house. What had I done, I wondered.

By the time I found her the screen she was sitting in front of showed the home page of Microsoft Internet Explorer. She moved the mouse around quickly, the arrow flicking here, there, click, click. Then the screen dissolved itself into bending and twirling patterns of cyberart. There was a spot flying around in it.

While she was calmly proficient in her efficient home office, with all the electronic gadgetry at arm's length, I felt I was not one hundred per cent welcome, but that made me want to stay. I confessed to being a phobic of webs, including the World Wide Web. She reeled off a string of swear-words.

'Mossies,' she spat. 'Arse-holes. We have come a long way from The Electronic Salon and, even Systers, bulletin-boards dealing womenstuff, exclusively female forums. Of no interest to men but they've got to take them over, don't they?'

'I know what you mean,' I sympathised as she manipulated the mouse and caught the gnat. It led to an on-going chat. 'How do you know how old they are? Or where they live?'

'You don't,' she answered. 'That's the trouble. I am trying to vet them using linguistic clues, the manner of language. I know for sure, some psycho is in here. Usually there are hints. Like a fellow, playing out his fantasies of being a woman can use an on-line name, say Molly. But they've got more subtle than that. Not only do they pretend to be women, they want to be lesbians and now, revolutionary feminists. Why? Don't ask me. Look at this.' The chat scrolled.

<BAC> The self-sacrificing saint is the female enemy of the female.

<BLUESKY> In the Middle Ages the women became saints to have sex with Christ, and how it actually turns out is self-mutilation, masochism.
<OWL> Song of Solomon, lust as spiritual union.
<BAC> How easily women fool themselves! BAF
<BLUESKY> They got so into it they could make stigmata happen on their hands and feet and side.
<OWL> The convents wanted to have a saint, right? Women could not go as far as men even in the church. So how they got their house on the map, was to have a saint, who could make things happen, by magic, by Christ's intervention, by miracles, so they all concentrated on the one of them who was prepared to go into paroxysms of faith, fasting, seeing visions, drinking the bath water of lepers and feeling the scabs go down their throats as a prayer, demanding holy communion so she could be in lust with the beautiful body of Christ.
<BAC> Are things so different? The sanctity of dirt, except the nature of the dirt has changed.
<MOP> Coconut Ice. The temperature has to be dead on. You need a cooking thermometer. Don't cool it in the fridge.

Chandra clicked on the print icon and in about ten seconds I had in my hands a hard copy of what we had just read on screen. She disconnected and backed herself out from her desk and led me from the room.

'Someone is spoiling our plans.' She whipped the page out of my hand. 'Which is a he? Which is a daddy's girl?' She was furious.

'I don't get it,' I admitted.

Her kitchen benches were uncomfortably low for a standing person. She put a kettle under the tap in the shortened sink and swung herself around to plug it in. 'Sit,' she ordered.

My taking a seat brought us to eye-level parity. The chair had the firm, worn-wood feel of a family heirloom and the table was solid and scrubbed. I waited, knowing whatever I had to say would come into the ignoramus category. Chandra looked at me with brown eyes like a magpie's, set deep in her handsome, strong-featured face, betraying no humour, but it was there. My instinct told me she was hiding something, suspicious of me.

'I'm an IT moron, okay?' I smiled, fishing for the problem. 'The computer? Drugs, drink? I wanted to get back to the level of confidence I felt began when we had dinner.

'Tea? Peppermint? China? Earl Grey? Indian? Or coffee?' She slammed the canisters down one after the other.

'I'll have water,' I said, getting utterly sick of wearing her temper.

Distrust was palpable in the air. She wasn't going to tell me what was really bothering her, so I talked about the girl who was a boy in drag. Who carries hankies these days? What did Dello and Maz call him that day? What was his pseudonym? You can be anybody you want to be in a mask, in cyberspace, while you are alive to act it out.

She said in a voice that rocketed me back to her presence, 'There is enough living to do, Margot! Why do people need to live others' lives?' She placed a cup of Earl Grey in front of me. 'Subversion and subversion.' It was all double dutch to me.

'Listen,' I begged, 'Please don't think I noticed, or would tell anyone, about the produce I just saw. I won't. I don't care.'

Chandra accepted my reassurance with an abrupt nod. 'Right-oh,' she said. 'That's good to know. Self-protection.' When she had squeezed her own tea-bag, she clicked her fingers as if she remembered that something had gone missing. 'But it is not a self being protected, is it?' Her hostility might have been suspicion of me.

'Tell me about your fight with Meghan?' I inquired.

'Meg and I had a disagreement, a passionate one. I knocked her out. Meghan's a flake. And a fake. Okay I'll tell you. It's about who she works for. Top secret, haha. Peddlers in human lives, more like it. I found out on the net. I faced her with it, and she denied everything. But then got so angry she could kill. I hate liars. All they have to do is deny. Except they're aggressive about it. I went through every detail of what this mob is up to and she denied it all, but she was losing it at the same time. Well how do I know? My facts came from the underground network, groups who work against trans-national corporations. Who do I believe? My friend of years? Or a bunch of do-gooding hackivists? She shouldn't have put me in that position. Do I choose personal loyalty or public principle? I chose the latter. And I punched her smug mug.' Chandra suddenly laughed. 'Boy, it was a rip-roarer!'

She opened a jar and offered me a dried pear. I took it and looked at it. A picture of female genitalia, quite beautiful. She took one for herself and ran her fingers round its lines. She pointed to a stained glass window which repeated the pattern.

'Meg did that for me. She was into lead-lighting for a while. When she is into something, she's totally dedicated. Then forgets it, off onto something else.' In Chandra, beneath the surface layer of crankiness and the secondary one of peace within herself, there was a smouldering rage. It would not take much to get her fired up. Her straight look and savage eyes would give anybody pause about wasting her time, but I couldn't help myself. I'm nosy by nature.

'Show me how that works,' I begged indicating what she had been working on in her office.

'No,' she responded, crisp as can be.

Offended, I said goodbye and left.

Before I was off the verandah, she was back typing and reading electronic print. Urgency, or addiction? I walked slowly through the luscious garden, remarking at the lustrous greens of silver beet and parsley and the smokier hues of lavender and coltsfoot. There was a macadamia nut tree here which had had time to grow and seasonal tomato plants on stakes in a row. Underneath the spreading fig were chairs and a table. Potsdam Harry, Spotty, was in his paddock. I got into my car feeling, I appreciate this place. But why was she so horrible to me?

Chandra cannot concentrate on her business until Margot is off the property. As soon as she is sure the Suzuki is gone, Chandra leaves her office to go into the garden. She recalls her mother's words: be careful what you wish for, you might get it. If Mary Smith were not monopolising the mob at Sofia's, she would go there. She will, she decides, but first she must change her mood, rid herself of the dismay she feels losing control of her website. Dragging herself along the paths between her vegetable beds, on a billy-cart adapted to a personalised kneeling tray, weeding, getting the thrill of killing cabbage moth, she dreads the implications of the immaculate structure she set up for revolution being taken over by a psychopath or sociopath, or anyone without her strict ethical politics. 'Vermin!' she utters, squashing green grubs.

. . . hell hath no fury . . .

Although Ian Truckman did not think he would need the street directory and atlas available on the marvellous computer on his instrument panel, as he is never lost, he does. He types in a street name in the city of Melbourne, and his screen lights up a page of Melways with a cursor flashing. A box appears requesting his present position. Keilor, he writes. Then he is told to follow the moving arrow. The sound card, once the truck is in motion, says in measured weird English, things like, 'A right turn is unavailable to freeway, advise . . .'. The White Virgin weaves its way through the western suburbs. 'Take a left at the intersection of Smith and Leanda Crescent.' Eventually he finds himself at the dead end of a lane in a maze of factories, facing an eight-foot cyclone fence. The computer tells him to reverse six metres and forward again, then to type GTX and enter. The fence slides apart into roller-gates with a laser locking mechanism. He must have a remote mounted somewhere on the cabin.

Ian Truckman has no choice but to obey. After he has passed, the gates return to an impression of an uninterrupted wire. He drives on. Shipping containers like giant-sized building blocks are piled and lined up in an area he estimates as at least five acres. He is mystified until a golf cart appears driven by a man in a black skivvy and white jacket who signals to him to follow. He does, wondering what a tanker is doing among all these square containers, but beyond them is a wharf. He drives along it until the cart stops and the man raises his palm, stopping him, then brings both hands to shoulder height, turns them and flaps him to park at a designated spot. There Ian is directed to lower the stilts of his trailer and detach the semi. Now rigid, without articulation, he is told to drive away. This is tricky. He backs his vehicle all the way to dry land. The golf-cart man follows his bumper. Truckman waits, after a three-point turn has him facing the way he came, for instructions. The guy tells him to go, and wait for a phone call.

Ian, who had figured the load was water, is now convinced. The gate opens for him to pass and closes behind him without any manipulations on his part. Whatever the operation is, it is huge. Not one of the containers had an identifying mark. The substance he transported from the north coast of New South Wales to the docks of Victoria is certainly illegal, probably drugs, hidden in a few thousand litres of water which they will now ditch. They must think him a fool not to work that out. A few million bucks worth of heroin was going to hit the streets of Melbourne because of his journey, because no way would they road-transport something they were putting back to sea. So, he has a handle on his boss and his job. He might ask for a hike in salary, not that he is unhappy with what he's got so far. Money of itself should make him happy, let alone the horsepower under the bonnet and the gigabytes on the dash. Now, through no conscious decision of his own, he is on the gravy train. It is so easy to have it all for the taking. He drives towards his mother's house.

In her converted tram amid the secondary growth of black wattles, Ilsa opens her new book, and her mind is in Vienna a hundred years ago. Virginia White, a kilometre away as the crow flies, cleans her shelves trying to find photos of Maria. At the third point of a roughly equilateral triangle, Judith, in her woolshed, opens an army-issue ammunition case where small white goods in shiny packets are neatly stored. She removes packaging from the never-used kitchen gadgetry, wraps each in cloth, rearranges the contents of the tin and closes the lid. In the firm cardboard cartons with graphics of juicers, blenders, electric jugs, toasters, she places heads of dope, pressed in plastic sandwich envelopes. After putting in a handful of rusty nails to lend the boxes weight, then sealing them up as if they have never been opened, she stacks them in a suitcase which she hides. Completing a rhombus on the cartogram of the north-western section of the inhabited reaches of Lesbianlands, Ci Amigdalos creeps up to the saddle where Hope solecistically murmurs garble.

Hope Strange is staring at a horse skull lying on a hessian bag.

'I'm a gypsy at heart,' Ci interrupts, intending to startle. Hope looks at Ci and sees a snake in the grass.

Hope holds the skeletal head. She says, 'Look, no teeth.' She places it with reverence inside a design of white quartz pieces, carefully laid out in a pattern, and searches the sky.

'So?' Ci has a canvas bag strapped to her back, but she does not reveal its contents. Her eyes are crafty. She arrogantly wanders around Hope's camp, angling for clues, ready with sly fabrications. Stealing from women on Lesbianlands is as cinchy as getting on well with clever use of flattery. Hope, however, is younger than she, and spinny with concerns of bones and stones, evidently unaware of her enviable grace. Ci instinctively hates her.

'For protection,' Hope explains, counting the hills.

'Protection against what?' Ci raises her eyes and catches sight of an eagle soaring.

'Aliens, hollow women, helicopters, spirits of darkness,' Hope answers.

'You're a nutcase.' Ci laughs, engagingly. 'But this place is full of crazies. You going to the funeral tomorrow?'

'Tartara Tartara. Hades, hell hath no fury. Tartara Tartara, like a woman's scorn,' chants Hope as she circles her rocks. Wind sings in the she-oaks. The moon is skinny and new in the blue. Ci is edgy, ready to be on her way.

'Why did you come here?' Hope indicates her home.

'Lesbianlands you mean?' Ci shrugs, 'Where else can you live rent-free? Do what you want? Live out your dreams? Get stoned?'

'Tartara tartara, didn't you hear it?' Hope demands.

Ci decides she is talking about the helicopter. 'Yeah, that belongs to the guy over, er, that ridge. His spread is bloody miles, a personal national park,' Ci tells Hope. 'You want to come tomorrow?'

'Yes. Maybe. I don't know.' She quivers like prey in the sights of the predator.

'If you get to the front gate in time, I'll give you a lift,' Ci rearranges her load and strides off confidently. 'Be there, a bit of communal ritual won't hurt you.'

Ci leaves a space in the air like an oxygen vacuum. The trees shiver. Hope is aware of entities in the elements and wonders if she has the courage to stay. Or go. She knows something is in store for her. The bush is full of unearthly noises. If she stays another minute at this site, she will be absorbed, she will be transubstantiated. She goes down to Rory's house, carrying her bed-roll. It is becoming dark. Fruit bats are moving in the strangler figs.

When I got to Sofia's the place was bedlam. A rainless electrical storm chucked lightning about in the evening sky. A Pajero with an opened horse-float was parked down the road. Not enough kerb-room for so many cars, some were double-parked along the nature strip. Number-plates from different states and territories. One or two burst into paroxysms of dog-barking when I walked between them.

The horse was in the garden. Tilly and a tribe of little girls were pulling at its rope halter. House and yard were as busy as a painting by Bosch or Breughel. Well-meaning acquaintances mixed with the closest friends weirdly crowded the limited space. Tarot cards were out. Keening, wailing, tears. Hugging. Agitated organisers rushed from one conference to another on the phone. Flowers kept arriving. Rehearsals of dirges and memorial ballads.

Poems being written and read. Collages of Maria's life on pin-boards. Columns of plastic cups, of throw-away plates and cartons of cutlery and cooking utensils cluttered the hallway. An ersatz familiarity flowed across persons, space and time coloured by the exotic. The unusual. A tall Negro woman in Balinese batiks glided around. Alison read palms with a mantilla resting on her hair. Barking lunacy all around. Chandra hobbled past me.

Sofia was raving. 'The liar in her lair, the slanderer, philanderer. Watch for the one who is everywhere but not there when you need her. She has the mind of a man. He is a bitch. Sweet as mustard, if you know what I mean.'

She grasped my arm with skinny hand and glittering eye like the Ancient Mariner who stoppeth one of three, I could not choose but hear.

'Only a fool would trust the snoop, who turns up in corners like a jack-in-the-box, nice as poison-pie. They troop off to their demonstrations of reconciliation as if they were not racist themselves to throw insults at the steel white virgin who has it in for single mothers and bludging boongs, who is like a mascot on the prow of a pirate ship full of rapacious, brutish thieves lusty for blood. Who is, herself, the sacrifice, the witch to be burnt at the stake. I need to go down to the cybercave, the lonely cage in the sky, and spread my thoughts across the world like a mole burrowing a maze for those who think like me. In virtual underground. A further circle of hell. They say the trillion angels are each of single species. We can't imagine that, except to suppose we are all one angel.'

She was high. I would not have been surprised if the sheer volume of personal auras hadn't lifted her above the milling throng. The most insane seemed those offering platitudes of condolence and commiseration. But I was here for Sofia.

'When not a body of flesh and blood, nerves, afraid of the prophylactic leakage of radiation which have got into our heads through the cathodes in electro-magnetic screens, I'm free,' she said, keeping her eyes on the African-American. 'Doom looms for Big Brother. A huge brother, a monolith with a Mount Rushmore face, teetering on feet founded in a honeycomb coal-mine, the very ore of which is ripped from the earth, with untimely haste.'

Yvonne passed a pair of patterned singing sticks to a tipsy Koori. Bossily, I thought. Sofia, still holding me, went on, 'Greed without so much as a thank-you. Big Brother is about to fall and squash us all. Any little individual who chooses a path for the greater good goes broke. Dies, perhaps. You can't know the spirits and have money too, Margot.' She let me go. Well, there was wealth, or the prospect of it, I thought, trying to assess the women I knew to be from the Lesbianlands. 'Taking.' Sofia was paranoid.

'Taking. From whom?' I asked.

'Our land,' said a fairly drunk Aboriginal. There was a didgeridoo among the assembled musical instruments.

Dello tried to lighten the mood by bursting into a funny feminist lyric. Cybil looked horrified, but it had the desired effect on Sofia. 'You lie, oh, you lie,' she sang. Her friends joined her in the Shameless Hussies' song. Some mourners patently disapproved, and others smiled softly.

What lights were on suddenly went out. 'Where's the fuse-box?' 'No, leave it, that's Maria.' Among other things, these were called out in the dusk. It seemed to get dark quickly in the blackout. Soon candles were alight and faces were cast into more melodramatic mien.

Sofia was beside me again. 'My suitcase carries my conscious life in words. I lug my suitcase everywhere. I'll have to push it down the street in a wheelbarrow like a laughing stock. Mad Rosie. I will have no home.' I could understand her distress, all her and Maria's things were vulnerable to plunder in this atmosphere.

'The mind of the madwoman flows like a stream through the landscape, seeping from the earth in individual springs, making a creek, a crik, a crack, then becoming a river. Watch out for the flood!' she warned me.

It truly was surreal. I had to get out of there, or I'd be next for the loony bin. Stumbling over the preparations for tomorrow, I went towards the front door. Outside it was just as crazy. Lightning still flicked though the windless air was warm and clear. The kids were shouting. 'Victoria, the horse was scared.'

Sofia followed me out the front door, lugging a heavy old port. 'I have rehearsed all methods and means to deliver justice,' she said. 'The devils or the angels can take over at any moment and weapons will come to hand. Beware, liar in your lair. Vengeance is mine.'

'Go for it,' I muttered.

On the porch, under a hurricane lamp, she unstrapped the leather belts. And said, as she took out a hard-bound book with gold motif and frieze, 'My mother would have wanted you to have this.' She handed it to me reverently and the gold lettering glittered in the flickering light. While being stunned by her words and her present, I thought there was meaning in her madness: everyone who had come would go away with something of Maria's. Sofia was curtailing possible pillage by proffering objects of significance. She was anchoring herself with the weight of Maria's possessions and her interpretation of Maria's relationship to all these people. The centre pole of the circus tent had fallen. As I held the gift, tears came to my eyes. Sofia had elicited genuine grief in my emotions and I pulled her towards me to cuddle and embrace her shaking, thin loneliness. But her body was stiff, as rigid as a board. She seemed to suffer my solace with a reluctant patience. We backed apart. Another guest came up the steps, immediately to be button-holed by Sofia. I said, 'See you tomorrow' and looked around, hoping to say something to Chandra before I left. She was with a group of women gathered around the fuse-box. They had a torch. They resembled, I don't know, a coven of witches? Lola pointed the light at her lap while Chandra worked, replacing the burnt-out wire. I touched her shoulder. She glanced up at my puffy eyes and rueful is the word for her smile. I left, hounded again by the sound of canine hysteria cooped up in a car.

The electrical storm was out to sea. I drove towards it, feeling, for once in my life, completely useless.

Hope finds Rory on the web.

'For the first month, Internet time is free. I would have to travel,' she tells Hope, 'if it weren't for this!' Then added, in explanation, 'I'm a stay-at-home by nature.'

Hope, grounded and reassured by Rory, says, 'I just used tarradiddle to frighten Ci away from my camp. I think she wanted to steal something.'

The chat page waits, the cursor blinking in readiness.

<DENGATE> Telecommunications assist our telepathy.

Rory doesn't want to leave the cyber-village. Geographic and social limitations are totally negated by the rise of online communities. But, she never knew it would be as exciting as it is. Hope is happy to share her enthusiasm.

'Look at the herstory of this,' she shows Hope. 'Women's Electronic Battalions, the web within the web.'

<u>Witches Entente Brooms</u>, 'web' and women have flown on sticks and now they grasp the concepts of instant transmission with ease.

<u>Wicked Ecclesiastical Bitches</u>, 'webs' danced provocative ecstasies claiming god or the devil entered us (it didn't matter which). 'Webs' have no trouble with impending doom. 'Webs' are not disturbed by murder of the enemy, nor by devious intrigue to subvert the course of his justice. His justice never served us. Not as a group. We are not a group, we are gropers in the freeze-us-out dark, groping about trying to find the overlay, the common blanket, which can warm our individual icy-lation. The coverlet. Succeeding is not believing, but knowing the covenant.

Hope reads with her, then asks, 'May I?' She sits on Rory's chair, and types, with all eight fingers and one thumb.

<EOEO> I have a broomstick to speed over continents.

Hope laughs. 'Let's find Tartarus?'

'Come again?' Rory pulls one of the dining chairs up to the old Chinese desk, and is entranced by the downright facility of the girl; she digs into lists, finds menus behind menus, chooses, clicks and the computer responds with a complexity of stored information, random memory, access to places and programs she didn't know it was capable of, not to say the whole wide world on-line.

'The sunless abyss below Hades, where Zeus imprisoned the Titans, you know?' Hope comes from a techno-Biblical axis foreign to Rory's practical and political endeavour. When in her short life did she have the time to learn all this stuff?

The night wears on as Hope discovers more and more witches on the web. In the old days they believed in tracks of electricity, lines of magnetism, grids of ley-lines within the earth, understood in all cultures, microwaves, patterns of energy, power. Electro-magnetic fields affect everything, and always have. Animals respond to them. They are getting choked by the hyperactivity of the global village. Hope's Tartarus is the hell-within-hell of the re-identification of the ley-lines, their eruption into common society through the clumsy progress of male physics, of naming, measuring and inventing machinery, harnessing the force, as it were, the marrying of ancient and contemporary witches. To wit, to know. Yet their communication creaks in the overcrowded band-widths needing more than ever telepathy to interpret the symbol, the suggestion, the meaning within the meaning, the poetic echo of forgotten chords in the dearth of shared belief systems.

'The tower of Babel, see?' Hope brings it back to the mundane dictionary of Western mythology.

But Rory needs words, even though, by now, she has gathered hell itself is not a hellish place, but something else, probably real, as everything was, apparently, something else. She is weary, tomorrow is a big day. She doesn't have time for Pagans and Warlocks.

'It is so easy for you,' Rory says, with not a little bit of envy. Hope clicks in and out of cyber-places with such speed, even going, at times, into the operating systems and software programs, Rory is worried she will alter settings or messages so that she will not be able to find her way around with her usual methodical, plodding technique. She suspects computers to be very individual tools. Hope, however, returns to the familiar desktop and suggests that she download what she wants rather than use up on-line time reading, demonstrates, tells her how much hard disk space she has left and asks would she like her to clean up the window a bit, create some short cuts.

'No no,' panics Rory, afraid she will lose something.

'Okay,' Hope shrugs, not the slightest bit concerned.

'Turn if off. I want to see how computer geeks do it.'

Rory is relieved when Hope goes through the procedure she usually does. She is not that much of an idiot. Just a slow old boiler. Chook trying to be an owl. Hope rolls out her thin mattress, climbs into her bag and is in the arms of Morpheus with the face of an angelic babe before Rory turns out the light and climbs to her loft. Hoots, scratchings, sounds of wings flapping and bats screeching in the thick foliage, instead of her usual reading, send her to sleep. The barking owl woofs twice.

In the thunderstorm which hit soon after I had gone to bed, I read *The Golden Notebook*.

33

The Golden Notebook by Trivia

A Diary

1

She, you and I walk abreast for a moment and in that moment cast one
shadow. The shadow of the trio ripples across the mat of grasses,
descends into the trench of tyre-tracks and, with ease, rides along the
rocky ledge. The land rises steeply upwards to our left above the rough
vertical made by the grader and, after the rutted horizontal, drops away
to the right. The deep green fronds of bracken and the lighter green
fronds of false bracken cover these slopes like repetitious curved brush-
strokes. Beneath the bracken, the bush is regenerating with ferns,
grasses, climbers, creepers, orchids creating ground covers and a
nursery of big trees, leaves dying and mulching, preventing weed growth.
Holding the dampness, rather than being tinder fuel for bushfires, the
pyromaniacal society believes. The shadow becomes one with the trees'
shadows. Although it moves, it is at one with the rooted.

I am all three. High-minded, foul-mouthed, and simply mediative,
vegetative: the one walking; the other talking; the third thinking—the
trivial self. She who speaks repeats and repeats. One walks, the other
sees. The view shows deep viridian gullies of rainforest giving way to
tall forest, dry sclerophyll eucalypt and pasture land on shaved
ridges. Like a backdrop painted in greying blues, the mountain ranges
seem to stretch higher and be denser as each dip reveals a further
rise until the clouds met on the horizon are small with distance.

You walk now off the road where drivers can go and begin climbing.

I am afraid to go with you.

A frosty shrub of a colour like *eau de nil* reminds you of the snow
country and you look upwards where the gums are sprung in three
trunks. You have walked through a shallow gully concentrating on the

placing of your feet. Now you look back and sigh, not only for the beauty of the ancient grass-trees, their spiky heads on twisted, leaning black trunks bent towards each other in timeless conversation, but also because the sigh was forced out of you.

We are walking because this is no place to dance. The dance occurs in the nervous system. The dance at this point is in the stillness of the landscape, in the ringing industry of the native life as countless insects play dead or leap with amazing agility or clap their wings together in contrapuntal code and birds' eyes concentrate to pierce their camouflage and disturbed wallabies suddenly thump through the scrub on long lower legs like a pair of sticks beating a carpet, rhythmically.

I did not realise I was dancing and lying to myself until I heard myself singing, 'this is no place to dance'.

If the light is perfect and you yourself are nothing but pure observation, you can see, to the east, the line of the sea, equivalently to the west, the flatness of the plains where the Range stops.

The space-ship.

There it is in broad daylight hovering shamelessly.

I feel the freedom here, the rarefied atmosphere. I feel the glamour, the enchantment of the female lands. Of course alien beings would come here! To a friendly place. My pack for some reason has become lighter. I am not afraid of the Bush, this is our land. Even though it cannot be possessed. It possesses. I am more likely to encounter a ghost than I am to meet a man. If I meet a woman, she and I will have the positive experience of making the journey and being here to share. But generally the women don't come this far. The western tracts of Lesbianlands are left to the wildlife. You make the decision with renewed energy. You want to go forward. Down. You have decided to walk the 'lands, you want to find the right place, the spot which speaks back to you. The northern end of the Campbell valley is swathed in low cloud banks. Somewhere down there in the mist is the mysterious far corner of our freehold, the boundary with State Forest. The immediate descent is sharp and rocky, manageable because of old cattle trails. You zigzag forward, losing the view. As the bush thickens so the land flattens a little as if you have found another ridge, but it keeps dividing, presenting you with choices. I am lost. In some places there are springs, puddles in the earth where water breaks the surface and

tadpoles blindly swim. Others, almost identical, are dry now. You have
to pause in your stride at the end of a stand of casuarinas. You are
faced with a hedge of lantana. If you crawl you can follow the paths of
wallaby or, once, cattle. Well eventually they must go down to the river,
one says, and you drop to your knees. We continue, looking for a
camping spot.

2

Such a cold night in September and you shiver. Nan says, 'It does
snow here, higher up. Sometimes.' . . . No chance of a dance, Nance.
Who said that? Truly, it was a voice in my head, but it was not my
own voice. No. I am clinging on. The copper rocks are blue. If you had a
mind to solve our financial worries willy-nilly a lorry load of this sent
to Sydney landscape-gardeners would do it. But the land is sacred. I
would be moving the spirits of ancestors from their resting place.

Money calls the shots. Always a call for money.

3

Widows Peak rises behind her, a jagged forbidding rock. The beak-shaped
mountain on our land to the north-west of Widows Peak, on which it
snows if there's snow around, is higher still and called, believe it or not,
Mount Ararat, on the maps. From where she stands she can see the
highway making its line through the pass in the Great Divide, some of
the pasture of Campbell River Station and across the central downs of
Lesbianlands. They do not know my camping gear was lifted from Army
Supplies in Stuart. I must move on to a more gentle spot where the bush
absorbs the threatening sounds. The walk has become something more
primitive, she notes wryly to herself as she crawls downward and forward.
A little fear rises, drying the mouth. As long as I descend one should be
all right. The lantana seems endless. How many cattle-ticks or paralysis
ticks or any sort of ticks are falling down her neck, I wonder. The only
thing that seems to grow with lantana is a savage thornbush. Skidding
now on loose soil and large stones on a sudden change of gradient, I am
falling. Tumbling with marginal control, I crash into barbed wire. There is a
path. You are with her but you do not feel very well. She is bold. She is
descended from the Amazons while you have amazing memory. I come
across a clump of Yucca filamentosa, Adam's Needle. Horrid plant. I
think I am cactus. Fucking finished.

We know there are no fences on Lesbianlands except those that separate ourselves from neighbouring farmers, and those built around kitchen gardens near dwellings. Tents for the most part. And a couple of old ones on the downs of Horses Hangout.

She, you and I struggle back the way we came, defeated by the barbed wire fence. You feel vulnerable, super-sensitive, and involved in our own drama. It's downhill all the way to my lover's arms. She favours the colours of ochres and tan. She wears a black Che beret with a red star sewn to the right of the centre, the felt flopping over the leather band on long, straight dark blond hair. She is dated, and proud of it, street-fighter of the 'seventies. But is that what I love? Her uniform? Her anachronism? But only one-third of me can love. I have come up here alone to sort myself out. Will camp one more night.

4

And sat that night on a flat piece of hillside amongst the blady grasses and allowed my soul to open to the past and the future and presence of the nocturnal chorus of mammals and birds and frogs and insects, I suppose, singing out and arguing about sex and food. The lights came silently at such velocity a less aware person would not perceive. I was not stoned nor am I in delusion. Struck by shooting stars which came to a stop to regard me watching them. Not a meteor shower. She, a part of me, hummed a deep melody in memory of a past life that haunts me to this place.

Now you smile: they are here.

Wow. They burn marks onto the ground to prove that my time in meditation beyond my own will, my own mind, is real. The spirit, I am told, is of finer essence than the soul, which in turn is finer than thought process and astral bodies are atmospheric shells. The ego floats through the warps of time and space until it attaches, an anchor catching the sand and rock, pinning a person to a time and place, the tail on the donkey. It seemed so sensible as the funny lights danced before my eyes and my ego dissolved into the collective mind like sugar in warming water. I closed my eyes and opened them again twice. At first they are still there, and in the second, when I am very tired, they are not. My girlfriend will think I am way off the planet.

5

Several days have passed, and nights with lights. I am living on water and sunflower seeds. Before Trivia I was Zola. Zola had taken for a surname the maiden name of her maternal grandmother, Zakharov, a Russian emigré. Zola Zakharov, a perfectly legal pseudonym. The passage of the white Russians from the revolution-torn capital was often through Siberia, into China, Japan and eventually Australia. Although Zola herself believes, and believed when she changed her name by deed poll, passionately in continuing revolution, the beloved maternal grandmother, Anna Zakharov, yearned in her declining years for the Chekhovian gentility of a culture, a country, a religion gone. The fibro granny flat behind the house in south-western Sydney was for little Zola an exotic cabin in a time-travelling locker.

She walked from the Formica-Laminex glisten of her mother's kitchen along the back path to a room (a converted garage) darkened by rich red brocades, heavily patterned floor rugs and tasselled tablecloths. The round table was crowded with photos of unknown, pompous ancestors dressed in fur with backgrounds of snow. The old lady had lost her mind by the time Zola, the fourth child in a family of seven, reached the age of reason, which was a pity as the little girl was agog with questions and curiosity. Instead she sat silently running her small square hands across the velvet, listening to undulating mumble in a foreign language and building walls of pretty tiles in games of senseless majong.

Beneath a long, narrow icon on gilded wood of a madonna in a warm shawl of deep blue and maroon dress with the child in green and gold, an angel either side of her ornate crown and halo, one holding a sword, one holding a cross, Zola became an iconoclast, a revolutionary, not because of Anna Zakharov's own beliefs but because the dear old thing in her senility had established a world in her garage which challenged that outside, the reality of the poorer suburbs of Sydney. The kid, Zola, had a secret and the secret was: it doesn't have to be like this. I confronted every teacher who tried to bring me into line in all the neighbouring schools with questions, or more specifically, the question, why? When told to sit down and do what I was told, or whatever, she, I, you, whoever unanswered and unsatisfied, resorted to the language of the streets and was soon expelled.

The days seemed mellow as I gave birth to another ego, Zola. In long evenings, she and you settled into an I, not Zola, while of a morning, Friesians with their white feathered friends stalking around their legs were picturesque. Mary's angels wiggled necks on the look-out for grubs exposed by the weighty hard feet of the beasts on the soft earth. Heavy-light pelicans preened on wooden jetties jutting out into the delta. Sun, moon, stars played with cloud formations. It was for me, okay. To take the name of Trivia, for humility and pride. My indulgence in sweetness was due to a resurrection as well, but I had not been dead.

Yet, Maria saved me.

The goddess, said my lover, walks among us, she of the many names. You entertained her in bed one morning with the litany of the Blessed Virgin Mary, for instead of Russian Orthodox little Zola went to a Catholic school. 'Holy Trinity One God, Have mercy on us Holy Mary, pray for us. Holy Mother of God, pray for us. Holy Virgin of virgins, Mother of Christ. . . Mother of Divine Grace, Mother most pure. . . Mother most chaste. . . Mother inviolate. . . Mother undefiled. . . Mother most amiable. . . Mother most admirable. . . Mother of good counsel. . . Mother of our Creator. . . Mother of our Saviour. . . Virgin most prudent. . . Virgin most venerable. . . Virgin most renowned. . . Virgin most powerful. . . Virgin most merciful. . . Virgin most faithful. . . Mirror of justice. . . Seat of wisdom. . . Cause of our joy. . . Spiritual vessel. . . Vessel of honour. . . Singular vessel of devotion. . . Mystical rose. . .Tower of David. . . Tower of ivory. . . House of gold. . . Ark of the covenant. . . Gate of heaven. . . Morning star. . . Health of the sick. . . Refuge of sinners. . . Comforter of the afflicted. . . Help of Christians. . . Queen of angels. . . Queen of patriarchs. . . Queen of prophets. . . Queen of Apostles. . . Queen of martyrs. . . Queen of confessors. . . Queen of virgins. . . Queen of all saints. . . Queen conceived without original sin. . . Queen assumed into heaven. . . Queen of the most holy rosary. . . Queen of peace.'

Your memory is impressive, Maria said to me as little Zola lay in her arms. We came to help build Lesbian Nation. It was her idea.

For me, Persephone, alive again in another spring, we left the dolphins to hear the mermaids sing. And goddesses may well be there.

6

Aliens, my goodness, we have seen and tried to read the marks, lines, short lines on the ground, burnt with no fire I know—a fire that crystallises the sand particles. Makes them green and iridescent. Like featherlight quartz.

Arrow-heads in different relation to each other. Chevrons and foreign punctuations.

7

Evil is not a term accepted in Lesbian Nations, because etymologically it comes from Eve and clearly places bad as female. Per se. To root out evil from the girl, the mother, the prostitute is the twisted motivation of many a murderer in movies, in history, in literature and court cases, accepted by critics, by academics, by judges and journalists as feasible. This is the world I left. I had personally to experience a holy war conducted against me to wholeheartedly embrace existence in the margin. I have begun hallucinating. Zola is dead. The body as beautiful in death, like the Morrigan, white with long hair floating outwards in the water. The next image put splotches of brown mud on her naked legs. Your own imagination saw the dawn across the wide river lighting the mangrove banks in red, her limp form caught in the roots beside water-logged debris buffeted by the out-going tide.

I died among mangroves, the lungs of the earth being choked by silt. Forgive me. I must move myself, my bones are poking out from my flesh and my joints are aching.

8

The words came out onto the page of the notebook Maria gave and named for me, out of me like blood from my face, off me like sweat from the brow, like blood from my wrists, squared my shoulders with the yoke of centuries, hardened my thighs for the hills I had to walk, to walk anywhere and I read it aloud one drunken night to the lesbian nationals gathered around and later looked in the mirror. Spring, summer and autumn had come and gone with women tearing each other's hearts out of their chests. In the hysteria of the fast and eating the bush food to hand, possibly magic mushrooms, she, you and I danced down the hills.

I have prised the quartzy chevrons from the ground and carry the lumps of rocks about with me. Found rubies, too. But I had done something very wrong. Panic attacked me.

Maria did not understand. She was not very impressed with the ordinary green quartz I held for dear life in my palm.

I thought I was special. I stopped by a creek and let the rubies go, fresh spring water flowing by my fingers.

Maria, you found me.

I told my lover when I came to and she wanted to believe me but couldn't comprehend why I called my watery blood gemstones. She thought I was a suicide, but I have lost my ego in the plural self.

I am trivia. Trivia dies. Trivia lives.

I had been to hell.

The cattlemen's fires burnt down the shelter I built with Maria. Green glass is in its place. And green grass. She took me away. I woke up in a motel room with a copy of Gideon's Bible resting on my chest open at The Apocalypse by St John.

9

Maria has left me alone. If I am too much for her, I am too much for anybody. For she is a strong and beautiful woman, and I hope my floating off to another plane does not disturb her karma. Whoever finds me please find her and give her this diary, dedicated with a deep love that goes beyond the grave. Beyond the vale of tears.

For Maria, yours always, Trivia.

34

. . . the funeral . . .

In the icy paleness before dawn, while Chandra is at her computer and Meghan travels to the airport, Margot wakes as if poked in the centre of her back by the forefinger of conscience. She looks out her bedroom window to see grey light flooding the eastern sky and reacts like a recruit at army camp, spinning out of bed to a type of attention. As Margot stretches each muscle and tendon of her body she remembers reading half the night. Weeping has made her sinuses gummy. Feeling the sharp tang of cold on her doona-warmed skin, she drops to her hands stiff as a board and presses herself through twenty fast push-ups, exchanging bed-warmth for blood-warmth. As she does a handstand against the wall, she sees a red eye flashing on the television screen. For the moment she thinks it is weird. Then she realises it is the message-blinker on her answer machine reflected from across the room, sparking warnings. She paces her hands out from the skirting board and her feet down the wall until her back arches as far as it can go, in which position the energies at the base of her spine act like a pocket of radiogenic rocks spreading heat throughout her frame. Upside down, blood rushes through her head, flushing her nasal passages. An exquisite balance between pleasure and pain teeters on nuministic experience as she inches her limbs closer together.

Having finished a few easier postures, she goes down her cute cement path to the outside loo. Wisps of fog hang in the paperbarks behind the fence. Stilled for a moment to listen, she thinks she hears the distinct sound of plate falling against crockery. As neither of her neighbours is in residence as far as she knows, it must be a lyrebird. Winter on the Paradise Coast is a subtle season, and autumn does have its mellow mystery. Morning crisp-ness suggests a coldness which never really comes. Deciduous leaves colour and fall as if the entire tree is dying against the background of native ever-greens. Because she is in an unaccustomed mood, Margot sits down at the end of her yard and stares into the space between her plot and the bush block behind. Doing nothing is uncharacteristic. Margot thinks when she is busy. Her mind nags on the word, waste. Waste of time. Rubbish and compost. Trivia. Little things, like cooking an old potato. The peel with its dirt and the edible flesh are one until the peel needs to be thrown away. The water which boils the white pieces is also tossed. Neither can be done away with before the process deals with them. Her brain box empties as the analogy works its logic. She catches herself realising her present vacancy is necessary. Yet, boiling potatoes can cause the house to burn down, taking with it all worldly possessions, computer, money, licence and cards, and may happen because the telephone rang. Indeed the telephone did ring, an emergency, a woman in distress. Maria. Margot has the sensation of having left something undone.

Her mind is tired, her emotions flattened by an enormity she has no words for, things she doesn't understand. Human life on the planet. The predicament of intelligence, awareness. The paranormal. All she knows of aliens comes from a TV program she watched recently. *UFO'S in Australia*, ordinary people telling their stories. She wrote as a note to the Featherstone file: 'I sat there and believed them, just for the sake of it. But no matter how hard I tried I couldn't figure the apostrophe. Is there only one UFO in Australia? No, because the one at Gosford was a completely different shape from the one at Narre Warren, which was different from the one on the road to the Dandenongs. Do UFOs own Australia? No, there is an unnecessary preposition. Conclusion, it is all bullshit.'

How dangerous is gullibility? Now, she remarks on the stubborn pedantry of her thinking only of the apostrophe. She remains seated, hoping to hear the lyrebird again. She hears, instead, the split-second timing of whipbird call and response. Suicides. Homicides. Accidental deaths. Autopsies. Words float through her brain. Bushfires. Arson. The young man who burnt down the historical cathedral in Parramatta got a light sentence because, the judge who gave it to him said, the boy felt no remorse. Her stillness absorbs thought forms, the information overload, the burden of nonsense attacking the psyche which seems to be in the air even away from the immediacy of the media. A persistent impression which she cannot find the words for keeps her in a trance. The connection, Margot grasps, is *The Golden Notebook*. Something in the diary is significant: unidentified flying objects? What was it that had a price above rubies? A man's soul? A girl's virginity? Maria's call for help had confused, yet gripped her.

The photo in Meghan's house Margot, an amateur photographer and developer of black and white prints, knows is a hoax. The snap captures high-beam headlights reflected in a rear-vision mirror, the two-lane blacktop of a highway in the background, giving the impression of a bright flying saucer hovering over a road at night-time. The negative was tampered with. Telltale signs of singular attachments have been removed. Such she thought, but now she doesn't know what to believe. Regarding Chandra, she feels on the threshold of a journey of an expedition into uncharted territory so far as her own life's experience goes. She has no idea where it will take her, what will be expected of her strength of mind, her sense of direction, her array of talents: what sacrifices? what gains? Sex would change the landscape. Provide a path. But she faces a dense jungle, a wall of living questions to which there are no correct answers. She cannot comfortably say Sofia is responsible for Maria's dying, nor Maria for Trivia's apparent suicide, but somehow she wants to get it right. To name the moment and move on.

Margot, having tied strings of rubbish together, composts them mentally. Like a siren in a factory, her phone rings. The bell. Communication technology tugs her back to work as surely as her athletic body demands exercise, care and expression of its potential. The answer machine takes the message. Inside, the piles of files remind her that she must have discipline. Before she deals with any of it, she cleans the house and gets down to some practical thinking.

The writer is not only Australian and female, but from the district and pretty familiar with the gurls. Chandra is convinced of this because she has discovered the Web address of the person who posted the recipes, which included the dope cake Maria was eating the day she died, and it leads to either the Annihilation Tragic or the clever hacker trying to take over control of her structure for the mobilisation of the Solanasite conspiracy. Whether or not this is one and same she is not at all sure, but her gut-feeling is not, ravers not usually being foot soldiers. Anonymity is a blessing and a curse on the Web. Theorists, generally, do not throw the bombs in bloody revolution. Furthermore, unable to catch the source of the glitches, she wonders whether the intruder is out to subvert the plans of the whole international network, or is attacking Chandra herself personally, through her site or, indeed, whether the whole thing is a prank or deadly serious. So far, all it's doing is making Chandra decidedly unsettled. To interfere with the superficial thing, her screen saver, requires nerdy know-how capable of plumbing the depths of the maze. As Chandra cannot figure out how to regain control of that, she has no way of knowing how deep the imposter, the meddling arsehole, has gone. Nor why. So she must come out of cyberspace into the real world of detection, reassess the character of her friends. She needs a private eye, and the odd thing is she has one right in the centre of her acquaintance. But she can't use her, she knows her too well. Margot Gorman would probably flush out the culprit; at the same time ten years' zealous work would go down the drain. Meanwhile Chandra has options to pursue and opportunity today to quiz women on their technical knowledge, on their attitude to SCUM and Valerie Solanas and to have a look around the mob to see who might have it in for her. Conceivably, there is someone in the community so adamantly opposed to separatist policy in sexual politics that he or she, happening upon the site, simply wants to destroy anything or everything that radical feminists set up. She gets on the blower, inadvertently, trumpeting her investigation.

An announcement in the departure lounge informs travellers of a delay, due to a few problems with the aircraft. Trouble with the Dash 8 to country towns is nothing new. Meghan Featherstone is used to it. She sighs, pulls her slim PC onto her lap, realises she cannot go on-line and plays with design of her homepage but, for several reasons, she is not feeling artistic. She is making a quick trip to attend Maria's funeral. She has to be back in Melbourne for a series of meetings starting Wednesday.

Chemicals, she writes, then looks around at her fellow passengers and their luggage. Almost everyone is sitting patiently. A couple of holiday-makers in matching canary yellow shorts take the seats beside her. She balances the laptop on the end of her skinny knees, tilted towards her relaxed arms. Fingers light on the keyboard, she stares them out when they want to chat or sneak a look at her screen. Businessmen reading magazines are similarly contemptuous of the tourists. One women in high heels and smart skirt-suit trots to the counter, has an argument, then anxiously paces. It is a long way out to the front of the terminal to go for a smoke from this backwater lounge in the huge building. Of course, she must make the trip for Maria's funeral. Fly in, fly out. Someone will miss her.

Meghan expresses her irritation in leg-jiggling. Escapist reading for her has not been written, yet. Virtual diversions, being able to say what she likes, give a fragile link to her social circle. Thoughts of where she belongs and what she really cares about distract her. The worried lady in a power-suit who fiddles with her gold lighter gives her an idea.

Nicotine, she types.

It is surprising how many gurls smoke, why? She, herself, is too busy. Most of the bush dykes are waiting for something to happen, except Judith, who lives what she believes. For all her talents, Meghan has never been able to keep to a tune, not even sing the national anthem. What made her fall for Jill in the first place was the effortless song bursting from her throat, vibrating the beauty of being, soaring in sound like a bird in the air. A purity rivalled only by silent maths which, of course, Meghan does have. When Maria sang in the protests, Meghan loved her too. Buddies into drugs, alcohol, disinterested in the civic duty of adult citizens, or mad, inspire Meghan to write her essays. Or chained to inaction by depressing poverty. Her sisters from the scrub hang about like the idle youth scaring the ordinary folk, as teenagers do. But that fear must be phobia because there is nothing to be afraid of. Unfortunately. Judith, on the other hand, is strong enough in her conviction to dress in the green, purple and white colours of the Suffragettes in the style of the second-wavers. Meghan remembers Maria with cigarettes, like Valerie Solanas, like Simone Weil, shooting the breeze, pursuing the feminist discourse.

Smoke is a social thing. Helps conversation? Cigarettes in their way contribute to the annihilation of female self as it seems to assert rebellion. Smoking in public places is something a respectable family does not like. The gang who drink also smoke cigarettes, and cannabis. While alcohol can be blamed for aggressive and destructive behaviour, the effect of smoking, nicotine, tar and carcinogens is less obvious psychologically, it being a together thing, a sit-down thing, a ritual, with approval overtones, probably generational, legal, cultural, certainly endorsed by film images. Apart from being a disincentive to exercise, it also suppresses extremes of emotion. Schizophrenics and manic-depressives smoke and smoke. They would prefer to smoke than eat or drink. Smoke affects the chemicals in the brain without making women particularly insane. The anti-nicotine campaigns do make them feel bad, but dedicated smokers like it regardless. The counter-revolutionary effect of smoking is, patently, the lack of healthy exercise, energy, passion, acceptance of guilt, and a measure of self-contempt in that women will do this to themselves when they know they are doing themselves no good.

Meghan tends to abstraction when she expresses herself. She has energy to burn. For the sake of air traffic control she cannot go online, even though, as she looks at the clock, now is the moment to check the market. So she raves and saves.

What about prescription drugs, pharmaceuticals? Anti-depressants, painkillers, Serapax, Valium, stimulants and amphetamines? Your doctor is a drug pedlar. Although it is okay to take them when prescribed, it still affects your personality. Calms you down. Enables you to cope with the regime that denies your existence. Heroin is 'drug culture'. The black market. The drug of drugs. Methadone just as bad. Counteracts heroin. Dangerous to take both? Too many gurls take heroin. They want to get out of it. Cocktailed and that's it! Annihilation: complete!!! Neutralise anger, pain. Perfect panacea for oppression. Dope the populace! Any threat to the hegemony is undermined. And financial and emotional resources are devastated. Loyalty shot. Heroin people become 'sick' and this brings all the rescuers to their service. Taking them away from the first principle of identity, getting to know and demand their own needs. Rescuers are so sanctimonious, but they also die. Yet political women are seen to be selfish or naive.

Tragic!

Meghan objectifies Maria's death and what she judged about her lifestyle. Again, the image of Judith ratifies her moralism. Song-birds, she muses. Soon she will be with Jill and her heart warms. She has a life-long companion, home fires, but her own happiness is not enough; who rules the world, or rather, what? Wealth? People don't, people's allegiance does, therefore, if women were to have power, it cannot be a group of diverse individuals united by an ideology, nor any idealism, but something simple like an agreed value-system which can include difference of opinion. Something to replace the fiat that money has intrinsic value. How could she ensure, had she the choice, that in making money available to women they did not just go out and kill themselves with it? She turns off the laptop and snaps it closed. The aeroplane is ready for departure.

For the moment she rides her own dragon. When she has time, Meghan swears she will study the basics for a community bank, maybe even get a law degree, but first, she has a job to finish, a point to make. What a blessing Chandra's website is! She will establish within it e-commerce credentials and a fund, perhaps an on-line female university, a shelf for the study of everything from a female viewpoint, architecture, prehistory, languages, military systems, music, current affairs, barter economics, the lot. And, she thinks, as she boards the plane, she will name it, She(se)lf, or something like that. She has not answered any of Chandra's emails but she digs the nickname. Meghan is the Annihilation Tragic.

Virginia parks her truck at the bottom of the path to Rory's, and cooees. Birds incorporate her call with a bit of extra chatter and a semaphore of wings: big-headed stick creature! where? where? get out of the way! down on your right! okay! okay! where are the chicks? here! here! is it gone? yeah! yeah!

Rory reaches for her Barbara Walker and reads, to Hope, that 'Universal Dike' was the Orphic name for the underworld goddess who received the soul of Orpheus. After Virginia joins them the three women talk about Eurydice.

'Sent by a serpent's bite to the land of death', Rory reads.

'Dike is another goddess name for Justice,' contributes VeeDub, sitting down.

'It occurs to me,' says Hope, 'that it's not such a bad thing to be called a dike then.'

'But the disparagers don't spell it that way. What they mean is toilet, I think.'

'Language is a fucken maze,' states Hope. 'Like dike is justice and hell, and us, toilets and serpents are bad, why, anyway? People don't deal with their own shit. Especially the rich. Maybe that's the whole answer.' While Hope is serious, Virginia and Rory can't help laughing at her chaotic logic.

Jill David knows the Qantas flight is late as she pulls the red Saab into the accountant's parking spot. She returns Rosemary's keys to the office manager and reluctantly climbs into her dinosaur of a van. She checks that her stuff in the back is covered and spends her time driving to the airport rehearsing her beautiful lies.

Rory has both hands full; in her left the phone, in her right the stone Hope gave her. The green-white pet rock soothes her arthritis, her tired eyes. She holds it instead of rolling a cigarette. Even though she lives in the bush she has indoor plants. On her desk is a maidenhair fern in a clay pot, a miniature forest if she brings her face too close to focus; it's ages since she has painted, or even brought out her drawing pencils. Rory puts down the stone. Covering the mouthpiece, she tells Virginia and Hope it is Chandra she is speaking to.

'Too many brilliant woman have killed themselves,' she says into the receiver.

Chandra in their short friendship has never been this curious. They trip through modern history and do not run out of names of scientists, writers, politicians, poets and painters of the female sex who have, ostensibly, gone mad. 'We must change that.' Dissemblance bothers both of them. Chandra saves going into detail until they are speaking in person, her immediate worry: is the Annihilation Tragic the mole?

'Actions speak louder than words. Lying for a greater cause, perhaps, can be excused,' says Chandra.

'What shits me about liars is they think you're a fool.' Rory plays with her red dog's ears.

Speculating on who might be subverting the game, they find themselves gossiping. Margot gets a mention, and Margaret Hall.

'Sofia learnt about computers,' Rory recounts.

'I know,' responds Chandra's rich voice. 'Sofia is smart; she could hold her own with the intelligentsia.' Chandra laughs. 'She would love it.'

'Margaret Hall had the job of helping beginners with the Internet at CyberCage. It's cheaper than the library. Customers there might be interesting. But I heard she isn't there any more.'

'Where's Margaret?' asks Chandra, suddenly urgent.

'She got a job in Sydney. I think,' Rory's inflection has a shrug in it. 'Where exactly? I don't know.'

'Perhaps, she'll be there today.'

After a pause, Rory says, 'I was worried about Maria.'

'Chandra and Maria did not get along,' Virginia tells Hope.

'Pretty Sofia is an absolutely delightful woman. I love her, but,' Chandra admits.

'What happened?' Rory knows from the grapevine it was more than fancy. 'You were close.'

Hope makes coffee and Virginia sits silently at the table, making eye-contact now and then, with each other, and with Rory.

'Nothing dramatic. She is fun,' says Chandra, 'we're friends.' Hope places a mug beside the stone on Rory's desk. 'But she's like a diet of too much candy. Her bedroom is draped with brocades and tassels like some movie of the 'twenties or 'thirties. She'd stand among the materials being Greta Garbo, in some moods, in some roles. Her clothes hang in a circle as if they were for sale at an outdoor market, all maroons and purples and velvet and velour. She'd tell stories about how her great-uncle was a grand archduke in Vienna when Vienna was the New York of the Western world. She amused me, but it was never serious. I mean I never told her my stories.'

'If Maria were less impeded by her weight or less lazy, do you think it would have happened?' queries Rory gently.

Chandra is circumspect. 'I wouldn't say she was lazy. She would run around and clean up after Sofia when she went off.' Both go quiet, as individually they recall the place as untidy and the glamour Sofia affected all but lost among the dirty cups and ashtrays. 'Last night Sofia was oscillating between being a grieving hostess or swanning smokily in doorways, a femme fatale. Over-generous. Women everywhere.'

'I'll miss Maria enthroned in her bulk in an armchair allowing it all to happen around her. It was a place I talked to people I hardly ever spoke to elsewhere. Anything goes. Went.' Rory turns in her chair to put both elbows on the desk and take the weight of her head in her hands.

Chandra says, 'Sofia demands ambience'. Her throaty voice carries a slight sob. Rory reaches for her mug of cool coffee, which she drains thirstily.

'There are times when Sofia is afraid of everyone,' continues Chandra. 'The front gate padlocked. Nazi troops have come to Austria and she must hide, no one is to be trusted. "They will look at my hook nose and think I'm a Jew!"'

'She doesn't have a hook nose,' observes Rory.

'I know. Her nose is actually a little turned up,' Chandra states. 'Retroussé.'

'Their relationship was like a vortex of drama into which other women were drawn, to then turn on each other, creating a complete psychodrama out of life as if lesbianism were a full-time job. A storm in a tea-cup. All fuelled with gossip, creating new bits of mischief, tossing in your tuppence worth. It made me so angry, the waste.' Rory wonders if she has said too much.

'Yes,' Chandra eases her mind. 'Better go. See you at the wake.'

'Right.' Rory puts down the phone and strides around before settling down with her closest neighbours. 'I don't really know what that was about.'

Then she says, 'We should think about going.' Feelings of anticipation, and yet not knowing what to expect, still them for a few minutes.

'Plenty of time,' says Virginia.

Hope prepares another brew.

Although Rory is wise enough to know that Chandra, so far, has kept a fair amount from her, thus the web-work must be pretty important, she feels she can trust Virginia and Hope so she describes what Chandra has shown her.

'The revolution might be gaining some reality, in the virtual world, at least,' she grins. 'The invisible cell of the wimmin on the net, murmuring of dissent. But Chandra's after information. I don't know what, though.' Rory savours the image of revolutionaries coming into her parlour to discuss action, practical problems, face to intense face. Whispering in case of spies.

Hope is happy to explain to Virginia the cyber-adventure of the night before.

Their dishes of prepared food covered and boxed, Rory's casserole, Virginia's potato salad, they join the exodus from Lesbianlands as gurls' vehicles gather on the river road to proceed in head-lit convoy.

The Campbells take the opportunity to pack their tools and Eskies, spikes, bolts, nuts, snigging chains, to trundle the old bulldozer down into Lesbianlands, to throw sleepers and thick milled boards on the back of the flat-bed, and, helped by a bunch of blokes told 'we're doing our neighbours a favour', as that's what country folk do, to spend all day on the witchy property. Safe in the assumption that the noise of crashing and crunching and cursing is unheard by feral gurls hidden in their homes, they work hard. The cacophony of intermittent chain-sawing and the constant drone of the petrol-generator echos in hills normally eerily tranquil with the quiet orchestra of flora and fauna listening and murmuring. They fell two grey gums, clean them of branches and crowns, lay them parallel across the creek, gouge out tight holes for the joists and secure the planks of black butt with six-inch nails, leaving a neat new bridge across the creek and an untidy mess in the scrub.

The Pearceville Mechanics Institute is not near the pub or the strip of houses along the ribbon of highway. Several miles inland, the hall is still used and maintained, with car-parking space and a single tarred, high-fenced tennis court in the once-vital village around the timber mill now practically deserted except for fallen-down mill-workers' cottages. The building survives as a venue for social activities. The hedge of hoary azaleas provides a carpet of pink and white petals in which the kids roll. Girls play and boys throw sticks for the dogs when they have been told to fetch fuel by the gurls who build a huge pyre in the paddock. At least two hundred women come to Maria's funeral from near and far, close in time, place and politics and distant in one or other of those. The Larrikin and Milt, with other bikers in ranks behind them, rumble up the dirt road like a pack of trained Rottweilers, coats shining, power contained, rest their machines on their stands in a line, take off their helmets and open their panniers to produce fresh vegetables which they carry in procession to the table. Cars keep coming all day. Each has brought something. Floral arrangements, fruit, a feast of food, rice, curries, stews, sandwiches, cakes, crackers, dips and chips. Pretty salads. Ice, beer, spirits and coke. Wine, coffee, tea, herbal drinks. Music on tape and musical instruments. Chairs. Cushions. Catering things.

When I arrived I parked beside two cars covered in the red dust of days' travel through the outback, and glanced at the number-plates, Northern Territory. Beyond them was Jill David's navy, rusty Urvan. I was surprised both by the amount of motor-bikes and the number of Indigenous women wandering about. I looked for Chandra's Subaru, and Rory's Guntractor. The red Saab? Close to the hall-door, as if it had been early, was Cybil Crabbe's shiny bubble of a car. Next to it the newish LandCruiser had its back open, inside a guitar case, bongo drums and something wrapped in a sari. The horse-float was stacked with hired chairs stamped RSL. Alison's Ford was there. But for the most part I did not recognise the vehicles. There was a motor-home with the stickers of Christian mission and extensive touring decorating its rear glass surfaces.

In the paddock gurls were feeding a fire with objects, clothes, papers from cardboard boxes which in turn were tossed into the flames. They were quite reverent, the rubbish detail dealing with the bits and pieces a person doesn't need any more, and no one else can use or treasure. I watched for a minute, and wondered what was going up in smoke.

Cybil and some other women were busy, unloading, arranging, sweeping. The first person I spoke with was Meghan.

She was scattered but she hugged me. There was a lot of hugging going on. I pulled away, clumsily asked, 'Where are your goats?'

'Oh they're fine, thanks.'

Not an answer to my question which was not, apparently, appropriate to her mood. I desisted from further inquiry.

'It's not only them,' she indicated an inoffensive elderly couple. 'It's the whole Christian hegemony!'

Obviously I had walked into the middle of an ongoing controversy over the rituals of grief. 'Their Lord isn't ours. Structures crumble and we've got no more than our own minds and our own kind to build a culture. Don't you find, Margot, the intensity of being among so many who loved, knew, even loathed Maria difficult?'

Not knowing what she was talking about, I made a face.

'What do they know of the vast potentiality of the woman's heart? What do they expect? Spinsters.' She walked off.

When I entered the hall, the atmosphere of suppressed tension was palpable. Heather Bishop singing 'If You Leave Me Can I Come Too' was abruptly stopped mid-phrase, and replaced with a morbid churchy dirge. Tiger Cat had changed the tape. She smugly looked for approval from the elderly couple, brushing her eyes past the Larrikin who, if her expression was to be believed, wanted to strangle her. All-out turf war over the music was prevented by the arrival of the hearse and the chorus of readiness as the casket was wheeled in and left in the centre of the room. I was not really aware of anything anyone else was doing after that. I sat cross-legged on a cushion, my hands resting one on the other, and didn't move, except for tears which had a will of their own. I was stunned by my weeping, overwhelmed by the pure feeling of sorrow. Even if I had wanted to I couldn't have seen people beyond shapes and movement. I was too taken up to be curious. Yet I could not have experienced this meditation without the presence of others, without the focus of the box and the candle flickering behind the fronds of fern or bracken, the trick of Maria being both there and not there. A state of answerlessness had me entranced, suspended in stillness, in total surrender for some time.

Grief at Maria's dying is sincere, both maverick and communal. She is in death even larger than she was in her life, that of a significant Australian radical lesbian in a milieu of her peers sharing a wave, making a wave, on the tides of time passing. The coffin arrives in the hearse at two o'clock, rolled out by the pall-bearers to rest in the hall for an hour. The suitably grave guys open it and leave. Lying in a silky shroud, the body is a human-sized earth mother, a supine shape of the Venus of Willendorf, crafted twenty-five millennia ago. Her face is exposed, serene and round. Along with the draped trestle table holding her valuables, vases of flowers, vessels of drink and wreaths, the hall is decorated with photographs stuck to the rough wood of unplastered walls. The pictures pan a biography begun before the Second World War and finished in the new century. From tiny white-trimmed brownish snaps of a babe in arms to those showing the unrecognisable girl in school uniform, through teenage moments in sporty tunics with family pets, professional shots of a debutante at a ball at an outback barn, the staged portfolio of her marriage in wedding regalia as artificial as can be, as a young mother in feminine curves of 'fifties styles in spotty dresses, then with daggy long hair and drippy skirts of her hippie stage, to the loose clothes in expression of freedom from brassieres and other restrictions. The majority are many interestingly angles of Maria as a women's libber, recognition of her protest, well-framed moments of pride in poses of power, accompanied by dozens of coloured rectangles depicting her in the bush, on the beach, overseas, at parties, in the desert, then documenting her increasing weight and widening friendship over the years, her gentle ageing caught by the haphazard presence of someone's camera.

Maria's mourners lament. The assemblage of many women who have shared so much hosts such a well of emotions it is as if a raging river is dammed for a moment. Members of her realm acknowledge her lifelessness with votive offerings, invocation and keening, with tears and dry eyes, with pause and reflection, with thought, feeling and emptiness, withal an appreciation of absence. Egos seeking meaning for themselves feel dwarfed by the magnitude of loss yet exhilarated by the importance of living. The reality of her corpse enhances psychic impressions of her spirit hovering, hearing, freefalling between worlds. Flying.

Maria's body is taken to the Crematorium, a low brick veneer building hidden in the newer suburbs of Port Water. The shiny surfaces and careful decorum of the chapel contrast with the anarchic lamentation out at Pearceville. Not all go to the ceremony. The hearse, a large powerful vehicle, once on the highway, disappears ahead of the gurls' cars. Some are lost in similar streets while Maria's corpse is turned to ashes. A few give homage, read messages, recall her life and say what she meant to them personally or go to the pulpit to weep uncontrollably. An a cappella group sings. White ladies officiate and usher. A psalm is read. Mrs Freeman talks about the difficulty of her child's birth in the hard years of the Depression. Finally, Maria's own voice on scratchy tape sings the congregation out within the allotted half-hour. Margot takes Chandra to the Crematorium in her Suzuki. They are silent returning to the wake. Sofia is not among the mourners at the cemetery. Nor has Sofia got herself entangled in the maze of parallel and dead-end streets. She is escaping from her grandparents, not far from the Mechanics Institute in Pearceville.

Because no one else was talking to them, after the ceremony, I went up to Maria's parents and introduced myself and offered my condolences. They had not seen much of Maria for forty years. They hardly knew Sofia. It was one of the biggest regrets of Mrs Freeman's life that she did not know her granddaughter.

'So what happened?' I asked.

The old man grumbled angrily, trying to dismiss me. I waited in their personal space until the woman decided to talk.

'It was a beautiful Christian wedding, and he was a good boy. We didn't, we couldn't, believe Maria when she told us, well, me really, that he battered her during the honeymoon. But it was true. She wouldn't listen to me when I said that was how men were. It is a wife's job to control her husband and that when she had children, it would all settle down. She left him before the baby was born. We knew it would come to no good. She had no money, but she would have nothing to do with us. Even when I begged her to give Sofia to me, if she couldn't manage, she refused. But she let her go with strangers! Oh, I find it very hard to forgive. God has given us grandchildren to love. Maria denied us that.'

'How?' I demanded of this soft, round old lady, who was as hard and sharp as nails. She, possibly, could control a husband, or be blinded to his faults.

'She gave her mother hell. Hell! She doesn't know the pain she caused,' he responded, from behind her shoulder, ungraciously.

'Calm down, dear. Maria is at peace now, in the arms of the Lord,' Mrs Freeman said piously, incidentally putting him in his place. He fiddled impatiently. She described the den of iniquity and squalor she found Maria living in with a babe in arms and laid down the law. Either she took the child or she gave her up for adoption. Eventually Maria took the latter course. Sofia from the age of one to some time in her teens was with a wealthy diplomatic family, she thought. I could see she didn't really know, but was firm in her righteousness in getting Maria's baby away from her. 'If she felt guilty then that was God's punishment.'

The milling lesbians among the roses and the metal plates on brick walls of the ashes of humans or standing in groups on the asphalt carpark were invisible to her, their solemnity, their sorrow, their love of Maria Freewoman completely ignored. Not by me. I saw how many there were, how big this funeral was.

'Well, Mrs Freeman,' I said, 'it's a pity you didn't know what a wonderfully kind and intelligent person Maria was, what a devoted mother and genial friend. She will be missed.' The predominance of their Lord was the tar and cement and regimented graves, not spiritual love. Not here, not today anyway.

Sofia journeys among ghosts in a world of her own making, neither truly historical nor intrinsically mystical. She mutters, exploring the derelict buildings to reconvene with the people who once lived there.

Although she accepts that she killed Maria, by wishing her dead, baking a cake, being born or having a pet, that is not the point. She must get one of these deceased hags to read her cards. The future dances like flame-shadows, looming agents of her destruction, but that is nothing new. Dear old women in the crinoline in cobwebbed corners with sneaky looks in their eyes know more than they have ever told, but Sofia is convinced they will tell her. She clears a three-legged table, yes yes, they would like it wiped. She spits and rubs it with the material on her elbow, with house-proud intention. The power of thought; it is the thought that counts. She rolls a forgotten stump from outside to sit at the table. She is ready for the seance. The dead are beautiful. 'You are beautifully dead now, Maria, in the congress of expired Amazons.' Sofia is reverent. 'The goddess whose image you aped, who lived a quarter of a million years ago plainly did not have to till the fields or walk about collecting water or gathering berries or digging roots from the ground. Queen of Willendorf sat still long enough for someone to knock out a sculpture of her. If there was one chubby duchess, there must have been many. Power women who were fed when hungry, probably didn't even lift up a fork, used their fingers.' Ladies in crinoline do not come to her table. Sofia realises she has dressed them all wrong. These bushwomen are insulted by her BBC drama costume for them. Sofia bows in frenetic apology and explains, 'I know you are hard-working, hard-talking millers' wives. Your knuckles are red, your skin blotchy, the cloth of your clothing raw cotton or something and you have not even got the time to wipe yourself properly.' She resketches a past in her mind and makes it a present and immediately the educated tenet of her tone changes. She and they engage in foul language and home truths for a while. She knows these women understand mercy killing. They have chicken, snake, heifer, baby blood on their hands. Sofia inspects their palms, 'Is any of this husband blood?' she inquires. Wouldn't she like to know! They are too cunning to be caught then, or now. 'Is any of it,' Sofia hesitates, 'mother-blood?' she asks. Her companions are horrified, they resound echoing, disappearing, 'No. Our mothers were our only friends.' 'Come back,' cries Sofia, 'don't go. I understand you lived and died in this backwater, and all your lives were full of travail, it doesn't make you ignorant, does it?' But, they are gone.

Sofia climbs the antiquated chimney to make a spectacle of herself against the western sun. She cooees into the air, but the sound does not carry. The defunct timber mill absorbs her words. The silver wood creaks underneath her, moves. There is danger. Sofia balances with two feet on the loose timber. Cars return from the crematorium. The wake is under way. She pursues the adventure of regaining the ground.

Virginia sees Sofia playing like a child on the unstable scaffold surrounded by a nimbus of madness. She does not panic. Untamed kittens slink in and out of discarded piles of stuff and rusted bits of machinery.

Heavy vibes in the night when Mars squared her Pluto conjunct Uranus, too much electricity, lightning, thunder, then a clear day, Alison paces a patch of shade as if trapped in a cage like a Sumatran tiger in a carriage on a circus train. The pupils and irises of her eyes roll out of her face leaving the whites to witness life around her while she wanders the universe of her brain, a solitary prisoner in a cell. Cybil, in contrast, resides in her curiosity, outside herself, at the centre of things, crying appropriately, constantly watching.

The sun sets, the new moon waxes in the west. By evening the embers are glowing inner potency and the campfire is surrounded by figures, moving shadows, coming, going and staring, murmuring, singing, calling. Gurls who are used to pushing back their feelings with recreational drugs are not without supplies. Fewer indulge. Although stoned, they keep the food up. They clean the hired dishes, cups and glasses. Rory resolves not to touch a drop of alcohol. She joins the teetotallers who have a pot of tea stewing. Everyone wants to be there for Sofia, but no one can find her. Libby Gnash is the one who is looking systematically. Unsuccessful alone, she organises gangs to find her. By the time Libby returns from her section of the search, Virginia has brought Sofia to the fireside.

Jill David's brown eyes are almost black with intensity. Milt and the Larrikin come back with several slabs of beer. Wilma Woods bots a bud from each city white woman she can find rolling joints. Em wraps her arms round her daughter, Serena, while Cassie and Venus play with Tilly. Maria has left behind her plenty of stories and the tone of these is her generosity and love of life, her tolerance and joy in others' happiness. Women who haven't spoken in ages choose each other to talk to.

Rory sitting beside Chandra says, 'I simply wonder what to do. Being a Solanasite, it's like being a revolutionary in fascist Spain. I like the idea, but when it means giving up the security of my existence, when it threatens to put me on the wrong side of the law, I get a bit edgy.' But Chandra directs questions at each woman who happens to come close enough: does she know the Web, if so, has she visited her website, okay then, what handle does she use?

Rory continues quietly. 'The thing that makes Valerie different from Christ is that she practised what she preached, or at least tried to.'

Jill David comments, 'She wasn't an assassin with kill skills.' She hands Rory a bourbon and Coke. They laugh as she imbibes.

'Christ couldn't practise anything, except throw a few miracles around which proved he was the son of god. I guess he died for the idea of himself.' Rory unfolds her rolling tobacco.

'They crucified him because he had all these people following him already, trooping around listening to his every word and writing it down because, indeed, it became the gospel,' Fiona jokes.

'Andy Warhol of two thousand years ago, sexually ambiguous and famous,' Rory throws out her hands, and grins.

Yvonne contributes, 'He was a leader of a revolutionary movement. How many people have died in his name? I would have thought Valerie was more your John the Baptist.'

'You can't make lesbians follow, they won't. I want to build things, not destroy them. Structure without leaders, as such,' Chandra is serious.

'You're a power freak, Wheels, get real,' Margaret Hall says sarcastically, materialising from the shadows.

Rory confesses, 'I know The Manifesto, our bible, by heart, and at times, in the middle of the night, when I can't sleep, the sheer splendour of her intellect keeps me awake,' Rory chants. 'Harmful types are: rapists, politicians and all who are in their service; lousy singers and musicians; Chairmen of Boards; breadwinners; landlords; owners of greasy spoons and restaurants that play muzak; "Great Artists"; cheap pikers and lechers; cops; tycoons; scientists working on death and destruction programs or for private industry; liars and phonies; disc jockeys; men who intrude themselves in the slightest way on any female; real estate men; stockbrokers; men who speak when they have nothing to say; men who sit idly on the street and mar the landscape with their presence; double dealers; flim-flam artists; litterbugs; plagiarists; men who in the slightest way harm any female; all men in the advertising industry;

psychiatrists and clinical psychologists; dishonest writers, journalists, editors, publishers, etc.; all members of the armed forces, including draftees and particularly pilots.' The effect is to make gurls around her raise their voices, all know Rory can be a bore.

'Particularly pilots. What we forget is Valerie had a great sense of humour,' Rory says, finally dropping her favourite subject.

Meghan wanders from the tight band around Judith's soft acoustic guitar to stand by the big fire. The dynamic of the group gets a bolt of electric antagonism as she and Chandra exchange a loaded glance. Rory asks her politely where she is staying.

'Have to leave first plane in the morning. So Jill and I are staying at a motel tonight.'

The new energy attracts other individuals and expels some. Virginia heads to the hall to find a drink. Cybil passes her going the other way.

Tiger Cat calls to the music group, 'Stop being so selfish. Let's have a sing-along?'

Margot opens a bottle of red wine. Virginia and she sit on the step and together toast Maria. Hope stops for a minute. VeeDub introduces her to Margot, who hears the New Zealand accent and recalls the birth certificate at the dairy.

When we went back to the Pearceville Hall, I pulled in beside the red Saab. I recalled the Larrikin saying I would be surprised at who deals hard drugs in Port Water and the impression I had that it was some respectable member of the crowd. Chandra and I were not in the mood to give each other our deepest thoughts. She wanted to get away from me for some reason. Camps had been set up by those who'd travelled far to stay overnight: a couple of little two-person tents; a larger tarp; a camper van. The hall glittered with candle-light. Women took each other to look at the photographs together to find themselves and remember what might have been forgotten. The tape was playing the Coors' 'Forgiven Not Forgotten'.

Rosemary Turner and Lola Pointless were there. I overheard them commenting that the relationship between Maria and Sofia was abusive because of the age difference. I informed them they were mother and daughter, and Rosemary shrugged, 'Whatever.' Lola glared at me.

I shared my bottle of wine with Virginia, who appreciated the vintage. She was sad. Maria was a good friend, a long-time friend. I said it was okay for her to get drunk at a wake. Others were intent on the same result. I grilled her about past times on Lesbianlands, about Trivia, about rubies, and when Maria was there. It was a very long story about emotional entanglements ten years ago, a Dickensian list of characters and plots within plots.

A fight broke out at the big fire. Tiger Cat was being beaten up for being a screw, a spy, and doling out deadly drugs. She was called a prick, a scab, a cunt, a fucking this and a fucking that. I don't like Tiger Cat myself and maybe everything they were calling her was correct but the Larrikin and her mates were going a bit far. I had to intervene, though it was difficult without hurting women I much preferred over the victim. However, Virginia, Rory and I did pull the assailants off. The mouthing went on, and the gist was if she wasn't working for the authorities how come she had pills to give away? For nothing. 'Currying favour, weren't you?' 'Weren't you?' 'Anyway they bloody killed someone!' 'We don't want your type around our campfire.' Both her eyes were practically closed from bruising. Cybil pressed a tea-towel of ice on them. And the poor ex-Gladiator was groaning from pain in her ribs.

Chandra suggested I take her home as she couldn't drive herself. Why couldn't it be someone like Cybil Crabbe or Rosemary Turner? But Chandra decided I was the right one. Dee and Rory helped her to my car and promised that they would get her vehicle back to town.

As I was driving through Stuart, I inquired, 'Where to?'

Tiger Cat, still with the tea-towel of ice held to her eyes, directed me off the major road to tarred tree-lined dark ones. I had never been to this area of five-acre blocks with big houses and long driveways midway between the rural town and the coastal one, away from the river. There were too many turns, I was sure I was lost.

Then she said, 'This one.' And pointed to a white-washed fence. A pony came into sight in the light of my head-lamps.

Now I had questions for her. 'What, exactly, are you up to? Is this your place? Are you living with some guy? What is the story with the pills?'

'For chrissake, Margot. Just open the gate, get me up to the house, and let me take a Mogadon,' she begged, miserably.

In front of the wooden gate, I turned off my ignition and calmly waited for an answer to at least one of my questions.

She groaned. 'I look after people's houses, okay? House-sitters, it's a thing on the net. You get to live free all over the country. They go on holiday, they have pets to be fed, burglars to be kept away. So here I am, feeding the pony, the pussy and the puppy while they take the kids to Disneyland. What do I know? I got references. I even mow their lawn. Open the bloody gate.'

Sucker that I am, I felt sorry for her. She was pathetic. I opened the pad-dock gate and drove through parkland to someone else's home.

When she was pulling herself out, I asked, 'Why are you hanging round the gurls, anyway?'

'Nothing else to do,' she said. 'The only thing in my life is keeping my body trim and going to the gym. Not much social fun in that, is there?'

Following her, actually helping her to the front door, I wanted to know about the pills she gave out at the Spiders barbecue.

She responded with a scoff. 'You think I'm going to tell you!'

'Why not? Got something to hide?' I let go of her so she could find the keys.

'You bet. They call me a bloody informant. What about you, Margot? Can you truthfully say you're not working with the cops?' She unlocked the door and let it take her weight. It was like being checkmated by a fool. I turned on my heel. I left the gate wide open and kept going, but a little bit down the road, I thought about the pony, and pulled up. It was very dark outside the car and there was scrub right down to the bitumen of the narrow road. I walked back gingerly and dealt with the gate.

It was so stupid, but trying to get back to the Suzuki, I got entangled in cobwebs. Cobweb after cobweb. It was all I could do to stop myself from screaming. Every which-way I moved, cobwebs. My skin was crawling, my car full of spiders.

When the gurls finally make their way to their homes on Lesbianlands, they are amazed to find the bridge back in order. Ti Dyer, for one, is glad when she sees it and sits in the lamp-light sharpening the teeth of her own chain-saw. Virginia and Rory are drunk, and Hope drives the Rodeo slowly, like a little old lady of seventy.

35

. . . like a bully . . .

Home, Ian Truckman can't believe they're happy to see him. Home-ground, square suburban block and everyone for miles around barracks for Essendon. His mother with a grin and red and black beanies and scarves hanging on hooks in the hallway; he hasn't been so happy for months. Pencil pines spaced like goal-posts. Green grass.

In Shopping Town he buys presents: at the hardware, weedeater, 3.3-kg petrol-line trimmer; at Toyworld, a jigsaw and cricket set; at Harvey Norman, games. His sister says, 'Oh Ian.' He mows the lawn, whipper-snips the edges.

Full of largesse, mobile hooked onto his pants; his big rig, White Virgin, parked in the street, he shows off his gadgets. Plays cricket with the kids and his brother-in-law. The men hit the pissy bowling for six and don't go out till they want to, rather dink the little ones over the fence to fetch the ball. They hoot. The whole family bellows. Nippers are great, he finds, you can yell at them and make them laugh. They're not that happy when he bowls fast and bowls them out, but they gotta learn the rules and what's what. His brother-in-law has to respect him because he has a job, money and a truck. He does what Ian says. They cheat. It's funny. When the youngsters get all sulky they tell them it's a joke. So they laugh. And yell.

Brother-in-law got retrenched. Hanging round the house with Ian's mother. 'What's wrong with his own?' Ian sits in the toilet, talking to the Bomber posters. 'The little nine-year-old calls him Homer. They call me something from the Simpsons too but I don't watch it, don't know what they're laughing at, so I wear it. I call him Homer and it's big deal. Make them wait a day or two before I start up the semi, just to listen to it purr. Show it off to the kids, my sister's kids. Had to be sure they wouldn't mess it up. We all sit up inside and say jeez, ah and wow. Uncle Ian this. Uncle Ian that. Let the kids have a go. They sit in there and watch one of their comic-book videos on my tiny screen. Keeps them quiet while we have a beer.'

Mrs Truckman at him about the grandchildren she never sees. 'Well you'd be bloody lucky.' The ex wouldn't let her within a bull's roar and she knows it but it makes the old woman cry. She asks him doesn't he care. 'Of course I do,' he says, but wouldn't really know whether he means it.

Then she susses him.

'What's wrong?'

Your mother sees through you like a sheet of bloody glass, he thinks. 'Nothing. What do you reckon? Nothing. Pay's coming in. Truck's going good.'

'Yes,' she says, 'I know, but what are you scared of?'

She's a witch, his mother. She's got the sixth sense. Ian flexes his pecs like a goon and says, 'People should be scared of me, not the other way around.' Then she's nasty. Turns into a nag.

'You always were a coward.'

'Was I talking like a coward?'

'No, like a bully,' she says.

Ian gives the lawn another mow and makes the kids help, heaping the clippings under the pencil pines inside the concrete rings Ian got for nothing from a bloke one time. Keep her yard tidy, as neat as a footy field. Beautiful.

He is waiting for the call.

36

. . . haven't got a clue . . .

My phone rang at about ten o'clock.

'You want to come fishing you better come now.' Lois gave her invitation in her unique fashion.

Half an hour later I was on the river with Lois and Thrust and Lois's sister, Mae.

Fish were jumping out of the water everywhere.

'The bream are breeding,' explained Thrust. 'The mullet's tasting good enough to eat, and plenty of them. Generally they are bait for blackfish.' At high tide, the river was a liquid mirror. The day still, cloudy. Lazy, satin circles rippled out. Why Lois was urgent was evident. A couple of dolphins broke the surface to catch the leaping fish. I must have told Lois dolphins were my favourites. Immediately they worked their magic. Contented, I grinned.

We, in a tin dinghy with an outboard motor, had gone quite close to town. Mae and Lois reacted to the diving dolphins with casual pride.

Mae is younger than Lois, and angrier. She talked about politics. The Mabo and Wik cases, women's secret business and the Hindmarsh Island bridge came out of Mae's mouth like a wall of atrocity. Then the Tent Embassy in Canberra. To Mae it was simple. 'This is our land. You stole it. Get out.' She tended to harangue, specifically the rural right wing where she saw the battle lines clearly drawn. I nodded and agreed. 'Ouch.'

Lois and Mae were different in character and looks but close because they were family. Thrust was busy with his line and bait, mumbling away to himself. Apparently the dolphins were his rivals. The women teased him and he grumbled something back, used to having the mickey taken out of him.

'The white virgin,' Mae went on, 'the plastic iron maiden. You see her driving around on television like the queen in an open car?' She made a wave with her wrist past her face like the royal brush. Both sisters laughed.

A dolphin jumped, grabbed a fish and submerged, appearing seconds later a hundred metres away blowing out air. I was thrilled.

'Fast heh?'

'You mob!' Mae yelled out and waved to people on the bank. They shouted back, reckoning the boat was about to get swamped.

'You watch out for yourselves,' she responded. Then to me, she continued. 'They, those whites, reckon they're are hard up and they resent it and they hate anyone who is worse off. They don't like it because we don't deal with it the same. We just sit on the dole all day with our hands out. Just because they're clipping their lawn with nail-scissors, they're better people, but they aren't and no one believes they are anyway, so all the time they are trying to prove it by pushing shit down everybody's throat. Some people are just born with hard nerves, just gotta tell everybody else what to do even though they don't know what it is without being told.'

Mae could talk all day. I sat back with a smile on my face.

'They put you in jail for stealing food for the kids up the Top End, no kidding.'

'Yeah, I heard that,' agreed Lois.

Thrust moaned about the turning tide.

Mae jerked on her short rod. 'Stupid if you ask me.'

Lois played a bite on her line. Mae wound hers in. I kept my eye out for more dolphins.

'They get hatred. They give hatred. And the men? The men want an excuse to kill. They can't kill people so they kill happiness. They got the guns and trucks and farms and, you name it, everything but not one of them has got happiness,' Mae said as she baited her hook, efficiently.

Lois reeled in her line dangling a wriggling fish off a clean silver hook, and showed it off. 'Yeah, working, telling everybody what to do.' Lois used her knife on the fish, and washed the blood off over the side.

'They reckon happiness is sitting around doing nothing, letting everybody else work for you. They pretend they're working all the time.' She flipped the cat-gut through the air in an S.

I said, 'I feel like diving in and swimming with the dolphins.'

'Not me,' said Lois. 'You wouldn't catch me doing that in a hundred years.'

Thrust whistled, 'You wouldn't want to, girlie. They see you as an invader, push you down to the bottom. They hold you down with their snouts until you don't breathe any more.'

'Shut up and keep fishing,' Lois asserted her authority.

'I am starting up this motor in a minute, so youse better move,' Thrust asserted his power, having control of the outboard.

As we puttered back up river towards the punt pier, I listened to Mae.

'White Australians are so stupid and so smug,' said she. I raised my eyebrow and glanced over my shoulder at Lois's loyal husband. 'I mean you and him too, and you know why, because, you don't know whose land you're on. You're ignorant. That makes you ignorant of a lot of other things. Just come and plonk down on any old bit of land and maybe pay a cheque for it or maybe not and say it's yours and then shoot at anybody who tells you different, well that's stupid. With the blackfellas, you got to find out whose land you're on first.'

There was not anything I could say.

'No one feels comfortable unless they are on their own land, that's why the people die of drink and hang themselves and that, because they know they are not on their own land. If you went over to China and proceeded to put your rubbish out and eat the surrounding vegetation and animals, blow out the hillside and make a dam and act like it was yours, that would be ignorant, wouldn't it? Say a polite Chinaman comes along and says, excuse me, sir, but that's my land you puking over, do you mind moving? You go, why? and he says, well sir sit down and I'll tell you why. The Anglo reckons, none of that, don't need education on what I don't know, and shoots him. So he makes damn sure he stays ignorant.'

'You're right,' I commented. Restitution of land to Indigenous people is absolutely necessary, but not my half-acre. I would have to think about this a bit more. She said, whose land are you on? But she didn't mean an individual. She meant a community, a nation, and with that, spiritual worth, non-ignorance.

Mae shook her head. 'After a few generations the opportunity has gone and now we got all these white people and other non-Indigenous ethnics coming begging, saying sit down, sit down, tell me what I don't know and my grandfather wouldn't let you tell me. We say, well if you've got a beer I'll sit with you, but I'm buggered if I know what to tell you. Then these liberal fellas start salivating and panting, anything, anything you got give it to me. You got dotty paintings I'll have that, thank you very much, and you got a didj, well I'll have a go at that too. This is cool, let's have a competition. Australia's too small for a competition. Let's have the competition in London and then an American can win, did jer ee doo, boo bop. When they took the kids away from the communities, they took away the possibility of feeling all right. Now everyone's unhappy and ignorant, and wondering what the shit to do about it. So you take a hit, you sniff petrol, you drink, or if you're a fat cat you buy this and you buy that and build an effing great fence around with a couple of Dobermans to protect it. Still doesn't mean you're not unhappy or ignorant. In fact it proves it, because you look outside and starving in the gutter of your very own street is your brother but you don't recognise him. You don't recognise him because you don't see him. You let him die so you can stay ignorant.'

Mae was going to go far. I said, 'Yeah, I don't know.'

'The truth is they have got no spirit and they don't want to know that.'
Mae pulled a beer out of the cooler. 'Want one, sister?'

'And because they've got nothing, they want everybody else to have even
less,' Lois added, refusing the drink.

I agreed. Property in my understanding is tied in with the value of money
and ownership. I have a big concept of theft and fair dealing. 'I understand
that England stole New South Wales in 1788. I do not see what I can do
about that now, apart from continuing to be right-minded according to my
own lights,' I said soberly.

Mae sank into silence. Thrust gave me a fish to eat. I was fulsome in my
gratitude. Lois grinned. I thought about my job for Lesbianlands and Trivia's
romantic disillusionment. When I got inside I wrote a note to myself: back
to Rory's; when?

Her house is full of strangers, therefore she will be stranger still. And they're
after things, not pearls of wisdom. In fact, they are killers. Nomads with
gonads attacking monads. She goes about naked to show she is human: 'Do
you like my new dress?'

'Put on some clothes, Sofia.'

'Why? Cockroaches have souls too.'

'Sofia, please.'

'Could do with an iron perhaps?'

Sofia is in delusion. Local gurls are not with her now, travellers are. They
take down the curtains and put them in the washing machine. They have
mops and buckets, and window-cleaning squeegees. They are busy people
with objectives in mind before they hit the road back to their own lives.
Dressing appropriately in towels and scarves, she repeats her tale to each
woman who comes, and sometimes to the same one twice, as if it is the first
time she has told it. Those who listen hear the jumble of imagination
pinned to a rather narrow base of personal experience, even though as a
child she went to Africa, Russia and South America. She had a nanny.

'After the meal, the meal of maize and gristle and a green herb like rocket,
the full moon forty-five degrees high in the sky, some women got to their feet
eagerly, feeling their skirts for leaves and twigs to brush off. Hermione
hesitated and stared at the fire. I was a girl. I watched her across the flames.
The women walked away in the moonlit darkness and the men chatted as if
nothing much were happening in the cutting hut. We wrapped ourselves in
carpets and held each other and slept until dawn. With her arms around my
young girl's body in such a fierce hug, she felt me. Hermione touched me,
until then I loved her. At first she patted and stroked and didn't see the tears

in my eyes. The other women slowly and efficiently packed up their beds and went outside to make a fire and sing some songs. The early morning sunlight came in shafts through the cracks in the rough walls.' Sofia babbles on, pulling jars of grains out of the pantry, gathering blankets, undoing the well-meant organisation of the good samaritans.

Mary Smith tries to hold her, to shut her up.

Sofia isn't eating anything, only drinking coffee and alcohol. Africa, the American, has no time for Sofia's racist madness. In her bag of pills for all occasions, she has the makings of a Mickey Finn. She makes the mistake of suggesting this solution to one of the Territory women. They, then, guard Maria's daughter, knowing that more poison in her system is not what she needs.

Before I set off for Penny Waughan's I spoke with Chandra on the phone for about an hour. We discussed my job, how I discovered the truth, how it must be more than simply asking questions and I told her some of my techniques but concluded, with a laugh, it is an inborn talent. I needed to know more about computers.

She said, 'On the net are hundreds of youth suicide sites.'

'Are they hidden or obvious?' I asked, pencil in hand.

'Depends on what you know already, really.'

'Hundreds of sites?' I wrote down a few as she called them up at her desk.

She told me about the gopher field and the password field then extemporised on the subject of young males today. 'Probably an underestimate. They have this friend, a computer. They're alone and depressed. Unlike me, fifty, a kid of the 'fifties, fed on sentiment, lachrymose schmaltz, for entertainment these kids are given psychopathic nutcases as models when they are vulnerable. Ghouls, Hallowe'en creeps who mean it with hook hands and axes and brilliant blades, and blood, blood everywhere. Violence is in their baby food. And they're more computer literate than their folks, who can maybe write a letter and do a spreadsheet of household expenses but have no real idea of how the net works. Cyberspace is outer space to them, while their kids live there, drumming up motives for themselves to be antiheroes. I'm talking Play-Station games and action videos, as well.' Chandra sounded though she hated males.

'Yes, but they say those games aren't so bad. Just the challenge of problem-solving,' I felt the need to argue. 'Anyway. Penny, his mother, teaches computers.'

'Doesn't mean she knows where he goes,' Chandra was into her topic. 'In his imagination.'

'Went,' I corrected. 'I'm interested in where he went in reality, as it happens.'

'Yeah,' she said vaguely. I had the feeling she was keying in things as she spoke to me. 'And they're going to put more policing pressure on parents. It's horrendous when you think about it. The computer is a friend when you are alone. I reckon when teenagers get together, they hike off down to the "drug store".' Chandra put on an American accent, 'And hang out, at the shopping centre, showing off how loose and cool they are. However, the lonely one has all these cyber-friends who have no facial expressions, who can't punch you in the arm or wrestle you to the ground, who can turn you off, who can romanticise themselves. The inherent frustration is siphoned off into obsession, addiction. To a type of fantasy. The funny thing is his virtual world is like Victorian fiction. Yet it is a whole world away from it all. A gone yet here world. It's very Gothic. If you're young, you need your peers, like you really do. Hence hundreds and thousands of suicide sites.'

I remembered how Neil frightened Tilly with a cape and make-up. 'What? Do they glamorise it?'

'They give recipes and methods and means,' she answered. 'How to do it without too much pain, or with heaps of drama, on costs and not being found out beforehand. Or if not so blatant, there is passive encouragement, support for the action, curiosity about it and each member grows in estimation as he comes closer to his decision. Imagine, a tiff, the hormonal big-dipper of despair and elation. Death has a fascination. For the adolescent male, apparently.'

'Many do it?' I dropped my pen, and sat listening to her voice. 'For the voyeurism of their cybermates?'

'Yes, lots. A great number. It is all very poetic. The big act of courage getting esteem from these peers is in going. Doing it. First, privately you have to whip a motive inside yourself or interpret the world you breathe in as hostile. Your mother. Your father. School. The girlfriend who rejects you is a favourite. And underneath this is real depression, the motive itself. Can you check his computer?'

'I suppose so,' I flipped a page of the notebook.

'Search through Youth Suicide,' she instructed. Chandra gave me a quick review of the lesson on what to expect if I managed to get to Neil's computer.

Suicide was, of course, a possibility. I wondered on my drive over to Canisteo Bayou how depressed he really was. Click on his Favourites menu, I repeated to myself, so as not to forget.

Penny Waughan's dinner table was set, with a cloth, correct cutlery, a bread and butter plate with a warm Italian bun in a checked napkin, a wine glass, a

Cabinet-Merlot with the $7.99 price still stuck on the bottle, all ready for one. A small card of anti-depressants was the only little mess in the classy tidiness. I suspected that would have been removed before she sat down to her formal supper. Her feast would be a pasta with a red sauce. A little salad was prepared with lettuce, tomato and olives, sprays of basil and parsley decorating. I thought it a nice honouring of herself and a nod of respect to the twenty-nine per cent of the Australian population, who live by themselves in their own place. Count me in, I couldn't judge. However, I could not avoid feeling the full blast of pathos in the sad nobility of it. When she answered the door she must have shrugged at my timing. Actually I thought she was dining a little early.

'Come in, Margot. Sit down.' The sitting-room in this house was beyond the dining-room though they were one large space angled away from each other by the position of furniture. She offered me a sherry, which I accepted as I sat on the three-seater couch. She poured the extra dry flor into tiny crystal glasses from a matching crystal carafe. She lowered herself into an armchair perpendicular to me and went about the ritual of lighting a cigarette. A jazzy blues track was playing on the CD at a low volume. I registered a few bars in silence but could not recognise the artists. The saxophone was the voice of the piece. I resisted the temptation to comment on the music. She made no reference to her dinner table. She was still breaking bread with the deceased Neil. He was in his room perhaps, a sense of presence altered time. The recent past was here as if it were sealed away by no more than a skin of Glad-wrap. But. There was nothing sentimental about this woman's strict and uptight mourning. I found it hard to fight back a tear as a particular riff in the jazz caught up the thread of her inner devotion, now a void. There was a thin crust between this piece and a full-on Negro spiritual with wailing and keening and unrepressed sobbing. I swallowed.

'It seems your son was a hero to his father,' I said.

'Neil was Nigel's son too. I have to remind myself of that.' She stubbed out her butt, continuing, 'I feel no comfort in the fact that Nigel will be grieving was well. Neil was much more like me. Not only in looks but inside. But yes, Nigel loves heroes.'

'Was Neil a hero?' I encouraged.

Penny looked at me and smiled. 'What would I say? Of course.'

'By that I mean, do you think he had the spine?' I changed key.

She nodded.

'Okay, let's take it from there. Am I interrupting your meal?' I was, after all, a professional PI.

Penny Waughan pushed herself out of her chair and went into the kitchen and called, 'I'll just turn it all off. It's only spaghetti bolognaise. I have to keep myself together. I'm tempted not to eat at all.' On her way back, she removed the pills from the dining table and put them in a drawer. Then she refilled our glasses with sherry from the decanter. Every movement was executed with slow care.

Spiral shorthand book on my knee, I asked, 'Do you think he was depressed? Seriously?'

'No,' she said without a beat.

'No,' I echoed her.

'What do you mean?' she asked as she sat again. 'Neil would not have committed suicide.' She was really indignant. 'He would not have done that to me.'

'Of course,' I pacified. 'A hero, in any sense of the word, does not kill himself, though he may take life-threatening risks. Because heroes have causes. A sense of right and wrong, a purpose.' Pursuing that direction, I went on, 'Where do we look for his cause? His crusade?'

Another cigarette, this one lit more urgently. 'Neil had nothing to be afraid of. He had his father's love and mine. Although he was spoilt, he was not ruined. He had our care and he had his freedom. What he did with his freedom I'm not exactly sure, but I could trust him. That is the horrible irony of his death. Neil was naturally cautious. He was sensitive, too. He would not put himself in danger because he knew it would hurt me terribly. He was mature. For fifteen.'

'Caution,' I said and wrote. 'Okay. I accept that. And from Nigel I accept that Neil was Luke Skywalker. I already know he was a computer whiz.'

'Of a weekend,' Penny gazed into the past. 'The boys would be in there jockeying the screen, and Lisa would come up and help me with the pizzas. I'd give anything to Neil, so I networked the two computers in the same ISP account. Lisa used my computer then, when she got sick of the all-male stuff. You know what teenage boys are like. Neil had his own email address.'

I figured that must be sometime back. 'How about lately?'

'Recently?' Penny frowned. 'He kept going out. He didn't mope or sulk. He had things to do.'

My mind was working fast and having a lot of trouble with my ignorance of the superhighway and its byways. I imagined the signposts lay in the hardware, but I did not have the language, nor did I want to push Penny into cracking through the fragile surface of her grief because I would not be able to cope with the shards. I did not want to shatter her. However, when I looked up I saw she was looking at me with a steely gaze, full of backbone and intelligence. She, on all appearances, had ended up better off than her husband in the financial disputes he had said were so acrimonious. So she had the grit in the awful emotional warfare. Maybe that was what she meant when she said Neil was like her inside.

'Can we check his email? Or is this not a good time?' I caught her steady scrutiny with mine.

'Well, now is as good a time as ever.' She got up, smoothed down her skirt and led the way. 'His room,' she said as she came to the desk, 'is a lot neater than I would have expected.' Indeed, all disks and piles of paper were squared off and dusted.

'What's that?' I asked, pointing to one of the bits of hardware that were not printers, or monitors, or keyboards.

'Which? Fax, modem, flatbed scanner.' She tapped the equipment and bent down to the power point. Again she was surprised. The electricity was on. There was a light on the multi-adaptor which had a number of plugs through the spaghetti junction of leads. She pressed one button on the main computer and everything whirred to life. She murmured. 'The cleaner doesn't usually disturb his arrangement. But, of course, she would know.'

It was much neater than last time I was here. Penny sat down and her fingers danced on the board for a second, while her eyes remained fixed to the screen which registered asterisks in response to her typing. No words, letters or numbers. The modem beeped out a telephone call.

NiNwalker Attention. Attachment download. Go NiN, this is really interesting.

We both read together. A number of messages attracted my curiosity and I suggested we print them out.

'You don't want all this advertising.' The pages came with surprising speed.

Penny frowned, as she moved on.

'They're asking for a password I don't have.'

'Try R2D2,' I said.

She did.

Penny worked the mouse. The screen slowly composed a graphic of a plant, and its botanical name. I did not recognise the name but the leaves looked like some kind of wattle. Penny tapped again and pushed her seat back. The printer ground out the picture of the tree. She slid back to the computer and brought up the index of Neil's email. 'Look at the dates,' she indicated, dismayed. Dew-like tears emerged from the corners of her eyes.

'Some of this came after he—' she hesitated— 'He died.'

I picked up the pile of paper. Among the firm bond was a limp shinier sheet. Again, Attention NiNwalker and a date after his death. It read:

As soon as you take DMT you need some cushions behind you because you fall over. Takes effect real quick, dramatically increasing heart rate and blood pressure. Tastes like burning plastic, but it's natural man.

I moved my gaze onto the monitor and Penny was reading about the same drug. She was crying freely now.

'Neil was not into drugs,' she sobbed. 'We talked about it. He had a heart-murmur. He wouldn't take something as dangerous as this!' She fisted her hands and spoke through clenched teeth. 'Neil was not robust. His heart, he knew. He wouldn't.'

Still holding the sheets of paper I'd picked up, I put my hand on her shoulder, 'I haven't had a chance to talk with Dr Neville. He's away on holidays. And the complete autopsy report is not available yet. But.' I pulled up a chair and sat beside her. 'Working from the premise that he was a hero, that he was cautious, that he was extremely computer literate, his fight may have been in cyberspace. We are looking for his crusade.' Removing my hand from her arm, I shuffled through the pages and came across a diagram. I showed it to her. 'Is this Neil's handwriting? A laboratory has been discovered in the country district around Port Water.'

Penny obliged me by looking, and affirmed as she shook her head in confusion, 'But I have no idea what it means.'

'It reminds me of algebra, perhaps a formula of some sort. What were those initials? DMT? These notes all seem to have something to do with it, and acid, LSD, crack, cut heroin, sugar, gelatine. But what bothers me is this.' I put the fax sheet in front of her and pointed to the date.

'Well, that warning is too late. Too fucking late.' She fiddled angrily. 'What was he doing?'

'I don't know, Penny.' I raised my eyebrows in ignorance. 'But obviously someone else has been using his computer.' That someone was Alison Hungerford.

Penny lit a cigarette. Her hands were shaking and it took her a moment. I hoped it would calm her. I collected the paper, found a folder, labelled it and asked if I could take it with me.

She nodded distractedly, whipping herself up. 'What do you know, Margot? What have you found out so far? Sweet FA, I'd say. What has this got to do with the women's clothing?'

'Don't get upset,' I ordered. She had been drinking and taking anti-depressants; her mood changed, her rage erupted

'Don't say that to me, you patronising bitch.' She exploded, screaming, abusing, smoking, sobbing and banging about the room. 'You've got no fucking idea, have you? You haven't got a clue about how it feels to be a mother who has lost not only her only son, her only child, but her best friend as well. We were close. He is gone. I miss him more than I can say. I don't know why I hired you. Why would I? It doesn't bring him back, does it? I just know someone murdered him. I feel it inside.' She collapsed into a huddle on the floor, keening like a banshee.

Guilty that I hadn't told her much, I felt a sudden twist of loyalties. I had not mentioned the women and their barbecue. Certainly not that Alison, her cleaner, was there. Their involvement truly bothered me, especially since I had the intuition that something fishy went on, from Cybil Crabbe. He was accidentally there, that I gleaned from Dello and Maz. Picking him up was a spontaneous move. They had no idea of his gender, his identity, not even where he had come from. I watched Penny rocking herself and howling like a dingo, paralysed by dismay, while my mind played ball. If it was murder, he could not be the intended victim. I knelt down beside Penny and fiercely hugged. I turned her around and pushed her face into my neck and resumed the rocking with her.

Penny was calming down in my arms. She began to pull away. I grabbed her in a bear hug and said, 'Yes, I don't know what it feels like.' Information, perhaps would be a better comfort, so I said. 'He was picked up as a hitch-hiker and taken to a party near where he was found, where I found him. The interim toxicology report on both him and Hugh Gilmore show the existence of drugs in their blood on the night. But, as I said, a full police investigation is not finished, so all the paperwork, including forensics . . . Well, it's not conclusive.'

She sat back on her heels and wiped her eyes, pulled her lips together in a narrow line. 'Oh no, Neil promised me . . .' She silenced herself, shaking her head.

'It is possible they were administered without his knowledge.' I sounded very formal but Penny sighed with some kind of relief.

'How close are you to your cleaner?' I asked, as I looked at a large poster of the Marilyn Manson group on the wall of the teenager's room, and another of a magician in a cloak with a white face looking menacingly Gothic.

'Alison? I don't know her at all. She is rather distant and formal and I am intimidated by her movie star looks. I pay her in person sometimes and she leaves. I know nothing about her. Should I?'

I lifted the fax sheet I had found in the bundle and wiggled it.

'The date? Who is it from? It might have nothing to do with Neil. Someone tore it out. Must have been Alison.'

Attention Mrs Beeton. Confirm toad. Witches' brew!!! Ditto white sugar. Big mess. Megacrap!! The village is riddled with corruption. Conscience is corruption. Copy?

I put it in the folder with the other printed emails and the graphic.

'Looks like she was using your son's computer for her own fun.' I tried to sound light, appealing to possible generosity in my client. Meanness disappeared from her thin mouth to a sort of self-criticism. Penny got up with energy, dusted herself down and lit a cigarette.

'The situation is embarrassing, you see. I am basically a very shy person. I come from a working-class family where work is honoured. My mother's house was a new pin. Alison is a natural aristocrat, the way she walks, carries herself, her accent! for chrissake. I'm never sure that my taste is to her liking. When I have time I clean up before she comes. But when the two of us, Neil and I, were here, and there were his friends, the housework got on top of me. Neil.' Penny could not stop the tears now the floodgates had opened.

'Of course,' she sobbed, 'I was suspicious.' She gestured the neatness and breathed out. 'I can't stay here any more tonight, Margot.' She quickly went through the procedure with the mouse until the computer rested on its exit line and switched it off. She went to the power point and turned off that as well. She unplugged the modem and the fax, with an attitude of that's that then. I had missed my chance to examine the Favourites menu so I had to figure another way to access this gate to cyberspace. I noted quickly with a felt pen: did P.P. know of N.W.'s heart condition? Grill Alison!!!

We went back upstairs. She offered me food. Just as I was refusing I changed my mind because I felt if I didn't stay she wouldn't eat. She poured the wine with a little apology about its quality. I don't have a problem with quaffing wine when the fare is spag bol done the Australian way. She had prepared enough for two. We ate. Afterwards we sat on the lounges and talked about drugs. Teenagers. Video games, and skateboards. She talked about Neil for hours. Nigel got no mention, even when we covered Neil's young years when Nigel had said he did most of the child care. She kept opening wine. I wanted to bring up the subject of their play with make-up and dresses but I did not find the opportunity. She kept repeating that she wanted to protect him, that she had to stop herself smothering him, depending on him. It turns out he had far more time to himself than most teenagers are allowed. A responsible latch-key kid.

When I got to my car I prayed I would not meet a booze bus on my way home. I didn't. Having missed the last ferry, I had to go the long way. I stopped by the little white cross and the plastic flowers lit by my car headlights and knelt down to give my respects and feel the fresh night air on my hot cheeks. Fairly drunk, at the site of Hugh Gilmore's death, I cursed myself for my incompetence. I hadn't asked Philippoussis who was heading the reconstruction team. An average of $80,000 is spent per fatal accident to give a report to the coroner, and the deputy coroner can direct the cops to do more investigation. Why were these two lads' deaths being treated so lightly? Where was that stuff about the plant, the drug, on the computer, leading? How far can I trust Philippoussis or his freedom to act fully in the cause of justice?

37

. . . a vertical drop . . .

In the rainforest, Virginia hears. 'Cooee, VeeDub. Cooee.' It sounds like an opera singer's vocal exercises, using vowels.

Judith Sloane is sitting at her table when she enters her shelter. In front of her are an unopened bottle of tequila and two other bottles of something in a paper bag. As Judith is as tight as a miser's purse-strings, the surprise makes Virginia smile.

'Hello. What's this?' she asks.

'We're going to the party,' Judith says, all innocence.

Virginia suspects an ulterior motive, and she is feeling seedy. She makes excuses. 'There will be no moon tonight. My battery's had it.'

'I have a torch. The wake is still happening. We should be there. Both the Tibetan and the Egyptian books of the dead . . .'

Virginia interrupts, 'Spare me.'

Judith insinuates that she has been meditating and that being morbid is not what Maria would have wanted. 'She needs her pals to help on her journey on the other side.'

Judith's nonsense makes VeeDub feel weary. In the galaxy of her home, she is a black hole sucking in energy like matter. However, she is under her roof and in the White family civility to guests was a must. For all her faults Virginia's mother was unfailingly hospitable, gracious to all and sundry. Most of the day Virginia has been sitting in her chair reading, and snoozing, vulnerable to influence in that she hasn't been driven or busy, rather hungover.

'Tequila?' Virginia picks up the bottle and has a look at the Mexican in his hat.

'Well, with an old soak like you who's stubborn, I had to bring an enticement,' Judith admits disarmingly. 'Have a jar and a jaw with the gurls, what do you say?'

The prospect of drinking with Judith alone against having a hair of the dog in broader company, incidentally taking her negative vibe away from her place, sways Virginia to say, 'Okay.'

The late afternoon sun burnishes the blue-green leaves and the slice of moon higher in the western sky give a sense of silver and gold to the spectrum. Birds collect about their nests, bickering. While Virginia is amazed by the brazen disregard of their past antagonism in Judith's invitation, they share custodianship of land, of residence, of habitat. They are attached like vine and tree.

Judith says, 'You know, I don't approve of your sculpture. Word will get out. It always does with this place. It becomes a magic Shangri-la to women all over the world. When they hear that there's this thing to be discovered deep in the rainforest, in the wilderness, they'll make expeditions. You're putting out bells and whistles and beating your drum saying "Here we are!" "Look at us!"'

'It's my work. I'm driven to do it.' Virginia feels helpless.

'You are just drawing attention to us,' Judith says confidently.

Virginia does not know why Judith brought it up, except to make sure Virginia has no kudos for being an artist, no greater role than any of the other gurls. Snake vine, clinging and curling, is as much a part of the forest as orchid, or dead man's toilet paper, the gimpie gimpie. They walk through corkwood, lilly-pilly, ferns, lomandra, acacia, coachwood and bracken. They cross the plateau and the paddocks. Judith strides like an Englishwoman on the moors. Following single file, having relinquished her plans for an early night, Virginia tells herself, 'after all we're sisters'. The hour walk is pleasant. Virginia's headache goes. She trusts Judith exactly as far as she could throw her.

Em, Ci, Zee, Bea and Kay are at the ex-farm-house on the hill. Gig and her new girlfriend put purple crepe paper on the verandah posts. Serena, Venus, Cassie and various younger kids are running about with some of the dogs, screaming. Dello sits in an armchair dragged from a shelter for the occasion. Olga is making hot potato chips in a wok on the open fire. True to her word, Judith fixes Virginia a drink which she soaks up like a dry sponge. Then she gets her another. Virginia supposes she should suspect funny business, but doesn't care. She is one of the gurls, she belongs.

Yvonne arrives, squats beside her and they chat. Yvonne is very knowledgeable. Virginia and she enjoy sparking off each other.

A mob from Stuart turns up with cartons of beer, nuts, take-away chicken, tubs of margarine and logs of white bread. Dello is given a huge box of chocolates, which she comments about to everyone but does not open. It is her birthday. Lanterns are set about the bush, large brown paper bags with sand in them set in black plastic plant pots, each with a candle to be lit when it gets dark. Dusk in the day, Autumn in the year, the B minor chord, the evensong of birds, company, a little alcohol in her system, Virginia feels harmonious wave-motions. But there's an irritating tic in her knee.

The stars begin to show as the blue deepens perceptibly. Emma and Helen have houses quite near in dry sclerophyll scrub with clay earth and black wattles and white cedars and tussock grasses. The number of children increases. Yvonne is replaced by Alison, in leopard skin, at Virginia's side.

They talk about the Internet. 'This woman believes in women violently overthrowing the present ruling class, transnational capitalism, and taking over the means of production?' Virginia asks, half-jokingly, as Alison recounts Chandra's concerns and clumsy questions of yesterday.

'She's not the only one.' Alison continues, 'Gargantuan accumulations of wealth in the hands of a few men at the expense of everyone else, mass propaganda pacifying whole populations with misogynist stupidities. It's out of control. Immoral, but what can we do?'

'Demonstrations against globalisation are starting to happen on the streets,' Virginia comments, idly. 'Synchronised by the Internet.'

'It is possible,' says Alison, 'to wage electronic guerilla warfare.'

'Revolution,' states Virginia, 'I believe in. Uncompromising hatred, no.'

'Anyway, Chandra kept asking, who is Mop?'

'That an Internet handle?' Virginia watches Alison nod. 'Well, I wish her revolution all the best, but I think it is unrealistic.'

'Do you now?' Alison grips Tilly by the hand saying, 'Come on, sweetie.'

Em and several women say, 'Say goodnight', and take the kids to the visitors' hut to bunk them down. Dogs find safe places to circle, soften and slumber. Beer in the baby's bathtub full of ice succeeds tequila as Virginia's drink. She does not want to eat. Premonitions disquiet her. The mood is quite different from similar parties of old, where there might have been drugs but there was music and wholefood cooked in cast iron on the fire. The mellow togetherness has been replaced by a cynicism, a toughness. The wake, now over twenty-four hours, is getting out of hand. Aggression.

A bunch of gurls start whooping, yelling and cracking whips. 'Go get her.' Dello is lighting a joint when they grab her. Roughly. They tie her up with leather straps. They carry her to a nearby tree and hang her from a branch by her feet and ankles and then start whipping, singing a profane version of 'Happy Birthday'. They give her the number of her years in lashes.

Virginia is horrified. 'This really is obscene.' Judith is beside her, disparaging the sadomasochistic tendencies among young lesbians, but her final words let them off. 'They needed to shock someone.'

'But you don't have any excuse!' Virginia is angry.

'It's a generational thing.' The measured cadence in her ear, cheeky Ci with her sharp, dark features catches her eye, Judith and Ci seem to be a team.

'It's abuse!' Virginia is affronted. 'You know where we've come from, Judith. You can't turn your back on your own rage.'

'They want to be like gay boys,' Ci teases. 'Everyone has a bum-hole. No one has a cunt any more.'

Maz is dragged into the darkness to be a part of the act. There are squeals and someone rushes back to grab a lit candle from a lantern on the ground. They seem frenzied. Bea and Ti are quietly heating up a teaspoon over a burning branch from the fire, noticing but not caring.

Virginia turns to Judith and says, 'I have to go. I am not a part of this. This is rape!'

Ci goads, 'Cool it, Beetle. Maz is enjoying it.'

'Well, I'm not going yet, and you're not taking my torch. Here, have the rest of the tequila.' Judith hands her the bottle which she grabs by the neck and skols. Every fibre of her being is revolted by what was happening with and to other women. The alcohol makes her nerve ends stand up, she wants to throw up.

The sadomasochists come back into the circle somewhat subdued. Dello, while grimacing with pain, expresses gratitude, 'Well, thanks gurls. I can't say it was a pleasure, but so far as pain goes, it beats self-mutilation with razor blades.'

Virginia stands up and asks, 'Has Separatism created space for women to do this to each other?'

No one answers her. They have shocked the old gurls. 'Party on, people.'

There is no dancing. The festivity is about getting out of it. Virginia lays her spine along the ground, bends her knees and rests her eyes in the stars. She drags her mind into play like a life-belt by thinking, trying to recall the analysis of Ti-Grace Atkinson which she read way back in the early 1970s. It was about the human dilemma: rationally our imagination requires freedom but there is always the limitation of the body; there is a shortfall between possibility and actuality. Ti-Grace, Virginia thinks, argued that man resolves 'his divine predicament' by cannibalising the consciousness of women, through the will to power. The female counterpart, should she be in control of resolving her own human predicament, is self-annihilation. Feminism has never wanted equality with men because that is appropriating the hierarchical and exploitative pattern. Men are not the only bearers of the social relations of male supremacy. Those into power are any subjectivities that are domineering and contemptuous. Separatism is about women making conditions for themselves that withdraw their female energies from the regimes of male supremacy, as much as they are able. If you include sex, and you don't have to because we can never achieve whole separatism and anyway it is not an aim in itself, it stands to reason, separatists are lesbian. But erotic domination, indulging in pain and inflicting it, is heterosexual in its worst meaning and value.

Virginia rises, her mental rigour sobering her a little. If she asked, someone would probably admit openly to wanting masculine power, or, if a bottom in the S and M duality, to wanting subjugation. Several of these gurls, ironically, are members of proud dykes calling themselves, The Neverhets.

The justification of coming to power does not rationalise this behaviour for her. It is past now. Dello holds court from her armchair and the noddy effect of heroin blanks out expressions on faces around her. Talk ambles on. There is no reflection in it, no motivation, no cause and effect, and few feelings enter the story of it. It will be a footnote while the plot becomes a secret. 'Keep it a secret, keep it alive.'

Virginia fetches a drink from the baby bath and returns to the shadows. Judith is asleep. Judith finds sleep easy. Virginia does not, even though her conscience is clear. Certainly not in this unsafe space.

Maz whispers to Dello and takes her seat. The women are lounging, sitting, squatting, smoking either tobacco or marijuana. Or both. Alison walks back into the circle.

Maz says, 'It reminds me, Ali. Remember? Suddenly we have to deal with death. It's with us all the time, but it's sudden.'

'Really sad,' says Dello. 'Two deaths in one month.'

'Maria and the poor kid,' Maz metaphorically takes the speaking stick.

Virginia lets her mind wander, trying to retrieve some comfort from her love of Cybil. She is too vibrant to daydream in company. She joins the conversation, forces her uncompromising position on them, talks about the things she wants to.

'Co-dependency, like co-counselling, like the ideals of androgyny, makes my lips curl.'

'Don't criticise Maria, now!' pleads Alison.

'But I cried my eyes out,' pleads VeeDub. 'I felt the loss so deeply. She was one of us, one of my belonging. My grief surprised me, I felt I didn't know her well enough. I didn't even know who she was sleeping with.'

Ci, still impudent, says, 'Go on, Beetle you do want to know. Tell her.'

'I was her lover,' Alison addresses Virginia fiercely.

Virginia is floored.

'But she put her primary energies into Sofia,' Maz expands.

'No. Why? She's not interested in who did this, who did that, are you,

VeeDub? You want to know why?'

'Oh, gimme a break.'

'Anyway, Ali didn't kill her.'

'Are you saying someone murdered her?'

The company shrugs. Someone mumbles, 'Maybe.'

Music becomes louder, suddenly. Acid house.

Two strong torches swing around the gurls like searchlights. They focus their lights on the users.

A constrained and vicious voice, 'Where's my packet of Drum? You smoked it didn't you? Now I get the dregs of Winfield Blue. I don't even like it. You bludge and bludge and you say you're going to pay us back, but it's always next cheque.'

'Oh, chill out.'

'Get over it.'

Jay is very angry. 'I think the Drum was the straw that broke the camel's back.'

'Ha ha.'

'Don't ridicule me. You've always got money for your junk but you've never got any to pay your debts.' It is said so loudly, Judith wakes up.

Yawning and stretching, she joins in, 'What about the rates?'

'So, it costs.'

'Fuck you, it costs! It costs you nothing. Because you scam here, you steal there and you borrow from women who are too kind to say no and probably don't have as much money as you do anyway, without any intention of paying it back.'

'We got our reasons, didn't have nice comfortable middle-class child-hoods like you, no sweet elocution lessons.'

Jay steps across and smashes Ti across the face with her torch.

Dello screams, 'Take your shit out of here.'

The thrashing goes on, Ti fights back. The aggressors fuelled by righteous anger and the victims taking the blows with sarcasm, screeches and curses rip through the night. Owls move from their perches and possums escape up the tree trunks. Maz pushes the fight out of the circle, but the four of them continue tormenting each other with maledictions and expletive-coloured character assassination as they go away down into the valley. Virginia feels an increase in her heart rate. She has no defences against what was coming into her, no valve system in her social epidermis to stop absorption of the behaviour of women to women. Heat builds up in her cheeks.

Sudden quiet. The mood mellows. Aftermath comments are dismissive.

Virginia gets herself more to drink. The darkness of the night has her jailed here, but even so she wonders why she stays. She sits on the arm of the armchair and asks, quietly, 'What happened that Friday night, Dello? A young girl died, right? Who was she?'

'It turns out it was a boy in drag!'

Judith crouches, arms around her knees listening.

Virginia asks her, 'When can we go?'

Judith doesn't move, hugging her calves as if she's cold, 'I want to hear this.'

Virginia says, 'You have great night vision, can I take your torch?'

'We'll go in a minute.'

'But the funny thing,' Dello continues, 'The really funny thing, is, Cybil took her/him onto the beach, we assumed, for carnal gratification. She wouldn't have known he was a guy until well into it.'

'Cybil?'

'Yes, Beetle, Cybil.'

Judith, in eliciting every detail she can, says, 'I was on the beach.'

'Well, what did you see?' Alison asks.

'Nothing.'

A thousand arrows pierce Virginia's heart. Although nearly all the candles have burnt away and the glow of embers throw red light onto a few close to the fireplace, she is conscious of blushing. Hot blood hits her face like lava from the erupting volcano inside.

'I love Cybil!' she explodes to shut their gossip up. 'On top of the vicarious whipping, the violence over money, the insult to my notion of community, the abuse to my sense of being a part of a lesbian collective, the disgust at being connected to such unwholesome self-wastage as is smack, I feel betrayal right in the middle of my guts. I know Cybil is perverse,' Virginia mutters ashamed. The red blood of rage starts pumping up her body. She breaks into immediate, all-over sweat. Her teeth clench, her hands fist, knees lock.

'It's true.'

Judith gets to her feet, mollified. Virginia would have become paralysed if Judith hadn't suggested they go home. The two follow the torchlight, showing rocks, tussocks and sticks like a piece of film, away from the scene of the gathering in silence. Virginia stumbles into Judith's heels. She is panting.

'I thought you were the Amazon,' Judith says, sarcastically. 'The great triathlete! You're drunk!'

The mockery spins her into tempest, she savagely pushes her back. Judith falls forward onto her torch. It goes out. In total darkness Judith hits Virginia. They punch each other and fall into an inarticulate wrestle, a savage fight, years overdue.

Virginia's body is as impervious to pain as the heroin girls', and Judith's abiding jealousy has her pulling her hair and head-butting her forehead and squeezing as many bruises into her arms as she shakes her. Virginia kicks and punches. Judith throws her backward, hissing through her teeth. Virginia in trying to regain her balance falls down a steep but short incline. She lies in a bowl of dead leaves. Judith goes. Judith can find her way better than any other woman on the lands at night. She has cat's eyes.

When Virginia finally feels the pains and aches, she begins to cry. She curls herself into a ball, bawling. She is not frightened even though she doesn't know where she is and it is possible in this country to lose yourself for days. The canopy blacks out the stars. Soreness alone is not the reason for her tears. The anger not entirely spent on Judith comes back with a vengeance when she comprehends Cybil's betrayal. Tears turn into a torrent. Irrationally, she wants to kill the alluring, transvestite boy who is already dead. The ferocity in the outer circle of her sisters on the land and then between Judith and her has invaded her body with cuts and bruises as her heart and mind tear each other to fragments. She feels her self-worth torn to pieces. She cannot anaethsetise herself against the pain of sexual betrayal. Fifty years on earth trying to reconcile the wild mind-soul with the unco-operative flesh to be in the present, she had become whole, for Cybil! And now through gossip she is flattened by the sword of her lust. Dismembered by the visualisation of the sensual Cybil casting her liquid eyes upon the young butch in a dress, enticing her away from the crowd, Virginia visualises her spinning her sexual magic, stroking with chubby hands, cunningly undoing her costume, seeking her private parts, finding a penis there, probably erect, and keeping on going.

Eventually Virginia begins walking. There is water beneath reeds. Swamp, a billabong she does not recognise. A night in the forest, scented darkness, she climbs. She turns around. And around. Dizzying herself, spiralling down, moving until she is exhausted and covered in fine threads of sticky cobwebs. Spiders crawling on her scratches and abrasions, she falls over on dry earth, begins to slip, and to lose grip. Virginia tumbles and knocks herself out. There is a vertical drop. A mine shaft. Or the burnt-out root-system of a huge tree. When she comes to, she is in a cave.

Book Six

transsexualism

Thursday Friday Saturday Sunday

Thursday's child has far to go

38

. . . the blood of the daughter . . .

In my dreams I fell like Alice through the looking glass, pursuing someone who kept disappearing around the next bend, being distracted by talking red herrings, mad hatters, benevolent dictators, despotic school-teachers and resplendent queens stripping to reveal cocks. Feeling that I had lost a vital connection, I got down to work as soon as was reasonable. Needed to arrange another trip to Lesbianlands. Interview a member of the Campbell family. Find Alison. Rory's number was engaged. Chandra did answer and I told her that I wanted to go out to Rory's. She asked could come with me. That was good. The weekend would suit her.

What was the nightmare telling me? I drummed my fingers by the telephone, thinking of people to call. Meghan's work number was answered by a male with an American accent responding cautiously and politely. Dr Featherstone's whereabouts were not known. 'I'll take that with a grain of salt,' I said. 'Excuse me?' he replied in the way Yanks have which means 'I beg your pardon'. 'Thanks a lot,' I rang off. I went back to her papers. The simple forgeries of her signature, money taken out of her accounts from different banks, at ATMs in different places on the same dates, not enough to make her notice in the short term, but she would eventually, by which time, I assumed, the embezzler would have got in her ear. Meghan's impostor jumped their gun a little so I became a fly in the ointment. From the evidence I had it worked out in total to be at least ten thousand dollars. But it could be more. A lot more, if she frequently received these sizy fees. I whizzed a conjecture through the calculator. There was enough of a clearly laid pattern for me to find an aggravating tip of the iceberg.

The accountant was hedgy. But she was probably that way with everyone. Rosemary Turner struck me as the type of person you needed to know the answers before you questioned.

More paperwork arrived in the mail. Whether it came from Meghan herself or the trickster who sent the first lot I had no idea. No covering note. In it was a photostat of a contract signed by Meghan and her witness, handwriting surprisingly similar, and for the Nadir Group of Companies, Seth

Friedan and Joshua Conrad. Meghan had given exclusive rights to her work to these people. She is called the proprietor and her work is defined as, amidst mystifying technical terms, laboratory and field analysis. In short, any discovery she made in her work for them as a forensic geologist was entirely theirs. In return, again couched in impenetrable jargon, she receives half-yearly lump sums to be paid into a merchant bank in Brisbane. I found out that Nadir Mining Explorations was a subsidiary of Falcon registered in Malta. I felt like Humphrey Bogart. I turned the manila envelope around in my hand. Same as the original, just as chaotic. I remembered the cap I picked up as ugly as hell and as common as muck with no glamour whatsoever. Evil is banal. But there are clues in the obvious and the coincidental. Nadir is a clue. I rang her lawyer. Ms Hardface informed me that Megs had changed her solicitor. She was now represented by Libby Gnash.

Nadir, the lowest point, beneath the observer, diametrically opposite the zenith. Hell as opposed to heaven. The pin-dense centre of the earth as opposed to the infinite surround of outer space. Dark as opposed to light. Mess as opposed to neatness. Confusion as opposed to clarity. Letting lateral logic apprehend the connections of where I had been and what I had seen, my mind ranged. A single locality, Meghan's place. I had been at the mid-point, the observation deck: Meghan and Jill at home sharing food, then mess, then neatness, both beyond the awareness of the couple. This bunch of stuff, I thus concluded, came from the raid. Definitely not from Meghan herself. I went through it again, and as the joint was left in disarray, a mad mess similar to the order of the these papers, I knew that whoever cleaned up was another person. Anyway Meghan was not in town at the time. Whoever it is was still forging her signature, therefore does not know of my arrangement with Meghan.

Apart from the contract there didn't seem to be anything else that was relevant: a lot of receipts for clothes, feed, household things, hardware, solar panels, incredibly expensive binoculars, dirty bits of paper, and a couple of snaps. Another one of the dodgy UFO, and a picture of the sisters, Meghan and Trina, about eighteen and seventeen years old sitting formally at a festive family table. The pupils of their eyes as red as rats' in the flash, both in white shirts of different design, Trina's frilly, Meghan's tailored, Trina's hair long, Meghan's short, both the same height, the same facial structure, and as skinny as each other. Trina has a cigarette. Meghan less slumped, but they are so alike they could be twins. The room behind them is very brown, bookcase, teak sideboard, a few Christmas cards and an understated silvery table decoration, and holly on a perfect pudding. Surprisingly unmessy for a Christmas snap, no children, no scrunched-up coloured wrapping, starched tablecloth. I got the feeling these girls were well-behaved in the strict formality of familial duty.

Nothing much was to be gained from staring at the photo. Except why was it sent to me? I searched through the junk for the handwriting that had flummoxed me. No match this time. Different forgers? I went back to the contract.

There was a vicious secrecy clause. Her witness was said to be Hope O'Lachlin. High on my hunches, I suspected that there was no witness, that Meghan, if it were indeed Meghan herself, had forged the witness signature. Hope O'Lachlin was a New Zealander whose birth certificate I had found. The gurl Virginia had introduced was too young and bald. Anyway her surname was Strange. Plainly this other Hope's name was being used. I flicked through the sheath of Dr Featherstone's papers with a impatient sense of annoyance and lethargy. The forged signature did not jump out at me as it had before. I rang my friend, the handwriting expert; she hadn't got around to it yet. I had cashed the cheque, but thought I kept a photocopy. Maybe I had put that scrap of paper in another pile, another file. I could not find it, therefore, it took on the proportions of being the key to the whole matter.

Classic: dissemblance, deceptions, disguises. Handwriting, voice on the telephone and, now I had a picture of Trina, impersonation was possible. Meghan Featherstone could, for whatever intents and purposes, be in two places at once. I should not forget the acting ability of Jill David, either. I was frustrated. Who was wearing hat? I wrote. Anything to do with M.F.'s work? Whereabouts does Judith fit?

The scribbles on the back of grubby receipts were meaningless out of the context of the time at which they were written. I thrust the untidy bundle of mismatched business back together and tied it into a labelled folder. Who has given this to me if not the woman herself? I cannot find out who is ripping Meghan off if I do not have the full picture, or, who wants me to think she's being ripped off? Someone must have all the information, or access to it. Knowing I had a clue and lost it made me talk this over and over to myself, ending up rationalising that any work I did on that job until further notice from the client would only thicken the plot and confound the mystery of where all this money had gone. Of course, Meghan could be involved in telephone banking, day-trading, paperless transactions which were, for me, like looking for substance where there was nothing but a hole. I picked the manila folder up and walked it to another place. I rang Libby Gnash and left a message on her machine.

Now Neil, the young white male, dead. White virgin? The pinched features of his mother, Penny Waughan, pleadingly needing answers, to appease her distress, for her intellectual comfort, to keep at bay the despair behind her eyes before it drove her to a kind of hopeless emptiness, at one with the sterile mansion. However, she is an energetic woman, one worth working for, whose son, her joy and pride, had been torn out of her life before a close adult friendship could begin. The basic pain of it was enough. I refuse to blame the mother for the son's deviance. He was a person in his own right; if he wanted to dress up in feminine garb it was his choice. Penny did not know about it. Did not endorse it, no matter what games they played together when he was younger.

Is there any relationship between the death of Hugh Gilmore and Neil? Too pure heroin on the market always brings a spate of overdoses, generally means the police have busted big-time, then skimmed and got rid of their cut on the streets within twenty-four hours. A multi-million dollar stash was found in the false bottom of a cruising yacht's dinghy. Why were you wearing women's clothes, boy? A party? Dress-ups? Was there a school function? Where had Neil been earlier that night?

The elders have left for the desert leaving the wealthy whites to take care of their own. Sofia is beginning to use language which shocks everyone. She has developed a hatred for the Negress who persists in hanging about with Mary Smith. She is recognising no rules of polite behaviour. She grabs women and holds their arms with a fearsome strength. 'Now she excited the girl. She dragged her arms, her hands, down her body and shook her forehead against her belly, then she put her tongue on the clitoris she was about to remove. She sucked with infinite tenderness because the erect clitoris was easier to hold and slice. With a power only known to women, a psychic ability to axe sensibility and get on with the job, with the sharpened stone. Irrationally, finally dissociated from herself, she jokes with the women, sometimes in men's hearing, about slicing off his member. But it's hollow laughter covering the trauma and tragedy each woman, everywhere, experienced at the very same age, crying, screaming and bleeding. The statuesque nanny who was like a highly paid model in her beauty and commanding appearance walked away onto the savannah with bloody hands.'

Sofia swans around the garden. 'With bloody hands,' she repeats as she pushes the sane women away. 'Stop watching me like screws.' They cannot pin her down, but they keep their eyes on her.

'Should we section her?' they say, keeping their voices low. Mary Smith has to go back to the city to work. Worried women whisper to each other, even so Sofia does hear them, for they, like she is, are saying the same sort of thing over and over. She turns mean. She is cunning. Although they galvanised into the busy activity of finding all blades, she has hidden a knife in her knickers and secateurs up her sleeve.

Suddenly she is competent. Compliant. Their relief is palpable. They boil water for tea in a saucepan.

'I'm just going to the toilet.' She knows they have been watching her. Like hawks.

'I am just going to throw up and piss, vultures. Vipers,' she hisses.

'Uh ho,' Mary is immediately on the ball. But too late. Sofia has locked herself in.

She calls, 'Sof, are you okay? Come out. Are you finished? I need the loo, now. I'm busting.'

All present know she has gone too far when she sings out, 'What can white women do with ties of blood? Slice the tie. And bleed from their fucking bleeding hearts.'

They put their shoulders to the door and burst the latch. Sofia is beyond dramatic effect, and quite into the sensations of self-harm, talking to the blood, getting it everywhere. Especially on her hands. She wants to pat their faces, baptise them in her blood.

'You know nothing, my children. Nothing. I bless your ignorance. In the name of the mother, and the nanny, this is the blood of the daughter, taste it, my sisters. Drink my blood and ye shall be saved.'

'Let's get her into Accident & Emergency,' says Africa. They grab her limbs, manhandle her into a car and take her to the hospital, where she is a bloody and raving lunatic and the medical profession deals with her straight away.

Sofia is locked up in a ward with bars on the windows, and force-fed drugs which make her dribble and shake.

Efficient women clean and seal the house and arrange with locals to have the lawn mowed and the mail collected. They fill their cars with petrol and take the roads north, south and west out of the town of Stuart.

Libby Gnash responded to my message with aggressive curiosity. It was ironic. She did not trust me, but, for all her pugnaciousness, on a gut level, I trusted her. I appealed to her stronger suit. The Fight Against Injustice. Would she help me in the Featherstone affair? There was nothing fair about this contract. I made an appointment for later on in the afternoon.

No sooner had I put the phone down then it belled. I picked up within seconds to be, again, greeted with the cutting off of the other end as I said 'hello'. The third time it happened in the past few hours. Images of Meghan's ransacked joint came to mind. My house could easily be burgled. If Meghan was away, who cleaned it up? What happened to the goats? As if I were psychic, I knew I had to do with the reason. I was not being paranoid. I was the object of the game. Instinctively, intuitively, I felt something or someone was out to get me; yet I didn't know what it was about. It could have been any of my three cases; it could have been personal; it could have to do with the past; it could have to do with the future. I felt a sensation of frustration, of fear. Certainly there was too much on my plate. I was afraid I was not competent to deal with it. In that instance, what had I forgotten? What have I overlooked? I have been meticulous. It was more than being overwhelmed by jobs. It was outside me, outside of control, somehow entering my nervous system. Awareness of high jinks in the huge continent of my ignorance made me search my home, restlessly looking for the clue, for the thing I had lost, or forgotten. I picked up the bottle of nux vomica I had not given Philippoussis. Of course, I couldn't trust him: what was I thinking? No way would they not do an autopsy on Maria's body. The circumstances of her death required it. By law. Yet they had released it for burial as if that were no big deal. Poisoning by cane-toad is so bizarre it would make the papers.

In the spirit of dealing with things, I rang Sofia's number. Mary Smith told me that Sofia had suffered a psychotic episode and had been taken to hospital and was in the care of Mental Health. The house had been totally cleaned and furniture put in storage. It really wasn't my business. Everything was under control. Without Maria, herself, calling on my assistance, I admitted that was right. The feeling about Maria, or even about Sofia's welfare, was in essence different from that which was troubling me. It was melancholy, not embattled.

If Meghan's place was raided, was her stuff at my place threatened? My security leaves a lot to be desired. I didn't want to jump to any conclusions. Forget it, I told myself. It might never happen. I wondered if I could keep the Featherstone file away from other things in my neat dwelling, make sure the possible home-invaders go for it and not destroy my things wantonly. Get paranoid, and you can't move. But I felt apprehensive. Something was out there, actively trying to upset me. And succeeding. As I was hiding it in the laundry behind the detergents and odds and ends in that cupboard, I looked at the stupid snaps of suspected UFOs. Although fakes as I had first thought, their existence fed my present dread. Fraudulent or not, what was I to make of them? Did someone want to send me mad? Believing in Martians invading the planet was not in my scheme of things. Yet, logically, I can accept the concept that humans are not the only conscious, mentally impartial, abstract thinking beings in the universe. It was the data that was ridiculous. These snaps were proof, rather, of another woman playing with my head: why? Folding the contract into my spiral notebook and putting that in my satchel, I covered the rest with a rag and put a packet of Surf and a bottle of cloudy ammonia on top. Whether I was being silly or wise didn't matter.

At the barbecue were—I picked up the biro—Maria, Sofia, Alison, Jill David, Alison's son, Maz and Dello, Spider-coalition dykes and poofters.

Someone driving a nice car. Rosemary Turner? Someone wearing a mining company hat. (Why did I suddenly imagine mining on Lesbianlands? Explosions.) Cybil Crabbe. The Larrikin was there, but left? Someone dealing, or distributing drugs. Tiger Cat big-noting herself. Judith Sloane on the beach. There were another couple of kids playing behind the group. I wondered if Margaret Hall knew anything. I rang Margaret and discovered she has moved to Sydney. I had to interview each one. For Alison I had Chandra's and Penny's numbers. As soon as I thought of Chandra the whole arrangement of my nervous system altered to a kind of pleasurable terror alert. Was this 'psychic' fear I felt no more than as yet unexpressed sexual needs? Pleasant anticipation of emotional engagement was closer to the tenseness, but not it exactly.

No excuse to ring Chandra now. And anyway, I felt it would distract me from the quest of the moment. I doodled a map of the picnic site, the sandhills, the beach, the road, the car park, the convenience shelter. Sketched cars in, from my shaky memory. Drew donuts in the square beyond the caravan park, wiggled a line for the beach, initialled in places where characters were. J.S. opposite the beach path to the picnic facilities. Interesting. Where was young Lenny? A chat with him alone would not hurt. 'Find Alison,' I read my own note. As I did I recalled she had been beaten, battered like a wife, and Tilly had old bruises. Was this what I had forgotten? Well, I had and Alison was important in relation to the material on Neil's computer as well.

Whatever, when I got up from my desk, I still felt nervous, incompetent, vulnerable. Above all, frustrated, half-way through a jigsaw puzzle with plenty of loose pieces, none of which seem to fit anywhere, too garish and diverse to make sense. Feeling I should be doing something else . . .

39

. . . kidnapped . . .

Virginia White finds herself in a void. She has fallen into the labyrinth during her night of the soul. She passes in and out of consciousness, spinning within a moment of time, suspended in the vertical ever-is of emotional intensity, images following one upon the other with such a fluid alacrity they are as contradictory as surreal paintings. Not words, nor memory, could capture them, let alone sculpture. She lies unmoving, with the moist rocky floor of the tunnel embossing her flesh, for so long speedy little spiders construct traps for other insects in the hair of her head. When her eyes open they see absolute blackness. Yet the brain is bright with the yellow sandy beaches of her childhood, the blistering burn on the soles of her feet, first she is tiny, then enormous. The tremendous clashes of colours in her husband's ties and shirts, his Melanesian skin, his swaggers of bold arrogance, his thoughtless expressions of violence and remorse segue into the covert schemes of others to make her unimportant.

Then, the need for survival jerks her into awareness. Alien slime covers her features, drips off proud skin. She is intolerably itchy. She has to find water to wash. She sinks into half-sleep again. A finer pain puts the physical irritation into perspective, oh god! Her distant self knows the goddess is unimpressed by filth and pain. She is incensed, enraged on behalf of the planet. The dead feeling of depression threatens to suck the life out of her being except for the ache of hunger and thirst. The rocks' jagged edges jade her nerves.

Time forgotten, she concentrates on her belly and throat. She relaxes for a second, probing the industry of the spiders about her forehead. Her rage goes. With eyes open seeing nothing, feeling about with her hands, she moves. She derives subtle comfort from the roots of a tree; the living thing having a closer than rocks', though not the same, relation to time as she. By habit she worries about what she should be doing, but none seems important. Money has no reality. The lover, depraved woman, hurts her more than any enemy could. Or deprivation. She carries that pain in her bosom even in the present predicament.

Vigour returns. She scrapes up a handful of the mud near her buttock, rubs it onto her abrasions and epidermal soreness. The relief is the absence of the tickling itches and stings. The mud begins to cake. She searches for more. Her body heat dries out the clay. Her attention catches on the intent to be motionless, to be unnaturally still like a woman her own age in a beauty salon somewhere with mud-cake on her face. She shares this crazy quietude with any number of women all around the world. She hears water. She must be disoriented, the sound contradicts her sense of direction. The trickle seems deeper in the labyrinth. However, she crawls towards it. The cave branches after she rounds the tree root she had been leaning on. Here she stops, on all fours to sniff and listen, proceed according to the information of those senses. Further down is another fork and a narrowing of the width. She must choose between what she could fit in and that closer to water. They seem man-made. She chooses water, but not in the open air. She, on her tummy flat as a lizard, is lying in a pond. Not clean, she is wet. She has to squeeze herself backwards. A cold shiver of panic turns into a hot flush as she gets stuck. Her rump strikes alarming resistance. Anxiety returns, this time heading for screaming, laughing hysteria. She must not give in, because sustained panic is a stupidity you can never live down because it is the self betraying the self and the consequences are quite long-term and exactly the same as those of any act of stupidity. Stupidity is too much of a self-indulgence. There will be no rescue anyway. She could be working silently in the rainforest on her ark or she could have gone further into the jungle where none of the others ventures. While she considers the impossibility of rescue she is deep-breathing and counting out the air. Colours start to occupy half her brain, the right frontal lobe suffused in violet, then slowly indigo to pale blue and lime green, yellow, one after the other the hues of the spectrum invade her consciousness. She hypnotises herself into sleep, or a hypersentient relaxation. Her spirit travels.

When she wakes, cold, shivering and swearing. She wriggles back to the pond to drink. Using a crocodile roll, she manages to face in the direction out. No panic this time, just cool, calculated survival and measured writhing. Beyond the tree root, there are several cavities, two of which show a faint glow of daylight. She stays a moment with the tree and surveys where she had gone mentally in the last few hours, coming up with a conclusion so banal she is almost disgusted with herself. Apparently, her relationship excludes friendship and work. Her work, the ship the world will never see depicting women trying to survive and express themselves, was thoroughly and contemptibly put down by her lover as a useless, pointless wank. Yet. The sculptured boat is her survival, even though only very recently a dead tree; bursting with life-size figures the barque her sense of freedom, transmogrifying into the women of her generation. That this needed to be done is indisputable. Not bought. Not sold. Extant. Standing. Driven inside, her lifting of her talents above the commercial gunk of the fashion, the fortune, the fame are hellishly difficult. Art is the shattering of the mirror we look at ourselves through. Friends neglected, torn to pieces for their inadequacies, their sacrifices, the ways they survive. Maria, forgone, for lust of Cybil. Not only neglected, criticised, judged. While she was criticising the women, the dykes, the feminists she knew, she was trying to find something. Her lover's horrid betrayal shows Cybil to be devoid of Virginia's projection upon her of finer motivations. Nevertheless the hook is in her gills, she struggles on the line. Cybil's hatred allowed Virginia to perceive things that by herself she might not have seen. Cybil annihilates her and Judith had to cop it.

Pushing at the walls, thrusting and dragging to lift herself against gravity, she emerges from the cave through the vertical air-hole of the mine into a tangle of bush, disturbed by recent blasting, fenced with hessian bags on sticks. She crashes her way through the prickly hedge, until she finds the creek. She follows its flow to a little waterfall and lowers her sore body into the rippling water where it is deep enough to wash herself in. Deeper than she needs, she floats on her back in a possible swimming spot with big boulders. An azure kingfisher watches from a branch. She looks up at the sky.

She takes off her clothes, gives them a rinse and hangs them on the vines and lets the water bubble over her body like a spa. She joins the Wampoo Fruit Dove in cooing. Feels silly, relieved, and terribly alone.

'Gotta go, gotta job. Got to be down past Footscray at five,' Ian Truckman tells his mother as he latches his mobile into his waistband.

He takes a piece of the kid's jigsaw for luck, to hang it off the rear-view mirror to ward off the aliens. It's a bit of blue sky with two hooks and two eyes and a speck of green tree.

At the warehouse, they release the trailer off its stilts and connect up the Freightliner. Michael is not on this trip. Once on the Hume Highway heading north, he mumbles his monologue. 'Strange seeing he kept track of me on the way down. I don't know, it drives heavy, this load. Haven't got a good feeling. Made me mum happy with some money, or at least it should have. She just wants to see my kids, asked whether I sent the ex any of it and what was her address so she could. Never got any answers to her Christmas card. Well what do you expect?'

He does not know what he is dragging back there. He wishes he did, because it would be safer. When he stops at Glenrowan Ian Truckman goes through his glove box for something to take with his coffee. 'Ned Kelly everywhere. Try some contact through the CB but nothing to say, not interested. Static interference. Take it easy, Ian. She'll be right, mate.'

When Virginia reaches up to retrieve her clothes from the overhanging branch, she is face to face with the barrel of a rifle. A man on horseback. He says, 'Wrong one.'

'Wrong what?' Virginia is not aware that her face, but not her naked body, shows her age.

'The wrong maiden in distress,' he removes his firearm from her face.

The stock saddle has a long stockwhip curled on the front pummel and the rifle is placed in a pouch where saddle-bags would be. The horse, standing in the water, extends his neck down to drink.

'Put those on and get up here,' the neighbour indicates the back of the saddle. Virginia is relieved more than anything. She puts on her wet clothes, uses the vacated stirrup and swings her leg over. She says, 'Thanks, Willy.'

'When did you discover the mine?' he asks savagely. 'How long have you known?'

'What do you mean?' Virginia retorts.

'I mean the gems,' spits Willy Campbell who, although tall on a horse, is a little man with a little brain. 'Did you find anything? What do you know?'

The witless questioning gives her time. Behind the tack on the warm flesh of the horse, she acts tough. Persephone, Artemis, Virginia.

The answer is forever. But she replies, 'Should I tell you? Would I tell you? I don't think so.' She feels light emerging from hell. Her knee throbs, her hip aches. She has bruised some bones. Something hard in her shorts digs into her seat. A cheap paper cutter is in one of her pockets with tiny blades and a penlike catch to attach it to the end of a sketchbook. She uses it for fine detail, like eye-sockets and creases beneath a cheek, around a mouth.

Suddenly she has to grab his waist as the horse climbs.

'Why are we going uphill?' she asks idiotically. 'I mean up so steep a hill.'

The sun is chased by the slim moon in the west. In the mountains after sunset, it is still light. They are going through the scrub, up a steep ridge. There are grass trees and large rocks, tufts of bladey grass. In her dreams all this vegetation was blue, bluish. White and black. They reach the top of the Widow's Peak. Then they descend into dusk. He urges his mount further. The path goes into a stand of thorns. He hangs down over his horse's neck. Virginia is smacked in the face by prickly, flinging canes, scratches upon scratches. Panic is an inch away. She lies back along the horse's rump, going downhill. Prone, looking at everything upside down. She has never been on this part yet it looks familiar and feels familiar. Here Lesbianlands borders

National Park, deep into the Great Divide. The sassafras is in full flower. A barbed wire fence. He orders Virginia off to undo the Queensland gate.

'I hate those things, they spring open and hurt,' she says. But she does what he says.

He waits, cynically watching, and then nudges his horse through. 'You're the wrong one,' he says again. 'You all look the same to me.'

'Which one did you want?' She carefully untangles the wires and, placing the stick in the loop at the bottom of the fence post, pushes with all her waning strength to latch the top to the post and restore the appearance of a continuous fence.

'About half your age. You're an old boiler. Scrawny and tough as a game turkey, I'd reckon. Get back on. You know what we call this place?' Virginia decides to ride side-saddle, hooking her second leg over the rifle pouch.

'No.'

'No Man's Land,' he sneers.

'Yeah, that's right,' Virginia says.

'No, I mean No Man's Land like in the war, like desert, like where you get shot at, where nothing can grow, where you get out of as soon as you can,' he explained seriously. 'Just sour ground.'

They come up to a cyclone fence behind which are earth-moving vehicles. 'Get off,' he commands.

Virginia complies, landing on a stone nearly spraining an ankle. He dismounts to tie the filthy rag from around his neck into a blindfold around her eyes. The horse crunches on gravel. Virginia is kidnapped.

40

. . . get away with murder . . .

Silverberg Planetary Defence Systems answered when we called Nadir Mining Explorations from Libby's office. Lola wasn't there. Taken aback, but quick, Libby asked for Josh Conrad in chummy manner. 'No one by that name.'

Looking at me and tapping the pages of the contract, Libby Gnash said, 'I really don't like this patent clause.'

'Come?' I wanted her to explain it to me very clearly. 'What about this Falcon set-up, in Malta?'

Little Libby grimaced, her eyes fiery with intelligence. 'Well, it suggests there is an umbrella organisation. What's the product, a mineral? drugs? The secrecy clause is a worry.'

'Why did you say "drugs"?' I was curious, because, even as an example, they had not occurred to me.

'Just something I read recently.' She tossed off the remark, throwing a gesture at the reading matter which surrounded her, without lifting her head. Law books, files, piles of briefs secured with pink tape, newspapers, torn-edged articles, statutes, acts, note-paper pads; something to read on every available surface, including the floor. The copier was buried. The opened drawers of the filing cabinet provided more horizontal space for flat folders. A colourfully busy screen of a computer suggested access to all there was to know via the World Wide Web. An office more in contrast to Rosemary Turner's I could not imagine, although they shared ingress through the same arcade. Posters on the wall were of old campaigns: 'say no no excuses'; and most were crooked. Several frames still leaned near the door, awaiting hanging. The picture I could see depicted a female of the Chinese red army nobly rounding up white leghorns on emerald and lime grass.

'What?' I demanded, thinking she would say something vague. Instead, she responded with exact names, such as erythropoietin, human growth hormones, perfluorocarbons and blood expanders now being traded along with narcotics, but not attracting police interest, beyond customs officers and sports administrators, and both the hard and the performance-enhancing drugs were big business, with the cover of real corporations, listed on foreign stock exchanges, registered somewhere else and financed with money laundered in the dirty gambling industry.

'That's why, the actual product, if there is one, is worth knowing. So,' she concluded, 'any dodgy company with no real officers, no people by the name of those who sign their contracts, is up to no good. I mentioned erythropoeitin, merely because it occurred to me and you're a triathlete. Globalised monopolisation of the freedom to do what you damn well like. George Orwell got it so wrong. Except for doping the workers with soma.'

Big Brother notwithstanding, it occurred to me that Libby already had this and other legal matters of Dr Featherstone's business under the wraps of her professional client confidentiality. I brought her back to the material of the legalised, apparent injustice on her desk in front of us. The personal nature of the previous case which saw us on opposite sides was in the past, water under the bridge; she answered my queries straight up. With some. No one trusts lawyers, but this contract, which she had not seen before, unified Libby and me against a common enemy. Bad people. Perhaps Maria's death brought us together a bit, enabled me to tell her about the Neil investigation, and my finding the Nadir cap in the toilet block.

'Private gyms,' she said, 'are main distribution points of illegal performance-enhancing drugs, some of which are legal in other countries.'

I explained who Sean was to me, without going into Tiger Cat's activities as I wouldn't have been surprised to learn that Lola Pointless and she were friends. 'He's a poofter and a man I trust.'

Libby accepted my recommendation of his character without argument. 'The homophobic witch-hunts in the press of rich libertarian paedophiles have grown way out of proportion,' she opined. 'A young man just says he was molested and he can get away with murder, pretty well. All he has to do is cry and act like a girl. Put his violence, his drug habit, his useless life down to what the old homosexual did. It is all believed. They put the guy in jail to taste rough justice and it's okay. The hatred is rampant. If indignation against molestation of girls were as righteous, what a safer society we would have! Instead such people as the New Right sanction violence as they quote the Bible and go around the country calling for a return of the death penalty!' She got off the high horse of her politics to ask, 'Is your trainer a conduit for illegal substances? Maybe he isn't, but his gym might be a place of exchange.'

Libby Gnash, a dynamo, was a glutton for information. Sean's hands have pummelled me, his society has amused me, psychologically he has been there for me before and after races, my trials of physical and mental endurance. I felt he was neither a paedophile nor a steroid pusher, but the fact that he has been acting strange lately, the presence of Tiger Cat and the opinions I had just heard were making him look fishy.

'Well, I'll get back to you, and Libby,' I said on parting. 'Thanks.'

When I entered the gym, it was eerily quiet, for the time of day. Late afternoon. I felt a bit like a mouse who has wandered out of her hole to find the kitchen deserted, folks left on holidays, leaving only the cat. She had changed her hair colour, and was heavily made up but I recognised her in the mirror, as I draped my towel over the equipment.

'You all right?' I asked Tiger Cat, warming up on the bicycle.

She didn't answer me. No one else came in. I shortened my routine. Why was Tiger Cat punishing her bruised body? She couldn't be feeling well. She had to be on something. When I went to wash my face, she was there in the doorway of the locker room, slits of yellow eyes gleaming. I ignored her. Whatever she was on, I felt I could handle her.

The vibe of deliberate violence. I looked up at the sky-light. What is it about ablutions areas? In a public toilet once a group of young black women felt like teaching me, a white cunt, a lesson. They threw a few punches, got damaged themselves. Tiger Cat moved, leaned her back against the door jamb and lifted a leg across to the other. Trying to buy some time, I buried my head in my towel. She said something about my body. I figured I could be imagining it. Sometimes the threat of injury can be sexual, especially with the likes of Tiger Cat, who I knew was into power that way. Whether she was butch or femme, bisexual or what, sex plainly motivated her. When I looked up she wasn't there.

'Sean's in the ballet room,' I heard. 'Sorry, aerobics,' she called sarcastically.

We shared a contempt for aerobics, maybe the only thing we really had in common.

I yelled, 'Thanks.'

Sean was polishing the mirrors that take up one entire wall. It looked as though there were lipstick streaks where he hadn't replaced the greasiness with gleam. Then I saw his face. It was black and blue. I stood still.

'What are you cleaning off, Sweetness and Light? Love letters?' I tried to joke. 'Threats?'

'Fuck off.'

'Are you going to tell me?' I asked gently. He had never been like this to me before.

'I doubt it,' he spat. And looked straight at me.

'What happened to your face?' I demanded with abrupt concern. I glanced about the room. Greenroom baskets over-flowed along the wall. There was a make-up case with its contents spilled.

'Someone mess up in here?' I maintained a jocular tone. 'I didn't know this room was used for anything but aerobics and kick boxing.'

'You don't know everything,' Sean Dark interrupted, showing none of the sweetness and light I knew to be there. 'Rehearsals are held here, regularly,' Although he is a marvellous cleaner I could make out a word on the glass. It must have been written heavily. Murderer.

'Who came in here, Sean? Who bashed you and trashed the place?' I was insistent. 'You're not a killer.' I went over to give him comfort.

'Don't come near me!' he screeched, brushing my fingers off his arm.

When queens get angry they really do scream. The pitch alone would send you back. I stepped forward. His bruised face was full of hatred.

'Two-faced bitch. Judas cunt,' he accused.

'Wait a minute.' I was aghast.

'You've been ratting on me. Once a cop always a cop, hey? Hey? You had to go and dob me in. While you go and play lady sleuth, I live in the real world. This, this, is the real world.' He gestured about a room chiefly dedicated to make-believe: body image, or theatre. 'You're working with the cops, I saw you!'

Nothing I could say. Instead I picked up some clothes and started putting them in costume baskets. Fancy-dress stuff. I recognised the tights worn by the youths at the Orlando dance. I folded, shook out, and got into tidying up. Silently helping.

Sean furiously rubbed the stains on the mirror. 'I don't deserve this. I never meant any harm by it.' He began to cry. 'I don't deserve this. All because of you. What have you been doing all this time Saint Margot, spying? Get out. Just get out. Leave that!'

Thus ordered, I dropped the large lacy bra on the polished floor. I could see why he was upset but that's all I could see. What part I played in it was a mystery to me. He seemed pretty sure of his information, though, and that means that someone has told him in confidence lies about me: I dobbed him in; I'm playing detective games; and I don't live in the real world. I had a fair idea who the slanderer was.

Charming, my reality simply obliterated by malicious gossip. I denied the accusations but I didn't argue. He was really afraid. It was him in the cop shop. Someone had bashed him up. Apart from theories, the only solid connection between any of it was lipstick. Lipstick on Neil and lipstick words on the aerobics hall mirrors, neither place lipstick should rightly be. I exited the room, verbal abuse following me down the stairs. No way was Sean Dark a murderer, but why would someone say he was? In such an intimidating way?

Tiger Cat was taking off in her car, a Hyundai Sonata that she won on her stint on *The Gladiators*. I shut the outside door of the gym. Then I saw the sign. 'CLOSED for cleaning. Normal hours resume tomorrow 7 a.m.' As I examined the handwriting, I noticed another sticky-tape mark on the glass of the door. Tiger Cat must have seen me arrive, removed and then replaced the note. Would she have been inside or outside? If inside, there is something going on between her and Sean with me as enemy. But, Sean wanted me to heed the note, because he had just thrown me out, definitely did not want me to see this disturbance. Tiger Cat, on the other hand, wanted me to go in. Therefore she wanted me to catch the physically abused Sean crying, clearing and cleaning. Pure mischief. So she was not inside before I arrived. If he didn't want anyone in there, and he wouldn't, he would have locked the door. There is a latch on the inside which does the same work as a key. I stood on the step and looked around. There was no evidence Sean knew Tiger Cat was there at all.

The RSL Club made a right angle with the gym, behind which were an indoor swimming pool and squash courts. A large car park bordered by a line of trees was in front of another larger car park serving the shopping complex. The gym, though a private enterprise, shared bricks and mortar with the RSL's facilities. There must be another entrance, I thought. I traced the wall around to my left and found a door that looked like a permanently locked fire exit. It was not locked. I opened it and followed a narrow dark passage behind the toilets and showers and was very quickly at the front door of the gym. Tiger Cat must have, or rather could have, seen my car, raced around here, ripped off the sign and ducked upstairs. She could have come to work out, seen the note, was obeying it and returning to her car, possibly, when she saw me arrive and seized an opportunity. The question is why? With such alacrity? Must be something. Or was she lying in wait? I let myself out of the gym for the second time, clicking the latch.

I had not had a good hard sweat and puff. Tossed my towel and water bottle in the back of the car as I sat in the driver's seat. A moment later, as if on a stake-out, DC Philippoussis pulled up in the unmarked police car. He told me to get in. We drove to the Police Citizens Youth Club in the spanking new sedan. He said it wouldn't hurt him to pump some iron either.

The PCYC gymnasium was abuzz with activity and chatter. The vinyl was torn, the equipment crowded and many of the weights old and marked in pounds and ounces. There was one other woman there, a teenage girl, boxing. Handwritten instructions were pasted on available surfaces. As soon as someone thought of something interesting to say or instruct, he had got out a felt pen, found any old bit of paper and put it up straight away. Diagrams of the human form with particular muscle groups emphasised in colour—amateur artwork on the faces and feet—had not been taken down for decades, as evidenced by the curling, yellowing edges. Youths in torn singlets admired themselves and each other as they dead-lifted, pulled, pushed and pumped with gadfly concentration, resting frequently to chitchat, performing and posing in front of inadequate mirrors. Rugby players pressed enormous weights with their legs or from their chests lying on their backs. Sean Dark's business, in contrast, was like an antiseptic kitchen, crisp and colour-coordinated, where health was an optional extra in a wealthy lifestyle. Sinister undertones of perversion completed the disparity with the good-natured politeness of unabashed male narcissism here.

Since becoming a triathlete I had not had to think too much about the cost of these things because Nike paid for both Sean and membership to his club as they did for my tracksuit and shoes. Suddenly it felt as if I was back home in class terms. The kids were friendly and the raw conceit competitive. I ran through my routines with no self-consciousness whatsoever and found all manner of gear that was so old-fashioned it was cute. Phil caught me smiling.

'Glad someone's happy,' he said, absolutely misunderstanding my mood.

With our feet hooked under a worn wooden bar on movable clinches to an angle with our heads lower, we worked our abdominal muscles in parallel unison.

'If you only knew,' I panted, starting to feel terrific. 'Had a problem with the Achilles tendon a week or so ago. Not too bad now. But I won't be competing for a while.'

Dissemblance was okay for now. Spies all about this place, but I wouldn't like Chandra or Libby Gnash to know I was here, in cahoots with the cops. 'You look worried yourself.' I sat up to change activities.

'Yeah. You know. Work,' he said nonchalantly.

'Did you get seconded to the coroner?' I asked as I walked over to the bench press.

'Not yet.' He let out a long breath. 'Working on it.'

Getting high on my own endorphins, I considered letting him know how much progress I had made on the Waughan case but did not feel free to talk. I left the equipment and lay a mat on the floor and began finishing with warming down stretches.

'Showers?' I asked him when I felt ready to leave. He directed me to the ladies'. Sharp needles of water ran over me, invigorating and refreshing. When I emerged, Phil Philippoussis was waiting for me. In the car he asked if I'd like a drink. The old cop culture.

'Sure,' I grinned. Like a crocodile.

We got a light ale each and sat in the beer garden of a pub in the back streets.

'So what's the story?' I asked, picking up the thought that the man wanted to unburden himself. Ever the detective. Always a woman.

'What's yours?' he responded, sharply.

'You mean?' I was a bit taken aback. Had he been on surveillance in the car park?

'Why you suddenly had to find another gym, of course. Apart from the desperate need to feel the state of your musculature?' You don't expect a sensitive New Age guy hidden in such a macho body.

'Okay,' I expressed giving in. 'Do you happen to know Sean Dark? My erstwhile trainer is accusing me of dobbing him into the cops, threw me out of his gym. But the most interesting part was the condition of his face when he said it. Not a pretty sight.'

'You think someone down the shop worked him over.' No question mark in his sentence.

'Well, I don't know. No, not New South Wales' finest?' Our eyes thrusting and parrying like a couple of fencers, I asked, 'What would I dob him in for? His place was trashed.'

'Was it?' He scratched his head, picked up the empties and went to get another couple of stubbies. I thought about my own question. What had Sean done? He could be dealing in steroids and so on, I supposed, but I do not know of it. He was the gayest gay guy I knew. All the damning information about him that I personally have, started today. Yet he wouldn't be the first Jekyll and Hyde I've known. The only other incident was seeing him at the police station. Phil returned with the cold de-capped bottles.

'Games,' he stated. 'Games with our glorious youth.'

'I didn't know anything about it,' I lied with measured indignation.

'Yep. Paedophile rings, according to my boss,' the detective constable confided. 'International conspiracy.'

'Oh come on? Harmless dress-ups?' I showed incredulity. 'Anyway, I thought the Crank was the Drug War Specialist!'

'That is his reputation. But he is not fond of gays,' continued Philippoussis. 'I can assure you, no one where I work rearranged your trainer's features.' He clinked my drink with his own. I nodded and frowned, then looked up.

'You know an individual with the moniker Tiger Cat?' Which of the three of us had he been watching?

He stared at me, asked. 'What does she do?'

451

'Good question. Mischief-making is a bit of a specialty. But not well enough herself to have done it,' I suggested. 'Who else?'

'Actually, I have no identification on this one, but there is a freelance spook about the place. Federal I think, but could be an overseas agency. All very hush-hush.'

'The Cat is not your subtle type,' I murmured. He must have interviewed her along with the others at the barbecue. 'Did you see her this afternoon? In the carpark?'

'Big girl is she? Big mane?' The DC smiled.

'Curls, fair from the bottle, and yeah, I wouldn't call her small. Has she any contact with the Crank or your DI?' I asked, and added, 'Changed her hair colour today. Actually.'

He rubbed his face from cheek to eyebrow, forehead, other eyebrow, down to cheek, then squeezed his nose and mouth, a cogitative procedure. After it, he looked at me with deep brown eyes which could express either intense self-interest or ideological passion. 'It could have been her who did him over. Your trainer and her? I'm not sexist in this regard. I think they hurt each other in a little fisticuffs.'

Unconvinced, I shook my head, 'My money's on Sean.' I grinned, 'She is, indeed the victim of a bashing. But it doesn't relate.'

We were not exactly in a secure enough environment for me to share details of Maria's wake, but I didn't have to as he said, 'The Crank is getting me to drag the bucket on our dead boys. I wonder why.'

'Curious,' I commented. Had he seen the note on the door, and waited?

'Considering his vendetta on paedophilia, it is strange. The other death was just crazy teenage playing chicken with danger and not winning. I had another look at the site. The yellow Charger was travelling.'

'Was he licensed?' I asked, noting he had changed the focus, incidentally conveying that it was Sean in his sights.

'Yep. P plate. I am not so sure about him. Bit of a petunia in an onion patch. Went off the rails after his mother died. She topped herself, just one of your ordinary sad stories. Constable McKewan said, motherhood killed her. Maybe he wanted to die.' If my man was going to talk like this, I was going to buy him another drink. I went to the bar meditating on the change in Philippoussis. Previously he thought at least two of the three deaths were linked. Now Phil was separating them into units with altogether different motives, causes.

'McKewen, let me guess, is a woman,' I said as I put the beers on the table and sat down. 'Don't you think something else was going on any more?'

'Of course!' he flipped back into the Pip I knew. The dog on a scent, trusting hunches. 'Of course, there is more going on.'

'I meant to give you this,' I said as I dug in my bag. I placed the homoeo-pathic jar between us. 'Nux vomica. Don't go telling me there was no autopsy of my friend, Maria.'

He pocketed the medicine.

'Strychnine. Routine in a suspected drug overdose. They've sent hers down to Sydney. It's in the queue.' He pulled down the corners of his mouth. 'Results in a couple of weeks.'

'An OD? After I gave you the kettle and everything?' I thought I'd got the police off Maria's case.

He laughed. 'Yeah, well, analysis might be interesting, but it's hard to beat cane toads and such.'

Not sure what to make of him, I asked, 'Will there be an inquest? On either or both of the boys?'

'Has to be. But when?' He swilled his drink. 'Vital facts. Reports from chemistry unaccountably gone missing. Plus other stuff.'

'Like what?' I could imagine, videos of the crime scene, forensic bits and pieces, whatever other detectives working on the case discovered, records of interview.

DC Philippoussis was not in the inner circle of the boys' club. I could see that now. He was lonely.

He mused, 'There is always your regular, everyday disrespect of the individual, murder by a hundred cuts and all that. He was a mate of your neighbour's son, Hugh. Lucky Sunshine wasn't in the car with him. They were, apparently, together earlier in the evening. Car was stolen. Responsibility scattered by the fan, but the shit don't stick. On the other hand, someone could have killed Neil Waughan.'

'Is that what the Crank's trying to suppress? The forensic pharmacist is a cop, right?' He was losing me.

'Don't know if it's suppression. Or whether they actually can't identify the substance. I would like to be assigned to the deputy coroner, see if there is a case for bunching the deaths together. Depends on what magistrate they get. Whether we have a full and fair inquiry, or a cover-up. Got to dance around in the ring for a while,' he said decisively.

'What do the medical certificates give as primary cause? Primary, secondary, related? Toxicology report?' I felt I was his partner, slipping into old ways. How long was he going to keep playing this game with me? Perversely, I did not mention the material I'd printed from Neil's computer.

'That is just it,' he said. 'Secondary cause, related conditions don't add up. You know fifty per cent of death certificates don't tally with how the person died. Primary cause, natural, heart stopped.'

Philippoussis gathered up the empties, and asked, 'One for the road?'

I nodded. We were both drinking more than was sensible, but why not?

'Where are the drugs on the list?' I queried conversationally as he sat down and we attended to the next beer.

'My own questions exactly. But, leave it son, go down to the marina, get lists on arrivals, departures, locals,' he quoted his boss. 'What is this guy on about? Paperwork disappearing. Putting me on wild goose chases after mariners. Do you know how many boats are moored in this harbour?'

'No, but I would be interested if you found anything odd.'

He shrugged, 'I could have done it by phone.' Indicating both keyboard and the Yellow Pages with his fingers walking and tapping on the table, he continued, 'The coroner's inquiry is the best bet for digging out the truth. I want to investigate, but unless I can work with the lawyers, there is no chance of an independent investigation.'

'What is the Crank's problem?' I asked rhetorically. 'Anyone better than you for the job? Working with the deputy coroner I mean?'

He sighed. 'They like to go with someone who has done it before. Maybe I look too ambitious. I need a homicide investigation under my belt. He knows that.'

'Too ambitious,' I repeated and raised my eyebrows. 'You don't want to give your senior officer any indication of your suspicions?'

'About him? Are you kidding?' The young detective constable was in a dicky position.

'No, I know what slime is like. You step in it. You smell it. But it slides away,' I reasoned. 'Once you know someone's shifty, you don't want to give them facts they can twist around and about to make their fabrications believable.'

'In a nutshell. If I can get onto the inquest team I owe my allegiance to the justice system. The pathologist is paid by the Health Department. If he smells a rat and the corruption can be traced to bigwigs in—' he paused. 'We could have an independent assessment here.'

I drank along with him, 'You want the magistrate to recommend suspicious circumstances?'

Encouraged, he agreed, 'I want the beaks interested. They were, after all, "accidental" deaths. The mortuary guys are bloody slack. They faxed the cause to the station. Do you know where I got it?'

'Nope,' I replied, feeling slightly drunk.

'Out of the fucking wastepaper basket,' he swore.

'And?'

'The doctors at that hospital are so damned tired, they're guessing. Blame the kids. These particular kids, who's going to look at malpractice?'

'You didn't believe the report? The death certificates?' I rode along with his indignation, his idealism.

'On the button. And I don't know why exactly. Related conditions, narcotics. Primary cause, bang on the head, crushed chest, secondary car accident. Primary cause for the Waughan boy, systems failure, sugar shock, secondary drugs, no diabetes et cetera in related conditions. Heart attack. Blah de blah, scribble.'

'Alcohol?' I gestured with my bottle.

'The scapegoat. Neither boy was drunk.' Philippoussis was now talking freely. 'My hope is the legal investigator is worth his salt.'

'Or her salt,' I corrected. 'Who is the deputy coroner?'

'It hasn't happened. The bodies are lying there in the mortuary and nothing is happening. If I can bring up the possibility of suicide, the magistrate has to be involved. That's my angle at the moment.' He finished his drink. 'Right Margot, got to go. You ready?'

I shook my head, 'No, mate, I'll walk back to my car. Clear my head. Get back to me, and hey, Phil, I'm a tomb. Let me know when you're on to it full-time.'

'Yeah. Intelligence-based policing, ain't it a joke?' he said as he left me sitting there.

With a sick smile, I waved him off. I hadn't told Philippoussis about the word, 'murderer', written in lipstick, being washed off by Sean Dark, but that could wait. And he hadn't picked up on my interest in the yachties.

The phone at the edge of the bar had caught my eye and I knew I wanted to ring Chandra as soon as possible. She was home. Some kind of amber light was flashing in the street map of my brain. Instinctive caution. I still felt queasy. Harbour news. Dates. I asked her if she could print out all the boat-stuff Alison sent from Neil's computer to hers. It would be interesting to see the material Philippoussis collected on the Crank's orders, but I did not want to help the Commander in case Phil's hunch was right and he was sending him off on a parallel scent that would lead nowhere but look good in court.

Ants climb into the butter again. Coming home from work, Cybil finds they have dug a hole in the fresh bread roll as well. Tiny, miserable brown ants, hunting around the griller, even in the oven, tracking like coolies along the landscape of walls and benches, appear as if born on the spot. Armies of conscientious creatures doing her cleaning for her are Cybil's enemy. Her flat is as grotty as inside her car, a shiny garbage bin on wheels. She feels a repugnance for herself, a shame. About the only thing which relieves this feeling is washing and polishing the duco. Generally after that she is too weary to attack the less glamorous task. Even if she would spend money on a cleaner she won't bring in someone who will judge her. Her bed is four-posted with genuine feather mattress and pillows, silken sheets and a mosquito tent. Her scented focus. The habit of cleaning is not ingrained; rather, for Cybil, it is a rare hysterical exercise in which lots of stuff is chucked out and flowers are bought to top it off.

Relationships with women confuse Cybil Crabbe. She wants an assistant. Mummy was Daddy's servant, or vice versa, depending on the job. Her parents, she suddenly realises, related by ordering each other around all the time. The measure of love equals the measure of compliance. Cybil had a happy childhood: she ordered harshly or she sweetly complied. All the family agrees on the importance of money and themselves as having a right to it, by fair means or foul, for instance, evading tax. Thus conversation in the one-child adult home is often of loopholes. Mummy and Daddy are partners in business, Crabbe & Crabbe, which was not a shop, a factory or an office. It bought property and ran at a loss. Daddy worked daily for a firm in the City and Mummy never went there. Cybil was not spoilt. Mummy and Daddy were strict, understanding the emotional dangers in her being an only child. Parents should not over-compensate with too many toys. Presents were rewards. Obedience was rewarded. The whole domestic structure was a balance of power relations.

Mummy, Cybil remembers, did have household help, a very old woman who was given a gift at Christmas, who, otherwise, discreetly came and went on a Wednesday when Cybil was at school and Mummy having her hair done before going to her bridge afternoon. As for herself, Mrs Crabbe flicked around the living areas with a feather-duster, screamed 'Take those things to your room!' and invested in a freezer, dish-washer, microwave as soon as they came onto the market. Cybil cannot remember seeing her operate the vacuum cleaner. The stronger recall is the make, Electrolux, and what the shares were worth. All a happy ordered life where the ledgers and the journals neatly tallied matched totals and god was in his heaven, until Cybil's secondary sex characteristics began to appear. At first Mummy was overjoyed by her little breasts and her early periods. After a couple of years, she began and kept mentioning how thick her knees and ankles were, and would always be. Cybil's legs are tree trunks. Nothing could have repulsed Mrs Crabbe more because it would never matter how slim her daughter kept herself, shapeless was shapeless. She had inherited her father's legs, but it was of no consequence on a man. In Mummy's moments of husband-hatred, she blamed herself for marrying him. As it happened, Cybil did not keep herself thin, she developed a big bottom and a certain coarse cheek to go with it. She ate chocolate when she was depressed.

Right now Cybil wishes that there was someone she could scream at about the mess. She has the words. She has the passion. She is, at heart, a perfectionist. She wouldn't mind rewarding later in the big soft bed with all the sexy wiles at her finger-tips and measured enthusiasm timed to mutual consummation. Cybil needs someone to talk to. She shoves a few things aside and finds her phone. She rings Mummy. They go through the litany of petty disasters that happen in the general course of events. 'Daddy is going senile, he left his milk boiling until the whole stove was a massive job and the saucepan had to be thrown out.'

'Is he really?' Cybil makes room on the lounge for Puddles, and lies back.

'Well, he is still catching the train at eight forty-three a.m. But they don't need him at the firm,' her mother's voice drips with contempt.

Mummy has a few sharp words to say about her bridge companions, especially the scorer who will never give up the pad even though she has to hang about four sets of spectacles around her neck and tries each of them on before she finds her reading glasses. Cybil has a rich laugh. Her mother amuses her. She will never be like her, god forbid. She responds with the catastrophes that have befallen her at work, and mentions in passing that a young lad had been murdered just after she had been speaking to him. Not that she knows it's murder, she just has to make it awful for Mummy to groan, to comment, to express her prejudices, so Cybil can be reassured that she is not like her mother. She tells her that he was dressed in girl's clothes. As Cybil recalls the hard surprise and the delicious climax she experienced rubbing the tip of his penis on her wet clitoris, her mother goes on about the teenagers in her local shopping mall staring at her waiting to bag-snatch her purse and how untrustworthy the Vietnamese and Turkish ones are.

'How do you know they're Turkish? Why not Lebanese?' Cybil herself does not feel racism. She grew up in a multicultural urban Australia. It is the nature of the nation and the food is the best in the world. You could choose any ethnic dish you liked and in the cities all you have to do is go out and have the real people cook it for you. She can tell the difference between a Korean and Chinese face. Listening to her mother makes her nostalgic for city-living. She says she has to go now.

Love-hate is the taste in her mouth as she replaces the receiver. At times when she feels the most passion for her, she hates Virginia. The Achilles heel of her sensitive heart, the uncompromisingly long fit limbs of her youthful fifty-year-old body, the foreign female independence, the lack of convention in her thinking, constantly surprises her, not always pleasantly. Combined with her pathetic need for affirmation, probably a class thing, or for support in her creative endeavours, which Cybil sees as a waste of time, the vulnerability is complete in itself, not for trade, does not fit in the tit and tat of rewards and punishments. It sits up like a victim and says, kick me, which Cybil did. Fuck me.

Which she does, with small satisfaction, because it doesn't alter the transaction. Virginia is not vindictive. Cybil gave her so much reason to be and she surrendered her pride. She wants Virginia to punish her. She says to her poodle, 'How can she when she doesn't know?' Cybil feels she has blown it with Virginia. If not now, later. The grapevine will put her with the dead boy, eventually. The joy of breaking taboos in clandestine secrecy deserts her. Cybil cannot imagine Virginia forgiving her. Virginia's righteousness would identify the transgression piteously.

Cybil, eyeing her phone, considers ringing Margot Gorman. Confession was always fun, sitting back watching the consequences, the drama of disaster. Instead of thinking about the fate of the lad, Cybil talks out her confusion to her dog.

'Bugger Virginia. Why she does love me? It is too pure, too idealistic. It makes me puke now that I turned myself inside out trying to hide my real self and think up words that sounded smart. Virginia's artwork is insanity. My mind was saying as my eyes were straying, where's the money in that? It is so remote even the land lesbians haven't seen it. She is wonderful. She is older. She has a tight bum and every muscle in her body stands out a little bit. She exists on cloud fucking nine. Doing a sculpture that no one will see, on a filthy black log the loggers left to rot. She showed it to me as if it were a beautiful thing, and it repulsed me. I just looked and shrugged and pretended I couldn't see as I wondered how my legs were going to carry me through the horrendous dripping jungle out of there. She blushed. Dig that! Blushed. She did not disclaim her work, which was what I was angling for, she cast those fucking deep eyes at me and shook her head. Then shepherded me down the hill, holding my hand when I stumbled over rocks and cooked me a great dinner. I could only be horrible. I can't control my fate. Does she know I am scared when I put a power look in my eyes that says, you dare? I don't believe she can still love me. Me? I mean it's the big league. That's what attracted me at the start, big league separatism, what was it about. At the party at the beach I could romance this sweet young thing into the bushes and do it. None of us knew her sex. What a fuck! But Virginia will call a spade a spade.' Cybil hates goody-goody stuff, and wonders if Virginia will ever ask her. 'Had I taken the young trannie into the bushes and done it? Where is the fun in that? If only he hadn't died afterwards!'

Cybil feels just as guilty about the mess in her flat. Now it is beyond the power and sex equation, uncharted territory for Cybil, who fondles her dog, muttering nostalgically, 'I doddled her dot until she came and then I stopped, looked at my watch, put on my clothes, scattered excuses and walked out the door.' Although Virginia did not cry, but looked at her with those intelligent eyes, so full of hurt and withholding dignity, Cybil had her where she wanted her. Cybil picks up a dish and hurls it at her wall, alone and scared, wishing she could turn back the clock to the luscious days with Virginia, the Amazon, indulging her senses.

But death is depressing. There is a block of chocolate somewhere. It is under some clothes near the computer. As it is at her finger-tips, Cybil decides to surf the net.

Chandra programs a hide and seek game in the maze of her wimmin site, to sift through the chatters in Cellar2. Using the same handles, the players earn points which at a certain level they can spend to become the mole or not as they choose. By quizzing them on an array of subjects, from the trivial and local to the historical and specific, the outcome is to get the others to reveal themselves. Her detective work here is far more successful than her face-to-face approach. With paper and pen she is matching the relevant pseudonyms with women she knows.

<WHEELS> Philosophising is not allowed; it's about what you know.

The key-players in their secret cell fall for her ruse as answering riddles is bait and hook. OWL is someone out in the bush. REDSHOES someone local. BLUESKY, BAC and MOP keep beating her, so she tosses in queries about the intrusion into her own website. As the night wears on, she becomes lost in her own fog and she herself is merely one of the players feeling around in the mist, thoroughly addicted to the game. Meanwhile she notes who in the game also chats on-line, trying to keep ahead and maintain control. Those rerouting multiple IP addresses are obviously the most suspect. She embeds a spider in the dubious laptops or on-ground computers to retrieve data from their hard-drives. She, Chandra, is also a sitting duck.

41

. . . the impossible separatist . . .

Virginia White is a trembling wreck. Her worst nightmare is being trapped in a lift in a city building. She is confined to a shed inside a cyclone fence deep in the wooded mountains of the Great Dividing Range. She tells herself not to panic. The essence of bravery is knowledge of fear. She has understood that woman's freedom is only with other women, that she can never be complete alone, and that loneliness is an annihilation of selfhood. Others break down the barriers. With all breakage pain is involved. She escaped the scenario of sitting with every conceivable thing money can buy, haunting singles bars, castigating herself for failing, watching television, getting fat, whatever, to find after all, she has a damaged, self-critical self. And she is not responding with courage. Involvement with other women to uncover her own identity, through intense relationship with the earth, pushing her boundaries, to realise her potential has led to this shivering coward. She quarried a hole in sheer rock-face to place a tank, made her own shelter, thought up a code of ethics, believing in her strength, in growth. Freedom. Respect. Her heroism is undermined. Trials met by the fragile ego, to survive without sustenance or comfort, all misunderstood, she is crying, not panicking. Absolutely bereft. The sufferer you never meet has no reality, neither has the goddess earth, as for the life in her veins, scraps of memory, race memory, genetic memory, spiritual memory, flitting alongside ego in the human condition, it is no good. Even comprehension of what she is is hollow. Emptied. How can she be locked up in her beloved bush freaked out? Her ego is not in her body, not at the moment. The concerns of individuals who are moulded by addictions, victims of circumstances, are but little dots in the distance. Caves?

Imprisoned. Castigating herself as misanthropic isolationist, the impos-sible separatist, caught by the short and curlies, feels her care for others evaporate. The abuse of the ozone layer, the effect on the climate does not bother her. Her lack does; it borders on despair. Theories that no woman is allowed to be free are no more real than being tied up. This bloody installation on Lesbianlands could not have happened without inside help.

'Nope. It was not that anyone started out evil. We simply did not know how to do it. Instead of letting questions reign, answers were hammered down with a gavel. Sentences. Statements. Prohibitions. And I, I too, wanted my way. We allowed space and protected our own. Space. If I have space, like a tree I can grow, and the vibe of grow is to know. But there were days to fill and not a moment to be wasted, learning, having about me books of facts, frogs, birds, reptiles, trees, sedges, orchids, an odd moment of contemplation, names were yet another safe haven from knowledge. If you could describe, identify, codify, make lists, you thought you knew, but did I? I found the carcass of an almighty tree. Was it madness? Was it inspiration, a shaft of light in the dark forest? The log had something to teach me. I had merely to educate myself by educing its secrets. I had left sculpture behind in the straight world. This sculpting was a process, not a product. It would never be seen, displayed, shown, praised or prized. I thought arrogantly as sweat made the handle slippery. Still there was more I needed to know. Then love, sex, undid me. Part of the full cornucopia of being, I could just reach out and take it, or I could leave it. How could it destroy my strength?'

Walls of green hardwood, padlock on a thick chain through a hole in the door, claustrophobia is not the only anchor Virginia feels weighed down by. She has no doubt who the traitor is, but there is nothing she can do. She does not have the freedom, besides which she is a snivelling, frightened wreck, screaming for release.

'I screamed. It is such simple torture. He tied me up. He did it with pliers, with wire. The panic rolled over me like a slow-moving breaker and dumped me in the wash of hopelessness. Who would care? Cybil would be glad to see me so small. Would Cybil care? Then I met despair. I let it roam like an eagle on the air above me. Who is worrying about me? Not Cybil. Is Cybil missing me? Faithless lover. I entered her realm: food and sex, champagne and bubble baths; passionate fights and passionate love-making; gratification. I could not give such pleasure without loving. Amazon wishful thinking. I will survive this, this restriction. The locked room alone would freak me, but I have no use of my arms. I cannot even bend one up to my waistcoat pocket to get the pen. There are two things hooked, that is right. I have a cheap paper-cutter there. One of those that have tiny break-off blades. This is going to take patience.'

Virginia uses her muscles to twist around and get the weapon in her hand, the plastic knife with its fragile blades, a pathetic sword. Her words flow on, hours pass, night and day.

The telephone rings in Cybil's flat. It is Judith Sloane, she has to meet. All oozy flattery.

'What's the problem with telling me on the phone?' Cybil is reluctant to dance to Judith's tune. If Virginia's back-to-nature ways are repellent to Cybil, and partly she had determined that was because she was a working-class girl at heart, Judith's downwardly mobile arrogance is obnoxious.

'I couldn't possibly do that,' whispers Judith. 'Not on this line.' Slimeball, thinks Cybil.

'Afraid of ASIO?' Cybil laughs.

'Well I am using Meghan's line and you know she works for the government.'

Curiosity playing a gut-line with her astuteness, Cybil agrees to a rendezvous. After she replaces the receiver, Cybil experiences a sudden surge of loyalty and recalls the time Virginia lost it with her about Judith. Some results of that tempest are still in the mess of her sitting-room. Cybil looks at her antique clock, automatically contemplating its value, sees time and, energised by unfinished business, dives into the job of cleaning her nest. It must be said that when Cybil Crabbe works, she does it well. 'Flowers,' she writes on her list.

As far as Judith is concerned, Cybil will learn for herself whether Virginia is right. She is inquisitive. 'Maybe it will be fun.' In a few hours her home is neat and tidy, just in case, and fresh sheets are on the bed.

42

. . . several loose ends . . .

After my swim in the creamy sea and a gentle jog along the pristine sand, I managed to get hold of Rory. She told me the bridge had been fixed, which, while she found it just as mystifying as its destruction, seemed to point the finger more decisively in the direction of the Campbells. They stamped their character on the style of the work. The job itself neat, the bush around destroyed, disregarded. She gave me Barb Campbell's address in Stuart. Then we arranged the details about Saturday. I'll be with Chandra. Good, great.

Taking the Neil Waughan file, I set out in search of Alison Hungerford. She was not at work. Penny's house on the canal was closed like a prison. Although those places have furniture for outdoor entertaining, they all looked inhospitable. Expensively secured. I walked along the concrete path past the miniature jetties. All that was left of the mangrove edges was mud. Seven black cockatoos, speaking to each other, flew over my head from a stand of radiata pines to the remaining cluster of river oaks beyond the development. Rain. The barometric pressure, indeed, did seem to fall. It occurred to me that I knew the fathers of her first two children, but who was Tilly's dad? Was he anywhere in the picture?

The Waughan file was a dead end until I found Alison to explain what the pages of print-outs I had taken from Neil's room meant. Dr Neville would not be back until next week. Fortunately, I had written notes from the Rory conversation in the yellow Spirax that was sitting on the seat.

The street for Barb Campbell was in quite a respectable looking row of identically designed houses with small porches and little sash windows in pastel expanses of fibro sheeting, uncluttered front yards with oleander and azalea shrubs marooned on mown lawns for the most part. Weeping bottle-brush and the odd tall gum which survived clearing from a former time provided a pleasant enough aspect. The back fences, I discovered, were almost non-existent as behind was an abandoned mill site with the black and orange residue of sawdust piles inhibiting growth of anything much except one rampant flow of nasturtiums and crops of Crofton, deadly nightshade, and the weed called 'farmer's friend'. A dominant blackbutt or ironbark shaded the wrecks of cars, some probably in working condition as bonnets were up and tyres pumped.

Whoever drafted these homes for the Housing Department had domestic fortresses in mind as ingress is achieved only through two narrow doorways, both easily barricaded. Receiving no response to my knock at the front, I boldly stormed the barrier of washing machine, washing baskets and auto-parts at the back. Inside walls a solid shade of light blue had not been painted for a generation or two. Neither pale enough to fade into the background nor dark enough to hide scuff marks, they boasted oily finger-prints and crayon drawings. The place was putrid with the housework of kids; that is, unmitigated mess. Games in progress and those forsaken had used whatever was to hand to create theatres of conflict, space stations peopled with Indians, cowboys, tanks, monsters or miniature kitchens and nurseries with Barbie characters and accessories relating to grossly out of proportion baby-dolls. A turf war over the main-room floor space erupted in violent screaming skirmishes too often for adult powers to attempt peace-keeping negotiations or bother with disciplinary measures beyond entering the foray themselves. Mostly, it seemed, they left the warring parties to it. And might won out. Survival of the fittest. Social Darwinism in a dwarfed world meant, in this case, at their stage of evolution, the overweight girl in garish pink ruled. The fittest was, apparently, the nastiest, the most stubborn and the biggest. Her girlfriends were the army that destroyed and laid to waste the homeland of her siblings' activities and colonised it with a tyranny Idi Amin would be proud of. The television was riotous with the robotic graphics and mechanical voiced phrases of a Play-Station contest. The bloke, his hands black from tinkering with an engine, made no appreciable difference to the atmosphere by his presence. He sat doing nothing, mesmerised by the flicker and crashes on the TV screen, possibly summoning up the energy, or waiting for it to occur to him, to go and wash his hands to enable him to do something. This, apparently, included speech.

Barbara Campbell, when she came in, had no time for me, whoever I was: one of the kids' mothers, a social worker, a truant officer, a do-gooder of some sort. She didn't appear to care about any other two-legged creature in the house either. With one arm she shoved aside the ineffable clutter on the kitchen table and opened the other, letting a tangle of leather strapping fall into the gap, and sat down. She hunted through the chaos and found needle, thimble and sturdy, string-like thread. From a chain around her neck, hanging between her breasts under her embroidered denim shirt, she retrieved a pair of half-moon glasses, balanced them on her nose and began threading a large needle. A cat daintily stepped over the remains of baked beans on a plate, whining for a pat, which she obliged with a facial nudge as both hands were occupied.

I spoke, introducing myself as a private detective.

She looked up, intrigued no doubt by a character who walked out of television drama. 'So what are you doing here?' she asked, then went back to sewing the bridle.

Flipping open the spiral notebook, I checked the details of her relationship to the Campbells with a lease neighbouring Lesbianlands.

'Willy's my brother,' she nodded.

'Basically,' I began, 'I'm investigating unexplained happenings on the women's-only property.'

She interrupted, 'The gurls are always seeing crazy things, like space-craft and the like.' The bit from the bridle clattered to the floor as she felt about for something. She left it there.

'Do you know them well?' I asked, easily. 'Can you tell me any particular names?'

'What do you mean? Like, who I know?' Now she bent for the bit.

'That would be helpful,' I encouraged.

'You sound like a social worker.' She glanced up over the top of her glasses. 'You got anything to prove you are who you say you are, because I am not giving any of the gurls' secrets away. So there. Even if you had a licence, I don't know what to look for. You're not a cop, are you?'

'Not any more,' I confessed.

'See,' Barb Campbell nodded as if she had won an argument.

'Look,' I laughed, 'I'm working for the gurls.'

Either my laugh or what I said made her more suspicious. Whatever softness she had firmed. Her hard face was cunning before it creased into a false smile. 'Why is that?'

Lowering my centre of gravity, feeling my trim strength, I said, 'You tell me.'

'Tell you what?' She finished her repair work and dropped it on the table with the rest of the junk.

The chubby girl in pink came into the room, was about to provoke her mother, but changed her mind and looked me up and down.

'If they put in any complaints about us lighting fires, we know exactly where to go with our information about them. They wouldn't like the drug squad out there, would they?' She said in the bossy tone I had heard her eight-year-old use a while before. The kid folded her arms, tough little cookie. 'You don't suppose those, you can't call them houses, have council approval, do you?'

Barb leaned her elbows on the messy board in front of her and stared me out. Body language and locus were telling me a lot: for some people the equation is so simple. I turned up the official tone. 'Perhaps you could tell me who fixed their bridge on Tuesday. I'm sure they are very grateful.'

'We did, of course. The whole family. And some neighbours. Did them a favour, so they don't make too much of a hullabaloo about fences, like that bloke Vanderveen. We're country folk. We can't afford to fix fences all the time. They've got thousands of acres, they can let a few cattle roam around. It's about the cattle, isn't it? Bloody greenies. Try everything, they will.' She got up and carefully picked the dirty plates from the assemblage of debris. 'Council could go in and bulldoze the lot. Don't know how many regulations they've broken, but it's got to be a few. Like, what's it called, you're not allowed to have more than one—shit, what is it?'

'Multiple occupancy.' I sighed as if it were all too much for me, and asked, 'You wouldn't know how the bridge got broken, by any chance?'

Barb shuddered like a horse and ran water into the sink. 'Nuh, Wilma and I were riding through one day, and we saw it. We said to each other, I said to Wilma, she said to me, Poor gurls, how are they going to get their cars across? So Willy and a few blokes, out of the goodness of their hearts, and they are good blokes, said, why not? Wilma talked with the Chinese one about it.'

Frowning, believing every word, I cried, 'But why would they do all that work for nothing?'

Barb Campbell turned around, amused, 'Well, Miss Private Eye, you don't know much, do you?' She laughed, a big ho-ho without mirth. 'They might earn a few drinks, around here, having been for a whole day in Lesbianlands. Most of the fellas are spooked, you know? They reckon they're witches. Deadmansland, they call it.'

The little cookie in pink piped up, 'They can. All they do is think it, and boom a tree falls down on your head.'

'Oh, right, okay. I get it.' Putting my notebook away, I finished with, 'So, Campbells fixed the bridge, but they didn't break it in the first place?'

'You got it.' Cunning came back into her voice. 'What did you say your name was? You could leave your address with me.' A double-blink, a thrust of the chin, and eyes sort of swimming to the ceiling, she had all the confidence of a despot prepared to slaughter his subjects.

Although I had a few business cards in my pocket, I shook my head and said, 'No way.'

Miss bossy busybody showed me out. Then the precocious little darling said importantly, in a conspiratorial whisper, 'But they can only do it to men. Females are protected.'

'Really?' The myth of the gurls' powers had evidently reached the level of superstition.

The pint-sized version of a plump matron, in answer, just stared at me and shut the door.

Alison could possibly be with her son's relatives. Taking the highway parallel to the coast, I saw the red, yellow and black Aboriginal flag flying in the breeze. Even if she wasn't, Lenny could give me some info on what happened that night. I stopped for a glance at the file in the Driver Reviver bay and was offered a free cup of instant coffee and a Kit-Kat. I sat among the travellers examining my rough map of the crime site. The red Saab belonged to Rosemary Turner. Who was the drug-dealing respectable gay person? Did that have anything to do with the free party pills? Now, where could the cap have come from? Jill? The connection there was Meghan's contract, same company. If it was Featherstone's, then, whoever went to her dairy-home could have taken it. Who wore it to the toilet? Why was it dropped? Someone was: careless? In a hurry? Carrying something else? Shocked? In the big motor I heard? Outside danger is statistically the least likely. Yes, I could have a few words with the boy, even if his mother wasn't there.

The settlement of Crossroads looked as unkempt as a garden devastated by pests. Bare patches, tussocks of native grasses, not exactly rubbish, dominated, though things had been left about, trustingly. An old BMX bike on its side, playthings, cricket bats, footballs scattered around like dogs' bones, empty drink containers near blackened planks and ash, make-shift seats carved from logs or appropriated from superannuated automobiles, goal-posts, useful for all five codes, at a list, painted white either end of a footy field discernible by vacant ground, a bit of slashing and flattening work making a dam-wall ridge one side and a dip opposite. Black kids in sports-bright colours and dogs in aimless constant movement made the place alive. A roadless big walking area connected the houses, a mixture of architect-designed open living spaces with interestingly shaped, energy-efficient roofs and wide bull-nosed verandahs with millers' shacks, grey with the weathered boards and rusty iron chimneys of yesteryear, and the stud-framed fibro boxes of some era in between.

In one of these lived Lenny's gramma. The same small sash windows that characterised the residences in Barb Campbell's street here were proudly glistening clean. Eventually I found Di Minogue. The pokey entrance was clear of clutter. Although as many kids were inside and more adults, there still seemed to be space for me. Short of a conference room, I had never seen so much seating in a place this size. Di's kitchen table was, at the moment, dedicated to the task of painting filo pastry with melted margarine. Fascinated by her skill, I watched her whip and flip sheets of the fine stuff from damp tea-towel to powdered chopping board without tearing, or swearing, which is what I do when I try to handle it. She was making her version of Chiko Rolls. The corn, mince and cabbage filling occupied a large mixing bowl underneath a gauzy umbrella even though there were no flies about. I was told Lenny was playing soccer with his father and other males of various ages. When I went out the back I recognised Violet and Daanii. A blue cattle dog was, apparently, keeping goal because every now and then the striker would aim his, or her, kick straight at it. A high ball came my way, I headed it back. Lenny and his father stood out from the crowd with the kind of looks that could charm the wicked, smiles that could part a fool from his money and other relevant clichés, such as butter wouldn't melt in their mouths. I played kick for a while, saying 'gidday' and answering 'how's it going?' with 'good'.

When I felt the tide turn to wondering what I was doing there anyway, I caught the ball with my hands. I explained, 'I need to speak with Lenny.'

His dad came too and we sat on the make-shift spectator stands overlooking the oval.

'I'm investigating the death of that kid the other night. Remember, Lenny?'

'Yeah,' he responded suspiciously.

His father, whom I had not been introduced to, butted in. 'When I heard Ali took Lenny to a scene like that, I slapped her about. Couldn't help myself. I was angry.'

Lenny laughed, 'But Mum hurt your arm, hey Dad?'

'So?' the pretty man shrugged. 'We were tanked.'

'Okay,' I sighed, 'Can I ask you a couple of questions, Lenny?' Pen and paper ready, I started with, 'Who was wearing a cap?'

He snorted, 'Like everybody.'

'Your outfit was cool, didn't you have one on backwards?' I had no idea whether he did or didn't.

'For a while. I lost it.'

'You lost it, you bloody mug,' said his father.

'It wasn't mine,' Lenny defended himself.

'What colour was it?' I wrote as I asked.

'Black.'

'Any writing on it?'

'I suppose.'

'He's not real good at reading, are you boy?' His dad was disarming.

'But you are good at noticing things, aren't you, Lenny?' I encouraged.

'Where did you get it?'

'Picked it up. Near the tree.'

'Yeah, what tree was that?'

Father and son exchanged glances as if I were really dumb. 'Where they do it,' Lenny explained.

'Who was doing what, Lenny?'

'Cybil was making out with Neil, dressed up as a girl.'

Shocked, I exclaimed, 'You actually saw that?'

'Pervert,' muttered his father.

'Yeah, and I knew it was Neil, 'cause I've seen him heaps of times.'

'Ali's a mongrel bitch,' his dad expleted. 'He,' he nudged his son, 'went with her and Iris cleaning sometimes. That kid was into some weird shit.'

'When, Lenny?' I didn't quite know how to put it, or in what order. 'When did you know it was Neil?'

'When I gave him back his cap. I says, "Here, poof, is this yours?" He was a white as a sheet, no, more like green. He grabbed it and ran. I think he wanted to throw up.'

'Anything else?' I asked. 'He was carrying?'

'Yeah, he had her panties in his hand. I didn't know he was going to die, did I?' Lenny looked concerned, and suddenly grinned, 'He went into the girls' toilets because I chased him.'

'And you don't go in there?' I clarified.

'Nup, never. He was safe in there.' He was looking at his father when he said, 'But I didn't know he was going to off himself.'

'Did you see anyone else in the carpark? Any vehicles coming or going?' For my own sake, I wanted my impression of a lorry authenticated.

Lenny described the scene perfectly, Judith Sloane's Mitsubishi Triton, the rigid semi, the odd vacancy when all the other cars were crowded on the roadside closest to the picnic area and no one on foot. He went back to the barbecue and mucked around until the shit hit the fan. Hiding how flabbergasted I was, I thanked them both and got up.

'Do you know where Alison is right now?' I asked before I said goodbye.

Both shook their heads and shrugged. We exchanged a wave and immediately after getting in my car, I noted down the answers to several loose ends.

43

. . . the grapevine . . .

Messages waiting in her mailbox. Email from Rory. >> CU w Margot, tomorrow? Chandra sends a quick reply.
>> Plenty to talk about!!

A disturbing stream of consciousness piece of writing is not, she decides, the Annihilation Tragic, though it comes up in her search for the mole, the tedious task of tracking, identifying and locating, through various engines. She has set up a firewall around the chat, sending out a bot to bring back information on all chatters operating.

>> they don't know my genius, yet they see it. i see it in their eyes, the recognition, then another look comes in and it says how can i use this to my own advantage. they change friends, gang members, closest allies become the worst enemies and then they are allies again, and if you don't forget anything, you are left on your own sweet pat malone. or, you pretend to be just like them, cool. and swing it, now the right environment for undercover agents to infiltrate, such as i to move about unmolested, unknown. i am as fluid as water, i flow. i reflect when i am still. i loosen false surfaces revealing true or false. i know martians and mutants. you're right, there is a narc i can smell her. a narc, or worse. there may be a murd ...

Oh the nonsense that bothers women. Chandra reads everything by anyone she pins to the area identifying herself as a Solanasite. She thinks this is Alison, as she is susceptible to psychological breakdown, but she glances down at her list of names: Margaret Hall, Jill David, Cybil Crabbe, Libby Gnash. Sofia is out of the picture, unless . . . And then there are the unknown OWL, BAC and MOP. Chandra is afraid of two things, infiltration by the police, constantly on the hunt for subversive activity, and the free radical, cancerous psychopath, within the conspiracy. She must prevent transgression, but she can't if she cannot maintain or retain control. BLUESKY is not in the district, the real world vicinity.

Chandra Williams is interrupted by an unexpected visit from Judith Sloane. She remembers the good work Judith did but—one being a Luddite subsister, the other well into the technological age—she never sees her these days. Since her fight with Meghan, especially, relations between them are decidedly cool. From the roneoed sheets to the rollicking bandwagon to the virtual village, Chandra has kept the faith of feminism, and enjoys a blast from the past. Another foot soldier for the revolution is always welcome. Unaccountably Chandra feels crabby. She is tired. The appeals for help, the dissemination of information, the demands of her email community have banked up. Chandra is placed in the network as a facilitator, a trustworthy crossroads; word can fan out from her office and maybe, even if it is as small as a blanket arriving where it is needed, the dispersal of information will achieve a result. Happy outcomes are also posted. Minutes are precious jewels. Judith never has any money, yet she somehow manages to make Chandra feel privileged to have her spend time with her. 'Too many bills.'

'Tell me about it.' Judith has entered Chandra's house silently. 'Give yourself a break and let's have a cup of tea. Would you like me to put the kettle on?' Judith asks.

'I won't be a minute,' Chandra responds, nodding.

Murderer. Alison suffers from multiple personality disorder from child-hood trauma. Sometimes Alison speaks of herself in the third person and some of her personalities are violent and irresponsible.

i wasted my affection on scum like you. your heart is in the wrong place. i feel deep betrayal from your death and from my friends.

This is loopy. Maria is dead. Chandra does not bother to answer Judith's call, 'Milk, sugar?' and keeps reading, entranced and baffled. She wants to see if the word 'murderer' is substantiated. Surely Maria died accidentally.

Judith is behind her again. She is very quiet.

>> and that is what it is inside of me, i want to be recognised not a consumer product we buy like big famous dyke singers. she doesn't have the heart. beware! she could blow our whole plan!

'It is extremely dangerous putting the Lesbianlands on the Internet, Chandra,' Judith whispers. 'We don't want to bring attention to ourselves.'

'No,' mumbles Chandra. For the first time she looks at Judith's face. She has make-up on. Mascara, lipstick, foundation, powder, the lot.

'What's that gunk on your face?' Chandra asks abruptly. 'Don't you know you're wearing dead whale?'

'Not any more. No animal was harmed in the making of these products. I know because I paid more to insure that,' explains Judith.

'I'm disgusted. Judith Sloane with make-up?'

'You are not still on about all that old stuff, are you?' She flicks her long hair back, and shrugs, 'Get over it.'

471

Chandra is bemused. She tries to reach the idealist she thought she knew, 'No. Immediately we let go, the revolution is lost.'

'Political correctness has become tedious, Chandra,' Judith says, with a touch of smugness, a touch of sarcasm.

Says Chandra, sighing. 'I am far from over it.' She spins into a turn on the spot, looking up at Judith with passion in her eyes. 'What happened to your face?'

'A fight. Your Lesbian Nation has turned to muck. It's every woman for herself,' Judith remarks bitterly. 'You can't have a revolution without violence.'

'You've become cynical, what brought that on?' Chandra leaves her computer, and wheels herself through her main room saying, 'We need culture, not nihilism.'

'Internalised sexual violence,' reckons Judith, walking behind her.

'I have never experienced sex as violent. Although, of course, I have had my heart broken,' says Chandra with artless honesty, inviting humour into the exchange.

The teapot and cups are ready on the kitchen table. Judith pours. 'One can always rely on your sincerity, Chandra. Plainly you need a girlfriend.'

Chandra laughs, 'Do I look like I'm denied the support of a little gentle loving and ego-stroking?'

'So you're getting it?'

Chandra makes a face, 'Who hit you?'

'Virginia.'

'You're kidding?' Chandra steers her chariot out onto the verandah and waits for Judith to bring her tea. She comments, 'When I was on with Alison, I saw her misery. As she hit out in aggression. At me. The daily indignity, the relentless leeching of self each demand and each act of masculine violence wrought. As mum number two, you can't know.'

'Well, I have felt betrayed by women who put their children first too, and I don't like it.' Judith states. 'Must be hard with a son like Harold?'

'Have you seen Alison, recently?' She takes the cup from Judith's hand.

'Yes, she was out bush yesterday,' is Judith's response. 'Harold's working out there, too, actually.'

'Is he?' Chandra asks, vaguely, reassessing her earlier conclusion about the writer of the narc rave: if Alison was out on the land then she would probably not access a computer, or be interested in writing that stuff.

'I think so.' Judith relaxes on the visitor's chair, tenderly touching her face to bring attention to her bruises. Irrelevantly, or possibly to stroke Chandra's politics, she opines, 'The nuclear family evolved to serve the industrial revolution, which shifted slavery to housewives and provided labour for the factories. The autonomy of women is only possible in First World countries that depend for their economic security on the slavery of Third World workers.'

'Was she okay?' Chandra is not about to get into ineffectual commentary. 'I mean Alison?'

'A bit stoned, a bit drunk. Why did you stop being with her? She is so sexy.' Judith's voice is sibilant. Chandra wonders what she is up to, why she is at her place, as she notices her clothes are fairly expensive, smart.

She replies, 'It was okay until the explosive, destructive tantrums. And the kids generally refusing discipline. Harold smashed the precious possessions to smithereens. Things flying everywhere. Mother and son in a power struggle, exhibiting violence. Her slowly absorbing this new abuse or loss into her system. Each one drags her away from her sense of herself and further away from the understanding of what a complete woman might be. Sexual relations are a little on the side.' She shrugs, 'Unfortunately.'

'You were committed to her?'

'I guess. Why did VeeDub have a go at you?' Chandra asks.

'Lesbian nation was a dream. Separatism is savage in the lesbian ghetto, as you well know.' Judith gazes across the garden, smirking.

'I was defending myself,' Chandra shakes her head. 'It was Meghan who was violent.'

'Self-protection?' Judith suggests. 'The truth is, Chandra, I don't know why Virginia belted me.' She gets up and leans on the rail. 'Will you show me what's happening on the Internet?'

Chandra shrugs, 'Why not?' They finish their tea and go into the office.

<DAMMIT> Annihilation of female selfhood is perpetuated by cowards like the White Virgin, creating myths and paranoia to achieve their required power. Like ethnic cleansing.

<BAC> It's the blokes who are using her. She is like a medium confessing the filth of the collective colonist-rapist brain, the ugly thought-form that is out there.

<DAMMIT> Actually when you really examine your conscience you have to ask yourself, are we sacrificing another woman, partaking in witch-burning?

The chatlines in <u>Cellar2</u> are open while Chandra's tracing software completes the task of chasing IP addresses. The muscles of Judith's guitar-playing fingers and weaving, spinning hands catch Chandra's distracted eye and for a moment as she feels uncomfortable. 'How is Virginia?' she inquires.

Judith says she doesn't know. By the time she leaves, Chandra's energy has been sapped. She stares over her paddock trying to whip it up again.

She watches Judith's new truck go out her gate, over the cattle-grid. She waits to see if it goes down the road to Meghan's. No. Then, she adds Meghan's name to her list of suspects. Rory, OWL?

Driving back through town I saw a bunch of gurls at the Telegraph.

The Telegraph Hotel took its name from a piece of Australian history famous to the fanatical few in the local heritage council. I did a job for the licensee who wanted to put an artefact, a cart with wooden wheels, in her beer garden to attract tourists with a bit of old world atmosphere and met opposition from the hobby historians. Although the Heritage mob knew the facts they were at loggerheads with the Historical Society. The one had the data and the other the bits and pieces, brown postcards, shaving blades, bottles, anything old. The tussle between those with the money and those with the relics consumed the energy of the enthusiasts. Repair, the threat of rust and upkeep worried the volunteers, so they latched onto my client's offer, while the other lot jealously argued it away. I guess they are not the only small group obsessed by internecine squabbles. The social organisation of the world is characterised more by the nature of small eddies of human activity than loyalty to broad ideals. Unified perhaps by taste, people stayed in circles of interest even when they were tourists on holiday. The old cart was no longer at the hotel. It was now on the little front lawn of the historical museum. The hospitality industry made its money and moved into the future.

The Telegraph's outdoor area reflected the coastal playground of Port Water with space-age sails and palm trees. The gurls, shaded by these, assimilated, seemed to choose their own eddy, which was in its way as strict as if they signed, paid and joined a constituted club. Dedicated drinkers, whose rules of loyalty and honour when broken consume most of the conversation, gossiped.

Sal Strauss, Wilma Woods, Xena Kia, the Larrikin and Milt were at a table in the beer garden of the pub, which overlooks the harbour of Port Water, the Sea Wall Sea World and the Lions park. I sat down with them. They were more subdued here, waiting for gurls from the land to turn up.

'Margot, you know Chandra won't have anything to do with an ex-cop.' I couldn't believe my ears. They were talking about my private feelings.

'It's true,' said Milt looking up from the racing form. I knew the Larrikin's contacts were far-reaching, but I did not expect this.

'Chandra,' the Larrikin insisted, 'flattened Meghan over something like baby-farming in South America. And multinationals rile her, right?'

'Here we have Margot smart as! in her Nikes with the subtle tick on all her gear, crisp, pure,' Sal plucked my T-shirt. 'And bought! While the company is exploiting women workers in poor countries. And children. Chandra would not approve of Nike, Margot. Their underpaid workers have to breathe in solvents that kill them, forced to work overtime, for a pittance, suffer humiliation and physical punishment and all the rest. She would say we should boycott their shoes.' Sal seemed to have a personal drum to beat; her irony had a bitter tinge.

'You were so proud of your Nikes, weren't you?' said Xena.

'Well, I didn't care,' responded Sal. 'They could have been Reebok, but they were great shoes.'

'Glue is glue. You can't get stuck without it,' Wilma made a joke.

Sal turned to me. 'Chandra could not go with either an ex-cop or someone in the pay of Nike International, regardless of the lust involved. Take it from me.'

'Here it is,' Milt found what she was looking for. 'They are Songstress in the fourth. In a quinella with Crestfallen. How's that?' She got up to place her bets.

'Who wants a beer?' I offered.

A session of gossip, casual observation; the odd question might yield something. I bought a round and asked for the docket. Expenses. Though on whose account I wasn't quite sure. Lonely Penny with her shiny surfaces was the type of woman who would love the give and take of family trivia about who is marrying who, buying presents at Christmas, but as far as I knew she had none. Family, for the Campbells, was everything, past, present, future, ideology, work, hobbies, possessions, values; one solid block. Sharp shards of difference threatened to cut the community of the gurls to shreds out of which, I guessed, new patterns of friendship would emerge. Resilient enough to withstand the dogged, ignorant dynamism of the Campbell bulldozer? I wondered. I went back to the group feeling the uncertainty of individuals bright as knives, treacherous as broken glass, for I knew the moment they mentioned it that I was in love with Chandra. And it was her passionate idealism that attracted me, as much as the chemistry between us. Yet they were right. I was paid by Nike. I was an ex-cop. Chandra could never be a hypocrite. She herself told me about her fight with Meghan. Meghan worked for the filthy captains of industry selling her soul, and in so doing, sold out women as well. Betraying solidarity between women Chandra could not forgive. I sat with such kin as I had, waiting for the gurls from the land, working. My instinct told me Alison Hungerford or Jill David would turn up.

Bikes lined up like horses at the rein-rail of a wild west saloon, helmets on the saddles in the centre of the street. The Larrikin loudly expressed the code she lives by. 'You scratch my back, I'll scratch yours. And know who owes.' She cooeed to the gurls who arrived. Yvonne and 'Ti for Trouble'. Jay, Dee, Dello and Maz. Milt wandered over and ended up talking with the bikie blokes.

Gig, driving Alison's car, pulled up. Tilly hopped out of the back, and Alison opened the passenger door. I drank full-strength beer. The enlarged group chatted about Maz's birthday party, rationalising some fairly disgusting sado-masochistic practice.

'It is as if I have found my inner nature,' Alison said.

'Not a pretty sight,' joked Dello.

'Call it self-hatred, but it's found its home,' Alison cried.

Xena asked, 'Yeah, where?'

'Coming to power,' mused Maz. 'I am a top with a slave and it is so easy! She is so willing, so guilty. I can't resist the temptation to tie her up.'

'I don't mind fantasising,' commented Ti. 'We don't mind that.' She reached out, but Yvonne pulled her hand away.

'I don't care if she hits up,' Yvonne gave as good as she got. 'It makes her so pliable. I adore stupidity.'

'She is proud of being selfish!' Gig stated.

'Apart from sticking it up the arm, she has got nothing to do except what I say. I understand lust, I understand passion.' Yvonne pulled Ti into a kiss. They moved away together and whispered under a palm tree. Then Ti returned and Yvonne hurried off.

I was not gaining much, but I stayed.

'Stupidity, that's it,' Alison snapped her fingers. 'It's dumb to be a genius.'

'What about you, Margot? Do you see your folks?' the Larrikin jabbed.

'No.'

'The ideal slave is a Christian with dreams of sainthood and admonishing the flesh and wearing hair coats and crowns of thorns.' Maz talked rubbish.

'Dream on,' said Dello viciously.

'You are, secretly, a good girl,' Maz teased.

Dello became angry. 'Well then that is the end of my ever really loving women. Cut.'

Maz continued, undisturbed. 'Love is impossible for me to even feel emotionally. Ever again. But I love feeling powerful.'

Xena said, 'You're full of bullshit.'

Gig wanted to know, 'Why is the violence never directed at the enemy, but at the lover or friend?'

Sal conciliated sarcastically. 'Maz is always talking about how women do each other in while happily doing it herself. You know lesbian relationships are four times more intense than het. One year equals four years.'

476

'Any more of those pills?' asked Alison. 'I want to dumb out. There is only one person who knows my genius. And I shot him.'

'Ask Larry,' said someone, while I wondered who Alison shot.

Xena stated, 'Marijuana saved my life.'

Alison looked well out of it. Grief. The company studiously omitted mention of Maria. Nor had they shown any shock over the confession of shooting.

'Women have different levels of tolerance, like the Cuban cigar after dinner.'

'To be stoned all the time means you are pretty much wasting your time,' judged Dee. 'This is cool if you've got nothing to do.'

'But sooner or later someone pays the tab,' Xena remarked.

'When they legalise marijuana, we should set up an industry, clothes, face cream, you name it,' Dee said enthusiastically. 'It's our future. The goddess plant.'

'Shut up.'

'Keep your voice down. We'll get busted. The drug warriors are all about town. Aren't they, Margot?' The Larrikin addressed me.

'It gives me the shits,' spat out Alison. 'What about psychiatric drugs! They make you into drongos.'

'You ought to know,' Maz smiled. 'Thought you wanted to dumb out.'

'Heroin started as a wonder drug,' Gig informed. 'In the laboratories.'

'I love it,' confessed Ti.

Dee completed the pair, 'And I hate it.'

'Why don't they give it to those who want it?' asked Ti.

'What I hate is the rip-off mentality,' Maz opined. 'You can't trust anybody any more.'

'People can get addicted to anything,' observed Dello. 'I reckon.'

Tilly was playing on the swings with holiday-makers' kids.

'Where did Tiger Cat get the pills that were given out on that Friday?' I suddenly asked Maz. 'Do you know?'

'They came from a bush laboratory somewhere near here,' Alison answered.

'How do you know?' the Larrikin barked.

'Read it on the net,' Alison replied.

I tossed in a lure. 'Tiger Cat. She's a narc.'

The Larrikin glared at me.

'Let's get it clear here,' Xena laid down her glass like a gavel. 'Do you know where we can get some more? Rik?'

'Eat your heart out.'

The Larrikin botted some coins to use the public phone in the bar.

Sparrows hopped in for the crumbs of potato chips. On the aqua water a flock of terns pursued a sturdy craft. Fat sea gulls squabbled near the fisherman's cleaning table.

'Hey, dig that. Judith Sly-bones in tête-à-tête with whatsername,' said Sal.

'Cybil, the cradle-snatcher.'

'Cradle-snatcher?' I wanted Wilma to expand, even though I had just been told by Lenny what Cybil had done.

'She doesn't care how young they are, I hear.'

'Do we, or do we not, have an item growing?' We all blatantly watched Judith and Cybil walk towards the park along the path on the sea-wall. Gliding on the water behind them, pelicans.

Cybil is suspicious of Judith. What does the hermit want with her? Her curiosity would only be answered by turning up, by having a meeting. Cybil is conscious of being watched as she listens to Judith's soft tones. Her ears burn. Margot Gorman is there. Although it feels deliciously covert, like boarding-school girls in the corners of halls, there are no walls. They are seen by eyes as wise as if they hear. Cybil is not listening. She is more comfortable as the watcher, not the watched. The secrets fall on deaf ears. She cannot trust Judith Sloane because she knows too much about her. All of it heard from Virginia White in Sunday morning pillow talk. Maybe truth is relative to each person's perception of it, she revises. From her own point of view Judith is probably none of the things Virginia said of her. While Cybil is insatiably inquisitive, she does have a strong faculty of discernment. While ready to take in hearsay, she wants the evidence of her personal impression. Cybil tries to walk away. Judith follows, speaking seductively.

'Will you have dinner with me?' The voice is husky, with attractive rounded vowels. Cybil cannot shake her, she has the insistent cling of a leech.

'Why?' She puts it rudely. 'Why should I?'

Judith will not take no for an answer. She is unfazed by rejection, convinced of her own significance. Her speech is a monologue. She has one idea, a purpose, all her energies geared its end. She hangs on until Cybil says, 'I've got an appointment, a conference, I have to go.'

'We have things to discuss,' Judith suggests conspiratorially.

Cybil nods. Despite her distrust, she names a place, and notes the pathetic satisfaction in her pursuer. For some people, getting what they want outweighs the way they achieve it. Fair, foul, flattery, cajoling insensitivity, outright aggression or bloody-minded determination they try, as if there were no meaning in the means. Cybil doesn't know why, but, instinctively, she dislikes her.

'Apart from that,' Judith smiles. 'You're quite gorgeous.'

Cybil says nothing and abruptly walks away, busily adjusting the padded shoulders of her ladies' shirt. She stops at the conveniences further down the park because she suddenly feels a shiver of fear. She checks her mascara. As she looks at herself, she admits that she needs Virginia. Not just anyone. But they are so alike. Perhaps Judith can become something for Cybil that is a compromise, morally speaking, and take away the loneliness.

Judith Sloane leans back on the grass in a pose, well aware that she is in view. She sits up, hugs her legs, looks at her scratches and pays attention to the sea-birds diving from a height into the shallows of the estuary. Then she takes out a tissue and wipes the make-up from her face. She marches up the hill to the beer garden, vaults the little brick fence and sits down at the table.

'You know what happened to me after the party?' The gurls shake their heads.

'Well, look. She indicates her yellowing black eye under the make-up. 'And there are more.' Her hands rub her ribs and she groans in pain.

'What happened?' asks Dee.

'Virginia, VeeDub happened. She turned on me and lashed out. She thrashed me and I hadn't done anything,' Judith, the innocent victim, is indignant.

Gig inquires, 'Why?'

Judith is tolerant, understanding, 'She hit the wall, I suppose and I was it.'

'Shit eh?' Wilma sympathises.

Margot returns with a round of drinks with Milt, who has fresh TAB tickets. She laughs genially. 'Been in the wars?'

'I don't think it's funny, actually,' Judith responds humourlessly. 'It has made my place feel unsafe, I don't know when she'll appear again, carrying the adze or the sharpened chisel she works with. The woman has gone mad. I am warning you. Her mind has detached itself from reality and is floating free. Why? She has always been jealous of me.'

'Are you drinking?' the Larrikin queries, genially.

'Of course not. I wouldn't even have their plastic orange juice. I'm not staying. Here look, up the back of my shirt? See?'

'Got any broken ribs?' Sal asks philosophically, 'Because if you have they will take ages to heal. I'd go to a doctor and get some strong painkillers. Make you feel better.'

'I might do that.' All look at her as she leaves them, carrying her hand-woven dilly-bag as if it were an Oroton purse.

'Looks like the Beetle clobbered the wrong snake,' Maz says. 'I shouldn't have told her.'

'Told her what?' Margot wants to know.

'Yeah, but who is Judith getting at, Cybil or the Beetle?' Gig ignores Margot's question.

'Both,' opines Ti. 'Stirring shit.'

'Why would she want to stir Cybil up? She is just her type,' Xena thinks.

'Maybe they are on-side, as you put it,' Margot observes.

'What's she up to?' Gig remains dubious.

'Why didn't you ask her?' Sal says idly.

'It's obvious,' Margot asserts. 'She takes you for a bunch of suckers. She shows you her bruises, tells you who did it, and Virginia's name is mud because you'll report the fact and it'll take off on the grapevine. And you don't even know if she's telling the truth or not.'

'What Judith should do,' Xena Kia opines, 'is sing more. Put on another concert.'

'Yeah,' agrees Wilma Woods. 'Good idea.'

'Give it a break,' scoffs Gig. 'She has locked her voice up in a bank vault.'

'Hey, Cybil would be the one to organise something like that,' Wilma continues her thought. 'Maybe that's what they were doing. Getting together some cultural activity for us gurls.'

'You wish.'

'One of the town gurls was into smack. Real cool and quiet about it,' Ti says.

'Who?' Margot asks.

'That's for me to know and you to find out, isn't it?'

'What about Cybil?' the Larrikin kids Margot. 'Could be her.'

'No. Too straight,' Milt reckons.

'Talk about straight and bent,' Maz interrupts. 'Like, take a line, there's only one straight one and how many bent? How many types of straight? How many types of bent?'

'We are all bent, airhead!' Dello exclaims.

'Got to go,' Alison groans. 'Where's Tilly?'

Dello brought Tilly back from the playground. The assembled drinkers seemed glad I took the sickest of them away. I do that sort of thing. If I'm around I can be relied upon. I needed more information about this laboratory that Alison read about on the Internet—as reliable a source as someone on the street, could be an expert, could be a bullshit artist. No knowing. The ethics of detecting concerned me quite a bit. Slander slid into gossip so easily. Judith was the expert. She wanted to show off her bruises while they were fresh because Virginia was responsible for them. It was a godsend and she was going to milk it for all she could get.

Alison was the most mercurial person I knew. She sat erect in the passenger seat. We left her car with Gig, and Tilly came with us.

'Devils, like fire, strangers, get inside my body, into my blood. I can feel it burning up, then nothing hurts. You wouldn't know the pain of nothing hurts,' Alison was trying to explain how mad she felt.

'Where to?' said I, waiting for instructions.

Alison, in response, asked me to take her to Chandra's. It was a good idea to get her to bed in the barn. She was silent for a long while.

As I slowed down to take the turn to Lebanese Plains, I finally asked, 'Who did you shoot?' I don't want to die guessing what I was too shy to find out.

'My father.' She spoke without the slightest qualm.

'Dead?' I glanced in the rear-vision mirror at Tilly, the image of her mother. She was looking at the paddocks, uninterested in our conversation.

'Oh no. He is a magistrate in a wheelchair. I was twelve. Nothing ever happened to me except my mind exploded. It was his betrayal of trust, not mine,' she screamed. 'What he could give me was lost. I shot to pieces whatever I was going to be. And gave my mother a nervous breakdown.'

Curiosity was stronger in me at that moment than any other emotion. 'Why are you so different now? Is it about Maria?'

'Just drive. I'm sick,' she ordered. 'I haven't eaten for days.'

The erstwhile equestrian helped me to get her mother to bed on the mattress under a cheerfully patterned doona in the barn at Chandra Williams' place. Tilly told me that Alison got sick now and then. She was certainly hot in the forehead when I laid my palm across it, and clammy. I left the young nurse carrying out instructions, drove my car up to the house, and explained the situation to Chandra. I took over some chicken soup, fresh bread, chamomile tea and Milo for Tilly, then went home. The half moon was high in the sky as the ferry chugged across the river. Out of the car, I let the stiff breeze blow up my fringe and cool my skin. I was exhausted.

Cybil, habitually a flirt and snappy dresser, anticipates her dinner with Judith Sloane with the suspicion that Judith wants more than her body. Cybil does not know what it is. She fears the worst.

Then, when they are facing each other across a table for two in a seafood restaurant, she tries to convince herself that now she is hearing the other side of the story. Judith says what she wants to hear. She bags Virginia.

'To put it mildly she thinks she is better than everyone else, but look at these bruises. She is just vindictive and as violent as the rest,' explains Judith, slyly glancing to gauge Cybil's reactions. No make-up now, her shiny black eye, facial bruises and abrasions would, if anything could, put her off her garlic prawns.

Cybil nods, seeming to concur on all points, although she found it hard to make Virginia go berserk, but, she remembers gratification the couple of times she had managed to get close. Judith's superior manner annoys Cybil.

'Why do you want to tell me all this?' she asks. Is that all you wanted me for? her bedroom eyes say. She feels she is being used, underestimated.

Judith shrugs mysteriously.

'Maybe you should just get over your jealousy of Virginia,' advises Cybil, and digs into the plate with her fingers.

'That's not what it's about. I thought you were a woman who would understand, who knows Virginia,' she whimpers. 'I feel really abused. I'm not going to let her get away with it. Not this time. We live in the wilds up there, no police. If women are allowed to go around bashing other women up because they don't agree with them, it's not safe.'

Cybil licks her thumb, 'I find Virginia quite moral and responsible.'

'Oh, I don't. She wants power,' claims Judith. 'She wants us to bend to her will.'

Cybil has known Judith's type all her life, and her projection doesn't fool her. 'I think she just wants to do her work,' she says, playing out the rope for Judith to hang herself. 'She's an idealist.'

Judith is very conscious of every movement. She carefully pours herself some water. 'Idealism is dangerous.'

Cybil coarsely guzzles her wine. 'Don't you mean ideology? Ideologues?' she asks, indifferently. She looks over Judith's shoulder at other customers, more interested in what they order than Judith's studied performance, although she does notice it. 'If you're not going to eat that, I'll have it.' Cybil covets the remaining rice-paper spring roll in the entree dish.

'No, that's mine.' Judith has been counting.

Cybil grins, and sighs, 'Tell me what really happened, then.'

'We were coming back from a party,' Judith has to speak with her mouth full. 'In the dark. No torch. Making our way home. And she just lashed out.'

Cybil is bored. Her eyes keep wandering to the swinging door to the kitchen. She watches the waitress.

'Virginia and I have known one another a long time and, you know what I mean, it's there all the time. Wednesday night her hostility broke through the surface.' Judith slowly, sanctimoniously, leaves the cutlery in the correct position for collection. 'Well,' she says, changing tack. 'I will have to retaliate to even the score. As I am not as strong as she, if it's an eye for an eye, she wins.'

Cybil rests her elbow on the table and her head in her hand, 'You mean idealism wins. Because Virginia wouldn't just hit you out of the blue.'

'Well, she did. She was drunk. Cybil, you don't need her. I'm warning you. She cracked. She'll come at you next. I'm worried for you.' Judith is seriously trying to seduce her.

Cybil recalls, as she looks straight at Judith, the appraisal Virginia made of this woman. Greed masquerading as monk, a miser on communal land tears the fabric of the collective. Virginia's biggest bone of contention with Judith was actually about the environment and abstract feminist ethics rather than personal animosity. Your closest neighbour is your worst enemy when deceit replaces respect for difference. Without truth, meaning and sincerity, said Virginia, and there was a fourth, something like relevance, you can only dictate. You can't have anything but struggle for dominance. Virginia is, Cybil concludes as she stares at the woman appealing to her, one of the least hypocritical people she has known. Especially women. Yet Judith is telling the truth, the bruises prove it. Uncomfortable, Cybil doesn't know what to think.

However, she parries, 'I don't believe you.'

Judith is shocked.

Cybil takes her elbows off the table to let the plates be cleared and, checking, appreciates the effect of her swordplay. She continues, 'You can tell me all the lies you like, and I might give you the benefit of the doubt. But I won't accept that Virginia hit you. Full stop. Not possible.'

Glancing through her swollen eyelids, incredulous, Judith shamelessly makes a pass, 'I could give you a better time, Cybil.'

'I'm sure you could,' she says, watching the waitress make her way from the swinging door past the other tables, carrying their main course. 'But Virginia did not beat you up.'

'But, it's true.' Judith is indignant. 'I really make her angry!'

'Frankly, Judith, I don't care,' Cybil thrusts. Steaming white rice is put on her plate. Abalone in green sauce she serves herself.

Something is being left out of the details of the fight which Judith describes, illustrating each blow to her body. Unlike Virginia, she is not giving Cybil her part in the event, her thoughts, her motivations. And that is deliberate. She must have provoked her. Cybil knows she could ask questions and receive answers. Liars are never lost for words. She tries one. 'Did you hit back?'

'No, I tried to protect myself!'
Judith, if she wants to seduce Cybil, will have to be more butch than that.

44

. . . the centre of the earth . . .

The men in the warehouse cast long shadows. Ian Truckman's questioning is silenced by, 'It's good money mate.' What they did with the trailer when he left it on its stilts at the docks is their business. His was home to see Mum and the sister's kids, play cricket, come away having nicked a piece of jigsaw for a good luck charm to hang off the rear-view mirror. The trailer he drags now is a tight rectangular package wrapped in khaki canvas, with state-of-the-art ratchet straps. Spraying the cabin with pine-forest fresh air, he says to himself, 'Good money, yeah.' He knows where 'good money' comes from.

Albury through Holbrook he pushes the rig flat chat on the clear Hume. The moon is a blade, swinging around from left to right of the highway. The night could be full of bones. The pressure pack falls out of his hand because of the sweat. The can is rolling under the pedals, so he slows the pace. Lights of a town. 'It's fucking Gundagai. Watch for cops. Don't answer CB. Shut up scabs, this rig can handle 140, no worries.' But the can is rolling round the floor and he needs to crap. 'Pull yourself together, Ian.' He has to stop at an all-night truck-stop, clean up in the shower, sit down for coffee and say gidday, what's your load? 'Yeah, I'd do that, if I knew the answer. Stop next one, Ian, my lad. I just got to lose that slick foreign sports-car. Stop it tailgating, passing, slowing, teasing, whizzing off and turning up again. It's not a car, it's a craft hovering eight inches above the road so as not to cause suspicion. It's only interested in me. What yer carrying, mate? What am I carrying for good money? Oh yeah, likely to admit it, sure. Not hungry anyway. Stopping, no way. Toxic shit. Guns. Don't know. Something illegal, I know that.'

Truckman is pulling this suspect material when Meghan frightens him travelling north between Albury and the Australian Capital Territory turn-off.

Meghan Featherstone chooses to take the Alfa Romeo to Canberra for the American. She has the kind of manic metabolism that scorns sleep. In Melbourne, they had arranged a meeting for six a.m. at the Brazilian Embassy assuming she would fly from Essendon with the rest of the team before midnight. However, the Yank, an automobile enthusiast who had bought the Alfa from a bankrupt in South Yarra for a price he could not refuse, needed someone to ferry it interstate. He mentions this casually. Meghan bounces in her seat, saying, 'Me, me. Let me.' Disingenuously. While the others shake their heads, her immediate superior smirks with a roll of his eyes to the ceiling. A practical man who knows how to handle his small bunch of specialists, he is a people manager. As a scientist none of the others approaches her intellect, but socially, Meghan is like a child. He does not treat her as a child. His intuition, educated by frank conversations with his wife, suspects this idiotic persona is an effective means of deflecting bothersome sexual harassment from her conceited colleagues, who are frequently humiliated when she dismissively demonstrates how slow they are.

Or maybe she is just naive. He leads the Australian arm of an international project which is top secret, involving several fields of science and study in locations all over the globe. While their clandestine activities are funded by various governments, most of their working capital comes from transnational companies convinced of the worth of their cutting-edge research. For continued confidentiality and avoidance of scrutiny from gubernatorial authorities such as taxation departments, money, channelled through a rack of holding companies, arrives in the workers' accounts from manifold sources. Above-board, no cash, the man runs a stable of talented, highly strung thoroughbreds. He has the job because he listens and watches, assessing the personalities equally as well as the material they present and analyse. That is why he is worth as much as they pay him. While ideology carried him through his science degree, his thesis a combination of zeal and plagiarism, his own expertise lies in human resources, fund-raising and diplomacy. To name the yet unnamed, to put God in His context, is his passion. To make the discovery, provide the explanation, which would eventually make him famous, is his destiny. While the scientists who collect data, experiment, conjecture and rationalise the findings are employees or consultants doing jobs from which they can be sacked at any time, or work in obscurity all their lives, he chooses. He is with the project right through. He has a hands-on, charming approach. He can talk money out of anyone, big money, for the biggest cause of all: the nature of man and the universe.

Meghan changes personality on the road. Meghan, the child prodigy, laughed to hysteria when the fair came to town. The ferris wheel was far too slow for her. The octopus, flying chairs, big dippers, the whizzer, the dodgem cars made her dizzy with excitement. When just a tiny tot she loved to be spun until she fell over. Her father, a mathematician, her mother a musician, both distant and abstracted adults seemed to find parenthood vaguely disgusting. Her sister, eighteen months younger, was and is driven by different demons. Where Meghan was fearless, Trina was controlled by anxieties. Trina would have tantrums brought on by terror in anticipation of what was about to happen, whereas Meghan would erupt into violence when emotionally disturbed and no excitement was scary enough. The father resorted to regimented discipline and the mother shrugged in domestic despair, turned to her piano and let the housework deteriorate until she got live-in help. The maid was a young German au pair with a taste for hair-raising games. Meghan fell in love, learnt German and French, and Trina's life became hell. Because Meghan pulled no punches when upset, everyone avoided upsetting her, which strategy was soon justified by her academic brilliance. Her parents recognised her prodigy and gave it encouragement and as much education as she wanted. The only relief Meghan had from the constant calculations in her brain, the mentality of learning one thing then having to know more, was the vertiginous daredevil escapades.

So her boss nods and the American tosses her the keys. He whispers *sotto voce* to his Australian counterpart, 'Can I trust her?'

'Should have been a racing driver, our Dr Featherstone,' smiles the man.

'I'll be in Canberra before six a.m.' Meghan promises.

The road gives her those precious moments of mental space she had achieved at the fairground in her young days. The car is beautiful, like riding a glorious hunter to hounds. She feels as aristocratic and glamorous as a countess in a James Bond movie. At Benalla she catches a semi-trailer whose South Australian number plate she recognises from a photo in her X-files. Targets for her mischief, UFO freaks, porn-surfers, rapists, cross-checked with registrations and driving licences identifying road-users who are vulnerable travelling, she decides to play. Her game is thorough. Her work requires her to have an extremely powerful torch. She has fibre-optic cable in her pack. She stops at a roadhouse, buys hot chips and sweets. Her tricks together on the passenger seat, she sets out to catch the lorry.

When the highway is shared just between the two of them, she tailgates him, flashing her long beam at hypnotic intervals. She knows she has a right bastard when he doesn't pull over to let her past. So she passes him suddenly on a left-bending curve and speeds away. Stopping ahead, she wobbles her piercing torchlight about through the back window until he is too close, then she darkens everything, to quietly bring up his rear later. She knows it's working when she times his speed from behind, flashing by him as he accelerates to 120. She reaches 180 kilometres per hour in the Alfa Romeo, all lights full on and screaming with the ecstasy of a roller-coaster rider on the down drop. She has fun all the way to the Federal Highway.

At the meeting she is refreshed and giggly, but loses her temper when someone presumes to order her to go to India next week.

'Get fucked. I'm not going offshore.' She is as temperamental as a chess champion. 'Not this month, boys.'

Her boss quietly says, 'Meghan, go get some rest. I'll be at your motel at eleven-thirty.'

In German, she utters something to effect of: 'I would not want to stay in this room full of sexist nincompoops if you paid me in rubies.'

The German responded in the same language, 'We pay you enough.'

Still in German, 'Oh? do you? Exactly how much? I want paper records. Of the Swiss account.'

'I beg your pardon?' Their amiable controller inquires.

'Nothing, just kidding.'

Dawn breaks at Goulburn for Ian Truckman, who pulls in behind the Big Merino, so proudly a ram. He reaches for the jigsaw piece, detaches it from his central mirror, kisses it superstitiously and puts it around his neck. The electronic message from his boss reassures him. Entering details into his logbook, he doubts whether the crates contain only what is written down. Dragging a tanker of water half-way down the east coast of Australia, delivering a million-dollar cargo, has taught him how smart they are, how cluey he is. He gets down, goes around the load yanking the self-clicking straps, tight and true. He locks up, has a shower and a shave. Orders breakfast. Rests. Waits. He has to ferry another bloke. He'll have the details. Truckman knew it; they wouldn't leave him by himself for too long. Mustn't show he's onto their game, say nothing, hear nothing, see nothing. They give him plenty of time to cogitate. Almost too long because Ian works out they're playing him for a fool. What do they think, he doesn't know a real UFO from some idiot in an Alfa Romeo buzzing around his rig like a blow-fly? Hannibal must have money to burn to go to all that trouble to exploit his weakness. He touches the missing bit of the kids' jigsaw at his throat, just cardboard and paper, a speck of individuality, right, they're having a go at his mind. Feeling sick on his stomach, having finished the bain marie selection on his plate, he hopes he has not caught a case of food poisoning.

'Clever dicks are fundamentally dull,' Meghan Featherstone murmurs as she flashes on her expensive slim-line notebook. She perches on the king-sized bed with its foot-deep mattress and half a dozen pillows and organises the results of her analysis in readiness for the visit from her hungry, ambitious

Solieri. Along with the hard scientific facts and the solid slivers of glass, she buries the mystery and places the nonsense in the mass of mind-boggling data in a stream of figures and formulas. She is ready to release her wild goose. The time is right. She hasn't slept. The printer spits out pages at the rate of thirty a minute.

Her boss comes. A rap on the door. As soon as she opens up, she is the very picture of driven genius, black rings under her eyes. The man resembles a television scientist straight from make-up. Ingratiatingly courteous, he takes a seat at the table. She overdoes her act of intellectual distress. She raves, appropriately distracted by the mental strain of higher calculus as she dumps reams of paper in front of him.

'Because of the maths of gravitation,' she says as she taps the column of numbers, 'it is assumed the earth is dense. It is too heavy to be hollow, right?'

'Physics proves this. Iron, lead, solid matter,' he recognises a couple of equations. Fe, relative atomic mass 55.847. Density 7.86 at 20 degrees Centigrade. For each known substance she has run the calculation almost to infinity. He shuffles the pages. 'What's this? Stone? Bronze?'

Meghan paces. 'But what do you make of it, Sol?'

He doesn't want it to be this difficult, but he does want to be able to articulate the abstract scholarship in media-friendly English. He packs the sheets into a squared pile, turns them over and lays his beautifully manicured hands on the blank whiteness. 'I can see you've done a lot of work, heating up matter to impossible temperatures, in the theoretical, why? What's the hypothesis?'

'No, what I've done here,' she reaches for the print-out. He won't let her consult them. He needs extrapolation, not detail, not jargon. 'But but,' stutters Meghan.

'From the top Dr Featherstone, and rustle up some coffee,' he orders.

She takes the kettle to the tap. He sighs, shakes his head and gets up to go to the bedside phone. From room service he demands freshly ground high-quality beans, an Italian glass plunger and demitasses.

'No, I do not want you to make it,' he barks into the receiver with crisp impatience. 'But we will have bottled water if we may.'

'At first,' Meghan complies with his request for the full story, 'I thought we had a strange, softish meteor, you know, something that would splat, as it were, on impact. That is not within the realms of sane thinking,' Meghan interrupts herself with a giggle. 'No no no, what I mean is, I was looking at the future. It could have been a space-craft landing, sort of hovering, blasting the ground with retrojets as kind-of brakes, turning the sand to glass. That wasn't it. But it wasn't far wrong. It wasn't that far wrong, the silicone has been baked. All except for the mysterious element.'

'That's what this is about?' He points at the mathematical material on the table.

'Well yeah, but none of it is right. I had to look at the past. Combine archaeological thinking with physics.'

'You've lost me,' he says patronisingly.

'No, I haven't. Don't be ridiculous. You picked it up straightaway.' She sits down at the table opposite him. 'Stone and Bronze?'

'So?'

'The Ages, you ninny!' Her tired eyes twinkle with the maternal humour of knowing more.

'Now, I wish I'd asked for the jargon,' he comments as he responds to the knock on the door and lets the busboy place the tray on the bench by the kettle. Silence until the hotel employee is out of earshot. Meghan is at his shoulder as he works making the perfect coffee.

'It's the mind-set, not the facts, that gave me the break-through. Well, not exactly. The future was a dead duck, right?, so the past. In the dictionary I read that in classical mythology the Iron Age, definitively human, is considered "the last and worst age of the world". It follows the Stone and Bronze.'

'This, plainly, is not your area of expertise, Meghan. How do you have it?' He indicated the coffee. 'Black?'

'Whatever,' she sighs, changes her mood as if offended. She pulls her briefcase out from under the bed. 'The molten layer under the earth's surface is an indication of how hot the centre of the earth is, but it cannot be hollow.'

He laughs. 'Show me that.'

Meghan hands him more of her work. 'Rutile, ilmenite, zircon, valuable, but not interesting.'

'What's this? Substance X?' He sips his coffee delicately.

'An inexplicable biospheric medium,' Dr Meghan Featherstone replies nonchalantly, opening the fridge door to cool down her coffee with milk.

He speaks, 'Should, of course, the glass have come from outer space, a bit of meteorite, perhaps, would that prove, or go some towards proving there's life, or was life, on Mars for instance?'

She shakes her head then nods. 'The first poser, for me, was it was too geometric. A perfect circle. What is truly round, Sol? To be accurate, a perfect half-sphere. Like a cut ball, five metres in diameter?' Meghan is paid well to teach him, so she is patient.

'How can we find the other component?' He examines the written material, intelligently. 'That would be a start.'

Meghan heaves a noble sigh. 'The only substance I know that eats glass is hydrogen fluoride, but it's incredibly toxic.'

'So we eat away the glass and find the biomatter?' Sol is a can-do man with resources at his finger-tips on his touch-phone. 'Is there a possibility that it's a fossil from earlier earth-life?'

'Use your brain man!,' Meghan scolds. 'Too integrated. Iodine vapour might work, if we find methane . . .'

'If not space-craft, what about earth-craft?' he interrupts.

Meghan snorts, 'I hadn't considered that.' She tosses a lump of greenish-white quartz in the air and catches it. 'About the weight of a cricket ball.'

'Methane cannot exist very long in the presence of oxygen without a biological source. Meteorites do not leave a perfect circle, nor do fossils or other dead relics of life as we know it,' he says, not taking any notice. Geologists always fiddle with bits of rock.

'I do not know about you, but it is pretty much proved to me that space-ships do not land on and take off from the earth's surface at will, although, a direct vertical rocket emission of nuclear-fuelled jet propulsion could explain, a, the glass, and, b, the circularity.' Meghan examines the uncharacteristic smoothness of her quartz.

'You're right, we'd know about rogue, non-government activity in that area. Private enterprise is shooting up satellites all over the place but we've got them all taped.' He closes the folder of geological data. Slaps it on top of the ream of the columns of mindless, brilliant calculations of computer software and wonders, again, where the hypothesis that set them running came from, and says. 'What's this gobbledegook about the Stone Age?'

Meghan takes a big breath, catches his eye before she says, 'What about Hell?'

'What about it?' He lifts himself off the chair.

'Beings living in fire at the centre of the earth,' Meghan grins. 'Very, very heavy guys. And so small you can hardly detect the carbon.'

'This is too outrageous! I know we live in a time of degeneracy and wickedness, but.'

'Exactly, beginning with the Iron Age,' Meghan posits triumphantly.

'I'm thirsty.' He flips a grapefruit juice out of the bar in the fridge, and offers her a drink with a gesture. 'I love it. You can properly say I am bamboozled!' He is sarcastic, 'Love it.'

'So,' Meghan doodles a circle. 'A bubble.'

'A bubble? As in blowing soap bubbles?' He looks at her drawing as he places the glass of juice beside the stone of similar colour.

'Yep. Of incredibly pure heat. Most of it, vapour. Think. Cross-section.'

She drinks his juice.

He sighs and gets another one. Then sits next to her. 'Okay,' he admits doubtfully.

'How come it appeared?' She scribbles in a few desert oaks and the horizon line of the desert. 'Did Atlantis have warning of its disappearance?' She drafts the crust of the earth with the different levels of strata in lines on a list, cross-hatching, dots, waves. 'We assume that the heavy nature of the centre of the earth is dead metal. Have you considered the possibility that life, not as we know it, could be heavier than matter as we do know it? This thing, Sol, has the structure of an excrescence from inside.'

'Heavier. Than black holes for instance?' He is sceptical.

'Oh no. Exactly calculable,' she reaches over and taps on the print-out. 'The centre of gravitation. The basis of magnetism. Mankind has only ever drilled down eight kilometres. We do not know that we do not have biological essences beneath that.'

'Run that by me again,' he requests, getting the picture.

'Do we know the chemical essentials of mentality, fully?' Meghan moves her hands in the air grasping for a concept. 'The material basics of—ah—soul?'

'Uh uh. I'm with you,' he assures her.

'The hypothesis suggests that a bubble, a pimple, has erupted from deep within,' she shows it with her pencil.

'Volcanic?'

'No, Sol,' Meghan says tiredly, 'I checked that initially, naturally.' She catches his attention with a serious stare. 'In your search for proof of the existence of god, how would you like to prove the devil?'

'Wow,' he leans away from the beam of her stare. 'This iodine vapour? Even, possibly, hydrogen fluoride can isolate this Substance X, right?'

'If we can incontrovertibly verify its bio-fossil component or pith, we can make a giant leap in the search for our reason for being,' Meghan says simply.

'My mind is blowing, girl,' he admits, reaching his arms up into a complete stretch. 'This is great. We may find a life force even more destructive than man!'

'Personally,' Meghan, having delivered her findings, seems suddenly bored with the whole business. 'I think that men came from one of the solar systems outside the Milky Way and invaded this planet. Whether or not for their own survival. Like Superman–Clark Kent,' she hesitates. 'However, they're rather like the cane toad, randy and poisonous, with no natural predator. A real exotic, extraterrestrial. Or like the domestic dog who interbred with the dingo, and made something worse than a wolf when it's at home. An out-of-control pest. With no predator, man is searching for an enemy, killing everything else.'

Her Solieri is greedily collecting the papers, including the doodled drawing. 'I'm not interested in your wacky personal beliefs, Dr Featherstone. What I want is Substance X, substantiated, named (I'll name it), identified, patented, organised, analysed. Carefully protected, knowledge of it cautiously marketed, and, when you're ready, open to authenticity tests by colleagues of world renown. Do I make myself clear?'

Meghan, the stressed and relieved consultant, acquiesces obediently. 'You'll find the test sample and the top-secret paperwork in a locked bag in my wardrobe in the living quarters of our Darwin base laboratory.' Meghan makes a bowling action with the weighted stone in her hand, then puts it down, crunches some paper into a ball and actually throws it with a stiff arm windmill at the wastepaper basket. Picks it up and does it again, loosening her shoulder muscles. He is packed up and ready to leave.

She grins. 'Now, Boss, I think I deserve some rest and recreation.'

'Sure, I'll ring you from Darwin. When I have had a good look at all this,' he feels for the doorknob.

'Just be careful who you show it to,' Meghan cautions. 'You don't want to be taken for a fool.'

'No way José! I'll be in touch.' He opens the door onto the plush corridor. She bowls a paper ball through it and acts silly. He shakes his head. 'Get some sleep. And have a holiday.'

45

. . . threatened to rape me . . .

The big black and tan dog greeted me with a wag of its behind. It had no tail. I smiled. As she had seemed pretty self-sufficient to me, I raised my eyebrows when Chandra asked me to lift her into the car. Sort of vulnerable in my arms, her upper-body strength carefully spread her weight evenly across my shoulders. She swung herself into the passenger seat like a pet monkey. Chook-feed in a bucket on her hip, Tilly waved us off with an arc of seed, knee-deep in a flurry of feathers.

This time, on the highway, I knew where I was going. A huge box of fresh produce topped by glossy silver beet leaves and bright red organic tomatoes sat in the bottom half of my rear-vision mirror. Every now and then, the human-sized head of the canine filled the reflection to look at the road ahead and catch my eye. We talked about odds and sods, asking each other personal questions in a way dykes have of getting to the essentials. Easy chatter in sweeping brush-strokes. My Achilles tendon injury somehow connected to my work on the death of a mother's son.

'"He was his mother's only joy",' I quoted.

'Thetis couldn't save her son.' Chandra inspired trust like a counsellor.

'Penny's devastated. I just wish whatever I do eases her grief,' I said. 'She wants answers.'

Chandra's smile creased the tanned face beneath the high cheek-bones and hard broad forehead. 'You've got a pretty good instinct in your investigations, Margot. What makes a good detective, lateral connections?' Chandra fished.

'All logical and linear with me,' I fibbed, omitting to mention the huge part hunches play in my work.

She laughed outright. 'You beguile with your sunflower looks. Here is the cliché incarnate! Margot's Achilles heel is an Achilles heel.'

'Yep. What you see is what you get!' Not exactly true.

'We both have secrets,' she said, as if she read my thoughts. On safer ground, Chandra gave her opinion of classic Greeks. 'Dionysus is like hippie men are now, wearing sarongs, exploring their femininity, dancing, playing the flute and driving women mad with their pretence, and Apollo is like the military, pure might. Achilles is definitely Dionysian, dressing up as a girl, Mummy's boy, but he is more of a poofter than your regular sensitive New Age guy, even though he fathered children when dressed as a maiden. They never give up sexual rights over women. They hang on to patrilineal descent. Achilles is vermin. Misogynist arsehole.'

My modern Greek-Australian mate was the macho man, but I didn't mention Pip to Chandra.

'And worst of all he killed and did despicable things to the body of the Queen of the Amazons, Penthesilea,' she remarked, viciously, reminding me of Rory and her guests last time I went to Lesbianlands. Also the word 'vermin' echoed in my head, said equally warmly by Vanderveen, the righteous environmentalist: if you believe something is vermin it is easy to kill.

'I have an old aggro Apollo to the north and wimpy greenie Dionysus to the south of my house. Who does that make me, Artemis?' I grinned at Chandra.

'Adonis was ripped to pieces by Artemis' dogs,' she said as I changed down gears to take the turn-off to the National Park.

Along the dirt road at a slower speed, I said, 'Speaking of pretty boys, do you think in a full-blooded matriarchy, the women in power had their fill of the most gorgeous youth of the land in springtime? For the rest of the year male adolescents were despatched to the desert to find their manhood through difficult initiations designed to let off their excess testosterone. I guess, a few lads wouldn't survive.'

She asserted, 'Men were not given free access to children or women. But they had to conceive,' Chandra affirmed. 'How do you think women would exercise power over other women? I don't think motherhood was as rampant as it is today.'

'That's a funny way of putting it.' I pondered the idea. 'Not all women are maternal, that's for sure.'

'What do you think about Lesbian separatism?' she probed.

'Separatist movements are a worry in this world where ethnic cleansing is the dreadful excuse for atrocities. Human rights violations—' I stopped because she wasn't listening. A mob of cattle sheltering in the shade of a gum on the flat of the road caused me to press my brake pedal sharply, bringing us up with a jolt. Myself and a cow gazed at each other. Then I turned to my passenger, mystified by what I must have done wrong. She had a closed mouth grin, a grimace, which she held a second before she met my eye with a twinkle in her own.

'Trust,' I finally answered. 'Power without oppression needs faith.'

The cows decided to move. I accelerated forward in a different, more cautious, frame of mind. Although my gut told me she didn't trust me, I felt the heart in my chest healthily beating. Happily.

Rory was ready to meet us in her Land Rover Guntractor, looking as pseudo-military as ever. The kelpie moved like a darting otter on the tray-back. Rory allowed me to take the boxes of food and the clothes bag while she carried Chandra to her truck. Chandra plainly wanted to be on the ground. Chemistry changed in the atmosphere. The divisible number two became the prime number three, an integer of a different colour. Unity or what? Fractions? The air was charged, fractious. Suddenly feeling discomforted I almost jumped back in the Suzuki to escape down the highway to the safety of the coast and a swim in the sea. I yearned to yell, 'Put her down, you stupid butch.' Irrationally irritated, I stood separately for a few moments, sorting the intense triangle. Rory fancied me, I fancied Chandra, and Chandra would probably go with Rory because she was politically up her alley, and that apparently mattered heaps.

The Rottie leapt onto the back of the truck with surprising agility. I pulled myself up beside Chandra and slammed the rattly door. The mood between the other two was sombre.

Rory addressed me. 'If you were surfing the net on your favourite subject, Margot, and you came across a site, say, called Cybergrils, what would you think?'

'Um, spelling mistake?' I replied.

'Okay. And?' she continued. 'Would you click in? And if you did, what would you expect to find?'

'A bunch of teenage geeks,' said Chandra helpfully.

'Right.' Rory kept the conversation rolling. 'Supposing, it was a spelling mistake, but then, it took on another meaning that was there all the time. Well? What do you reckon?'

'Steak and chops,' I joked. 'Q and A sessions at the cop shop. Truckies' meals.'

'Not a laughing matter,' Chandra tisked her tongue and motioned towards plants, saying, 'Look at all that stinking roger.' The weed looked to the un-trained eye like marijuana.

Rory had a point to make. 'Well, it has have something to do with girls. Lesbians?'

'Girls claiming their space in the technology revolution,' Chandra put in, lightly.

'What's the point of asking me? I know bugger-all about cyberspace.' I got out to deal with a gate.

By the time I was back in the vehicle they were exchanging information with so much mutual knowledge that clarifications did not need to be said. While I was madly curious, I kept mum. Explanations would come in their own good time. Once I let it go without trying to interfere, I quite enjoyed being bounced along next to Chandra, not having to socialise. When we passed the gate of Lesbianlands I sensed a change in nature. Chandra fell into me and let me right her back into position. On the fence was a sign NO MEN ALLOWED. TRESPASSERS PROSECUTED. Then SHOT ON SIGHT was added on a piece of cardboard lower down.

'Wilma must have been through recently.'

'Which Wilma?' I asked facetiously.

'Not Wilma Woods, Wilma Campbell,' Rory fired, not offering an explanation of what gave her the impression that Willy's wife had been through.

Rory hardly addressed a word to me during the jaunt towards her place, although she was not impolite. Rory is a direct, no-nonsense person. She did not try if she didn't have to. Chandra stared straight ahead. I had the definite feeling that I was supernumerary; that they had business with each other which could not be conducted while I was in earshot. I tried to probe, suggesting lightly that secret women's business via the superhighway must be pretty dangerous, so many phonies and hackers lurking. I was shooting in the dark, but their rigid reactions, an emphatic freeze, gave me the feeling I may have hit the spot.

At the new bridge, I said 'Let me out here. I need to interview some gurls. Lesbianlands' problem doesn't seem to be your priority right now. I guess it's mine.'

Rory stopped her cumbersome truck immediately. Chandra told me that food would be on the table in two hours max. I waited for her smile, or even that spark of mischievous humour, but her eyes were shaded, dark pools. Still water running deep. Taking my notebook and pen, I slammed the creaky door closed. They rumbled off. I took the downward path. It forked at a creek. I walked beside it for a while.

Instead of easily finding someone to ask questions of, I heard accusatory passion splitting the murmuring ambience of the bush. I stayed hidden, sitting with my back resting against a tree trunk, my notebook in my lap. Trying to repress my own resentment, in the weird character of this place, my anger was expressed by other voices.

'You're a liar!' I idly took dictation.

'It is beneath me to explain the plain and bloody obvious,' someone said.

'There's nothing I can do if you don't believe me, is there?'

'When a liar says she's a liar, she is lying.'

'I'm not lying,' the voice pleaded.

A gurl I did not know came through the trees, stopped, turned and shouted. 'Get fucked, you're breaking my heart.' Then they resorted to shrieking obscenities which you wouldn't have had to be nearby to hear.

'You're a coward, Pam. All for a bit of pussy. You shouldn't muck around with them!' The distant voice yelled.

Pam was a shorter, younger version of Beetle, the triathlete, with a lower forehead and dark chestnut hair. She had a pygmy possum in her shirt and talked to it. 'My Poss, she wants to get away from me, but my guts are churning, frenzied and frantic. How do you get on with women? Hey, Poss? The piper comes with his intentions to ecstasy hoping to make you, to make you a fool, an addict, a beggar, and the woman comes all flirt and kindness, dressed in the rainbow colours of confessions contrived to make you trust an easy goodness as you give away your freedom, blaming me. My sin was. Okay, she can blame me, Poss, and punish me as much as she likes, but I'm right. Too good to be true gurls, dark as sewers sucking at your springs of fresh water, your generosity. Braininess is worthless without compassion, and I am a liar, whereas her jealous rages are truth, Ruth. True as death and gluttony, and the lie that prostitution is the oldest profession. Just because she is a woman doesn't mean you can't become her sex slave or she can't be brutal and odious and cruel and all the rest. Men are happy to share their values. Poss, I didn't lead him on. I just wanted a good time for a change.' What she said gave her an idea. She stood up and shouted, 'A destruction upon your houses!' She calmed down, 'But that is not what I want. Now I see the fear in your face. It's okay, Poss, my little friend. The fear in my face excited her as much as it excited him.'

Pam turned around and caught me writing. She walked up to me. 'How can you tell the truth when there are no words for the magic of nature?' Pam asked, as if in the middle of a conversation with me, whom she didn't know. 'Now I can give up, slough the lot. Her actions are reactions to bloody gossip. You want to see my house?'

'Sure,' I accepted.

We walked across the creek, which, lower here than at Rory's, if indeed it was the same one, ran quite broadly, a shallow stream. Pam talked to herself, to me, to her possum, to the trees. 'I am to blame. I must be deadly.' Pam was one of the gurls who hardly emerged from the bush, and when she did, apparently, she went to the local pub and got drunk. While she was easily twenty years younger than Virginia, the softer features of her face were worn with the travails of the rustic life-style. Incredibly skinny, she walked with a stoop.

We stopped. She pointed to a big old native fig. In the shadows of its branches and hanging roots, I could identify, after a second, a rope ladder between the flat buttresses.

'You live in a tree?' I was amazed. 'A cubby house?'

'Yeah.' Her fireplace, pots, billy and plates, however, were on solid ground. Corner ropes tied to convenient trees stretched a tarpaulin slung over a cross beam resting in the forks of two planted poles into a roof, protecting the utensils from rain. Untie the knots, slip out the ridge-pole, pull off and fold the canvas over the neatly packed essentials and one would see practically nothing. A truly demountable kitchen. Pam dropped to a cross-legged sit and rolled tobacco from a leather pouch, still talking aloud. Amid chattering to herself, she suddenly asked, 'You are?' Her piercing eyes looked straight at me.

'Margot,' I answered.

'Margot, you're the detective. You want the culprit. He is in her bed dressed as a woman. The culprit,' she said the word several times, liking it. Pam saw my curiosity at how she shared her life with the frogs, birds, possums and thousands of insects. 'Have a look if you want.'

The rope ladder attached to the bough and floor-joists came up to a hole, then you crawled. I climbed into her wooden kennel perched in the arboreal growth. Her living quarters contained no more than a foam mattress and bedding, a fruit case beside it on which was a candle and a book on magic, and low rough shelves made of the same. I was examining the home of a real tree-dweller. Tidy, bare, a monk cell. Would-be windows and doors opened on to the trunk and limbs of the fig, making the branches a lounge, roomy with sitting-places, nooks and crannies.

'Far out,' I called.

At home in the forest, I'd heard Pam was a capricious thief, and, as I looked down, I saw her as pretty attractive. She didn't answer. I was a witness to Pam, nothing more. Or rather, I, like all about her, was an extension of her-self, her environment, her mood. But I did need to know what was behind her culprit rave. I descended to earth.

'What do you mean "he is in her bed dressed as a woman"?' I asked slowly.

'Cocks in frocks,' she muttered. 'Even naked. I live in my own world, but it's a really real world. Look at it.'

'Why was Gig so angry with you?' Standing, I reached down for my pen and paper.

'Jealous. It's too dangerous to tell everyone who you fuck with. I'm always scared. But I didn't lead him on. I don't do it with men.' Pam shrugged. 'I don't like men.'

'Which man?' I pressed.

She sighed. 'Like Willy Campbell threatened to rape me, right? The gurls have got to protect me and when I go out there's always someone with me.

I don't have a car, I don't drive. Don't have any money. Nothing. But when he came in here, I was shitting myself. He was looking for me. I'm the one he wants to rape. Anyway, he wasn't on horseback, he had a bulldozer and I saw him smash the bridge. But I ran away. I just told her then and she went ballistic.'

'Hang on, hang on,' I begged. 'You actually saw Willy Campbell drive the bulldozer over the bridge? Why didn't you tell someone?'

'How could I when I was hiding? No one can find me when I am hiding. But it's true.' She mumbled on some more about being called a liar and admitting she was a liar because it was too dangerous not to be.

'Well, I believe you,' I consoled. 'Now tell me, after you saw him breaking the bridge?'

'It was so scary! But he didn't do it deliberately. I didn't know dozers could move so fast. And the noise!' she exclaimed, and shivered in recall of it all. 'Chucking sticks of dynamite all over the place.'

'Okay, can you say where he went after that?' I inquired, hopefully.

'Dunno, but kind-of up the road to Ilsa's or off towards the plateau, you know, where Hope is living, but there's a gully to the west of that.'

'Other women heard the explosions, too.'

'I reckon.' The pygmy possum emerged from its cosy pocket. She patted it as it nestled into her neck. 'It was too crazy. Who was going to believe me?' The way she talked, full of internal drama, even paranoia, crying wolf and muttering on, it was easy to understand why she would not be believed.

'Where were you all this time?' I queried. Pam had missed the meeting, and all that had occupied the lives of the others in the meantime, a dance, a funeral, parties.

But she was not going to reveal her secret places. Pam had the instincts of a feral and the furtive gleam of a wild dog. In some ways she was right. Gurls did not want to know more than they could deal with at any one moment, and, if she came to their camps to say there was real and present danger when everything was dangerous to Pam, why would they listen? Usually, I supposed, they did not take Pam seriously, apart from sometimes cuddling her when she crawled into their beds. But I had got a rough idea of where to go next in my hunt, the track to Ilsa's. I said the usual polite things and went upwards to find my way to Rory's place.

The beginning of the waterfall was a narrow creek finding its way past flat rocks which seemed to invite you to lazily lay your body down. The view was a wonder to behold. Steep gorges, hanging rocks and dense patches of rainforest, and in the distance, pure hill-lines coloured in with pastel purple. The track I chose wound its way down into the bewitching feel of close jungle. The crystal sounds of water and birds piping to each other, rustles here and there, the heady smell of fecund growth and mulch filled my senses. I had no choice. I had to go where I would be a leech's delight.

After Margot leaves their company, Chandra begins to express her concern about the free radicals infecting the carefully set-up honeycomb of rooms within rooms of her website. Having got to Rory's hanging cottage and unloaded the boxes and bags, which Rory does while Chandra admires the bush and the building, over a cup of tea, they discuss face to face the vulnerability of the conspiracy to misuse. Chandra says, 'We know it is someone who knows our community, whether or not it is a he or she in the meat.'

'So,' Rory is down to business, 'we discard those who are not techno-literate.'

Chandra frowns. 'I don't know whether we're looking for two or three people here. One, the raver. Two, the betrayer. The Tragic.'

'Why can't they be one and the same?'

'Who knows?' Chandra mutters. 'They'd have to have a split personality.'

'Is the Annihilation Tragic a Solanasite?' Actually what is disturbing Chandra is not at all clear to Rory.

'No,' Chandra is using Rory as a sounding board. 'The net is anarchic, we have to change the strategy to allow revolutionaries to act in any way they feel fit. But how do we prevent transgression? There can't be unified action. But there's got to be boundaries?'

'I've thought about it and I don't want to be involved in the killing of any person,' confesses Rory with sincerity. When Chandra says 'we', she realises, she means 'I'.

'But how can we control it?' Chandra sighs. 'The structure facilitates the spread of ideas based on the passion of Valerie Solanas and the early radical feminists, who believed they could change the world. I cull the bags of hot air. I'm my own web-master. But, someone's come over the top of me. I did not anticipate, or formulate any mechanism to contain, really odd-ball, destructive activity.'

'I don't know if you can force everyone to agree with you.' Rory puts her criticism mildly. 'What would our major objective be, anyway?'

'If we attacked the money-markets, the banks for instance, down the line that would cause suffering of the poor, even suicide. Homicides out of desperation, because the fat cats will hand it down,' argues Chandra.

'As a member of a loose non-hierarchical organisation, how far is one responsible for the actions of others in the same cause?' Rory questions, rhetorically. 'It's as much about means as ends, isn't it?'

'Yes, and about individual conscience. A veritable monster,' Chandra exclaims. 'Such a perfect idea.'

'It was, I mean, it is, brilliant, Chandra. I think you've got to have faith in us participants,' Rory pleads. 'The ideals themselves intrinsically have ethical constraints.'

She acknowledges the compliment, and relaxes a little. 'I don't know about you, Rory, but I believe in loyalty to the philosophy. In practice. As integral to our updated manifesto. I'd choose loyalty to principle over loyalty to persons, including friends and lovers, given the instance they are in conflict.'

'Such dedication to the cause!' Rory jibes, doubtful that she agrees. 'Even if you could control membership to, say, a knowledge of the manifesto, you still have different interpretations of what is effective. And what is unacceptable.'

Although their conversation is abstract, it is potent with the intensity of hungry, selfish needs. They are like tennis players hitting balls over the net of Margot's absent presence, using the skills of their intellect, the high standard of their political commitment, to keep the game going.

'Remember the recipes?' Chandra pulls a handwritten page out of her handbag and reads, 'Mouldy Rice Bread; Black Coal Chapattis; What Pip Does With Eggplant; Sofia's Dope Cake; V.W.'s Anything Patties; Camp Oven Stewed Veg (fresh); Chandra's Strawberry Jam and Victoria Shackleton's Fried Tomato Sandwiches.'

'Strange,' Rory comments. 'Who's Pip?'

'The Tragic herself,' decides Chandra. 'Perhaps?'

'A mischievous imp. Let me guess, ah? Alison?'

'No,' Chandra shakes her head. 'Impossible. She's been out of it since Maria's funeral.'

'Sofia, then? She could have access, I mean, it is vaguely within the realms of possibility.' Rory tries to imagine what it is like for those with mental illness, locked in a ward. What are they allowed?

'Who is visiting her?' Chandra has not yet made the time to do it herself.

'A few,' Rory displays how in touch she is. 'Jill David for one.'

'Well, she could carry in a PC,' Chandra reckons. 'Jill loves gadgets.'

'Yes,' Rory accedes. 'I hope Margot's not lost.' She picks up the printed recipe pages.

Chandra pulls her callipers towards her seat, fits her arms in place and goes to examine the little exercise book Rory has hanging with a pencil. It is a record of those using the phone-line.

'Victoria and jaffle-irons do not get on,' Rory confides. 'Always in a hurry with a tendency towards shortness of temper, Vee's stomach's good mate is her heavy skillet. She is a vegetarian on principle, being an animal rights campaigner. Her better self is in constant battle with her salivating glands which respond to the thought of juicy steak and the smell of take-away chicken. So she puts thick sliced tomatoes on the inside and lavishly butters the outside and fries her sandwiches.'

Chandra flaps the call book. 'OWL has got to be someone here!'

Rory rubs her tummy as she says, 'Whatever, it's made me starving. Mate, thousands of lesbians have come through these lands, and met most of us. There are no Judith recipes. I'll get some grub together.'

46

. . . truly terrible . . .

Time passes. Virginia's nights are mooned by the bleak neon from the man's phosfluorescent torch, days by rays of sunlight through the gaps in the wooden slats, bars of restricted light. Apart from Willy's, movement about her is the size of spiders and rodents on the floor of rough boards, but he is the low-life. At first she focuses on him. She sees his leer as ghostly, his bandy legs in tight riding strides or baggy old tweeds three sizes too big held up with dangling binder twine, hears his phlegm-filled smokers' cough. She regards her jailer, in turns, as some kind of saviour, as ignorant, puny, ugly, as less than human, as the devil, as snivelling, perhaps equal, never superior, notwithstanding the chain. Virginia treats the male ego carefully. He has the keys of the padlock. She suffers bouts of hunger, agonising filling of the bladder, fits of rage, defiant dignity and discipline, sublime boredom, torture by thought and heavy heart as the hours roll across her like a Sisyphean ball. She is tied into a canvas-covered sleeping-bag with wire.

Tin-snips release her. She drops into a squat of relief without looking at him. Humiliated. He watches. Cold panic paralyses her. Tired, in pain, she wants to relax but his irritatingly physical power over her reflects deeper fear of violent ignorant criminal stupidity. Men lock women up. The petty circumstance concentrates her thoughts on wider issues, she feels guilty, embarrassed, has hot flushes. The fence in the middle of Lesbianlands is her fault. She knows their borders pretty clearly, but has not ranged much since starting the sculpture. Certainly not since Cybil.

She curses herself. Any bush-walker could have found it, Jeff, her brother, in proper boots with a water bottle and energy bars, but the gurls, VeeDub included, are too totally involved with themselves and each other. Meghan, perfectly outfitted, hikes all over the ground when she comes. She would have known, but Virginia is too busy. She knows the lay of the land, has a good visual memory and understanding of contour lines, but the last aerial photo she saw was taken about five years ago. There were no huts here. Her thinking is repetitious. The bag is over her body not her head, but the many branches of her intellect trap her in distractions. It fixates on an exhibition in the small gallery in Stuart where she showed clay renditions of found natural objects, things of universal abstract beauty, a piece of driftwood on the beach, the gorgeous lines of mountain profiles, mysterious shapes the size of beer cartons; even a cloud. Only several walking sticks sold. Framed prints and sketches reiterated what she was trying to say, to see, the cloud, the driftwood, the branch, the mountain range. The craft of the cerebral. But her concession, the size, a cartable, a buyable, a gallery size, made the whole thing too cute, too precious. All the gurls came. Virginia was their comic creative clown, the butt of witty comments, yet her lecture on the aesthetics of her work, sculpture, was serious, and reaction hostile. The lack of anything recognisable, representational of female or animal, struck Cybil, particularly—a stranger then—as repugnant. At the time Virginia was magnanimous, she mistook her interest for constructive criticism; was the disciplined artist a self-indulgent lesbian?

Later she wanted her body and to share in her being. The rehashing of that event which came and went, a pimple of creativity on the face of the community with Judith singing, others' painting and skits of theatre, is intermittent through Virginia's days and nights. At times she starts sawing away at the swag with the little paper-cutting blade, using her sense of touch and dexterity. A crazy zen activity. Pale lime dawns against gunmetal purple evident through the spaces in the hardwood shack, speediness and sleepy insomnia, intersperse with patches of her past which are so immediate she feels she still has the choice. Cybil seduced her and she fell in love, fell into the riddle of irony, the need for knowledge of woman through intimacy with a woman who is not there, who thought her exhibited work was something she could pick anywhere in the same way as adults think they could scribble and make art like children. Virginia tried to teach meaning and gave her the best piece, the profile of the mountain range, and Cybil said it looked like mud to her. Virginia set the work against the sky on the rail of the balcony, taking into account light and dark, but Cybil was stubborn. Around the same time Judith's voice was the holy grail, the chalice of feminist art, song. Orange daylight in lines on the floor of her primitive jail mock Virginia's magnificent ideal, freedom.

Rewriting the past with fabrication is better served by the fleeting pleasures of performance, the moment that cannot be recaptured. Myth-making, Virginia searches for the growth in the inadequate memory, the continuum of truth, and soon traces the machinations of Judith's deceit. She carefully gropes, then violently rips open the bag and climbs through the hole, leaving the zip parts spliced together. Time for action. This time she will kill her. She sold their land, or part of it, to the men. And the lazy indifference of the gurls enabled her to do it. Judith has been allowed to control the books, the deeds, the paperwork, for years, because Virginia and the rest had more important obsessions.

As for Cybil, she is grateful for her hurtful acts. If the clay exhibition had happened in the city, a few people would have come and gone with high-brow notions of women and wilderness. Theories of freedom, the adventure of creativity, the dreams, the uncharted imagination, the mighty tree wrecked on a reef, in the forest, dripping with the fairytale ambience of deep greens and luscious luminescence in the fungi, Virginia sees as tunnel vision. Sexually channelled through lesbian reality, she simply investigated female imagery not as beautiful, just lovely cunts, arm-shapes, thigh-shapes, breasts, forming out of the boles and branch-joins as opposed to the phallic reach of Gothic cathedrals and the merits of spires. Wet places. Cybil's ignorance of Virginia's purpose is iniquitous, criminal annihilation of her cultural effort. Savage and sophisticated beyond any degree of will that Virginia can find excuses for, Cybil's primitive act with the boy was truly terrible. But where does it measure against Judith's cold-hearted sell-out of women's land? Her calculated hypocrisy?

Virginia finds a hole in the wall of the locked shed and pisses through it standing up, as she and her brother had done. When they were nine, in her prepubescent year, the twins pissed everywhere. Until now, Virginia had forgotten that. Her bruises are healing. All the abrasions have firm scabs.

Given both are kidnapped, trapped, what is the difference between a mad woman and a sane one? Virginia feels released from the routine of daily needs. The plastic cheese and white bread that Willy gives her, she rations against the onslaught of the next pang, having one or two mouthfuls at a time. She drinks some water from the plastic soft drink bottle and places it on a noggin. In blackness is enlightenment. She is pathetically pleased to be standing and cannot understand how she spent so many hours curled up, sleeping in the corner. She feels she had taken the first steps towards responsibility and Judith's evil is banal, yet horribly dreadful. And Cybil's blow to her emotional being in causing such agony lessens the power of her enemies.

How many days have passed?

She lies down on the mattress and pulls the ragged bag over her shoulder and sleeps.

Gun-shots.

When she wakes, Virginia feels ill. Not only is it the sudden change of diet. The abhorrence she has to digest, what is happening on their land, is worse than processed cheese. Her anxiety goes to her stomach. She couldn't eat, anyway. Facts, suspicions, fear, philosophies, horrors worry her energetic metabolism, though her body is robust.

The feral pigs are human males. 'Swine.' There is a high cyclone fence enclosing an acre of bare clearing, probably the result of early logging endeavours, recently dozed on the side of a hill. A patch of natural growth lower down is tussocky, bladey grass, dry sedges. From the air, if you were flying low and coming from a particular point on the compass, you could just make it out. Did it appear suspicious to Vanderveen, in his helicopter last weekend? Two bulldozers, a tractor, parts, front-loading buckets and blades, log-snigging chains and slashers. The equipment could be stolen property. She has worked out it is Saturday, and there is a lot of activity. The generator is in use. ATVs. All-terrain vehicles, an army eight-wheel-drive transport, covered in fatigue-dyed canvas. They park it in the shade. Willy Campbell is the only one Virginia sees on horseback.

When let out of her shed, Virginia feels like a lone POW. Camps are forming down the hill. Bales of hay with targets painted on cardboard attacked. Bullets hit the flattened beer cartons. Each new set brings guns and starts firing them. Then they stop practising to get drunk. It is a men's gathering, but instead of spears and drums, they're playing with beer and weapons.

Virginia watches and waits to assess what is going on, a temporary camp. She overhears a man in a suit talking to Willy. 'Ground magnetic surveys point to the presence of a rich major volcanic gemstone reserve, could explain your alluvial rubies.' A perverse niggle in Virginia is eased to hear the metallurgist because it makes sense of her night in the cave. It is a mine shaft. Gurls have picked up gemstones from the creek, some alluvial rubies, some strange white quartz, but Wilma Woods and Zee Minogue will not allow a rock of any sort to be moved. They say their ancestors live inside them. When a friend of Rory's tried to take home an ordinary rock, she fell into a supernatural fit and did not recover until she had returned it to the exact place she found it. Men, unfortunately, have a different view. Ground is wealth and under the ground, rubies.

Because it is covert, the men are plainly, with this installation anyway, out of line, liable to legal charges. However, mining rights overrule freehold title. The motive is greed, buried treasure, riches for the digging. But who are the others innocently sizzling sausages and playing country music, guns out of sight? Making a hillock of beer cans, these good ol' boys would love to take on the army. And fight for their right to import and keep for themselves highly sophisticated military assault weapons, automatic pistols, rocket launchers and high-tech bows and arrows. Self-loading rimfire rifles of more than ten rounds. Pump-action shotguns. They have their politicians to whip up prejudices so they can shoot. Virginia, the kidnapped, is the spy behind enemy lines. The ignorant white man needs to be protected, against what? Virginia herself is a scrawny old bit of insurance.

47

. . . to sabotage your site . . .

Food was indeed on the table when I entered the marvellous dwelling perched on rock, with the music of water falling down various gradients all around. But a lusty argument was going on. Four hands struggled over the small keyboard of the laptop, competing to press a key or prevent such an event by grabbing a finger or slapping a wrist. I stood at the door and laughed.

'I tell you this is the mole!' Chandra was adamant.

'It can't be,' responded Rory. 'Look at what she says!'

'That's all very well,' conceded Chandra, frustrated in her attempt to type a letter by Rory's pushing her hand away. 'Look, I know this better than you. It is how we got to this message!'

'There is no way the writer of this is attempting to sabotage your site. No way!' Rory was having the last say, and leaned back in her chair and folded her arms across her chest.

Chandra shot her a clenched-jaw shake of the head and withering look. Speaking to me, she said, 'Margot, see that exercise book hanging by the door. Read out who has used Rory's telephone line in the last couple of weeks.'

While I was flipping pages, Rory impressed her opinion. 'So, she was clever. What does that matter? The more the merrier. If she's the got the technique, well and good.'

Chandra stressed, 'But, if I don't have control, I feel decidedly uneasy.'

In the notepad was a scribbled list of names and dates. Beginning at the end I read, 'Ci, local. VeeDub, local and Sydney. Hope, local, a few. Judith!' I looked up and made a face. 'Yvonne, Dee and Gig,' I finished. Over the page, I found Ilsa's name and no date. Chandra hand-wrote, and I went over to look at the screen. The other two moved away.

... you can't own land ... you can only take a loan of it for a moment and for that time you should care for it in return. a sacred task ... legally it is our property ... top layer, anyway ... mining rights ... the whole world should be worried! ... beyond the lantana infestation, behind the thorny hedge where the bush was merrily regenerating itself possums and dingoes were playing out their lives and the birds were eating the honey of native flowers or berries ... that European bees and bulbs were rare here ... orchids, staghorn ferns in the trees and maidenhair flourished along the creeks ... parrots were cracking the seeds, and new growth sprouted ... as the bush grows taller, the secondary growth is killed by shade ... wild boar dug out the roots ... the wishful thinking ... lesbians are overwhelmingly concerned with personal problems ... enough land to let the weeds be outgrown ... even the greenie gurls who have come to pursue their passions have rarely penetrated the backblocks ... bush regenerators don't stay for long periods. artists, arseholes and dreamers stay ... too dispiriting, we should warn visitors, they could get lost up here, more gullies than you think and not all of it bush ... a real mind fuck, telling lies to yourself ...

So I gathered that one of Rory's fellow Lesbianlanders had used her computer and Chandra needed to know exactly who. They did not want to let me in on the in and outs of their dispute, so instead of answering my polite queries, they called me over to the table to eat. They weren't saying much so I told Rory about my talk with Pam. 'She knew all the time.'

'Yeah, well, no one takes much notice of Pam, sometimes she's there, sometimes she isn't. I haven't seen Virginia for days. It happens out here.'

The meal was simple. Noodles and salad, crisp biscuits and dip. Metaphorically rolling up my sleeves, I tucked in.

'Willy Campbell drove his bulldozer across the bridge too fast. He didn't think, because he could have gone through the creek. Therefore, he was in a hurry. Seen by Pam heading towards Ilsa's,' I said with my mouth half full. Pushing my Spirax and pen across to Rory, I suggested she show me where Ilsa's is.

Rory drew another of her beautiful maps on a clean page, arrowing the related positions of Virginia's, where Hope is staying and Judith Sloane's paddocks to Ilsa's home and the winding road up and over the hill.

'There's a gully there, south-facing, cold. No one goes there. It's a gentler slope from the back, you may be able to get through Vanderveen's property, or State Forest.' She indicated where and handed it back. 'Willy's lease, Crown land is there.' She pointed.

'Okay,' I said as I took it. 'That is where the explosions were. Probably. Barbara Campbell affirms the family fixed your bridge, but denies they damaged it. She could, of course, be telling the truth. That would mean her brother doesn't tell her everything. But. The feeling I got was that these Campbells have no secrets with each other. And plenty with the outside world.'

Checking the hand-drawn map, Chandra joined in with, 'I find it hard to imagine that Judith did not hear the dynamite. She is the closest. She could have located it. Or Ilsa.'

'Well,' replied Rory, 'even though it's not obvious in the two dimensions, there's a high rocky hill here.' She pointed between Ilsa's dam and Hope's plateau. 'Not quite as high as Widows Peak, but of the same inhospitable vegetation. Sound would start echoing, but you're right about Judith's. If she were home, she would have known exactly where the blasts were coming from. And she couldn't have mistaken them for falling trees like the rest of us.'

'Either she wasn't home,' I deduced, 'or she was cognisant of events. Right?'

The strings of sight made a tight triangle, creating unified ground in our three-way glance. After a second or so, Rory said, 'She's a hard case, but I cannot countenance her being that bad.'

'Judith's an old politico,' opined Chandra. 'She must have been away.'

'Every time it happened?' I inquired. 'Does anyone have a record of exactly when these big bangs occurred?'

Rory shook her head.

'Well,' I slapped shut my book. 'I've got a bit of work to do.'

Because I would be back far too late if I walked both there and back, Rory thought it best if she drove me across to Ilsa Chok Tong's tram and dam. Chandra was keen for a ride through the hills. If I went home via Hope's *pied à terre* on the plateau, on foot, as actually there was no other way to get there, we could all meet at Virginia's, where they planned to visit next, and I could get another ride from there.

'Is Ilsa Chinese?' I asked, as we rattled back along the track.

'Ilsa is as Australian as you and me on her father's side,' Rory responded, stopping as she changed the four-wheel-drive down to lower range, then proceeded to grind up another rough road. 'But her mother is Swedish.'

The country dramatically changed as we curved down to the left. While eucalyptus grew in the incline, it was more sparse than the rainforest behind us. The bush we faced was composed of shorter trees with thick foliage, dense stands of she-oaks and wattles. Chinese-Swedish Australian Ilsa's retreat was cute and exotic. A quaint twisted chimney puffed smoke out of the front end of a carriage, merry curtains rucked sweetly in the windows. Down the hill a little was a small lake with rushes and lilies and waterfowl. The path along which Chandra could swing quite easily on her crutches was bordered with collected stones, blue copper rock and red jasper. Ilsa herself, having withdrawn as thoroughly as Pam from the rough and tumble of barbaric civilisation, seemed physically the better for it. Her face was unlined, her lithe body straight and winsome as a reed, yet her social skills were, if possible, rustier.

No one thought to ask Ilsa if she had negotiated with the Campbells. Although Barb was not interested in giving names, I retained the impression that their fixing the damaged bridge had been okayed by one of the gurls, one with Asian appearance. Grey gum was used in the new bridge, Ilsa told us, but she was more interested in big-winged creatures she could not identify. 'The Paradise Riflebird, the ordinary Chough, something I think is the Forest Raven, or the Torresian Crow,' she went on solemnly. 'The blessed thing was not a Glossy Black Cockatoo or any other type of black cockatoo.' She continued hunting in her bird book, and, after dismissing all the owls, with admirable academic impartiality, she doubted for a moment whether they were avian at all. 'A variety of bat?'

When Rory brought her attention around to the cause for our visit, she was terribly shy. It was painful, I decided, and left it to her fellow Lesbian-lander. Her trips to town for provisions were as regular as clockwork, but definitely she had not heard the explosions in the neighbouring gully. 'But then, I wouldn't. Echoes. Except, you remember Rory, the one at the end of the meeting. Now you have convinced me of the exploratory activities, and I will take your conclusions as true and correct for the purposes of further induction, it absolutely stands to reason that miners would be interested in the earth beneath our feet. We are sitting on a goldmine. Not only gold, but tin, copper, zinc and gemstones, most valuably, rubies.'

Her personal disinterest was dumbfounding. She went on to explain the Act relating to propriety of potential mineral wealth, which knowledge, if it were my place, would worry me a lot. But she had pigeon-holed it as a matter of curiosity in the cabinet of her reserve. God forbid that she would have to deal with people. So paralysed by our presence, she did not think to offer us a drink. I went outside to get myself water from the tank and gazed at the rearing hill which screened the offending labour. An intimidating climb to say the least. Then it occurred to me why Willy was in such a hurry to cross the bridge when he could have safely gone through the creek. His having recently fixed the other bridges, the machine was probably on that side of the property. He had to get his bulldozer to the site while Ilsa was shopping. If he bothered, he would have a rough idea of her time-table. Because even if echoes disguised the blasts' location, the sound of the bulldozer would be heard and remarked upon by this resident as he would have to pass quite close. After the main drag through the plain, and up past Judith's, this was the gurl he would have to consider. Wilma and Barb had been in on their horses, seen by Hope, casing out the place? Giving the all-clear, gurls gone to, perhaps, the dance? That left only Hope, apart from Pam, who could have witnessed the intrusion.

As soon as Rory and Chandra emerged from the anchorite's bolt-hole, I needed to step on it. Stopping at a fork in the road, Rory explained the routes to the plateau where I was headed. The shorter distance was already in shadow, the other still in sunlight. Affirming that I knew my way to Virginia's once I was in the vicinity of the creek which became the waterfall near Rory's, I said, 'See you later.' Chandra's mind was all over the place. She remarked on the beauty of the landscape while being chauffeured from house to house in the relative comfort of Rory's otherwise rugged vehicle.

When I had made the far ridge in fairly good time, I found strange signs burnt into the ground. I felt I was at a scene from Trivia's diary. Like arrowheads the signs made a pattern on the flat ground in two-foot-wide lines, making a square into three equilateral triangles. Peculiar geometry for a house plan. Further down there were the ruins of a four-sided dwelling. The poles supporting the roof were sooty black and silver. The corrugated iron was brown and bent. The once-whitewashed fireplace looked as if it had been sculpted with hands out of cowshit. Beside the cot, a tin trunk served as dressing table. I opened it. A couple of toilet rolls, a box of candles with three inside, articles of clothing, a towel, the sinus-burning pong of mothballs, leather working pouch and another exercise book tooled with the words, *Golden Notebooks*. Further writings of Trivia? Hope didn't seem to be about, so I made myself comfortable among the tussock grasses and read under the trees as I waited for her.

These were happier times for Trivia. Beautiful descriptions of Maria and lesbian love, simple, lyrical poems. Then Hope returned. The sun was setting, though sunset at sea-level would be later. The moon was half-full, high in a clear blue sky. The third skinny isolated gurl of my day sank down beside me gracefully. She tactfully lifted the leather-bound book from my palms, and opened it at the back.

'Look at this,' she breathed, her voice full of wonder. There were five pages of drawings. Surrounding each illustration was text in Trivia's handwriting. 'I've seen them, too,' she said softly.

In the bewitching dusk, I sat with an elfin Hope, possibly madder than either Pam or Ilsa, but much easier to be with. The picture she showed me was called 'Upstanding Formal Alien'. Height 1500–1600 millimetres, clothed in fine-woven robe. Her helmet, like a dog's head, was the same in each; wings, hidden in the first, featured in the other four; one Pegasus-like, a rearing four-legged winged creature with a fish-like tail; another fully flying with the limbs invisible; another on all fours, very like a dog, height 400–500 millimetres; and the final one, standing, unrobed, displaying full wingspan, two metres, looked vaguely familiar, like something Egyptian.

There were copious notes about them, including descriptions of a landing craft which was drawn as a sphere which breaks open to a bowl, similar to those plastic ones you buy for pets.

Yang's comments : after the fear comes the question, why are they here?
: sometimes you just have to accept that you've lost day
: they probably don't   : they touch your head under your hair
  think like   at night
  we do.

Yang calls them "chevrons" & imagines that their language form, like the original Chinese
is composed of sticks; straight lines : ∨ ∨ ∨ ∧ ‹ ∧ ∨ ↗ ↗ ↗ ∇ ‹ › ›‹ →←
《 》 《 ∨ ‹‹‹ › ‹ ∨ › ∼ ∼ ⌒ ⊓ ⊓ ⊑ ⊒ ◩ ◪ ⌂ ⌓ ◳ ◲ ﹌ ﹌
‖ ⫲ ‖‖ ‖‖‖ ⊓⊓ ⊓⊓ ⋿ ⊡ ⏃ ☖ ⌘ ⌻ ◉ ⧖ ⧖ M.

'It lands on the ground like a beach-ball,' explained Hope. 'They're really light. All this material weighs nothing.' She read, '"In their own galaxy they are pure mind, not soul, not spirit, not perfect." Where is it?' She flicked her eyes over the text. '"They have noses and ears like dogs so that they may know through these senses . . . The double chevron in the position of the third eye operates like a micro-chip for interstellar communication . . . Helmet-heads adapted for planetary conditions, carefully devised, incredibly clever computers of superflesh hardware . . . Ears can revolve . . . Translucent circulating fluid, no elimination process." Um, it's here somewhere. "They don't have substance as we know it. They can imagine. On earth they need mists or water to project their images." Yet, ah, hang on. "Wings, mixture between bat-wing and feather. . . . They invented all this from an observation station on Venus. . . . Trunk musculature like that of a snake, all bones interlocking vertebrae." Here is what I want to read to you: "Their skin is like seal's fur. Their eyes are like eagle's, except for the third eye which can appear human. Their tails are like aircraft rudders and necessary in various positions for balance. The only design feature they took from human beings, apart from head size, is opposing thumbs on the end of all four limbs." Somewhere it says, they have to land at high altitudes, something to do with oxygen. Hey?' she exclaimed eagerly. 'What do you make of that?'

'Notes, for a novel?' I suggested. 'A feminist sci-fi? Trivia was a writer.'

'But I told you. I've seen them,' Hope was trying to convince me with the strength of her conviction. 'I can show you where they landed.'

She was so sweet and keen and young, I wanted to indulge her but I am an honest sceptic. 'I bet it's over in that gully beyond Judith's, behind the escarpment near Ilsa's,' I said.

'How did you know?' She was flabbergasted.

Shrugging, I grinned. 'Just a wild guess.' Hope had verified the destination of Willy Campbell's bulldozer in my speculations, anyway.

Disappointed by my lack of faith, Hope insisted. 'But they've taken Virginia.'

'I beg your pardon?' I expostulated. 'What do you mean?'

'Her house is like the *Marie Celeste*. Cup on the table. Food ready to be cut and chopped, pot waiting. Been like that since, um, Wednesday. Like she just walked out to the woodpile and never came back. Disappeared, like in the Bermuda Triangle.' Hope described something my bullshit detector discerned as likely to be true.

'How do you know she didn't go into town on the spur of the moment, saying, like, bugger it, do it later? Urgent business?' I tested.

'Virginia does heaps of sudden trips to Port Water, but never does she

515

leave her house like that. I know,' Hope said definitely.

'How?' I encouraged her confession.

'Well, I go down there to read when she's not at home. I've never asked her, but I don't reckon she'd mind.' Hope's confidence was pretty well backed up by what I thought of Virginia. She wouldn't mind and Hope would find some interesting reading matter in her library. Not considering for a second that she had been taken by aliens, I wondered where she was.

I said, getting up, 'I'm going there now.'

'Yeah,' concurred Hope. 'But Virginia won't be home.'

Scrambling through the understorey towards the sound of the waterfall, every now and then I saw a wider vista. At one stage I could look down upon Rory's establishment, the telephone tower, various solar panels set on poles at angles and a disc glinting blue in the moonlit dusk.

Virginia's vehicle is in its spot. Chandra and Rory exchange shrugs. Rory cooees up the track towards the place where she knows she is working the log. No answer. The vegetables on the chopping board look tired and limp. They wait a while then return to Rory's.

The sun has gone off the solar panels. They see each other as shape and gesture as they sit on the darkening deck. The bush around them is quiet except for the occasional squeak and squawk as birds hustle themselves into nests. Fruit bats begin to become active. The two women are quiet in the dying light, breathing air dense with life force.

Realising Chandra has issues with power, Rory does not take up their earlier disagreement. Instead, asks how she became so good with computers.

'Started with bulletin boards in Melbourne,' Chandra says. 'It was exciting. Weren't many women in my Users' Group, but those there were smart. One of them ended up making money hand over fist trouble-shooting software. Wonder if she's a millionaire yet.'

'Different choices?' Rory suggests. 'Different politics?'

'No Internet then,' explains Chandra shortly. 'Fixing software was a lot of leg-work.'

'I see.'

'Mm, most of the time she was in her car, going to factories, banks, places, I don't know. I couldn't drive then.'

They go inside, chatting. When Rory begins lighting her candles to augment the weak halogen globe, Margot walks in.

'We thought you were lost,' lies Chandra cheerily.

'Yes,' agrees Rory, although neither of them had given her much thought since they had set her down on her way to Hope's.

'I was for a bit.' Margot displays some scratches, 'But I finally found the creek. I kept the sound of the waterfall close to my left.'

'What a girl scout!' Chandra moves about with one crutch, hurling herself into the lounge chair by grabbing its arms with her hands and pushing up and twisting in fast motion.

'Where have you been?' asks Margot. 'Did you see Virginia?'

'No, actually.'

'She wasn't there.'

Neither Rory nor Chandra know what to make of Virginia's absence yet, but they do not take Hope's explanation seriously.

'We'll go up again in the morning. Have a proper look,' Rory states.

'Good idea,' Margot sits in the armchair opposite Chandra. 'I've been reading Trivia's *Golden Notebook.*'

'Trivia. I remember her,' comments Chandra. 'She was a writer. Wasn't she? About five years ago.'

Margot puts on her tracksuit top, asking, 'Wasn't Maria her lover?'

'Me too,' Rory's abrupt non-answer silences Margot and Chandra. 'I'm afraid truth got stranger than fiction.' Rory keeps talking, 'Innocent not ignorant. She was streetwise but she could not understand the non-creative mind: why would you pay money if you could make it yourself? Why would you sell your soul to buy something when you could live in poverty and know something? Her imagination got the better of her.'

Margot smiles in the candle gloom at Chandra, willing Rory to talk on, open up, while she keeps her own thoughts on hold.

'She built before I did.' Rory speaks from behind the kitchen bench where she is preparing vegetables by the light of a small electric lamp. 'When it burnt down it broke her heart. And her spirit.'

'So many delicate things are so easily abused,' Chandra remarks clumsily.

Rory describes Trivia's place. 'A wooden frame and steel chests, poles, excellent roof with tank attached and no walls higher than half a metre, on the plateau. A long hole in the ground, a cemented dugout, rat-proof. The walls were canvas awnings. The fireplace was mud brick rendered with cow manure. Campbell's cows had the run of the place then.'

Chandra jokes, 'Were you on with her before, after or during Maria and she?'

'Before. Not for long. Maria was her last lover. Trivia cooked kidneys like Harold Bloom in *Ulysses*, she said,' Rory reminisces as she puts the washed lettuce from a tea-towel into a large glass bowl. 'Brain food. Mostly she was a vegetarian.'

'What happened to her?' Chandra asks.

'Killed herself. Slit wrists.'

Margot confides, 'I read her diary after Maria died. Sofia gave it to me.'

Rory continues, unhearing, 'Trivia allowed everything, even the most way out beliefs. She gave them credence. She indulged women. She had faith in them.' Rory stops her work to look into space. 'She was almost a chain smoker without it affecting her voice or her ability to scamper over these hills.'

'Did her mother call her Trivia?' inquires Chandra.

'No, she called herself that.'

'Writers are pretentious because they pretend there is another world composed of words and impressions and comment that is important. Escape is their work,' opines Chandra.

'Like cyberspace?' Margot has a dig.

Rory sets the table with plates, knives and forks, and puts butter and bread, cheese, tinned salmon and salad in the centre. She puts a match to Tilley lamps and the room brightens moodily.

'Trivia said making up reality was her profession. Amateurs at it on the grapevine sent her into a rage like a flame-haired raven talking nineteen to the dozen. Maria was smitten. She took her to hospital. The medicos were hopeless. Over-worked, incompetent. I don't know. We went to a motel, her doped on pethidine. Maria distraught. She woke, saw the Gideons and died. She was born six years too early.' Rory gets up to blow out the atmospheric candles as if they irritate her suddenly. 'Hope quotes the Bible, too.'

'And,' says Margot, 'she believes that Trivia saw aliens, and she does too.'

Chandra asks, 'Who's Hope?'

'Hope O'Lachlin?' Margot hears her own slip of the tongue, glances at Rory and runs with it. 'Could that be her surname?'

'No,' Rory shakes her head. 'At least I don't think so. It's Strange. And she is a very strange girl, I suppose, she does remind me of Trivia, a bit.'

Margot finds her bottle of wine and a corkscrew. As she reaches into the cupboard for glasses, she insists, 'But what happened to Trivia to make her do it?'

'She said something about aliens. She was calling her blood rubies. I wasn't much help. I thought she was going mad. Anyway, it was down to Maria.'

'The chain of instances in another person's life that are another person's life don't seem to be attached to a main trunk unless you make up a psychology for them,' Chandra grins as she reaches for cheese.

'Well that was as clear as mud.'

Margot feels there is an importance about Trivia and the mystery of the past of Lesbianlands and wonders what it has to do with now. She encourages Rory's memories.

'It was late August, there was a frost. Extremely unusual though not unknown here. She had planted lilly-pillies and pawpaws because she felt she could live on those fruits if she had to. They went black.' Rory sips her wine and frowns at a wall, remembering. 'There were neat clusters of dried grains and pasta varieties always at her house, canned food, carefully sealed packets of herbs and spices and dried peas and dried mushrooms. She could always cook you a meal. No, she wasn't mad. The aliens was the only truly weird bit.'

'If she was practising for survival, don't you find it ironic?' Chandra puts it.

But Margot is intrigued. 'Why did she call her blood rubies? Anything to do with the geology up here?'

'Not only Ilsa,' assures Rory. 'Meghan also reckons we're sitting on riches beyond measure.'

'Doesn't mean you have to plunder the earth,' argues Chandra.

'We won't.'

'You're not sad? For your loss I mean?' Margot's eyes search for Rory's through the shadowy light. 'I think you should check your books, though. Judith didn't show me them all.'

'On with the story, Rory, the trauma?' Chandra heaves herself up, finds her sticks and flops her legs into position before she takes her weight on her forearms.

'The frosts burnt the leaves. There were about three in a row. They burnt her berries and the big flat leaves of the pawpaws and the tomatoes that grew in her compost pile. Then the westerlies came and battered her place on the plateau. Then the fire. Trivia tried to be spiritual. She dredged up archaic symbols from the arcane, subtly changed them and placed them round about carved them on trees made rock cairns and dry stone walls. Everything was triangles, hence the name.'

The wine-bottle being empty, Rory pours some port from a cask into little glasses. Chandra goes outside and comes back in.

'The fire leapt from the crown of one tree to the crown of another and Trivia's place was burnt, including the frost-dried fruit trees. No one could find her. The front of that fire was ten kilometres swirling in circular winds burning and re-burning. Trivia talked about the putrid taste of her own saliva as waves of fear and panic and pure heat swept through her. She was alone with it for more than forty-eight hours. When we could we rushed up and surveyed the damage. Her face was black, her lips were red raw.'

'She had survived but she was traumatised?' diagnoses Margot.

'Maria just couldn't handle it. Trivia had to be all strong and giving.

Suddenly she wasn't. She was just as in need of care as Sofia. We came in with provisions and we fought the remaining fires which smouldered away in the middle of logs. Beautiful trees fell in two and lay pitiful on the cracked black earth. There were animal skeletons here and there. The bush had become an open space in a black and white movie shot in a northern winter. Trivia was at first high with her survival and the new knowledge of terror. She went to the creek looking for rubies, or hell she said. She was never the same.'

'Did you still love her?' asks Margot gently.

'I will never get over my grief. I don't often speak about it,' Rory says toughly. 'But my real pain started earlier. When she ditched me. For Maria.'

Margot, Chandra and Rory talk until they are too tired for more, and go to bed.

Chandra and Rory were having a pretty stiff argument when I woke up at a late hour for me.

'You shall be judged by what you do, not by what you think others should do.' Rory sounded exasperated.

'Do I detect a bit of the old Catholicism, Rory?' asked Chandra with a touch of sarcasm.

'All right. "By his friends shall you know him." Like that one, do you?' Rory was as menacing as someone backed into a corner. I lay still, listening, trying to determine the cause of their discord. Chandra must have released the pressure because their voices dropped. I heard the words, 'scum', 'sanction murder', 'responsibility' and 'the capitalist system', so I assumed the whole thing was political not personal. I got up and stretched, rolled up the sleeping bag, lifted the mattress and rested it against the wall, giving them time to get the idea that I had returned to the land of the living.

'Trevia was the Roman name of the Greek goddess, Hecate of the three ways.' At breakfast, freshly toasted muesli, biodynamic yoghurt, tinned juice and Oolong tea, Rory and Chandra went about my further education in a jolly fashion, showing off. Weather, company and foreboding atmosphere, the day had a quality of verve where you need to be ready for surprises. Or shocks. The intense payload of this triform friendship would, I sensed, require nerve, be valuable, and worth it. Whatever.

While it seemed to have helped Rory talking about what happened to the real person, the writer of the 'she you and I' diary, I learnt that the goddess's three-faced images received offerings of cake, fruit and money for protection in journeys, for healthy childbirth and bountiful harvests. She ruled springs and mountains. The corruption of Trivia to the modern meaning of trivial was, according to my elders, the patriarchy's attempt to belittle matriarchal cults by rendering unimportant established rituals and customs. They talked about Kali and Mut and the Morrigan. I listened and took in the delights of the leafy fresh air. It was as late as ten before we cleaned up and got on with the day. They had computer work to finish while the sun was on the solar panels feeding them direct electricity, so I walked up to Virginia White's house unaccompanied.

Its emptiness did not exactly have the Bermuda Triangle piquancy I expected from Hope's description. Her presence was too strong. The bed was made. I guessed it was a hurried but intended exit. Gestures like the screen put in front of the fireplace, the pushing of the vegetables under the colander with a rock weighting it down, though disturbed and knocked awry by possums, showed she meant to go for a while. The cabin felt similar to the last time I was there when Virginia turned up midway through my inspection of her home. And sat down for a chat.

A book was left open, spine up, by the chair. I read this piece of text:

> The conflict, therefore, is not between females and males, but between SCUM—dominant, secure, self-confident, nasty, violent, selfish, independent, proud, thrill-seeking, free-wheeling, arrogant females, who consider themselves fit to rule the universe, who have free-wheeled to the limits of this 'society' and are ready to wheel on to something far beyond what it has to offer—and nice, passive, accepting, 'cultivated', polite, dignified, subdued, dependent, scared, mindless, insecure, approval-seeking Daddy's Girls, who can't cope with the unknown, who want to hang back with the apes . . .

I flipped over a few more pages before I dropped it back where I found it.

SCUM will kill all men who are not in the Men's Auxiliary of SCUM.

When I replaced it, I remembered that Hope had admitted to reading time there. Not exactly the kind of propaganda to thrill the cockles of my heart, but I felt my unerring nose had happened upon an explanation of the argument between my mates.

I left Virginia's as I had found it and walked up a narrow, wet, yet rocky track which wound its way deep into the rainforest. Not a people-friendly place. I sensed the slithering of snakes and feared choking by thick vines hanging like ropes. It reminded me of American movies about Vietnam where the jungle is set with booby traps. You take one wrong step and whoop, you're gone, either down a hole or suspended in the air caught by your ankle. There were no reassuring sounds of chopping or chain-sawing, or even dog-barking. Just the relentless carry-on of things that don't care whether you live or die. I felt more oppressed there by the palpability of what I couldn't see than anywhere else I had been on Lesbianlands. Wherever her sculpture was, Virginia herself was not here. Of that I was certain. I turned around and walked slowly back to Rory's as my Achilles tendon started giving me hell.

Rory, Chandra and I had chunks of chewy camp-oven bread with tomatoes, lettuce and soft cheese, by the creek down from where the trucks were parked on the road. A little circle of blackened rocks marked this spot as a frequently used one. Rory threw together a twig fire faster than well-equipped campers can extract, hook up and light their gas burners, to boil the billy, to wash our lunch down with tea. All very wholesome. Glad of the prosaic picnic, I quietly watched a pretty little red and black bird duck in and out of the trees whistling sweetly. The other two settled into reminiscences, apologising to me, saying this need to share the past must be their age. I nodded and asked the name of the bird. Rory pointed out the parasitic bole on the branch of the dying tree, 'It's a male mistletoe bird. The female is just as pretty but much more subtle and could be easily mistaken for any little brown bird in the scrub.'

With our things packed and dog in the back, we left Rory and got in my Suzuki. I could see in her face that Chandra was not finished remembrances, so I asked questions as I drove along the dirt road. Her mother was a champion horse-woman with a winner's attitude to hard work and discipline. She applied this strength to her daughter's condition and together they worked out ways to not only cope but to enjoy life and be cheerful. The great achievement of that time was at a gymkhana in the Under-thirteen Show Jump when she did a clear round in her side-saddle over two-foot-six fences and won a ribbon. It was not only the ribbon, however, that thrilled her as a kid, it was the wholesale appreciation of the crowd. Everyone there had stood to watch. They lined the white rail fence. When she finished they cheered as she rode past them. She saw their joy for her, some with tears in their eyes. She received congratulations as if, like her mother, she were an Olympian. After that she became part of the landscape for the showy set, doing as much as she could about the stables. Surgery was dangerous. Instead of going straight to orthopaedic surgeons, she and her mother consulted broadly, especially the physiotherapists in the public hospital. There they all worked on developing her hip movement. Upper-body fitness went without saying. Her mother did not indulge invalid habits except as a necessity. Brothers and sisters, a couple of each. Father, in the background.

'He couldn't cope with my disability. Or he didn't want to. All I remember is his carrying me now and then and my mother having a go and then giving up on him,' Chandra explained.

'Now?' I prompted. 'Family?'

'I keep in close touch with one sister and in formal contact with the others and their kids. My mother died suddenly, of undiagnosed breast cancer, when I was nineteen.' There was real sadness in her voice.

'It must have been an awful shock.' I took my eyes off the road to look at her.

'It was.' She gestured right. 'Go down there. We will swim in the waters of Lethe.'

'What's that?' I asked pleasantly, anticipating more education.

'Nothing. I'm just talking about living in the present. My mother was the best, and I am glad she died quickly at the age of forty-five, because she was beautiful then, really stunning, and the undiagnosed bit, well it's just her. She left me the legacy of her tremendous care and thoughtfulness when I needed it, sadness, devastation, loss. Then I had to make my own adulthood, exactly as I chose. They say necessity is the mother of invention,' she laughed with a tinge of bitterness. 'Two years of grieving, bordering on clinical depression, then I was twenty-one and women's liberation had begun. Black liberation, gay liberation, disabled liberation, it was all stirring, and I was there.' She pointed to a gap in the trees. 'We're here.' I stopped the car in the shade.

She began taking off her clothes and said through the cotton of her T-shirt, 'Not far.' The casualness of her response to a question I didn't ask silenced me more.

Chandra has a body which is like the mismatched halves of a child's cut-out game. The upper half tanned and strong-boned, mature. Her lame legs are not ugly. The thighs are thin and white and held together. I guess I was staring rudely. Operations throughout her childhood failed to separate them.

Opening the driver's door, I tumbled into pre-exercise stretches as a way of covering the growing chaos in my mind, her sudden nakedness, and the silly words which sprang forth, like, 'What are we doing?'

'You don't have to take your clothes off yet. Carry me down to the river. Down that track there. It's quicker than if I take my sticks.'

'Okay.' I moved forward to lift her undressed, unabashed form.

It was quite a steep slope down, but the river, when we got there, was deep brown and shaded by big trees with exposed root systems. I wouldn't say I was particularly psychic but the black pond was spooky. A sudden depth and sluggish movement in a flowing river, where one could drown, being caught by debris underneath and held down.

Chandra tapped my shoulder and directed me to a spot where she could reach a branch that overhung. As I disrobed, I watched the schizoid body monkey-bar along the limb, swinging hips with flexible tight abs. The white, thin legs clung together as if the thigh-bones fitted into each other with a slight twist. She hurled herself into the water like kids do from dangling ropes. I stood calf-deep on the rounded river rocks, looking for the place to execute a shallow dive. I was surprised by regular splashing and glanced at Chandra. She held my attention. Her preferred stroke was, apparently, the butterfly. Her working hips and muscly abdomen meant her lower half moved like a dolphin, and her powerful arms thrust her shoulders and chest out of the water effortlessly. I don't know why I expected her walking disability to extend to swimming. It didn't. Her whole body moved in a unified undulating motion. I stumbled over the rocks and eventually fell into the river. She went under the surface of the water then. Unlike the sea, the texture of fresh water had a soft embrace, like satin, and each stroke was silky. My freestyle followed Chandra's butterfly at a fairly even distance. Then I turned into backstroke to look at the trees, leery of floating leaves and sticks, swimming snakes. A fascinating network of roots held the dirt of the banks together, in some places making portals to clay caves. Platypus holes? Maybe, wombats'. Neither past nor present but something to do with time was dragging me to the mysteries of things. I sighed and floated in an effort to relax. Chandra surfaced and circled, overarm, backstroke, in one place, speaking to me when her mouth was in the air.

'I am the river mermaid, and you are the summer Amazon. Please, if ever we become lovers, be like my mother.'

She dived beneath me.

When I went under and swam in wave motions, copying her, I forgot everything until my body had to come up for air. We made love in the water, front to front with our hands, and floated on our backs afterwards, day-dreaming, and giggling with a crazy embarrassment if we caught each other's eye. She did not seem aware of the ghosts which were so real to me. I was sure their bones were still there, beneath me in the sludge, veiled from view either by the thin membrane of time or the aqueous layers of the pool. She kissed me, then I carried her wet body back to the car. We dressed and let our clothes dry us.

The trip back to her place was speedy, electric with possibilities. Would we become regular lovers? Did I really want that? Chandra, I thought, had not made up her mind either. While she wasn't short on compliments of my physique, I felt she was containing me at a point of tension, as dressage-riders keep the power of their horses curled around the bit in their mouths. Apt image, okay. Okay.

We both, it seemed, had so much to do we said goodbye with the briefest of embraces, as if, after our intimacy we had to run away from each other to think. I returned to my home, musing about the *Golden Notebooks*, hideous flying creatures of mythology, Hope's aliens, pan-like Pam's soliloquy, the intellectual Ilsa's denial, Virginia's disappearance, and the subtle emanations of death from the pond Chandra called Lethe.

. . . too drunk to get an erection . . .

Virginia decides she will drink lots of water, so her system can be cleansed and diluted. Dense forest abuts part of the perimeter fence, lilly-pilly berries and wild figs litter the ground. Indignation rather than fear obsesses her. She feels a slow simmering rage.

The rape has been attempted. He was too drunk to get an erection, then fell on his knees and tried to make her come with his tongue. She was having a shower when the assault occurred. There is a drum of water, which is filled and fed through a hose into an old tin can with nail-holes in the bottom. In pathetic burlesque the plastic curtain with tropical fish on it defines the place downhill from the shed beyond the tank. Her neighbour locks his cyclone gate so that she is secure inside and so is his gear. Incidentally, he locks the gun lobbyists out.

He snuck up saying, 'I promised you this. Even though you're the wrong one. Wrong one on two counts. The other old girl, she's a mate of mine, a partner, though she says she doesn't hold with too many guns. The young one simply ain't you, she's the one I promised it to in the pub. They were joshing me, bunch of lousy sheilas, do anything to get their nails into drugs. Big mouths. I don't like being teased.'

Virginia stood still, wet and goose-bumped as he undid his fly, unsteady on his feet, possibly because of the rocky ground in the half-night. More likely too much alcohol.

'That's what it is all about, isn't it? Drugs. That's why you girls want to go feral in the bush. I know,' he said. 'But you'll do.' Willy Campbell's arms are very strong. He thrust and banged and started swearing as his member was not behaving in the manner he required. The half-moon in the cold sky is studied by Virginia as she shakes her head at the stupidity of the male sex. He entered her with his tongue, both his hands pushing the cheeks of her buttocks. Virginia resisted coming by looking at the trees trying to name them, thinking about wood, her breathing became jagged. Her senses were threatening to swamp her mind. She persisted in the effort to think, examining the branches of the eucalyptus, thin arms in the failing light, white mahogany, turpentine, blackbutt, tallow-wood, corymbia. Then an idea struck her and sucked feeling away from cunt and clitoris. His vigorous, sensuous exertion proved fruitless and he gave up exhausted.

Even so, he was proud of himself. 'I'm good, aren't I? I'm good,' he proclaimed. Virginia wiped her face with the scrap of towelling, an old beer mat, within reach. She pulled on her pants and khaki shirt as he sat on a rock and rolled a cigarette. A bit of candle was waxed to the tank stand. She gestured towards the biggest tree about twenty-five metres away, with bark just visible.

'Is that a tallow or white mahogany, do yer reckon?' she asked, in no way giving recognition to his violation.

'Tallow-wood. You could get a fair bit per cubic metre for that fella.' He is still calling this land ours? Virginia remarked to herself.

'Yeah,' she uttered, 'we might.' She lit the candle with his lighter. His thick lips had a mean sneer. After about an inch of forehead, greasy hair shot straight out of his scalp. He would watch his drinking. Next time would be full-on rape. He had unfinished business.

'Tallow, good,' she said.

'Yeah, beautiful springing waxy wood.' Willy like most locals knew his timber.

'Green, it would have quite a whip in it I should imagine,' Virginia checked.

'I suppose,' he said as he got up. The half-moon went weak behind wispy clouds in the now blue-black sky.

'Would you like sausage tonight?' Hospitable, harmless country folk, ha!

'No thanks, nothing. I'm on a hunger strike.' Virginia reminded him of the situation.

He took it as a joke. 'That makes you cheap.' He walked away.

Black cockatoos flew to a parliament of fowls gathering in the casuarinas on Vanderveen's property. Virginia recalls what they called her at school, Olympic high-jump material. The tallow-wood grows close to the fence. She thinks of Emma George and how she pole-vaults four metres something. The pen and the little blade in her pocket, whether used or not, is always there. He has forgotten to lock her up in the shed, securing the cyclone gate instead. She inspects the soil near the tree and finds a long, straightish branch. She sits down and cleans it of twigs and forks. Then sleeps.

In the daylight, she skins off the bark. The heap of hay-bales left over from the target practice comes into her vision. But she has decided to vault over the fence, landing in the dense lantana that covers the steep drop on the lower side of the enclosure. The keep. She has thrown herself into lantana before and gone tumbling down. After the pain of love she has contempt for other pain, and her enemy. Contempt for your beloved belies your heart. Seeing she came second in the triathlon, she rates her chances. Virginia practised pole-vaulting with Jeff many years ago. Pole-vaulters pace, utilising a little leap in each step as they get closer, they slam their pole into the ground and fly. To clear the loose spirals of barbed wire on the top of the fence she needs to leap over two point four, maybe three metres. They must have something valuable here already.

She tests her pole for faults. It is nice and green, strong about a hand-width diameter at one end and narrower the other, and about a metre taller than Virginia. She holds it like a lance at a knight's tournament so she can balance and sprint. She will have only one try. She looks for a place to jam it in. If it breaks, she is gone.

Think positive, she tells herself. I am shit-scared. He will come again this evening, or even sooner.

The fear gets Virginia's adrenalin pumping so thoughts for survival reign. She has been numbed for four days, injured and bruised before that. But she is fit now, lighter. She steals away from sight of the camps, the smoke and drunken blabber, beyond the spiky tea-tree bushes. She examines the hay-bales in case climbing is the better option. But it would be too obvious and too arduous moving them. If she visualises vaulting rhythmically in detail, she can do it. She runs, sprints, paces. She jabs the pole into the dirt, throws herself over the fence in a high-jump flop, and lands on her back in the lantana whose shallow roots disengage from the crumbly ground. The weed and she fall down the steep gradient. Virginia grasps the prickly spines, dragging them with her for harsh cushioning. She comes to a halt in the buttress of a fig. Stays there.

Rory, driving home on the major road through Lesbianlands, encounters Ci on horseback, with another rider, a lad, breaking the rules. She stops to remonstrate. Ci answers her back.

Rory screams, 'I am not responsible for your ignorance of lesbian ethics!'

She stands on the tray of her truck. Ci looks like the gypsy she is with a bandanna tied around her forehead. Their dogs take the opportunity to show each other smells in the immediate vicinity.

'You cannot bring a man onto women's land!' Rory is almost in tears.

'Who says?' says Ci cheekily. 'I'll bring whoever I like to my place.'

'No,' hollers Rory. 'This is female space.'

'He is only a kid!' Ci excuses herself carelessly.

'It doesn't matter how old he is. He has the rest of the world, why bring him here?' Rory argues, stamping her foot.

'Because it is where I live,' Ci replies calmly. 'Why should you worry? We're not going anywhere near your place.'

'That is beside the point.' Rory sits down heavily on her tin tool case. The kelpie, Tess, leaps up and comes to her knee. 'Ci, it took us so long to establish Lesbianlands as a male-free environment, money, work, meeting after meeting. You can't just be so cavalier.'

Ci is all innocent concern. 'Look, Rory, we won't be long. We will just ride in and out, okay?'

'It is not okay, Ci,' answers Rory, defeated.

Ci moves her pony forward, 'I built my house. I paid for the materials. I am an anarchist and I'll fight for it. You can't tell me what to do.'

Rory runs her hands through her hair, 'Anarchy, you little twerp, is about responsibility.'

'Try and stop us.' Ci kicks the pony and pulls him up at the same time, making him circle the vehicle.

'How can I do that?' Rory asks. 'You know I can't.'

Ci bends her horse. 'Look, it's business, okay? In and out again, that's all. Well, maybe a cup of tea. He's not staying over the night or anything.'

Her genuine love for her sister-Lesbianlanders keeps Rory begging, 'Ci, what if all of us did it? Brought our brother, father, nephew, mechanic, carpenter in?' She argues, 'You might trust him, but he could be another woman's enemy, rapist, whatever. And if you suddenly make new rules, or rules for yourself, there's nothing stopping you changing them tomorrow. Let's say, it's not regulation, but a tradition. We want to build a tradition. Consider the future, consider the model we are trying to set up. Just so women know there is a place where men can't go.'

Ci is not impressed with the plea, 'I'm not sleeping with him, don't be stupid. And fuck tradition.'

'You didn't even hear what I said!' Rory is distressed. The boy on his pony in the big stock saddle smirks, quietly watching. Rory attacks him, 'Why can't you respect us? Just turn around and go.' She stands and addresses Ci. 'Please don't do it. Have you asked anyone, Fi? Gig?'

'No one was going to know. Anyway, it's my life and I have a right to choose,' Ci finishes aggressively. She kicks her horse and the boy follows at a canter. A little further up the road they take a track to the left into the bush.

Rory makes her way home in a lather of fury and despair. She really wishes Virginia were around to unburden her woes, and, if she were truthful, they would include the unrequited, quite hopeless, suit with Margot Gorman.

When she is alone, she turns on her computer. Rory's face flushes and her body is bathed in a sudden sweat. She is embarrassed. She clicks a few changes and hooks into a menopause chat-line.

I feel great, she reads. I've been taking hormones since I was thirty-five and I'm fifty-seven now. When I went off them for a month, I was impossible. Anger. Tears. Irritable.

Someone else writes, It's just part of the process of ageing, like losing eyesight, hearing. You take something for diabetes. You take something for heart pain. Well, hormones are just natural.

The words appear on the monitor thick and fast, each woman having her say.

And they're very good for osteoporosis and arthritis.

Another puts in,

They have helped me keep my looks. I don't have any argument with them at all.

Rory watches the chat roll on as tears come down her face. No one raises any objections to hormone replacement therapy at all. These women should be in the pay of the Chemical Giants, they are advertising for them. She logs on and types, <RORY> How much do they cost? Her question is ignored. As she reads the anecdotes of one individual after another, she feels all the beastly menopausal symptoms they describe: irritation, impatience, hot flushes.

<RORY> They discovered ERT around about the same time as Valium, don't you think there might have been some kind of conspiracy, to shut up the little lady, seeing they couldn't give her laudanum any more?

She is incredibly angry with Ci, but she is savage at everyone for betraying women in the little ways they do. The ladies on-line are now angry with her. In the freedom of her splendid isolation she feels pressured, and that alone, gets her dander up. The answer to her question eventually comes in the form of a question,

Are you in a Health Fund?

To which she responds immediately with,

If I were in a Health Fund, I would certainly be paying for these 'natural' things. Someone is paying some laboratory somewhere else to package them in plastic and little cardboard boxes with a company name on it. Any of you got shares in that company? I bet you haven't.

Taking on middle-aged women proselytising about replacing estrogen, she feels like Valerie Solanas, blazing at stupidity, barking at Daddy's girls. These horrid obedient women are like the drug pushers in her community. Except they truly believe they are giving helpful advice, cheap. She slumps, owning her intellectual loneliness. While she needs friendship, she needs compromise like a hole in the head. She types:

Hormones are not like hearing, or hearts, or arteries, eyes. Indeed these things are not like each other. Women's ageing should not be automatically pathological. You are just putting off 'the change' and until you are mumbling, grumbling nannas. Too bad if you haven't got nice children and grandchildren! But you do have your Chemical Company, and don't worry darlings, he will provide a whole tray of things for you to take you away from the reality of yourself. Signing off.

She clicks out, runs her mouse around a bit more, reads the marijuana websites and scans information about Du Pont disparaging the plant which before and during the Second World War was used for clothing and building and all sorts of things. Du Pont maligned it so that plastics could take over. Instead of feeling gratified that she is not wrong, Rory feels depressed. The mighty mind of man has yet again successfully conspired for destruction of the earth and humanity against reasoned constructiveness and freedom. Business deals like Ci's split the foundations of her own lifestyle.

Rory loves the forest. She knows she loves the forest as much as she loves her bitch, Tess. She has built here. She works here. She knows the names of most of the birds and trees and ferns and animals, even rare species. Yet, she cannot feel that love without sharing it with other women.

'Where the fuck is Virginia?' Rory yells at the scenery. She expected her the day before yesterday. She still has not arrived. Rory feels rejected, dejected. They really must talk about Judith, about Willy's intrusion. Money and men and male violence. Marijuana. They need to ensure the integrity of Lesbianlands against the selfish wiles of the women. It might not be Judith, but Ci who consulted with the Campbells. For all her obsession with the awful Cybil, Virginia is trustworthy. Rory sets out to find her, first in the truck. Then on foot.

Rory goes along the top road and then crosses the hills to Virginia's shack along a path through the higher rainforest. It is much damper than she expected. On the facing slope she can see through the trunks of large trees a surprising woman shape, like the figurehead on the prow of a boat. As she progresses and comes across other angles of Virginia's huge, mostly hidden sculpture, lit by enigmatic patches of the sun, she finds if she takes one more step it disappears into nature. Several times she back-tracks and almost cannot see what she had seen a moment before. As she descends its implausible seclusion mystifies her more.

At Virginia's she finds no sign of life. She leaves a long clearly written note, begging her to come and discuss the things, finishing with 'please, please see me soon'. She considers climbing up to her ship, remembering the report of the work close up from Hope Strange, but she is not in the mood.

She knows Virginia isn't there. Nor is she in town, as she is unlikely to have gone in someone else's car.

Rory drives up past Ilsa's, tracing the tracks of the bulldozer. The wall of lantana with the struggling wattles and white cedars growing up through it makes her sigh. They are crushed and flattened at one or two places. She has not penetrated this part of their bush and has had no wish to. She stands at the head of the dark gully and sees rounds of disturbed earth, circles of singular blasts, strangely symmetrical. Eerie.

On the road on her way back home, she comes across Dee, Fi and Kay, who are stuffed into the front seat of a little Rocky. She wants to grill them about the troubles in her mind, but she finds her emotions too intense to communicate easily; had they seen Virginia? No. The three of them are polite and nodding. Willy Campbell was around but that was a while ago and way down the other end of Lesbianlands. They say it's great having the road back in action. They saw Willy's brother-in-law at Pearceville.

'Stumpy tried to make us go along to the rally next week,' says Fi.

'Oh yeah. Might go. Could be funny,' Kay puts in.

Dee says, 'We gave him a hard time.' The three laugh again, 'He said what we really needed was a good screw.'

Rory makes a face. 'How disgusting!'

'Yeah, he threatened Helen. Gunna straighten her out with real manhood!'

'Ti nearly flattened him.'

'You weren't drinking with Stumpy in the pub?' Rory marvels aloud, and silently asks, where do they get the time? 'Why do you bother?'

'Not in the pub, we shared a beer down at the lake. Bit of a lark, really. He's scared of us,' informs Dee, proudly.

'What's to be scared of? Stoned, stupid and useless,' Rory mutters. She wonders how dangerous their indolence really is, to her, to the land.

As she turns off her motor, and listens to the nattering of birds in the dark density of leaves, Rory has the distinct feeling that Margot and Chandra are together and she has no hope. A thought-form from outside flits about her consciousness like a moth. A butterfly, a flighty suspicion, as clear as crystal. Chandra is her friend and she likes her, yet she feels ashamed and jealous. She doesn't feel strong enough to know the truth. Rory wants one woman to be personally loyal to her. Her, her meagre, ravished self. She is thinking about Margot Gorman and her shyness becomes a red cheek. A sweat. She is besotted. She presses the numbers and Margot answers. Rory is lost for words. She longs to ask about Chandra and her, but ends up being practical, saying, 'The bulldozer tracks go all the way up to where we thought they would. And there are holes in the ground in the gully. I promise we will pay you. When we've got a result.' She splutters.

Margot says, 'Tell me that again, I will get a pen.' Rory holds the phone, feeling perplexed; plainly for Margot this is a business call. 'That's all?'

'I can't find Virginia. I've looked everywhere. Spent hours.' Rory tells Margot about Ci.

'I thought gurls up there could be isolated for weeks.' rejoins Margot. 'Sounds like Ci's business is dope. It wasn't Harold, was it?'

'No.' Without meaning to, Rory sobs. 'I'm sorry. I'm sorry, Margot. It's just. I feel. Lonely, I guess.'

Margot is open. 'Come and visit. Come with Chandra, tomorrow, no, the day after. Any time. Okay. Okay?'

'All right.' Rory puts down the phone and paces about her lovely house, weeping. Virginia and she are of an age. Their paths in life have run parallel through the tosses and turns of the last three decades. They share Chinese star signs. They rely on each other, even though Virginia's creative devotion seems to Rory, an artist herself, far too extreme. And Cybil is a shocker. Rory cries middle-aged lady's tears on her verandah, waiting for her friend to show. 'Please, come. Come.'

Ilsa, not having satisfied herself as to the identity of the big-winged birds, sets herself a hide in a crag of the rocky hill and watches at dusk. She is rewarded. From out of the bush all over the hills black cockatoos rise with their squeaky, human cry and their lazy, strong flap, all flying in the same direction, fill the sky. It is a wonder to behold.

Roz Small has an affinity with crows. She has raven hennaed hair and black clothes. Her face is as pale as the moon. She likes to be awake at night. During the day she stays inside, sleeps or sews. She lives under canvas Bedouin-style on a flat piece of land which was graded for a communal longhouse not yet built. It is gravelly. The poles are hung with laces and stained glass shapes in copper foiling. Big on symbols and very artistic, Roz has embroidered the word, Emania, on the curtains of her doorway and appliquéd screen prints of Celtic wolf-hounds to guard her entrance. Her own dog is merely a blue heeler bitch called Dormath, who alerts her to the presence of ghosts and the nearness of death.

The waxing moon is overhead, calling her out. She sees the wisp of cloud, and predicts rain. Her friend is Nicole Montoya who is camped, at present, in Victoria Shackleton's functional stud-framed stable along the side of the road. After sitting in the air watching winged shapes fly over the mountainous horizon for a while, they convince each other that it is okay to be about. When the moon is high in the night sky, Roz and Nic decide to go where the road takes them.

They come to Judith's farm and mistake sleeping sheep for boulders. The house is in shadow and darkness. No one is at home, so they go inside. Nicole ignites a lantern. Beyond the shadows of the spinning wheel and the stark upright chairs is a hanging frame. Ever interested in fabric and cloth, Roz takes the lamplight closer to examine the rack.

'Hey, check this out, Nic.'

'What?'

'Well, weren't these the clothes and gear that Gig said that Hope stole?' Roz giggles. 'Stole, I dig that word. Here's a stole. Cool.'

'You are not wrong, sis. I recognise this stuff,' says Nicole as she picks at pieces of fabric. 'Fuck, hey! Why?'

'Whatever.' Roz loses interest.

Nicole shivers. 'I don't get a good feeling in this place.'

Roz, in fact, a solid and tough gurl, likes to make a show of being afraid. 'Me neither, let's go.'

'You want to steal them back?' Nic asks. 'I don't mind, I'll take them and . . .'

The senior of the two, Roz says, 'Dunno. No. Not a good move.' Dormath is under her feet, trying to hide. 'If she's got these then she might have other stuff. Why don't we organise a raid? Get more gurls, you know?'

Nicole nods. 'You never want to come here when Judith's here. I didn't think it'd be worse when she's not,' she reckons.

Roz Small agrees. 'It's truly creepy.' Blowing out the flame and replacing the glass, she falls over the cat as she moves. Its mew of protest is blood-curdlingly shrill. 'I'm outta here.'

Book Seven

money

Monday Tuesday Wednesday Thursday

Monday's child is fair of face

49

. . . spiralling into the fifth galaxy . . .

Directions on his IT network have sent Ian Truckman, smoking again, off the Pacific Highway to the road to the west of the ranges. Manoeuvring the large articulated vehicle through the Barrington Tops, he creates a problem for every car coming in the opposite direction. He has to slop into the expanding puddles as the rain beats down. Although he is supposed to control his own access to his communication systems, or at least feel in control of it, he does not. The bloody thing switches on when it wants to and runs sentences and words he can make no sense of. Someone is sending him mad. He has the sweats.

Nonsense crackles through the CB. Vector, lector. Static, he can't quite hear, so he talks over it. 'My man, give me a low ten and high five. My man. What do you expect? Me to lose my hat? Couldn't do it. Shook my head. Lips sealed. Screen, TV. Screen, monitor. Right inside, Scania? Can ya scan ya. Need some eye-drops. Gotta job to do.' Ian Truckman wonders what all that rubbish was about. He drives the latest Freightliner. The Scania's gone. But that is the word trapped in his mind. He is being scanned. He knows. Small episodes of insanity unsettle him, but he drives. He finds some savage purpose in himself. 'To frighten you, my pretty white virgin, my little dragon, puff of my cigarette.' He watches the wispy genie in the stream of smoke and nearly leaves the road.

Ian, who has a big-breasted Barbie painted on each of his doors, thinks he would feel a lot better if he could get a girl in his clutches. To bring back reality. To bring back sanity. He eases into a resting bay. To see himself as the powerful man he is, the ordinary bloke, he needs to assess the size of his rig. A simple young female will bring his humanity back to him, reflect his essence.

As soon as the ignition is turned off, the computer screen bursts to life. But he sees his hand move this time. He is doing too many things at once. His left hand doesn't know what his right hand is doing. Heaps of sightings, meteorites raining down on earth like pennies from heaven, four-billion-year-old rocks!

The scrolling stops and the screen flashes message. Ian keys in his password.

Route B. Got to pick up a bloke. Roger, got it. They've been sending him code messages that were bullshit as far as he was concerned. No sense. Like off the planet. Had him worried there for a while. The way it suddenly turned up on his screen seemed like it came from out of space. Truckman cannot, truly, understand. Too much information, communication coming one way, Ian hasn't got a say.

One of the mischievous bugs from outer space, which flow into the earth's atmosphere over the Antarctic where the protective ozone is torn asunder, being eaten away by the methane gas and fluorocarbons among other emissions of modern human practices, thriving in the greenhouse effect of global warming, enters the system of Ian Truckman where it flourishes. While Mr Frank Zoltowski calculates the kilometre-long asteroid, AN10, will come within 39,000 kilometres of the Earth in 2027 instead of the comfortable 30 million, knocking out satellites and creating dust storms and disaster, while the magnetic poles are preparing to switch, the driver of White Virgin, Freightliner FL112, is infected by a virus giving him galloping Alzheimer's disease.

Smoke in the roadhouse not in the cabin, too dangerous considering the load is guns. Ammunition. Crazy but he does not know how so many fags got lit. He gets the feeling they know every-bloody-thing.

The bloke is at the roadhouse and boy! is he a bruiser. Ian mutters as he paces along the trays of pre-cooked food, pretending to be at the counter, but glancing. 'Big fella. Got swastikas tattooed to his arm skin. Pretty faded like they were done a long time ago. He's old. Much older than me. Bald but hairy elsewhere. Still wearing blue singlet, no Yakka stay-pressed shorts for him. I look neat as a businessman beside him but he does the recognising. He's got the rego of the Freightliner and her name, White Virgin, written on a bit of paper.' He says his name, 'Bruce.'

Bruce is a talker. He talks like he knows everything but he's fishing for information. Because Ian doesn't know, he is not saying. 'I drive my truck,' he responds, happy to be the silent type.

'Know where we're going, mate?' enquires the big, genial fellow.

'You tell me,' Ian says suspiciously, 'Bruce.'

Bruce shrugs, 'Yeah, well, you know enough. Nice rig.' They climb into the truck.

Ian is arrogant. 'Should be. Gets looked after.'

Bruce continues chattering, 'Reminds me of what my dad was up to in the 'thirties round Bega way.'

Ian, not hearing, says, 'That so?'

'Shooting practice,' Bruce claps his hands. 'Right to bear arms, bushies and bikers.'

Ian has to concentrate on the task of transport.

'Show of strength, there's a few truckers coming I heard,' Bruce expounds. 'You gotta say, that's power.'

Ian likes this guy, he loosens his tongue. 'Been on my own in my cabin for too long,' he chats.

'By the way,' Bruce says, dragging a bit of paper out of his shorts way down there under a load of fat, 'I got a map.'

'Good.' Ian suddenly feels remarkably sane. 'I just had the general direction.'

'That's right, north,' Bruce directs, stabbing the sheet with his greasy forefinger. 'We take a right off the New England Highway, then we go deep into the wilds.'

Ian sees his free hand reach for the paper.

'What's your weapon, mate?' Bruce folds it away.

'Just a Ruger rifle,' Ian answers simply, trying to maintain control.

'You're kidding me?'

Ian grins. 'Of course I'm kidding you, Bruce. I'm not invited to this bivouac as far as I know. I've got to deliver on the coast.'

'The bloke that owns this place reckons he has found rubies,' boasts Bruce.

'Fair dinkum?' exclaims Ian, reckoning a mate with this mouth couldn't be anyone's secret agent.

'They are sitting underneath the ground sat on by a pack of sheilas. Just has to get an exploration licence and they're history. Reckons gem quality worth about $10,000 a carat,' Bruce impresses his driver.

Ian changes gears to experience the power of his engine. 'Keep going. Bruce, you're good company. Settles me down. Gives me direction. You know what you're doing,' he mumbles.

Ian Truckman, the silent, efficient type, with another man beside him, is in command of his semi-trailer, speeding heavily, riding high.

The monitor mounted on the cockpit of a dashboard flickers to life.

'Hey, what's going on?' Bruce freaks. 'You got whatchercallit, hackers? Computers aren't safe, mate.'

'Not that,' Ian explains uncertainly. 'Aliens.'

'Stone the bloody crows!' Bruce slaps his beefy thigh. 'How'd you do that?'

'New technology, mate. Keeps you up to date. Something to do with the satellites,' Ian assures him. 'With cyberspace up and running extra-terrestrials can communicate. Finally,' he adds.

Bruce has met some weird types in his time, but you take them as you find them.

You don't need a million dollars to buy a boat, but it sure helps. For the craft that will propel you to the dizzying heights of the moving and shaking jet set -- and see you rubbing fenders with the world's best -- it has to be big.

The words accompany a graphic of a motor cruiser.

'On-line shopping, Ian?' he asks

Bruce watches the screen for a few more minutes, expleting his incomprehension, then gets bored and looks at the paddocks of the Western Tablelands through the windscreen.

'Do any hunting, Ian?' he asks, because he just can't stop talking.

'No, mate, not for a while,' Ian settles the pace at 105 km/h.

Bruce is a disingenuous, rural man. 'There's a whole hill of trees gone since I was out this way last.'

'That bother you, Bruce?' Ian condescendingly inquires, because he is aware of exactly what is happening. 'This is just the beginning.'

Bruce gets comfortable, ignoring what he has quite clearly heard. 'They call it die-back. They don't even know what it is. Gum trees just turn up their toes, one after another or all together. Could be a pest. They don't know.'

'You think their fuel don't burn?' Truckman gives up and reads the road-sign out loud. 'Armidale, fifty.'

'Right. I gotta make a phone call, can you stop?'

'Don't need to, Bruce. Here use this.' Ian hands him his mobile.

'You got the lot.' Bruce takes instructions and makes contact with his fellow shooters. 'You know the Shell?'

'Out of town?' Ian verifies.

'Yeah. Rendezvous. We're right on time. They said you were reliable, Ian.'

Never short on compliments when they're needed, Bruce.

'So, I leave you there, right?' Ian hides his dismay.

'That's about it, mate,' avers Bruce. 'And thanks,' he says from the ground before he slams the door. Then he waves.

'Yeah,' Ian nods grumpily. There is a network of arrangements going on, movements on the roads, in the sky, on the sea, out in space. It is all connected, monitored. Maybe they even care if he's sick, Ian is just a pawn in their game. No choice. Feeling dizzy. Seeing things. The highway is a ribbon in the breeze.

Virginia scrambles through brambly bush, feeling for thorns, instinctively, responding to the contours of the land. Flat backdrops to her self-involved drama of the last year transform beneath her feet into the three dimensions of reality. She progresses as shakily as if she rode a whale in mountainous seas. Owls above her move from tree to tree.

The moon sets. Darkness is complete. No stars. A damp, chilled air pushes through her clothes, her skin. It is not wind. It is night being thrust forth by the coming day, the last hurrah of black cold. She steps gingerly on leaf and loose stones, skidding, righting herself, banging into branches, hopelessly blind.

Streaky light infuses the sky. Ghosts scurry like the nocturnal animals in a hurry to find their sleep and day birds begin to squeak. As wary as a phantom in this wondrous changing of the guard, she witnesses the slow diffusion of colour.

Then dawn, like a silver-golden sword, strikes the highest crowns, conferring the honour of hard-edged life. Of light.

Of sight. Then, after a few moments marvelling, she finds it commonplace and takes bearings and heads towards her home.

The first recognisable feature in the landscape blows her mind. Her vision discerns her gigantic sculpture. Though still magnificent wood, her Amazon ship in the forest is a mish-mash of confused images. As if she could not tell the difference between Sappho and Penthesilea, it's neither on an island nor beyond the Trojan Plains, not horse nor barge, neither primitive nor civilised, but crude and abrupt, embryonic, whimsical, incredibly naive. Heavily bereft of dynamism. Embarrassing. She laughs at her own rudimentary efforts to form art so arrogantly self-reflexive. So desperately big. She knows the galley and the bunks. She climbs the deck. She finds a place to rest, but cannot sleep. She just relaxes. The irony that her over-reaching ambitions resolve themselves in the mundane gratitude that this is so remote and inaccessible she will avoid the vigours of exhibiting flattens and amuses her. Apart from the joke that she has tricked the critics, her mental efforts take her nowhere. She is exhausted. Too tired to close her eyes. She feels absolutely nothing.

Strange lights appear in the morning sky. She hallucinates an upright being with wings alighting on the prow. It stands like a small human in a helmet, and the wings become a cloak. She hears it speak. It is not words. It is music, fixed tones and sequences, very high-pitched like bats, but measured.

Sounds involve her while her sense of sight abdicates its fierce throne in the hierarchy of her being aware and becomes disfocused so the bush dances in shimmering impressionism: the fall of Rory's axe, a 747 overhead, an odd howl, and beyond the immediate birdsong and bustle, gurls' dogs' barks. It is philharmonic. Virginia White wonders if she has reached Mary Daly's experience of quintessence, spiralling into the fifth galaxy, realising the archaic future.

50

. . . seduced by idealism . . .

A squall came in from the east but it didn't keep me inside. After a jog, my foot was really sore. I needed my trainer. Even though I'd as easily accepted Sean's betrayal of trust as he had what he saw to be mine, I had to get back in touch with him for a number of reasons. Faith between the sexes can collapse without warning. He could not have really meant that I'd snitched on him. Who did then? He said I dobbed him in. What did he say exactly? I can't remember for the shock of it. He just turned on me. Tore off his sheep's clothing and showed his wolf-teeth. Sweetness and Light swore at me, Sean Dark threw me out of the gym. I'm afraid it's *sayonara* boy, you are just as misogynist as the rest of them.

But, by the time I'd showered, I changed my mind. I rang Sean. 'How are you, mate?'

'Changing colour,' he said sulkily, referring to his bruises.

I decided to be tough. 'Was not me who said anything about you to the cops, so, what was that all about?'

He cleared his throat, 'I heard from a reliable mouth that you were in cahoots with a dee.'

I sighed. 'Nothing to do with you, but.'

'Sure.' He sounded dispirited.

'No, true,' I assured him.

There was silence between us for a couple of seconds, then he said, 'Can't speak on the phone, Margot.'

Faking impatient good humour, I demanded, 'What the hell is this all about, Sweetness? I am in the dark, Mr Dark.'

'At least you sound like the same old Margot,' he laughed.

Lying, I proclaimed, 'I am the same old Margot. Let's get together.'

We made a time and place.

Judith Sloane thought that seducing Cybil Crabbe would be a walk-over. She can rely on her sexual charm, though normally not needing to do more than tease. She has the number of Meghan's private extension.

Meghan Featherstone, while an object of fun, is her rock, her pedestal. There for her, always. The sincerity, warm-heartedness, within the eccentricity, is appreciated by Judith, perhaps more than by anybody else. Meghan, however, is uninterested in anything Judith has to talk about. Judith disconnects with a feeling of dissatisfaction. She leaves the house with a cursory glance that everything is as she wishes it and gets into her Triton with its purple bumper stickers: 'my other car's a broom'; 'practise random acts of senseless kindness'. Judith's loyal admirer is taken up with her own affairs. Her relationship, her work, her finances, her fads, whatever, are more gripping than her star-struck adoration of the singer she never slept with. Yet Judith, used to using her vulnerability, had only rung Meghan to touch base, to keep in contact with the mirror on the wall that told her she was the most perfect of them all. But the reflection fails her today. Judith's practised flirtation techniques, her silky voice, do not have Meghan playing along, assuming the secret recognition of each other's worth with a laugh, an okay, oh yes, of course. She is totally distracted. Simple Featherstone affirmation would do. The words need not even be true provided Meghan states them.

Judith now curses her for the very honesty she needs. She hears thunder in the violet cloud to the west. Violent fulmination in her car sounds hollow; she cannot see her face in the rear-view mirror. She adjusts it but the light is bad.

Judith drives through the town of Stuart, impatient and irritable, taking the back streets. Her scheme to do with Cybil died without being born, clever as it was in theory. Trying to move Cybil was like talking a boulder into moving itself. Judith is pissed off, yet her vehicle travels smoothly. The skyscape is dramatic with impending weather.

When she comes to the right turn into the Warrumbingle Highway, she hesitates to click her seat-belt into place. She is amazed she has to wait for a convoy of trucks, motor bikes, farmers' four-wheel-drives, all travelling at the same speed. A sign reads SHOOTERS' RIGHTS. They are enjoying themselves, bipping their horns. The back of a Bravo ute carries a bunch of young men openly displaying their firearms, and another is draped in the Australian flag. A shiver of genuine fear horrifies Judith; then she is excited. She U-turns and goes up the dirt track to a farmhouse. There she asks if she might use their telephone. She pays fifty cents, and gleans the information she needs. When she is back on the highway she travels slowly, enjoying the disturbance from the comfort of her car. She gets to the upper Campbell before the eruption of weather. She stops at the mailbox.

Judith Sloane is a closet snoop. If there is a postcard to someone else she reads every word, bank statements she holds up to the light, or, if she knows the gurl is not in the lands, she simply opens the envelopes to get the information. Personal letters she tends to leave alone, afraid the karma would come back on her. She doesn't want others to read her mail. Although surnames are hardly ever used in the community, they're necessary for dealing with the institutions of the patriarchy: the NRMA; the Department of Social Security; Tax; Police; magazines and newsletters; the local council. Someone has written all the surnames of the gurls; Judith reads them again.

The post has just been delivered. She takes up the bundle and one by one tosses the envelopes back. She is looking for hints as to who is as clever as she and any communication between the others and this company which was coming to mine. Although the prospect for mining rights has been advertised in the local paper, the gurls seem to have paid no attention. Usually she let off the crackers of distress, but this time it's true. There was real dynamite and there will be more of it. For Rory, there is only a letter from her mother. That's strange, notes Judith, her mother only writes once or twice a year, now two in a week. Family tragedy, great, Rory might be off for a while! Judith hears a car and strolls nonchalantly away from the mail box with no letter of her own. A post-office box in town is where her official correspondence comes. She parks the Triton in the Christians' tractor shed and makes her way into Lesbianlands on foot.

If my imagination were a painting, right now, it would be one of those confused landscapes where roads lead nowhere, human faces loom too large, and little explosions take place on the horizon in the background. With my sanity sending me mad, my emotions were reacting to an information overload which threatened to swamp me. Whether it was the expansion of media coverage available to us in Australia or whether indeed there was a log-jam of disastrous events backing up on each other, it seemed to me this Monday morning the world was hurtling towards wholesale catastrophe: earthquakes, floods, mud-slides, volcanoes, tornadoes, blizzards, cyclones, global warming, both hot and cold temperatures all reported in superlative terms, breaking previous known records, exceeding all means and measures to cope, exacerbated by territorial wars where neighbours were burning and bombing each other's houses and rendering viable cities into scenes of destruction with civilians running for cover beneath the sporadic firing of sniper bullets, forced out of their villages at gun-point, speaking from some foreign land in broken English about rapes, massacres, unspeakable atrocities. Watching the news, reading the paper, being in touch was like Orson Welles' *The End of the World* and *The Day of the Triffids* rolled into one, yet worse, for, taking into account all the sensationalism, it was happening. Underneath each audio-visual thirty-second grab or photo with minimal journalistic text there were so many films and novels of individual suffering that one's heart-strings would be frayed to shreds. Alongside that, taking equal space, serious corruption of officials, the fatuous frivolity of wealth being spent in ridiculous ways, manic shots of stock exchange frenzies, and straight-faced reports of money markets and financial indices, before the sport and weather. The oscillation between El Niño and La Niña was carefully monitored in an ongoing graph to which you could get addicted if so inclined. The hole in the ozone layer was expanding, eating away at the earth's protective atmospheric shield. It mattered to me.

The rain they had predicted started. The last major flood of the Campbell River was thirty years ago, thus the next one was due. With all the clearing and development and increased population in the valley, more dire consequences were expected. Hail hammered the roof for five minutes. Although this storm would pass, the forecast was for extended precipitation. The downpour should have eased my mood. Instead it sought the depressions in my own person, making puddles, dispersing my focus.

Sparring with my punching bag on the verandah, dancing through the pain in my foot, my meditations zoomed from the ozone layer to my secret fears of the man in the truck. I thrashed that delusive paranoia with left hooks and right jabs at the leather. I had to get over it. I had work to do. With physical exertion I could excrete nonsense in beads of sweat. Not to say the emotional trepidation of getting involved. I had the energy of a flea.

When I got to my desk, the shorthand notebook and the computer screen seemed too small to handle the breadth of my ignorance, the scrappiness of my knowledge, the loose threads of my investigations, so I hunted around for big paper and a packet of coloured felt-tip pens. The cramped neatness of my office would not do, so I swept all condiments, cups, cutlery, fruit and jam off my kitchen table onto the sink and bench, creating chaos so that I might dig to a deeper order. Superficial organisation has in the past distracted me from the vital value of confusion. It was self-discipline for me not to wash up, get out the vacuum cleaner, shine the windows, rid the house of daddy-long-legs' cobwebs, polish silver, bake a cake. I could not afford the time for housework nor to please myself by mere tidiness. I scrubbed the toilet bowl anyway.

Finding the roll of butchers' paper, I tore off roughly a metre and laid it down like a story board. Characters, places, plots and motives. Who I knew, what I knew, where I had been. Suspicions, insights, gut-reactions. What I didn't know, where I hadn't been, players I had not met face to face. Dr Neville, I wrote, beginning my list.

Places. I had not been to 'the hornets' nest', for instance, which is a block of run-down flats where smack-addicts hang out and speed, dope, ecstasy are available. Drugs had a part in this, played by a shadowy figure who the Larrikin implied was respectable, either a user or dealer, or both; not a complete stranger to me. I could, for instance, imagine Cybil slumming it. Gut-reaction to her was that she was hiding something from me personally. Then there was Rosemary Turner, who had the eyes of a death adder and the body of a dowager.

Motives. Yes, and money. Money had a role in it all.

There were those I simply did not trust. Jill, Tiger Cat, Judith. I felt I could discount Judith on the question of drugs, but not money. Tiger Cat seemed to have nothing to do with money, or if she did, whose? Jill liked the poker machines. I had to stop my mind at this point from flying off into fanciful scenarios. It was too easy to presume everybody I didn't like as capable of deadly deeds.

What was the aftermath of Maria's death? Who was handling her estate? With Sofia incarcerated, who was looking out for her interests? Those out-of-towners at the funeral seemed to take control. I, myself, saw that Mary Smith pinned to the eyeballs; she was as underweight as any junkie, but very respectable and articulate. An employed city-slicker. I hoped at this stage that Libby, the lawyer, was Maria's executor because, for all her feistiness, she would be fair and reasonable.

But how did I know this? While among my list of characters there was an honest lot, with money you didn't know that higher purposes wouldn't motivate ostensibly illegal activities, law-makers on the whole favouring the rich and powerful. The manuscript I read snatches of at Virginia's, the SCUM Manifesto, advocated taking on the status quo. Well, that's what I gathered anyway. While someone like myself might be amused, more fervent types might truly hate the patriarchy. And hatred, certainly, is cause of much destruction.

Not wanting to consider Rory and Chandra in this light, though it was plain they were up to something they didn't want me to know about, I wandered outside in the rain, now a refreshing drizzle. A sharp, vibrant rain-bow arced across a battleship-grey background. Beautiful! The mailman passed. In my post was this month's Spiders Coalition Newsletter. I flicked over to the photo page. There were snaps of the Orlando dance and one or two of the barbecue. Jill David with her arm around Rosemary Turner laughed into the flash. Of course, that weekend Meghan Featherstone rang me from the desert. I wondered if she knew of the intimacy between her girlfriend and her accountant. Pictures of Margaret Hall and Alison

Hungerford reminded me that Rory and Chandra were not the only women I knew who were messing around on the Internet.

If one were to conduct guerilla warfare against one's perceived enemies, the global electronic village would be the place to do it. The terrorist tactics of the animal rights extremists or the anti-nuclear movement's heroes were cases where your passion to save the defenceless or the planet would override fears for your own safety and lead you to action outside the normal strictures. Perceived enemies could include such transnational companies as the conglomerate that, for instance, Dr Meghan Featherstone sometimes works for, or, indeed, governments with inhumane policies. A conspiracy of committed revolutionaries using computers was a possibility. Why even myself, if I acted upon the feelings of despair I had this morning, could be persuaded to behave illegally in a good cause. I have the kind of middle-level intelligence that recognises that those brainier than I can see and feel things beyond my ken. Which awareness could lead, I supposed, to desperation. Or acts of bravery.

The wide scope began to overwhelm me. Back to my great untidy page, I scribbled. Lesbianlands—rubies? I flicked open the Spirax. Details of my conversation with Hope rendered little, except the suggestion of another general motive for destruction.

Madness.

Campbell's greed for mineral or gemstone wealth was understandable, as was his threat to the fragile Pam of rape. If Pam had not hidden out in the hills, but had communicated earlier what she had witnessed, would it have made much difference? That speculation was pointless. Her actual behaviour expressed the depth of fear his, probably casual, intimidation inspired. One cannot, in judging another woman's actions as inappropriate, then dismiss it. Mad or not, Pam was real. Her experience valid. Quite comprehensible, in fact. This horrid, taboo-breaking show of masculinity was more reasonable in my appreciation of the data in front of me than the suspicion of a conspiracy of radical women driven by indignation at incredible unfairness and cruel injustice to murder of men. Why did that explanation seem more probable when the other, while not explaining the same incidents, was more logical? Why, in short, were gurls mad and blokes and families sane?

Virginia White seemed to me, when I spoke with her in her house, as one of most interesting and level-headed persons I had ever met. Yet, of course, she has to be mad, chipping at a log in the hostile jungle away by herself. She had less of a crazy turn of eye than Chandra in whose hands I would put my life. What's more, when we raced she was competitive with her mind on the job, a basically healthier attitude than Rory's. Rory was so beset by worries and responsibilities that she put aside her art, her creative outlet. Yet, at Virginia's chair, her reading matter urged criminal operations as opposed to civil disobedience to hasten the women's revolution. And, I felt, Virginia was the type to act on her beliefs.

All this musing was beside the point of my investigations. Males made more sense as culprits. To stop my own lunacy as I tried to assess the females, I wrote down the names of men, apart from Willy, in proximity to Lesbianlands. Alison's son, Harold, and Vanderveen. Harold was helping harvest the crop of marijuana in the National Park and Vanderveen was of the stamp of environmentalist who would shoot all vermin, the sort who sees the world's multiplying human population as the major threat to the planet. Regardless of whether it was someone's precious moggie or not, that man was capable of dispatching all cats. If the gurls on Lesbianland stepped out of line, these two forces, the black market and the holier-than-thou ecology fanatic with all the wealth of the white market in his power, would squeeze them out. Either could easily take their land, or make their lives miserable. But the present enigma was neither black nor white, it was grey, the dubious Campbell family and its murky ally, one of the gurls themselves. To that there were two questions: who? and why? Was the mining legal?

Money, drugs, madness were words I had circled with each coloured Texta I had worked with on my butchers' paper, which was now looking interestingly chaotic.

Because my heel was jagging from my boxing exercise and because I glanced at my notebook and saw the conversation with Chandra from our drive in on Saturday and because the Spiders' newsletter photo page was open on my bench, I wrote Achilles, and circled that. As the Greek hero was of no use by himself, or as himself, I wrote what he represented. Transsexism in this context. That brought me to other males. And, finally, back to the beginning: Neil, the transvestite youth. Strange as it might seem, radial lines from him seemed to connect everything. Police, poofters, Sean, porn, paedophiles. Philippoussis. I did the washing-up and got on the phone.

Proud of my page with its bright words and lines and ragged edges, I carried it without creasing or folding to my office and stuck it on the wall above my desk. The abstraction was alluring. I gazed at the unfinished piece of scrap, like a painter, realising I had never worked like this before. Usually I chased detail and arranged data with algebraic precision, facts, deduction, cause and effect. This sketch was schematic. I picked up my pen and added more. Pertinent or not, I wrote: relationships—sex & love.

There was a community of gurls; whether they believed in aliens, like Hope and Trivia, or Amazons, like Chandra and Virginia, they practised politics, conducted romances, were victims of betrayal, seduced by idealism or suffered its inevitable underside, disillusionment, as if their culture was as real as that of any other village. Yet, like Virginia's sculpture, like their illegal, hand-made dwellings, like interest groups in cyberspace, like colonies of life in the misty ranges, it was invisible to normality. There wasn't a pigeon-hole to put them in, or, if one did, one was kind of wrong. They were neither freaks nor spinsters, neither married partners nor bag-ladies, not unified by utopian visions of building a new state nor truly alienated from society as outcasts, as witches or animists, neither terrifying nor harmless. There simply wasn't a term to describe the vivid and troubled mob.

I looked at the word madness and remembered Sofia in the bin, Alison on Neil's computer, the flash of crazy secrecy in Chandra's eye and Hope in the sanctuary of Lesbianlands, replacing Christian fellowship with the congress of aliens. Meghan came to mind as one hanging off a tight-rope strung between two worlds, the mountains and the desert, in her dank south-facing place. I memoed: Jill? Trina? Then I rang Dr Neville's surgery.

The Annihilation Tragic's latest essay is entitled: <u>Money</u>. Chandra reads it on the printed page.

Money is god, and violence is the archangel sitting on the right-hand side and poverty sits on the left, both trials of annihilation of the female self because they are so obvious, ubiquitous. And women are enchained. Money is sacred. Money is divine. To transgress this belief is to be immediately punished by poverty or pain. It is impossible in this world to live without knowledge of them. Women know. A poor man can spend the family's last dollar on himself, especially if he is a drinker, if he is a gambler, plunging the women and children into destitution. The pathos is classic. The same man feels he has a right to violence because he is upset. I don't care how much remorse there might or might not be, the fundamentals are taken for granted. Money requires belief. But there is always a punishment. In middle-class divorces, often the woman is left with little of the money and care of the kids. The need for money is paramount but it is only a belief. A religion. Poverty is a real fear for women. Put up with violence, aggravated assault, sex under duress, pushing and shoving, forced watching of misogynist television, or pornographic videos, daily humiliation, you name it, all will be appeased by the hope for, if not the acquisition of, money. Win the lottery! Money is the god of the pope, the god of the queen of England. Without money there is no power.

Wealth can actually make women unhappy. What does the rich bitch buy? Painful cosmetic surgery? We have to believe in money for it to work.

Just like god. Fear of poverty equals greed for money; fear of male violence equals need of protection, from whom? The absoluteness of these oppressions is the point. In the lesbian community, the god money's police are probably other women, realists! But money is addictive; if you believe in it you can never have enough. Money is kinder than almighty god, but an infinite gulley-trap nonetheless, the more you have the more you need. Hence colonialism, of countries, of country-side and women's bodies. The original theft, essential plunder, must continue eternally. Conserved. Conservative aggression. It is a closed circle. You take. You own. Use violence. Make others pay. Revolutionary thinkers have no action they can take because potency is negated by poverty, and activist revolutionary lesbian feminists have too much to do as well as fear for their lives.

This woman's anger soothes Chandra. She is sorry her email address is defunct.

Chandra rolls back from her computer on her fat wheels with such a thrust she is through the door. Although she would like polished wood floors, she has serviceable rubber linoleum of an institutional greyish colour. She picks up her rolling tobacco from the kitchen table and goes onto the verandah.

After taking in the heavy character of the sky, Chandra skims down the page.

Greed is a disease, there appears to be no cure for it. A woman who does not see the revolutionary future of women as important, even if it is only intent and dreams, does see money as the thing she can have. Money as power. Daddy's girl is likely to spend it destroying herself, readers, I am going to kill riches. If I don't succeed, who cares? Don't underestimate the strength of womankind, hell hath no fury like a woman's scorn. Not, as he said, like a woman scorned. Hell is alive and well, Tragic.

Alison parks Chandra's car and wanders across the yard, looking white-faced and sheepish but the weather excites her. She is refreshed, chatty and sane. Tilly is safely at school.

Chandra gives Alison a run-down on her weekend, the bulldozer tracks, the bridge, Margot's job, Ilsa's description of the ownership legalities and the gemstones. She is about to confide her feelings for Margot when they are interrupted by the telephone ringing. It is Rory. Frantic about the missing Virginia, but arranging to come with Chandra to Margot's tomorrow.

Back on her verandah, Chandra speaks. Alison listens. Lightning, sudden stunning rainbows. Now wind.

'Judith Sloane is a miser. The meanness of misers is legendary. It is not only habit, it is the staff of life, the measuring stick, the meaning. They are secretive, misers, and so they need to be. It is to Judith's benefit to let every-one think she is poor.' Chandra says the words as if she is thinking of some-thing else, something she cannot find the sentences for.

Alison nods, 'What I've noticed is she manipulates people.'

'Hang with me,' Chandra continues. 'Let's say she is a miser. And a liar. The huge void in Judith's centre gets bigger. A part of the miser's mentality is envy. Judith is envious of Virginia White's talent.'

'She tried to make me sing with her once, or we did a few rehearsals. She's got a lot of talent, but she was terrible to work with. Yeah, I guess it was envy. Didn't really jam, didn't like me singing too high.' Alison trills a bit of melody, and laughs. 'We had an argument about music in the end. Her material was so turgid.'

'It drives her crazy that Virginia can be so complete in herself as to want to create for no return. Yet she sees her as a non-realistic weakling.' Chandra seeks Alison's eyes, 'You know what I mean?'

Alison does. 'Anyway there's only one of her songs that I like.' Thunder claps.

Chandra grins and shakes her head, 'Why someone like Judith Sloane hides in Lesbianlands is the same why classic misers go through rubbish bins. Her miserliness makes her monk-like. She sussed the gurls long ago, and stayed, while wave after wave of idealism has come and gone. Rory has also stayed, through sheer stubbornness and conviction. Rory is a fact of life for Judith, one largely ignored. Everything Rory does makes pedestrian sense. The good-hearted pragmatic. But Virginia.'

'Gives her the shits,' affirms Alison. 'Rory doesn't bother her. Why? Because she's given up her art.' More thunder. The breeze freshens.

Chandra reckons, 'Margot just might nail her.'

'By the way,' Alison comments. 'I've figured what Neil intended to do when he went out that night.' Her voice is drowned.

Chandra keeps talking on the subject she started. 'And then there's Virginia's disappearance.'

'Purely coincidental,' is Alison's opinion.

'Through Judith,' Chandra synchronises her thought paths, 'we have the link to the penetration of Lesbianlands.' She snaps her fingers. 'I must tell Margot. The wasteland valley no woman bothered to go in is where they blasted, except, I bet, Judith has crops hiding in there. When VeeDub starts her sculpture, Judith feels she has to do something contrary. The more positive her reflection becomes, the more negative she gets. She fraternises with the chaps, okay? There is money in it for her. "Money is god",' Chandra quotes.

Alison remarks, 'They wanted to go into the rainforest and bring out staghorn and orchids, but she said she would not let them, saying the other women would not allow that. Dig this sky!'

Chandra reasons, 'But really it's because the road to get there is too close to Virginia or Rory. I am guessing all this, but it makes a lot of sense. If they created a new track out the back and came in from the other river valley, they wouldn't have been caught. Why didn't they do that?'

'Didn't have to. They had inside help.' Alison smiles and says, 'She must be getting cheeky because if they've fixed the road through Lesbianlands, they mean to use it.'

'They must have a licence.' Chandra backs her chair. 'Well, I don't know it's Judith. It's easy enough to pay any one of the women, put so much money in an account number she gave them, they could take their rubies and no one could do anything.'

'Willy Campbell threatened to rape Helen, I think. Or Pam, can't remember. There's gurls out there wouldn't mind being stoned all the time, if they could afford it,' Alison says, bitter with recent experience.

Chandra frowns, 'Perhaps Rory is right to be worried. He could have got Virginia. Two birds with one stone. He was born in that bush. He knows every ridge and landmark. Since his threat, say, he has taken to riding in the lands, sneakily. He wants to get the woman he has been told, by his spy, could create trouble,' Chandra speculates.

Alison nods, 'Gurls have got cocky.' She shivers.

'He gets a lot of credence among his mates in the pub for this invasion. But the gurls make fun of him, they give him a hard time. Then he resolves to rape one of them one day. And does it.' The rain comes on to the verandah on the wind.

'You know that little creep, his brother-in-law?' It starts to pour.

'Rory saw Judith driving up to Willy's one day. Judith knew about the bulldozer.' Chandra convinces herself, as she rolls to shelter.

'No one will believe it's Judith, not when they can point their finger at the users,' Alison shouts.

'Exactly, that's why she's so sure of herself.' Chandra cries, 'Will you look at this weather.'

Alison rubs her arms. 'Holding the sword of the law over their heads by a single thread to show the perilous nature of their happiness, à la Damocles, is one thing, but he was going too far. Threatening rape. The gurls won't back Judith,' she says loudly.

'No, Judith has been in and out of the lands a lot lately, she said.' Chandra completes her version of events, 'So Rory doesn't discover what is really going on. Gets Margot in.'

Alison asks, 'Do you reckon Margot's a good detective?'

'Too good for my liking,' Chandra states, recklessly.

Alison senses that the vibe of affection, even intimacy, has entered Chandra's life. So she warmly suggests, 'What I think Margot needs is a feminist text to read.'

Although Chandra understands Alison to mean that if Margot is going to be close to Chandra she'll have to bone up, she firmly dismisses the idea. 'It could be dangerous if, in the course of her investigations, she jumps to the conclusion that theory could easily translate into action thirty years later.'

'It's okay, Chandra,' Alison assures her. 'I know about the Solanasites.'

'Thought so,' Chandra thrusts her chair into a spin. 'Let's go inside.'

'Better!' Alison follows her. 'But I really do reckon you should confide in her your deepest passion. It's one of the things that makes you exciting, Chandra.'

'Flatterer,' she scoffs.

Nikki, the Rottweiler, occupies the one comfortable chair in the lounge-room and Alison really wants to sit down in it. Chandra commands obedience and the large bitch slowly retires to her sheepskin in the bedroom. Alison mentions her son, Harold, and Chandra sighs, realising she will have to move into her counselling mode.

51

. . . all very plausible . . .

Sean and I walked safely away from any eavesdroppers along the breakwater in the wind that was scattering the showers, casually talking.

'Yeah, who?' I asked.

'Al the Pal, Alison,' he answered. 'She reads palms. Nice chick.'

'I hope you don't call me fowl when I'm not around. I know Alison,' I said, and added, 'Sort of.' We strode into the teeth of the easterly. 'Let's get down to brass tacks, Sean. What is going on?'

He caught up. 'You ever been to the Mardi Gras?'

'Only as a cop,' I mumbled, looking at the spitting sea, saw its expanse and recalled how the Celtic song that Alison sang had seemed to pierce the veils of time. She must have presented yet another face to Sean as he was sure she was a Gay Coalition lesbian. I assumed, however, differently.

Not about to get into the many facets of Alison's character, personalities whatever, with Sean anyway, I asked, 'Sean, why did you think I put you in? And for what?'

'Hold it right there,' he grabbed me. 'He told me it was a woman. Ex-cop.'

'Who?' I moved out of his grip.

'Crankshaw,' he whined.

'The Crank?' What, exactly, did the Commander know about my dealings with Philippoussis? 'What do you know about drugs? That's his specialty.'

He didn't answer, but said, 'I gather he hates a poofter more than anything in the world. Scum of the earth, we are.'

We took the cliff path and I shouted, 'I thought you didn't indulge. You told me you were a radical celibate!'

Sean's voice began to shake. 'I never ever touch them.'

I stopped and faced him, 'Who?'

'Boys,' he admitted. 'Youths.'

The air was tense with salty spray and negative ions as if the barometric pressures of land and sea were at odds. I stood still to breathe in more, turned towards him and said, 'Let's walk.' I gestured up to the old lighthouse on the highest part of the foreshore. We passed conscientious older people looking after their health, and younger types with dogs. Lads, the mirror-cleaning, the lipstick, Neil's body, tick-tocked through my head as I paced out.

'Who wrote "murderer" in the hall, Sean? Not that I believe it.' I don't think he heard me.

From the white-washed relic of white man's history, we climbed halfway down the cliff-face. It seemed as though we had the wild Pacific Ocean to ourselves as we settled onto a couple of rocks. A perilous position, but I didn't want us even seen together by whomever. Here, an inch or so away from a nasty fall, Sean and I had to trust each other. We were both fit. When I looked at him I could see it was not me he was really afraid of. In fact, he looked more secure at the edge of sheer rock than around people.

'Okay, all of it,' I demanded.

Sean relaxed into his explanation and, oddly, started with the Mardi Gras. Before the first one, when he was arrested, homosexuals used amyl nitrate to enhance the sex experience; then they began experimenting with designer drugs to unite the two highs, speed, dope, LSD, until they came up with Ecstasy, which is the ideal dance-party drug. With E, the warehouse-rave organisers had the perfect chemical. It kept the punters dancing all night, it kept them happy and controllable. If not raided they made a load of money. I had no idea Sean knew so much about drugs, except of course, steroids. I said this.

He expanded. 'I don't really, well, not for a long time. This is all just theorising. I don't know. A group of friends of mine, one a school-teacher, all with the same tastes and the same respect for boundaries, decided on a style of entertainment all our own. Like, Bazza's the drama teacher at the High, and I have the hall. We never touched the boys or gave them drugs, only a bit of grass, but that was frowned upon and certainly not in my aerobics hall. What we did was fun. Dress-ups, games. High camp shenanigans, quoting Oscar Wilde, Jean Genet, you know, wit and culture. These boys, like, needed it. Needed to know they weren't alone, that there was an honourable and long tradition behind them. It was education. James Baldwin. Socrates. For Christ's sake, our intentions were noble.' I could tell these thoughts had been running around his head over and over, probably disturbing his sleep.

'The boys, Sean?' I prompted.

'The pick, the cream,' he eulogised. 'Their intelligence and their beauty. It was my fantasy come true. I don't know if they had sex with each other, but none of the adults did. That was our solemn vow, and I kept it. I don't any more. Look at these.' He pointed to the healing shiners on his face.

Staring out to sea, I asked, 'Where did you score those?'

'I refused sex with a guy,' was the reply.

'Assault and battery,' I named the crime. 'Did you charge him?'

Sean shook his head with the same resignation and lack of litigious bottle you see in many women, the power and connections of the attacker too much to take on.

Still looking straight ahead, I pressed, 'Was one of your boys, by any chance, Neil Waughan?'

'Uh huh. Yes. May he rest in peace,' he sobbed. Sean's tears moved me. I bit back my own sentiment.

'Why does everything turn to shit?' Sean screeched at the waves crashing beneath us.

'The Friday evening before the dance on Saturday, was that a dress-up day?' Now I looked at him.

He nodded, 'School sports day.'

'So?' I urged. A sea eagle rode the air currents.

'Two of them came, asking if they could use stuff. They had a plan, to walk through town as girls they said. But,' he said. 'Bazza and I were busy with the Elizabethan costumes. They just wanted modern stuff, chiefly make-up.'

'Who was the other boy?' I asked, snuggling into the shelter of the cliff as the wind increased.

'Hugh,' he confirmed my suspicions. 'Oh, he chickened out at the last minute. Neil was totally disgusted. They left together about five. Like a straight couple. They were up to something.'

'And,' I sighed, 'you didn't see them again?'

'No,' he snapped.

Sean was falling into a fug of self-pity, so I shot my question sharply, 'Did you know Hugh died as well?'

'Yes,' he answered slowly. 'Well, it must have been the Cat.'

Giving up I rationalised, 'I had no idea you were into that so, no, it wasn't me. What did the cops want you for?'

'To harass me. Crankshaw. Filth,' he spat. 'I got the impression he was not sharing his intelligence with his colleagues.'

'How did you get that impression?' I interrogated.

'Just the way he shut other dees out. He reckons paedophiles use young boys to experiment with new designer drugs. He was trying to say that was what our group did. But I told him we were clean.' Out on the wet coastline I could see the petulant Queen Elizabeth the First gliding around with her courtiers on roller-blades in the wind-reddened face of my friend, the queer. 'Not that he would understand the word.'

Although I felt I didn't need to ask, I inquired, 'Did he believe you?'

Sean sparked up a bit. 'Doubt it. But I have no idea. There were times when I thought he was onto a real gang of predators, if so, I'm with him. Give homosexuals a bad name, they do. But he is on the wrong horse, heavying me. My phone's tapped. Well, he won't find anything. I don't have those connections.'

'The distinction might be a bit subtle for him,' I commented, knowing the Crank to be of the old school. 'Did he ask you to go undercover by the way?'

'Beg yours?' He glanced suspiciously up at a single-engine aircraft making its slow way along the coastline, flying low.

'Nothing,' I muttered. 'He depends more on informers than proper coppers. There is, probably, another group out there without your ethical stance. Neil, and maybe, Hugh, got involved with them as well. Probably too trusting. Too young. Who was your assailant?'

'Tow-truck driver by the name of Paul. Forget you know anything about him, he would squash you like a beetle, Margot. Long criminal history,' confided Sean. 'There must be some alliance between him and the Crank because, otherwise, things don't add up.'

'Why was Tiger Cat hanging around your gym all the time?' I asked, 'Any link between her and your guy, Paul?'

Sean meditated on the roiling sea beneath us, and mused, 'How am I going to keep the business going with all this aggro? She is some pill freak! I think she raided my cabinet but all she would have found was Sustagen and astringents. Then she offered me deals on human growth hormones. Incredible, like she wanted to distribute illegal gear through my establishment, but she really didn't have a clue what it was about. Not that I do.'

I laughed, 'Is it possible the Crank is upright? Using her?'

Sean made out he was taken aback. 'Actually, could be I suppose.' Sean shook his head. 'She's harmless, I reckon. She didn't dob me in, now I think about it. Talking with you has made me feel better, Margot. I wasn't myself with all the fear. What the Cat was on about was pathetic. She's crooked all right, but dumb.' He nudged me. 'Both of us bent queers but straight as arrows.'

Not as close to him as he would have liked me to be, I protested, 'But Tiger Cat is so in love with the power of being surreptitious, the idea that you could have been defending your virtue would not have occurred to her! She wouldn't even think the term outside the context of a lawsuit.'

'She's a scout for a gay and lesbian community bank they're trying to set up in Sydney. Anyone who entrusts their savings to her needs his head read. She's on commission,' Sean divulged as if he had just remembered.

'Money!' I exclaimed, 'Knock me down with a feather!' I put that small fact on hold. It could be helpful elsewhere. Shaking my head, I noticed there was a fisherman's goat track along the side of the cliff. 'I take it you didn't invest?' Complete dismissal of Tiger Cat was not going to help me. I wanted get to the bottom of the boys' deaths. The Crank being onto a paedophile ring rang true; it explained his treatment of Philippoussis, who was fundamentally a good heterosexual man, not grubby enough to infiltrate. Hardened slimy crooks would see him coming, and he would get nothing from them. Pip didn't even think his trips to the marina were worth much. There was all that stuff on Neil's computer that Alison had kept going, which in context could be very useful.

'Anyway, she's left town, I'm told.' Sean was speaking. 'You know I really believed it was you, and I felt hurt. But now I see he was being clever in not actually naming you.'

'Well, he lied, Sean. It probably pissed him off, you being a red herring and all,' I concluded. 'But the lads probably thought they could insinuate their way into the lion's den.'

'Things must be getting hot for a couple of kids to be a threat,' he muttered. 'Though they can turn on you.' His bitterness bit through the biting wind.

'They mess up your aerobics room? Hugh's friends? Neil's friends? Your youths?' I was convinced I understood the rocketing testosterone of adolescents, from sensitivity to aggression, from loyalty to hatred. 'Don't fancy that teacher's chances in this district.'

'Bazza? No,' confirmed my trainer. 'He's leaving. More's the pity.'

It started to rain. As we left our rock roost, Sean and I had a choice.

'You or me?' I pointed to the goat track.

'How is your Achilles tendon?' Sweetness and Light was full of concern now that he had unburdened himself of his own troubles.

'A vulnerability you might say. A blessing in disguise. I'd like you to get me back to fitness over the winter,' I said, feeling a nostalgia for the simple focused life of the athlete.

'Signed your new Nike contract, yet?' Sean, the small businessman, was on the ball.

'It's in my in-box. Haven't dealt with it yet. Nor have I done anything about the audition, yet. Been busy the last couple of weeks.' I made excuses.

'You should.' He looked up at another aeroplane beneath the clouds. 'I'll take the low road and you'll take the high road and I'll be in Scotland afore you.'

'And the rest.'

'Be careful.'

'Take care.'

We parted, both better off for having cleared the air between us. I made it to my car before the rain really hit.

Flicking through my notes as to the aims and objectives of my day, I decided on my next destination. Dr Neville was actually a jolly, harassed and popular GP. His waiting room was warm and full of tiny tots, all playing happily in a well-stocked pen of sensible toys. Their mothers flicked through a generous stack of expensive glossies which combine quite interesting articles with fabulous ads targeting the power-suited woman in black and white with a spot of colour, the perfume, alcohol, jewellery on offer. I didn't manage to finish reading about baby-farming in South America as he was prepared to squeeze me in between two appointments, at reception, while checking the state of hysteria behind me with a sweep of his eyes.

After that, I drove to the cop shop. Front desk directed me to an entirely new set-up for the Detective Constable I wished to see. Different building. Different atmosphere.

The autopsy conducted on Maria proved her death was accidental, Philippoussis told me. Adamantly. 'Absolutely accidental.' He murmured, looking vaguely about at the as-yet-unpacked boxes on the floor, 'I mean who would deliberately put a toad in a kettle?'

'Indeed.' Sofia, Cybil, Jill, Libby, Alison, I was not about to speculate. Any of the junkies, Maria herself.

'Unfortunately,' he continued, 'she had been in proximity to both Hugh Gilmore and Neil Waughan the night they died. And the possibility that, Hollywood style, someone was running around murdering people has to be scotched, formally.'

With an office to himself, a change had come over my man. He was altogether more comfortable. His phone rang. Philippoussis held down the mouthpiece and said, 'One of your friends.'

'Who?' I wanted to know, but he wouldn't say.

'Seems like your Tiger Cat has done a bunk,' he said.

'So I believe. She is a member of an Internet group called House-sitters. She's been living rent-free for yonks. Probably just moved to another,' I said. But I wondered, 'Why would she leave the area?'

He was nonchalant, unforthcoming. 'Why not?'

'They pay a couple of hundred a year and when people go on holidays, they move in, look after the cat, mow the lawn and take in the junk mail. Suits both parties,' I said, playing for time. 'She could have got another one here.'

'Wonder who gave her a reference,' he said, as if he knew more about her shady activities than I did but didn't consider them important.

'All of them, probably.' He handled some papers on his desk with a finalising gesture. He stood up to fish files out of cartons. Myself? I kept the conversation going. 'Neil's doctor said he had a heart condition. Nothing particularly serious, except he had to watch his intake, keep his stress levels down. Apparently, too much adrenalin, even, was risky.'

We compared notes and hypotheses. Philippoussis' change in confidence was caused by his secondment to the Coroner's Office. Now he was independent of the Crank and answerable to the magistrate. The deputy coroner turned out to be a go-get-'em, young female solicitor, with brains, energy, body, the lot. Perhaps too ambitious to be loaded with a policeman for life, let alone Greek in-laws. But for now, Pip was happier than I'd known him. For some superstitious reason, he thanked me for it. He was out of the octopus reach of intelligence-based policing. The other detectives had had to hand over their work and there would be a full inquiry into Neil Waughan's death. Shuffling a manila folder, he found a sheet which listed Neil's regular medications: the kid was on Valium. I glanced at other pages, some with photographs attached. CID had done a better job than Phil had previously indicated. Hugh Gilmore was a classic disillusioned rural male using heroin at the age of sixteen, into a bit of petty thieving, one hospital admission, overdose. He was the link to the paedophiles in the motor cruiser. The police had noted sightings of the vessel, but it was not registered at the marina. They had not, from the papers I was going through, anyway, the information I had, that Hugh and Neil left Sean Dark's gym on the night in question in fancy dress. There was one other person who might have conveyed that detail.

'Was Catherine Tobin an informant, Phil?' I asked, mentioning her drug-habit and her hanging around Spiders Coalition events canvassing for investment. I needed hard fact. 'Her file?'

Philippoussis obliged by leaning over and tapping the keyboard of his computer. He ran down her data sheet with his eyes, saying, 'Unofficially, you could say. She was in a relationship with a gay liaison officer in Sydney. Though prior to that she is not known to be into her own gender, so to speak. She left the department a good ten years before that after an unsuccessful sexual harassment charge, which was generally believed to be trumped up. More a case of entrapment. Not a popular girl by all accounts. But seems to be able to talk her way into schemes. Up here, no, she wasn't a snout. I did check it, because you told me to, Margot.' He looked up and grinned at me. 'Vanity is her thing. Body-building. She is funded a little by an organisation that wants to set up a Gay Bank, a home mortgage scheme. She does recruit investors. They aim to provide cheap housing.'

'How could such noble-minded people trust someone like her?' Wonders will never cease.

'Oh, they haven't actually done anything yet. It's all on paper. At this stage you wouldn't know whether it was ridgy-didge or bodgie. Catherine Tobin, aka Tiger Cat, just hands over names and details, addresses, phone numbers, whatever. The finance is handled further down the track.' Philippoussis clicked out of the software I recognised, plainly wanting to get on with his unpacking.

At the door, as I was about to leave, it occurred to me to ask, 'How does CI fit into all that?'

He finished our session with the curious detail that the Fraud Squad was keeping its eye on a certain member of this Gay Bank Collective because of previous history.

'Interesting,' I thanked him and left.

Rory switches off her electricity. She does jobs outside and checks the weather and covers her solar panels with anchored tarps. Still worried about Virginia, she does her housework and stacks her chopped wood inside. Hope Strange appears. She tells Rory how she saw Judith on the ridge, with her face battered and bruised, walking home.

When Rory asks her, Hope says, 'Judith Sloane's injuries are a product of the bad vibes on the land. Malevolence certainly.' She goes on with what Rory decides half-way through is a lot of rot. 'Said she was kicked by Virginia, knocked out, disorientated. I didn't believe her.'

Rory laughs at Hope's earnestness. 'Something was seriously bothering her? Do you think she got bashed by a bloke? Dee said they were threatening, and a lot are turning up, bikies, truckers and so on.'

'The bruises were a few days old. She was acting so weak, I helped her back to her shack and lit the fire.'

'Should I go up, do you think?' Rory asks without meaning it. 'If I was to go out, it would be to find VeeDub.'

'We've got to find her before it starts to rain,' Hope urges, 'Judith thinks I'm round the twist. I must be. I have a very clear idea of what the aliens look like now, and how they disguise themselves in mobs of black cockatoos.'

Hope's description of the aliens is so graphic, Rory doodles drawings while she talks. 'Hey, you did good. I must bring down Trivia's pictures, and compare.'

Thunder in the distance claps Rory on the back with a hearty appeal to her sense of responsibility. 'Come on.'

Hope is keen. 'Before I thought aliens got her. But they didn't.'

They drive the mile or so up the rugged track to Virginia's turning circle. The keys are inside the Rodeo, and seeing those, Rory inquires, incidentally, 'Can you drive, Hope?'

'Of course. I drove you home from the funeral. Why?'

'Because, even if we don't find her, we'll have to get the vehicle out before the storm hits.'

The Mental Health Unit of the local Area Base Hospital was signposted, along with Physiotherapy and Social Work, in quite a big wing. There was some kind of community group having a meeting in a large room to the right. 'Friends of Schizophrenics', I read on a sandwich board as I went down the stainless corridor.

The psychiatric nurse ushered me to Sofia's room. Jill David was there. She sat calmly, listening to a drugged Sofia rave. 'If it benefits women at all, it benefits whores and courtesans. And only financially, unless they are perverts. The infantry grunts are women, you bet, god's police, the down-trodden, wife-beaten, Bible-bashing, it's hard-for-me-so-sure-as-hell-it's-going-to-be-harder-for-you-if-I-have-anthing-to-do-with-it type of woman.'

'So we get bugger-all,' Jill said.

'I am not black, I am not Vietnamese, I am not a Korean car company, but I am blessed with being different. I cannot take these psycho drugs any more because the chemical companies are trying to poison me, and it is not my earthly body they want to destroy. They want to destroy my mind, because I know who it is. They have destroyed my mind. They've done it.'

Jill leant over and took her hand, 'It's okay, Sof.'

Listening to them politely for a while, eventually, in a pause, I asked, 'Where's Margaret?'

Sofia replied, frowning. 'They've taken her away. I have to get a computer of my own. If I don't I will go off. If they don't take me as well.'

'She left. Got a job in Sydney,' said Jill. 'I think.'

I was certainly seeing Jill David in a better light than I had before.

'Some sick chick there,' spat Sofia, implying her ward-mate.

'She's not that gross, Sof,' Jill eased.

'This is a catacomb,' confided Sofia. 'I'm in hiding. Chat-line interface, lists, email, MUDs, multimedia. Living maze. Choose another option. Acronyms, the Internet is another language. How do you know really what they're saying. They nearly got me. Sucked in,' shouted Sofia. 'Women at the well, come. Come. We must revive Etruscan. Etruscan is a language in which all the symbols and signs are known to man but no sense can be made of them. Women at the kitchen sink, wet nurses. Cyborg, lesbian Etruscan.

Watch out for the greenie friends too wasted to care about political action other than the legalisation of marijuana use.'

Jill gave me a complicit look of tolerance. 'Never mind,' she comforted.

'Another white magic substance. And we are talking about a lethal white substance,' Sofia gestured towards the RN who was distributing medications.

Sofia winked at me, 'Sweetened condensed milk, Margot, with the international Nestlé label. No. Is this our poison?'

'What do you mean?' I conversed, taking a leaf out of Jill's book.

'Okay, where has the icing sugar got to?' Sofia demanded of the sister. 'All the men are dead. They begin to stink. The women buried them in their backyards. Maybe it is just the men of women who have backyards who are killed. No, all. The others use public parks for burial grounds.' She was speaking loudly, telling the professional in uniform a tale as if she had asked her a question. 'So,' she continued, 'they have just gone. Slowly the infrastructure of the modern world breaks down because there are no, say, linesmen, repairmen. Women have not been trained to fix electrical cables etc. My story is called *night of the shovels and spades*. Let's make it happen!' She whooped, an ineffectual revolutionary.

'Maybe the San Andreas fault goes too, and a tidal wave rushes across the Pacific and wipes out East Coast development,' commented Jill, entering her reality.

'The Earth pulls her lips apart. It is liquid fire in the centre. Under the skin.' Sofia threatened to become obscene. 'She angrily swallows what falls in. Or erupts.' Sofia stared at me as if she had forgotten what she wanted to say to me, and shook her head. 'Erupts, right?' she continued, wanting to keep talking. 'Leaves dead stone? Salt. A pillar of salt. Let's kill the white man. The white man has no right to appropriate what he does not understand, but he does and he places upon it an analysis which presupposes the pre-eminence of his sexuality.'

Jill sighed, 'Which is so boring, endlessly, tediously boring.'

'It's more than bloody boring, woman. It's a matter of life and death,' said Sofia angrily. 'Crete teaches us that it's wise having a piece of string to enter the labyrinth with. Tunnels. Burrowing away, making new pathways. A string of words, hypertext, piercing hype, shovelling shit, whatever, getting in, killing the Minotaur and getting out scot-free. Cyberspace is just the place.'

When the sister came with her ministrations, Sofia made it known to us we were dismissed. She took her medication without argument, allowing the nurse to mother her.

Jill and I left. Outside, I stood beside her as she pressed the key-ring and all the locks on her rich friend's car spring up at once. Another rain squall hit. I moved quicker than she and was sitting in the passenger side when she closed the driver's door, staring at the car-phone. It rested on its cradle between the front seats. I didn't say anything because the instrument brought back the sense of panic I felt when I used it to contact the police.

'So, Margot,' she began. Hesitated, then confessed, 'You've worked out, I'm having an affair with Rosemary Turner.'

'I guessed, when I visited Meghan's house in Lebanese Plains and noticed all your things gone,' I fibbed. The rain came down like a wall of water, enclosing us in the claustrophobic space of the Saab. I raised my voice a little. 'I saw your picture in the Spiders' newsletter. Do you want to explain?'

'Which part? Everything has changed since Maria died. For me, anyway.' There was a new honesty about Jill. Previously she had been quite difficult to be alone with: liars' silence charges the atmosphere in a way I find oppressive. Yet I know it is only my intuition speaking.

'Why?' I asked.

'Well, I always thought Maria was madder than Sofia, I suppose. But it was death stalking her with his sickle,' she explained enigmatically. 'I've got a feeling he hasn't finished with us yet.'

The rain eased and a crack of sunlight speared the thin shower. Her very dark brown eyes gleamed mischief, humour. I sighed, 'Let's start with Meghan. What's going on there?'

'She's coming back tomorrow. I'll tell her then. I didn't want an argument at Maria's funeral.'

Their relationship was not really what I was interested in. I reached into my bag and pulled out my notebook. The pen was still attached. I flicked pages, gathering focus. I told her, 'Someone, not Meghan, wanted me to investigate her finances. Then after I had dinner and stayed over, Meghan herself employed me. When I realised you were into the pokies, I thought you would need more money than you probably have. So, you being a good mimic, I wondered whether it was you who pretended to be Meghan. Then I went over one day and the place was a dreadful mess. The next time it was spic and span.'

Jill nodded as I spoke, and looked at me when I paused. 'Trina turned up and threw one hell of a wobbly. Now, that woman is totally crazy. Judith was there. But she had no finger in them pies, and, well, I left them to it. Came back a week later and cleaned up.'

'Trina, Meghan's sister?' I turned to a new page and scribbled, 'Judith?'

Jill watched me work, and remarked, 'You know, I'm envious of you, Margot.'

'What?' I exclaimed, shocked, I think, by her levity.

'I wish I could work at what I love,' she said, simply.

'Instead of using your talents breaking hearts, I suppose,' I commented.

'There are no parts in straight theatre for me. Not any more. A neurotic, a saint, or a prisoner. When a performer can't perform, what does she do?' There was a decided note of self-sorrow in her voice.

'I don't know. Do you think Judith could have imitated Meghan's voice?' I asked, and added, 'If it was Trina, why did she do it?'

'Because she hates me.' She took on a frown of appropriate seriousness. 'She found out that I was gambling. I don't know how. Maybe I told her. Maybe she saw me, but personally, I think she is the one ripping Meghan off. Hangers-on all over the place. Judith's another one.'

I went for the jugular. 'Did you steal from Meghan?'

'Depends on your definitions of give and take,' she sparred. 'I won't now.' She drummed her fingers on the steering wheel, reminding me that Rosemary Turner was also a player.

'So Trina had some cause to suspect you?' I pressed.

'I had it bad, for a while there, Margot. All I could think about was getting to a poker machine and blanking out. If I couldn't feel risk, taking a character I played to the edge, then I got the rush of, what is it, fear?, losing money. You know, dry mouth, clammy hands, the roller coaster of hope and despair. I don't know.' She looked for sympathy, for understanding, and met my direct gaze. 'Now and then I dipped into our joint account. Meghan wouldn't notice. Wouldn't mind. Trina suspected and then ransacked the place for evidence. Meghan must have left some papers up at the Brisbane place.'

'Can we talk figures?' I suggested, fiddling with my pen. 'How much? Say, a ballpark number?'

'Three thousand, tops.' Jill David shrugged, sad, a little bit depressed, but not guilty of anything she considered excessively immoral. 'Two and a half, maybe, in dribs and drabs. How pathetic! Look at Sofia. Now Maria's gone. Can't blame her any more, can we?'

I cleared my throat. 'Do you love Rosemary?'

She shook her head. 'No. She's easy. Comfortable. Normal. Ordinary. It doesn't matter how bad I am. The naughtier the better.' She barked a mirthless half-laugh.

Sunshine was now glistening on the wet surfaces. Rosemary Turner's car-phone, it suddenly occurred to me, pre-dated mobiles. That's what it was about the Saab, with its central aerial; it reminded me of unmarked police cars. And established drug dealers among other businessmen.

'Easier than feminists?' I sought clarification.

'Yes,' she confirmed. 'Much.'

Snapping closed the spiral pad, I continued conversationally, 'Do you remember grilling me about feminist texts I had not read? How sarcastic and superior you were?'

'Don't come the guilt-trip, Margot. I have enough already,' she pleaded.

'The SCUM Manifesto interests me now.' I made a play of academic disinterest but she wasn't fooled, as I hoped, indeed, she wouldn't be. Nevertheless she complied.

'So you've discovered the Solanasite Conspiracy? I wondered why you were asking about Margaret Hall.' She grinned. Another cloud brought another downpour. 'Ah, the blessed revolutionaries of cyberspace. Babes in the post-modern woods.'

'Come again?'

'Old dears clunking into the new technology with their old-fashioned views hoping to change the world,' she revised.

'Chandra doesn't limp in cyberspace,' I said indignantly. 'Nor, I imagine, does Meghan, but she could not be a Solanasite. She and Chandra fell out about politics and practice.'

'That, Margot, is where you are dead wrong. Megs is a Solanasite all right.' Jill turned her black-brown eyes with their cynical glitter to my eager blues ones and smirked. 'Her methods are more subtle and more effective, that's all.'

Laughing light-heartedly, feeling for the handle in the door, I scoffed, 'Amazons, right? Warrior women. Penthesilea's revenge and all that? A joke, is it?'

Jill pulled down the corners of her mouth in a world-weary expression of 'been there, done that, moved on' and her last self-sorry comment was, 'I don't want to end up where Sofia is.' Which I took to mean if you take things too seriously they will call you clinically insane. I could have said, no, Jill, you look after number one and you'll be okay, but all I did say was 'thanks,' and 'goodbye'.

Sometimes when clouds scud across the sky and the sun breaks between the high precipitation and the low miasma, it is as if a yellow electric light has been turned on and suddenly the wetness is infused with brightness. That was how the weather was when I waited in my Suzuki Sierra outside the block of flats they call 'the hornets' nest'. I was acting on a hunch, relaxing into surveillance. My hunch was that Tiger Cat had not left the area. Now I knew that she did not have the might of corrupt police behind her and was more likely to be connected to lesser forces whose devious methods I would probably be able to protect myself from, my simple question could elicit a reasonable reply. I did not see her in the waspish comings and goings I observed. My intuition, however, was not far off, for Cybil Crabbe's irides-cent little bubble pulled out of the underground car park within twenty minutes of my stay at the kerb.

Slumming it, I knew it! She drove like one who learnt to drive in the suburbs on an automatic, all accelerator and brakes, whizzing down the straights and stopping sharply at corners. I followed, making myself obvious, eventually bipping my horn and gesturing. Neither of us was prepared to leave her vehicle. I didn't want to be left standing while she took off, and she had good reason not to cave into my demands. If she was the 'respectable' dealer, it wasn't my business. I tried to convey this with smiles and open palms. She must have been confused because the merry game meant I chased her into a cul de sac, a residential court shaped like a key-hole, from which she had no escape except to smash into my fender. We stared at one another through our windscreens for a moment; then she reached down and emerged from her car opening an umbrella.

When she stood at my window, I said, 'I hear that you Cybil took advan-tage of Neil among the banksias and sand-dune grasses.' She answered with an almost imperceptible nod, and I asked about the state of his health at the time. 'Did he come? Was he sick? Sweaty? Hyperventilating?' How was his heart? I really wanted to know.

She prevaricated for a while as my questions sliced through her artifice. Realising I knew a fair bit already, she told me candidly what happened between them. 'Afterwards I was so shocked by what I had done, I returned to the circle and buried my head. I was blind, deaf and dumb, catatonic. I just sat there, invisible, a shadow, dissociated. Until you came, looking spare and shocked yourself. You ran off. The police came. I was anchored, cemented to my spot. When people started leaving I had to move and when I moved I raced to my car and sped along the dirt roads. I couldn't bear to be among the crowds at the punt. I went the long way, going so fast I could have killed myself. But I didn't.'

'No, you didn't,' I said, thinking of Hugh Gilmore as I identified the second car that was the first to pass my place on the fatal night. 'And you never saw him again?'

'No.' Her eyes beaded with small, unwilling tears.

The vulnerability of a hard, sensuous woman was fascinating. There was something real about Cybil Crabbe after all. Perhaps it was the recognition of self-disgust. She stood still while her umbrella dripped, waiting to block my censure with whatever skill she could muster. I thought I am not judge and jury, merely an investigator. 'Did you notice a yellow Valiant Charger? Suped-up vehicle? Driven by a kid?' I queried.

'Yes, they were doing donuts in the next beach entrance, where the surfies go. I had taken the wrong dirt track. A group of boys, about three cars. They looked pretty high, self-destructive, manic. I remember thinking, watch it fellas, there'll be cop-cars about any moment. And yeah, I think one did follow me. A lunatic night. Is it only a month ago? There was a big moon. I heard him crash. Behind me. I slowed down then, and drove home trembling. I've been trying to forget ever since.'

'Tragic,' I commented and reached for my ignition key. I started my car, pressed the clutch and reversed into a driveway. She seemed frozen to the spot, a squat statue. I drove away.

The heaviest rain did not come until I was on the ferry, and there it was dramatic and drenching. The phone belled as soon as I got home, and Chandra's voice filled my ears with her conviction that Judith Sloane had betrayed the gurls and the principles of Lesbianlands and was in cahoots with Willy Campbell. It was all very plausible as good stories from the imagination are and I asked, 'Why?'

'Because she is a miser,' she answered. Then added, defensively, 'And Alison agrees with me.'

'Okay,' I said blithely. 'See you tomorrow, yeah?'

'You know I'm bringing Rory?' She sounded in two minds about that, which made me grin.

'Of course,' I replied.

Chandra is thinking of Margot Gorman. She talks nineteen to the dozen and Margot listens. She realises, in the security of her home with her plants and animals, how much distrust she has incorporated into her romantic relationships with women. Burnt too many times. But she was right, inspired? Trust has to be the mortar of the edifice of a gynarchy. It is physical between them, that is, intensely emotional. Urgent, promising wonders. Yet partnerships cause incidental caucuses which, no matter how great your intentions, bring settled tactics to the general forum; this is counter-productive to the revolutionary cause. Chandra has seen couples destroy collectives over and over again in her time. She, herself, has been culpable, both in the blush of love and in the agony of the break-up. Chandra takes it deeper, into the veins of her very self. The happiness of sharing your worries, your work, along with the minutiae of your trivial days, having a load lifted off your heart and your time lightened by sparks of anticipation or the smiling, cuddly presence, is so seductive all the world thinks it is the be-all and end-all of possible pleasure. The pressure, however, to right wrongs, to make a difference, to pursue a path with meaning towards a non-hypocrisy in oneself, to actually act on your beliefs, or if you can't do anything, think anyway, comes to a serene contentment that can cope with any circumstance. The violin string between indulging your capacity for joy and knowing the real limits of your worthiness, usually a strain, out of tune or stressed to snapping point can, conceivably, be tuned. But Chandra is not stupid enough to think such tension is easy. And she is quite aware of the inflexible ideologue in herself, and how, in love, that wall can become a ton of bricks. For the chemistry of sexual attraction to taste as sweet as the rare fruit it is, she would have to display her strength of mind and conviction. A secret kept from the one who shares your bed causes moral cancer, festers to tumours of self-disgust, eventually. But pillow talk is terribly dangerous.

How far can she trust Margot? How much can her lap and shoulders take? While talking on the phone she was listening for clues of Margot's intelligence, and got nowhere. What she did understand was her kindness, her rigorous sense of justice and fair play. Chandra lets herself admit she is overwhelmed by Margot's guilelessness, her beautiful structure of body, the turn of her ankle, as they say in Victorian novels, the articulation of her muscles, veins, sinews, bones; and the way she uses her strength to accommodate Chandra's disability without arrogance. When they swam together, it was all swirls. The climax in the water was quick, replete, clitoral. Chandra is, at her age, only interested in relating to free and independent women. She doesn't want to fall into co-dependency. Again. She wants honesty and strength. She thinks about this. The addiction of love comes over you and your principles fly away. Everything goes on hold as if an irrational goddess demands loyalty to another realm; all you do for your lover is dressed in sacred raiment with an odour of goodness. To her cost, in the past, Chandra thinks, this was not necessarily blessed with rightness. But who knows? Activity pursued in the arena of love or with the aura of love usually compromises her. So as not to hurt her lover a lesbian will often, simply, change her mind. Go along with behaviour or beliefs otherwise unconscionable. Chandra snaps her fingers and sighs. Wisdom from life and wisdom from logic are both very well, but wisdom from the feelings throws an almighty spanner in the works. She knows she cannot trust Margot Gorman. She would never trust an ex-cop, a spy or someone in the pay of corporations that lay rainforests to waste and exploit the labour of women and children.

So Chandra concludes, rather ruefully, as she yanks out weeds in the steady rain, that she must exercise self-control, will-power, over the urges that her very passionate body will ache to satisfy in the near future. The expectation torments Chandra. She pulls her callipers into position, stops, watching the clouds break up in the south-east, before she makes the strenuous effort to get erect. The sticks sink in the mud. To get to her feet, she says ironically. Keep your feet on the ground, Chandra, she admonishes herself. Unless she can change her, she must not fall in love with Margot Gorman.

The sun set, the moon had risen, but at dusk today you wouldn't have known. Half-light, half-dark hung in the cumulonimbus air, forcing a look at the clock to tell the time. I was waiting for a reasonable hour before I opened a bottle of wine. I leant back on my desk chair with my feet on an unopened carton, the Featherstone manila folder on my lap. A couple of deposit receipts puzzled me. They did not relate to her known accounts. I wanted a drink. I wanted to taste different reds. I glimpsed the untidy scribblings of the morning as I swung around, deciding to give in and break open the boxes. As I came back with the corkscrew, and stared at the metre-square butchers' paper, it occurred to me to ask: how much is in the Lesbianlands account? Rory's phone was dead, so I cracked a fruity chambourcin. I looked up Trina's address in St Lucia and dialled directory for the phone number.

Although the timbre of her voice was identical, it soon became evident that Meghan's high-pitched engaging enthusiasm was, in her sister, obsessional, mad. The matter of money sent her into a spin. 'Where is it? She can't have sunk it all into that dreadful place, what's it called? Lebanese Plains? Cedars of Lebanon mean something biblical. I guess, started by an inbred colony with fundamental Christianity. Whatever, it was creepy. Jill's a parasite. She was so angry, I'm afraid she'll send up a bunch of girls to bash me or throw me out. That's why I haven't got back to you. I've been lying low. It's about time you rang up, by the way. I was giving you a lunar month. Judith Sloane was there, going through things. Jill called me psychotic, a leech, a moron, told me to grow up and I said, look who's talking. When I accused Jill of having gambling debts she was lying about, Jill well and truly lost it. Sheer violence. She accused me of going through all Meghan's papers, of stealing, of sneaking. I came in in the middle of something between her and Judith, and something about Jill discovering Judith there when she came home.'

I interrupted the flow, 'Trina? Trina, listen! Do you think that Jill is stealing from Meghan? Is that why you employed me?'

'Meggy is a fucking consultant, isn't she? She should be a bloody millionaire. Anything to do with money and they turn up like vultures, feral bludgers. I've been protecting Meghan for years. How come she doesn't own this flat?

Tell me that, tell me that. Then all I'd have to pay is the rates. It would only take one job and she could pay it off, but she doesn't. She said she can't. Where is her money?' She kept talking while I swilled the chambourcin, '97 vintage, across my palate and taste-buds. Then I held the receiver in the crook of my neck and pumped the air out of the bottle and stoppered it.

Before I delved down for another grape, another wine, I said, 'Maybe she has discovered better things to do with her money than supply her sister.' I didn't expect her to listen to me. Or if she did, to hear what I was saying. I rely on my canine sense. Dogs, because they have no words, can always scent the truth and its absence. What about Trina? It was an old story in Meghan's relationships, I imagined: her sister and her lover hate each other. So they fight, so? The truth was, both wanted money for nothing. And so did that other ex, who never gave me her name.

Trina suddenly demanded. 'Where are you coming from?'

'What?' I jerked back into the communication. A paper chase is usually like a game, a logical maze. Right from the beginning this one had led me into the asylum where the insane reign.

'PI Gorman,' Trina continued. 'Here's a fact for you. Judith was telling porkies.'

'What do you mean?' I obliged by inquiring.

'Pork pies, lies. She told Jill she wasn't snooping and she was. She was planting evidence and she was taking stuff. But who listens to me, I'm just the crazy heterosexual sister. I can tell you're not listening to me. Why did you ring? You haven't heard a thing!' she accused.

'I am afraid you're wrong, Trina. You have disabused me of many fanciful notions by what you've been saying. I think you're right. Both Judith and Jill took some of Meghan's cash, as you yourself have. You've explained to me the complete mess of these documents, the petty pilfering, the odd parts of the country. The wild goose chase.' There was no way, I thought, of knowing whether this woman was suffering a clinical mental illness or merely neurotic, but Megs would keep providing her with a safe house. All I could figure was her hysteria had gone now I had put her on the spot, and I waited for our telephonic connection to be broken because I had a lot of work to do and a lot of wine to taste before the night was out.

'Well, I'm not paying you,' she said peevishly.

If I went through the seven deadly sins, searching for a motive, I reckon avarice would loom large, but with Meghan Featherstone, I felt I had to seek its opposite. 'Fine,' I replied. 'Goodnight, Trina.'

52

. . . organised paedophile ring . . .

Virginia, weakened, exhausted, finds her own bed. When she struggles out in the morning, she discovers her car is gone. Her home is dripping, in the midst of the thick cloud, which at a lower altitude would be rain. From moon-shadow through the tangled streams of dreams to day-fog, she shifts in a netherland of no clarity. She is emotionally emptied, physically fasted to an ethereal plane where disfocused meditation is reality. She is lost in her own environs. Apart from water, she ingests nothing. Hunger has no grip, no grab. The fruit and vegetables on her bench, disturbed by possums, are limp, if not completely eaten. The jar of chilli powder and the tomato sauce bottle are on the floor with scratches on their lids. The remains of milk coffee in the cup on the table is scummy with mould. She shrugs and goes back to bed.

After about five hours' sleep, during which the hemispheres of my brain continued thumping ground strokes at one another, I woke feeling seedy and on the ball. My work-space pulled me like a magnet a pin. The fan in my computer whirred loudly and lap-wings made a racket running around the lawn. I turned on the printer, called up my files, read, reassessed and restlessly made a cup of tea. Needing to wash the positive ions off my electrified skin with a burst of surf, I pulled my wetsuit off the rack and paced down to the beach. I gingerly broke the breakers. My toes turned blue but soon I was fish-kicking under the rollers which were biding their time then coming in high. I let the oceanic energy toss me about in the spit of its spending on the shore. Then I waited for the next and used the white water like a spa. I eventually swam out beyond the bar to the flatter sea and floated on the hills and dales of waves, and thought.

Of Rory's matter. The telephone call I made to the Campbells, trying to find out whether a mining lease had been acquired, was worse than point-less. I aroused suspicion. They kept handing the receiver to each other, told me nothing and used their voices continuously to ask me who I was, not associating me with the one who saw Barb. But like her, they said, it was none of my business as I didn't live there. They had made a neighbourly arrangement with the gurls. Which one? They wouldn't say. The gurls were interchangeable as far the Campbells were concerned. They feigned ignorance of surnames, implying that my using such identification only proved that I was a complete outsider and had no right to interfere. I asked did they know that Virginia White had disappeared?

'What car does she drive, dear?' Wilma Campbell had asked in motherly tones. My want of description on this score elicited cocksure dismissal like an iron fist in the glove of apologetic sympathy. The Lesbianlands' maelstrom in a tin mug was a storm of personal drama, invisible to the greater world. With interwoven roots, it was hard to see the wood for the trees, or the trees for the wood, to single out the individual who traded with the Campbells, or the weed in the native balance of the bush.

Rory, in contrast to Wilma, sounded flummoxed by her friend's absence. It was amazing they were of the same species on the same planet, let alone living within a couple of miles of each other and fairly similar to look at. Their essential difference made those sci-fi movies of aliens taking human form seem believable.

The sea rocked me in its cradle, vigorously. King tides were predicted. I recalled Chandra saying she wanted me to be like her mother. As I never knew the woman, how could I possibly ape her, or even try? I summoned up an image of this horsewoman, understated, in her hunting hat with a bit of scarf rhythmic in the wind of her mount's gait. Her spine was straight, her eyes ahead; invisible geometry dotted lines from her eyes to the horse's ears, pricked and erect, the spines of the two creatures maintained a living right angle together; the tip of the toe, the point of the knee, exact alignment. While nothing was static, all contained tremendous strength and discipline. There was no padding in the shoulders of her jacket, yet squared perfection in the movement and rhythm was easy, like music. I changed from back-stroke to freestyle. The flowing tail, black and shiny, of the horse was the only loose thing apart from the scrap of scarf in the whole outfit, echoing the motion, expressing the compressed power of the high-kneed forward pace and suggesting the relaxed impression of the carefree seat of the rider in the saddle when, in fact, all muscles were engaged. The long hands in their gloves were soft on the reins, yet the fingers laboured. The gait changed from a collected canter to a simple elongation of the whole order. Swimming with cupped paws, hurling what water I grabbed backwards, feeling my shoulders revolve and my hips roll, it bothered me that I forgot the name for the colour of a horse when its body is reddish brown and mane and tail black. I must be in love because I wanted to go through Chandra's childhood photos. I swam and it came to me: bay. I knew there was a connection between the horse and the sea. I wondered where the name came from as I imagined in another aeon riding a porpoise from place to place. The dressage of this long-dead mother gave me the clue to Chandra, her holding back, her lust for power, for justice, for freedom of movement, yet keeping it contained and, although she could be playing me for a fool, teasing, she wanted command of a lover, or love itself, as much as she wanted me. I appreciated her speculations on Judith Sloane's miserly motives.

For a silly moment on the beach I forgot my injury and started to run. I felt the pain stab like an arrow, tripping my step. Yet I pranced in the sand, on my toes, keeping heels out of it.

After the exercise I felt sick. My brilliant liver demanded pure beetroot juice. Naturally, I did not have any raw beetroot in the house. Thrust had a luscious-looking garden. I was so desperate I used the phone. Lois answered. I didn't get a chance to say why I rang. Lois had a pressing piece about cousins staying in the house, and how they were going to make trouble. I could hear aggressive language in the background.

'Who you talking to, sister-woman?' The politics of the have-nots, justified hatred?

'Shut up, it is none of your business anyway. Better not come round here, Margot, this is a radical mob. They can smell cop, and you're not hard to pick.' Lois dropped her voice. 'It is not their Murri mum that makes them a worry, Margot. They got a bugger of a Yugoslav father.' She was trying to tell me something about serious violence. I overheard a male voice demand again who I was.

'It's just one of my clients, why can't you shut up and let me conduct my business?' she yelled, then, into the mouthpiece, she said, 'they bloody don't have to come here and stir up us mob. I got customers and stuff.'

'Crikey,' I said with absolute sincerity and added, having no thought as to what I could do, 'you know where I am if you need me.'

As I put down the phone, I remembered that the rally was on today. Militant Aborigines I did not expect. Shooters Party and biking clubs, yes. Ignorant racists gathering around their mascot, the televisual plastic celebrity, nicknamed the white virgin, were ready for scuffles. We really didn't need the land rights lobby playing into their hands by providing them with the publicity of conflict. When I read newspapers I prayed the degree of political, religious, ethnic clashes in other parts of the world would not come here. Not the bovver boys of soccer hooliganism in England. Nor guns in every household, like the United States. This was easy-going, she'll-be-right Australia, but I'm afraid, like all pleas for divine intercession in human affairs, it was wishful thinking. I had offered my help on automatic impulse.

Before nine when she has important business to do, Rory goes through her correspondence, re-reading a sensitive, almost shy, letter from her mother, and checking her bills. The ISP account, though not that much money and crammed with all sorts of offers of services, details the hours she spent on-line. She frowns. She finds her diary and justifies the dates in columns. Someone on the land used her computer with her password when she was not here. Her rocky perch of a house is impossible to lock. She invites communal access to her facilities, asking only that women log their phone calls in an exercise book with a pencil on a string near the door. There is a tin with change for cash, or records of what's owing. Suspicion of her sisters does not come naturally to Rory. Virginia always pays up when the bill arrives. Hope, so facile with the technology she could take computers for granted, might not even know that she was required to note expenses she incurred. But, actually, it could have been any one of the gurls.

Rory, for all her independence of mind and spirit, is dependent on Social Security for income. By nine-fifteen, she is on the telephone quietly going mad with annoyance. No matter what she does, sitting there, impatience builds up like molten lava under the crust. She tries to think up something to do, a yoga exercise holding the handpiece? Even philosophising doesn't work: how can nonsense be tamed? How can the hysteria of frustration be used? Telephonic efficiency is sending everybody crazy, including the people who work in the call centres. The power of witchery to force things to happen in your favour is smothered by the boring procedure of bureaucracy. She has to get through. Music is interrupted by a recorded message that informs her that if she doesn't hold on she will lose her place in the queue.

The stone that Hope gave her gleams with its own light, an interior white glow. It fits into a fist: she could smash someone's face in, with an enhanced punch, but Rory has to be very angry to be at all violent. Although she weeps for the plight of street kids and wants to change the world, she knows that revolt leads to bloodthirsty excess. In short, she could never be Madame Defarge with a front row seat at the show of the guillotine's falling blade, filling baskets with heads. Her copy of Solanas' treatise is within reach. She trawls its pages for the comforting intellectual passion, and wonders what sort of urban terrorist Valerie might have been had she a cadre of dedicated followers, or indeed use of satellite communication systems and underground networks of women who agree. Rory puts SCUM on the pile of things she must take to town, all the official papers she has of the Lesbianland Collective. Judith has the bank books and access to the vault where the deeds are held. Finally Social Security talks to her in person and she notes the time of the appointment.

One person's sense and purpose can look like nonsense to another.

Glancing at her red dog's yellowish eyes ever-ready to go for a walk or leap onto the flatbed of the truck, she decides to go on-line for a little while. Full of hot air, some of these women. She clicks the Stein code of hypertext, prepositions, articles. There are only three in the chatroom she wants. Who is truly revolutionary and who is, at heart, a lachrymose reformist? The truly cruel thing we know about women is the way they pull each other down; nurturing females failing to nurture each other?

Rory believes real courage does not involve killing. It is about living and goodness, practising what you preach. Not designing drugs for children: what are you women doing?

<MOP> Well, let's raid this lab and grab the sweets, then the means of destruction are in our own hands anyway.

<BAC> Crumbled and powdered chalk? Fine sugar and glucose?

Rory frowns as she reads. She types 'MMIMR'; signalling private chat. There she gets a mobile number to ring, written in a jumble to resemble a car registration. Beneath the symbolic language of white food is the code for action, and right now she wants to know for sure whether her cyber-co-conspirators had anything to do with the accidental or deliberate death of the lad who dressed as a girl. Are any of her comrades vicious enough or mad enough to take the life of a contemporary Achilles, some mother's heroic son, as Valerie Solanas took a shot at Andy Warhol? She, herself, is too fundamentally decent. However, she does need the information. She speaks on the phone.

'Something to do with kids?' she asks the woman whose voice she doesn't recognise.

'A new generation of party drug was disguised in candy. Yeah, boiled sugar, so the guinea pigs, the lads, didn't even know they were eating narcotics.'

'Reminds me of the alcohol they're pushing these days, that look and taste like soft drink but are almost as overproof as rum,' Rory expands.

'Yeah. Looks like sweets. Old fashioned granny-made lollies.'

'So? What? They invite boys around, go fishing, surfing, give them toys, say they want their bodies, for a little play, when actually they're monitoring the effects of the concoction?' Rory takes notes.

'Right, they move up and down the eastern seaboard, targeting holiday spots. The laboratory this month is in Port Water.'

'What's our interest?' asks Rory, the Solanasite.

'Nothing. It's common knowledge on the grapevine.'

'Good.'

'In sisterhood.'

'You too, bye.'

Rory rings Margot and conveys all the information she has, barring the network of Solanasites. Tess's wild barking transforms into a yelps of welcome. Rory goes to the window to see Virginia picking her way through the trees under a battily broken black umbrella. Long legs in big gumboots, an old brown oilskin making her rucksack into a humpback, she walks slowly humming the first bar of 'Singing In The Rain', without the verve of dance or happiness, more like the drone of some insect. However tuneless, it is music to Rory's ears. She laughs through tears which sprout in her eyes as underground springs break out of craggy hillsides Ah friendship, she sighs.

Outside on the porch where VeeDub disrobes, Rory says, 'Hi, where have you been, you bloody old mole?'

'Lost and found, you might say,' grins Virginia. 'Up and down. In the ground and all around, and here I am, Rosaleen, Josephine, Penelope.'

'What the hell are you talking about?' Rory lifts the pack off her back, shakes out the coat and hangs it on a rack. She is so pleased she fusses busily.

Virginia examines Rory's blotchy clay-red face with her intense eyes but the beetling brows are wide on her forehead. She opens her arms for a warm hug and holds Rory till her shuddering sentiment rises and falls, until she becomes still. They break apart and go indoors, words tumbling and somersaulting in acrobatic interruptions and effortless assumptions of care and communication.

'Where's my vehicle?'

'We're in for a flood.'

'Got any grapes or an apple?'

'You're as skinny as a stick.'

'I am, Rory, I am, accountable,' Virginia states, as if it is an explanation for everything. She pokes about Rory's fresh food bin.

'Hope drove it to the front gate.'

'Accountable, Rory. No excuses. None.' Virginia finds an apple and sinks strong teeth into it.

'I haven't seen you for a week.' Rory sits heavily at her dining table. 'You've been gone.'

'A week, is that all? It seems an age.' Virginia fills the billy, finds matches and lights the gas, saying, 'I've been gone an age.'

'I've got to go into town later. There have been developments. They're mining on our land. I'll have coffee, not tea,' Rory remarks as she notices Virginia shaking tea-leaves into the pot. She gets up to locate her percolator.

'I better have tea. Coffee might be a little too heavy on my nerves,' Virginia sits down and lets Rory take over preparations of their beverages.

Rory rattles the biscuit tin. 'Oat-cakes.'

money

Virginia nibbles the one she takes, and compliments her friend, 'You make a nice Anzac bickie, Rory. Yes, I know. Mining. Willy's got a fenced-in yard up the top. Full of heavy machinery. Padlocks. The lot.'

'No kidding? Fuck.' Rory repeats the swear-word several times as she grabs the billy with a cloth and pours. 'Fuck, fuck, fuck.'

'And that's only half of it,' Virginia explains.

After they have exchanged information, worried and reassured each other, Rory rings Margot.

Looking at the time, she says to VeeDub, 'I'll drive you to your car. Hopefully it's okay. The creeks are rising. We had better go.'

'Cool. We've got to look at the bright side. I'm lucky I fell down the hole last week and not this, heh? Their excavations are so primitive, they'll fill up with water for sure.' Virginia chats as Rory collects her bills and books and bags. 'You taking the SCUM Manifesto for any particular reason?'

'Why do you ask?' Rory responds with a question. 'Don't I always have something to read?'

'Oh, I forgot to tell you,' Virginia says as she watches Rory fold her laptop into its case. 'I surfed the Internet a couple of times when you weren't home.'

Rory stops, amazed. 'I didn't know you even knew how!'

'My brother, you forget, builds the bloody things. Or did.'

'Yeah, yeah, but I didn't think you were interested.'

Virginia White laughs because she simply can't explain to the dogged, pragmatic Rory the possession of wings. She hugs her again, and says, 'Let's go.'

'Wait, you bugger. How did you know my password?' Rory is indignant, and mystified.

'Easy,' VeeDub smiles. 'Practically everybody uses their pet's name.'

Instead of treating my liver, I attacked my hangover with raw egg and hot sauce. After speaking with Rory, I rang Philippoussis. No chump with the technology, my man. As soon as I gave him the lowdown on the plant, he was on to it. He said he would get toxicology into gear, retesting stomach contents. But sugar was hard to detect, being quickly absorbed by the bloodstream. More for the magistrate to deal with at the inquest. How was the deputy coroner? Fine.

I rang Alison at Penny's. She asked for the details of the detective's email address to send across as attachments all saved correspondence with the Boy-lovers, both hers and Neil's. Plus the graphics of the plant. Ask Penny. I warned her they would probably come to look at the Waughans' computers and, while she was forthcoming with what she had discovered, she thought it best to get out of there and send the stuff anonymously. Neil had found out the <u>Whymen</u> web address was an organised paedophile ring with links to the drug trade. She confirmed there was a cruiser up in the mangroves.

I got back to Philippoussis to tell him to expect electronic mail, and although I'm no expert on hardware, software and the Internet, and what is where exactly, I said, 'Neil's PC might be worth a look.' In this exchange, I recommended police look for Tiger Cat. As she was handing out freebies at the gay and lesbian picnic, that is where he could find a sample of the pill. Reassured that he had little or no interest in the other women at the barbecue, I asked if he thought the Crank was kosher, after all. Now we knew a new drug was being made in a laboratory in these parts, with paedophiles providing candidates for singular scapegoats. 'Or money,' he said. 'Two birds with one stone.' Ha ha. Whatever, Catherine Tobin was the courier to the scene of Neil Waughan's decease. Although I didn't like Cybil Crabbe, I didn't want her roasted while genuine evil bastards got away scot-free.

Meghan Featherstone sees a pure green as people are said to see red when they are angry. Jill David is relating to someone else. If they weren't in the Arrivals lounge of a country airstrip, she would have smacked her. Jill's desertion is dressed in moody blues, sinking head and pearly tears. While actually sincere with fear, the actress in her could have performed the part with equivalent outward signs. Meghan does not appear to hear the rest of the conversation that assures her that the goats are with Judith's friends up on Hippi Sitti plateau. Navy-grey clouds lurk behind the smoky hues of mangrove trees. She rushes along the edge of the tarmac to the hangar where her car is parked.

Driving out to Lebanese Plains, furiously speaking to her emotions, the music on her CD blaring, Meghan's sight is sharp. Yellow leaves stand out in relief, skinned gums are peachy pink and lemon streaks in the scrub, last year's bark on the forest floor soaking up the rain, too wet to be a bushfire threat, just yet.

'Jealousy, you jade dragon breathing flame,' rails Meghan. 'Burning self. Stupid emotion clutching the guts, depressing the nervous system, bringing frowns down from the crown, crinkling skin, grabbing a slimy hold like some goo from sticky elsewhere, not respecting boundaries, taking over everything. Rendering the lot yucky. All thought sucked into quicksand. Jill, you are without morals! You have brought a strong woman down. This is horrid, annihilating pain, you bitch! Jealousy could drive a girl barking mad. Because. Simply because there is no answer, no getting rid of it, just languid songs whining about not going out. Self-destructive fucking jealousy.'

She replays the scene of her homecoming over in her head, from touch-down to let-down, word for word. She remembers exactly what Jill told her about Judith and Trina. But Meghan, feeling so absolutely betrayed, is not inclined to believe anything.

Chandra Williams is on her horse outside the local store getting her shopping handed up to her and packing it into her saddle-bags. Meghan does not stop. She does not wave. She takes the gravel bend at speed.

'Yet, one bit of my mind knows, Jill and Rosemary could be having a ratshit time. There is no guarantee they are not really spooking one another. Self-hurting women are nothing new. That cow Turner is too smug for self-harm; all feminism means to her is her personal advancement. Masochist Jill, she'll have you for breakfast. Masochists, addicts, think they're only hurting themselves, but they are hurting all of us. Is it only jealousy I feel? I grieve for what you have lost. Me! I could be constructive, whereas you, Jill, you are plainly destructive. Gives you heaps to weep about with no responsibility. I have been there for you. Taken the tab. You want to see me squirm so you say you are really happy, having a great time. You sex junkie. Don't feel sorry for me; pity I don't need. My distress is denser, broader. You only worry if the blame can be placed on you, then accuse me, when, in fact, you project your faults onto me! And succeed. My feelings of self-immolation make me welcome danger.'

At her parking space overlooking the creek, Meghan checks whether she could drive all the way home. The stream is muddy, swirling, making eddies and strange moving surface puddles. A risk, yahoo. She reverses, accelerates and bumps the undercarriage of her low-slung car. 'Get over it. First one ford, then the bridge. I am so over it! but wishing you cared.' Her car is skidding, sliding. 'I think you do care. It is just that I am too intense. That thieving sleazy mongrel is the opposite, lazily saying sweet nothings, certainly not challenging truth.' Meghan is losing control on the greasy clay. The fat mags are slipping sideways. 'Facts are harder than the pleasure domes of gambling and drug-dance frenzies. Dream on. Pretend. So why am I so jealous?' She guns the motor. The back wheels spin, spitting grass and mud behind, until careless fury and engine-power have her fish-tailing across the turf. 'I don't know what I'll do. Oh fuck the enemies in our bosoms. I hate this hurt. Jill, Jill, why do you do it to me?' The on-road tyres in off-road conditions are like skis in melting snow, but Meghan, eventually regaining control, manages to bring her car to a halt near her house.

The half-renovated dairy is perfectly clean. Meghan sees Judith's work in the cell-like order. Pretty flowers picked from the paddock in a vase are dandelion, lantana, scotch thistle and Paterson's curse. Everything put away.

'What a well-meant bloody nuisance!' Too many vacant surfaces. A note on the table. The names and address of the goats' whereabouts, saccharine wishes in yellow on purple like the daisies of fire-weed and morning glory, with kisses and stars, such a lot of effort on such a small thing. Judith had done no more than give Jill the phone number of the couple, but she intended to milk her serendipitous intervention for all its worth. The drawers where Meghan's papers and photographs are kept in a rough and ready fashion are neat. Envelopes clipped together to be used again. Meghan sighs. She will never find anything unless she goes through it all, tossing, making a vital mess.

No cat, no dog, no goats, no lover, no homeliness. Meghan gazes out on the miserable day and stares at the silvered bits of hardwood planking Judith brought to make a pigeon coop so that they could home messages to each other over the hills. Judith never even got as far as bringing a pair down in a cage to fly back to Lesbianlands. A glance in a book was probably all she knew about training homing pigeons. If Meghan herself had glanced in that book, or Permaculture magazine which is what it was, the birds would have been into their schedule within the week. But, Meghan realises, all she did was buy the original parents and acquiesce to a lot of utopian, atavistic visions. The half-built pen is ghostly. Deadly nightshade with its black berries grows through the rolled chicken wire. She lets her eyes roam across her piece of real estate, as she stands at her bedroom window, trying to revive her vision for this place.

Canines guard the gates of hell, but Meghan is more partial to felines. A devil-dog appears on the edge of her consciousness. She focuses on her driveway. Chandra's hat, horse, side-saddle and person come over the brow of the hill. Meghan stares at her, the straight back, the elegant flop of her useless legs, the riding crop, the classic arch of her mount's neck. The obedient, huge dog lopes along with laughing, savage teeth and lolling tongue. 'That woman is together while I am in a thousand pieces.' When she hears the 'cooee', Meghan descends her ladder.

'Are you okay?' Chandra asks, 'You were driving like a maniac.'

Chandra has come to make sure she arrived safely. The fact that Meghan drives that way most of the time seems to have escaped her memory.

'I guess,' Meghan replies suspiciously. Chandra knocked her out last time they were this close to each other.

'I'm surprised your car made it up that hill.' Chandra indicated the erratic tyre marks.

It is not raining. They talk outside. When Meghan was away Chandra had had a visit from Trina, her sister, who was psycho, according to Jill David, who had thrown her out. Meghan nods. In her own account Jill was a heroine. Trina had walked over to Chandra's, and told her. Meghan asks why Chandra took Trina's side in the brawl. At this minute, she enjoys a bit of malice at Jill's expense. Before, she would hear nothing against her. This among other things jostles for room in Meghan's capacious mind as she offers Chandra a drink, is accepted and passes her a glass of tank-water.

Chandra sits high on her stocky horse. Meghan's eyes are level with her waist. Since their last encounter, their violent disagreement, relations are so cool, warming would take some effort.

But Meghan is abrupt, 'When Jill threw Trina out, what was my sister's story?'

Chandra is watching her dog with a frown, 'Pardon?'

Meghan glances at the animal that is perfectly still, like a cat, concentrating on something invisible. 'Trina?'

'Well, I can only say what Trina said. I mean there were accusations I didn't necessarily take on board because she was obviously distressed.' Chandra is circumspect.

'Why didn't you tell me?' Meghan demands irrationally.

'You wouldn't have listened. And, why would I? I was just an ear, a counsellor, not a gossip. Besides we weren't talking,' Chandra says off-handedly.

'Right,' Meghan is aggressive. 'I'm listening now.'

'She said she was convinced that Jill was stealing from you. Large sums of money.'

Tears appear in Meghan's eyes. She tries to force them back by pursing her lips.

Nikki begins panting again, and drops her ears. 'I didn't make any evaluation either way. It did her good to talk. There was lots of stuff. About your childhood. About her envy of you. How emotionally cold your parents were. How you succeeded and she didn't. How you bought her a flat in Brisbane. How Jill accused her of bloodsucking. Sibling rivalry weighed on her mind. My advice to her was to do one thing,' Chandra speaks gently.

'What was that?' Meghan demands, in a much harsher manner than she intends.

'Oh, not any precise thing. Just one action which would make her feel better. You know, to get it out of her system. It was no good her stewing on it, grinding her teeth to stumps, not eating, chain-smoking, tying herself in knots. I didn't care what she did, I said, it could be anything at all, provided it expressed what she felt and what she thought, put the problems that were eating her up inside out there in the world so that she could deal with physical monsters, rather than ghosts of the past and suspicions, and so on.' Chandra's hands on the reins are still as if her whole posture was studied, ready for an explosion which if it scared her mount would not shift her from her seat. 'I gather from Margot Gorman she wrecked the place.' Chandra grins; after all, once they were friends who understood each other. She senses a vulnerability in Meghan that could go either way, to volcanic eruption or soggy dissolution.

The horse stamps his foot, trying to rid his legs of a large fly. Chandra moves him to a patch of luscious-looking grass, then gives him his head, hooking the reins over the pommel and folding her arms. Meghan follows, pensive.

'I've done everything I can for my sister,' she says defensively.

'I must say,' smiles Chandra, 'you and she are very alike, both string beans.'

'Trina is eighteen months younger, one inch taller and skinnier. Always has been. Fragile,' Meghan parrots. Suddenly, she shivers. Both women look out to the west where shifting cloud hides parts of the mountain ranges.

'I know, but your voice. And the way you both speak, you could be mistaken for one another,' Chandra observes.

'She's crazy,' Meghan says.

'Maybe you need her to be crazy so you can be rich,' comments Chandra, bringing up the bitterness between them.

'What a load of manure!' Meghan dismisses Chandra without much conviction.

Chandra shrugs her shoulders. 'Where are your goats? I don't see them.'

'Someone is looking after them. Did you hear about Virginia White bashing up Judith?' Meghan touches the neck of the grey horse.

'Yes,' responds Chandra. 'No one has seen Virginia for days. Personally, I don't trust Judith. If Virginia hit her, there'll be a good reason.'

'Tomorrow, Chandra, perhaps I could come over?' Meghan's voice is brittle, weak. 'I could use a friend.'

Chandra pulls Potsdam Harry onto the bit. 'Well, I know you and Judith are thick.' Glancing up at a laden cloud, she says, 'I'd better be on my way.' She whistles her dog. 'Sure, I suppose, tomorrow then.'

'Yes,' Meghan concurs vaguely, as horse and pedestrian walk a few steps abreast. She opens the door of her car and pops the boot. Chandra sees the flash laptop balancing on top of bags and gear of all sorts and wonders whether Meghan mucks around in the IRC of the Solanasites.

Chandra gees her horse into a slow canter up the slope, and her dog bounds behind.

The candidate for the coastal electorate is a woman who says she is just a nervous housewife. Her off-sider for the country seat is a gun-toting primary school headmaster with a big hat. Neither of them has the size and colour, the glamour, of the white virgin herself. All three walk along the streets of Stuart, with their entourage, shaking hands.

Xena Kia, having painted ferocious Maori coils on her forehead and cheeks, waits for her friends at a table outside Greasy's take-away, drinking tea. Ci and Jay pass, saying they will be back in a minute. They have to go to the chemist. Gig and Nicole have promised to bring Zee from the pub. Wilma Campbell's weedy brother, Leo Smithie, is handing out leaflets, running ahead of the party, an officious, unofficial scout. He smirks as he lays the mauve and green flier down in front of her.

Xena growls, 'You really are a plain little man, Stumpy.' The features of his face pushed in by a hand which did not reach the chin, he is a physically unfortunate guy with long grimy hair. Even the celebrity is taller than he is.

The white virgin, bright light of the ultra-Right, is, in person, exactly the same as she is on television. She is totally at home. Xena is taken by surprise.

'Mind if I sit here?' she asks, and sits down. 'We are not a racist party.' Three camera crews are following her. Farming couples in buffed-up hats are thrilled to catch a glimpse of her, and come over all shy when she recognises their salt-of-the-earth quality in banal phrases. Less self-conscious rural folk call from a distance, 'Good on ya, darlin'!'

She orders a cappuccino and a slice of lemon meringue pie. Xena is caught in the lens. The politician handles food with the confidence of the Country Women's Association and doesn't choke, as Xena does, on her mouthful of drink.

Gurls behind the press corps are having a great laugh.

When Xena gets up to leave, having not said anything, she is engaged in conversation. 'You have to agree that it is not fair that multinational companies are taking our wealth out of the country.'

Xena is stuck for words. The woman is looking into her eyes earnestly. She is a happy, humourless woman, with no evident internal worries. A puppet perhaps, but relishing it. 'Australians haven't got a chance when the government allows Canadian pork to flood the market.'

Kay comes up to the table, punchy for political discussion. 'We might agree with that,' she says, putting her arm across Xena's shoulder. 'But we do not agree with your solutions. Come on, Xena.' As she moves away, Kay, opportunistically for the cameras, shouts, 'Pigs are housed, anything from 20,000 to 100,000, in hot horrible sheds, unable to even turn around, unable to ever lick their piglets, unable to move in any direction, never to ever to see the sunlight, to feel fresh air waft across their beautiful pink bodies.'

'Canadian pork is flooding the Australian market,' the personality repeats, not to be outdone.

'It's disgusting,' Kay continues her tirade in a very loud voice. 'And cruel.'

Gig, Zee and Nicole have come from the pub and are making a scene with the young men from the media. But the journalists do not film them; the best photo shot was the white virgin with Xena, in her face paint, and they have got it. Meanwhile the object of the verbal abuse turns her friendly attention on the girls who serve her and the small business people who want to shake her hand. Kay keeps it up as she walks down the high street. 'You are mainly interested in the economics of the situation, as inhuman as the farmers who keep the pigs in the sheds. All their lives. Until they're slaughtered!'

Gig yells for the hell of it, 'You are creating your power out of myths and paranoia, you don't care who really gets hurt. What you call simplicity is slovenly ignorance.'

Zee chips in, 'What have we done to you?'

Xena, not alone any more, chants, 'Cowards. Cowards, pick on the blacks and the single mums. Pick on those weaker than yourself.' The unruly protest satisfies the candidates, their leader and her minders. They smirk, clean-cut and polished, ordinary Australians, as opposed to riff-riff with bad language.

Gurls take their attitude off to the beer garden of the hotel where Kooris and visiting Murris are gathering; all settling in for a session. They sit outside so the publican will not complain about their dogs. Sometime during the afternoon, Zee, having made new friends and met up with cousins from Walgett, waltzes out to their table with the news, 'You know what? That lot are charging ten dollars to get in to her sermon. If we all go, it means they get a hundred bucks or more for their bullshit. Us mob aren't going.'

'That does it, gurls!' states Gig, 'For our demo. Not getting my money.'

Out-of-town police circle the block in white cruisers with defining red and blue top-lights, waiting for trouble, ready to grab drink-drivers and brawlers.

53

. . . international female conspiracy . . .

Making a Philippoussis-type coffee and sweetening the oily black with heaped teaspoons of sugar, I settled down to read what I had written during the night and printed in the morning. Called *Notes towards the end of the Featherstone investigation*, it addresses Meghan.

Prior to meeting you in person

Haphazard, incomplete paperwork arrives in the mail. I am engaged to find out who is embezzling your funds. Job confirmed by telephone. Though confused, evidence shows you do earn a lot of money, and that withdrawals from your accounts take place at several different places in Australia at the same time. There is no share portfolio or anything to indicate where the bulk of your probable wealth resides. I am told there is a discrepancy, and there appears to be same. I find out that:

a) Someone impersonates you; who? She must sound like you and be able to forge your signature. Katrina Featherstone, Jill David, or, at an outside chance, Judith Sloane. I assume your sister, being close to you in age etc., could do it; why? Jill is an actress, excellent mimic and has access to your documents, cards etc., but, again, why? Discovered later, it appears that Judith Sloane practised imitating your signature. Why?

b) Proof that you are down a sum, 50 grand? Possibly more. Confirmed by accountant, Rosemary Turner. Documents, however, incomplete and client unco-operative in providing more. Suggestions by accountant that you have a habit, e.g. cocaine, in which case, you impersonate yourself to maintain secrecy and throw blame, whatever. Is Turner capable of embezzlement? Morally, professionally, yes; but I get the feeling she hasn't got a clue where your money has gone. And she'd like to know.

c) Two things: who employs me? & where's the dough? While Katrina may have impersonated you, it is unlikely she took the money. Handwriting expert (report & invoice enclosed) analyses signatures

586

and written notes. Katrina signed your name but did not forge your signature, while there is one (possibly two) competent counterfeits for fraudulent purposes. She has no motive and no need, as you already support her to a large extent. Similarly Jill, except for one thing: she has an expensive habit. Gambling. My observation is, also, that she likes the good things in life, e.g. flash cars. At present, with assistance of Rosemary Turner, applying to be declared bankrupt. Implication: she has other debts, unknown to me, unable and/or unwilling to pay. As she has no other income than unemployment benefit herself, I believe she is capable of siphoning your cash. She likes a sugar-mummy.

If, for instance, Judith's the culprit, is she in conspiracy with Jill David? If so, what are they up to? As both are secretive types with a tendency to lie, I doubt it. Also, while both could be in your house when you are not there, hence take what they like, why would either engage my services? My intuitive guess is Katrina Featherstone, being poorer, hence sharper about money matters, in familial loyalty sicked me onto Jill David, who had a great thing going leeching your accounts to support her diversions until this investigation. The upshot of same is the pilfering has to stop, and if she goes bankrupt, she doesn't have to pay debts incurred.
So Katrina succeeds in upsetting Jill's apple-cart.

Post our meeting
The plot thickens: why do you now employ me when you didn't in the first place? Together we could have found out who impersonated you, nutted out why, and either you tell me or you don't tell me what happened to your money. But you are more unco-operative than your pretender. Then:
a) your house is ransacked;
b) you change solicitor;
c) I find Hope O'Lachlin's birth certificate -- no use by itself, where is her passport?; elsewhere her signature forged;
c) house cleaned up and goats gone;
d) further documentation: i/ contract ii/ insurance papers;
e) UFO photos.

Something is going on
The way your house is ransacked, in anger, suggests a personal/emotional motive, not professional, not fiscal, pointing again to Katrina (or possibly Jill or Judith). I discover the photos. The UFO photos are fakes (whatever they mean!), hence nonsense. Hope O'Lachlin's fake signature appears on contract, which means either you or Jill or someone, is establishing a

false identity: why? You have the best motive, since it invalidates an extremely exploitative contract with one of your employers, a conglomerate group of companies, including Nadir Mining Services. Change of solicitor = change of moral character, from slack shyster to tireless campaigner, indicating cessation of corruption, or perhaps, legal action by ex-girlfriend wanting some lolly -- in which case you would need a good female advocate, not a bad, male one. Why not a seeker of truth and justice in the first place? Because you, Meghan, have/had something to hide viz. phoney Hope O'Lachlin signature. According to contract you earn heaps, and the omission of documents, including deeds, and further insurance papers that would give me an idea of what you really own, there is a lot more money missing. Up to or more than a million dollars over the years could be unaccounted for, and probably not my business as plainly you are in control of that and you are my client. It does explain why you didn't give a fig for Jill's pilfering, even though to Katrina it was a lot of cash.

However, if it is not yourself, that leaves a) Rosemary Turner b) Judith Sloane c) Hope O'Lachlin, unknown character born 1961, can't be Hope on the land who is more likely b. '81. But birthdate could be tampered with; were you born about '61? There is at least one non-kosher 'Dr Featherstone', and I don't think it is possible to forge your own signature. If it were, why on earth do it?

As your detective, I advise: sack the accountant, not a totally loyal woman, but she (as yet) does not know your full financial picture. Jill has been observed driving around in her red Saab; make of that what you will; Jill says she will tell you of their affair.

Judith Sloane is a sly customer and I wouldn't be surprised if she nicked the Hope passport from your place; but who nicked it in the first place and why? Is it real? Who is she?

I don't know. You probably do.

Finally, a coincidence. A Nadir Mining Services baseball cap was discovered by me at a possible murder site. Whatever you're into, Meghan, I hope you're not in too deep. By the way, I discount the cocaine theory ...

Hugely dissatisfied with myself, I chided me. Margot, do not ever again work after dark with a skinful of red wine. There is too much doubt. This was not a neat piece of Virgoan work. I needed Auntie, to separate the major threads of my personality, astrologically. My Scorpio rising suspected dark mystery while my Gemini moon wanted to invent glib scenarios. There was a truth beneath it all, but beyond me. Because I was just one person, a triathlete, with three investigations going nearly a month, my failure felt too overwhelming. I filed the page, squared off the folders, dusted the computer keys and went down to the sea.

The Pacific Ocean hit the nine-mile beach, tatting foam into dirty white lace at the edge of billowing jade silk. While the sand was a kind of beige, the sea was almost khaki under the filthy grey sky. A curlew disappeared into foot-holes, rushing this way and that after invisible food. Instead of giving me perspective, both the sandpiper and the ocean made me aware of my clumsy size—neither insignificant, as all this beauty, this nature, was reflected on my retina and recorded in my brain, nor big enough to embrace what I was conscious of with serenity. I, like the prawn-trawler heading for port, was an object, a construct, ploughing my way with the motor of free will through the tides of fate, pathetically different in colour and kind and selfishly deter-mined to get somewhere. My destination, for the moment, was the surf. And I threw myself in for the second time in a day. What made me so sure Meghan Featherstone was not a cocaine addict? She was manic and moody enough.

Rory allows Chandra to chauffeur. Nikki and Tess share the back seat. Usually liking the slow throb of her idiosyncratic truck, on arriving at Chandra's, she eyes the Subaru and is convinced by Chandra, whom she can't help seeing as handicapped, that it is okay. Chandra hates condescension. On the way to the coast, to Margot's, Chandra notices Rory quietly crying. She continues steering, not asking the reason for her tears.

Rory has a letter from her mother she hadn't opened until she got into Chandra's car. She'd picked up her mail on the way out of Lesbianlands, thrown the envelopes in the glove box and followed Virginia's speedier vehicle along the dirt road.

'Do you want to hear my mother's letter?' Rory offers.

'Sure,' Chandra assents. 'Why not?'

'"Dear Roslyn",' she reads, '"How are you? I hope you are fine. I was refused Communion today! and it has made me very angry. Tom, your brother, and his partner, Kim, are members of the Rainbow Sash Movement. You know I always hoped Tom would turn out to be a priest. Now I under-stand why he could not. He is too honest! I have been taking the sacrament all my life. I never questioned my belief, as you well know, dear. We the Irish-Catholic Australians, even as we starve, have the Faith of Our Father's Holy Faith in our veins. We have our roots in the Church. Tom was always a saintly boy. It is God's irony that a girl from a family of thirteen should have only two children, both of them homosexuals. 'Gay'. Such a strange word. But the Lord works in mysterious ways to trick us to salvation.

'"So, I put a rainbow sash about me, one of the parents. I love St Pat's Cathedral. I go there too rarely. Your Confirmation day, Mary Louise's wedding, and when Tom was in a choir one time. It is surprising how seldom a Catholic parishioner from Preston goes to the Cathedral of the Diocese of Melbourne. But our Archbishop gets my Irish up, my girl. His sermon was all about how homosexuals are exactly the same as adulterers. He certainly does not know my children! Now Archbishop Mannix was a different kettle of fish, since he was a stubborn Irishman and lived to a ripe old age because he walked ten miles twice a day!

'"Roslyn. This man can steal my Blessed Eucharist! We were all refused the Bread! I have never been refused Holy Communion in my life. To think that one would have to lie, to disguise oneself to take the Body of Christ!

'"You can't take the politics out of an Irishwoman no matter how hard you try. It just goes to show. We weren't in chains for hundreds of years for nothing!"'

Chandra interrupts, 'What is your mother like?'

Rory doesn't immediately answer. She is in reverie. Roslyn O'Riordan, she hears the rolling rr's of the Irish nun as she calls the roll, slapping her black leather strap on her thigh in arhythmic emphasis, rattling her large rosary beads noisily, looking for any excuse to deliver corporal punishment. Rory was toughened by that strap. There was an orphanage above the classrooms. The nuns' sleeping quarters were in the attics of the convent. The orphans were called boarders. Not many 'boarders' had families to go home to in the holidays. They were mostly weak, white and craven kids with Pommy accents, though a couple were of Aboriginal descent. Day scholars also had accents, Lithuanian, Hungarian, Latvian, displaced persons at the end of the Second World War, but most had lost them by the end of school. The Irish-Catholic Australian kids should have been the elite of the priest-ridden parish school where those in positions of power were of their ilk, were it not been for the perverse divisiveness of that religio-genetic condition itself. All the nuns had straps attached to their girdles and used them freely. One had to be impossibly pious. Rory, a broad ruddy girl with a brother far weaker, was anything but pious.

'I am remembering primary school,' she says aloud to Chandra. 'The only subject considered important was RK, religious knowledge. Our days were peppered with moral questions. One I'll never forget. "Is it better, when you are asked to do something, to say, yes and do it, or say yes and not do it, or say no and not do it, or no and do it?" The nun was always trying to catch us out. I guessed it was a curly question. They must have sold those straps at

Pelligrini's with their special and individual handles. Margaret Mary's handle was silver, while Sister Colomba's was folded leather, a kind of flat, fat-centred figure of eight. Anyway, I knew the answer. I was so certain I thrust my hand into the air nearly propelling myself off the seat, pumping enthusiastically, dying to get in first. She pointed at me. With the handle.

'"It is best to say no, and to do it, because then you don't have to do it if you don't want to, but you probably will," I said, knowing I was right.

'"Come up here, you smart alecky red-head. No wonder the folk of Innisheer'll not go to sea when a red-headed woman crosses their path on the way to the currach. Wait at the side of the platform."' Rory puts on an Irish accent, and continues the anecdote.

'"Class?" she asked.

'The pious girl, a full-blown hypocrite at the age of seven, Raelene, opted for the first response, "Sister, it is best to say yes and do it." She sat down, knowing she had said the correct, though glaringly obvious thing. Her gratification was what Sister was going to do to me.

'"Maureen? What do you think?"

'"If you say no it might be because you can't do it?" Maureen was considered the most intelligent girl in the grade.

'"Now, little people, are you being honest with me, now?" The nun enjoyed herself with these kinds of posers and went through the whole class without revealing the Right Answer.' Rory recalls clearly getting more cuts than the boy who said, guessing, that it was best to say yes and not do it. When asked why, he rationalised, 'You get into less trouble if you say yes.' Although she got the strap practically every day of her schooling until the age of twelve, generally for sticking up for one of the boarder-orphans or her younger brother, this particular day stands out in her memory. 'I stood in front of the class and she hit me on the palms of both hands, and the backs of both knees, for being honest. She caned me for being true to myself.'

Rory tells Chandra the story, without self-pity, not seeking sympathy. Her tears are for her mother, not the powerless child. 'The only thing they wanted to teach was craven obedience.'

In answer to what her mother is like, Rory shrugs. 'I guess, I see something of her in all my lovers. They kind of expose a little bit about each other. Or me. She pretty well describes herself in her letter. She loves her church. She has church clothes and house clothes. Goes to the shops in either, depending on her mood. Tom is your ordinary wussy poof. But he wouldn't contradict Mum when she offered her opinion.'

Chandra's station wagon, an automatic with a manual accelerator, is quiet enough to conduct a reasonable conversation in. Rory enjoys talking of her family, a fact of life she all but ignored in her thirties and early forties.

'Tom and Kim are great to Mum now. She hated Women's Lib in the same way Dr Mannix hated Commies. That's when she and I split asunder. But it is a buzz, this letter. She has finally hit the barricades.'

'What age is she?'

'Eighty-four? Five?'

'Really?'

'My parents didn't marry young. And stayed at home with their parents until they did. Mum has only recently taken to writing to me,' Rory says, softly. 'I guess I'll answer this one.'

'Oh yes. It's a great letter,' Chandra encourages. 'Get to know her, Rory, before she dies.' She pulls into the queue for the car-ferry and they watch the barge on its cable dawdle towards them. Rory lets the dogs out to sniff along the grassy verge. Sun is behind ice-cream clouds which stand out against steel-dark ones stunningly. Pelicans glide about the sticks of oyster leases. One sits on top of a pole. Terns are busy.

'Before we get there, Margot's I mean.' Rory blushes as she attempts to word what she has to say. 'I should admit that I've got a candle lit for her.' She glances at Chandra. 'Guess I should put it out?'

Chandra presses her lips together, grimaces and looks straight back at Rory. And shrugs. The Rottweiler and red kelpie return to the car on recall, leap in, happily grinning as Chandra starts up the motor and they clunk onto the barge.

In the laundry I washed the salt out of my wetsuit, thoroughly. I hung it on a rail in the bathroom and shower. I was walking through my house naked when I heard a car. I dived for my clothes in my bedroom which has a window onto the front yard. Chandra's Subaru. Two women, each with a dog. They were early! I fumbled for a T-shirt and draw-string chinos, neither ironed, both with no buttons or zips. Rory leant against the passenger door, sniffing the sea like an animal discerning something in the air. Chandra must have told her she didn't need any help and dear butch Rory looked a bit miffed. I sauntered out bare-footed and wet-haired. Chandra fell into my hug. The muzzle of her bitch nudged my leg.

'What colour was your mother's champion horse?' I asked into the hair behind her ear. She thrust me away with both hands on my shoulders, pushed me into a position she could look into my eyes.

'Margot, what a question! My mother had several champion horses: a grey, big ugly fellow who could jump a mountain; a brown almost black thorough-bred with long white socks; and a pretty bay mare, my favourite, but far too spirited for anyone but Mum to ride. All those were champions because she was a champion. We had plenty of other horses and some won led classes. The bay mare's father was a champion stallion. I could keep talking about my mother and her horses until the sun sets in the west. But Rory is here.'

I apologised and gave Rory a sisterly embrace. I patted their canine companions one after the other. We went inside. 'Virginia turned up.' Rory's voice was low, pretending the chemistry between Chandra and me was of secondary importance to her. 'By the way,' she said, 'I think there is something happening next door.'

The observation interrupted trivial chatter. Chandra sat in a chair, next to which was my unanswered mail: the invitation to do the advertisement and my Nike contract.

'Nothing like someone else's troubles to get away from your own,' philosophised Rory. 'Come on.'

It was a command. Tess obeyed and I, too, followed her out.

We stood together on the concrete path in my backyard listening. The old fellow to my north was yelling abuse. Although not swearing, each of the words he did use belittled his wife. He had no doubt she was his chattel. The thing that had been niggling me since he was last here, at least a fortnight ago, slowly dawned on me.

'She has been there all that time,' I said to my friend. Rory did not know what I was talking about. He was telling her off for not answering the mobile phone he had given her as a present.

'Where is the mobile phone?' he demanded.

I told Rory I remembered it ringing. 'When I saw her on her back step one day she rushed inside.'

'A gift that was intended to keep her in check when he was not around, meaning he could be a jailer at the same time as being free himself,' grumbled Rory. 'Screws are in jail too. Most of the time.'

'I could have assured him she has not been so much as out the door,' I explained, but it made me angry that the woman had not protested before. She annoyed me with her pathological timidity. I blamed her. My mind was rapidly changing. He was becoming frantic about the whereabouts of the bloody gadget.

He now called her dirty within our hearing.

'Oh for god's sake, no one could be cleaner,' I muttered as we listened. He called her sexually promiscuous. She was plainly a far more alluring character in his imagination than in reality. However, we heard no peep from her.

'I'll string you to the back of the Pathfinder and drag you along the road until you tell me,' he threatened, sounding ludicrous.

'Does this happen often?' Rory asked me.

I shuffled. 'She won't talk to me.'

He shouted, 'I don't have a rope in the car, but I do have cable.'

Rory made a face. 'I want to get a look at this jerk,' she said.

The strangest thing about the house to the north of mine is that it has roller doors closing off its front verandah. These were rarely open more than a metre from the ground. Brick veneer walls were broken only once in each room with small aluminium windows. I had not seen it as quite the fortress it was until now. The highly polished four-wheel-drive was parked at an angry angle to the inappropriate garage doors.

Chandra, her guard-dog at heel, was already swinging herself into their driveway as Rory and I came along. We made three abreast behind him and stopped in a line. While the red dog ran about, the black and tan hound was clearly at work.

Chandra spoke in her ordinary voice. 'I know from my experience in refuges that blokes like this are real cowards. The older they get, the more cowardly.' Betraying her anger, she shouted cruelly and loudly. 'Don't blame your soft dick on your wife.'

Rory used a quieter, more sinister, tone. 'And it's not her fault. Nothing is her fault.'

'You pathetic old fart,' both yelled in concert, as if rehearsed.

Nikki kept an eye on her mistress and the man, but didn't growl or move from her sit-stay. I saw the cream faux lace curtains in one of the windows tweak aside and the old woman's face, a vision of fear, peeking out. The roller doors were locked with a padlock a little way open. He attempted once to drag them up then said to himself, 'I've got the spare set in the car, under the seat in a little metal box.'

Rory murmured, 'Boy! are we in Cloud Cuckoo Land!'

I asked, 'Did he hear you?'

Chandra nodded towards the window. 'She did.'

When the old man turned around and made to shove past us, snarling, Chandra jabbed him in the prostate with her right-hand carved snake. Knowing the strength of her upper body, I winced with his pain. She transferred her weight and slapped upwards with her left. She had done this before. I was shocked by such focused hate. He saw the dog and was genuinely scared. He doubled over. Rory prevented me helping him. It was so instinctive I hardly knew I was doing it. She pulled me back.

Suddenly the side window opened and the wife turned banshee. 'Takes a cripple to beat you, you old shrivel-cock. Give it to 'im. Have a go, you bitch. Finish 'im off. 'Ave a geez in the woodpile. Show it to 'im, cunt.' Then she slammed the window shut with a snap lock.

Rory strolled off down the side of the house. After taking a moment to absorb this insanity, I ran to the woodpile. There was the cell-phone on the chopping block, having had the worse end of a furious axe. Rory, coming up behind me, laughed.

'Let's drag him round to have a look. And hope she keeps hopping from window to window to see.' My emotions were so confused, I was swept up by a warrior woman fantasy of retribution. It was something to do. Something physical. I rushed back around the front, to find Chandra standing over the old codger, leaning on her sticks, panting. Nikki shadowed as I lifted him up, turned him round and frog-marched him to the woodpile. Rory was keeping one eye cocked for the twitching of nylon lace. Chandra hobbled on her three inadequate pegs, keeping pace with me and the gentleman of senior years. It was getting hilarious. We all wanted to see his reaction to the state of his 'present'. He was, impotently, infuriated. But careful, because of the dog.

A back window slid open, 'Give the gimp the axe. 'Ave a go, cunt. Takes some sheilas, Herbert, soft-cock, limp-dick, pain in the fucking arse. Millstone. Life sentence. Lock me up in a loony bin! Maybe there they will let me get my teeth out.'

'Oh Christ,' expleted Rory. 'She's driven mad with pain.'

'Okay Herbert, tell us about the last conversation on this poor little ex-gadget. Tell. What was said?' I toughed in police-speak.

'Nothing. I just rang. I rang once or twice a day. If she didn't answer I had plans,' he boasted.

'Okay, she answered, and?' I demanded.

'She wasn't telling me what to do,' Herbert proclaimed, defiantly.

'She said she needed to go to the dentist, didn't she?' Rory put the leading question.

'Ethel has been saying that for about two years. Nothing new in that.' The ignorant old bastard!

'Maybe the pain-killers ran out?' I suggested. I could feel Chandra, beside me, fuming.

He counted on his fingers. 'Yes, that would be correct. Two days ago to be exact.'

Having let him go, looking at the mangled mobile, hearing the piping of Eastern Spinebills in the forest beyond the fence, sizing up the situation and making no sense of it, I asked, 'What do we do now?'

Chandra could, quite happily, have clubbed the bloke to death if the look on her face was any indication, but she kept her canine killing machine in check with a soft murmur. Rory, whose interest was plainly in the woman, grinned and nodded towards the house. 'At least she's having a good day.'

'Yeah, but what do we do?'

The old man turned pathetic, pleading. 'It costs too much . . .' he started.

'Nice car,' Chandra was irate. 'Bet you never drive it over sixty kilometres an hour. Why don't you just trade it in on something less expensive? Her teeth can't cost that much.'

Selfishly pedantic, he explained, 'They count your cash, you see. You can't get them on the pension any more. You have to put the money in goods and property. If you are worth something, what have you worked all your life to have in your retirement, they don't pay your dentistry any more. They did.'

'You never listened to what she was saying.' Chandra showed no sympathy for him.

Rory sighed, 'Chandra, cut it out. She likes you.' Rory nodded towards the curious curtains. 'Because you're a gimp. Go and try and get her out of the house. Margot, have you got any pain-killers? Herbert, have you got the pain-killers?'

'Of course, but I wasn't going to tell her that, until . . .'

'Yeah, we know,' Rory interjected. 'I'll get them. They're in the Pathfinder, right? Under the passenger seat?'

Herbert was obsessed with money, with retirement funds, with roll-overs and negative gearing and government decisions and bank charges. By standing there with him I had opened the floodgates and he yabbered on. If not talking he would be making noise with his lawn-mower, as if his whole existence was in an echo-chamber. I watched Chandra, the 'gimp', limp along with the help of her unique callipers, her obedient hound on alert, at heel. I felt no fonder of Rory for using the word, and I loathed the woman in the house for her prejudices. A magnanimous tenderness for Chandra flooded my sympathetic nervous system yet I felt rebuffed by her strength of conviction and her attitude of superiority to me. Indeed, her violence. I was weak and hopeless. My can-do approach whittled away by want of achievement of solid outcomes, a bunch of lacks assailed me as old Herbert kept up his ear-bashing. No real direction held me to the spot I was standing on, listening and not listening, watching and not watching.

Chandra was having no luck with the petrified pensioner. They stood either side of the locked backdoor, calling each other names. Rory made her way inside from the front or the side door. She was standing at the sink filling a glass with water. An Amcal red and yellow paper bag sat on the sill of the window. She reached for it, removed the prescription drugs, read the labels of about five containers, chose one and removed pills from the bubble pack. She surprised the old lady by appearing behind her in her bush hat with its covering of badges, her ample army shirt bulging at the pockets, tablets in the palm of one hand and water in the other. The door opened. Rory and Chandra had a quiet conference.

Rory came over to me and began talking. 'Haze and Daze are friends of ours.' Chandra joined us, releasing her guardian from duty. Nikki snuffled the woodpile on the scent of a lizard.

'Haze and Daze?' I repeated, 'Sounds like two women behind a fog of marijuana smoke.'

'Hazel and Daisy actually.' Rory went on to explain, 'They're a pair of women with a mission. You can't talk to either of them about anything else but their work. They're kind of reconstituted nuns, if you like. They have a passionate friendship and run a kind of half-way house, a general factotum of a place for those in need of aid. They keep themselves busy. They even run suicide workshops.'

'Rehabs.' The little kelpie joined the big dog in the hunt for the reptile and both women called them off. 'Out of it!'

'Haze and Daze do things for people. Sometimes get funding, sometimes don't. Anytime you go there it's full on.' Rory spoke to Chandra.

Of the old chap beside me, I said, 'I think Herbert needs to see a doctor in case Chandra did any damage, and Ethel needs that dentist.' I wondered why my friends ignored me. They had started chatting irrelevantly.

Rory ruminated, 'It's just that it's an effort to go there as a friend. You get swamped with the details of human tragedy, on every level. It's like walking into a box of tangled wool. But they can get things done.'

'They do,' said Chandra, 'but I'm not saddling them with him.'

Rory addressed me. 'Chandra wants to take the wife there, because neither of us think she will get her dentistry straightaway. What to do with Herbert, though?'

'It's not a good idea to separate these two, is it?' I considered. 'They've been a couple for too long. I mean, who's going to pick up the pieces?'

'A life of torture,' disagreed Chandra. 'Haze and Daze to the rescue.'

Rory opined, 'I don't have my car. What do you say to me driving the big beast out the front here and you and Chandra following?'

'No,' I objected. 'He'll have conniptions.'

Chandra grunted, 'Oh, I don't care about that.'

'I do.'

She stared at me, her face flushed. 'What do you care about him?' she demanded. 'He's already dead.'

'He is not!' was my riposte. I strode off.

Rory dealt with the bickering elderly couple.

My emotion erupted in self-defence as Chandra followed, attacking. She and I screamed at one another. Neither of us made much sense. She was mad at me for letting the situation next door get so bad. She said I had pricks in my head as she whistled her guard-dog into her car. 'Men are useless and harmful objects!'

The fight continued inside my house.

'And what are you doing, taking money from these murderers?' Ferociously, she picked up my contract and tore it up. That made me furious. I gave as good as I got. Sexual attraction, exciting, titillating closeness, turned into violent disagreement. I was not going to let her dictate my work.

'Lord save me,' I exclaimed in despair. How could something that was so nice transform into this ugliness? I tried to pacify her, but her temper was a wonder to behold. She tore me to pieces with her tongue as I went out and thumped my punching bag in frustration, yelling, 'It's my bloody business how I live my life!'

'That's the trouble with you post-feminists,' she spat. 'You only care about your own independence. We said the personal is political, and you all took that to mean the political is personal, fucken individualists! You sell your souls and say it's your business. Well, your comfortable life-style, PI Margot Gorman, is paid for by women elsewhere who have bugger-all to start with. What you do personally affects every other woman on the planet!'

As if the weather-goddess wanted to weigh in on her side, lightning fired flashes at the earth, and thunderbolts cracked. Storm-winds began disturbing the trees. I had to shout to be heard. 'How could you tear my contract up?'

Chandra started being sarcastic, and hobbled inside and took the audition letter into her hands and ripped that up too. How dare she? My silence was eloquent as I watched where the pieces of my correspondence ended up. Too proud, too incredulous, to gather them while she was there, I took umbrage that she judged me.

Her passion exploding, I was blasted by a barrage of political correctness which stunned me, and left me feeling sorry for her. She exited my house on her sculpted sticks, her weapons, her weakness, spoke to someone else and slammed the Subaru door.

When I heard her car start, I retrieved the bits of paper and took them into my office, where I sat and puzzled. I banged my forehead on the keyboard of my dead computer in resignation.

'It's okay,' I heard behind me. Rory was in the doorway. 'She is just very angry. She'll be back.'

'That doesn't mean I'll be here,' I croaked. 'What did you do with them?' I meant my neighbours, Herbert and Ethel.

'Oh, she's in charge now. I made her take Valium and Panadeine Forte. Gave them both some medicinal brandy I found in the truly dreadful lounge-room. They'll go to the hospital. While not kind, he's plainly used to taking orders from her when his welfare is at stake.'

Rory's ginger hair was flattened into an unattractive part in the middle by the constant wearing of the hat, which she now held in her hand. She carried a brief-case, as well. Solid around the hips where the army pants stretched to accommodate feminine bulges, in earthen colours, generally bulky all over, she was of a piece, whole. She reminded me of a dolphin. It must have been her eyes. Tess licked my hand. Rory convinced me to have a cup of tea. She calmed me down, talking about the history of Lesbianlands, the personalities of the women and how they had tried to put radical lesbian theory into practice there but that was much harder than anyone could imagine. She reckoned they had achieved a lot if you looked at the positive side, but there was danger in being romantic about it.

'Real danger,' I said. 'You have someone like Judith Sloane who, if all my suspicions about her are right, can appear to be a right-on sister with colourful, angelic ideals, while, in fact, she is a mean, bitter miser who is selling you out.' I made a zipping motion indicating an outer persona opened like a suit to reveal hidden character.

She nodded sadly, and asked me if I had read Valerie Solanas' manifesto. I told her I had glanced through it at Virginia White's when I went looking for her.

'Margot?' she queried, getting up from the kitchen table, finding her attaché case and popping its lock. 'Can we get down to some work? I am worried. If we can't trust Judith who is treasurer, we're in deep shit.'

'You want me to find the proof to nail her?' We went into my office. Rory pulled up a chair and sat down beside me at my desk. We both looked up to my colourful notes. Rory read a bit, then gestured toward the manila folders.

I took a yellow lined foolscap pad from the drawer. And told her how difficult it was getting information out of the Campbells. 'Also,' I added, patting the Featherstone file, 'I think she is an accomplished forger.'

'We need two signatures on the cheques.' Rory sounded desolate.

'Yours? And hers?' We shared a nodding realisation. 'Your beautiful script would be a piece of piss to copy, if you don't mind my saying.'

Troubled by the far-reaching implications of criminal skill combined with treachery, even the horrible worst-case scenario of her signing away the deeds, we worked on the Lesbianlands problem until we heard the return of Chandra's motor vehicle. Ignoring that I summarised, pencil in hand. 'Virginia White disappearing, did that have anything to do with bulldozer and unexplained explosions? What do we have on Judith Sloane apart from her strange behaviour? Her fight with Virginia? Her lying and generally acting uncharacteristically, and Chandra's theories of greed and collaboration?'

Rory related the story of Virginia's return, her cryptic descriptions of being lost and found and the existence of heavy machinery padlocked into an enclosure hidden in the wilds.

Chandra leant on her crutches and rested her weight on the door jamb. She seemed somewhat mollified. Her hair was wet, making her face seem bonier. Her excellent skin was high-coloured. Her deep-set eyes glared at Rory's open case. A copy of the SCUM Manifesto was all that was left inside it.

'You haven't told her about the Solanas site,' she accused Rory.

'Plainly I miss a lot not being on-line,' I said lightly. Rory reached down for her copy of Valerie Solanas's manifesto.

'Not yet,' she replied, calmly.

The atmosphere in the room was tense and thrilling. Rain hit the tin roof. I was in for a roller-coaster ride.

'What is SCUM?'

'SCUM is the bible.' Rory said.

'The bible?' I looked at the slim volume in her hand. As books go, it was about as different from the leather-bound, gold-embossed, fine-papered millennial best-seller as you could get, short of junk mail and give-away leaflets. The binding, staples, had burst and the cheap paper was so stained and discoloured, the words and sentences themselves must have kept it together.

'Well, the new testament. The manifesto of the only true revolution,' Rory expanded, handling the tract with reverence.

'You have to have eyes to see.' Chandra's sarcasm was back. She jerked herself off the wall, swung around and assisted herself into my sitting-room to, I assumed, take the weight off her arms in a chair.

'The reason I was going to tell you about the site that Chandra mentioned,' Rory began, lifting her voice over the sound of the downpour, 'had to do with your investigation into the murder of the young lad dressed as a girl.'

She had my attention, but her own concentration was disturbed by the patent disapproval of Chandra. We came to an impasse. I have a nose for dissemblance, and I suspected all along that something was being kept from me by these women. The carriage of communication stopped at the top of the big dipper, engine failure. I frowned at Rory, willing that she take the plunge, release the brake, but the silent, fuming Chandra had power over both of us. I got up and, passing Rory, went to join Chandra in the other room. Rory came. I stood in front of the chair and looked down at those defiant, intelligent eyes. Rory took a seat. Professionally a problem-solver, I paced, mechanically, dirty bare feet on the gritty floor. The thunderous precipitation eased. The ensuing silence begged conversation. Where to start? It was up to me. The floor was still that of a holiday house, a weekender up the coast, away from the real world, my home. Sand under my soles. Words failed to meet the demands of emotional intensity. Their eyes followed my motion and I caught each's gaze again and again. I, personally, was important to both these lesbians. Their knowledge and their love, in conflict, stilled their tongues. I felt sinewy, strong, and terribly ignorant. The golden tan of my forearms was caught by a sudden shaft of sunlight. The drying fringe of my fair hair was irritating my eyebrows. I flicked it aside. I grinned as I could suddenly see why they wanted me in their commercial, yet another blue-eyed beauty exhibiting the healthy values of our sporty nation in the sun, surf and sand.

'Let me guess then.' I sat on my coffee-table, knees apart, facing them both. 'From the bit I did read of this treatise, I gather that men are the enemy. And boys who dress as girls are just as bad because they are the like the hero, Achilles, who hid among the maidens and eventually massacred the Amazons, desecrating the corpse of their queen. Because Rory indicated this site, this SCUM Manifesto might have something to do with the murder of Neil Waughan, I deduce that, whatever is communicated between contemporary Amazons in cyberspace, the outcome could be deliberate assassination. Of the enemy. Men. Boys. In the name of revolution. Well, let me tell you, Neil was not murdered, though his death was probably caused by one of the lesbians at the barbecue. It was not an execution. But that does not free this Solanas site thing from probable intention. Guilt. The Internet is a world wide web, political slaying of the enemy could be happening anywhere. Not only your violence today, Chandra, but your evasion several times in my company, makes me wonder whether you might not have both the passion of conviction and the wherewithal to have, in fact, acted upon it. Your distrust of me, which I take personally, is more probably seated in what you perceive as my alliances, with the police, and with international corporations. Capitalism, post-feminism, post-modernism, I don't know, something you hate. It is almost as if you think I prostitute myself for the almighty dollar. Or worse, I am singly responsible for the exploitation of the workers in Nike's factories in Asia. Furthermore, you are capable of destroying your own friendship ties for what you reckon is the greater good, as evidenced by your treatment of Meghan Featherstone.'

Rory turned a harsh glance in Chandra's direction and placed the manuscript on the table beside me as if it was hot. I picked it up and began fanning its pages. 'So what is the story?'

Chandra had not crumbled under my attack. She had been assessing me, taking in every word and reading my logic between the lines. Now she gently expounded, 'The Solanasites are intellectual and compassionate women trying to figure out a way to effectively make the world a better place. Most of it is discussion.'

'But lately,' Rory interrupted, 'we suspected a loose canon was rolling out of control.'

'She, or he, worried us. Identity is hard to determine. Everyone has pseudonyms.'

'But this one, we worked out by the way she writes, the way she speaks, comes from our own area, or visits here. I dunno. A possible psycho.'

Chandra took over the explanation. 'She is Australian and local, of that we're sure.'

Sceptical, I pulled my legs up into a more relaxed seat on the table. I was prepared to listen.

Chandra said. 'I scanned the visitors to my several sites, chasing down their location. Not all who post bulletins are of the revolutionary mode, but those who are should recognise each other. We had established a code, a language beneath language. It was working. Now for the mobilisation: how to implement policy? Who, of these theorists, was in action.'

'Hang on.' I palmed my hands as if on point duty. 'What do you mean by "action"?'

Rory piped up. 'There were all sorts of ideas about subversive activities. We could run a prostitution racket to finance our subversive activities. The sex industry is the one thing patriarchy demands and assumes control over. Not my notion, you understand. They wanted to spike a male-only product —shaving cream? Jock-straps? Silk ties? Razors?'

'Condoms? Inside, of course,' Chandra joked.

I did not laugh. 'We are not man-haters.'

'Who are you kidding?'

'Sorry, slip of the tongue,' I parried. 'Money?'

'Well, yes. That was obvious.' Rory reached for her flimsy little 'bible' and read, ' "There is no human reason for money . . .' da da. "But there are non-human, male reasons for wanting to maintain the money system." Then she goes on to detail what.'

'You can't have your beloved structures, your collective circles, your better world without dealing with everything, and everybody needs money. That includes how we treat the environment. Sustainable development.' I felt emotionally, physically and intellectually exhausted. Languidly, I folded off the coffee-table and stretched on the floor before I stood.

Rory rose as well. She handed me her precious little book and pleaded, 'Margot, please read it. Every word, from the beginning.' She looked at me with such a selfless, caring warmth I wanted to swim into her arms.

I said, 'Okay.'

They prepared to leave.

'You don't trust me,' Chandra commented as she hobbled to her car.

'You don't trust me either,' I countered. I dearly wanted her to respond to me with the affection Rory had shown. 'I can't stand not being trusted. I'm trustworthy for chrissake.'

She rattled her car-keys. Both dogs barked, eager for movement of any sort. She would not catch my eye, or cuddle.

'Like, for instance, I don't know whether you pull away from me because I smell bad, because I am not really your cup of tea, or because I am not a man-hater.'

'Ditto,' she muttered.

'Well, I'll never be like your mother.' I stood back. I was suddenly angry.

'I didn't know I pulled away from you,' she said, settling into the driver's seat.

'Oh, get a grip. Think I can't read subtlety? According to my senses, you should be eager to see me again.' I didn't care what I said. 'To do anything.'

'Sure,' she replied simply.

'Come for a swim, bring Rory along. I don't care. I fucken don't care.'

'You care too much, Margot.' Chandra smiled slightly. 'You are a perfectionist. And why should I trust you when you might have no conception of the ethics of what I am doing? When you, should you be given the facts you demand, see the action as wrong? I know you, Margot, I know you enough to know you would do something. You would fight wrong according to your own lights.'

'Do you mean you are engaged in activities I would see as criminal? And how well do you know me? How?' She still had a slight smirk about her large, wide mouth which made me want to smile as much as I hated her for it. She was winding me up. Yet another drama-addicted dyke. 'Get over it.' I was wallowing in those slimy waters myself. I wanted to shout and swear. But I would not cry.

Fiercely I looked at Chandra, I wanted to be truthful. I frowned. 'I want a lot of things from you, but I think I can deal with this by myself. You come with Rory if you want.'

'Have a swim?'

'Yes.'

'Back-stroke?' she teased, showing her earthy side.

I waved to Rory as the station wagon backed onto the road. It was hardly dark, as the moon shone brightly through a break in the cloud.

The Subaru with the disabled parking sticker stops on sandy gravel, overlooking the ocean, not far from Margot's place.

'The sea frightens me,' says Chandra.

Rory watches it batter the cold sand. Open frankness is her ideal, but she is in a position where direct manner is impossible. Rory has chosen to give Margot, an outsider, the axial clue and she has to face Chandra who knows what she has done. 'Dangerous,' she comments. 'Especially when four-metre tides are expected.'

Chandra has no more told Margot of her dread of the Summer Amazon's element, than let her in on the conspiracy of the Solanasites. 'I am the river mermaid, a fresh-water fish,' Chandra says, boasting. 'The sea is not natural with me. I can swim because my mother was wise and I was in a pool before I could walk. I could never walk.' She changes the subject. 'Unreflective as Margot is, non-reader, non-thinker, she is not stupid. She has a nose for bullshit. The scent of crap or something wrong in the air and Margot's head goes up, eyes engage and, if you could see them, her ears would prick up like a cattle dog's.'

'Yes, I agree,' Rory states. She moves her head around, assessing the climatic atmosphere outside the car.

Chandra stares at the boring simplicity of the horizon, a silver line, single colour, different shades, different textures, the dramatic sky, the surface of water. 'Give me trees.'

Rory senses Chandra's stress. The Solanasite project is facing its first real test. 'The international dyke conspiracy, the calling of the bluff of the Rightists' foreboding begs the question, can women, *en masse*, cold-bloodedly kill? If women had done as Valerie suggested, immediately after she suggested it, simply left men, refused to have anything to do with them, it need not have come to the matter of destruction. Murder is asking a lot of women,' she says.

'But some have to be proud, vicious and arrogant enough to do it,' Chandra counters. 'Otherwise, the Amazon is betrayed and Achilles continues to dismember Penthesilea's remains.' Although no two days are the same, all time is now. This storm is threatening. A shower at sea causes a dramatic rainbow to appear like half a question mark on the deep grey cloud behind.

'Do you think the betrayer in our midst is a dedicated traitor or a trickster?' Rory asks.

Chandra looks Rory up and down, frowning. 'We cannot know this irritant, this bug, this virus, is not a man.' She turns away, having seen the ill-lit shape and profile rocking between faith or indecision. 'The meddler could be a Daddy's girl, simply out to make trouble.' Chandra puts her fist on the gearstick. 'Penthesilea led a band of warrior women whose intent was war, whose training was war, whose life-work and enjoyment in life was war. Where in the entire global village to find such a battalion again? We, to achieve the freedom of women, must have an army.'

'Yeah, but,' Rory demurs. The spectrum disappears. The sky darkens.

'Otherwise, the whole damn thing stays an uneven playing field in the battle of the sexes. Which is not a joke,' Chandra argues. 'Not a silly British-American comedy. Not a fantasy. It continues to happen. I could kill a man today, I could spill blood. Because Trojan wars appear to have been won and lost, the victors have prescribed the status quo, changed reality to suit themselves and convinced just about everybody this is how it is. It doesn't mean the war is over.'

'I don't think so,' Rory mumbles, staring out at the navy-blue sea, inhospitable in the ghostly light of approaching rain. 'The mummy's boys, like Christ, like poofs and drag queens, like high camp opera buffs and fashion designers, like the hippy whippy tree-sitters and all the devotees of Carl Jung and men's movement jocks claiming their female side, have androgynised the warrior woman. She is invisible. Okay, we are invisible, which makes cyberspace the excellent place for our meetings under a full moon of revolutionary intent. A brilliant concept, but I don't think you could kill anyone, Chandra. At least I hope not.'

'Don't be so sure,' Chandra says ominously. 'Our enemies may have found us. They would have no compunction in killing us. The ultra-Right is convinced, as we are, of the operability of an international female conspiracy, they just have it twisted by their all-encompassing prejudices. Assisted by Jewish banks and Russian mafia, for goodness sake!'

'A lone sociopathic genius, I reckon,' Rory remarks. 'That's who's playing in your website, rerouting others' stuff through glitches. Challenging your role as web-master, that's all.'

Chandra, herself, cannot see how it was done. 'We romanced about the ultimate controller, said that she was a wealthy woman coming out of the Bahamas or Norfolk Island. At other times we had her floating around the world on a big yacht, migratory, or with a personal Lear jet. A techno-birdwoman. Even a female cosmonaut in a rogue space station orbiting the earth was suggested. Possibly beings from another planet could take the rap. We had no proof of any of that, but we had to lay down the scent, shock them, scare them, have them chasing a hare of the wrong colour. We have to be so absurd only a female can follow the real path. No Dionysian, smart-arse pretend-woman could sort the imaginative from the real. Because lies are their bread and butter, how could they?'

'You've obviously gone more into it than I have. Who do you mean when you say we,' Rory asks, 'yourself?'

Chandra says, 'We fucked up as much as we could, to use Valerie's term. It didn't take heaps of equipment. They have no proof of anything on the Internet. There are no bodily chemicals, no scent.'

'Margot might be able to smell it out, even in cyberspace,' Rory continues. 'But I like her, Chandra. I wanted her to get a picture of what we are about.'

'No,' Chandra chides, as she feels the courage seeping out of her purpose. 'There is a sub-site buried in alien web pages for the warrior women who call themselves evil.'

'Alien web pages?' Quiet lightning sparks out at sea.

'Yes,' Chandra affirms wearily. 'Like the Elvis fan club. All sorts.' She wants to live, to have fun, to enjoy what she has made of her life. She wants to fuck, eat, drink wine, ride. Go out with Margot, listen to music, picnic on the grass, but she has worked herself into a revolutionary lather, painted herself into a serious corner where she must wear the dark clothes of the assassin and hide in the shadows. She knows in her mind it is guerilla warfare, but her heart wants the joys of love, to frolic in the garden of delights. Rory, Chandra realises, hopes to bring Margot up to their level of understanding, expertise and commitment in the future, but, she reasons, that it's relatively impossible. Logical equations make it most unlikely. Margot is reading the manifesto as a piece of evidence in her trail of detection.

Chandra pulls herself together, smiles at Rory and says quietly, 'I'm glad you gave her SCUM to read.'

'What a relief that is,' sighs Rory. She rolls a cigarette.

'Stay at my place tonight.'

'Thanks.'

'What say we pick up some Chinese or a pizza?' Chandra suggests as she gets her station wagon on the road.

'Great.'

54

. . . what they wanted to know . . .

Hot flushes flash on her flesh as if electric circuits short in the brain in her skull. Virginia cannot diagnose the cause, post-traumatic chemical reactions or menopausal symptoms. Her mind shuts down, then comes alive with sparking verve. Her sense of self is an unintelligible static.

There was no welcome from Cybil. No bed for her there. She drives to the long beach away from the suburban sprawl of the tourist-retirement town and intends to sleep in her car. The night is wild with shooting stars and king tides crashing. The moon rides scudding clouds. Sheet lightning floods the busy dark with sudden illumination, devoid of thunder. She feels she is facing some abyss, but her pain is not a void. It is a throbbing, thumping energy, a solid awareness in her guts. She is restless, no drugs, no alcohol, no cigarettes. The sand, when she ventures out, is crisp beneath her feet. She strips to embrace the discomfort of freedom, the bare essential of being, and throws herself into the breakers. The waves lift her high as they peak and roll. The activity of light in the white, roiling foam shoots through her skin like a spa beyond spas, draining the weariness from the marrow of her bones. She needs all her strength, and it is just enough, to not be thrashed, dashed and dumped. She is on a knife-edge between freezing to death and being too hot to handle. As there is no comfort, no warmth, no cool, and she does not seek it. She emerges, salty and wet, simply alive. She is not calm, nor mad. She is disintegrated and of a piece, standing, like a surviving soldier erect among the fallen in the smoking spoils of a battlefield, as she dries herself with her T-shirt, owning nothing but the experience of some kind of journey which involved no travel. Indeed, she could travel if she wished. There is no duty to anything, certainly not to material possession, nor even the weighty art she felt bound to. Or love? Well, if the beloved can hurt you so much, so casually, so carelessly, what is there to be afraid of? No enemy could inflict this agony and physical pain doesn't touch it. Starting from an appreciation of desolation in the thoroughly personal through the sagacity of living, there is, Virginia thinks as she picks up a handful of sand and lets it run through her fingers, change. Whatever.

It is still night-time when she starts her car. The tuned motor of the diesel engine surrounds her like a doona of sound, easing the chill in her heart with soft gratitude. She drives along the rutted roads, through low-lying coastal bush, slowly, knowing that serendipity follows the drama of a feeble wisdom. Margot Gorman lives near here. Virginia looks for houses amid the paperbarks. Then there are three. A light burns in the middle one. An aqua Suzuki Sierra sits quietly beneath a free-standing carport. Two bikes hang beside it under the roof. After a pause of consideration, wondering what she can give in return for bed and breakfast, Virginia turns into the yard and parks the Rodeo on the lawn. Her fellow triathlete is busy at work in a small room with a desk, computer and angled lamp, frowning over reading matter. VeeDub steps back into the darkness and lets out a dog-maiden cooee, the vocal signal of a gurl's approach. Margot meets her on the verandah at the front door.

The yell did not startle me, as practically every other human noise would have at that time of night. The call of one's own kind. Virginia White yelped, a poor forked creature seeking shelter from the storm, but arrived like an answer to my prayer for help. I had come to the part in the manifesto which says: 'If SCUM ever strikes, it will be in the dark with a six-inch blade.' I highlighted it and went to the door. She asked what I was doing and I told her. I took her to my office and she studied the chaotic map on my wall. She was impressed. Complimentary. But most of all, she helped me interpret the hypnotic, enraged, fluent manuscript. Few women, she thought, would take Valerie Solanas's suggestions literally, while every woman would agree with the gist if she were at all honest with herself.

'When the Solanas site started up,' she explained, 'the Solanasites were trying to revive the strategic side of early 'seventies feminism. Most of which was theory, a way of seeing. The discourse borrowed its methods from all sorts of disciplines. Science, art, all philosophic and political opinions. They took on everyone: Freud, Marx, Darwin, biology, theology, archaeology, philology, everything. Social criticism and grassroots action continued and continues to this day.'

'Feminist studies at the universities?' I asked, and she shook her head.

'They turn out to be very small worlds indeed.' Virginia eyed the carton of wines I had begun tasting. I fetched a couple of glasses. 'When the Internet expanded,' she continued, 'the non-tenured ethical feminist had a means of spreading her word, started net-working with like-minded. Where were they to go? What were they to do? At first Chandra's site was full of hot air, but it existed, which was great. For several years, they just raved to each other in the chat rooms. Mainly whinges. Older feminists losing their academic jobs. Women's Studies graduates starving them out. That sort of stuff.'

I looked at a label, pulled the vacuum cork, sniffed the bouquet, offered her a smell and poured. She nodded and went on. 'While there were more jobs for women than ever before, there weren't enough. You're talking a lot of female intellectuals here, hungry for their own culture, digging up the past, re-writing history, un-covering, dis-covering, re-covering. Again far fewer were being published than had things to say, stories to tell, insights to share. Each had in common the feeling that Valerie Solanas had said something personal to her when she first read her, and to a lesser extent Ti-Grace Atkinson. But the fervour, instead of burgeoning as it had in their hearts, shrivelled out there. People, both men and women, calling themselves feminist were undermining feminism. Radical thought became decidedly uncool, old hat. Lipstick and shaved legs were back. Post-modernism, sado-masochism, alliance with, among lesbians, gay men and transsexuals, women claiming pornography for themselves. Like, we needed whole institutions, universities, galleries, political parties, to cover the breadth of ground we had to to catch up, culturally. Solanas had put it all, in a way, in her little tract. So the Solanasite network snaked out through the Internet. All sorts of women, from academics to refugees, all identifying, as you have here, the fundamental forces of oppression; money and poverty; male violence and fear; actual war; madness; nonsense; drugs; pornography; feminised men.' She paused. 'Nice wine.'

Swirling it over my taste-buds, I agreed. I had chosen one that would go well without food.

Virginia talked on, 'All wanting to do more than put a Band-aid on damage. The Solanasites always take a female point of view. They needed each other. They got each other through the web. It felt good, sharing. But they had to work out what to do. Last time I logged on they were still at it, though the codes had deepened, and it seemed to me, older women had been joined by considerably younger ones, cyborg street-fighters. New generation.'

'Okay,' I sighed, gesturing to my butcher's paper on the wall. 'How does that affect me?'

'Well,' she got up and pointed. 'The Meghan investigation, for instance. If she's a Solanasite, this money that's missing could bankroll a project, or be there for female intellectuals who no longer have a job and can't pay their rent, or be channelled to women in need wherever. Or, Meghan could be working . . .'

'She is a Solanasite, Jill told me,' I interrupted.

'Well, if she's working for a transnational and she is a Solanasite, then she

609

will be "unworking".' Virginia picked up the skinny volume and began trying to find the place. 'Solanasites either "unwork" or,' she read, '"withdraw from the labour force", but that's not the bit I want. Listen to this. "Love can't flourish in a society based upon money and meaningless work: it requires complete economic as well as personal freedom". . . . Ah, here it is, "SCUM will unwork at a job until fired, then get a new job to unwork at."'

The penny dropped. But I asked, 'You don't think this is all madness? Lunacy?'

'Of course not. Solanas was brilliant. Madder men have ruled the world on stupider ideas for yonks, with,' she added, 'disastrous results.'

'But how would she do it? She's a forensic geologist, a consultant. I mean, wouldn't it be dangerous?' I said, as I picked up a pen and found my notes.

'The more powerful your position, possibly, the easier it would be. I don't know. I took the other option.' Her voice became reflective, a little sad.

Scribbling, I conjectured, 'She would have to be clever. But we know she is that. She could just throw into her report a piece of information that sabotages the whole deal.'

'Or,' Virginia augmented, 'she could lay a scent in a mischievous direction and have their hounds hunting a phantom hare. If she were clever, as you said, she could leave them standing with egg on their faces, say, having a lot of research which proves that aliens landed at points with latitude and longitude carefully recorded.' She laughed, 'Meghan could have fun, unworking, in the scientific arena, a lot of which is nonsense already.'

'I reckon you've hit the nail on the head. Thanks.' I smiled, looking up from my note-taking and saw Virginia was really tired. 'I'll find you a mattress.'

When I went out to trundle the sofa into a spare bed, she did not follow me. After I had made it up and moved a light to within reach of the pillow I returned to ask if she would like a cup of something. She was looking at the chaotic diagram of my cases, spun out and pale as if shocked.

'What's the matter?' I asked.

'Did Cybil kill the transvestite boy?' She said the question as if it were entirely possible; as if she, Cybil's intimate, considered her capable of murder.

'She may have caused his death, but,' I began.

Her tan skin was pale, bringing out the steely streaks in her dark hair like a gossamer cobweb. Her eyes reached new depth as she stared at me in horror, saying, 'You get what you wish for, Margot, and it is the opposite of what you really want.' She went on to explain. 'Penthesilea's revenge, in banal, grubby reality. The young Achilles, like a black widow spider's mate, dead after sex. I wished for her to realise some truth about herself, to face the moral laxity in her sensuality, her use of sex, her despair. And now she must, and now I'll have this knowledge, always, a hollow shadow across my sense of joy, where a healthy ego should be, a friend, an ex-lover. A changing, growing person.' She sighed, and moved away towards the lounge-room. 'I almost prefer that he had been deliberately killed, by a Solanasite, who knew what she was doing. Oh my goddess,' she said, as she lay on the prepared bed, 'I hope Judith's all right.'

The regrets were not enough to keep her awake. I turned off the light and went into my office, switched on the computer and edited the Featherstone report. I felt I earned my sleep.

In the morning, Meghan reassesses the state of her heart and wonders how Margot Gorman is getting on. She is glad now that Trina pretended to be her to get the detective to look into her finances to rile Jill. For once, Trina has done her a good turn. Having an instant coffee outside in the goatless paddock, amid the verdant grey stillness of the day, everything is changed. In the autumnal equipoise of temperature, there are no shadows. The sodden, south-facing block anchors her, sucks her in, challenges Meghan, a protean person. Complements her.

She takes a walk. The water-table is high. Beneath the tangled carpet of kikuyu, her footfalls squelch. Violet skies hang over the west mountain range. Frogs agreeably croak. Meghan's mental and physical energies compete with the twang of her heart-strings, urging her to her new fad, her next thing. She feels free of the burden of Jill, her depressions, her demanding frustrated talents. Fuck artists, get a real job. She listens to the amphibians, slaps mosquitoes and remarks on the squawk of the young butcher birds. They hop around the top of the unfinished pigeon coop keeping an eye out for frogs to catch, to belt to death on a branch and hang in the naive, savage pride of nature. Meghan, an admirer of raptors and snakes, conceives the next target of her enthusiasm. Ecology. She will make a wild-life sanctuary, a non-people-friendly regeneration of her place. She'll plant koala trees, rip out the exotics, revive the indigenous seed source, study the subject, know it all, do it perfectly. Released from the squalid compromise of Jill's addiction and the financial drain, she goes back inside, refreshed, ready to clear up a few things.

Fifty thousand looks like a lot of money to Trina, who like all the Featherstones is rigorously honest; Meghan has made it overnight. The tidiness of her papers in the drawer intimidates her, while she knows she must look through them and check what is really missing. First get rid of the mortgages: pay off St Lucia, for Trina; close the joint account and fix up the rest of the loan on Lebanese Plains. On-line to the banks, it is all so quick, freeing up stock, selling some shares, transferring money, day-trading off the Nadir bonus, out of mines into sustainable energy companies and other sunrise industrials.

Meghan finds the personal difficult. Jill is cheating with Rosemary Turner. She can't believe it. 'Trina might be mad but she is not dumb,' she says aloud. 'And, although she has a problem with me, she is loyal. She would not go off her tree unless there was something.' Meghan, now savagely motivated, makes a working clutter of the sterile tidiness. Her bodgie space-craft snaps, from a previous job, are gone. That is odd.

Whatever the report and bill from Margot Gorman, Meghan writes a generous cheque, sticks a Post-it note on it with the word, 'thanks' and seals it in an envelope, which she addresses. She emails Libby Gnash to instigate invalidation of her contract and make it known to her employers that she will no longer be available for further consultancy. She also instructs her to get onto partner-before-Jill, ask her price and pay her with the proviso that she have no more harassment, no contact at all. 'Bargain with her,' she types, 'she'll be cheap.'

There remains now for Meghan to clear it all up with Chandra Williams. Her creeks are too swift for her low-slung car. She sets out in her bushwalking gear, full kit.

'Caroline, my first lover and sister-in-law, calls us the Spartan twins,' Virginia White was talking about her family, over coffee and heated-up frozen croissants. When we woke, it was late morning in a grey day and we were both hungry. 'She's a classics scholar.'

She was really enjoying the brunch. Second course was coming, eggs, toast, fried tomato. I squeezed the juice of fresh oranges into a catching jug.

Gurls, I had learnt, only talk about their families when a level of camaraderie has been reached. The straight society talk that stuff all the time. And the lesson was a savage one, the death of Maria. Before that, I wasn't trusted. So, as I poured the OJ into glasses, I appreciated Virginia's chat as confidence in me as a person, a growing, changing ego, a lifetime friend. Yet, I had not offered similar information. If I did I would do so quite guardedly.

'Jeff and Caroline have three kids. Two boys and a girl, Cally. Cally's still in her teens. Both boys are in their twenties, both married. If Jeff has grandkids, I do. I mean they're mine too. And he does. I am a great-aunt.' Virginia downed the orange juice and attacked the truckie's plate I put in front of her.

'My mother's maiden name,' I ventured, 'is Norman.'

Virginia laughed so hard I was glad she had swallowed her last mouthful. My standard joke was funnier than ever, so I, too, was sputtering. When the gush of amusement died to a ripple, she suggested I take a look at my Viking heritage. We talked for another hour, covering many subjects easily, so quickly, it was incredible to feel so broadly understood in so little time. The Lesbianlands issue was the least resolved and most disturbing of my jobs, but getting Virginia's particular perspective, while it was entirely personal, enlightened me. It opened a wide landscape with past-present-future dimensions, even as it was peculiar. The fight was on to save the property, though Virginia didn't like the term. 'We don't, can't, own land,' she said. 'The title just means we have a right to protect it.'

We stood together in my office, speaking of anything, of everything, as the updated Featherstone report came through the printer.

'Lori Heise, in the US, Dallas, I think, has done a world-wide report on domestic violence, all cultures, huge,' Virginia gossiped about the grapevine aspects of the Internet. 'Years it's taken, and one in three women suffer abuse.' But that was not the point she had to make. 'One in how many, do you reckon, are like me?'

I reassured her that there were heaps of lesbians, millions of great-aunts, and that every woman in the world was unique.

'Yeah, okay.' She accepted my invitation to stay another night, then she reckoned she might make a trip to get to know her nephews' children while they were still babies. 'Years pass at such speed, I could lose the precious moment without noticing.'

She went about her day, and I sat down to write out a report for Penny Waughan.

Meghan Featherstone does not find Chandra Williams alone at her home. Alison Hungerford is there. Rory O'Riordan and her whippy red dog, Tess; all are on the verandah.

Alison is laconic with the effects of psychotropic drugs.

Chandra's Rottweiler softly growls. 'Who's that, Nikki?'

The conversation collapses under the barrage of kelpie yelping as Meghan mounts the steps. She takes off her coat and squats on an upturned milk crate.

Accepting a cup of tea, she begins her reconciliation with Chandra by telling the three the story of her proof of hell. 'Beneath the volcanic layers it is not hot, the molten lava is a reaction, chemistry.' Her audience is appreciatively stunned. 'What men can't measure, they can't know.'

'True.'

'Unless they name and calculate, formulate and pin down, it simply doesn't exist, except as god. So I gave them the devil, Prometheus Unbound, and said it was promethium, a trivalent element, with some mysterious car-bonesque constituent that could indicate life.'

'Nonsense, right?' Chandra is suspicious.

Rory pulls down the corners of her mouth. 'I don't find it too far out. Nearly all interpretation of data is bound up in belief systems. While we push the envelope of discovery, in all scientific fields, how they make sense of this flow of fact is radically conservative.'

Alison nods, and comments dreamily, 'Gurls going forwards and back spending their energies on vain quests for meaning, for a meaning which is beyond our realm of reason to start with, irritate me.'

'Exactly,' agrees Meghan. 'I found genuine research was being discarded because it did not fit the paradigm. Not only in my own area, but every-where. From work in Antarctica to analysis of moon-dust, from dinosaurs to the cutting-edge genetic engineering, good data was going down the gurgler, because it didn't accord with what they wanted to know. Read, believe already. So, instead of going "ooh ah, you won't believe this!", I go all serious and make out the conclusion is indisputable, because it does fit in the con-structs of their faith. I dressed the bullshit in reams of valid data.'

Chandra is excited. 'The conspiracy is working.'

'But,' worries Rory, 'that is not male-specified. It turns us on our own. Nonsense, meaning. It'll fuck up women's heads just as much. Probably more. If that hits the newspapers, men will be sceptical and women will fall for it.'

'So?' Meghan shrugs. 'Of course, I had to have a mystery to start with.'

'Is it revolutionary?' Rory remarks, uncertainly.

Chandra shakes her head. 'But you're not in control of it.'

'Actually, that's what I wanted to talk with you about, Chandra, in person,' Meghan appeals, getting up and leaning over the balcony-rails before she turns.

Alison opines, 'I'm picking up aggro vibes.'

Neither Chandra Williams nor Meghan Featherstone take much notice of the other two as they stare at each other. Repair of fractured friendship, forsaking feelings of betrayal and renouncing patterns of thoughts, the habits of enmity, requires considerable emotional maturity. Even strong women have few reserves to call upon. Especially fractious lesbians, intent on autonomy, vulnerable to self-doubt, find it hard to accept the implied criticism of their worth.

'We could spend hours revealing secrets, exchanging strategies, putting our heads together, going over the ground of our individual journeys in cyber-space,' says Meghan, 'but that betrays our faith in each other. Furthermore, the Solanasite is only one head of the Gorgon.'

Rory says, with laughter, 'Athene, the death goddess. They tried to disguise her roots in Libya, where she was Medusa. I like it. I love it.'

'Yes, chop one off and another will appear. It's a bigger monster than you know, in more disguises than you can pick. You attacked me, having no idea what I was doing. I watched as you fished for sisters.' Meghan confesses to meddling with Chandra's screen-saver.

Nets entangled, lines crossed, Chandra and Meghan argue about the on-going conspiracy. Neither Rory nor Alison can interrupt as it is way over their heads. Far too intense.

'You try to control everything,' Meghan insists.

'I work really hard,' says Chandra in a voice low with menace. 'For absolutely no recompense!'

'I know!' Meghan's voice is high, squeaky. 'And it is really good, too. But, you can't make women behave, believe, exactly as you do.'

'Instead, just let them burn and destroy so I can meditate on the coals, hoping for a phoenix to arise?' Chandra is fighting a rearguard action. Her utopia is in tatters. The redefinition Meghan is asking of her is too much. She has to have her hands on to see how things work: knowledge is power.

Virginia experiences ineffable sadness as she says to Cybil, 'It's a real shame you're too damaged to love.'

The flat overlooking the beaches, sharing a street address with motels and holiday units, where there was passionate love-making and mess, is uncomfortably clean. 'You feel truth, you can't think it. Death, loss, annihilation, the word is feel, to know. To value.'

Cybil Crabbe's stare is as blank and unexpressive as the results of her new broom. Even Puddles, the poodle, curls neatly in a fresh, cane dog-bed.

'I loved you so much I couldn't function. It made life impossible.'

With all her cheek and courage intact, Cybil struts into her kitchen, obliterated. She stands in the middle of the shiny tiles paralysed by her own stubbornness, trying to work out what to do.

'Virginia,' she says when she finally decides, 'I will tell you what happened, but first we must start with my father. Daddy loved me so much he couldn't keep his hands off. If I threw a tantrum I could get anything I wanted.' Cybil's resolve to confess her betrayal to Virginia dissolves. 'I can't take it. It's like I don't belong to myself when someone loves me too much. I belong to them.'

Virginia sits cross-legged on the couch, her elbows on her knees, her hands on her heels, her facial features fierce as she assimilates the substance of what Cybil is saying.

'I just never knew what it was, exactly.' Her despair is palpable. 'Everything is nothing.'

Virginia unfolds her long body and stands, preparing to leave.

'For Maria's sake, will you give me a hug?'

Virginia cries for the loss of Maria, among other things, and because tears are easy, in Cybil's arms. Then she is restless, she doesn't want to stay. She takes her leave of Cybil, crisply. Strangely grateful for the hurt, she is gentle. Almost cheerful. Cybil keens like a banshee as Virginia skips down the stairs.

55

. . . drop-dead gorgeous . . .

Chandra was reluctant to swim in the sea. For all her cyber-activities, her loves, her prejudices, her hobbies, horse and garden, her disability, her politics, she was fragile. Her freedom to be herself was to do her own thing. It would be pretty freaky having no leg strength where the rollers break on shore. It made me melt with feelings of care and protection.

The swim date was off. Fair enough.

She accepted my invitation to dinner out, though. We discussed what sort of restaurant we wanted: seafood, Italian, Thai, a big red steak or delicate Japanese sushi. Fancy having a smile as broad as Chandra's, a large forehead so full of brains! I am intimidated. I'm just an ordinary dogged Virgo-dog who knows her erogenous zones are dying to be touched. Sister, don't try to be smart. Stunned for a minute by questions I had not considered, I stared into space, remembering Maria. 'When women fall for each other,' she had told me in our first conversation soon after I arrived in the Campbell River valley, 'they are expected to be perfect and are for a short time. Nothing can be found to be wrong with her because, at that stage, all your dreams come true: love without violence, tenderness, beaming attention, humour, understanding, someone to do things with, to enjoy, to share and show off, preen, prance and be gorgeous. You're in love with yourself. You're entertaining and original. She's not threatening, and there is lots of beautiful sex. Later ethical decisions must be made about staying together and giving things up or forcing restraint or sacrificing self. Questions to understand about responsibility and giving attention to another's problems. Or moving on to another without changing one's behaviour or view of oneself.' At the time I listened politely, now I knew she was right. What I feel for Chandra is of a different order altogether. With Broom I was a shallow, good-time gurl. With Chandra I could expect to find hidden depths of myself. A real me. I needed to be free.

Now I was desperate to finish the business with Penny. I had as clear an idea as I ever would of what happened to Neil Waughan. I banked on the probability that she would be home. It was late in the afternoon when I got to Cannisteo Bayou. I took the footpath along the canal and crossed the lawns. Ants were making tiny tepees of dirt in the grass so that when it rained water wouldn't fill their holes, flood their homes. I tried not to flatten their work with my feet and walked slowly.

She was on her private jetty, lighting a cigarette. Lightning flashed in distant skies. 'Penny?' I called for her attention.

She turned around. 'Margot, I was just thinking about you. Is it over?'

Giving her the envelope, I said, 'Well, it is in good hands now. Detective Constable Philippoussis will present a pretty full report to the coroner at the inquest.'

A plastic chair leant against a plastic table. I righted it and took a seat. She puffed as she read. When she finished, she said, 'He always had a weak heart.'

'A lion-hearted boy, he wanted to fight evil,' I comforted. 'He found evil in a group of men he discovered preying on lads. His friend Hugh, and Hugh's mates, were being given toys and pocket money, which they seriously needed as they were poor, unlike Neil. All they had to do in return was make themselves available.'

Mrs Waughan braced her face to voice an obscenity. 'For sex?'

'That's what they thought and that's where Neil made his mistake,' I clarified. 'Oh, they used them all right, and abused them. Made them think they were filthy old poofters who couldn't resist the beautiful youths and would pay. Hugh and his friends probably hated them as they obliged them and were bought off. I don't think Neil was into hatred.' I saw my job at this point as an adjunct to her healing process. 'I think he was too clever to think he could fight paedophilia.'

Flattery wasn't what this brittle, unhappy woman wanted. She was out for blood.

'No,' I affirmed. 'He discovered on the Internet an international group, into every sort of filth, some of whom travel around in an ocean-going cruiser, testing new hazardous drugs on the boys they prey on. They haunt holiday towns where their boat wouldn't be remarked upon, and there is high unemployment among the locals, chiefly young men who should be employed. Or gainfully occupied in some way. While into drug-running, gun-running, prostitution and child pornography, they were looking to invent the new up-market party pill. He found out the yacht was in Port Water. He contacted Hugh to find out how he could safely infiltrate. Together they decided that the queers would fall for him dressed up as a girl, or possibly think of him as a girl and leave him alone.'

'What could he have done?' To stop too fierce feelings, she lit another Light. 'What was he thinking?'

The mansions along the canal seemed sparse of people, as if each housed a widow or widower or an elderly couple silently waiting for the annual disruption of grandchildren. 'He wanted to get the bad guys,' I reckoned. 'Sink their ship. Do reconnaissance. He may have had a plan to sabotage their electronic navigation gear, or find out how he could in the future. I don't know.'

She nodded, eagerly. 'Yes, he would have understood any electronic equipment. He could have made a bomb, he knew how. But how was he going to get away with it?'

It was easy to imagine how well she got on with her son. I guessed, 'To the teenage mind, fuelled by Hollywood movies of heroism, a disguise was a protection of some sort.' While I knew firearms were available through the Internet and recipes for homemade explosives, nothing like that was found either in Hugh's car or at the scene. Neil himself was carrying so little, identification took some time.

Spits of rain spotted the murky surface of the dredged mangrove swamp. Instead of going inside, Penny's movement raised a permanent umbrella and we sat ourselves beneath it. I continued. 'He never got there. Argument among the boys. Let's say, Neil tried to tell the others not to take the drugs, and they said, "Get real", or whatever. They may even have forced Neil to have a pill or he may have had one later at a barbecue he ended up at. They had a fight, tossed Neil dressed as girl out onto the road and drove off, high themselves. He was picked up by lesbians who thought he was a girl. He didn't tell them otherwise. He ended up at a gay beach party, harvest moon or something. His disguise, conceivably, made him imbibe more alcohol than he was used to or smoke dope or take a party pill. Plus, by this time he is overwrought, tense and possibly close to panic. What was wrong with his heart?'

The miserable weather darkened the sunset. 'Ectopia, morbid displacement. If he got stressed it would have an irregular beat, not life threatening.'

According to my theory it was. I took a deep breath, believing that truth was better for grieving mothers than superficial sympathy. 'He may have had an orgasm which put more pressure on it. Anyway he went to the toilet to throw up, and, died of a heart attack. Or at least, that is probably what the inquest will determine. Although, they might say it was system failure from toxic substances. Then, I don't know. The magistrate may recommend charges be laid. Normally the amount of chemicals found in his blood would not cause a problem, except for the ingredient they were trying out. But analysis shows he had no more than one pill and others I've spoken to didn't find it very powerful.'

'Will Philippoussis get these men?' she asked vengefully.

Taken aback, I frowned. 'I gave him all the information that Neil collected, the name and anchorage of the yacht or cruiser, and allied connections. Charts, etc., history of other ports of call. He had quite a dossier, some of it useful to crime-fighters. When the task force arrived to investigate the scene, the other boys, who were skylarking further up the foreshore, took off in cars that were either stolen or hired for them in adults' names. Hugh happened to go by himself along the way that doesn't include the ferry ride. Perhaps he was scared of the police, and killed himself taking a corner too fast. These men, as you call them, would not be able to operate as arrogantly as they do if it weren't for corruption inside the system. Now that Phil is working with the deputy coroner, it is possible some will be caught.'

Southerly gusts angled the rain into our shelter. She snorted.

'Your son died trying to be a hero,' I emphasised.

'There's a storm coming,' said Penny Waughan vaguely. The rumble of thunder made her speak louder. 'So,' she sighed, gathering cigarette pack and lighter. 'What do I owe you?' Before we ran into the house, she secured the umbrella shut and placed the plastic chairs against the matching table so water would run off their backs.

It was too strange to think of money. Payment didn't matter. The outdoor furniture on the clipped lawns, seats leaning two-legged into tables and the phoney trees folded down like bats' wings ready to be opened into instant shade were desolate, and repeated all along the canal. If there weren't so much tar and cement, bricks and mortar, water would not be so alien. I felt a failure. The neat hard edges of these human dreams belied habitation. The weather moved in. One or two lights came on in windows. Penny's place was dark behind us as we stood in the garage. There were more living beings in a graveyard.

'I don't know, a few hours. I don't think I've done anything much. All I can hope is your memory of your son is better for knowing, that's all.'

'Yes, perhaps,' she murmured as she closed the roller door. She wasn't satisfied.

In the house, I stood at the floor-to-ceiling glass looking out. The moon must be up, but muddied by cloud. Street-lights were smudgy blots in the dusk.

'I'll be able to sleep,' she said harshly. Or hoarsely. I turned around to watch her finish the sentence. 'If you do something about this laboratory.'

Shocking me, she slapped the envelope on the palm of her hand with a smack. 'You have all the material. You know where it is. Are you going to accept this state of affairs? Police corruption? Accidental death? Neil's plan to sabotage their navigation systems, or plant an incendiary device, or whatever it is, was aborted. Through no fault of his own. I can assure you, Margot

Gorman, he would have worked it out to the last detail. The formula will be in his computer files. He recorded everything.'

There was life in these sterile mansions after all. A few days ago I would not have thought it possible, but now, yes, I could do something if I wanted to.

'I would like to know more about this activity off the coast,' I acceded simply, putting a sinister overtone on the word 'activity'.

'Good,' said Penny Waughan, the efficient teacher. She went over to the sideboard and flicked on a lamp which lit a tree of pottery cups. Her cheque book was in her handbag on a chair nearby.

'I'm happy now,' she said as she wrote her signature. 'I have a new cleaner.'

Evidently she was aware of a tidiness and dustlessness that I wasn't or she would not have thought of it.

'Oh? Really?' I was surprised. 'Alison doesn't do it any more?'

'No. She put me onto a wonderful Aboriginal woman who sits down and chats with me. Iris. I find her more friend than cleaner. She brings me presents.' She smiled for the first time since I'd known her.

A natural gossip, Penny told me that Alison had had a breakdown. She actually laughed when she said, 'She never did much cleaning, anyway. Paid Iris, apparently. Here you are, Margot. And thanks.'

Five hundred dollars. I folded the cheque into the back pocket of my black jeans and stepped forward, opening arms for a warm hug. Grief over-whelmed me; we both wept. I would have more to do with Penny Waughan.

For the minute, I was eager to get home as I was flooding and smelling of blood. My period had come three days early. Virginia's dual-cab ute was in my yard. Tow-bar and roof-racks I noticed. A fan of caked red earth behind each mud-guard, chassis high off the ground, windscreen glistening clean, pearling the raindrops. No bumper-bar stickers. VeeDub was exciting to have around the house because one didn't know what she would come out with next. I told her the gist of my meeting with Penny Waughan. Her lively mind took it all in, and up a notch or two.

'Action stations!' she barked, like the second mate on a ship.

I made a couple of phone calls. When I was having a shower, she walked into the bathroom, incidentally gathering the dirty clothes on the floor and putting them in the laundry basket, saying, apropos of whatever was going on in her head, 'You know the Christian tenet "by your friends shall you know him"?'

'What?' I yelled.

She repeated it, and continued, 'Well, for us.'

'Gurls, you mean?' I decided that there was no embarrassment in letting her watch me wash my naked form, and, scrubbing my knickers, listened.

'Yeah, I've often thought about that,' she opined, leaning on the steamy mirror.

'But this is hardly the time for theological theory. We got work to do,' I shouted.

'For us it is, "by her family shall you know her".' With that she left me to my ablutions. There was some kind of collective consciousness happening here because that was a reflection, a sort of meditative echo of the exchange we'd had over brunch. I let it play in my head like a theme in a concerto taken up by the orchestra. As I was drying myself I called out for her to go to my boxes of wine and choose some. Half-dressed, I made another phone call.

'Hi, Lois, can I speak to Thrust?' I knew my voice was abrupt but she recognised urgency when she heard it and called him.

The fisherman took his time but his explanation was clear and I scribbled notes with a rough map of the estuary on my pad.

'By the way,' I said, 'are you using your dinghy tonight?'

'Of course not.' He was amused at my ignorance. 'Never fish when the moon is coming up full.' I thought it was the weather.

A delicate request, I asked could I borrow it for the night. I used too many words, reminding myself that tradesmen hate lending their tools, but these people are generous to a fault. Ten minutes later I was in the passenger seat of Virginia's car driving through the rain, giving directions. Both my push-bikes were installed under a tarpaulin on the tray, along with wetsuits, raincoats, towels and sweaters. We stopped outside Lois's cottage, bipped, then VeeDub backed the ute towards the garage. The boat-trailer was ever-ready to be lowered onto a tow-ball. Thrust strolled out and rustled up a can of petrol in case we needed it, shaking his head.

'Bad evening,' he commented.

'Yeah, mate,' I concurred. 'Big tides predicted.'

'It's the water coming down the streams you want to watch. They got an inch up the mountains. We're in for a flood. Mark my words.' This taciturn man could talk about the weather till the cows came home, always with a lugubrious spin. Perhaps it was all he thought about, and the infinite mystery of marine life in his immediate vicinity. However I did not have time.

'Thanks,' I said. 'We probably won't use it.'

As we pulled up at the punt-port, the last of the cars was rolling onto the ferry. We just made it.

My romantic dinner with Chandra transmogrified into a council of war at a large round table with a lazy susan in the middle. Six different Chinese dishes, predominantly seafood, a cauldron of steaming white rice, chopsticks, little bowls and tinier identical ones for weak tea made the board look as busy as our business. I called for wine glasses.

Present were: Chandra in her wheelchair; Rory, who had ordered Mongolian lamb which proved more popular than expected; Alison, looking puffy; Meghan, who gave me a cheque which reminded me I had left the other one in my black jeans; Virginia, who in raiding my cellar had come up with a reliable Riesling and a cheeky Merlot; and myself who had downed a Naprogesic for menstrual cramp but was otherwise pumped. We had the restaurant to ourselves except for transient customers who doorsat until presented with stacks of containers in plastic bags to take away. Incurious they were, probably thought 'girls' night out', not amazed by a pack of Amazons plotting. Nevertheless, I noticed I was not the only one among us to check. Remarking on that, I said, 'I still have the feeling that Tiger Cat is hanging around.'

'Prowling,' joked Alison.

Agreeing that food was the immediate consideration, we ate as we tossed around ideas as to what to do. The laboratory was situated at the edge of the airstrip. The cruiser was moored in the mangroves somewhere near there. Probably, we reckoned, tied up to the wharf of an oyster shucking shed. As the banks of the delta are muddy there would be a pier of some sort.

'If I were them,' conjectured Rory, 'and my electronic gadgetry was aboard-ship, I'd weigh anchor and come ashore in a row-boat.'

The way she said it had us in stitches. 'So,' she continued seriously, 'I'm keeping my operations separate: technology at sea, chemistry in the lab. It's a hangar, is it?'

'Not really,' answered Meghan. 'There are a few warehouses along there. For hire. The company rented one for me to put my car when I'm on a job. I still have the key, actually. If you had a small plane you weren't using you wanted to keep under cover, I suppose you could call them hangars. But, basically, the ones down that end are for storage. The Flying School and a couple of charter companies have the bigger ones, you know? The road to the left? You take the right to the car park?'

She was interrupted by Alison exclaiming, 'Lo and behold!'

'Speak of the devil.'

'When witches get together they can magick up anything,' Rory put in as we all listened to Catherine Tobin at the counter ordering Honey Prawns, Crispy Lemon Chicken and a large Special Fried Rice to go.

'Not eating alone, either,' calculated Chandra.

But it was Virginia who led our charade. 'Hey, Tiger Cat,' she greeted. 'Sister triathlete, how are you going?'

'Pull up a chair,' I invited. I formally introduced Dr Featherstone and

Chandra Williams, saying, 'You've met Rory and Alison?'

Tiger Cat did not want to join us. She said, 'Hi,' reluctantly and stayed where she was. But she had no dignified choices; either cop a dozen eyes staring at her blush, or pace up and down outside in the rain. Even as thick a skin as the Cat's could not resist our attention. Rory lifted her out of her misery, almost physically. She went over, grabbed her arm, brought her to our table, kicking a chair into her path, and genially offered her a beer.

As Rory was twisting the top, I attacked, leaning forward, conspiratorially, 'When I was with my DC friend the other day. In his office. You know he's working for the deputy coroner? Anyway, he took a call. I don't know what it was about, but he said, and I quote, "one of your friends". What did he mean?'

Chandra was horrified. 'You're not a police informer, are you?' she asked Tiger Cat, who could not withstand the onslaught of her indignation.

'Not me,' she squeaked a specious laugh. 'You want to know who that is?'

Half a dozen heads nodded eagerly.

Tiger Cat relaxed. 'You'll never guess.' She took a swig of beer from the stubby. 'The Larrikin.'

We took in her smug satisfaction of grassing on a grass without comment. Her food arrived at the counter. The discreet Asian woman left it there and returned to the kitchen.

Alison broke the look-lock with, 'Cool drugs you were handing out at the Spiders' barbecue. Got any more?' She would have convinced me she was stoned, but Tiger Cat's yellow eyes greasily slid from left to right, ending up on her dinner next to the cash register.

Meghan who doesn't drink, smoke cigarettes or marijuana, or indulge in heavier drugs, hissed, 'Got any speed?' She whipped a twenty-dollar bill out of her wallet and pushed it towards the bottle, saying, 'You deal, right?'

Rory groaned, 'Put it away, Megs.' But she picked up the currency note and played with the money. 'Tiger Cat gets them for nothing.'

'Well, that is really curious,' Chandra said. 'Because I always thought, and it's only my opinion, that individuals in the drug scene were really mean. Like they kill people who don't pay. I often wonder what they do with their money, you know? Like apart from paying each other to kill each other?'

Virginia frowned in agreement. 'Power, it's about power, Chandra. They don't care about money, per se.'

'No,' argued Chandra. 'It's about money.'

They kept this up while Rory grinned at Tiger Cat, daring her to get up and leave us. There was a meal for two on the counter, and whoever that other person was they would be expecting their Chinese hot. But the Cat was hypnotised. Alison took out her pouch, got up and said, 'I think I'll have a joint.' She went outside.

'You are in a cleft stick,' I said to my academy colleague. 'You know me, honest as the day is long. You told Sean I was a snout.' She was about to object, because it wasn't true, but thought better of it. 'Well, I have a couple of choices here. Like you.' I pushed my chair back. 'Either, get you charged.' I walked to the front of the café, picked up the bag of take-away and looked out the window. Alison came in the door after that, telling me there was a man waiting in a car.

'A man!' I exclaimed as we returned to the table. Alison nodded and I finished my sentence to Tiger Cat, 'Or you tell me the truth.'

'The whole truth and nothing but the truth,' piped up Meghan.

What a dill, presumed the eyes of the Cat.

'There's power over,' debated Virginia.

'And power of,' Chandra interrupted.

Rory joined their play-acting. 'But it is all cowardly.'

Placing the plastic bag between my elbows on the table, I rested my chin on the heels of my palms. 'I'll let you go back to him, with the food and with a neat story about a bunch of friends wanting a chat, giving you a beer, whatever, when you explain how you managed to acquire free pills so that you could glad-hand your way into the gay and lesbian community of the Paradise Coast, either to whip up investment in your girlfriend's banking enterprise or to pay for your own habit, and why.'

'How and why,' she echoed, realising that suddenly all the artifice of my friends had dropped into attentive silence. 'What do you want to know?'

'Your friends, the rich paedophiles?' I stabbed in the dark. 'Tell us about the Friday night two boys died.'

The thing about self-serving liars is they are generous with information they think is not going to hurt them personally. 'In the afternoon,' she began, 'there was to be a party on the yacht. It turned into a fizzer because the lads didn't turn up. The millionaire guy had ordered some fresh meat, boys he hadn't met before and wouldn't meet again. It's getting hairy for those chaps these days. They've got to stay anonymous. He gets someone to move his yacht from port to port. He arrives by plane, usually with some mates. The deal is, boys introduce boys, and disappear. They're pretty well compensated, but the kids know nothing. He's a real arsehole with a hell of an operation. Treats everybody like scum. He was furious. Arriving and nothing doing. Made the trip for nothing.' She laughed. 'Gets back in his plane and flies away. Everyone's shitting themselves, heads will roll. Anyway, one of my contacts gives me a call. A bunch of pills have no place to go. Like they're not on the market yet. No one will touch stuff they don't know. Like it's got to be GBH, heroin or whatever. You've got to know what you're taking. He assured me they were okay, just had not been established. Didn't have a name. Never will take off, in my opinion. They're still working on it.'

'You picked them up, where? You knew this Spiders do was happening and you thought you'd spread them around?' I urged her to continue.

'When this bloke says they're harmless, they're harmless. He's a hell of a chemist. I trust him on that score. He's a weasel, but a wizard in the lab.'

'You wanted to get in with the gays so you give out free drugs, thinking that would be good PR?'

'I was not targeting people who didn't use. Everyone had a good time with them, at the barbecue and the dance. As for getting investors in the bank, I was not so successful. Different clientele.' Tiger Cat gazed at me brazenly. 'You can't get me for dealing, Margot. They were free. And if anyone comes forward and pins me, I'll deny it and they won't have proof.'

'Who's at the factory now?' Meghan shot the question sharply. 'Tonight?'

'How many people are on the boat?' fired Virginia.

'Quickly,' said Alison. 'He was looking impatient.'

Catherine Tobin aka Tiger Cat gave us the information we required. The guy opened the door, searching the place. She held up her stubby with admirable bravado and indicated she was coming. I handed over the munchies I had hostage. And she left in a hurry.

The waitress-cook reckoned the chief eating had been done so she cleared the table. We took advantage of the space. I redrew the map of the estuary, filling in the airport, the roads, the track down to the oyster lease and shucking shed, the probable position of the cruiser. Where the party was to be and Neil's exact intention were matters of conjecture. But we agreed the yacht was the safest and most obvious place. The pederasts fly in, victims already on board, food, crackers, drugs and grog, courtesy of the providence of the captain; they motor off for fun and pleasure, completely free of scrutiny either at sea or in the harbour or up any of the arms of the Campbell River delta. Easy, so easy. But what, in this scenario, was master Waughan going to do? Were the girl's clothes to get him on board to be chucked off when the boy-lovers arrived, having tampered with the electronics, navigation gear, electrics, computer? Or was his costume a matter of ignorance, thinking he would be more attractive as a transvestite? Did he think they would not expect a girl to have his expertise or warlike intent? The answers were somewhere. Meghan's laptop PC, with an internal modem and digital connection, was impressive but not nearly as much as she was herself utilising its keyboard and calculating power to test our hypotheses. Chandra suggested we needed access to the hard drive of Neil's computer. Meghan passed her mobile phone to Alison to ring Penny and get her to have a look. I reckoned Penny would be only too keen and probably proficient enough to comply. We agreed to assess the boy's plan on its merits, and if it was unworkable, do a bit of sabotage of our own invention.

'Hi, sweetheart,' Alison cooed. We all did a double-take and frowned questions at each other. 'Are you, darling? That's good, isn't it? Okay. See you in a little while.' She took the handpiece away from her ear, read it face up and pressed a button. Then she explained, 'Tilly and Lenny are with Iris and they're all at Penny's. Tilly's watching cartoon connection on satellite TV. I've got to go over there.'

'That's better, actually.' I brought out my notes. 'You're familiar with his Internet connections if we need them. You can keep contact with us telephonically. And Penny could help. She definitely wants revenge on these predators. You could work together. She knew her son, how he would think, how he would feel. She was convinced he would have a clear plan written down.' I reached down for the print-outs. 'Having not studied these in this light, with this objective, anyway,' I shrugged, 'I don't know.'

Chandra picked the pages up, glanced at them and handed the folder over to Meghan, whose razor-brain sliced through the sheets with the odd nod and mm.

'Know what questions to ask?'

Meghan said, 'Ah ha.'

Alison collected her things and stood up. 'Better go. I'll be more with it when I'm sitting down in front of the screen, when I'm a totally mental being. Right now, I'm stuffed.'

Meghan closed the folder. 'Have you been through his desktop?'

'Not all of it. There are a lot of games I wasn't interested in. I didn't take any notice of the school work either. What the hell is Iris doing, taking my kids over there? I'm paying her for baby-sitting.' Alison frowned. 'They should be asleep.'

I recalled the crowded Minogue household, the empty Waughan one, and said, 'Penny needed a friend.'

Alison left the restaurant. Chandra remarked, out of the blue, 'Even if that two-legged line of snot did tell the jock, we're all right. He wouldn't believe we were going to actually do anything.'

'Because we're a pack of raving lunatics,' explicated Rory. 'And we are. We bloody are.'

'Too right,' commented Virginia. 'On a night like this.'

On the footpath, in the quiet mid-week town, businesses had closed shop.

One cab cruised. A couple of night-strolling tourists browsed the flood-lit window displays under awnings. They dallied. When I saw that they were reading prices and looking at coloured pictures of houses on the real estate agents' strip, I ceased being suspicious of them. Chandra's Subaru station wagon and Virginia's four-wheel-drive with a boat trailer attached stood out in their parking spots. I noticed Rory was wearing my Nikes, not her bush boots.

'Where's your car?' I demanded of Meghan. She responded with the uncanny reading of my mind that Virginia showed, explaining that her creek-crossings were too dangerous, that Rory had picked her up in her truck, and that 'it's okay, Margot. I have my key-ring.'

'Good.'

'And on it is the key to what my boss calls "the Port Water godown".'

The last time I had been to the airport, it was to meet Vanderveen in his private helicopter. I vaguely remembered tin sheds towards the mangroves.

'It has electricity, yeah?' I was showing signs of nerves. 'So you can just take the Subaru into it, and shut yourself in?'

'Margot,' Chandra pulled my arm, and I looked down at her. She grinned, 'Do you think that was necessary?' She pointed at the twelve-foot runabout comfortably hooked to the back of VeeDub's car. The pair, I thought, were serenely at home in this shire. One wouldn't be surprised if an identical outfit turned the corner into the bare street right now, five minutes to midnight. She was laughing at me.

So was Virginia. 'You should see what else she has brought. Wetsuits, the lot.'

Rory was impressed. 'Goggles, flippers, spear-fishing equipment?' She reached into her commodious pockets and pulled out a white stone. 'I have this,' she skited as if it were a weapon. Meghan examined it professionally and gave it back with no comment.

'So you three are in the godown. Virginia and I park at the terminal, so as not to arouse suspicion. Then we ride the bikes down the runway, rendezvous near the lab, okay? And take it from there.' There are two strips perpendicular with one another: the major one for commercial craft and the lesser one for charter and private planes and helicopters. The intersection of the roads to these two activities occurs immediately after the gate. It was quicker to get to the warehouses via the tarmac, and, I determined, less obvious, there being no lighting there. Security was sure to be about.

Seventeen-year-olds with their probationary licences in their first cars buzz Alison as she drives her old brown Falcon along the wide empty streets to the canal development some kilometres from the town centre. Two Datsuns drag her off from a lonesome traffic light, with high acceleration in the low gears and lousy mufflers. The wet road gleams straight in front of her. She floors her right foot, six cylinders beneath the bonnet respond; within a couple of hundred metres, she overtakes the second. Adrenalin rush. The series of roundabouts ahead with their planted palms challenges her to take on the first. She speeds up to the tail-light, then, changing down, with high revs, weaves into the right lane of the semi-circle, leans into the altered camber, then, gearing to the superior power of her car, leaves them for dead. By the time she gets to Penny's she has assumed the character of a lout in her head. Her speediness is arrested somewhat when she sees Lenny asleep on the leather divan and Tilly snuggled up in a doona, sucking her thumb, her wide eyes tired and entranced by an animated version of an adult movie—*Men in Black*—on the TV screen. She murmurs motherly words to her beloved daughter and kisses her hair. She does the same to her other child, and grins at the adult women, who stand and wait.

'Black coffee is what I need, if we're going to do this,' states Penny.

'Plenty of sugar for me,' accepts Alison, as she goes to settle down at Neil's desk.

Readily sharing involvement in the task, Penny offers Iris her bedroom. Checking that Lenny is fine where he is and turning off the television, Iris bundles up Tilly, doona and all, carries her to the boudoir with its en suite and lies down on the expensive mattress.

Normally, I do surreptitious jobs by myself, my way, with thorough preparation, a thermos of warm tea among other tools in my box of tricks, everything in its right place and my body fit for the unexpected. Now, not only was I encumbered by help and assistance, physically I felt like shit and didn't really know why we were doing it. Too tired from two nights without full sleep, the blood sloughing off the walls of my reproductive organs stabbing pain like the knives the Little Mermaid felt when she exchanged fish-tail for legs and the damaged Achilles tendon giving my heel curry, I wasn't up to commanding a team. On the other hand, I was running on adrenalin and analgesics and whatever other chemicals kick in when more than usual is demanded. Bereft of the necessary talents, skills, information and womanpower by myself, I was thrilled by the danger, pointless or otherwise. Relinquishing control, letting the decisions fall into consensus, I, consciously, gave up direction as one of my tasks. I knew no more than anyone else, had no better idea of strategy nor what was in store. Virginia drove slowly, easing the trailer over the bumps and pot-holes with the rattle of tin in the galvanised steel, while Chandra had zoomed off like someone with a train to catch, neither attracting undue attention from the traffic unit on patrol.

'I should have secured that petrol can,' I muttered.

Virginia's calm at the wheel inspired the trust one would like to feel for a comrade-in-arms or a fellow castaway on a raft of folk facing survival at sea. Knowing that released another feel-good chemical in my brain. I checked behind us and saw moonlight glint on the outboard motor.

'A break in the weather.'

The rain had stopped. Clouds parted, but hung like mountainous seas frozen in the sky, stalled above the earth by barometric pressure. It seemed the moon was moving with the grace of a ship under sail. There were two vehicles in the air terminal car park, locked late-model company cars. The first flight was due at dawn. I took the mountain bike, Virginia the road-racer. She kept to the tar and I traversed the puddly grass, but we arrived at roughly the same moment at the group of storage sheds. Rory materialised from the shadows in my quiet shoes and showed us into the godown through the small side door.

Chandra was in her wheelchair already. The rest of us stood for our confab. There was nowhere to sit anyway. Although these sheds were windowless, a narrow line of weak yellow light had indicated to Meghan that Tiger Cat was probably right. Someone was working in the one three doors down. They did not make drugs in this cleverly obvious place during the day. Rory, one of those rare individuals who could whistle a Manhattan taxi from Queens, would go on cockatoo duty while we raided the laboratory.

'First, we should ring Alison and Penny,' Chandra said.

'No,' disagreed Meghan. 'Get into the factory first, secure it.'

'Why?' Virginia asked Chandra.

'Why?' I asked Meghan.

Rory, more used to meetings of this sort than I, folded her arms and looked from face to face like a chairperson, ready to step in and mediate, if necessary.

Chandra replied, 'They'll be waiting for contact. We don't want them to go sleep, or have nothing to do.'

Meghan's explanation was more manic and circuitous but I gathered that she was aching for the action to start and wanted to set up her PC portable at a desk with chair, preferably a high stool and bench where she felt comfortable and could fully concentrate. Rory considered the options and supplied the compromise. With herself as the go-between, with her various whistles and bird-calls, hiding midway near the wall of the vacant depot outside, she said Chandra should stay with her car in the shed, ring Alison apprising her of our situation with an update, reassuring Penny and her that we would be back in touch, and then be ready for signals should strife erupt. Meanwhile Virginia, Meghan and I could do the commando bit. There was only the weasel in there doing his chemical wizardry, assuming our informer had told the truth. Meghan was bursting with excitement as if the vendetta were personally hers. Virginia's energy was quiet and menacing. I glanced down to see if Chandra was at all miffed, but her eyes twinkled, appreciating the intelligence of the division of labour, that aims are accomplished step by step and they also serve who sit and communicate; networking was her specialty. Rory, tossing her lucky stone, rehearsed her wordless vocals, attaching meanings to the sounds for procedures following all possible contingencies. I missed my thermos of tea because my mouth was dry.

We moved according to plan and snuck up to the pedestrian door of the hangar with its tell-tale sliver of light. Virginia shocked the daylights out of me by savagely banging the tin wall while I was bending forward to examine the latch with my pencil-torch. Fortunately, the heavy-duty chain was hanging loose with its pendant padlock. The weasel, if he wasn't already spilling his powders in panic, would be frightened out of his wits by the caterwauling of Meghan that accompanied VeeDub's racket. Meanwhile, I quietly jemmied the door. Silence came in tempo with the impact of a kettle-drum beat the second I released the catch. Stillness while we counted, calming our breath; then, it was positively Beethoven, the way Meghan slowly pulled the steel chain across the jagged metal of the hole, link by link. I kicked open the door. Sure enough, he was shitting himself. Wonder-woman in triplicate swam before his eyes.

His weapon was out of reach. It was a self-loading .32 calibre pistol, for which no licence can be obtained; absolutely illegal. A quick look at the magnification in the lenses of his glasses calculated with the degree of difficulty in hitting a moving target with such a firearm—unless he practised by day in a games gallery, which was possible—had me moving towards it. Virginia went directly to him. Meghan, swinging the chain like a bikie, walked around the walls examining the contents of the shelving. He didn't know who to watch. The factory was a neat set-up, with workbench and stool, Bunsen burner and test-tubes, white stuff and pharmacy scales, his cigarettes and hand gun, under a low-slung pool table light on a pulley. Cupboards with narrow brackets riveted to the shed walls had fake tin doors. In the darkness of the front of the hangar, mechanics' tools were in a mess around a vintage aircraft in pieces. All of the offensive business could be demounted in minutes to take the appearance of the garage of a fanatical enthusiast. Indeed, the weasel himself could act that part with no character affectation by slipping on the greasy coverall hanging at the ready on a standard coat-rack. With the looming Virginia staring him out, threatening to whip off his spectacles if he moved his eyes, I had ample opportunity to grab the gun and remove the clip. Meghan lost it and started smashing bottles on the concrete floor. Indecision, more than sticky faeces, more than continuing fear of us, held him to his seat. Plainly invasion of his premises had happened before, would happen again, and we were not the cops. His workshop was inherently dangerous. He knew that.

'Piss off,' he said.

Meghan, with no thought for the consequence of her action, took offence. She whirled the chain and smashed him in the head with the padlock. Then she took a bottle of ether and put it in her pocket, saying, 'We might need that.' Her icy foresight was in stark contrast with her out-of-control temper of a moment before.

'I heard you had a violent streak,' I wailed, as I went to examine the body on the floor. He wasn't dead.

'Remove it,' ordered Dr Featherstone, the boss. Then she found behind the coat-stand a broom and proceeded to sweep up the glass she broke.

Virginia and I dragged the limp form out to Rory, who picked up his feet and the three of us carried him to the godown. Chandra had rope in her car. When I returned to the hangar, Meghan had rearranged the laboratory to suit herself. It was functional. I frowned in wonderment. The shelves were clear, Bunsen burner, test-tubes and pharmaceuticals were nowhere to be seen, and she was wiping the bench with a cloth.

'Quick work,' I commented. 'Why did you do that?' I asked unhappily.

'It's all in there,' she indicated a big black garbage bag. 'Gun too.' She dismissed me. 'Don't trust cops.'

The clip was in my pocket. I hauled the rubbish into the darkness by the plane and left it. The three others arrived as Meghan was fastidiously scrubbing the seat of the stool with disinfectant. Virginia took the PC off Chandra's lap and laid it on the bench. Rory reported only one movement on the drome. Night security firm checking the doors of the terminal and the Flight School hangars. 'He had a torch and flicked a calling card at each place he stopped. Not a worry. Not doing any more work than paid for, apparently.'

'Nevertheless,' reckoned Meghan. 'Time is of the essence.'

'It's just too cocky by half to leave that weasel alone all night without support,' I agreed.

'No,' said Virginia. 'Yes, they are cocky. But they will have back-up.'

Rory returned to her post. If bad guys turned up I didn't know what she could do apart from whistle in the dark. Chandra pressed out the numbers on the mobile. Meghan brought her computer to life. Virginia and I stood sentry, each privately figuring a plan of action if Rory whistled interruption.

The snatches of the conversation I caught both between Chandra and Alison and between Chandra and Meghan conveyed to me that Alison, or Penny, had found the ingenious co-ordinate geometry of Neil's sabotage plans in his geography home-work. He had a map of the east coast of Australia with all the known shipwrecks described in degrees of longitude and latitude. He had downloaded safe passage navigational routes from international shipping, hobby and professional fishing and cruising yacht club sites. Then, apparently, he'd written a program to alter the database of the highly technical, electronic mariners' compass software for both operating systems. So that if he got fifteen minutes on the cruiser's computer, he could make the skipper on the high seas think he had plenty of draught beneath his vessel when in fact he was heading for shoals. He had factored in a complicated virus that would make correction of the course completely confusing, creating reefs and coral islands where there were none. If the steering was computerised, his formula was fail-safe, because the only way the seaman could get out of it would be to go entirely manual with visual input, should he find out in time.

Meghan was relatively impressed, but 'it's such a boys' thing, isn't it?' she kept saying.

'Couldn't we do something more simple and practical?' inquired Chandra.

'Of course,' the scientist responded.

'Well, what are we wasting time for?' asked Virginia, from the doorway.

'Aw,' Meghan demurred. 'He's given me some ideas. A clever little, thorough little nerd, he was.' Meghan's rash behaviour was beginning to give me the shits: what an arrogant spoilt brat!

Chandra used that beautiful phone-speaking voice of hers to wash firm flattery of her son's ingenuity and righteous passion over Penny Waughan's sore heart, and signed off with, 'thanks, we'll need it.'

Rory's whistle, car coming, on road, turning left, triggered swift movements. Meghan pressed one key on the laptop, and closed it. Virginia threaded the assault and battery weapon through the hole in the bent door, holding the cleaned padlock. Meghan had a moment of indecision about the light, but Virginia could not have been following the intrigue of Neil's cunning because she had figured out how to close shop and nodded. We were in darkness. VeeDub quietly opened the door. Chandra was first out. Meghan hurried to push Chandra through the long, clinging grass behind the neighbouring building. Car wheels splashing on the tar made my bowels quake. Needing my pencil torch to illuminate the work of her dexterous fingers, Virginia manipulated the chain through its hole in the jamb from the outside and managed to press the arch of the padlock inside, linking the chain together quite tightly. As we crept past the weasel's parked car, VeeDub squatted beside a back tyre, took off the cap and stuck a matchstick in the valve and let it down. Sensibly, she replaced the cap. A large black-winged creature flew across the moon. Rory hooted, car stopping.

Virginia and I heard it and skedaddled to the shade of the next door depot, flattened ourselves against the wall and held our breath. Two men sat in the front seat of the tow truck, their faces registering surprise as one popped his door and the cabin lamp revealed their expressions. Whatever Virginia thought, she was right about one thing. They discerned no light under the side-door of the workshop, no chemist inside. They circled the car and found the flat tyre.

'You got a key to the padlock, Paul?'

'No, mate. The lazy little shit has rung up someone to pick him up.'

'That could be so, but why not us? We're his minders.'

Paul considered the younger chap's logic, but wasn't having a bar of it.

'Girlfriend, what's the bet?' Plainly Paul and his partner were not senior to the pharmacist in the organisation, otherwise they would not be guessing about his personal life.

'Hey,' called the younger guy, rattling the chain. 'He's locked it from the inside.'

'Well, that's it, isn't?' Paul returned to his truck, as oily in the diffuse moonlight as the wet tarmac behind. Light misty rain began.

'What do you mean?' The fellow asked.

'They're at it, aren't they?'

'I never remember no mattress in there.'

'Who needs a mattress?'

'What about the puncture?'

'Cool it, kid,' Paul pulled rank. 'We'll come back in half an hour, let them sleep.'

'If they haven't got a mattress, how come the light's out?' The younger fellow was reluctant to leave with questions unanswered.

'Why haven't they got a mattress? You don't know they haven't got a mattress. If you worked in a place like that, at night, would you have a mattress? Of course, you would. They got a mattress.'

'Okay, all right, but what about the flat?'

'We'll fix it for him,' Paul said. 'Not a problem. Give them thirty minutes.'

The side-kick had another look at the car. Virginia and I squeezed back further.

'Slow puncture, probably doesn't know about it yet.'

He returned to the now low rumbling tow truck and got out of the drizzle. They revved off to the end of the macadam and along the dirt road to the river. Thunder clapped in the distance. We had half an hour before they returned, and discovered our work. They went towards the oyster jetty. The building storm was even more of a threat to dare-devil schemes. I swallowed another pain-killer and took up the rear as we five entered the dark godown.

Meghan said, as she switched on the light, 'I want to get on their boat.' The moans of the chemist presented us with an immediate problem. He was hog-tied on the cement floor. I felt more in a bind than he. The Subaru could not leave this shed until the tow truck and the minders had gone, but they wouldn't go until they were satisfied he was accounted for. I longingly gazed at my bikes, wanting to escape, riding all the way home on my own if I had to. But I wasn't alone.

'Enid Blyton eat your heart out,' said Rory.

Virginia and Meghan laughed. Chandra and I caught each other's eye. 'Tiger Cat did not mention the bruisers,' I said.

Virginia recalled that she did say the skipper of the cruiser was sleeping on board. 'I reckon,' she remarked, 'that they are going to pick him up, because there is a storm coming, a flood warning they've just heard, or something, and they are doing what they are paid for, minding.'

'Fucking fizgig!' expleted our captive.

'No, she's not,' I contradicted. 'Your man in the tow truck is. I saw that vehicle in the police yard, privileged parking spot.'

Meghan fiddled with the information on the screen of her computer, balanced on the bonnet of Chandra's car, with her fingers and her brain-power, seemingly uninterested in the victim of her blow. Rory went over and examined his wound, feeling for fractures in his skull.

He said, 'Yow. Ouch.'

Virginia picked up my wrist and looked at my watch. 'We're running out of time.'

'Won't be a minute,' Meghan responded as if spoken to.

'What exactly are you doing?' I asked.

'Less than five,' she muttered.

'Five what?'

'Minutes.'

'For what?' I was getting exasperated with her and very nervous.

'What Neil was planning to do in fifteen Meghan can do in five for better effect,' Chandra explained.

'Forget it. I'm ringing Philippoussis,' I decided. But Chandra wouldn't release her grip on the mobile.

'Call in the cavalry,' joked Rory, in hockey-sticks tones, still in the mood of the Famous Five. She really did not understand the danger we were in. I did. I did not want my friends hurt, or killed, either of which could happen, within twenty minutes. I walked over to my racing bike and began wheeling it to the door, putting the responsibility for their welfare squarely in Chandra's hands.

'Hang on,' Virginia begged. 'Wait.' She turned to Meghan and asked, 'Why is this so important?' She gestured to the computing.

'If we bury their destruction inside their own equipment, set it to work only at sea, with no outside input, no telephone calls, no emails, nothing can be traced. I can disable the pilot and their automatic transmission—possibly, if it's electronic, the rudder as well.'

'And how do you intend to get aboard?' Virginia insisted, 'And then up to the poop-deck.'

'I'll get to that. Margot's brought wetsuits, as well as a dinghy. No problem,' Megs said vaguely as she memorised her formula and closed the laptop. She put it on the front seat of the Subaru.

Virginia smiled, 'You are way too focused, Meghan!'

'What about him?' Rory gently kicked the knee of the weasel. Meghan handed her the ether.

'What about them?' I almost screamed, expecting the tow-truck boys to be back at any moment. I put my foot into the pedal-case and began scooting in preparation to swinging my leg over the bar and haring off for help. But once on the tarmac I didn't press on. The wind was up. The storm brewing. Thunder getting louder. Lightning stepping closer on its erratic electric stilts like a magnificent daddy-long-legs of fire. No lights or automobile movement over near the mangroves. I really wouldn't leave my sisters to face the music, so I decided to scout and rode slowly across the airstrip. I heard a cry behind me. Chandra, in her wheel-chair, was racing towards me, body crouched, elbows flying. I circled and saw in a flash that the mobile phone was still on her lap.

'I'm coming with you,' she panted as she whizzed by me.

We were tiny creatures under a big, booming sky, fast-moving beings with steel wheels. But the lightning was several kilometres away. We stopped where the bitumen ended. In the obliging, sporadic luminance, we saw the mantis of a tow truck near the dark shucking shed and two figures on the pier. Chandra handed me her telephone.

'Ring him now,' she said. There was in that second such respect for me and such trustworthiness in herself I went breathless. I did, as she assumed, remember his number.

'He's probably in bed with the deputy coroner,' I commented as I waited for him to pick up his receiver.

'I'm at the airport, Pip,' I explained. 'With a bunch of bad guys about to kill us. Well, they will if you don't get here quick.'

I told him exactly what I was seeing, the motor launch pulling into the pier and where he would find the lab. The guys were taking their time securing the multi-million-dollar vessel to the pylons. I thought, shit, we've got to move.

'Margot?' I heard Philippoussis as I threw the phone at Chandra's knee. She pressed the close call button and we made off back to the warehouse.

Virginia and Rory carried the bound bloke to his car and left him in the back seat. We would hole up out of sight behind the Yale lock of Meghan's godown, keeping mum and listening. It was several minutes before I noticed my mountain bike and Meghan herself missing. But I was hushed when I opened my mouth. The tow truck's engine we heard as it came to a stop outside the hangar. They were still arguing loudly about immaterial things.

'You go prawning three days after the full moon!'

'Three days, you reckon?'

'Exactly. All up and down the rocks, you see the fires of prawners eating their catch.'

A third voice had joined the debate.

'Well, that gives me a few days to get the gear together.'

'But they catch flathead near the oyster leases, prawns are further down.'

'Yeah, you done spinning, Paul? like fly-fishing from moving boat?'

'It's the storm I've got to worry about,' the skipper confided.

'Fishermen don't like the moon. Rather be out there with a searchlight when it's pitch black.'

'Hey, the chemist is in his car!' The young off-sider's voice yelled. 'He wasn't there before, Paul, was he?'

Paul evaded the question, preferring to stay cool. 'Flathead have spikes. That's what I know about them.'

'He's out cold!'

'Don't eat an oyster in a month with o in it,' said Paul, as we heard him break a rifle or shotgun and clamp it back together. 'Never break that rule, son.'

'The door to the factory's been jemmied,' the younger chap informed. Paul himself was prowling around the depots, rattling doors, checking shadows. 'Bolt-cutters in the tool-box.' His voice was loud, and terribly close. We froze into ice statues. He wanted to be at the lab when the other guy opened the door, curiosity getting the better of caution, he left off rattling our doors. As they investigated the disappearance of the lab set-up, I squatted and prayed for the cops to arrive.

Meghan Featherstone is leaning the bike against Virginia's ute when a Highway Patrol car turns the corner. She places the bike in the boat and climbs into the back and hides under the tarp. She lifts the edge to watch the police stop at the gate. When the uniform is back inside, the cruiser dims its lights and proceeds as quietly as possible. They circle the airport car park, then stop at the junction of the roads. In the distance, Meghan sees, in a flash of lightning, another, the large white four-wheel-drive with its red and blue toplights, making its way along the dirt track at the other end of the aerodrome property, a powerful searchlight flashing its beam forward and back.

'Estuaries. Oyster sticks, racks under them.' She thinks, 'I was born with a caul. Where's the wetsuit?' Hiding on the tray of someone else's pick-up, feeling around for a latex body-suit she is not sure will fit, thinking that at least it will protect her from the lightning she fears more than the bullets of men's guns, she is obsessed by the chance to get back at someone who deserves the worst the best way she can; a fairly brilliant plan, detailed down to the last specific factor.

Driven by the dynamism of its logical progression, amazed by the dramatic beauty of its execution, arrested by a circus outside, Meghan realises she is a maniac. If she doesn't do this, she will have no catharsis. She is enthralled by the thrill, but stilled, having to take stock, and for her it is like hitting a rock. She does not want to face her ludicrous self. She wants no mirror, no lens, no self-reflection or criticism. She just wants to do it, to be within the experience, to feel the hysteria. To do it, to get out, to dive into shark-infested waters, swelling with the debris of upstream flood, to challenge the fates, shake her fists at the gods, is a dream, whereas to be silent and staid is a nightmare. She parts the tarpaulin. And ducks as the sirens of more cars arriving present the reality, a ho-hum drug-bust of petty crims and their pathetic greed and incomprehensible stupidity. Lights and sounds and a thunderstorm. She cannot bear inaction a moment longer. She wants to see if she'll survive. She needs the high. She sneaks out of the hide and retrieves the bike.

The Annihilation Tragic rides. She rides through the wind and rain to the far side of the airstrip, then along the fence to the track. Onto the jetty and there is the boat, battened down. She jumps on deck. There is nothing she can do, the poop is locked, the underdeck likewise. She tries everywhere, but there is no way in, no tools at hand, not even to smash the glass.

The long-wheelbase LandCruiser pulls up. A tall dark man and Margot Gorman walk along the wharf. Meghan dives into the swirling river.

With Rory, Virginia and Chandra it wasn't hard to wait in silence. While we were worried about her, Meghan's manic energy was not missed. We were tense but we were calm, as if each of us had spent time alone without moving a lot, and were thus practised at not fidgeting. I noticed Virginia relax her wrists and turn her palms open. Rory clasped and unclasped her greenish white stone. Chandra went through a series of finger exercises as I go through stretches of my hamstrings et cetera. I was so tired a yoga posture was just what I needed. I stayed in the cross-legged asana, with my right hand on my left, simply sitting.

When we heard the sirens, Rory tossed her stone and we played catch. There were a lot of male voices. When I heard a female, either Constable McKewen or the deputy coroner, I thought it was cool to emerge, as Phil Philippoussis wouldn't be far away. The others could do what they liked.

Three patrol cars and the LandCruiser blocked the tow truck and the weasel's BMW. To the first uniform I encountered I said, 'Detective Constable Philippoussis about?'

'Over there,' he directed me.

'Ta, mate.'

Phil in his adidas tracksuit was not the most senior man. He introduced me to his detective sergeant, a serious-faced Christian-looking chap, and to the deputy coroner, also in a tracksuit. She was drop-dead gorgeous, intelligent, friendly and competent. As it wasn't her patch—there wasn't a dead body—she genially said she was along for the ride, but it was plain she could have been boss if she wanted to. The plain-clothes unit was from her office. Paul, if he was the Crank's informant, had been bagged by the wrong crowd. I gave them a potted history of the last few hours, showed them the rubbish bag Meghan had filled and handed over the clip from the automatic. In explaining the state of the black-market chemist, I tried to make light of Meghan's behaviour. The weather was beginning to look really filthy. I inveigled Phil to drive me over to the boat, which they would have to commandeer anyway. 'It's a matter of urgency, Pip.'

When Meghan saw us coming towards her on the jetty, she turned around and did a running dive into the moving river. She swam about a bit in my wetsuit and eventually came back to the pier. We pulled her out by her arms, and she said, 'I needed that.'

'You could have been killed,' said Philippoussis.

Meghan replied, 'Precisely. But I wanted to get those arseholes.'

Phil assured her that he would inform Interpol and impound the cruiser. He checked the mooring and slapped some SOC tape about the place. I picked up my bike and put it in the back of the police vehicle. Meghan was shivering but exhilarated. It had been quite a night for her, but she was still frustrated. 'I don't trust men,' she muttered.

When we returned to the line of warehouses, I discovered that Virginia had ridden my other bike back to her car. We checked out with the sergeant and waved to the deputy coroner, who smiled, 'See you.' Chandra drove me across to Virginia waiting at the wheel, with her head on her hands, sleepy. There were only a couple of hours till dawn, and we had to take the dinghy back to Lois's. So I worked out, everyone could come to my place. If Chandra slept with me and Virginia allowed Rory the other half of the sofa double-bed, then Meghan could have the floor with the couch cushions, we'd be right. We trundled along the back roads through the mangroves, paperbark and tea-tree, across the bridge to the north, past the bend where Hugh Gilmore died and the little white cross with its plastic flower wreath still stood, home.

56

. . . arrayed in purple and scarlet . . .

Judith Sloane examines her treasures in the woolshed. She handles the valuable contents of her cashbox, her payment of rubies, and slowly lets them run through her fingers into a hand-painted silk scarf. Another electrical storm flickers in the distance. Spinning the combination lock of the little safe, she places it in the rusty chest. The domed tin lid falls with a clatter. The noise annoys her. Judith finds herself without allies, without friends, but it is not her fault. Padlocks secure on the antique trunk, the boards of the false floor replaced, she shifts bundles of fleece. Although she has no lover, she has pounds of heady dope in the shiny boxes of small white goods, kitchen gadgetry she has never used.

The Koori from Kempsey was not much more than a one-night stand. Although Judith milked the fling for all its politically sound connotations in the gossip mills, she would not lend her the Triton. She allowed herself to be bought a beer, fed a meal, even considered buying a pair of decorated singing sticks, or led the family to think she did, but was horrified at the thought of them all piling into her expensive vehicle, pristine with carefully contrived vibes coming from little silver statues of goddesses and occult talismans.

Under more floor-boards is the crate of presents, women's artwork, appliquéed jackets, crude carvings, finger-form pottery, mobiles of feathers and sticks, shell necklaces, stained glass designs in copper-foiling, paintings, pictures in watercolour, crayon and charcoal; proof of how much she is loved and admired. Many women have adored her.

But now, she cannot remember who did what. Judith is not interested in opening the shoe boxes where hundreds of photos of sheep, pigeons, cows and horses, portraits of women with smiles and guitars, postcards from all over the world are squashed in so tight the corners are coming apart. In an old leather suitcase, strapped with a rein, are things she did with her own hand to give, but couldn't part with. She looks at those: a hand-woven wall-hanging, a knitted vest, several cards, bits of tatting and crochet, clay pieces, homemade parchment from recycled paper; much of the work unfinished. On top of the moved and replaced planks she arranges junk, tools, some old, some borrowed and not returned, a galvanised bucket with a hole in the bottom, a new block-buster handle.

The storm is brewing in the north-east. Judith checks the appearance of the hovel with a tug here, a toss there, like a fastidious window-dresser, and leaves a set for a scene depicting the careless innocence of subsistence. She has now more money than she ever dreamed possible. No work on the planet, short of international stardom, could have earned her so much. She has no need to suffer fools gladly.

Judith Sloane assumes it would have been easy to seduce the sexually amoral Cybil Crabbe, a push-over. She has never had trouble getting lovers. In her mind she had her already, a partner to travel with, see the Barrier Reef, sail around the Whitsundays, after all the toil, spoil herself with the good things in life. And it would have been a nail in the coffin of Virginia White. So much clever planning, being as cunning as she could, the gift of Virginia's violence exactly what she hoped for, turns, with such a banal and abrupt dismissal, to dust as dry as ash in her mouth. She doesn't believe it. Refusal hadn't bothered Judith much before as she could slither away with her secrets to meditate in privacy at her wheel, appropriate the rejection as her own and re-emerge with smooth stories, to tell the truth in confidence that it was her choosing, actually. She could use flattery to charm whomever she wanted.

Clouds rear heavily behind the circle of hills that surround her place as she tramps from one shelter to the other. Wet weather generally wraps her in its cocoon. Her shack is away from the threat of falling trees, but there is no honey in the jar. Two cans of dolphin-friendly tuna and one of no-brand pink salmon do not provide the comfort she should expect from food, even mixed with potato mash and beans from her garden. She sits down to spin at her wheel, hearing the bleating of her flock as they hunker down together under the red cedar and the turpentine at the rocky knoll in the paddock. As shepherds are said to talk to their hats, she starts an erratic rave.

'The spiders are colonising my space. Their gummy traps take up more and more room.' Old webs dangle from the corners of her dwelling. Gusts have thrown up bits of unclean wool to hang suspended in the sticky dust, getting dustier. Her flock of black sheep are brown. The loose tufts have faded to reddish tan, an uncomfortable in-between. The older bits are greenish. In her meditation Judith perceives Virginia as her dark side. 'No one has sympathy. I scratch and spit to defend myself as I am torn and tearing. Savages. Culprits of civilisation and its victims whine and scheme.' The spiders are silent. Black cockatoos screech, rain and rain. Their lazy wings lope like big-boned athletes, arrogant, powerful parrots flying from casuarina forests and pine plantations. The sky blackens with wings and brumous winds.

Judith grimly grits her teeth until her jaws ache. Her calm craft belies the crabbing of her claws as she grasps the fibres. She is hungry. The groin muscle flexes and loosens as her foot on the pedal increases its rhythm She is the picture of the classic witch of history in the wickedness of her industry. 'I flee their fires, lit by a flaming torch, the bearer encouraged by crowds yelling in rapture for another's pain, mobs waiting to witness agony, to watch agony, the self-righteous spectators vicariously torturing each and every one of itself. I smell the flesh burning. I am one of the crowd. Without pain, whispering betrayal, using lies to survive. Howlingly afraid of death, willing to throw the blame at the flames, bleeding with frenzy, drunk and alive, crazy. In my dreams, in my meditation, I am gutting myself, angry and passionate; outside, I am cool, disinterested, mysterious. Smoky voice and silken hair. Silky voice and smoken hair. No one knows my soft long locks are dyed, that my one personal extravagance is exclusive hair products, hugely priced. No one knows I'm going grey. How can success turn so absolutely to such distress? I am restless, unbearably restless. I don't know what to do. My imagination was based on witches, wonderful witches, now I am haunted by visions of witch-burning. Time has warped and I am there. No one is here, but I am surrounded by accusatory fingers pointing as saints hoist me up on the rack. They poke at me. Aliens from other times have invaded my humble hut, caught me at my wheel, as if they have been hunting me down the centuries. Escape.'

Judith has pure Anglo-Saxon heritage. English is the patois of her native soil, where her, her mother's, her grandmothers' and ancestors' umbilical cords are buried. Words cannot fail her. The language is her birthright. English names what she knows, and is as guiltless as she as it renders irrelevant tongues which speak of things outside the shop-keeping mentality. But Judith Sloane with this grasp of clarity has used her fluency to build castles in the air, to entrance and entrap, and above all, to fool herself.

She can't remember exactly when she starting deliberately lying. Perhaps it was when she came to Australia and had to disguise her snobbery to get on the peace wagon of politics where the band was playing. Being true to her roots became unconscionable. While others were crudely calling for liberation with narrow vocabularies and clumsy syntax, she fell into habits of manipulation. At first she stooped from superior grammar to be understood but she sounded like a genius and they made her a star. Maybe the land itself, so geologically ancient, so murmuring with ghosts, mocked her sophistication, or, perhaps, the native people still communing with their spirits, with their hunting and their gathering, their culture struggling against the noble European heritage turned her away from speaking the truth.

With the bullfrogs calling for more rain, Judith leaves her humpy. She is in need of honey and her car is garaged on the other side of the river, only a walk away. After striding across the paddocks then along the road, pursued by a whistling down a long corridor without a hint of echo, Judith pushes her way through the bush on a narrow track she knows well. The eerie sound of other-worldliness is distinctly in her ears. She feels an unholy cathedral about her. Walking very quickly to the gate on air-soled boots with advanced climbing treads, her passage is silent. Her plaid shirt tied round her waist by its arms until she reaches the road, she wears her vest and moleskins.

Every moment or so, she handles the little pouch of gems and touches her wallet in her hip pocket. She is driven by the need to hide her wealth at the same time as have it. She wants to be done with Lesbianlands now, to be walking away with her treasure, autonomous, anonymous. No one is around. Even the dogs are sleeping. Let them lie. The looming weather, of course, has shooed the gurls to town. Nonetheless, she follows her habit of passing their places noiselessly by her own slightly divergent tracks. Surreptitious skills learnt in a dangerously sarcastic childhood and honed in a clever adulthood, she can be as still as an Hopi shaman. Her footsteps on the ground make no sound. Apart from honey for the moment, she also wants to be transported to the counter of the bank, requesting a box in her name in the vault.

But the whistling continues in her ears with its aggravating lack of echo, ringing on her drums. She can hear nothing else. Currawongs open their beaks and lift their throats but she cannot hear them. A butcher bird in front of her stands on a low branch, dipping his head and carefully performing his beautiful call. It doesn't penetrate. The distant thunder booms, impending like doom. She hears that, she is not deaf.

Judith Sloane becomes hot, unbearably hot. She perspires. It is muggy. No wind in the pre-storm air, not a breath. She takes a sidetrack, aiming for the river to cool off. The clouds build up, black and brutal. Thunder rumbles. Not a zephyr. No rain. The mountains of the Great Dividing Range close in. She is so hot. Her throat is dry. The path climbs. It shouldn't. She wants to go down. In her hurry to leave the house, she forgot her water bottle. More thunder. Overhead. She takes the next track down. When she finds the river, the bank is sheer. She is parched. Salty sweat is irritating her skin. She struggles along the water's course until she can slide in. She holds the pouch of rubies in her fist and skids as the skies crack.

Hard sudden rain pelts down. Mud beneath her feet. She has no footing, she slips over the bank, into the creek. It is deep. Thunder is deafening. Lightning is close. She looks at it with horror, marking time, out of her depth.

A shaft of electricity, a jagged snake of sharp sparks, strikes the conducting water. Judith cramps in shock. Her body shudders. Seconds later she is dead.

The precipitation is as dense as five thousand years of women's tears. Hail strips gurls' vegetables and fruit trees. The springs that feed the Campbell River all open their faucets on full, fill the streams and get them flowing fast. It doesn't let up for hours. Rory's house on its stilts is marooned, the creeks roar and rise. Her swing bridge is swept away. Logs dislodge. Trees on the banks are torn out by their roots. Top soil shifts beneath lantana thickets. Land slides.

The rain was a mighty waterfall surrounding all and sundry. My yard was so soggy there was no other way to the loo than along the concrete path, and that was slippery.

After she and I had returned the boat and trailer to the yard of Lois and Thrust, picked up a litre of milk at the shop, some fresh rolls and the newspaper, Virginia had coffee and muesli and was on her way. What a big, strong woman, with a practical bent and a lust for life, a brilliant mind and a sense of compassion and humour! 'Safe journey, friend,' I slapped her back in a sisterly hug, and grinned. We all waved her off through the curtain of drips from the guttering of my front verandah.

When I begin a love relationship, I cease to need to write. Communication is all showing, not saying; displaying and being, not describing and reflecting; and anyway, who has the time to sit alone and put it down? A gear changes. Time is needed for the precious little things in the company of the beloved. Life goes into overdrive and you cruise along; everything is in the present tense. You're travelling. The landscape's changing and you are at your destination. Each moment is delicious and unique, full of history and mystery. Each passing fancy is magnified to magic, as if a zoom lens is attached to your eye bringing the close-up closer and blurring the background into a magnificent impressionism of colour. Oh dear.

I just loved everybody. Well, all those who stayed in my home anyway. If I could sing I would sing. Rory and Meghan fought over sections of the fresh paper for the few moments it was a folded thing, Rory, eventually, getting the news and Meghan, the business pages and sport. I gave Chandra breakfast in bed. When I went back to the kitchen for refills from the teapot, each had her elbows on the open broadsheet, page two in Rory's case. They were in earnest discussion about the nature of money. If I hadn't had Chandra to go to, I would have enjoyed joining in and, no doubt, I would have learnt something. Such an embarrassment of riches!

Alison phoned and we all talked to Penny. Four stories she got. A squared-off picture of the events of last night was more than I could give by myself. I was chuffed. She wouldn't get better than that. Then I remembered the cheque in my pants and recovered my payment from the laundry basket. The rain was steady and hard. When we had all showered, there was one urgent matter on the agenda, according to Meghan. The rest of us didn't mind.

Hope Strange stands beneath the tin roof that Trivia erected, walled by sheets of water. She hears the big waterfall roaring as well as the sound of new ones and the crashing of trees. The pelting is deafening overhead. The sun goes dark. The black cloud pauses theatrically and passes. Thunder and lightning pursue their path before the ferocious wind. The storm moves on its way, leaving steady rain.

'Chapter 16, verse 18, And there were voices, and thunders, and lightnings; and there was a great earthquake, such as was not since men were upon the earth, so mighty an earthquake and so great,' Hope shouts, almost laughing, ever-remembering the Bible-bashing since birth. 'Whatever, whatever, whatever,' she continues. 'The cities of great nations fell. Da da. And the woman was arrayed in purple and scarlet colour, and decked with gold and precious stones and pearls, having a golden cup in her hand full of abominations and filthiness of her fornication. Ah ha, MYSTERY, BABYLON THE GREAT, MOTHER OF . . . um, and when I saw her, I wondered with great admiration.' Hope strides like an actor in the role of a preacher performing to the weather as if her open cabin were a proscenium arch. 'And the angel said unto me, Wherefore didst I marvel? I will tell thee of the mystery of the woman, and of the beast that carrieth her, which hath seven heads and ten horns. Yeah yeah, yeah yeah,' Hope is quite suddenly infinitely bored. So she knows the Apocalypse off by heart, so what?

Later on in the day, when the rain eases a bit, she dresses in an oilskin. Keeping to high ground, circling the gullies, she enters the rainforest and approaches the sculpture from above. It is not there. She wonders if she is lost. The bush has reconfigured itself. The creek is unrecognisably wide and raging like a torrent. It is dangerous to descend any lower. She goes to the top of the waterfall, which in itself is a moment of splendour in magnificent wilderness. She can't get to Virginia's house, or Rory's, so Hope squishes her way across the high ridges to Judith's. No one is home but spiders, pigeons cooing their loft and sheep huddled together under a couple of trees in a bundle looking like boulders.

She lights the fire and hunts about for something to read. There in the book-case in a box like a book is a stack of passports. English, South African,

German, Australian and one from New Zealand, her own. Hope O'Lachlin. With her date of birth altered. How bizarre! She finds an Agatha Christie paperback, snuggles up in the sheepskins and reads out the rain, when hungry eating tinned fish.

Rory, Chandra, Meghan and Margot are all in the one car, the Subaru station wagon. Tess and Nikki are in the back. It's crowded.

'Well there's no way I'm going to get in for a few days,' Rory comments from the passenger side of the front seat.

'Nope,' agrees Meghan.

'That's okay. You can bunk down in my barn as long as you like,' Chandra offers. Margot gazes over the speckling cloth of water that was a grazing paddock. Wading birds high step and spear food while the dairy cows crowd on an island of raised earth. She must get back to photography soon, she muses.

The women are going for lunch at a macrobiotic café up on Hippi Sitti plateau where there's an art exhibition. But first they are checking on Meghan Featherstone's goats.

After she turns off the highway and as they begin the hairpin bends of the steep climb, Chandra remarks on the crazy driving of the trucker in front of them. All four are fascinated.

'Well we won't be passing him, that's for sure, not on this road,' Chandra says firmly.

'Look at that!' A motor-bike leaning into the corner coming down narrowly misses the big white semi-trailer. All the lights on the cabin begin flashing like Christmas decorations.

'This bloke's crazy!' Rory reckons.

'Maybe he's scared,' mutters Margot, quite frightened herself.

'Amber caution lamps, blinkers, headlights and tail-lights, stop-lights and backing lights, how can they all go on together?' wonders Rory.

'Oops, okay, he's turned them off now,' Chandra enters the mood.

Margot is, uncharacteristically, a bundle of nerves. The others can hear terror in her voice. 'Don't you think it would be a good idea to stop and let him get away?'

'Yeah, but where?' accedes Chandra

'There's a look-out up here a bit, not far.' Meghan points.

'Meanwhile, let him get ahead,' croaks Margot.

'Okay,' Chandra says. 'Don't get your knickers in a knot.'

The path of the Freightliner is chaotic. It is fortunate Ian Truckman is having to drive slowly in low gear; he has no hope of keeping to his side of the road. Cars coming in the downhill direction pull out onto the shoulder to let him pass.

'Here it is. On your right.' Meghan tells Chandra.

Chandra turns into a scenic parking bay which would give a great view of the Campbell River valley and the escarpments of the Great Dividing Range. Margot gets out and tosses a raincoat over her head and shoulders. In front of her, the wooded cliff is precipitous, showing the tops of pencil palms, palmettos and ancient gums of wide girth.

'Wow!' Chandra winds down her window filling her senses, 'I'm glad we had to stop here. It's wonderful.'

'Is that the river,' exclaims Rory. 'I have never seen it so wide!'

'It used to be like that before they cleared and irrigated,' says the now keen ecologist, Meghan. 'But in this weather, you couldn't tell the sheep from the goats.'

'Listen,' yells Margot. The horn of the semi makes a racket like an intermittent siren. They look towards the piece of road they can see further up. The truck comes into view weaving erratically. 'He's not going to make it.' Margot jumps back in the car.

Beyond the verge of the road there is a sheer drop. A stubby fence of corrugated white tin is all that separates the horizontal camber from the vertical decline. The truck hurtles through it. White Virgin is airborne before it plummets into the bush many metres below. The rig bursts into flame and the petrol tanks ignite. Several explosions occur one after another. The acrid smoke makes the rain smell dirty. Chandra shuts her window.

Ian Truckman is incinerated.

'Thank the goddess for this downpour,' says hard-hearted Meghan. 'Means he won't start a bushfire.' The conflagration is snuffed. The detonations cease. The wreck turns into a smoking blackened mess of twisted metal. Meghan, Margot, Chandra and Rory leave other road-users to do their civilian duty, but, in discussion, agree that nothing can be done anyway.

The juggernaut ended up is pretty well inaccessible. Witnessing the death by fire and the love in her heart burns an abiding phobia out of Margot Gorman's system.

They decide to eat before they search for the farm where Curly Cue and her sisters are staying. Lentil burgers, zucchini quiche, baked brown rice, stuffed mushrooms, cottage cheese, alfalfa sprouts, green tomato fritters, paw paw smoothies, mineral water, garden salad. They have the place to themselves. Pottery and craft of varying levels of talent crowd shelves along the wall and are for sale. Watercolour landscapes share the walls with horrid oil-crayon abstracts. They are waited on by a large man with a white beard and long pony-tail who talks about climate changes.

When he returns to his cooking, Meghan rudely asks Margot and Chandra, 'How was it?'

It is Rory who blushes, Margot notices. Chandra is lusty and cheerful in reply.

Unaware that two things, amazingly, floated during the storm, they enjoy their afternoon. Meghan's goats are happily housed in a tractor shed, munching lucerne hay.

The wool on the backs of Judith's sheep gets wetter and wetter.

The boat floats. As the creek rushes down to river, in the gloom of continuing rain, the Amazon ship catches tangles of vicious vine and drags out lumps of lantana. The adzed log spins in the whirls and curls, destroying gangs of weeds, dislodging pockets of darkness, embracing she-oaks and wattles, opening up new possibilities for enjoyment of landscape and sky. Eventually it lodges between two boulders in a curve of the creek, the prow high over a swimming hole of the future, the aft in an incidental waterfall quite close to where Virginia escaped from the cave. The exploratory mines fill up.

The body of Judith Sloane surfs the cataracts downstream. Jagged branches and exposed roots tear the clothing off her limbs until the corpse is naked. The little leather sachet of rubies sinks to the floor of the tributary and, avoiding the currents, settles among the pebbles. The corpse gets dragged down by snags, and stays caught beneath the surface of the deep pool in the dark bend of the river which Chandra told Margot was the waters of Lethe.

Coming to the end of her journey when the moon is rising just before dusk, Virginia is at her nephew's home by the kids' bed-time. They are three and four and a half.

'Read us a story without a book, Auntie Gin.'

'Okay.' Virginia leans in the doorway, and begins, 'When you go to sleep, you'll find a dream and in that dream there is a stream and in the stream there is a fish and in the fish there is a wish . . .'

Other Books by Spinifex

Figments of a Murder
Gillian Hanscombe

"A rich and robust satire of feminist politics combined with a murder mystery." — Anne Coombs, *The Australian*

ISBN 1-875559-43-4

Fedora Walks
Merrilee Moss

When the ghostly Fedora interrupts Julie Bernard's morning coffee in Brunswick Street, Julie's life is set to change. An out-of-work PI, Julie is seduced by Fedora's French accent and beautiful hats, but soon discovers that wearing beautiful millinery is a dangerous activity. A satirical take on lesbian crime fiction, with a mix of fantasy and otherworldly theatricals, Merrilee Moss makes us laugh out loud.

ISBN 1-876756-04-7

Ballad of Siddy Church
Lin van Hek

"She writes like an angel giving the devil her due."

— Keri Hulme

ISBN 1-875559-61-2

White Turtle
Merlinda Bobis

Co-winner Steel Rudd Award, 2000
Winner Manila Critics Circle Award, 2000

Alternately mythic, wistful or quirky, Merlinda Bobis' tales resonate with an original and confident storytelling voice.

ISBN 1-875559-89-2

Rumours of Dreams
Sandi Hall

From the author of the highly acclaimed *Godmothers* comes a new and startling novel.

"Move over, Matthew, Mark, Luke and John: this is a Gospel for the new millennium." — Denis Welch, *NZ Listener*

ISBN 1-875559-75-2

The Falling Woman
Susan Hawthorne

Top Twenty Title, Listener Women's Book Festival

"A remarkable lyrical first novel that weaves together such disparate themes as the mystery of epilepsy, love between women, and an odyssey across the Australian desert."

— *Ms Magazine*

ISBN 1-875559-04-3

Goja: An autobiographical myth
Suniti Namjoshi

This powerful meditation, part autobiography, part elegy, deconstructs the glamour given to wealth and power, and celebrates the quest for love.

Goja is a beautifully written, sensitive work by an extremely intelligent author. This one should be on everyone's shopping list. — Caroline Lumley

ISBN 1-875559-97-3

Building Babel
Suniti Namjoshi

"Suniti Namjoshi is an inspired fabulist."

— Marina Warner

A unique book which invites the reader to explore ideas on culture and contribute to the Babel Building Site on the Spinifex website: http://www.spinifexpress.com.au

ISBN 1-875559-56-6

Feminist Fables
Suniti Namjoshi

An ingenious reworking of fairy tales from East and West. Mythology, mixed with the author's original material and vivid imagination. An indispensable feminist classic.

Her imagination soars to breathtaking heights . . . she has the enviable skill of writing stories that are as entertaining as they are thought-provoking.

— Kerry Lyon, *Australian Book Review*

ISBN 1-875559-19-1

St Suniti and the Dragon
Suniti Namjoshi

An original imagination full of surprises from Beowulf to Bangladesh.

I can think of plenty of adjectives to describe *St Suniti and the Dragon*, but not a noun to go with them. It's hilarious, witty, elegantly written, hugely inventive, fantastic, energetic . . . With work as original as this, it's easier to fling words at it than to say what it is or what it does.

— U. A. Fanthorpe

ISBN 1-875559-18-3

The Bloodwood Clan

Beryl Fletcher

The Bloodwood Clan is not only beautifully written but incredibly thought provoking. It raises questions on relationships between communities, cultures, men and women and between women themselves. — *Essential Magazine*

Fletcher is quickly establishing herself as one of the boldest and most inventive talents in contemporary New Zealand fiction. — Jennifer Lawn

ISBN 1-875559-80-9

The Silicon Tongue

Beryl Fletcher

"One of the best reads I have ever had. I couldn't put it down, gripped in the exploration of intersecting lives, rejoicing that women in their seventies can fly in cyberspace." — Diane Nason, *Hot Gos*

ISBN 1-875559-49-3

The Iron Mouth

Beryl Fletcher

Top Twenty Title, Listener Women's Book Festival, 1993

"The language is a lyrical delight . . . One is compelled to read on to find out what is going to happen . . . as they play the games people have played for thousands of years." — Marion Findlay

ISBN 1-875559-22-1

Cowrie

Cathie Dunsford

"There is freshness, humour and honesty in the writing . . . it both charms and enlightens." — *Canberra Times*

ISBN 1-875559-28-0

The Journey Home / Te Haerenga Kainga

Cathie Dunsford

"This is a lesbian fantasy dripping with luscious, erotic imagery." — *NZ Herald*

ISBN 1-875559-54-X

Manawa Toa / Heart Warrior

Cathie Dunsford

With sensuous writing and a deep knowledge of the traditions, the reader can feel the rock of the sea, taste the food, and fear the attacks on the peace flotilla as it approaches Moruroa Atoll.

"The imagery is superb . . . I recommend this book to anyone who cares about Aotearoa and our future."

— Chris Renwick, *City Voice*

ISBN 1-875559-69-8

Another Year in Africa

Rose Zwi

"A tender, richly detailed and engrossing novel."

— Elaine Lindsay

ISBN 1-875559-42-6

Safe Houses

Rose Zwi

Winner, Human Rights Award for Fiction, 1994
Top Twenty Title, Listener Women's Book Festival, 1993

Set against the escalating violence of the last years of the Apartheid regime, it tells the story of three families—black and Jewish—who are inextricably bound by love and hate, hope and betrayal.

ISBN 1-875559-21-3

Last Walk in Naryshkin Park

Rose Zwi

Shortlisted, NSW Premier's General History Award

". . . uses the words of survivors, archival material, interviews, documents and photographs to create a powerful testimony, an act of remembering life as well as death. It's a moving, vital, devastating and inspiring work."

— *Gleebooks Gleaner*

ISBN 1-875559-72-8

Imago

Francesca Rendle-Short

ACT Book of the Year Award, 1997

"*Imago* is a great restless read, punchy and quirky and indescribably tender."   — *Diva*

ISBN 1-875559-36-1

I Started Crying Monday

Laurene Kelly

Fourteen-year-old Julie starts crying on Monday when things go badly at school. Worse is to come.

ISBN 1-875559-78-7

Too Rich

Melissa Chan

"One of the best Australian whodunnits . . . the characterisation is superb, the style elegant." — Ray Davie, *The Age*

ISBN 1-875559-02-7

If you would like to know more about Spinifex Press,
write for a free catalogue or visit our home page.

Spinifex Press

PO Box 212, North Melbourne,
Victoria 3051, Australia
www.spinifexpress.com.au